A TEXT BOOK OF

ARCHITECTURAL PLANNING AND DESIGN OF BUILDINGS

FOR
SEMESTER – II

SECOND YEAR DEGREE COURSE IN CIVIL ENGINEERING

Strictly According to New Revised Credit System Syllabus of Savitribai Phule Pune University
(w.e.f June 2016)

Dr. A.D. PAWAR
M.E. (Constru. Mgt.) Ph. D.
Assistant Professor,
NICMAR, PUNE CAMPUS
Formerly, S.T.E.S.'s, SKN – SITS
Kusgaon (Bk), Lonavala, PUNE.

Mrs. V.S. LIMAYE
M. Tech. (Civil), M.P.M.
Associate Professor,
Civil Engg. Deptt.
Sinhgad College of Engineering,
Vadgoan (Bk.), PUNE.

N3562

Architectural Planning & Design of Buildings (SE CIVIL)   ISBN 978-93-83750-90-0

First Edition	:	**January 2017**
©	:	**Authors**

Published By :
NIRALI PRAKASHAN
Abhyudaya Pragati, 1312, Shivaji Nagar,
Off J.M. Road, Pune – 411005
Tel - (020) 25512336/37/39, Fax - (020) 25511379
Email : niralipune@pragationline.com

☞ DISTRIBUTION CENTRES

PUNE

Nirali Prakashan	:	119, Budhwar Peth, Jogeshwari Mandir Lane, Pune 411002, Maharashtra Tel : (020) 2445 2044, 66022708, Fax : (020) 2445 1538 Email : bookorder@pragationline.com, niralilocal@pragationline.com
Nirali Prakashan	:	S. No. 28/27, Dhyari, Near Pari Company, Pune 411041 Tel : (020) 24690204 Fax : (020) 24690316 Email : dhyari@pragationline.com, bookorder@pragationline.com

MUMBAI

Nirali Prakashan	:	385, S.V.P. Road, Rasdhara Co-op. Hsg. Society Ltd., Girgaum, Mumbai 400004, Maharashtra Tel : (022) 2385 6339 / 2386 9976, Fax : (022) 2386 9976 Email : niralimumbai@pragationline.com

☞ DISTRIBUTION BRANCHES

JALGAON

Nirali Prakashan	:	34, V. V. Golani Market, Navi Peth, Jalgaon 425001, Maharashtra, Tel : (0257) 222 0395, Mob : 94234 91860

KOLHAPUR

Nirali Prakashan	:	New Mahadvar Road, Kedar Plaza, 1st Floor Opp. IDBI Bank Kolhapur 416 012, Maharashtra. Mob : 9850046155

NAGPUR

Pratibha Book Distributors	:	Above Maratha Mandir, Shop No. 3, First Floor, Rani Jhanshi Square, Sitabuldi, Nagpur 440012, Maharashtra Tel : (0712) 254 7129

DELHI

Nirali Prakashan	:	4593/21, Basement, Aggarwal Lane 15, Ansari Road, Daryaganj Near Times of India Building, New Delhi 110002 Mob : 08505972553

BENGALURU

Pragati Book House	:	House No. 1, Sanjeevappa Lane, Avenue Road Cross, Opp. Rice Church, Bengaluru – 560002. Tel : (080) 64513344, 64513355,Mob : 9880582331, 9845021552 Email:bharatsavla@yahoo.com

CHENNAI

Pragati Books	:	9/1, Montieth Road, Behind Taas Mahal, Egmore, Chennai 600008 Tamil Nadu, Tel : (044) 6518 3535, Mob : 94440 01782 / 98450 21552 / 98805 82331, Email : bharatsavla@yahoo.com

niralipune@pragationline.com | www.pragationline.com

Also find us on f www.facebook.com/niralibooks

Dedicated to…

" Our Beloved Parents"

…Authors

PREFACE

It gives us great pleasure in publishing this text book on "**Architectural Planning and Design of Buildings**" for the students of Second Year Degree Course in Civil Engineering. This book is strictly written according to **New Revised Credit System Syllabus** of Savitribai Phule Pune University (2015 Pattern).

As per the policy of the University, Engineering Syllabi is revised every five years. Last revision was in the year 2012. New revision is coming little earlier, as university has introduced **Online System of Examination** from year 2012.

As per the **New Credit System**, the **Online Examinations** Phase-I will be conducted based on First & Second Units and Phase II on Third & Fourth Units. The **Online** examinations will have objective types of questions with multiple choices. End Sem. Theory Examination will be based on all the six units and that will be conducted in traditional way and the Theory Course will have 4 credits.

Questions from previous papers of the University of Pune are included at the end of each chapter. It is our objective to keep the presentation systematic, consistent, intensive and clear presentation of concept through explanatory notes and figures. So we are sure that this book will cater for all your needs for this subject.

Main feature of this book is, **Complete Coverage** of the New Credit System Syllabus with large number of **Worked (Solved) Examples and Exercises.**

We have given Separate Book of Multiple Choice Questions (MCQ's) which will be very useful to the students especially for Online Examinations.

We take this opportunity to express our sincere thanks to Shri. Dineshbhai Furia, Shri. Jignesh Furia, Mrs. Nirali Verma and Shri. M. P. Munde and entire team of Nirali Prakashan namely Mrs. Deepali Lachake (Co-ordinator), who really have taken keen interest and untiring efforts in publishing this text.

The advice and suggestions of our esteemed readers to improve the text are most welcomed, and will be highly appreciated.

Vinayak Chaturthi

Pune   **Authors**

SYLLABUS

Unit I : Town Planning and Legal Aspects (08 Hrs)

(a) Town Planning : Necessity and evolution of town planning in India. Development plan and its importance, Objectives and Contents of DP, Land use zoning, Introduction to different zones of land in town planning, Requirements of various zones, Height zoning and Density zoning.

(b) Legal Aspects : Role of Plan sanctioning authority, 7/12 abstract, meaning of different terms of 7/12 abstract, Form 6 and its types, Concept of TDR, List of documents to be submitted to local authority, Procedure for seeking Commencement and Occupancy Certificate, Various NOCs required.

Unit II: Architectural Planning , Building bye laws and introduction to Green Buildings (08 Hrs)

(a) Principles of Architectural design relation between form and function, utility, aesthetics. Necessity of bye-laws, plot sizes, road width, open spaces, floor area ratio (F.A.R.), concept of V.P.R. Marginal distances, building line : control line, height regulations, room sizes, Area calculations (built-up area, carpet area etc.), Rules for ventilation, lighting, Vertical circulation, Sanitation and Parking of vehicles.

(b) Green Buildings: salient features, benefits, planning concepts (site selection, orientation, sun path and wind diagram etc.), Rating systems (LEED, GRIHA etc.)

Unit III: Architectural Drawing and Safety Aspects (08 Hrs)

(a) Introduction to Architectural drawing : i) Line plan, ii) Developed Plan, iii) Elevation, iv) Section, Selection of scales for various drawings, dimensioning, abbreviations and conventions as per IS 962, Elements of perspective drawings, parallel and angular perspective of small building elements.

(b) Safety Aspects: Fire load, grading of occupancies by fire loads, Evacuation Time, fire escape elements, Need for earthquake resistant structures, planning considerations, disaster management.

Unit IV: Building Services (08 Hrs)

(a) Noise and Acoustics – Sound insulation, Acoustical defects, Reverberation time, Sabine's formula, sound absorbents, planning for good acoustics.

(b) Ventilation – Necessity of Ventilation, Natural ventilation: stack effect and wind effect, Thermal Insulation, Mechanical ventilation and its types, air conditioning systems.

(c) Lighting – Principles of day lighting, design of windows, artificial illumination, SC, ERC, IRC, Daylight factor, Solar energy systems for lighting (BIPV).

(d) Plumbing – Water storage tanks at ground level and on terrace (capacity), Plumbing systems, various types of traps, Fixtures and Fittings, Rain Water Harvesting etc.

(e) Other services – Telecommunication, Electrical, Smart services and Waste management etc.

Unit V: Planning of Residential Buildings (08 Hrs)

(a) Functional requirements of Bungalows, Twin bungalows, Row houses, Ownership flats, and Apartments.

(b) Developed Plan, Elevation and Sectional Elevation of above mentioned categories.

Unit VI: Planning of Public Buildings (08 Hrs)

(a) Functional requirements and planning of industrial buildings, commercial buildings, School, Colleges , Hostel, Auditorium, Restaurant/ Hotel building, Primary Health Center/ Hospital, Shopping complex, Sports complex, Vegetable market, Post office, Bank buildings etc .

(b) Dimensioned line plans of above public buildings.

CONTENTS

Unit I : Town Planning and Legal Aspects

Chapter 1 : Town Planning — 1.1-1.12

1.1	History, Necessity and Evolution of Town Planning in India	1.1
	1.1.1 Necessity of Towns	1.2
1.2	Importance of Safety, Services and Amenities	1.2
	1.2.1 Safety	1.2
	1.2.2 Services and Amenities	1.3
1.3	Development Plan (DP) and its Importance with Reference to Living, working and leisure	1.5
	1.3.1 Living – Working – Leisure	1.7
1.4	Land Use Zoning	1.8
	1.4.1 Objects of Zoning	1.8
	1.4.2 Advantages of Zoning	1.9
	1.4.3 Aspects or Ways of Zoning	1.9
	• Questions	1.12
	• University Questions	1.12

Chapter 2 : Legal Aspects — 2.1-2.50

2.1	Township and Role of Plan Sanctioning Authority	2.1
	2.1.1 Procedure for Township Project Approval by Plan Sanctioning Authority	2.3
2.2	Formation of Co-operative Society	2.6
2.3	Formation of Apartment of Ownership	2.10
2.4	7/12 abstract	2.11
2.5	6-D Form	2.17
2.6	List of Documents	2.21
2.7	TDR	2.30
	2.7.1 What is TDR?	2.31
	2.7.2 Why Reservation of Land is Necessary?	2.31
	2.7.3 Who is Eligible?	2.31
2.8	Commencement Certificate	2.35
2.9	MSEB	2.39
2.10	NOC for Roads, National and State Highways	2.40
	• Questions	2.50
	• University Questions	2.50

Unit II : Architectural Planning, Building Bye Laws and Introduction to Green Buildings	
Chapter 3 : Architectural Planning and Building Bye-Law	**3.1-3.28**
3.1 Principles of Architectural Planning and Design	3.1
3.1.1 Planning for Utility	3.5
3.1.2 Planning for Aesthetics	3.7
3.2 Necessity of Bye-Laws	3.8
3.2.1 Basic Definitions	3.9
3.3 Development Control Rules for Plan Preparation	3.11
3.3.1 Plot Size	3.11
3.3.2 Means of Access	3.12
3.3.3 Open Spaces	3.13
3.3.4 Floor Area Ratio (F.A.R.)	3.14
3.3.5 Marginal Distances	3.16
3.3.6 Height of Building	3.19
3.3.7 Provisions Regarding Room Sizes	3.20
3.3.8 Lighting and Ventilation of Room	3.21
3.3.9 Drainage and Sanitation	3.22
3.3.10 Parking	3.23
3.4 Building Line and Control Line	3.25
• Questions	3.27
• University Questions	3.28
Chapter 4 : Introduction to Green Buildings	**4.1-4.28**
4.1 Introduction of Green Buildings	4.1
4.1.1 Planning Concepts of Green Buildings or Eco-housing	4.1
4.1.2 Salient Features of a Green Building	4.7
4.1.3 Site Integration	4.9
4.1.4 Benefits of Green Buildings	4.9
4.1.5 Environmentally Friendly, Non-Toxic Paint	4.17
4.1.6 Green Roofing	4.19
4.1.7 Use of Insulating Materials	4.22
4.2 Cost Effective Housing	4.25
• Questions	4.28
• University Questions	4.28

Unit III : Architectural Drawing and Safety Aspects

Chapter 5 : Introduction to Architectural Drawing 5.1-5.58

(A) BUILDING DRAWING

5.1	Introduction	5.1
5.2	Types of Drawings	5.1
5.3	Use of I.S. Specifications	5.2
5.4	Graphical Symbols	5.4
5.5	Scales	5.8
5.6	Title Block	5.8
5.7	Line – Plan	5.10
5.8	Development of Line – Plan	5.11
5.9	Plan	5.12
5.10	Elevation	5.13
5.11	Sections	5.13
5.12	Schedule of Doors and Windows	5.18
5.13	Area Statement	5.20
5.14	Abstract From I.S. - 962 – 1967	5.22
	5.14.1 Size of Drawing Sheets	5.22
	5.14.2 Size of Drawing Boards	5.23
	5.14.3 Margins	5.23
	5.14.4 Title Block	5.23
	5.14.5 Numbering of Drawing Sheet	5.24
	5.14.6 Reproduction of Drawings	5.24
	5.14.7 Folding of Prints	5.24
	5.14.8 Reinforced Concrete Work	5.26
	5.14.9 Colouring the Plan	5.26
5.15	Detailed Drawings	5.27
5.16	Methods of Preparing detailed Drawings	5.28
	5.16.1 Drawing Foundation Plan	5.28
5.17	Roof Plan and Terrace Floor Plan	5.29
	5.17.1 Roof Plan for Pitched Roof	5.30
	5.17.2 Roof Plan for Flat Roof	5.31
5.18	Site Plan	5.31
5.19	Other Details	5.34

(B) PERSPECTIVE DRAWING

5.20	Introduction	5.34
5.21	Important Terms in Perspective Drawings	5.35
5.22	Principles of Perspective	5.36

5.23 Types of Perspective ... 5.39

    5.23.1 Based on Position of Object with Respect to Picture Plane ... 5.39

    5.23.2 Based on Number of Vanishing Points ... 5.40

    5.23.3 Shades and Shadows in Perspective Drawings ... 5.41

5.24 Method Of Drawing One Point Perspective ... 5.41

5.25 Method of Drawing Two Point Perspective ... 5.42

• Questions ... 5.51

• University Questions ... 5.58

Chapter 6 : SAFETY ASPECTS ... **6.1-6.34**

6.1 Introduction ... 6.1

    6.1.1 Fire Safety ... 6.2

6.2 Classification of Buildings Based on Occupancy ... 6.2

6.3 Fire Load ... 6.3

6.4 Factors Affecting Fire Development ... 6.5

6.5 Pattern of Fire ... 6.5

6.6 Fire Severity ... 6.6

6.7 Fire Resistance ... 6.6

6.8 Some Common Construction Materials ... 6.9

6.9 Fire Resistant Construction ... 6.9

6.10 Means of Escape ... 6.18

6.11 Fire Detecting Systems ... 6.21

6.12 Fire Extinguishing Systems ... 6.21

6.13 Introduction to Earthquake Resistant Structures ... 6.21

6.14 Earthquake Loads ... 6.22

    6.14.1 Roofs are a Major Load ... 6.22

    6.14.2 Walls are a Major Load ... 6.22

6.15 Other Loads to Consider Include Building Contents, Especially Where The Building is used for Storage, Machinery and Water Tanks ... 6.22

6.16 Resisting Earthquake Loads ... 6.23

6.17 Specific Activities Associated with Earthquake Emergency Response ... 6.23

6.18 Earthquake Resistant Structures and Techniques ... 6.25

    6.18.1 Shear Walls ... 6.25

    6.18.2 Purpose of Constructing Shear Walls ... 6.25

    6.18.3 RC Shear Wall ... 6.26

    6.18.4 Plywood Shear Wall ... 6.27

6.19 RC Hollow Concrete Block Masonry Walls ... 6.27

6.20 Steel Plate Shear Wall ... 6.28

6.21 Moment Resistant Frames ... 6.28

6.22	Advanced Earthquake Resistant Design Techniques	6.29
	6.22.1 Seismic Dampers	6.30
	6.22.2 New Breed of Energy Dissipation Devices	6.31
•	Questions	6.33
•	University Questions	6.34

Unit IV : Building Services

Chapter 7 : Noise and Acoustics   7.1-7.46

7.1	Introduction	7.1
7.2	Effect of noise	7.1
7.3	Comfort Standards	7.1
7.4	Properties of Sound	7.2
7.5	Measurement of Sound	7.3
7.6	Behaviour of Sound in Enclosures	7.5
7.7	Reflection of Sound	7.5
7.8	Noise Classification	7.6
7.9	Sound Insulation	7.7
7.10	Noise Control	7.7
7.11	Requirements and Conditions of Good Acoustics	7.13
7.12	Sound Absorption	7.14
7.13	Sound Absorbents or Acoustical Materials	7.14
7.14	Classification of Sound Absorbents or Acoustical Materials	7.17
7.15	Requirements of a Good Acoustic Material	7.18
7.16	Acoustical Defects	7.18
7.17	General Principles and Factors in Acoustical Design	7.22
7.18	Acoustics for Various Types of Buildings	7.23
7.19	Sound Level Measurements	7.28
7.20	Constructional Requirements for Different Building Services	7.33
	7.20.1 Electrical Services	7.34
	7.20.2 Switch Room	7.35
	7.20.3 Energy Meters	7.35
	7.20.4 Layout and Installation of Wiring	7.35
	7.20.5 Telecommunication Services	7.36
	7.20.6 Entertainment Services	7.37
	7.20.7 Air Handling, Conditioning and Air Heating	7.37
	7.20.8 Vertical Circulation: Lifts and Escalators	7.38
•	Questions	7.44
•	University Questions	7.46

Chapter 8 : Ventilation   **8.1-8.22**

8.1   Introduction   8.1

8.2   Comfort Factors for Ventilation   8.2

8.3   Systems of Ventilation   8.5

8.4   Air conditioning   8.11

8.5   Comfort Air conditioning   8.11

8.6   The Cooling Load   8.15

8.7   Components of Air Conditioning System   8.17

8.8   Air Distribution System   8.20

8.9   Systems of Air Conditioning   8.21

•   Questions   8.22

•   University Questions   8.22

Chapter 9 : Lighting   **9.1-9.20**

9.1   Introduction   9.1

9.2   Principles of Good Lighting   9.2

9.3   Illumination Levels Recommended by the National Building Code of India,
      For Various Types of Visual Tasks   9.2

9.4   Daylighting   9.4

      9.4.1   Designing for Daylight   9.5

      9.4.2   Daylight Factor   9.7

      9.4.3   Components of Daylight Factor   9.7

      9.4.4   General Principles of Design of Windows for Good Lighting   9.10

9.5   Orientation of Buildings with Respect to Lighting   9.12

9.6   Artificial Illumination   9.12

      9.6.1   Necessity of Artificial Lighting   9.12

      9.6.2   Types of Artificial Lighting   9.13

      9.6.3   Design Considerations for Artificial Lighting of Interiors   9.13

9.7   Solar Water Heating System   9.15

•   Questions   9.20

Chapter 10 : Plumbing   **10.1-10.24**

10.1 Introduction   10.1

10.2 Water Supply Requirements for Buildings   10.1

10.3 Storage of Water   10.2

10.4 Layout of Water Supply and Drainage System   10.4

10.5 Plumbing System for Waste Water   10.5

10.6 Rain Water Harvesting   10.16

•   Questions   10.24

Unit V : Planning of Residential Buildings

Chapter 11 : Planning of Residential Buildings — **11.1-11.42**

11.1	Planning of Residential Buildings	11.1
11.2	Site Selection	11.2
11.3	Types of Structure	11.2
11.3.1	Comparison Between Different Types of Structures	11.3
11.4	Arrangement of Rooms for Residential Buildings	11.4
11.5	Size of Rooms for Residential Buildings	11.8
11.6	Planning of a Residential Complex	11.9
•	Important Points	11.12
•	Questions	11.12
•	University Questions	11.39

Unit VI : Planning of Public Buildings

Chapter 12 : Planning of Public Buildings — **12.1-12.40**

12.1	Planning of Public Buildings	12.1
12.2	Types of Buildings	12.1
12.3	Group B: Educational Buildings	12.2
12.4	Group C: Institutional Buildings	12.7
12.5	Group D: Assembly Buildings	12.10
12.6	Group E: Business Buildings	12.13
12.7	Group F: Merchandise Buildings	12.16
12.8	Industrial Buildings	12.18
12.8.1	Data Required for Steel Fabrication Shop	12.24
12.8.2	Data Required for Vehicle Service Centre	12.25
12.8.3	Data Required for P.V.C. Pipe Unit	12.26
12.8.4	Prestressed Concrete Pole Factory	12.27
12.9	General Buildings	12.29
12.10	General Guidelines and Some Common Units which are Needed in Public Buildings	12.34
•	Questions	12.36
•	University Questions	12.38
•	**Sample Question Paper for End. Sem. Theory Exam.**	**P.1 – P.2**

Chapter 1
TOWN PLANNING

1.1 HISTORY, NECESSITY AND EVOLUTION OF TOWN PLANNING IN INDIA

A town is a settlement ranging from a few hundred to several thousand (occasionally hundreds of thousands) inhabitants, although it may be applied loosely even to huge metropolitan areas; the precise meaning varies between countries and is not always a matter of legal definition. Usually, a "town" is thought of as larger than a village but smaller than a "city", though there are exceptions to this rule.

The ancient remains of the towns in India dates back to 3000 B.C. Urban civilizations arose on the banks of rivers e.g. in India, in the Indus valley, Euphretes and Tigris in Asia and the Nile in Africa etc. India has an ancient history of refined urban planning which could have been popularized and been more effective than Chandigarh in terms of providing a more identifiable set of concepts and practices for its urban citizens e.g. Udaipur in Rajasthan, Fatehpur Sikri, Hampi, Vijayanagar and of course the ancient Harrappan townships come to mind.

In general, today towns can be differentiated from townships, villages, or hamlets on the basis of their economic character, in that most of a town's population will tend to derive their living from manufacturing industry, commerce, and public service rather than primary industry such as agriculture or related activities. Today some consider an urban place of fewer than 100,000 as a town, even though there are many officially designated cities that are very much smaller than that. Development Control Rules under a Development Plan and provisions in the National Building Code of India are controlling the structure of the town and its growth.

Classification of Urban Centers: UDPFI GUIDELINES (1991)

Classification	Plain areas Population range (in 000)	Nos.	Hilly areas Population range (in 000)	Nos.	Local authority as per 74th CAA
Small towns	Less than 50,000	2820	Less than 20,000	134	Municipal Council
Medium towns	50,000 – 5,00,000	560	20,000 – 80,000	20	Municipal Council
Large city	>5,00,000	89	≥ 80,000	5	Municipal Corporation

1.1.1 Necessity of Towns

Any human settlement behaves as a living organism and hence it depicts "**origin, growth and decay**". Sir Patrick Geddes emphasized upon organic character of the town and suggested integration of "Folk, Work and Place". The success of planning the area is judged by the appreciation by all sectors of public. The success also lies in the sustenance of the area. The rapid race of industrial development and rising aspirations lead to urbanization trends. On the other hand, modernizing rural India was also not such a straightforward thing. It meant a transformation of agricultural practices that have not only depleted natural resources such as water and quality of soil, but also have displaced people in a massive way, often pushing them into cities to continue living in wretched situations.

Following are the main objects or ideals of planning the area viz beauty, convenience, environment, health etc. Beauty can be derived by systematic arrangement of natural and manmade entities to facilitate many functions in day to day life. Basically, it involves distribution of land for various purposes (zoning). Then finalizing different layouts, preserving natural character and providing supportive manmade structures are the different tasks.

Planning the streets and spaces around building, preservation of soft landscape, architectural control on all sorts of structures are the main considerations for beautification of an area.

Convenience on the other hand, can be judged by the amenities provided to the people may be "Economic, Social, Recreational etc." in the form of cheap electric supply, job opportunities, proper locations of industries, facilities to commercial areas, transport facilities, adequate water supply, easy disposal of wastes, parks, playgrounds, cinema halls, shopping centers etc.

Environment affects all the activities of the residents. Any settlement represents a big psychological globe for the occupants. Providing an environment which will produce cumulative positive effect considering physical, social, perceptional, economical, cultural needs of people is a difficult task in front of planners. Proper synthesis of natural and manmade environment is essentially to be carried out to fulfill it.

The main objective of health is to use the land for right purpose for betterment of the society. This can be achieved by division of land in various zones and avoiding the encroachment.

The other aspects to be considered in detail are as follows:

1.2 IMPORTANCE OF SAFETY, SERVICES AND AMENITIES

1.2.1 Safety

In India, the North has been invaded number of times and the areas are reconstructed many a times but the Southern towns have maintained the town planning intact. In the past, fortified towns were very popular for safety but now-a-days a defense town is specially established. A military town has to serve different functions than civil town hence it is to be planned to suit the changed activities such as training requirement, ammunition etc. It differs from civil town in following aspects e.g. population density (lower), employment, function, housing, social groups, living status (individual), work places. The administration of this military town is under Cantonment Service.

Many activities are being organized in towns. For smooth and safe operations of these; special care taking supports / bodies are needed. Safety aspect for the following few cases is of utmost importance.

(a) Accidents: We all are rushing to our work places from our residence. Hence, we must be ensured about, safe to and fro journey. Along all types of transportation routes many accidents are taking place daily. For this special check-posts with medical facility, police squad, mobile vans are to be provided, the information of which is to be displayed at suitable places. Regular checking and maintenance of the routes is required which will help in reducing the total count of accidents. Also, public awareness to obey traffic rules may serve the purpose.

(b) Safe Drinking Water Supply: To avoid health hazards it is essential to provide pure water supply to the citizens confirming the standards laid by WHO.

(c) Waste Water Treatments/Sanitation Facilities: Kitchen and toilet waste must be treated and the effluent with necessary care is to be disposed off. Also, the waste from industries and agricultural area is to be treated first. Reuse and recycling will reduce the pressures on pure water supply.

(d) Theft: Today's family size has been reduced with both partners working. Hence, most of the time the houses are locked. In this regard "Intelligent Homes with special security services" will prove to be beneficial.

(e) Disaster Management Cell: During any natural hazard people are to be safeguarded for which establishment of this cell is most important. The supporting hands or teams for this are doctors, police, NGOs, food-water suppliers, volunteers etc.

(f) Safety at Important Places: All of us are aware of the facts about the attacks on Taj Hotel Mumbai, World Trade Center, America etc. As such places are famous worldwide, adequate precautionary measures are to be taken to safeguard such important features. Also, some of the dilapidated structures of historical importance are to be strengthened so as to add grandeur and beauty to the area. Constant checking, closed TVs etc. may be some of the ways to safeguard the places.

Likewise, many other aspects are to be taken care by; like child labour, woman harassment etc., but the proven fact remains with us is that this is not the question which is only to be solved by Government but self attitude towards this will play an important role.

1.2.2 Services and Amenities

1. Services

In our cities, basic services, such as clean drinking water, proper sanitation, roads and other public services, are in decrepit condition. Absence of quality public transport, traffic problems, land grabbing, settlements, illegal constructions, theft, and kidnappings have ruined city life. However, it is essential to take care of the residents by providing daily services confirming with the minimum requirements mentioned in UDPFI guidelines.

The growth of town is based on the cater; that the Government is providing for the area and the occupants therein.

Now-a-days to attract the residents to individual's project for purchase of land or houses many ultra-modern amenities like convenient shopping centers, club, steam and sauna, gymnasium leisure facilities at their best are provided. Also with modern amenities like a school, convenient shopping centre and 100% power back up are provided within a big project. Some special services like waste collection and disposal, vermiculture and gas supply through pipe lines, energy saving techniques etc. are also responsible for attracting the people towards typical project.

For smooth working of the areas Town Planning Department and Municipal Councils/Corporations should work for the betterment of the area. Following sketches depict the hierarchy in the department with required engineering support.

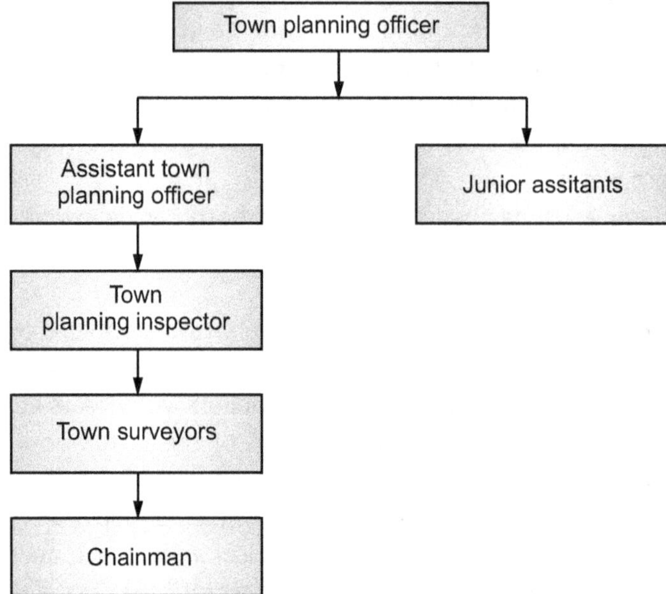

Fig. 1.1

Hierarchy of planners where junior assistants are involved in collection, analysis and synthesis of the data.

2. Amenities

"Amenity" means roads, streets, open spaces, parks, recreational grounds, play grounds, sports complex, parade grounds, gardens, markets, parking lots, primary and secondary schools and colleges and polytechnics, clinics, dispensaries and hospitals, water supply, electricity supply, street lighting, sewerage, drainage, public works and includes other utilities services and conveniences.

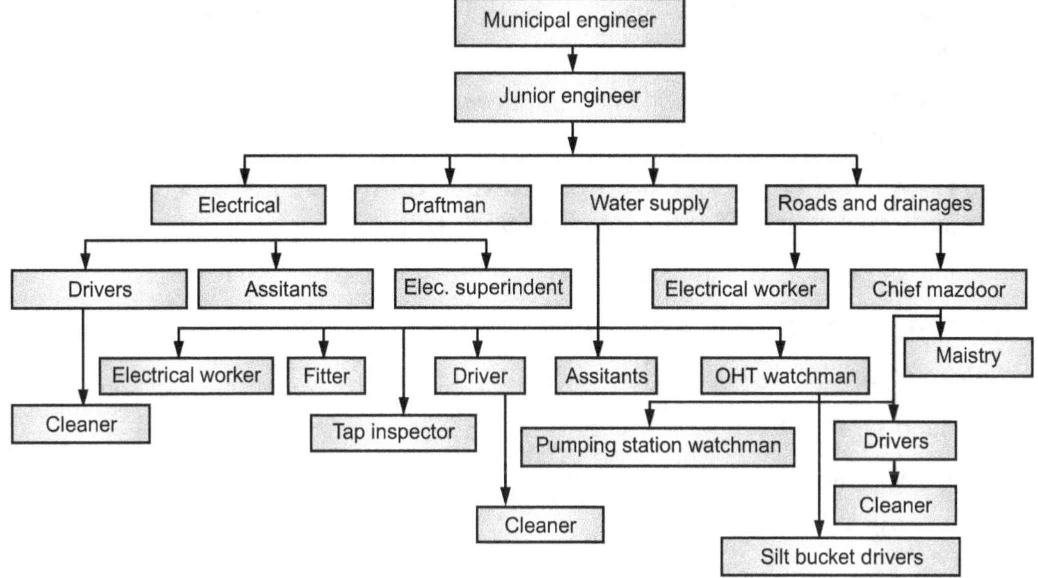

Fig. 1.2

Engineering Support: City Engineer / Municipal Engineer is the head of the tree and a special position of Development Engineer (Junior Engineer category) is responsible for implementation process.

1.3 DEVELOPMENT PLAN (DP) AND ITS IMPORTANCE WITH REFERENCE TO LIVING, WORKING AND LEISURE

The word, "development" has been defined in Planning Acts as carrying out of any building, engineering, mining or other operations or over or under the land or making up any material change in its use or in the use of any building standing on it.

It can be defined as a plan for the development or redevelopment of the city. It aims at comprehensive development of an area.

Objectives of DP

- Serving as a policy framework to fulfill the needs and aspirations of the community.

- Promoting larger interest of society.

- Bringing effective co-ordination between physical, socio-economic, cultural and political forces that are responsible for formulating the structure of the society and the technical means to regulate it.

- Formulating long range and short range programs with a common developmental thread in them.

- Creating a total environment which is functional, efficient, healthful and aesthetically satisfying the needs of human activities.

- To provide a framework for planned investment and phasing and programming of implementation process.
- In general, DP will help in providing the following aspects to life which may be seen after effective implementation of D.P.

Parameters of Quality of Life in Urban Dwellings (which may be expected after effective implementation of various proposals of DP)

- Safety (against accidents, thefts, social and fiscal crimes)
- Means of livelihood for every citizen
- Housing facilities for all
- Pollution free atmosphere
- Water supply – Minimum needed with assured good quality
- Sanitation – sewage disposal
- Storm water drainage
- Toilet facilities for everybody and facilities of clean public toilets
- Solid waste disposal
- Well surfaced roads with walkways free of encroachment
- Adequate and evenly located parks and gardens
- Market facilities at nearby locations (especially for commodities of day to day needs)
- Medical facilities (Hospitals, pharmacies)
- Education facilities from primary to college
- Good public and private transportation facilities intra city and inter cities
- Entertainment centres, cultural convention centres, public libraries
- Sport grounds for youngsters
- Recreation sports in and near the cities
- Adequate parking areas
- Well controlled traffic arrangement
- Reduction of disparity (disparity results in crime)
- Harmonious atmosphere within the religions and healthy social atmosphere
- Clean and healthy eateries (affordable to all categories of people)
- Good hotels for stay of outsiders (affordable to variety of categories)
- Uninterrupted energy supply (electricity, gas, petrol / diesel etc.)

- Policy and provisions at various locations for extra care of senior citizens and disabled.
- Quick response from police and medical centres in case of emergency
- Disaster management plan and preparedness.

The Act that support and implement DP is Maharashtra Regional Town Planning Act, 1966. The period for which projections are to be considered is of twenty years and the Master or Development Plan for the said duration is prepared.

General Stages Involved in Preparation of DP:

- Declaration of intention to prepare a plan.
- Consultation and eliciting public suggestions for planning purpose.
- Carrying out surveys (natural, land use, population characteristic, economy, traffic and transportation, housing, utility, community facilities etc.) and identifying the issues associated with an area.
- Draft proposal preparation and discussion with authority.
- Hearing the suggestions.
- Finalizing the proposals (with republication in case of major changes).
- Submission to sanctioning authority.
- Scrutiny and approval.
- Implementation process.
- Periodical evaluation monitoring and review.

Necessity of DP:

- To control haphazard development and make the area sustainable.
- To control the development of industrial cluster.
- To curb the migration of rural population indirectly.
- To cut down the problems arising from overcrowding of the area such as shortage of houses, water supply, traffic congestion, inadequacy of open spaces, insufficient public amenities etc.
- To develop the linkage between regional plan and other short term action plans.

1.3.1 Living – Working – Leisure

In simple way, a building can be very well described as an enclosure which is suitable for a human being to move in. Architectural composition for a building conveys the expression of the building through the visual impact.

Every building in its own has some peculiar character associated with it. Character grows out of the function of the building. This functional character is better understood or appreciated when form of the building follows function. An integrated approach or rationalization of functional character and personal character is the essence of the design. The sole of the building is in the genuineness of the design. It is different for different buildings and as such every building is unique in it's design. Man has to utilize the building for different purposes with broad categories as Living – Working – Leisure. Hence, the design is finalized; based on these and the proportion and disposition of the human figure.

Living: For all buildings where the main character is stay of persons, for certain specific duration is expected; more emphasis is given on horizontal and vertical lines indicating tranquility, peace. This is practically to be considered while planning and designing residential buildings, hospitals, hotels etc. Calmness is achieved by more horizontal lines. Also, the elevational treatment given indicates warmth (e.g. old residential buildings, Taj hotel etc.).

Working: The utility of such buildings is on hourly basis and hence proportionately power and dynamism is expressed through the external appearance of the building.
(e.g. corporation buildings, corporate office buildings).

Leisure: Sometimes peace, sometimes enjoyment, sometimes essence are the objectives of such type of structures hence the design has to reflect all such characters (e.g. theaters, gymnasiums etc.)

1.4 LAND USE ZONING

In broader terms, the utility of the land can be sensed in two ways;
1. Profit making
2. Non-profit making.

In the first category, belongs all the sites developed for residences, offices, industries etc. whereas in second belongs to the land which is developed for non-profit making purposes such as roads, parks, playgrounds, educational buildings, government offices etc.

The zoning is defined as the regulation by law of the use of the land and (or) buildings and of the height and density of buildings in specific areas for the purpose of securing convenience, health, safety and welfare of the community.

1.4.1 Objects of Zoning

(a) **Futuristic Planning and Development:** By considering the projected population and needs of the same as well considering the aspirations of the residents in a particular area one may utilize the land skillfully.

(b) **Co-ordinating Different Public Amenities such as Transport, Water Supply, Drainage, Power etc.:** Once the existing facts are analyzed and futuristic projections for various developmental parameters are analyzed then a rational solution for the problems can be given which is based on legal provisions of planning and plan enforcement.

(c) Effective, Sustained, Balanced Growth of an Area: Economic backing for the development is provided by the Government, or special planning authorities or otherwise. But achieving self sufficiency for the proposed development is an important aspect of zoning. For which a detailed survey, synthesis, analysis and solution are the important steps involved.

1.4.2 Advantages of Zoning

- Minimum damage due to fire, natural calamities, disasters etc.
- Controlled future development.
- Public amenities with proper surroundings; thus giving cost effective and space effective growth pattern.
- Improved Community Health (no overlap for the zones).
- Population density regulation.
- Economic upgradation of an area.

1.4.3 Aspects or Ways of Zoning

(a) Density Zoning

There is no direct control or restrain on the number of occupants in a particular area. But there are some indirect means of control. These are:

- Specifying marginal distances.
- Restricting the height of the building.
- Specifying minimum size of allotment for each house.
- Limiting number of houses per unit area.
- Specifying ratio of total site area to the total built up area (concept of FAR).

(b) Height Zoning

The essence of the height restriction is based on the climatic factors, type of the building, zone type (utility wise).

Its advantages can be summarized as:

- Control on Central Busy Area activities.
- Pleasant look for a particular lane or an important street if uniform height is used on the same.
- Avoids dominance of tall buildings for getting the light-ventilation advantage at the cost of adjacent less heighted buildings.
- Control on land value.

(c) Land Use Zoning

It clearly indicate the uses to which the area is associated. The major categories are:

- **Residential (40-50%):** This is the largest occupied area of the town. The main objective of this zone is to provide the residents peaceful, healthy and hygienic surrounding. Hence, its location is on upstream of industrial area on windward side.

The other important aspects for location are: nearness to market place, parks, playgrounds and away from noise, smoke, nuisance.

Various types of buildings are planned here depending upon the class of the mass.

- **Commercial (2-5%):** The main objective of this zone is to provide various services/facilities to nearby residential area, such as banking, shopping, offices, godowns etc. Hence, its location is preferably near the traffic centers abutting the roads.

- **Industrial (2-25%):** Light industries and factories using electric power and the minor industries such as bakery, dairy etc. may be allowed in vicinity of residential area but those producing undesirable waste and pollutants are to be placed away from residential zone but near to the available transportation routes.

- **Institutional / Public-Semipublic (15 – 20%):** Schools, colleges main government offices do fall under this category.

- **Transportation:** This is an important area as it is responsible for the growth of the town at the same time is responsible for serve the daily needs of the residents. Traffic management in itself a big topic to deal with. The main objectives are smooth and easy flow of the traffic, provision of safe, convenient, rapid and economic transport facility for men and material, to increase the overall carrying capacity, to reduce the delays etc.

- **Recreational (Remaining %):** All recreational facilities like parks, playgrounds, cinema theaters, town halls, restaurants, library stadium etc. fall under this category. These units are normally scattered throughout the town instead of clubbing them together.

(d) Other Ways of Defining Zones

- **Vacant:** Within this area partial built up but unoccupied areas are seen. Mostly situated on outskirts of the development.

- **Open Spaces:** Under this category many recreational areas lie; such as sport grounds, play grounds, parks etc. In case of neighbourhood plan minimum required area is 10%.

- **Agricultural Land:** This zone is basically related with land producing food in direct or indirect way. Thus, actual area under agriculture and all the other related areas such as forest land, marshy land, barren land, nurseries etc. fall under this category. The basic requirement of this zone is water supply, irrigation facilities, transport route and nearness to market.

- **Green Belt:** A belt purposefully provided on the periphery of a town to limit its growth. The purposes served by this belt are provision of parks and play grounds, picnic spots, recreation grounds, poultry farm or nursery, it assists in shaping up of town, fruits and vegetables can be cultivated in this area etc. In such areas, no specific construction work is permitted except few like gymkhana, swimming pools etc.

- **Public Utilities:** Basically, this component of the zoning is representing the physical structure of the towns as many services are to be suitably located and designed. The main aim is to achieve maximum efficiency. The public services are of following categories; water supply, sewerage, refuse disposal, storm water drainage, public transport, electricity, fire stations, hospitals, health centers, gas, educational institutions, parks and play grounds, telephones etc.

- **Informal Sector in a Town:** Many parameters may be called as parasites of a developed town like slum and squatter areas or haphazardly grown areas because of Gunthewari fall under this category.

- **Special Economic Zone (SEZ):** A zone which is representing a geographical region that has economic laws that are more liberal than country's typical economic laws. SEZ allows the Government to experiment with radical (in Indian context) economic reform in a sufficiently large geographical area (minimum size 1000 ha) but on localized basis without the difficulty of introducing such reforms at the national level.

Broad Objectives of SEZ:

Earning foreign exchange and contribute to exchange rate stability, boosting the export sector, job creation with raised standard of living, skill introduction to local human resource, introduction of new technology, development of backward regions etc.

Colour Code for Zoning Demarcations:

Sr. No.	Category	Description	Colour code
1.	Residential	Plots used to build structures for residence like houses, hostels, dharmashala etc.	Yellow
2.	Commercial	Offices, banks, Government buildings, storage houses, nursing homes, theatres etc.	Dark blue
3.	Industrial	Service industries, light industries, heavy industries.	Violet/ pink
4.	Open spaces	Sport grounds, play grounds, parks etc.	Light green
5.	Agricultural	Actual area + nurseries, marshy land etc.	Dark green
6.	Transportation	Communication routes of all categories + allied areas and telephone	Grey
7.	Utility and services	Water supply + treatment plant, drainage/sanitary facilities, electric power	Brown
8.	Water body	Lake, river etc.	Blue
9.	Public – semi public	Institutes, religious centers etc.	Red clubs

IMPORTANT POINTS

- Town planning concepts.
- Necessity of Town Planning.
- Development Plan
- Land use Zoning.
- Types of Land use Zoning.
- Objectives of Land use Zoning.

QUESTIONS

1. Write a short note on evolution and necessity of towns.
2. State and explain the aspects to be considered while planning the towns such as beauty, safety etc.
3. Write a short note on services and amenities in the town.
4. Explain the hierarchy of Planners and Engineers in the development of town.
5. Explain the activities living, working and leisure in detail and mention different types of buildings and use of the same for the said purpose.
6. Write a short note on land use zoning and mention the requirements of each of them.
7. State different objectives of D.P. and parameters of quality of urban life.
8. Explain procedure for preparation of D.P.
9. Explain the need of townships.
10. Explain the role of Plan Sanctioning Authority for townships.

UNIVERSITY QUESTIONS

Dec. 2014

1. Elaborate the term land use zoning and mention the requirements of each of them. (Minimum 4 zones).
2. Write a short note on land use zoning and mention the requirements of each of them.

May 2015

1. Write a short note on land use zoning and mention the requirements of each of them.

Dec. 2015

1. What is the importance of safety, amenities and services for town planning?

Nov. 2016

1. What is Development Plan? State its importance.

Chapter 2
LEGAL ASPECTS

2.1 TOWNSHIP AND ROLE OF PLAN SANCTIONING AUTHORITY

A new concept in the field of planning, which is responsible for the development of an area around an urban centre. Maharashtra Government has passed the resolution in the year 2004 for the said purpose.

Concept paper on this aspect was widely accepted in International Infrastructure summit in 2002, which was organized by Government of Maharashtra in collaboration with Maharashtra Economic Development Council.

There is a dire need to promote private investment in housing sector to facilitate housing at reasonable price and also to create hassleless environment for the residents. This need arises from the fact that 50% (or even more) of population of India is forecasted to be living in urban areas by 2041. Hence, a step towards fulfillment of this demand is essentially to promote integrated townships.

Policy Decision for Promotion of Townships:

- Physical and social infrastructure to be borne by private developers.

- 100% direct foreign investment for development.

  In November 2005, S.T. Policy was announced for Pune District and in 2006-07, township policies for whole states are in place including corporation and councils.

- **Applicability:** Gist of policy – general Applicable in Local bodies and area under it and in R.P. area in Residential as well as in agricultural zone.

- **Area Requirement:** The minimum land required shall not be less than 100 acres (i.e. 40 ha) which is unbroken, uninterrupted with access road of width 18 m.

- **Declaration:** The area declaration is through MRTP Act, 1966. If it is under R.P, then section 18(3) is to be followed whereas if area development is under DP then section 44(2) is followed.

For Infrastructure Facilities

All the infrastructure facilities are to be provided and maintained by the developer of the area. e.g. 140 lit/cap/day of water supply, inside road planning development and maintenance.

Drainage and Garbage Disposal

The least possible D and G is to be pass on to municipal corporation for which reuse, recycle eco-friendly techniques are to be implemented.

Power: Developer himself shall ensure about continuous and quality power supply. Back up generators for supply may also be employed for the said purpose.

Environment: Without major changes for topographical features and hampering ecological systems environment is to be protected. All the land is to be put for different land uses namely:

General Norms

- **Residential use of Land:** Total use is of 60%, 10% of which are of 40 sq.m. tenements.

- **Commercial:** Proper distribution within the area is essential as it caters for the adjoining urban areas.

- **Educational Area:** Within the area, considering pattern of projected primary to secondary education facilities are to be provided (preferable at walkable distances).

- **Public Utilities:** Utilities play an important role in common man's life and these are to be located suitably to serve the residents considering aspirations and need. e.g. Electric power substations, bus stations, fire brigade, sewage and garbage disposal etc.

- **Transport and Communication:** The main access to area shall be minimum 18 m wide and the road work within the area should satisfy prevailing bye-laws with minimum width of 9 m.

- **Service** Industries**:** Suitable locations offers other than residential area without environmental pollution impact.

- **Amenity** Space**:** 5% of total area, which is to be evenly distributed and within which markets, essential shopping, townhall, libraries etc. are to be suitably placed.

- **Health** Facilities**:** Main objective is to provide P.H.C. within the area, but one way go for hospital location if projected population is more.

- **Parks,** Gardens **and Playgrounds:** Minimum 20%, exclusive of open space layouts.

Development Control Regulations

(A) If Township is Developed within:

- Residential Zone:

    FSI of 1.0 of gross is provided in RP and corporation areas.

- Agriculture – No development Zone:

    RP – 0.5 with 50% open area.

Additional 0.5 may be allowed with premium of ₹ 500/sq. ft. or by referring ready reckoner of the area, whichever is more.

- Corporation - FSI – 0.2, additional 0.80 ………. (same as above)

(B) Planting the Trees:

- Residential zone - 150 trees/hectare to be planted and maintained.
- No development zone – 400 trees/hectare.

(C) D.C. Rules:

For the areas, regional plan rules and local body regulations are applicable.

2.1.1 Procedure for Township Project Approval by Plan Sanctioning Authority

1. Locational Clearance by the Government.
2. Letter of Intent from Collector.
3. Final approval by the Collector in consultation with Deputy Director Town planning.

1. Locational Clearance

To be submitted to Government with copy to be submitted to Director, Town Planning.

Following document are to be submitted:

(a) Ownership and development rights.

(b) Village map indicating the boundaries of the said township.

(c) Part plan of R.P. / D.P.

Scrutiny: Checking of the above said documents and on site is to be worked out within stipulated time of 90 days and within this survey the following points are to be detailed in:

- Character of the land (continuous, broken, unbroken etc.).
- Command area of irrigation.
- Water bodies and forest areas.
- Historical monuments/Archeological sites.
- Land ownership (To clarify about disputes if any).
- NOC of irrigation and other departments.

The Locational Clearance is granted by issuing notification in Gazette by the Government. If the entire ownership is with the developer then township shall be declared under sections 18(3)/ 44(2) of MRTP Act, but in case of partial ownership (of minimum 50%), procedure under the sections 20, 37 is to be followed.

Validity of locational clearance is for one year and if can be renewed after submitting the application to the Government.

2. Letter of Intent

The developer shall submit the application in prescribed format to Collector/ Municipal Commissioner with the following documents attached the rein:

- Ownership and development rights with 50% ownership of land, tribal land if any.
- Environmental clearance.

The scrutiny procedure for the above said submissions is worked out within 45 days within which and letter of intent is to be given the validity of which is for six months and which can be renewed.

3. Final Approval: To Collector / Municipal Commissioner

For getting the Final Approval the following steps are to be carried out by the developer:

- Submission of layout plans of entire Township area, sector wise detailed building plans and details of phasing.
- Agreement with bank guarantee of 15% of its development cost.

The approval is granted by the Collector, in consultation with Deputy Director, Town planning.

While approving all the documents, are thoroughly scrutinized for the following aspects:

- Amalgamation of land.
- Layout (Road hierarchy, Ventilation areas, Open spaces etc.).
- Building plans.
- Land utilization.
- FSI statement.

Appeal: An appeal can be filed within 40 days in case of any aggrievence by the order of Collector / Municipal Commissioner, to

- Director Town planning – (R.P. Area).
- The Government - (Municipal Corporation).

Implementation and Completion:

- Basic infrastructure to be completed to the satisfaction of the Collector / Municipal Commissioner as per the relevant phase.
- Total span for completion is of ten years.
- Occupation certificates for individual buildings are allotted by the Collector / Municipal Commissioner in consultation with Town Planning.
- Final completion certificate for the scheme is granted in consultation with Town Planning Department and after producing NOC from MPCB, Forest Department and Chief Fire officer.

Interpretation:

Any dispute arose, is to be referred to the State Government, where decision is final and finding.

Special concession for Townships Projects are as under:

- **N.A. Permission:** The procedure is automatic, no separate permission is required.
- **Stamp Duty:** 50% of prevailing rates of Mumbai Stamp Act.
- **Grant of Government Land:** Land to be leased at market rate to the developer.
- **Relaxation:** From Mumbai Tenancy and Agriculture Land Act (condition of being agriculturist is removed).
- Exemption for Ceiling of Agriculture Land.
- Exemption for Ceiling under ULC Act, 1976.
- Partial exemption for Scrutiny Fee.
- **Floating FSI:** Within the township, Floating FSI is permitted. Unused FSI of one plot can be used anywhere in the whole township.
- Development charges: 50% of the normal are charged.
- For star category Hotels, Hospitals and Multiplexes concession to property tax is offered.

Latest Status of Township Projects:

The Government has given Locational clearance for 14 projects. Out of these four has got final approval and the schemes are running phasewise.

In Pune, ongoing townships are:

- Blue Ridge: Hinjewadi, IT-park.
- Amonara: Hadapsar.
- Nanded City: Sinhgad road.
- I–Vel City: Jambe.
- Magarpatta City.

Characteristic Features of Magarpatta City:

Following sustainable systems are provided within the area:

- Solar water heaters
- Extensive Greening of City
- Rain water harvesting
- Vermiculture pits
- Use of Eco-friendly materials (recycled) – like Flyash, City farming.

Others Civic Amenities:

- Magarpatta City School
- Gymkhana
- Shopping Area
- Gardens
- Cafeteria.

Socio-Economic Status:

- The model has established a different model for urban settlements of workspace and residential in same premises.
- Migration or displacement of the original land residents has stopped.
- Lifestyle is upgraded.

2.2 FORMATION OF CO-OPERATIVE SOCIETY

The Maharashtra Co-operative Societies Act, 1960 provide two definitions namely:

1. Housing society means a society the object of which is to provide its members with:
   - Open plots for housing,
   - Dwelling houses,
   - Flats.
2. Housing society, the object of which is to provide, in case of open plots, houses or flats already acquired by its members, common amenities and services.

Life within a housing co-operative is based on common management and sharing. Such management is intricate and different. The relationship thus established creates a bond between members, which inspires them to undertake further activities and social life on a shared basis.

The essence of the co-operative movement is that the people concerned should themselves look after the management of their affairs including economic betterment and social welfare.

"Co-operative Society" under Section 4 of the Maharashtra Co-operative Societies Act, 1960 means a voluntary organization formed with the object of promoting mutual aid, economic interest or general welfare of its members in accordance with co-operative principles.   As laid down in this Act or these Rules, the Registrar may refuse to register that society if it is likely to be economically unsound or which may have adverse effect of development of the Co-operative movement.

Procedure of Formation of a Co-operative Society:

To form a Co-operative Society, **Section 6 of the Maharashtra Co-operative Societies Act, 1961** lays down the conditions for registering a society which is among others, that a minimum of ten members would be required to own the various units in the building. These persons should be from different families.

Also, these persons should be competent to enter into a contract under the Indian Contracts Act 1872.

Every developer has to form a Co-operative Housing Society at one point of time or another. With the limited amount of options available with regard to management of the affairs of the building i.e. (a) Condominium (b) Private Limited Company and (c) Co-operative Society, (excluding the unrealistic rental housing), it will not be an exaggeration to state that in atleast 90% cases particularly in Mumbai the Promoters and/or the Builders have formed a Co-operative Housing Society. The flat purchasers normally do not know the basic requirement for Registration of Co-operative Housing Society. It is here that apart from the statutory obligations cast upon the builder, the builder as a friend, philosopher and guide of promoters helps in forming a Co-operative Housing Society.

Earlier, unless the registration proposal was signed by 90% of the flat purchasers, the society could not be formed. Now, even if 60% of the total number of flat purchasers is willing to form a Society, then the Co-operative Society can be formed.

The Society has to be registered with the Registrar of Co-operative Societies. The application for registration has to be made in **Form-A. Under section 8 of the Act,** 1960 states that for the purposes of registration, an application shall be made to the Registrar in the prescribed form and shall be accompanied by four copies of the proposed bye-laws of the society and such registration fee as may be prescribed in this behalf. The application should be signed by at least 10 persons (such persons being a member of a different families) and who are qualified under the said Act.

The procedure for Registration of a society begins with electing a Chief Promoter in a meeting of the Promoter who has the authority to sign the necessary documents on behalf of the promoter members and open a bank account in the name of the proposed Society after obtaining the necessary permission from the Registrar.

The Chief Promoter will apply to the registrar for reservation of name of the Society of the proposed society and permission to collect share-capital. The name once reserved is valid for 3 months. He will then deposit the collected share money in the bank account of the proposed Society. This has to be done only after receiving the name reservation from the registrar and after collection of the necessary share capital.

The application for registration should be accompanied with the scheme showing economic feasibility of the proposed Society, bank balance certificate, and list of persons who have contributed to the share-capital and the entrance fee of the proposed Society.

The registrar will enter the particulars in register of application maintained in **Form "B"** and give serial number and issue receipt in acknowledgement of the same.

Afterwards, if the registrar is satisfied that a proposed society has complied with the provisions of the said Act and the rules and its proposed bye-laws are not contrary to this

Act or to the rules, he shall within 2 months from the date of receipt of the application register the society and its bye-laws.

The Other Documents Necessary for Housing Societies are as follows:

The person who has legally acquired or intends to acquire a plot or flat in the proposed Society can join in application for registration of a Society. The following procedures have to be fulfilled:

- The documents pertaining to the purchase of land/building.
- Title clearance certificate.
- Sanctioned/Proposed plan and layouts for construction of building / houses.
- Proof of payment of stamp-duty and registration of documents.
- Certificate from the architect showing the scheme of construction.
- In case of Builder promoted Societies, **Form-Z** and for others **Form-X** is to be submitted.
- 60% of the total members should join in the Registration Proposal.

(i) Registration is optional in the case of a flat owner to another person in a registered Co-operative Society. This is because under section 41 of the Maharashtra Co-operative Societies Act, 1960, any instrument relating to a transfer of shares in a society is exempted from compulsory registration.

(ii) A flat owner to another person in an unregistered society, registration is advisable. This is because registration of a document safeguards the interest of a purchaser.

In the Rules framed under the Act known as Maharashtra Co-operative Societies Rules, 1961, the Registrar classifies the societies under section 12 and Rule 10 where housing societies is classified into three categories:

- **Tenant Ownership Housing Society:** Where land on which the houses are built and constructed is obtained either on lease-hold or free-hold basis by the society for the joint activities of the members.
- **Tenant Co-partnership Housing Society:** It is a housing society, which holds both land and building either on lease-hold or free-hold basis and allots the flats or other premises in the building to its members.
- **Other Housing Societies:** It consists of (a) House Mortgage Society (b) House Construction Societies.

Every society must make by-laws regarding the object of the society, privileges, rights, duties and liabilities of members. And such society cannot legally incur any obligations not directly connected with the furtherance of these objects. The objects for which a society is formed should be clearly, definitely and exhaustively set forth in the by-laws as provided under Rule 8 and section 10 of the Act. Any act which is beyond the objects specified in the by-laws is ultra vires and void and if thereby any loss is incurred the official responsible will be personally liable.

The Validity of Membership in Co-operative Society:

In order to become a member of the society, a person has to comply with the provisions of by-laws of a society besides complying with the provisions of Section 22 and Rule 19.

For instance, a housing society may require any declaration as to the holding of any other premises in the area of operation of the society. Whether a particular person is validly admitted as member of the society or not is to be seen by the Registrar and not by the Co-operative Court under section 91 of the Act.

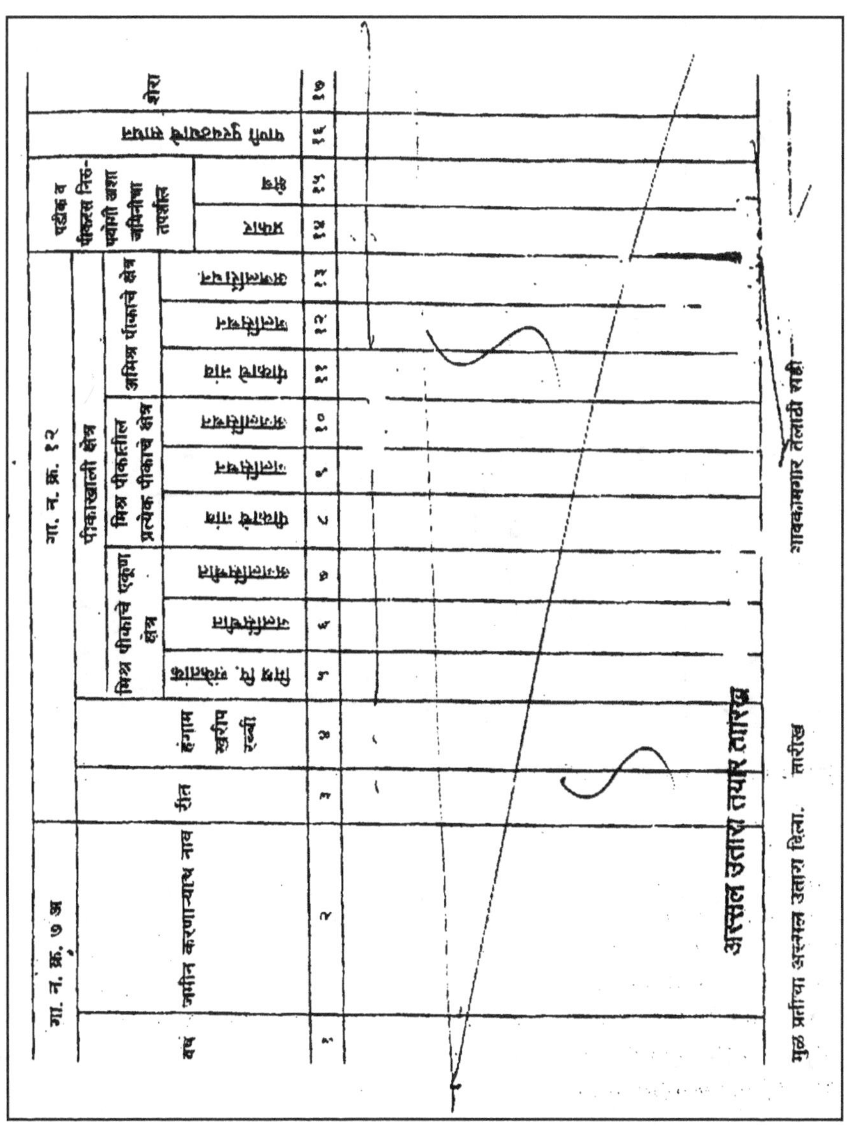

Fig. 2.1

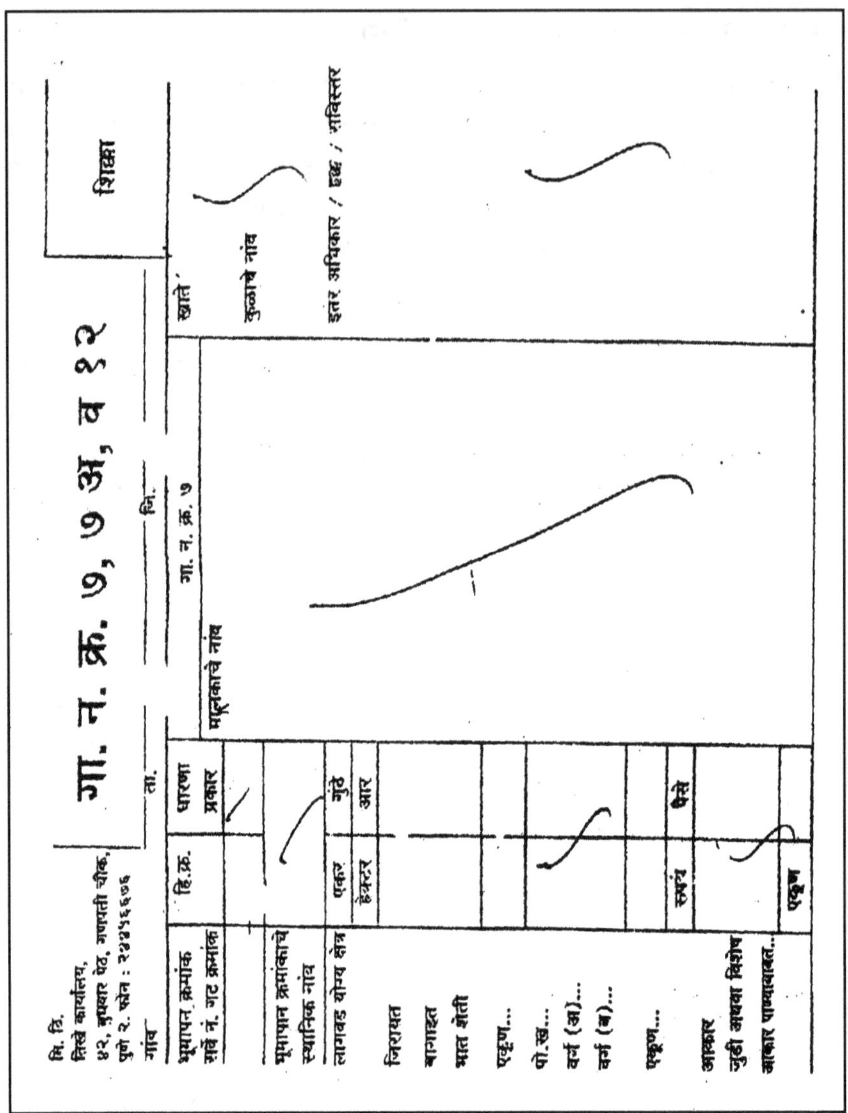

Fig. 2.2

2.3 FORMATION OF APARTMENT OF OWNERSHIP

The Maharashtra Apartment Ownership Act, 1970 provides for the ownership of an individual apartment in a building and to make such apartment heritable and transferable property. **An Apartment** means a part of property intended for any type of independent use, including one or more rooms or enclosed spaces located on one or more floors in a building intended to be used for residence, office, practice of any profession or for carrying on any occupation, trade, or business or for any other type of independent use and with a direct exit to a public street, road or highway or to a common area leading to such street, road or highway. In respect of apartment ownership, the legal title of the flat as an object, along with a proportionate share in the common areas of the building and also proportionate share in the land on which the building stands, vests in the apartment owner. That means, the building belongs to jointly but each apartment owner has an independent right to his apartment to the exclusion of others. Whereas, in the case of ownership flat, the title to the building and the land vests in a co-operative housing society or a limited company and the flat owner is not a owner of the flat in real sense but he has only a right to occupy the flat. This is a species of property, which is heritable and transferable. In case of Maharashtra Ownership Flat Act there should be atleast 10 members for forming co-operative society and in apartment ownership there should be 5 apartments in one or more building. In case of Ownership Flat Act or Co-operative Societies Act the assessment of the flats will be in the name of owner of the land or builder or the society and in case of Apartment Ownership Act there will be separate assessment in respect of each apartment and its percentage of undivided interest in common areas and facilities. In case of Ownership Flat Act, there will be registration of Co-operative Society or Pvt. Ltd Company as contemplated under section 10 of MOF Act and in case of Apartment Ownership Act declaration is required to be made in prescribed form before the Magistrate as required under the Act. All transfers of apartments by the sole owner or all the owners of the property (being an owner or owners who has or have executed and registered a declaration in form "A") to an apartment owner and subsequent transfers from an apartment owner to his transferee shall be by a Deed of Apartment.

In the case of the first Deed of Apartment the party of the first part shall be either the sole owner or all the owners of the property who has or have executed and registered the Declaration in form "A" and the party of the second part shall be the apartment owner. In the case of subsequent Deeds of Apartment, the party of the first part shall be the apartment owner and the party of the second part shall be his transferee.

2.4 7/12 ABSTRACT

The Village Form VII-XII is a combine form incorporating village forms VII and XII. kept together. Village Form VII is an index of all the rights by survey numbers and survey numbers whereas village form XII gives details of crops, fallows, survey and boundary marks. It is a combined form. The upper part is form no. VII and the lower part of V.F. No. XII. The village Form VII-XII is as shown below:

VILLAGE FORM VII

Record of Rights

(Adhikar Abhilekh Patrak)

[Rules 3, 5, 6 and 7 of the Maharashtra Land Revenue Record of Rights

and Registers (Preparation and Maintenance) Rules, 1971]

Village: Hamadabad　　　　　　　　　　　　　　　　　　Taluka: Satara

Survey No.	Sub-division of Survey number	Tenure	Name of the occupant	Khata No.
191		Occupant Class I	Shantabai *alias* Kanta Bhandu Kadam (1) (107) [(1) Hirabai Ramchandra Shinde 0-8=0.	127 Name of the Rent tenant ₹　P ....
	Local name of the field Cultivable area	H.A. 1 29	(2) Kalavati Dharmaji Shinde 0-8-0] (127) Ganesh Parbati Dhane	Other rights: Dattatraya Pandurang Dhekne recovers the maximum rent of ₹ 20 Area of 0.28
	Total　　1 29 Pot Kharab (uncultivable) Class (a) ..... Class (b) ..... Total　____ ₹　P Assessment　　8.69 Judi or special assessment		(156), (157)	assessed of ₹ 1.81 is shown in the name of Government. The transaction of 156 and 157 is against Consolidation of Holdings and Fragmentation Act(1). Boundary and Survey marks

VILLAGE FORM XII

Register of Crops

[Rules 29 of the Maharashtra Land Revenue Record of Rights and Registers (Preparation Maintenance Rules, 1971)]

Year	Season	Code No. of mixture	Details of cropped area										Land not available for cultivation			Remarks
			Mixed crops area		Pure crops area											
					Constituent crops with area under each											
			Irrigated	Un-irrigated	Name of Crop	Irrigated	Un-irrigated	Name of Crop	Irrigated	Un-irrigated	Nature	Area	Source of Irrigation	
1	2	3	4	5	6	7	8	9	10	11	12	13	14	15
			H.A.	H.A.		H.A.	H.A.		H.A.	H.A.		H.A.		
1968-69 Kharif			... ...	0.60	Groundnut ...		0.45	Chillis ...		0.02				
			Coriander ...	0.02										
Rabbi			... ...	0.61	Rabbi ...									
			Jowar ...	0.40										
			Kardi ...	0.03										
			Wheat ...	0.03										

A Combined Form:

This is a combined form of Record of Rights and Register of Crops. It consists of two parts (i) the upper part which in effect is an index of Village Form VI and (ii) the lower part which provides statistics of cultivation including crops and fallows. But for few exceptions listed hereafter, no change can be made in the upper part unless and until an entry is made and certified in the Register of Mutations i.e. Village Form VI. As soon as a mutation is effected in Village Form VI, the Talathi should make pencil entry in the concerned village Form VII. As soon as the said mutation entry is cancelled or modified, the pencil entry should be rubbed out and modified entry made in pencil. Immediately, after the entry in the Register of Mutation is certified, the Talathi shall record it in ink in Village Form-VII. The pencil entry facilitates checking during crop or other inspections on site and protects public against cheating by suppression of all accomplished transactions.

Authorities for Effecting Changes:

Changes in survey number, Hissa number, area including Pot-Kharab and agricultural assessment are supported by the Akarband, Kami-Jasti Patrak and Akar Phod Patrak or Hissa Form No. XII issued by the District Inspector of Land Records. Changes in tenure are made under orders of Government, Collector or other competent authority; changes in Khata number are made by the Talathi once in ten years and changes in the name of the owner and tenant and other rights are brought about by certified entries in the Village Form VI. Seldom does the local name of the field changes.

General Instructions to be Followed:

The following general instructions are to be followed in maintaining Village Form VII:

- No words, figures and names in Village Form VII shall ever be erased.
- The names, words or figures which are no longer to be retained shall be struck out by a single line drawn through them, so that the original is still quite legible.
- The new names, words or figures shall be written underneath that which has been struck out or if space is not enough then at the side in such a way that it is quite legible for what the new matter is substituted.
- The entry number in Village Form VI upon which change is based shall be written against new name, word or figure entered or omitted.
- If a new name or figure thus inserted is again altered by a further mutation, the same process is repeated.
- If the mutation simply removes a name not putting anything in its place, then it is struck out as in (b) and (d) above, nothing is to be added.
- Use only one page of form for each parcel of land viz. Survey number of Sub-Division of a Survey number including a Hissa.
- Use stiff covers, for these books or volumes and the pages or forms by strong laces, so that the pages can be turned over.
- Divide the village map into suitable blocks of about 100 to 150 holdings or so, number them, write up the Village Form VII in respect of them and bind them in one volume as instructed above.

VILLAGE FORM XII

Register of Crops:

The Village Form XII is also known as Register of crops. The crops grown in each agricultural season every year are required to be shown in this form. Every year when the crops are grown and standing in the fields, the Talathi is to visit the village for the purpose of crop inspection and making entries in the crop register. For this purpose the Talathi is to fix a date at least seven days in advance and arrange to inform the villagers of the fixed date. He will publicise his visit by beat of drum or other suitable method, requiring villagers to be present in their fields and evidence the entries being made in the Register of crops. The Talathi is also to give intimation of his visit to the Village Panchayat Sarpanch 'if any' and through him request the members of the Village Panchayat to accompany him (Talathi.) On the date so fixed, the Talathi shall visit every field in the presence of the villagers, the Sarpanch and the Village Panchayat members who may be present there and make entries in the said register. The Talathi is to allow the persons interested to see the entries so made.

After the enquiries made by the Talathi the Circle Inspector or any other superior officer is to visit the village for verification of the entries. Such visiting officer is to give prior intimation about his visit and after making due enquiry has to correct entries found to be incorrect.

Instructions for Maintaining Village Form XII:

- Care should be taken properly to distinguish between fallow and Pot Kharab and grass and fallow, crops in Pot Kharab should not be shown.
- But if considerable cultivation is noticed in Pot Kharab of Class (b), say 0.506 hectares i.e. five gunthas or more, then Talathi may make note of the fact and add this to the other cultivation in unassessed land and other lands not intended for cultivation shown in Village Form XI.
- While writing up the crops statistics, the Talathi should first attend to the Pot Kharab and fallow areas; and then the grass or grass and babul, if any. But the areas of these should not be finally entered at the first inspection if there is any likelihood of the area thereunder ploughed up and cropped in the Rabi season. The area under improved seeds should be distinguished by putting the indicative letter I.S. against it.
- Next to this, attention should be given to mixed crop. To save clerical labour, the Talathi should record at the beginning of each volume of Village Forms VII-XII the standard composition (Code No.) and the name of the mixture being used in writing the crops statistics.
- After completing these entries, the Talathi should count and note in the 'Remarks' column any fruit trees old enough to bear fruit of the following kinds which are scattered over the field: Mango, Tamarind, Jack, Coconut, Tad and Date Palms. He will also count and note the following kinds of fuel trees, if any, scattered over the field:

    Babul, Neem, Khair, Dhavdar and Anjan.
- He will also note the trees, the cutting of which is prohibited under the Maharashtra State Felling of Trees Act, 1966, and rules thereunder viz. Tamarind, Mahuva, Jack fruit, Khair and Teak trees and under the Maharashtra Land Revenue (Prohibition of Cutting of Trees) Rules, 1968.
- If at any time, it is directed to count any other trees, it should also be done. But when the whole or a distinct portion of the field is entirely set apart for growing pala or fruit trees or fuel trees, then the area under those trees will be given and not the number.
- Authorised crops in unoccupied land or land not included in survey number or in unassessed land leased for reclamation etc., as well as crops in Government land encroached upon should be brought to account.
- Similarly when alluvion or diluvian is noticed the Talathi should note them in the 'Remark' column for taking action when statutory limit is exceeded.
- Diluvian is fallow but crops in alluvion, before it becomes assessed area, are disregarded. Crops sown but failed, but not sown again will be accounted as crops.
- But when sown again, the first crop is disregarded and crops sown again are shown after keeping a note to the effect that "crop of failed".
- They will however, never be treated as two crops. All crop reaped more than once should be accounted for as second or third crop, if they are all sown and reaped in the same area.

- Another important point to remember is about the lands under the command of the Pat but have not grown irrigated crops. For the correct accounting of crops in these lands, all officers concerned should pay special attention to the proper maintenance of this record.
- In order to know the total area under green manure and the cropwise area benefited by the green manure, the area of the crop grown in the green manured field should be marked by the letters G.M. in bracket against that crop.
- It is not necessary to total the form, as the total of the cropped area is taken below Village Form XI.

Entering Area of Fallow Land:

In columns 12 and 13 of Village Form XII area in respect of fallow land is to be shown. There are eight kinds of fallow lands which are to be shown separately. Which are as follows:

Un-cultivable Follows:

- Forest-Lands under Government forest as well as private forest in a village should be taken into account for mentioning area thereof.
- Hill and rocky tracts, desert area, rivers.
- Non-agricultural lands, viz. area under buildings, roads, railways, burial grounds, military camping grounds, water sources etc.
- Lands kept fallow for certain period i.e. (five years or more).
- Grass lands and used for grazing cattle.
- Lands other than forest consisting of useful trees.
- Other fallow lands i.e. lands kept as fallow for a period from one year to five years.
- Current fallow i.e. lands, kept fallow only for one season (Kharif or Rabi) in a year.

Different Sources from which Water is taken:

In column 14 of the Village Form XII the different sources from which water is taken for the purpose of irrigation should be noted. These sources are viz.

(a) canals, (b) tube wells, (c) wells, (d) tanks, (e) bandharas, (f) rivers and nallas.

In respect of sources viz. canals, tube wells and wells, Talathi should ascertain after enquiry on the spot whether the particular source belongs to Government or private person. Where water is lifted through electric pumps or oil engines such information should also be entered in this column whenever any crops is grown with the aid of any irrigation, the kind of irrigation should be written against it.

The classes of recognised irrigation are:

Tanks, wells, pumps (steam or oil engines working on river banks or wells), Government canals, private canals or Pats, lifts (Dhekudi).

It would suffice, if only initial letter, instead of the whole word is written over the irrigated crop e.g. T, W, S, P etc., when more than one method is used then the irrigation should be classed chiefly according to the source of water i.e. from tank or from a well; but if from a public river, then according to the method of appropriating it. Wells often supplement Pats; the crops should be classed as under Pats but (W) added to indicate Motasthal aid.

2.5 6-D FORM

Village Form VI is a diary of mutations. A record of changes in the record of rights in respect of all the particulars are shown in this form. These particulars are expected to be written in detail as required under Section 148 of the Maharashtra Land Revenue Code and the rules there under.

VILLAGE FORM VI

Register of Mutations

PHERPHAR PATRAK

[Rule 10 of the Maharashtra Land Revenue Record of Rights and Registers
(Preparation and Maintenance) Rules, 1971]

Village: Hamadabaj　　　　　　Taluka: Satara　District: Satara

Serial No. of entry	Nature of right acquired	Survey and Sub-Division numbers affected	Initials or remarks by Testing officers
1	2	3	4
157	Date of mutation　　Date of receipt of 11-7-69　information 4-7-69	Gat. No. 191 (one only)	Consolidation Transaction is in Contravention of Consolidation Act and should be reported
	Sale (1) Khatedar Shantabai Khandu Kadam (2) Tarabai Ramchandra Shinde (3) Leelabai Dharmaji Shinde have sold undivided share of three annas and nine pies in a rupee to Baliram Parbati Dhone for ₹ 1,200 on 2-5-1969		Notices have been served Certified (Sd.) Circle Inspector 7-9-69
	Registration No. 3782 Date of intimation of mutation on the interested parties 11-7-1969 Date of intimation of certification	Date of publication of mutation on notice board 11-7-1969 (Sd.) Talathi	

Who is Occuptant?

The person who actually holds possession under a claim of title shall be recorded as an occupant or a Government lessee as the case may be. If there is a doubt as to actual possession the person with the strongest title should be recorded.

How to File Mutation Papers?

Every vardi, order, or authority upon which an entry in the register of mutations is made should be kept in a file; where they can easily be found. Akarbands and Kami-Jasti Patraks should be kept with Village Form I. Registration extracts in continuous file in the sequence of months and written reports, mutations, orders and other correspondence about mutations filed in sequence of the entries in Village Form VI.

VILLAGE FORM VI-A

Register of Disputed Cases

[Rules 5(2), 16 and 25 of the Maharashtra Land Revenue Record of Rights and Registers (Preparation and Maintenance) Rules, 1971]

Serial No.	Serial No. in Mutation Register (Village Form VI) or rough copy of Record of Rights	Survey No. and Sub-Division No.	Date of Receipt of objection	Particular of dispute with names of disputing parties	Decision of officer
1	2	3	4	5	6

VILLAGE FORM VI-B

Register of Fines under section 152 of the Maharashtra Land Revenue Code, 1966

Entry in village Form VI	Name of acquire of right or holder of document	Order of Tahsildar as to fine to be levied	Number and date of receipt
1	2	3	4
157	Shri. Sahebrao Anna Dhane		....

VILLAGE FORM VI-C

Register of Heirship Cases

Village: Hamjabad   Taluka: Satara   District: Satara

Sr. No.	Name of deceased occupant or other right holder	Date or approximate date of death	Old Khata No. in Village Form VIII-A	Names of legal heirs	Names of the heirs out of column 5 in actual possession	Order of Tahsildar as to who should be entered as occupant and/or in the other rights column	Entry in Village Form VI embodying decisions the other
1	2	3	4	5	6	7	8
3	Shri. Bapu Govindrao Dhane		18 7-4-1969		Sons: Age 1. Shankar 34 2. Ganesh 25 3. Dinesh 17 4. Dinkar 10 Daughters: 1. Indubai Shrirang Yadao 30 2. Sakubai Kisan Kadam 23 3. Kashibai 21 Bhiku Kadam 4. Yashoda 12 5. Radha 55 (Widow)	Shri. Shankar Bapu Dhane (as manger of joint family)	No. 167
					Out of these, Shri Shankar is the manager of Hindu un-divided family.		

VILLAGE FORM VI-D

Register of New Sub-Divisions (Hissas)

Village: Hamjabad   Taluka: Satara   District: Satara

Mutation entry in Village Form VI	Survey No. or sub-division No.	Nature of change required in map	By whom done and date
1	2	3	4
161	23	123	Hissas measured on 25-12-1971 by Shri. P.H. Deshpande, P.H.S. Measurer (Sd)
		H. No. 1 .. Shri. Vasant Ram Sharma H. No. 3 .. Shri Laxman Ram Sharma H. No. 2 .. Smt. Shantabai Wife of Ram Sharma	(P.H. Deshpande) Dated 25-12-1971
168	18/2	A. 18.2	Hissas measured on 20-11-1972 by Shri. M.G. Choudhari, C.S.Z. (Sd.)
		B.	(M. G.Choudhari) Dated 20-11-1972.
		H. No. 18/2A .. Shri Sitaram Rajaram Shinde	
191	101	H. No. 18/2B .. Shri Tukaram Rajaram Shinde 1 2 101 H. No. 1 .. Shri Sitaram Rajaram Shinde H. No. 2 .. Shri Balku Dhondu Pawar	

(**Note:** The above entries are illustrative)

Subsidiary Registers:

The four subsidiary registers, viz. (i) Village Form VI-A-Register of Disputed Cases, (ii) Village Form VI-B-Register of Fines-under-section 152 of the Maharashtra Land-Revenue Code, (iii) Village Form VI-C-Register of Heirship Cases, and (iv) Village Form VI-D-Register of New Sub-division (Hissas); are simple, self-explanatory and easy to maintain. They facilitate correct entries in Village Form-VI, apprise public of their obligations to assist Government in maintaining an accurate and up-to-date Record of Rights and ensure that the survey records on which the Record of Rights is based are also maintained up-to-date.

2.6 LIST OF DOCUMENTS

Alongwith the plan, the following documents are required to be submitted:

- Notice to execute the proposed work in the standard form.

- Undertaking from the architect in the standard form.

- Extract from property register stating the details regarding the owner and land.

- Plan from the city survey office showing boundaries of the plot and adjoining survey numbers.

- Certificate regarding area of the plot given by a corporation or town planning department.

Resubmission: If the plans comply with the requirements of the rules and bye-laws of the sanctioning authority and the code of town planning scheme, they may be sanctioned in due course, otherwise they may have to be resubmitted as per instructions of the Authorities after complying with the same.

General requirements regarding plans, notice, certificates, undertakings, qualifications, and so on by different plan sanctioning authorities such as corporations, municipalities and others are indicated below.

1. Documents and plans

2. Number of copies

3. Owner's notice to execute the work

4. Undertaking from the supervisor

5. Building completion certificate

6. Qualifications and the experience for licensed surveyors, architects, engineers, clerks of works, structural designers, and plumbers.

7. Extracts from the property register card.

1. Documents and Plans

The following is an extract from building rules and bye-laws of municipal corporation. The person intending to carry out the work shall send, along with the notice to be given, the following documents and plans:

- Correct plans and sections of every floor of the building intended to be erected which shall be drawn to a scale of not less than (10 mm = 1 m) and shall show the position, form, dimensions and means of ventilation of and access to the several parts of such a building and its appurtenances and the particular part or parts thereof, which are and those which are not intended to be used for human habitation and in the case of a building intended to be used as a dwelling house for two or more families or for carrying on any trade or business in which a number of people not exceeding twenty maximum be employed or as a place of public resort, the means of ingress and egress. Such plans and sections shall also show the depth and nature of the foundation and the proposed dimensions of all the walls, posts, columns, beams, joints, all girders; and scantling to be used in the walls, staircases, floors, and roof.

- A specification of each description of work proposed to be executed and of the materials to be used. Such specification shall include a description of the proposed method of drainage of the building intended to be erected and of the sanitary fittings to be used and also of the means of water supply and shall, if necessary, by the commissioner, be supplemented, by detailed calculations showing the sufficiency of the strength of any part of such a building.

- A block plan of such a building which shall be drawn to the scale of the largest revenue survey map at the time being in existence for the locality in which the building is, or is to be situated and shall show the positions and appurtenances of the properties, if any, immediately adjoining the width and level of the street, if any, in front and side of the street, if any, at the rear of such buildings, the levels of the foundations, and the lowest floor of such buildings, and of any yard or ground belonging there to and the means of access to such buildings.

- A plan showing the intended line of drainage of such a building and the intended size, depth and inclination of each drain, and the details of the arrangement proposed for the ventilation of the drains.

- Undertaking from the person who is appointed to supervise the execution of the work.

Plans and sections to be submitted to the corporation under the provisions of the act and the building bye-laws and rules should be drawn and signed by the surveyor, engineer, architect or structural designer licensed by the municipal commissioner.

The description of the works set out in the plans must comply with the requirements of the building bye-laws.

The structural drawings and the structural calculations which are to accompany the plans shall be prepared and signed by the structural designer licensed.

2. Number of Copies

- Three copies of plans for buildings in "gaothan" areas.

- Four copies of plans for buildings in agricultural lands.

- Five copies of plans for buildings in town planning scheme areas.

One of the above plans shall be signed by the Municipal Commissioner when signifying his approval or otherwise of the plan and shall be returned to the person by whom the same was furnished.

- If found necessary by the commissioner, it shall be incumbent on every person whose plans have been approved or otherwise, to submit amended plans for any deviations he proposes to make during the construction of his building work and the procedure laid down for plans therefore shall apply to all such amended plans.

- Every plan or amended plan mentioned above shall be coloured with fixed colours as follows:

  Block Plan: The proposed work is in red; the existing work is in black grey or neutral tint and the open spaces are uncoloured. Work to be removed is to be clearly shown on the plan.

  Plans and Sections: Proposed work in white lines if shown on blue ferro prints and in red lines if on white coloured prints.

  Deviations: In red, if shown on blue prints and in black, if on white prints. Brick work, Wood work, RCC work, or steel work shall each be differently specified.

- All the drainage work and drainage lines shall be shown on original and amended plans in distinguishing colours together with the location of the sewer trap chamber and the depth of street connections.

3. Owner's Notice to Execute the Work

Typical Notice
XXX Municipal Corporation

Notice under Section _______ of the XXX Provincial Municipal Corporation Act, 1949.

No.

Date

To The Municipal Commissioner,

XXX Municipal Corporation,

XXX

Sir,

Pursuant to the provisions of _________ of the XXX Municipal Corporation Act, _______, I hereby give you notice that I intend within the meaning of that section to execute the following work:

- Description of the proposed work.
- The purpose for which the work is intended.
- Dimensions of the work.
- The name and address of the person intended to be employed to supervise the work.

- Name and address of the contractor, if any.
- The description of walls, whether stone or brick masonry, the nature of mortar to be used.
- The depth of the foundation and whether it is to be taken upto murum or hard rock strata.
- Information about the projection of the balcony, whether it is on the municipal land.
- How is the disposal of sewage water provided for?
- Whether the land on which the proposed work is to be erected is owned by the person giving the notice.

I hereby acknowledge to have perused the building regulations contained in Chapter XV and schedule Chapter XII of the XXX provincial Municipal Corporation Act, _____, and the bye-laws made under the said Act.

Yours faithfully,

Signature and address of the owner of the proposed work

XXX (Name of the town)

4. Undertaking from the Supervisor

The following undertaking from the person who is appointed to supervise the execution of the work should be submitted to the Municipal Commissioner along with the notice.

To The City Engineer.   Date

XXX Municipal Corporation, XXX.

Sir,

With reference to the notice under Section _____ of the XXX Provincial Municipal Corporation Act, _____ , Submitted to you by Shri. _____________________ for the execution of the work _________, I wish to inform you that I have agreed to supervise the execution of the work mentioned therein.

Yours faithfully,

Licensed Surveyor   L.S. No.   _________________

Licensed Engineer   L.S. No.   _________________

Licensed Architect   L.S. No.   _________________

Licensed Structural Designer　　　　　L.S. No.　＿＿＿＿＿＿＿＿＿＿

5. Building Completion Certificate

(a) Certificate from the architect to the Corporation/Municipality

XXX Municipal Corporation

Building Completion Certificate

I do hereby certify that the following work＿＿＿＿＿＿＿＿＿ has been (insert full particulars of the work) supervised by me and has been completed to my satisfaction, that the workmanship and the whole of the material used are good; and that no provision of the Act or the bye-laws and no requisition made, condition prescribed or order issued thereunder has been transgressed in execution of the work.

The drainage works in relation to the construction work mentioned above have been completed in accordance with your drainage rules and bye-laws and a certificate prescribed under rule＿＿＿ of schedule from Shri. XXX, a licensed plumber is sent herewith.

Signature

(Date)

License No. ＿＿＿＿＿＿＿＿

(b) Certificate from the Corporation to the Owner

XXX Corporation,

＿＿＿＿＿＿＿＿

No.＿＿＿＿＿＿＿　　　　　　　＿＿＿＿＿＿＿＿

Dated

Occupancy Certificate

(According to XXX Municipal Corporation Act of 1949)

From

The Assistant Engineer,

＿＿＿＿＿＿＿＿ Corporation,

＿＿＿＿＿＿＿

To

Shri. ＿＿＿＿＿＿＿

Address _______________

With reference to your application, dated _____________ for permission to construct a building _____________ at plot No. _____________ the Commencement Certificate No. _____________ dated _____________ _____________ was issued to you.

With reference to the completion certificate, dated _____________ issued by your architect and submitted to this office, permission required to occupy the same building is hereby granted as per _____________ Provincial Municipal Act.

XXX Sd/

Assistant Engineer

_____________ Corporation

6. Qualifications and Experience:

Definitions:

1. Words and phrases which are used but not defined-herein shall have the same meanings as are assigned to them in the XXX Municipal Corporation Act, _____ referred to in these bye-laws as the "Act".

Qualifications of a Licensed Surveyor:

1. No surveyor shall be granted a license by the Commissioner as required by Section _______ unless the said person possesses the qualifications and experience as prescribed:

   (a) A degree in civil engineering of any University or a diploma or a degree in architecture of any University or Institution recognised by the Commissioner.

OR

   (b) Associate membership or membership of any institution which is considered by the Commissioner to be equivalent to a University Degree in civil engineering or architecture.

OR

   (c) A diploma in civil engineering of any University or institution which is recognised by the Commissioner with practical experience of at least one year of work connected with the survey and building construction.

2. Any surveyor who has been granted continuously for a period of five years immediately preceding the date on which these bye-laws come into force, a surveyor's license by the Municipal Corporation of the city of XXX or who has at least five years practical experience of work connected with the survey and building construction work, may

be granted a surveyor license by the Commissioner, provided he passes the practical examination held by the City Engineer for testing the merit.

3. No architect or engineer shall be granted a license by the Commissioner as required by section ____ unless the said person possesses the qualifications as prescribed:

   - A degree in civil engineering or a diploma in architecture of any University or institution recognised by the Commissioner in this behalf.

     OR

   - Associate membership or membership of any institution which is considered by the Commissioner to be equivalent to a University Degree in civil engineering or architecture.

   - A diploma holder in civil engineering or equivalent, holding surveyor's license for at least 10 years before these bye-laws came into force, if he is able to produce sufficient evidence of his having done structural engineering work for the ten years.

4. No person will be granted a license by the Commissioner to work as a structural designer for carrying out the works of design and execution of RCC.

   A diploma holder in civil engineering or equivalent who is already holding surveyor's license continuously for the last seven years previous to the passing of these bye-laws.

Qualifications of a clerk of works:

5. Any person who intends to work as a clerk of works may obtain a license from the Commissioner under section ______ if he produces a certificate from a licensed surveyor of having worked under him for a period of five years to the satisfaction of the licensed surveyor.

Qualifications of a Licensed Plumber:

6. (i) No plumber shall be granted a license by the Commissioner as required by ______ unless the said person holds a Degree or a Diploma in Civil Engineering or Sanitary Engineering of any University or Institution recognised by the Commissioner.

   (ii) Not withstanding anything contained in clause (i), any person who does not possess the qualifications prescribed in clause (ii) may be given a plumber's license by the Commissioner, if:

   (a) He was granted a plumber's License by the Municipal Corporation of the City of XXX continuously for a period of five years immediately preceding the date on which these bye-laws come into force.

       OR

   (b) He has extensive practical experience of not less than five years.

Provided that the Commissioner may, before granting a license to such a person, require him to pass a theoretical and practical examination.

The Architects Act, 1972 (No. 20 of 1972):

An act to provide for the registration of architects and for matters connected therewith was passed by the Parliament in 1972. The objects and reasons stated were, "Since independence and more particularly, with the implementation of the five year plans, building construction activity in our country has expanded almost on a phenomenal scale. A large variety of buildings, many of an extremely complex nature and magnitude, like multistoreyed office buildings, factory buildings and residential houses, are being constructed each year. With this increase in building activity, many unqualified persons calling themselves as architects are undertaking the construction of buildings which are uneconomical and quite frequently, unsafe, thus bringing into disrepute the profession of architects. Various organisations, including the Indian Institute of Architects, have repeatedly emphasised the need for statutory regulation to protect the general public from unqualified persons working as architects. With the passing of this legislation, it will be unlawful for any person to designate himself as an "architect" unless he has the requisite qualifications and experience and is registered under the Act."

Other professionals like engineers will be free to engage themselves in their normal vocation in respect of building construction work provided that they do not style themselves as architects.

Application for Registration:

According to this act, "Every architect who desires to have his name entered in the register shall submit an application in form No. XI, together with documentary evidence about his eligibility for registration accompanied by a draft of ₹ 50/- (Present situation) in favour of the Secretary, Council of Architecture, New Delhi, for issue of a certificate of registration and the certificate of registration shall be issued in Form XII.

Form No. XI

Application for Registration of Architects

The Secretary

Council of Architecture

New Delhi

1. Name in full (in block letters)
2. Father's name
3. Nationality
4. Date of Birth
5. Residential address

6. Professional address

7. Particulars of qualification (supported by attested copies)

8. Date of commencement of profession/service.

9. Whether practising independently/as a partner/or employed

10. Period of residence in India

11. Present address on which communication will be made

12. Any other particulars.

I hereby undertake that if admitted as a registered architect, I will be bound by the provision of the Architect's Act, 1972 and the rules and regulations framed thereunder or that may hereafter from time to time be made pursuant to the said Act.

I also enclose a draft of ₹ 50/- as registration fee for the year ______________

Yours faithfully,

Encl. List of particulars endorsed.

Form No. XII

Council of Architecture of India

Certificate of Registration under sub-section (7) of Section 24 and sub-section (4) of Section 26 of the Architects Act, 1972.

Certificate of Registration

This is to certify that the name of Shri./Shrimati ________ has been entered in the register and his/her Registration No. is ________. This certificate is valid from the ________ day of ________ 20 ____ to the ________ day of 20 ________ inclusive.

Renewals

Signature of Registrar

List of Additional qualifications.

Given under the common seal of the Council of Architecture. This ________ day of 20 __________

President

Secretary (Seal)

Extracts from the Property Register Card

City Survey: Poona, Taluka: Poona, District: Poona			
Survey No. (Shivajinagar) 560	Area (ha) (0.34)	Tenure (final plot) 26	Particulars of assessment or rent paid to the Govt. and when due for revision
Basements:			
Holder in 19 origin of the title (so far as traced)			
Lessee			
	City Survey Office SEAL		
Other encumbrances Other Remarks			
Date	Transaction	Vol. No.	New Holder (H), Lessee (L) or Encumbrances (E)	Attestation
12.4.44	As per partition deed	120	H Kiran Joshi	Sd/- Tahsildar
5.11.68	As per sale deed amount ₹ 4,32,450/- From: Kiran Joshi	S(2) 4350 – 9.4.67	Vidya Co-operative Housing Society	Sd/- Tahsildar

2.7 TDR

The main occupation in ancient time was agriculture and people used to live in villages. After mechanization was introduced, town and cities were developing and becoming more populated. Cities became more populated because people migrated to cities in search of education and jobs. As development was increasing rapidly, more and more multistoried buildings were built. To control haphazard growth of city, local bodies (corporations) introduced certain bye-laws and Development Control Rules (DCR). Due to development in the area employment is increased and thus enhancing per capita income, hence living standards of people is increased. On the other hand, due to urbanization, the pollution in air, water and land is increased to a very large extent.

2.7.1 What is TDR?

In Development Plan, reservations are shown against a number of public utilities. In view of limited financial resources available with the utilities and consequently the paucity of funds for such huge compensation, the State Government have introduced the concept of Transferable Development Right. Before introducing this concept the municipalities used to compensate the land owners in terms of money as per Government value of the land. The utilities may now be upgrade / expand their services and provide better amenities to the citizens.

With this concept if any land owner hands over the possession of the reserved land to the Municipal Corporation free of cost without any encumbrance, a Development Right Certificate (DRC) will be granted to the owner to construct a built up area equivalent to permissible FSI of the land handed over by him/ her on one or more plots in the zones specified. The Municipal Corporation has a mandate to regulate the activities pertaining to Transferable Development Right.

2.7.2 Why Reservation of Land is Necessary?

The main purpose of reservation is to provide facilities to public. These facilities include basic facilities such as school, hospitals etc., recreational facilities such as play grounds, gardens etc., essential services such as fire brigade, vegetable market, water treatment plants, waste water treatment plants, etc.

2.7.3 Who is Eligible?

The owner of the plot which is reserved for a public purpose or road construction or road widening, in the DP and for additional amenities deemed to be provided in accordance with modified DCR excepting in case of an existing or retention user or to any required, compulsory or recreational open space, shall be eligible for the award of TDR. Such award will entitle the owner of land to FSI in the form of DRC which he / she may use for himself / herself or transfer to any person.

Development Rights will be granted to owner or a lessee only for reserved lands which are retainable / non-retainable under Urban Land Ceiling Act, 1976 and in respect of all other reserved lands to which the provision of the aforesaid act does not apply and on production of a certificate to this effect from the Competent Authority under the Act before Development Right shall be to such extent and subject to such conditions as Government may specify. Development Rights are available only in cases where development of a reservation has not been implemented.

Land Development: TDR granting and DRC handing is worked out only after the reserved land is surrendered to Municipal Corporation free of cost and free of encumbrances after leveling of land, constructing a compound wall of 1.5 m height, providing street light, access road by the owner is completed and Municipal Commissioner is satisfied.

Issue of DRC: A DRC shall be issued by the Municipal Commissioner himself as a certificate printed on bond paper in an appropriate form. Such certificate will be a transferable and negotiable instrument after due authentication by him of all transactions etc. relating to grant of DRC. Other important aspect is transfer of name in land records.

Documents to be submitted for availing TDR:

- 7/ 12 Extract

- Fher Far (change of Ownership + other)

- Power of Attorney

- ULC Order (NOC)

- Search and Title Report

- N.A. Order

- Original Site Plan

- Zoning Demarcation

- Zone Certificate

- Demarcation

- Architect Area Certificate

- Tax NOC

- Six files to be submitted: To TDR department, Road department, Legal department, Bhoomi and Zindagi department, Bhoomi praman, D.P. Department.

Creation of TDR: Plot area minimum: 500 sq.m / 5000 sq. ft.

Zones: A, B, C (PUNE CASE)

(A) Congested zone (FSI – 1.5 to 2.0) in core of the city. TDR is generated here but it is not applicable or cannot be loaded on the plan within this area. Hence, it can be used in lower zones.

(B) Semi-congested zone which is peripheral to A zone. Development is proper and area is accessible from outside and within.

(C) Non-congested and on the outskirts of city limit peripheral to B zone.

Utilization of TDR:

Development rights shall not be used in A zone and some other congested area. Development rights shall not be used on plots for housing schemes of slum dwellers for which additional FSI is permissible and the areas where permissible FSI is less than 1.0.

Development Rights shall not be used on the plots fronting on arterial road with 30 m width in zone B. It can be subjected on rest of the area to other regulations.

Transfer of area: A to B OR C, B to B OR C, C to C only.

Development Right Certificate may be used on one or more plots of land whether vacant or already developed or by erection of additional storeys or in any other manner consistent with these regulations, but not so as to exceed in any plot a total built up FSI higher than prescribed.

(a) The FSI on receiving plots shall be allowed to be exceeded not more than 0.4 in respect of TDR available for the reserved plots.

(b) The FSI on receiving plot shall be allowed to be exceeded by further 0.4 in respect of TDR available on account of land surrendered for road widening or construction of new road from the very said plot. For utilization of TDR minimum width of road is 6 m.

Priority List for Generation of TDR:

Phased annual programme is open to public for utilization of TDR in the form of DRC (as per DP references) and used after receiving plots and in case of emergency utility may be completed initially and then DRC etc. is finalized. Following are few examples:

- DP Roads reservation already committed by authority during past years.

- DP Roads reservation responsible for improving circulation pattern.

- Reservation for essential municipal service such as fire brigade / water / sewage plants / vegetable market / burial / crematories etc.

- Parking reservations that can be developed by Municipal Corporation for multistoried parking lots.

- Reservation for transport.

- Shopping center which will yield high asset to Municipal Corporation etc.

Priority List for Utilization of TDR:

This shall be made available to the public in the office of Deputy City Engineer (DP).

- Grant of TDR in case where lands are under acquisition (request for the same is to be made to special LA OFFICER – for the cases after 30 September 1993-TDR introduction and acceptance).
- Possession of the land has been delivered without having received part or full compensation under MRTP, BPMC Acts.

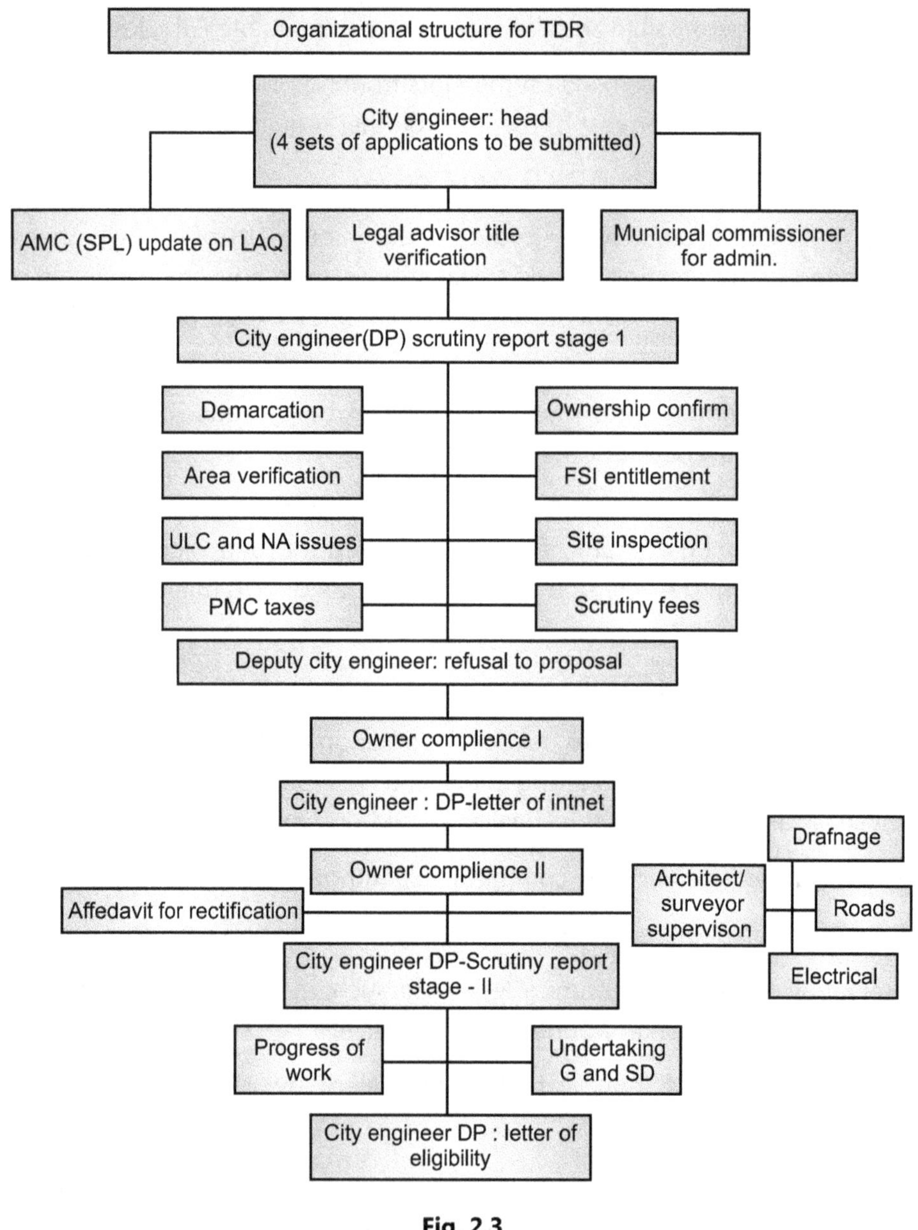

Fig. 2.3

2.8 COMMENCEMENT CERTIFICATE

1. Format I:

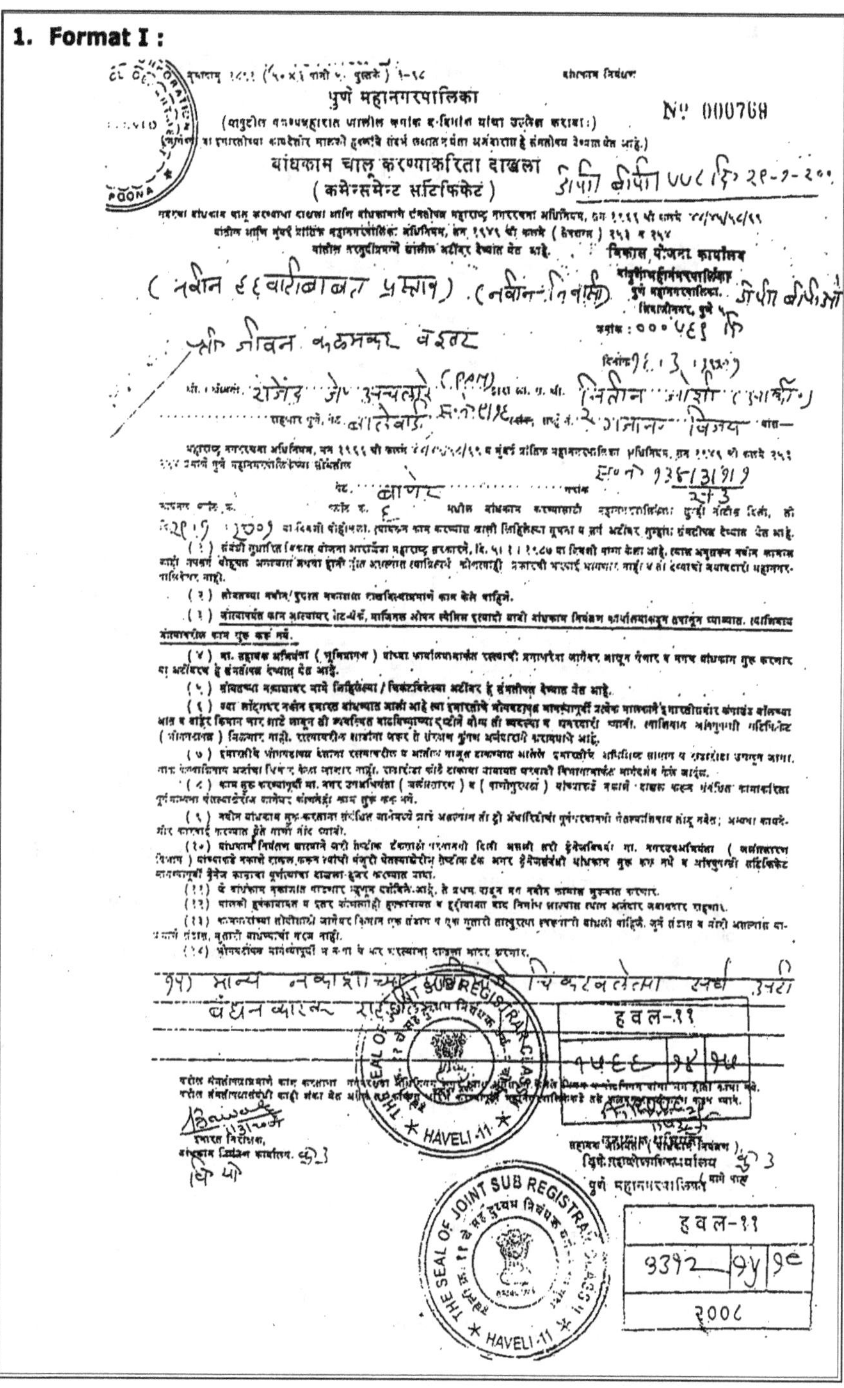

2. Format II:

---

2. Format II :

LONAVLA MUNICIPAL COUNCIL

Date :- 16/05/2007   No. ENG/BP/ 25/2007-2008 /527

Form No. 2 (Rule No. 5)
COMMENCEMENT CERTIFICATE

Subject :- **Proposed construction on land bearing, CTS No. 186/ F & 186/6 'A'
Bhangarwadi, Lonavla , Tal:- Maval, Dist:- Pune**

Lonavla for Shri/Smt,   **Mrs. Geeta Ashok Agrawal
C/o Virendra K.Parakh, Architect
7, Vardhaman Society, Lonavla 410401**

Reference :- Application / Letter dated 7.5.2007

From **Shri.Virendra K. Parakh
Architect
7, Vardhaman Society,Lonavla 410401**

Commencement Certificate under section 45 of the Maharashtra Regional Town Planning Act 1966
is hereby granted to :
**Mrs. Geeta Ashok Agrawal
C/o Virendra K.Parakh, Architect 7, Vardhaman Society, Lonavla 410401
For construction on land bearing CTS No. 186/ F & 186/6 'A'
Bhangarwadi, Lonavla , Tal:- Maval, Dist:- Pune**

Lonavla.as per the accompanying plan as amended by this office in green on the plan & on the
following Conditions :

1. That the commencement Certificate shall remain valid for period first year from the date of issue and there after it shall lapse.
2. That the applicant owner shall intimate the commencement of the construction work to this office in writing in advance.
3. That the applicant owner shall give the advance intimation to the collector of Pune Revenue Branch before commencing Non-Agriculture use of land.
4. Plot/land shall be demarcated on site before commencement of the work from city survey officer , Lonavla / T.I.L.R. Vadgaon.
5. If the existing trees comes under Proposed building prior approval for tree cutting to be obtained from L.M.C.
6. This Municipal Council will not supply water for construction or drinking purpose.
7. That the construction work shall be carried our strictly as per sanctioned plan and as amended by this office in green on the plan. If during the construction any departure from sanctioned plan is intended or way of internal or external changes , prior sanction of the L.M.C. shall be necessary. A revised plan showing deviations shall be submitted and the procedure laid down for the original plans heretofore shall apply to all such amended plans. Any works done in contravention of the sanctioned plans , without prior approval of L.M.C. shall be deemed as unauthorized.
8. The owner through his licensed Architect shall give notice to L.M.C. on completion of work upto plinth level , No progress above the plinth shall be carried out unless plinth is checked and approved by L.M.C.

Contd ...2...

---

9. All Building material shall be stored exclusively within a building plot. The stocking of materials and details on public roads / highways shall be prohibited except with special permission of L.M.C.

10. No temporary construction shall be permitted without prior approval of L.M.C.

11. If the electrical H.T. line is passing through or near the plot necessary N.O.C. of the concern Authority shall be submitted L.M.C. before actual commencement of the work on site.

12. If the plot is abutting on the Mumbai – Pune National Highway or and Railway line , necessary N.O.C. regarding set back distance from the concern. Authority shall be submitted to L.M.C. before Commencement of the work.

13. The structural design of building shall carried out in accordance with structural design chapter of national building code of India.

14. All material and workmanship shall be good quality confirming to Indian standard Specifications.

15. Plumbing ,sanitary and electrical work shall be carried out as per the requirement of Indian standard specifications under the supervision of authorized Licensed Holder.

16. Adequate fire fighting equipments shall be installed.

17. Copy sanctioned plan shall be made available on site whenever requirement by L.M.C. and Police Authorities.

18. The owner shall be pay necessary octroi for buildings material time and is liable to show / s submit all necessary accounts as and when required by L.M.C.

19. The owner through his licensed Architect shall give notices to L.M.C. regarding completion of work in prescribed form and shall be accompanied by three sets Record plan. The built up structure shall not brought into use without occupancy certificate of L.M.C.

20. All portions of the building shall be used for the specific purpose as shown on the sanctioned Record Plan.

21. That the L.M.C. is not responsible for any Government ,Technical ,Privet Ownership ,Area & Boundary disputes.

22. If it is noted that the information plan and other details supplied by the applicant is false or wrong the commencement of occupancy certificate shall stand cancelled & applicant will be liable for action under such consequences as maintained in relevant provisions of chapter IV of the Maharastra Regional Toning Act 1966 and the sign reserve the right to revoke or modify the permission granted.

23. Display board showing all details of development viz permission No. and date ,plot No. C.T.S. No./R.S.No. ,Plot Area ,Built up area sanctioned Nos. of tenements ,Name of the developers Architects etc. shall be erected at prominent Place on site.

24. At least   trees to be planted in the plot.

25. Provision of rain water harvesting (i.e. conservation, augmentation & recycling of water) shall be done on site.

No. ENG/BP/ 25/ 2006-07

Date : 16/ 06 /2007

Chief Officer
Lonavla Municipal Council

To ,
Mrs. Geeta Ashok Agrawal
C/o Virendra K.Parakh, Architect
7, Vardhaman Society, Lonavla 410401

C.F.W.C. to :
1. The Collector Of Pune (R.B.)
2. City Survey Officer ,Lonavla / T.I.L.R. Vadgaon (Maval)
3. Building Inspector ,L.M.C.

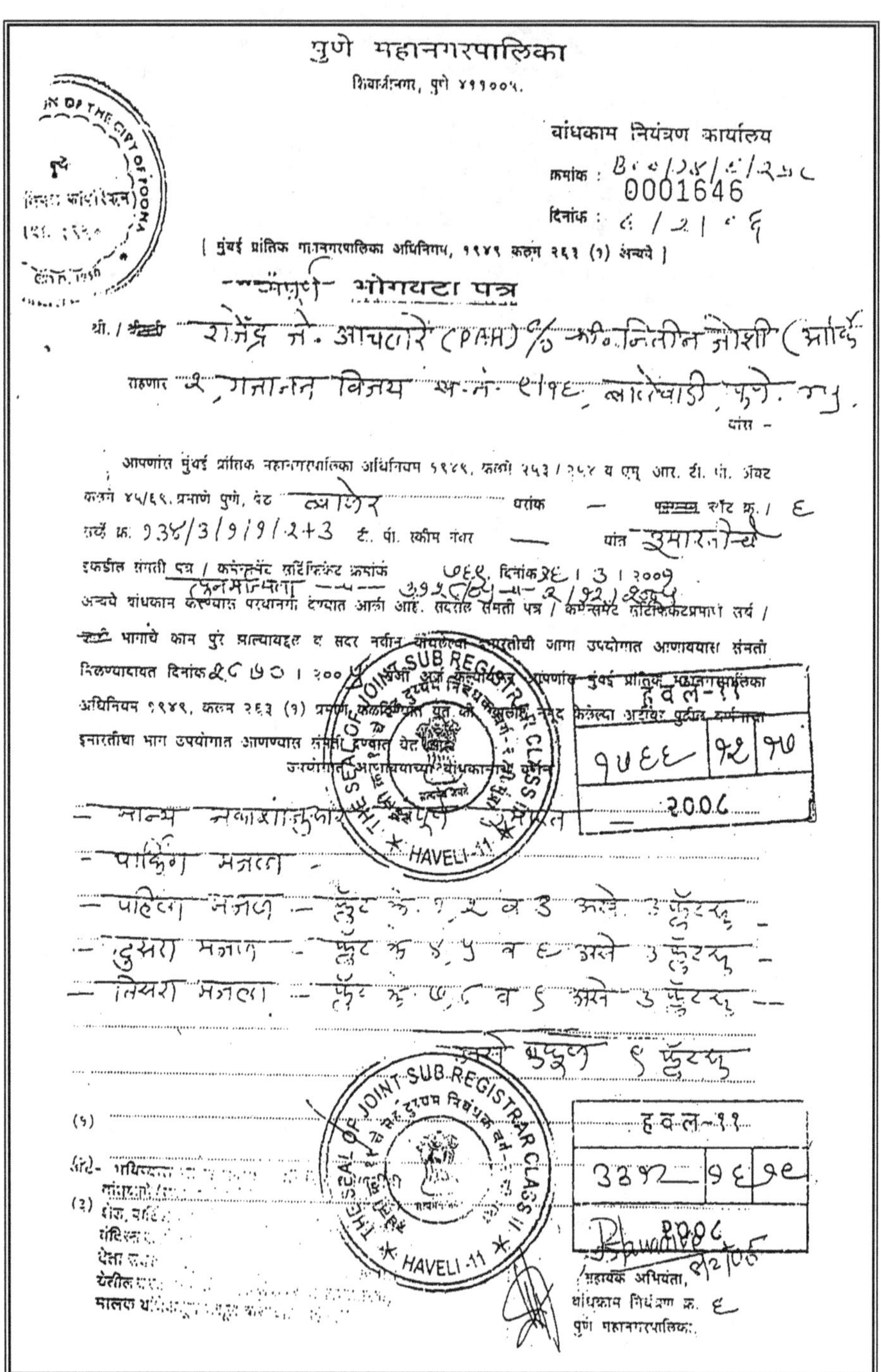

2.9 MSEB

FORM - X

प्रपत्र - एक्स

१) पूर्ण नांव : *आचढरे अशोकिट,*

    मावळत्या ग्राहकाचा पेशा / व्यवसाय :

    आणि पूर्ण पत्ता :

२) नवीन ग्राहकाचा पेशा / व्यवसाय आणि पूर्ण पत्ता : *श्री. प्रशांत सुभाषराव पाटिल*
अनुदाभ:— न्याख्याता (Lecture)
फ्लॅट. नं. ५ , गौरवी अपार्टमेंट, नाठेवाडी फाटा

३) विद्युत शक्ती जोडून दिलेल्या स्थळांचा पूर्ण पत्ता : *पाबुणढक मुढा S.N. १३४/३/१/१/२/३*
ब्लॉर, पुणे—४५

४) स्थापित यंत्रसामुग्रीचा संक्षिप्त तपशील भार
    ग्राहक क्र. व मीटर क्रमांक : *3.७ KW*
    ग्राहक क्र. 160220174589
    मिटर क्र. 9000064859

५) कारखाना किंवा उत्पादन इत्यादीचे स्वरूप : — *घरगुती*

६) व्यवसायाचे हस्तांतरण नोंदणीकृत विलेखाव्दारे :
    झाले की कराराव्दारे असे नसेल तर त्याची
    अंमलबावणी कशा प्रकारे झाली ?

७) विद्यमान मालकाची (म्हणजे मावळत्या ग्राहकाची) :
    स्वाक्षरी व तारीख :

८) नवीन ग्राहकाची स्वाक्षरी व तारीख : *१०/०६/२०१८*

९) विद्युत पुरवठा परवाना धारक किंवा अभियंता : दिनांक
    किंवा प्रभारी अभियंता यांचे अभिप्राय

१०) सुरक्षा प्रतिभूति ठेव म्हणून भरलेली रक्कम
    रूपये —————— पावती क्रमांक ——————
    दिनांक —————— प्राक्कलन क्रमांक ——————

११) (असल्यास)——————

2.10 NOC FOR ROADS, NATIONAL AND STATE HIGHWAYS

Commercial centers, residential complexes, factories etc. are increasing day by day along the road side under the jurisdiction of Public Works department. The proposals for approach road are received from public. On Scrutiny of the proposals, if found suitable the permission is granted by the Chief Engineer. After obtaining permission it is necessary to make agreement in the prescribed form. The required documents, conditions and general procedures are as follows:

1. How and Where to Apply?

If it is adjacent to National Highway then - concerned Executive Engineer of National Highway Division. If it is adjacent to the State Highway /Major District Road/Other District Road/Village Road then - Executive Engineer Public Works Division/Zilla Parishad (Works) Division.

2. Which Documents are Required with Application?

(A) Documents:

- Application from Owner.

- NOC for non-agriculture of land (Copy of NA permission from Revenue Department).

- Plot ownership document.

(B) Plans:

- Index/Key plan.

- Part of village map showing survey numbers in which private property is located.

- Layout plan/site plan showing details of construction, proposed approach road, C.D. works etc.

- Access plan showing the position proposed approach roads, exact chainage of proposed approach road, position of existing approaches on both sides of proposed approach road, land width, building line, control line, centre line of road, carriageway / formation width, C.D. works etc.

- Cross-Section of approach road.

- L/Section of arterial road for 300 metres on either side of proposed access.

- Detailed plan of C.D. works and trap drain with cross section.

- Existing access plan.

- Plan showing drainage arrangement at approach road.

3. Who Takes Decision on the Application?

(i) National Highway/State Highway/Major District Road

The Chief Engineer,

Public Works Region Ministry of transport

New Delhi.

(ii) Other District road/Village road

The Superintending Engineer

Public Works Circle.

4. Expected Period to Take Decision:

Three months approximately.

TO BE FILLED BY THE APPLICANT

To,

THE EXECUTIVE ENGINNER,

____

____

____

Subject: Access Permission for approach to Private Property Abuting on National Highway / State Highway / Major District Road.

Sir,

Kindly find enclosed herewith the proposal in prescribed formats for permission to take approach road from N. H. / S. H. / M. D. R. In km. No.__________ of __________________ road section of N. H. / S. H. / M. D. R. No. ____________ for access to private property belonging to ________________________________ in survey no. __________ / gat no. ________________ of____________ village, Taluka. ________, District ___________, in triplicate.

It is requested to please accord permission for the said access.

Thanking you

Yours faithfully

(Name and Address of the applicant)

D. A.: Checklist and drawing in triplicate and other documents in single.

PROPOSAL RECEIVED ON

Details to be furnished for obtaining access permission for approach road to private property.

Name of Applicant with Address

____

____

____

Sr. No.	Item	Information to be furnished by applicant	Comments SDE/DE/SDO
1.	Location of the proposed road (km. ___ & Chainage ____).		
2.	Whether within municipal limit or out side municipal limit and place?		
3.	Traffic intensity on road in MT/Day, PCU and CVD, (At the nearest count post).	Do not reply	
4.	Width of road and land width available.	Do not reply	
5.	Whether there is a divided carriageway or other wise?	Do not reply	
6.	The distance from center line of the road to the plot boundary of the private property in metres (Front and Back).		
7.	The proposed construction will be used for residential purpose or non-residential purpose.		
8.	If non-residential, mention the purpose of activity (attach the development plan sanctioned by competent authority duly attested).		
9.	The distance between tangent point of the curve of the said road and that of proposed approach road in a direction parallel to the center line of the road (For arterial road it should not be less than 500 m in Urban area and 750 m in Rural area.)		

contd. ...

10.	The width of proposed approach road. (This shall be adequate to enable safe operation of the vehicles). It should be 7.50 m to 9.00 m according to category of main road).		
11.	The radius of the access for entrance and exit road with the highway (The ruling radius of curves being 30 m and the absolute minimum 13 m).	Do not reply	
12.	Whether the private property is in plain and rolling country or in hilly terrain.	Do not reply	
13.	If on plain and rolling terrain whether it is on level ground? If on hilly terrain whether slope is less than 5%?	Do not reply	
14.	Whether vehicles entering or leaving the private property would be fully visible to the traffic using the main road?	Do not reply	
15.	Distances of building line, control line & private property boundary from the center line of the road (Attach plan).		
16.	The type of cross drainage work proposed to be provided to allow road side drainage (pipe culvert / slab culvert) (Attach plan).		
17.	If pipe culvert is provided, give the diameter of pipe (It shall be 750 m diameter (Minimum). The diameter of the pipe shall be suitably made higher to cater the road side water flow efficiently).		
18.	Is the catch water drain (as per the sketch attached) provided and its details are shown in layout plan submitted with the proposal? (If not, the proposal will not be considered).		
19.	Whether the private property is affected by land acquisition proceedings or alternative improved alignment?	Do not reply	

contd. ...

20.	Whether tree cutting is required due to proposed approach road? If yes, give details and permission for cutting/ rehabilitation (Show such trees on the location / site plan).		
21.	Whether the NOC for non-agriculture of land is obtained from the Revenue Deptt.? If yes, mention No. and Date.		
22.	Whether the following document and plans are attached with the proposal? (if any one from the list is missing the application will be rejected).		
(A)	Documents: (i) Application from owner. (ii) NOC for non-agriculture of land (copy of N.A. permission from Revenue Department.) (iii) Plot ownership document.		
(B)	Plans: (i) Index / key plan. (ii) Part of village map showing survey No. in which private property is located. (iii) Layout plan / site plan showing details of construction, proposed approach road, C.D. Works etc. (iv) Access plan showing the position of proposed approach roads, exact chainage of proposed approach road, position of existing approaches upto 500 m along highway on both sides of proposed approach road land width, building line, control line, center line of road, carriage way/formation width C.D. works etc. shall be shown in different colours and distances on the plan. (v) Cross – Section of approach road. (vi) L/Section of arterial road for 300 m on either side of proposed access. (vii) Detailed plan of C.D. works and trap drain with cross section.		

Notes:

1. All plans should be signed by the owner.

2. The plan will be signed by the Deputy Engineer and Executive Engineer while submitting the proposal.

3. For the reference of the applicant the following plans are attached with the check list.

   (i) Existing access plan.

   (ii) Plan showing drainage arrangement at approach road.

4. The owner / owners (Licensee /Licensees) will have to enter license deed as per Annexure – I enclosed.

LICENCE FOR THE USE FOR NATIONAL HIGHWAY LAND

* Here enter details of premises i.e. land revenue no. etc.	1. Agreement to construct an approach road with necessary provision for drainage to *______________________________ ______________________________________ ______________________________________
* Here enter name of National Highway	______________________________________ abutting on the ________________________________ boundary of * ____________________________ in kilometer ___________ in Survey No. ____________________________
* Here enter full details of the party in whose favour Licence is issued	of the village _____________________________in the Taluka of ___________ of the ____________________ District. An agreement made this ____________________ day of ________________ between the President of India (hereinafter called the Government which expression shall, unless excluded by or repugnant to the context, including exclude his successors in office and assigns) of the one part and * ________________________________
* Here enter the name of National Highway	hereinafter called " the Licensee" (Which repugnant shall, unless excluded by or repugnant to the context, include the said Licensee's successors, heirs, executors, administrators and assigns) of the other part.

contd. ...

	2. Whereas the Licensee's has applied to the Government for permission to construct on the Government land an approach road with necessary provision for drainage to his property abutting on the boundary of *____________ in Kilometer _____________ in the ____________ Taluka of the ____________________ District, more particularly described in the Schedule annexed hereto and shown in the drawing attached hereto (hereinafter referred to as "the said premises").
	3. And whereas the Government have agreed to, grant such Permission on the terms and conditions hereinafter mentioned.
	4. Now, this agreement witnessed that, in consideration of the terms and conditions hereinafter continued and on the part of the licence to be observed and performed, the Government hereby grants to the licensee permission to construct an approach road with necessary drainage works to the said premises as per approved drawings attached subject to the following terms and conditions.

SCHEDULE

(here type the schedule refereed to in clause 2)

In witness whereof this agreement is executed in duplicate by the parties hereto on the dates mentioned below their respective signatures.

Signed by shri.

(Name in full)	For & on the behalf of
The Licensee	The President of India
The constituted attorney	Under secretary to the
The licensees	Govt. of India
In the presence of	Ministry of Surface
1. Name in full (Signature) With designation	Transport (Roads wing)
2. Name in full (Signature) With designation	1. Name in full (Signature) With designation
	2. Name in full (Signature) With designation

N.B.: Wherever alternatived such as "at " his From their Licensee Divisional has etc. are given only Licensees Executive have applicable portion should be typed in the fair licence deed.

For Office use only

To,

____

____

____

Subject: Access permission for approach road to private property abuting on national highways / state highways / major district road.

Ref.: Your Letter No. _____ Dated __/__/__.

Dear Sir,

The application submitted by you is found to be incomplete, hence it is returned herewith. The following remarks may be complied and the application may be resubmitted

____

____

____

Yours sincerely

D. A: Proposal in original Executive Engineer

____

____

____

For Office use only

No. 1

Proposal for permission to approach road from N. H. / S. H. / M. D. R. For the private property of ______________________________________ on N. H. / S. H. / M .D. R. in km. _______ of __________________________ section.

CERTIFICATE

1. The nearest existing approach road connecting on_____________ (N.H./S.H./M.D.R.) is beyond _______ m. from proposed approach.

2. The nearest C.D. Work on N. H./ SH/ MDR is beyond ______ m from proposed approach crossing N. H. Way.

3. Portion upto 200 m length on either sides of proposed approach is straight and the road banking is not more than 0.6 m.

4. The proposal fulfils the requirements of IRC- 62, 1976.

5. There is no obstacle like other approaches or accesses, C.D. Works, Big road, side trees etc, road in curve, road in high bank or road in cutting in construction to this proposed approach hence the permission may be granted.

Sub-divisional Engineer / Officer

Sub. Dn. ____ .

For office use only

No. 2

CERTIFICATE

Certified that the standards adopted in the case of proposed construction of approach road for the access to private property of ___________________ km. No.________ of ________________ Section of N.H./S.H./ M.D.R._____________ Location near ___________________ village in District _________ are as per IRC. Specification No. 62/1976.

"Guidelines for control of access on Highways."

Executive Engineer,

____

For office use only

Letter of Permission

Government of Maharashtra
Public Works Department
Public Works Region

Chief Engineer's Office,

Ph. No.

No. D-2 (HDM) /Approach Road / Dated ___/___/___

To,

The Superintending Engineer;

____

____

Subject: Access Permission from N. H. / S. H. /M.D.R. No. _____________

In Mouza ____________________ S. NO. ______ in km ________

To M/s _________________________________ grant of

Reference: ____

____

With reference to the letter cited above, access permission from N.H /S. H./ M.D.R. NO. - -------------- in Mouza ----------------------- Survey No. ---------------------- in km No. -- ---------------- for the private property of Messer's _______________________ is hereby granted subject to the conditions as laid down in Government of India, Ministry of Surface Transport, New Delhi's letter No. N.H./III/P17/75, dated 30/10/80.

The approach road and the cross drainage structure shall be constructed as per the rules. The road top level of the approach road shall be as shown in the approved drawing. The agency shall give guarantee to maintain the level of the approach road top as per the approved drawing. The permission for the approach road is granted subject to the following conditions:

1. For Urban area, any construction within the private land of Licensee /Licensees shall not be done within 6 m from the road boundary.

2. For rural area the proposed residential construction should not be done _______ m from the centre line of N.H./S.H./M.D.R.

3. For rural area the proposed Non-residential construction should not be done _______ m from the centre line of N.H./S.H./M.D.R.

4. Adequate drainage arrangement in the proposed construction shall be made so that the surface water should not flow over the highway / road.

D. A.: Set of

Proposal 2 Nos.

Chief Engineer

Copy to Executive Engineer, _________________________________

_________________________________, for information.

IMPORTANT POINTS

- Objects of zoning with its types.
- Aspects of zoning, its types, other ways of defining zones.
- Objects of DP, parameters required for quality of life, stages involved in preparation of DP and the necessity of DP.
- Procedure for formation of a co-operative society, definition, documents necessary for housing society.
- Instructions required for maintaining village from XII, VII, VI D form. Utility of the same.
- General requirements: For plan submissions, No. of copies, Owner's notice to execute the work, undertaking from supervisor, building completion certificate, etc.

QUESTIONS

1. Explain the working strategies in case of co-operative housing societies and apartments.
2. Write a note on 7/12 abstract, its importance and meaning of every terms on it.
3. Explain the utility of 6-D form.
4. Enlist the documents to be submitted alongwith building plans.

UNIVERSITY QUESTIONS

Dec. 2014

1. Write a short note on TDR.

May 2015

1. Enlist documents to be submitted for Seeking Commencement Certificate and Occupancy Certificate.

Dec. 2015

1. Explain the role of plan sanctioning authority for Co-operative Housing Societies and Apartment.

Nov. 2016

1. Enlist documents to be submitted for seeking commencement Certificate and Occupancy Certificate.
2. Explain the following

    (a) TDR   (b) FSI

Chapter 3
ARCHITECTURAL PLANNING AND BUILDING BYE-LAW

3.1 PRINCIPLES OF ARCHITECTURAL PLANNING AND DESIGN

Alongwith the planning principles studied in the subject BCEE. (like Aspect - Prospect Economy).

The design of a building needs a programme and organised process. Process at every stage from sketching the plan to the completion of construction. And the result of whole process is a architecture - a completed building - which will possess an expression. It is the space organisation for utility to facilitate function. The resulting structure is an architecture, the process behind it, is also an architecture. For architectural composition of a building, following principles are considered:

1. Unity
2. Mass composition
3. Contrast
4. Proportion
5. Scale
6. Accentuation and Rhythm
7. Materials for the exterior
8. Expression.

1. Unity: The meaning of word 'unity' is 'oneness' but it is not that oneness represented by a single thing but it means harmony among elements; the elements, which cannot split apart from each other. It is that expedient of composition which gives coherence to the parts and integrity to the whole. The unity of architectural composition lies in concept not in the units or elements and therefore to maintain unity in architectural composition some central or focal idea providing an interesting accent is created. The focal idea may be a major mass placed either centrally or to balance the asymmetrical composition. It may be a lavishly treated main entrance, a tower or a vertical element dominating the rest of the composition.

The duality and competition destroy the element of unity. If a certain form is divided into two parts by an architectural feature or treatment creating two separate elements of equal shape and size, the unity is broken. Duality and competition because of repetition can be relieved by introducing an accent to dominate the composition, as shown in Fig. 3.1.

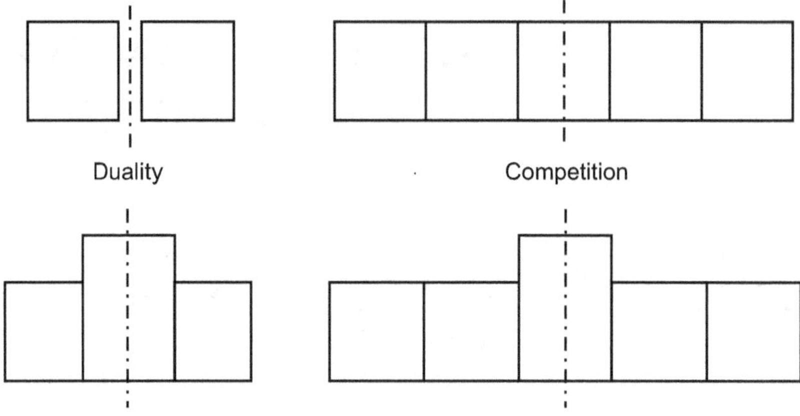

Fig. 3.1: Duality and competition relieved by dominating accent

2. Mass Composition: In architecture, mass refers to the visual effect of a body. The three dimensional visual quality of a body is its mass. Mass has some relation to the size of a body, but none whatsoever to its weight. On the basis of proper balance in composition, harmony and weighted adjustment of different masses can develop and satisfy the viewer with reference to relative importance of the various elements of the design. The balance may be either symmetrical, nearly symmetrical or asymmetrical. Fig. 3.2 shows horizontal and vertical mass and their arrangement to achieve architectural composition.

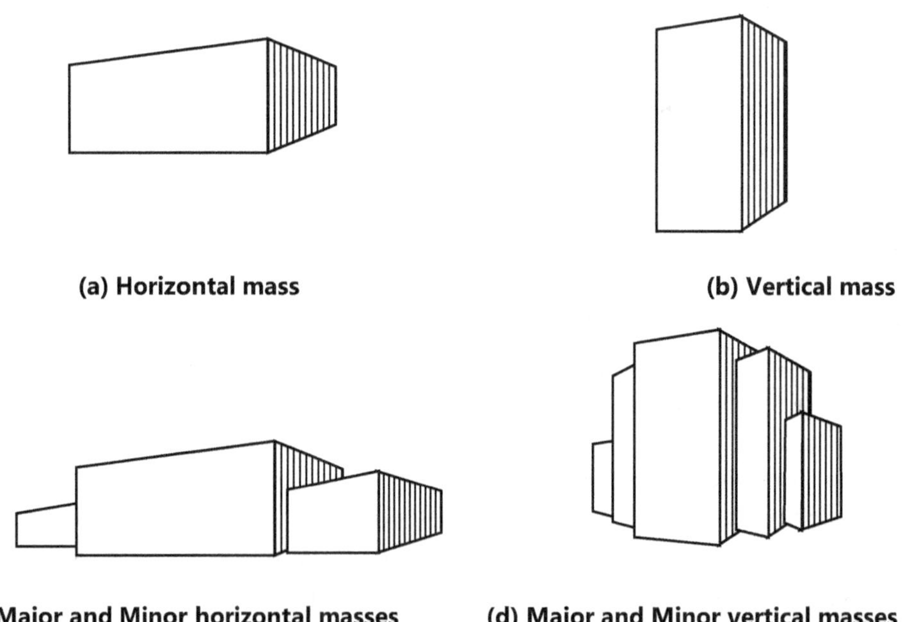

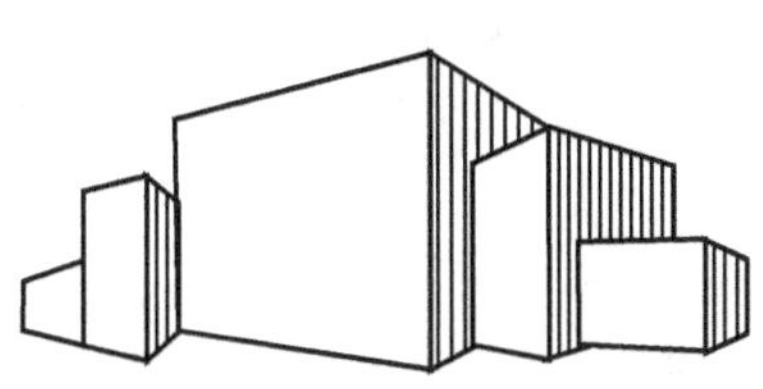

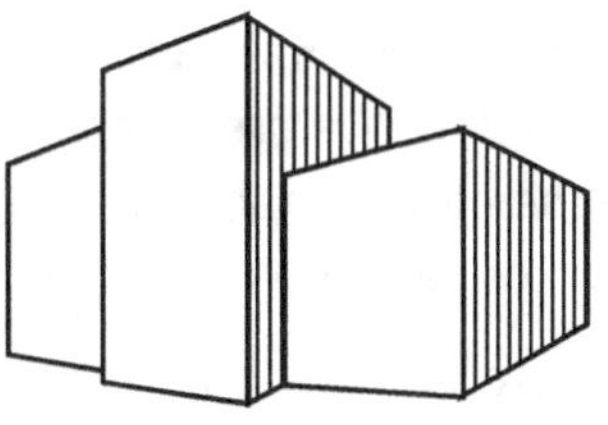

(e) Horizontal and vertical masses   **(f) Unsymmetrical but balanced masses**

Fig. 3.2: Mass composition

3. Contrast: Mass composition with harmonious unity should create interest in the design so as to catch the attention of the observer. Monotony may reduce interest. Hence, the essential requirements to avoid monotony is contrast. A well conceived contrast of form size of tone and of direction may result in serious harm to unity which is the first principle of composition. It is, therefore, necessary to make use of contrast with much restraint for the purpose of developing aesthetic sense and maintaining unity with variety. Contrast can be achieved in mass, in space, in mass and space, in surfaces, in colour, with light.

4. Proportion: Mass composition is the result of arrangement of various elements in proper proportion with each other and that with the compositions as a whole. Proportion is entirely a matter of relationship. It is not the actual size but the relative size of one form to another. Unless the proportion is correct to the scale of conception, it would be violation not only of conception but it will mislead the perception and do harm to the character of the building. For instance, if a giant sized door is provided to a residential building, it would confuse about the purpose of the building.

5. Scale: The proportion is not merely a matter of relative dimensions but the result of scale also. In architecture, scale means the proper relation of several parts to one another and to the whole from aspect of size. The "Intimate scale" is used to suit the needs of man. The size of doors, windows, staircase, steps (rise, tread) etc. should suit the user and create a feeling of comfort and ease. On the other hand "monumental scale' is used to create an effect of grandeur and grace, so as to impress the observer. By providing wide treads, wide width of staircase, graceful height, large size of columns and comfortable height of ceiling, this scale can be achieved.

6. Accentuation and Rhythm

> **Accentuation:** After viewing any space (internally and externally) a person always has a special feeling about a particular element. This feeling is because of the impression, emphasis, rigidity, firmness, function, decisivity of that element. This emphasis of the element is termed as accentuation.

> **Rhythm:** Any repetitive occurrence of a particular pattern is called as rhythm. Rhythm may also be created by successive decrease or increase in the dimensions of chosen pattern.

7. Materials for Exterior: The elevational treatment creates basic visual impact on observer's mind. We are aware of the fact that functional aspects can be seen or emphasized through the elevational, treatment given to the building. Hence, while selecting the materials one must concentrate upon this factor.

The character grows out of the function as we know and this can be achieved through unusual perfect combinations to fulfill the need of the exterior. As such the end result is that the building can be immediately recognized as temple, school, hospital etc. Simplicity in design, proper choice of the material and its disposition are the key factors to achieve the character.

For example: Corporate buildings are associated with glass façade these days, whereas marble is normally preferred for temples. Stone masonry work or block work is usually preferred in case of huge public buildings.

8. Expression: Expression represents the creation of the building and represents the harmony through colour code, shapes, lines etc.

Internal and external expressions are looked upon differently. Exterior deals with physical form and external feature but internally it is represented by interior spaces and disposition.

Exterior expression is related with façade treatment, vertical and horizontal lines etc.

Mass, proportion, rhythm etc. all are responsible for expression as it is the visual effect.

"Expression in building is thus not only reflected but also educative, with building being the most immediate and continuous physical environment of man. Architectural expression strongly shapes man's psychology and influences his esthetic sensitivity".

By, Architect, Heinrich Engel

Book, The Japanese House.

Other Principles:

Form: Definite forms appeal to human eye is a fact as they can readily perceived and understood. 'Form' refers to the shape of the building arrived at as a result of the functional requirment of the programme.

Man found different forms from the observation of nature. Discontinuity and continuity is the characteristics of natural forms. Angles and polygonal forms expressed discontinuity, whereas circles and curved lines and surfaces represent continuous forms.

Posts, beams, panels and trusses are constructed as discontinued structures and these structures are then integrated with continuous structures in the form of vaults, shells, or other curved surfaces. The real aim of architectural composition is to integrate forms and materials of the structure.

Aesthetics: A practicable synthesis of all principles of planning with due thought to the site and climate may result in a structure which may be a mere utility, devoid of any aesthetic sense. Aesthetics is purely subjective, a personal apeal to one's feelings, knowledge and experience. "Aesthetics is a branch of philosophy. Its aim is to search and uncover the elements and factors of the beauty.

Beauty demands aesthetic considerations at every stage and step of the process in creative architecture. These considerations constitute the spirit of architecture, aesthetical revealment is the overall effect of composition. It may be the composition of plan or exterior of the structure. The effect of aesthetics is related to the (i) architectural composition, (ii) interior design and (iii) landscape architecture. The main principles of architectural composition are (i) Unity, (ii) Mass composition, (iii) Contrast, (iv) Proportion, (v) Scale.

Function: It is the function of the building which primarily dictates the plan and forms. The functional character in architecture results when external expression of the building is the manifestation of internal function. It is the result where "form follows function". Functional design deals with the development of plan composition to facilitate in purely practical way the purpose of the building. Sizes are decided according to the requirements in accommodation and rooms are grouped in their functional sequence. For instance factory buildings are planned according to their functional sequence and plans are made very simple. Current architectural design is interplay of materials, methods and functions with forms determined by materials almost as much as by function. Every element may express its own function and altogether the function of the building as a whole.

Planning for Utility and Aesthetics:

Building represents an enclosure wherein many activities are conducted. For satisfactory working and performance of the occupants it is essential to provide better working environment within and outside of the building.

Planning can be viewed or judged by considering the function and form of the building as well as the feeling that we are getting from the utility of the building and aesthetics. Function, form, utility and aesthetics can be depicted through the submission drawings and working drawings.

3.1.1 Planning for Utility

The word utility encompasses the utility of the entire layout; the infrastructure provided within the layout and also the utility of the building and within the building itself.

Utility of the Layout: The layout of the area indicates the approach roads, internal roads, positioning of the buildings (residential, commercial, industrial, educational etc.), marginal distances, etc. Also, other important features within the layout are locations of security office, water storages, drainage facilities, electric substation and supply, gas connections etc.

For finalizing the layout many aspects are to be considered by an Architect and Landscape designer, viz.

- Prevailing D.C. Rules.

- Climatic variations, solar path.

- Soil characteristics and site exploration (For topography and other natural characters).

- Owners choice.

- Material availability and characterization.

- Optimization techniques, maximum and deliberate use for natural resources.

- Functions to be performed by the occupants.

- Sequential operations which will be indicated through connectivity matrix etc.

- Location of site, total number of occupants, frequency of visitors, guests etc.

- Sensory and cultural characteristics of the place etc.

A **bubble diagram** will help the designers in many ways in this regard. This indicates models of physical space and its utility for various aspects (on % basis also it can be finalized), program requirements or existing conditions. The main use of this bubble diagram is in representing the relationships between various components in plan. Different bubble diagrams for the same area represent different relationship possibilities and one of them is finally approved.

While planning an area one must concentrate upon:

- Approach and departure

- Entry and egress

- Movement through order of spaces

- Functionality of and activities within the spaces

- Qualities of light, colour, texture, view and sound.

Services within the Area: A preliminary topographical survey is essentially to be carried out to check for the contour patterns. This will help in finalizing the road pattern as well as to decide the locations for storage reservoirs, water supply and drainage layouts, treatment plant (if any) etc. Also, considering the entry and exit, nearness to mains etc. electric substation, telephone facilities, checkposts etc. can be located properly.

Utility Concept as Applied to a Building:

A building can serve many objectives and hence there is a basic difference while planning for a residential building, a commercial building, an institutional building or so. Hence, in other words form of a particular building is related with the functional behaviour of the building.

Thus in case of functional utility one most concentrate upon:

- Size specifications, owner's requirement and funds availability.
- The purpose and scope of the building.
- Prevailing bye-laws.
- Grouping of different units depending upon the function and number of users.
- Details about furniture requirement and its disposition.
- Roominess (of the area).
- Flexibility: Accomodative and adoptable use of the space helps in opting relative changes.
- Due care for sufficient provisions of sanitation, ventilation, light, cleanliness and maintenance provisions (alongwith appropriate technologies, Refer green buildings and other relevant paras).

Every possible check can be established at every level and many flow diagrams and line plans may be drawn by the architects considering grouping, circulation, orientation (aspect – prospect), privacy, elegance and economy.

Also, other parameters are checked such as cost/m^2, cost/m^3, FAR etc. and then the approval from the owner is obtained.

3.1.2 Planning for Aesthetics

Aesthetics of Built-form

Usually proportioning systems as adopted in architecture go beyond the functional and technical details of architectural form and space and provide a different dimension called as "Aesthetics".

Aesthetic experience from a built form is altogether different than what we feel while observing a natural landscape. In natural landscaping, one may observe the following points like colours, texture, rhythm, proportions, projections etc. whereas in case of built environment in addition to above; aesthetics can be better understood by balance, symmetry, asymmetry, disposition, maintenance etc. In case of aesthetics which is related with buildings following factors play an important role, that are associated with architectural composition.

- Unity
- Mass composition
- Contrast
- Proportion
- Scale

- Accentuation and Rhythm
- Materials for exterior
- Expression (Refer principles of Architectural Planning and Design)

Working Drawings

Drawings to be submitted to Corporation/Sanctioning Authority:

- Site Plan – Block plan and area statement.
- Ground floor plan, first floor plan, basement floor plan, terrace plan and car park plan; scale: RF 1/100, i.e., 10 mm = 1 m.
- Elevation – Scale RF 1/100, i.e. 10 mm = 1 m.
- Sections passing through staircase, WC, bath etc. giving details upto the foundation.
- Schedule of doors, windows and grill work.
- Schedule giving notes for type of construction, foundation work, RCC work etc.

3.2 NECESSITY OF BYE-LAWS

A well planned and architecturally designed layout may have to be abandoned because the design does not benefit the statutory requirements in one or other respects. With all liberties in planning and designing, an architect has to shape and trim his layout if need be so as to make the resulting plan to the mark of the rules and regulations enforced by the concerned authorities. There are building regulations and bye-laws laid down by the Municipal authorities in their jurisdiction. In other areas similar statutes are made applicable by the Town Planning authorities. In Rural areas the Revenue authorities are concerned with this.

These regulations dictate upon:

- Lines of building frontages,
- Built-up area of buildings,
- Open spaces around buildings and their heights,
- Provision as to size, height and ventilation of rooms and apartments,
- Water supply and sanitary provisions,
- Structural design or sizes and sections.

The knowledge of the regulations and bye-laws, which influence the building design, needs to be considered as a sound basis for the professional architects and the students as well. While giving the details of structural elements, according to the rules and regulations, certain additional details are given here. This will help students in providing suitable sizes and sections without going in for detailed calculations. However, it is advised that students should calculate and design various members as far as possible.

If bye-laws are not followed, development will take place without proper amenities and healthy environment and all construction activities will aim at only making profit. Therefore, building bye-laws are necessary for the following objects:

- Building bye-laws help the architects or the engineers in planning developmental projects.

- Bye-laws help in carrying out systematic growth of various parts of locality and avoid haphazard development.

- Building bye-laws ensure safety against fire, pollution, health hazards and building failure.

3.2.1 Basic Definitions

1. **Act:** It shall mean:

   - The Bombay provincial municipal corporation Act - 1949.

   - The Maharashtra Regional and Town Planning Act - 1966.

   - Urban land (C and R) Act - 1976.

2. **Balcony:** A horizontal projection including a handrail or balustrade to serve as a passage or sitting out place.

3. **Basement or Cellar:** Storey of a building below or partly below ground level.

4. **Building:** The word building shall have the same meaning assigned thereto as under the B.P.M.C. Act 1949.

5. **Built-up Area:** Area covered immediately above the plinth level by the building or external area of any upper floor whichever is more excepting the areas permitted in the open spaces.

6. **Building Height:** The vertical distance measured in the case of flat roofs, from the average level of the ground around and contiguous to the building to the highest point of the building and in the case of pitched roofs, upto the mid-point between the eaves level and the ridge. Architectural features serving no other function except that of decoration shall be excluded for the purpose of ascertaining height.

7. **Carpet Area:** The net floor area of all habitable rooms within an apartment excluding the area of walls.

8. **Chajja:** A sloping or horizontal structural overhang usually provided over openings on external walls to provide protection from sun and rain.

9. **Courtyard or Chowk:** A space permanently open to the sky, enclosed fully or partially by building and may be at ground level or any other level within or adjacent to a building.

10. **Detached Building:** A building whose walls and roofs are independent of any other building with open space on all sides as specified.

11. **Development:** 'Development' with its grammatical variations means the carrying out of buildings, engineering, mining or other operations in or over or under land or water, or the making of any material change, in any building or land, or in the use of any building or land and includes redevelopment and layout and sub-division of any land, reclamation; 'to develop' shall be constructed accordingly.

12. **Drainage:** The removal of any liquid by a system constructed for the purpose.

13. **Enclosed Staircase:** A staircase separated by the fire resistant walls and door(s) from the rest of the building.

14. **Existing Building or Use:** A building structure or its use existing authorisedly before the commencement of these rules.

15. **Floor Area:** It shall mean covered area of a building at any floor level.

16. **Front:** The space between the boundary line of plot abutting the means of access / roads / street and the building. The plot shall be deemed to front on all such means of access.

17. **Habitable Room:** It means a room constructed or intended for human habitation.

18. **Occupancy:** Principal occupancy for which a building or a part of building is used or intended to be used.

   - **Residential Buildings:** These shall include any building in which sleeping accommodation is provided for normal residential purposes with or without cooking or dining or both facilities.

   - **Educational Buildings:** These shall include any building used for school, college or day care purposes for more than 8 hours per week involving assembly for instructions, education or recreation incidental to education.

   - **Institutional Buildings:** These shall include any building or a part thereof which is used for purposes such as medical or other treatment or case of persons, informity care of infants etc.

   - **Assembly Buildings:** These shall include any building or a part of a building where groups of people congregate or gather for amusement, recreation, social, religious, patriotic, civil, travel and similar purposes.

   - **Business Buildings:** These shall include any building or a part of a building which is used for transaction of business for keeping of account for similar purposes.

   - **Office Buildings:** The premises where sole or principal use is to be used as an office or for office purpose; which includes, administration, clerical work, handling money, telephone and telegraph operating and operating computers.

- **Industrial Building:** These shall include any building or part of a building or structure in which products or materials of all kinds and properties are fabricated, assembled or processed.
- **Public Building:** Except where otherwise defined means a building owned and used by Government or Semi-Government or public registered trusts for public purposes.

19. **Parking Space:** An area enclosed or unenclosed, covered or open, sufficient in size to park vehicles, together with a drive way connecting the parking space with a street or alley and permitting ingress or egress of vehicles.

20. **Plinth:** The position of a structure between the surface of the surrounding ground and surface of the floor, immediately above the ground.

21. **Plinth Area:** The maximum built up covered area measured externally at the floor level or the basement or of any storey whichever is higher.

22. **Room Height:** The vertical distance measured from the finished ceiling/slab surface. In case of pitched roofs, the room height shall be the vertical distance measured from the finished floor surface upto the mid-point of the sloping roof.

23. **Row Housing:** A row house with only front rear and interior open space.

24. **Semi-detached Building:** A building detached on three sides with open spaces as specified. Provided, however, that semi-detached construction will be permitted only when the intention is to save construction cost by having one common wall and when the two buildings in the two adjoining plots are designed jointly.

25. **Site or Plot:** A parcel / piece of land enclosed by definite boundaries.

26. **Storey:** The portion of a building included between the surface or any floor and the surface of the floor next above it, or if there be no floor above it, then the space between any floor and the ceiling next above it.

27. **Tenement:** An independent dwelling unit with a kitchen.

28. **Volume Plot Ratio (V.P.R.):** The ratio of volume of building measured in cubic metres to the area of plot measured in sq. metres and expressed in metres.

29. **Width of Road:** The whole extent of space within the boundaries of road when applied to a new road, as laid down in the city survey map or development plan or prescribed road lines by any act or law and measured at right angles to the course or intended course of direction of such road.

3.3 DEVELOPMENT CONTROL RULES FOR PLAN PREPARATION

3.3.1 Plot Size

As per the development plan, a site or plot is a parcel, or piece of land enclosed by definite boundaries.

Following are the rules for various types of zones.

Residential and Commercial Zone:

(Excluding weaker section housing schemes undertaken by public authorities).

The minimum size of plots in residential layouts shall be of 50 sq. m subject to the following further provisions:

- Plots having area upto 125 sq. m shall be permitted only for row housing schemes and the width of such plots shall be between 4.5 to 8 m.

- Plots having area between 125 sq. m to 250 sq. m shall be permitted only for row housing or semi-detached housing and the width of such plots shall be between 8 to 12 m.

- Plots above 250 sq. m shall be permitted for row housing, semi-detached or detached housing and the width of plots in this category shall be above 12 m and no dimension of plot shall be less than 12 m.

The above rules will also apply to sub-division schemes layouts and building construction pattern in commercial zones.

For special housing schemes, for Low Income Group and Economically Weaker section of society and slum clearance schemes, the minimum plot size shall be 20 sq. m with a minimum width of 3.6 m or the size as prescribed by Government from time to time.

Industrial Zones: The width of plot shall not be less than 15 m and the size of plot shall not be less than 300 sq. m.

Cinema Theatres / Assembly Halls: The minimum size of plot for cinema theatre / assembly buildings used for public entertainment with fixed seats shall be on the basis of seating capacity of the building at the rate of 3 sq. m per seat or as prescribed by Government from time to time.

Mangal Karyalaya: The minimum size of plot shall be 1000 sq. m.

Petrol Filling Stations:

The minimum size of plot shall be

(a) 30.5 m × 15.75 m – for petrol filling stations without service bay.

(b) 36.5 m × 30.5 m – for petrol pump with service bay.

3.3.2 Means of Access

Every building existing or proposed shall have public or internal means of access. Any building shall not in any way encroach upon or diminish the area set apart as means of access. The means of access shall be clear of marginal open space of at least 3 m from the existing building line. The plot shall abut on a public means of access like street / road. If it is not, then the width of road shall be as per the following Table 3.1.

Table 3.1

Length of means	Width of means of access in m	
of access in m	When development is only on one side of means of access	When development is on both sides of means of access
Upto 75	5.0	6.0
150	6.5	7.5
300	8.0	9.0
Above 300	11.0	12.0

For all industrial buildings, theatres, cinema houses, assembly halls, stadia, educational buildings markets which attract large crowd, width of road shall be as per the following table.

Table 3.2

Length of means of access in m	Width of means of access (minimum) in m
Upto 200	12
Above 200	15

The length of means of access shall be determined by the distance from the farthest plot (building) to the public street. The length of the subsidiary access way shall be measured from the point of its origins to the next wider road on which it meets. In case of U-loop, the length shall be considered as half the length of the loop.

Intersection of Roads: At junctions of roads meeting at right angles or at less than 60°, the rounding off shall be done as shown in the following Fig. 3.3 and 3.4.

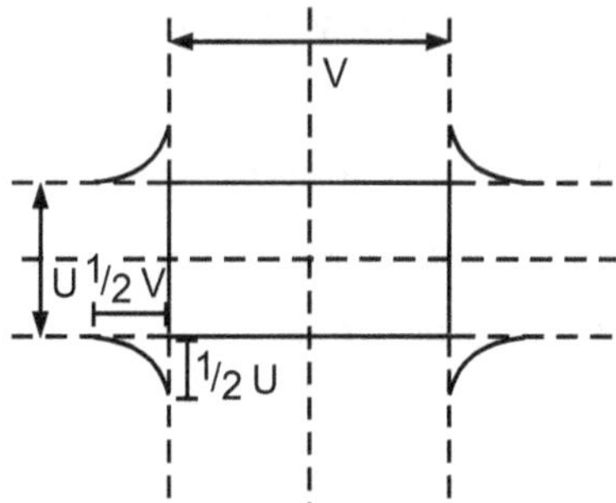

Fig. 3.3: Rounding off intersections at junctions

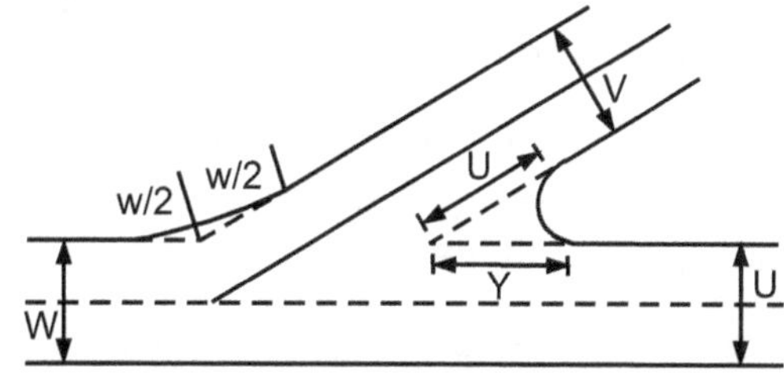

Fig. 3.4: Rounding off intersections at junctions

3.3.3 Open Spaces

In any layout or sub-division of land admeasuring 4000 sq. metres or more, 10% of the entire plot area shall be reserved as recreation of space which shall as far as possible be provided in one place. In case of very large layout, distribution of total open space in the various sectors may be allowed, provided that no such space at any place admeasures less than 200 sq. m. The shape and location of such open space shall be such that it can be properly utilized as play ground. The minimum dimensions of such recreational space shall not be less than 7.5 m and if the average width of such recreational space is less than 24 m, the length shall not exceed 2.5 times the average width.

For the open spaces having area 570 sq. m or above, a two storeyed structure having built up area equal to 15% of open space shall be permitted out of which 10% built up area shall be allowed on ground floor and 5% on first floor for the purpose of pavilion or Gymnasia or other activities which are related to open spaces.

If the open space is not directly approachable from all the buildings in the layout, an independent means of access having minimum width of 5 m shall be provided.

3.3.4 Floor Area Ratio (F.A.R.)

To maintain designed population in different parts of the city and to avoid haphazard growth of the city, local authority lays down certain controls on F.A.R., height of the building, total covered area, tenement density, Volume Plot Ratio (V.P.R.) etc.

Floor area means covered area of a building at any floor level. The quotient obtained by dividing the total floor area on all floors excluding exempted area by the area of plot is called floor area ratio or Floor Space Index (F.S.I.)

$$\text{F.A.R. or F.S.I} = \frac{\text{Total covered area on all floors}}{\text{Plot area}}$$

1. For Calculation of Covered Area or F.A.R. Following Areas are Excluded

- Projections for cornice, chajja, roof or weather shade having width less than 0.75 m.

- An unenclosed canopy not exceeding 5 m in length, 2.5 m in width in the form of a cantilever and having a minimum clear height of 2.1 m below the canopy.

- In residential buildings, a balcony at roof level above floor of a width 1.2 m measured perpendicular to the building line having maximum $1/3^{rd}$ length of perimeter of building and 10% of the floor area of each floor.

- Parking lock up garages having height upto 2.4 m.

- A basement or cellar space under a building constructed on stilts and used as a parking space, air conditioning plant rooms.

- Electric cabin or substation, watchman's cabin of maximum size 1.6 sq. m, pump house, garage shaft, fire hydrants, electric fittings, water tanks.

- Stair case room, lift rooms above the topmost floor, architectural features, chimneys.

- Well, plant, nursery, water pool, uncovered swimming pool, platform round a tree, fountain, bench, ramps, compound wall, gate, overhead water tank on top of the building.

Different rules are framed for congested area relating to the existing congested areas specified in the development plan and existing Gaothans of villages included in the municipal limits. The permissible F.A.R. shall be 1.5 for purely residential building and 2.00 for building with mixed residential and commercial use. The permissible tenement density shall be 250 T/Ha.

In case of buildings, having residential and commercial use, the commercial use will be permitted only on ground floor. The F.A.R. permissible for residential use is 1.5 and commercial use is 0.5. In case of educational, public health and charitable buildings in congested area. F.A.R. shall be 1.5. But under special circumstances, F.A.R. equal to 2.25 is permitted.

Permissible F.A.R. for buildings in areas other than congested area is given in Table 3.3.

2. Area Measurement of a Building

Following definitions explain various forms of building coverage:

Covered Area:

It is the ground covered above plinth. Area occupied by compound wall, uncovered porches, is not included in the covered area.

Plinth Area:

It is the built up covered area measured at the floor level of a building.

Following areas shall be included:

- Areas of walls at floor level excluding plinth offsets, projections beyond claddings when building consists of columns.
- Internal shafts of sanitary installations less than 2 m^2 in area, air conditioning ducts, lifts.
- Porches and other cantilevers provided.
- Area of Barsati at terrace.

Following areas shall not be included:

- Lofts.
- Internal shafts of sanitary installations greater than 2 m^2 in area.
- Unclosed balconies.
- Towers, turrets and domes unless they form a storey.
- Architectural bans, cornices.
- Vertical sun breakers.

Floor Area:

It is the usable covered area of the building at any floor level.

Thus,   Floor area = Plinth area – Walls

Following areas shall be included:

- Doors and other openings.

- Internal pillars and supports.

- Plasters along the walls exceeding 300 m^2.

Following areas shall not be included:

- Plasters along the walls less than 300 m^2.

- Fire places projecting beyond face of wall.

Built-up Area:

It is the area covered by all floors of a building. It includes everything covered under roof. Area occupied by balcony, staircase is excluded from the built up area.

Carpet Area:

It is defined as actual area of usable room at any floor level (Literally means the area where carpet can be laid). It does not include sanitary accommodations, verandahs, corridors and passages, stores in domestic buildings, staircases, and shafts for lifts, garages, air condition ducts and plant room.

3.3.5 Marginal Distances

As per the building regulations, spaces open to sky should be left around the buildings. This open space is useful from the following aspects: (a) to meet light and ventilation requirements, (b) to facilitate fire fighting operation, (c) to serve the purpose of future expansion of streets, (d) to reduce noise level and entry of pollutants in the building by planting trees, (e) to reduce loss due to fire in case the adjoining building catches fire.

The open space left between the street and building is called as front margin, open space on back sides is called as rear margin and on sides is called as side margin.

In congested areas front margin, for residential buildings facing roads 4.5 m or more in width shall be 1.5 m. For shops and commercial buildings, minimum front margin shall be 2.25 m. For educational, public health and charitable buildings, a clear open space of 3 m all around the building shall be provided. Provisions for open spaces applicable for areas other than congested areas for residential buildings, residential cum office or shop buildings permissible on plots are given in Table 3.3.

Table 3.3

Far. front/Rear/Side Margins/Tenement Densities/Heights to different categories in Non-congested residential zones

Sr. No.	Description of Road	Mini-mum plot size in m²	Mini-mum fron-tage in m	Minimum setback from road front in m	Minimum side and rear open space in m	Maxi-mum permi-ssible Ground cover-age in m²	Maxi-mum height permi-ssible in m	Far	Tenement Density/ Maximum No. of storeys permissible	Remarks
1	2	3	4	5	6	7	8	9	10	11
1.	National/State Highway, or road as specified by the Municipal Commissioner	750	18	6 m from the D. P. road line.	Half the height of the building minus three subject to minimum of 3 m (side and rear)	1/2 or 1/3	18 m	1	250 Tenements per Ha/G + 7 or G + 6	
2.	M.D.R.O.D.R. and other roads 24 m wide and above	600	18	4.5 for purely residential tenements and 6 m for other uses on groundfloor.	Half the height of the building minus three subject to minimum of 3 m (side and rear)	1/2 or 1/3	18 m	1	250 Tenements per Ha/G + 7 or G + 6	
3.	Roads of width below 24 m wide and above 15 m.	500	15	4.5 for purely residential tenements and 6 m for other uses on groundfloor.	Half the height of the building minus three subject to minimum of 3 m (side and rear)	1/2 or 1/3	18 m	1	250 Tenements per Ha/G + 7 or G + 6	
4.	Road of width below 15 m and above 9 m.	250	12	4.5 for purely residential tenements and 6 m for other uses on groundfloor.	Half the height of the building minus three subject to minimum of 3 m (side and rear)	1/2 or 1/3	12 m	1	250 Tenement per Ha/G + 3 or G + 2	
5.	Road of width below 9 m and above 6 m.	250	12	4.5 for purely residential tenements and 6 m for other uses on groundfloor.	Half the height of the building minus three subject to minimum of 3 m (side and rear)	1/2 or 1/3	12 m	1	250 Tenement per Ha/G + 3 or G + 2	

Sr. No.	Description of Road	Minimum plot size in m²	Minimum frontage in m	Minimum setback from road front in m	Minimum side and rear open space in m	Maximum permissible Ground coverage in m²	Maximum height permissible in m	Far	Tenement Density/ Maximum No. of storeys permissible	Remarks
1	2	3	4	5	6	7	8	9	10	11
6.	Road of width 12 m and below.	125 250	8 to 12	3.00	side margin 2.25 m of 2.25 m only on one side in case of semidetached rear margin 3.00	1/2 or 1/3	10 m	1	250 Tenement per Ha/G + 3 or G + 2 (i) G + 1 (ii) G + 2 with side and rear margin of 3 m.	In case of categories 6, 7 and 8 marginal distance of any building shall be minimum 3.00 m from peripheral boundary of the layout.
7.	Row Housing on Roads of width of 12 m and below.	50 125	4 to 8	3.00	side margin 2.25 rear margin 1.50	1/2 or 1/3	10 m	1	250 Tenement per Ha/G + 3 or G + 2 G – 1	
8.	Row Housing for Economically weaker reaction/ Low income group.	20 50	4	1.0 m from pathway / 2.25 m from road boundary.	side margin 2.25 rear margin 1.50	One full plot area after leaving areas under set backs	10 A	1	400 Tenements per Ha. size of the tenements should be between 20 and 30 sq. m.	

The provisions regarding built up area, permissible F.A.R. and open spaces for buildings other than residential buildings are given in Table 3.4.

Table 3.4

Type of building	Maximum permissible F.A.R.	Built-up area (maximum permissible)	Minimum open space
1. Educational buildings	1.0	1/3rd of plot area	6 m on all sides from boundaries of plot.
2. Institutional buildings (Hospitals, health centres)	1.0	1/3rd of plot area	6 m on all sides from boundaries of plot.
3. Cinema theatres, assembly halls	1.0	–	Front set back 12 m side and rear open space 6 m.
4. Public entertainment halls, Mangal karyalaya	1.0	1/3rd of plot area	Front open space 12 m side and rear open space 6 m.
5. Buildings in commercial zones	1.5	Half of plot size	4.5 m along peripheri.

When a building abuts two or more streets, the setbacks from the streets shall be such as if the building was fronting each such street.

3.3.6 Height of Building

The height of building is decided by two factors; either by the width of the street on which it fronts, or the minimum width or rear space. The height of the building is measured upto the tie beam in case of pitched roof and upto the surface of roof in case of flat roof. In case of pitched roof, the pitch is not expected to exceed 45 degrees or the height of parapet by three feet in case of flat roof. No plinth or any part of a building or out-houses shall be less than 30 (60 cm according to some authorities) above the determined level of the central part of the abutting street or foot-path, or the highest part of a service lane or any portion of the ground within 3 m distance of such a building. A Table 3.5 below gives a typical example of building heights with reference to street widths.

Table 3.5

Sr. No.	Width of street	Height of the building
1.	Upto 8 m	Not more than $1\frac{1}{2}$ times the width of the street.
2.	8 m to 12 m	Not more than 12 m.
3.	Above 12 m	Not more than width of the street, and not more than 21 m.

The height of the building with respect to the rear space is fixed by two imaginary lines – the horizontal line and the diagonal line. The horizontal line is drawn at right angles to the road, through the centre of the front line. The location of this horizontal line is taken at the higher point along the line. See Fig. 3.5. The diagonal line is drawn in the direction of the building at $63\frac{1}{2}$ degrees from where the horizontal lines meets the rear boundary. No part of the building is allowed to project beyond the diagonal line except that for minor part such as smoke chimneys, turrets etc.

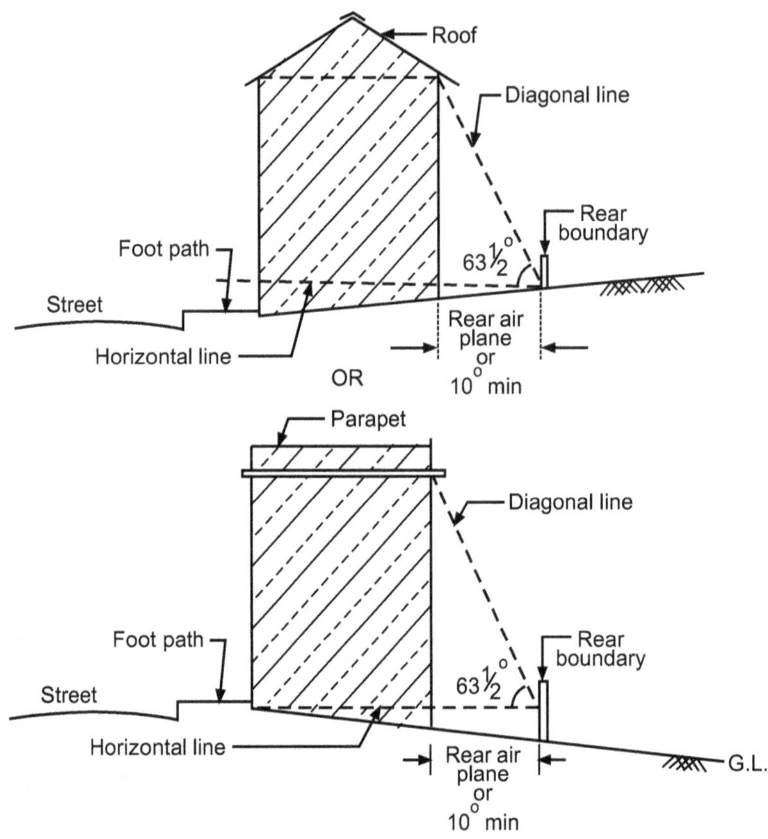

Fig. 3.5: Height of buildings with reference to rear space

3.3.7 Provisions Regarding Room Sizes

(a) Habitable Rooms

Size: No habitable room shall have a floor area of less than 9.5 sq. m except those in the hostels attached to recognised educational institutions where minimum size of a room shall be 7.5 sq. m. The minimum width of a habitable room shall be 2.4 m. One full side of a habitable room in which windows for minimum light and ventilation are provided shall abut on the required open space.

Height: The height of any room for human habitation including that of kitchen shall not be less than 2.75 m measured from the surface of the floor to the lowest point of ceiling.

For centrally air conditioned rooms, the height shall not be less than 2.4 m.

(b) Kitchen

Size: The area of the kitchen shall not be less than 5.5 sq. m with a minimum width of 1.8 m. If the kitchen is also intended for use as a dining room, the minimum floor area shall be 9.5 m with minimum width of 2.4 m.

Every room to be used as a kitchen shall have means for washing of kitchen utensils which shall lead directly or through a sink to grated and trapped connection to the waste pipe. Window of area not less than 1 sq. m opening directly on to an interior or exterior open space shall be provided.

(c) Bathrooms and Water Closets

Size: The size of bathroom shall not be less than 1.8 sq. m with a minimum width of 1.2 m. The minimum size of water closets shall be 1.1 sq. m with a minimum width of 0.9 m. If it is combined bathroom and water closet, the minimum area shall be 2.8 sq. m with a minimum size of 1.2 m.

The height of bathroom or water closet measured from the surface of the floor to the lowest point in the ceiling shall not be less than 2.2 m. Every bath or W.C. shall be so situated that atleast one of its walls shall be open to external air with the size of opening not less than 0.3 sq. m in area. Bathroom and W.C. shall not be constructed directly over any room other than water closet, washing place, bath or terrace. Bathroom and W.C. shall be enclosed by walls or partitions and surface of every such wall shall be finished with a smooth impervious material to a height of not less than 1 m above the floor of such room.

(d) Store Rooms

Size of a store room in residential buildings shall not be more than 3 sq. m. The height of store room shall not be less than 2.2 m.

3.3.8 Lighting and Ventilation of Room

All habitable rooms including kitchen shall have, for the admission of light and air, one or more openings, such as windows, fan, lights, opening directly to the external air or into an open verandah not more than 2.4 m in width.

Where lighting and ventilation requirements are not met through day lighting and natural ventilation, the same shall be ensured through artificial lighting and mechanical ventilation.

The minimum aggregate area of openings of habitable rooms and kitchens, excluding doors shall not be less than 1/8th floor area.

For ventilating the spaces for W.C. and bathrooms if not opening on the front side, rear and interior open spaces, shall open onto the ventilation shaft. The minimum size of such ventilation shaft are given in Table 3.6.

Table 3.6

Height of building in m	Minimum area of ventilation shaft in sq. m	Minimum side of shaft in m
Upto 12	3	1.5
18	4.5	1.8
20	6	1.8

3.3.9 Drainage and Sanitation

There are some regulations for minimum requirements for water supply and sanitary conveniences for different types of buildings:

(a) **Residential Buildings:** There shall be one bathroom with a tap, one water closet and one sink per dwellings. The minimum requirement of water shall be 135 litres per day per head.

(b) **For shops and Commercial Offices:** There shall be one water closet for every 25 persons, drinking water fountain for every 100 persons and wash basin, one for every 25 persons.

(c) **Hotels:** There shall be one water closet per 100 persons for males and 2 for 100 persons for females. There shall be urinals one for 50 male persons.

(d) **Educational Buildings:** There shall be one water closet per 30 pupils in nursery schools. For other educational institutions, 1 W. C. per 80 boys and 1 W.C. per 50 girls shall be provided. There shall be 1 urinal per 20 boys. Separate W.C. and urinals shall be provided for male and female teaching staff. The requirement of water shall be 45 lit. per head per day for day schools and for boarding schools 135 lit. per head per day.

(e) **Hospitals:** There shall be one water closet for every 8 beds, 2 wash basins per 30 beds and 1 bathroom for every 8 beds. In addition, there shall be separate water closets and urinals for male and female administrative staff. For hospitals, requirement of water shall be 340 litres per head per day.

(f) **Government and Public Buildings:** There shall be one water closet for every 25 male persons, one for every 15 female persons. There shall be one urinal for 7 – 20 male persons and additional one urinal for every 20 male persons. The requirement of water shall be calculated at the rate of 45 litres per head per day.

(g) **Cinema Threatres and Auditoria:** There shall be 1 W.C. per 100 persons for males upto 400 persons and additional W.C. 1 per 250 persons above 400 persons.
For females, there shall be 3 water closets per 100 persons upto 200 persons and 2 additional W.C. per 100 persons if the number is more than 200. There shall be one urinal for 25 male persons.

Separate wash basins for male and female persons at rate of 1 for every 200 persons shall be provided. Separate urinals for male and water closets for male and female staff shall be provided. The requirement of water shall be 15 litres per seat of accommodation.

(h) Industries: There shall be one water closet per 15 male persons and additional one for every 20 persons. There shall be one water closet per 12 female persons and additional one for next 13 female persons. There shall be urinals one per 20 persons and additional 1 for every 20 persons. Drinking water requirement is 30 litres per head per day.

3.3.10 Parking

Parking spaces for cars scooters and cycles shall be provided to each building depending upon the type of building and number of users. The space requirement for motor vehicles shall be 2.5 m × 5 m, for scooters - 3 sq. m, for cycles - 1.4 sq. m.

Table 3.7 shows provision for off street parking space for vehicles.

Table 3.7: Off street parking space

Sr. No.	Occupancy	One Parking space for every	Congested Area			Non-congested Area		
			Car Nos.	Scoo-ter Nos.	Cycle Nos.	Car Nos.	Scoo-ter Nos.	Cycle Nos.
1.	Residential (i) Multi-family residential	(a) 1 tenement having carpet area more than 80 sq. m.	1	2	2	1	2	2
		(b) 2 tenements having carpet area between 40 sq. m. to 80 sq. m.	–	2	4	1	4	4
		(c) 4 tenements having carpet area upto 40 sq. m.	–	4	8	1	4	4
	(ii) Lodging establishments, tourist homes, hotels with lodging accommo-dation.	(d) Every five guest rooms.	2	2	4	3	4	4

contd. ...

	(iii) Restaurants	(e) For Grade I hotel, eating houses, 18 sq. m. of area of restaurant including kitchen, pantry hall, dining rooms etc.	2	2	2	2	4	4
		(f) For Grade II and III hotels, eating houses etc. for an area of 80 sq. m. or part thereof.	–	4	8	1	4	4
2.	Institutional (Hospital Medical Institutions)	Every 20 beds.	3	2	4	3	4	4
3.	Assembly (theatres) cinema houses, concert halls, Assembly halls including those on colleges and Hostels and Auditorium for Educational buildings.	40 seats	3	5	10	3	10	10
4.	Educational	100 sq. m. or fraction thereof the administrative area and public service area.	2	2	4	2	4	4
5.	Government or semipublic or private business buildings and Auditoriums for Educational buildings.	100 sq. m. carpet area fraction thereof.	2	2	4	2	4	4

6.	(a) Mercantiles (markets, departmental stores, shops and other commercial users).	100 sq. m. carpet area fraction thereof.	2	2	4	2	4	4
	(b) Wholesale	100 sq. m. carpet area fraction thereof.	2	2	4	2	4	2
	(c) Hazardous building	100 sq. m. carpet area fraction thereof.	1	2	4	1	4	4
7.	Industrial	Every 300 sq. m. or fraction thereof.	1	2	4	1	4	8
	Storage Type		1	2	4	1	4	8
	Plots less than 200 sq. m. (any use)		–	2	4	–	2	4
	Plots less than 100 sq. m.		–	2	4	–	2	4

3.4 BUILDING LINE AND CONTROL LINE

The line upto which the plinth of a building adjoining the street or an extension of a street or future street may lawfully extend is called as **building line**. It includes the lines prescribed, if any scheme or development plan or under any other law, in force. The line refers to the line of building frontage which is known as set back or front building line.

Control Line: In case of buildings such as cinema theatres, factories, commercial concerns which attract large number of vehicles should be setback a further distance apart from the building line. The line upto which such buildings can be constructed is known as **control line**. The distance of control line from centre of adjoining street or road may be about one and half times that of building line. The distances of the lines of building frontages is decided by the category of the city zone in which the site of proposed building is located. In the development plan, the present width and future likely widening of each street and road is marked. The minimum distance from the centre line of road is prescribed for the line building frontages. The space in front of the building helps in future widening of the road, reducing noise, dust from abutting buildings and preventing creation of blind corners at the intersection of the streets. This space also helps in maintaining open spaces for air, sun etc.

Table 3.8: Distances of building and control lines

Type of Road	In open and agricultural country		Ribbon development along approaches		Actual limits in urban areas	
	Building line m	Control line m	Building line m	Control line m	Building line m	Control line m
1. National and state highway	30	56	18	30	30	45
2. Major district roads	24	45	9	15	15	24
3. Other district roads	15	24	6	9	9	25
4. Village roads	12	18	6	9	9	25

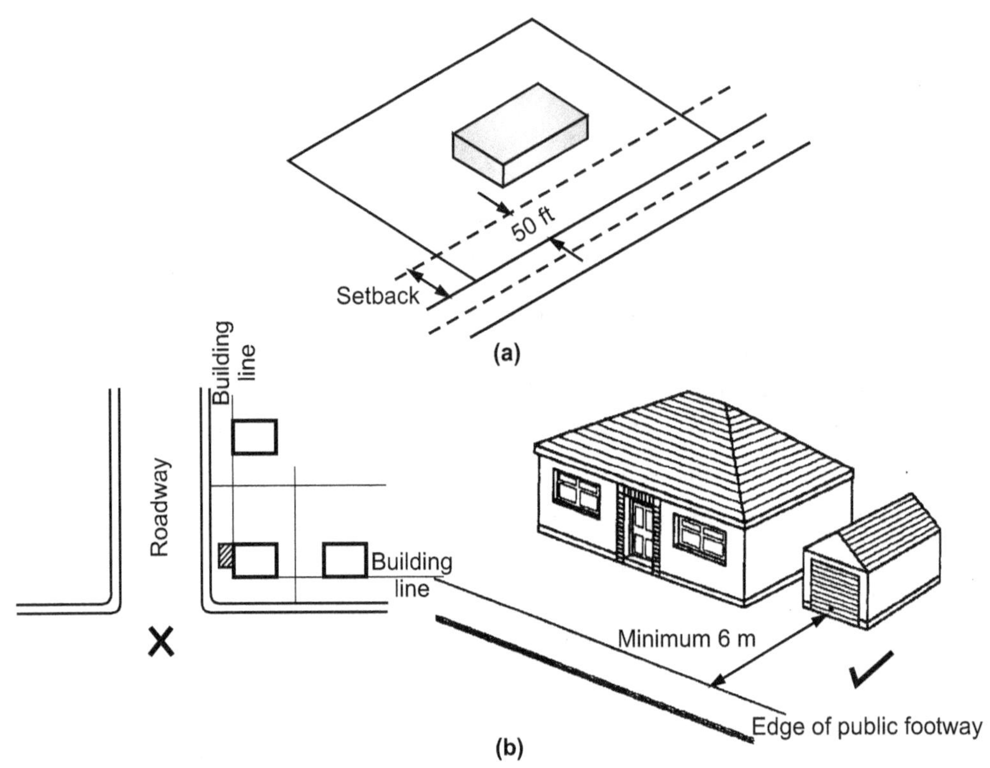

Fig. 3.6

IMPORTANT POINTS

- Necessity of Bye-laws and basic definitions used in projects.

- Area measurement of a building :

  1. Covered area 2. Plinth area 3. Floor area 4. Built-up area 5. Carpet area.

- Height of buildings for different rooms.

- Requirement of drainage and sanitation for different buildings.

- TDR its definition, eligibility, documents to be submitted for availing TDR.

- Principles for Architectural composition of a building with its points.

- Salient features of a green building.

- Site integrating with respect to green buildings along with types.

QUESTIONS

1. What are the objectives of framing development control rules?

2. What are the criteria for minimum area of plot?

3. What is F.A.R.? What are the areas exempted while calculating F.A.R.?

4. Why open spaces around any building should be left?

5. What is building line and control line?

6. What is FAR? State its necessity.

7. What is building line and control line? Explain their importances.

8. It is decided to plan a single storeyed hospital building. Enlist the essential amenities and areas for the different units. Explain also, with sketch, how you will apply principle of grouping, while preparing a flow diagram.

9. Enumerate the various area calculations in building and explain any one in detail.

10. Explain the necessity of building byelaws.

11. What is the difference between built-up area and carpet area?

12. Explain any one of the following:

    (i)   Building line and control line. OR

    (ii)   Rules regarding height regulations of buildings.

13. Explain the following terms with sketches:

   (i)   Building line.

   (ii)   Control line.

   (iii)   Marginal distances.

14. State the byelaws regarding road width and height of building.

15. What is Floor Area Ratio (FAR)? State which areas of construction are excluded while calculating floor area ratio.

16. Write a detailed note on building line and control line. Mention its distances for all types of roads.

17. Discuss the importance of built-up area, plinth area, and carpet area.

UNIVERSITY QUESTIONS

May 2014

1. Explain the following principles of architectural planning with suitable sketches : Privacy and Roominess.

Dec. 2014

1. Differentiate between building line and control line by drawing a suitable sketch.

2. Explain the important aspects of layout of water supply and drainage systems.

3. Explain the following principles of architectural planning with suitable sketches : unity and accentuation.

Dec. 2015

1. Explain various rules for lighting, drainage and sanitation as per building rules and bye laws.

Nov. 2016

1. Explain the following principles of architectural planning with suitable sketches: Prospect and Roominess

Chapter 4
INTRODUCTION TO GREEN BUILDINGS

4.1 INTRODUCTION OF GREEN BUILDINGS

The concept of Green Building is essentially based on the premise that economic development and urbanization need not go against the flow of nature. Green Building principles reflect through the complete building life cycle and are aimed at reducing impact upon the environment. The essential element of green building is to make the most efficient use of resources such as energy, water and material, and to ensure that the building maintenance activities do not burden the environment.

It is now being increasingly realised across the world that the benefits of sustainable design are not limited to the environment alone, but can rather have a significant effect on your bottom-line as well. Well designed sustainable design systems go a long way in reducing operational costs by avoiding resource wastage. Besides, adopting the sustainably approach creates improved goodwill within the consumers and the corporate world at large.

4.1.1 Planning Concepts of Green Buildings or Eco-Housing

Eco-Housing: There is an urgent need to address the great challenges of our times: climate change, resource depletion, pollution, and peak oil. These issues are all accelerating rapidly, and all have strong links with the building industry. Eco-friendly construction can not only help to create a better outdoor environment, it can also help to build a healthier indoor environment. Green building is not only a wise choice for our future; it is also a necessary choice. The construction industry must adopt eco-friendly practices and materials that reduce its impacts, before we reach a point of irreversible damage to our life supporting systems. The industry needs to take its own initiative and find alternative ways to build, using green, renewable energy resources, and adopt non-polluting practices and materials that reduce, recycle and reuse, before it is too late.

A carbon footprint is used to calculate the amount of damage caused by an individual, household, institution or business to the environment through harmful carbon dioxide emissions. Reducing carbon dioxide emissions is seen as essential to sustaining the environment and can be achieved in two ways: **Reduction of Carbon Dioxide Emissions and Carbon Offsetting.**

There are many ways that companies and institutions can reduce carbon emissions. Here are just a few which may not only reduce carbon emissions but in turn improve overall efficiency of the houses.

- Enacting a recycling policy.

- Enacting and promoting a car-sharing scheme amongst its employees.

- Encouraging employees to walk or cycle to work.

- Educating employees in the need to reduce carbon emissions.

- Reducing the need for air travel.

- Reducing the use of electricity.

- Developing new methods of work and manufacturing that are less harmful to the environment.

- Other forms of carbon offsetting include investing in organizations that promote awareness of environmental issues and supporting sustainable technologies (such as solar or wind power).

- Use of locally available materials

- Use of daylight for sustenance

- Use of reclaimed materials

- Use of Environmentally Friendly, Non-Toxic Paint

- A Green Roof

- Use of insulating materials

- Adopting new developments: Environmentally Friendly Concrete

The list is endless; here few from the above said list are detailed in and the students may work out for the remaining areas on their own.

(a) Eco-house
(b) Wind power
(c) Day light
(d) Stone-Bricks
(e) Local material
(f) Reclaimed material

Fig. 4.1

Wind Power

Wind generators are generating a lot of interest right now, offering the first small wind generator commonly available for the home. We need to dramatically reduce the emissions from the fuel and carbon we use, and wind as well as solar is one of the energy sources in plentiful supply, that we are learning to use.

Harnessing Energy From Wind

Wind generators work by having their turbine blades, usually three, rotating in the wind, turning a copper coil inside a magnetic field, which in turn creates an electrical current. Clearly the stronger the wind the faster the blades will turn, hence the importance of siting the generator in a high, exposed place, where wind is continuous, or as continuous as can be expected.

Electricity created inside this unit, the current, can then be fed through the system directly into the grid, via a grid tie inverter, which converts the currents voltage.

Solar Energy

- Passive solar energy heating for cold climates, and passive solar cooling for hot humid climates.

- The term "Passive Solar Energy" means that basic physical concepts (such as sunshine, warm air rising, and cool air falling) are used to Heat and Cool a building, without the need for fans, water pumps, or other "active" mechanical equipment. Using solar radiation to Passively Heat Air and Water is very easy and inexpensive to do.

- Using the sun's solar energy for Cooling and Dehumidification in a hot humid climate, (where the night time air is too warm and contains too much water vapour to use for direct ventilation), is a challenging engineering problem.

The Importance of Recycling

Many people simply dispose of unwanted or used and consumed items without giving it much thought. They simply don't bother to consider the consequences of their actions. For example, things like batteries and electronics items often contain chemicals where, if they end upon a landfill site, they will eventually seep through the bottom and pollute the ground water. This results not only in the contamination of our water supply but also contamination of the soil in which we grow our food. Once in the food and water supply chain, these chemicals are impossible to get rid of so we are putting our own and future generations supplies of food and water and our own and future generations health at risk. Simply put, by not recycling, we are diminishing energy, water and other natural resources that mankind relies upon which is why we should get hold of a list of going green tips, which we can follow as well as doing some research on the green products which are available to us.

Lighting accounts for around 15% of the energy bill in most homes, and around 25% in commercial buildings. It is supplied by electrical power plants using fossil fuels, and is responsible for a significant percentage of carbon dioxide emissions, a leading cause of global climate change. Because of this, the building industry has targeted lighting as a key element in sustainable design, and there is now a global movement to develop and implement lighting solutions that meet people's needs and concerns, and address environmental regulations. One must concentrate upon the following factors.

Daylighting Design

The most sustainable lighting is natural daylight. It is not only a free renewable resource but it also has well-documented health benefits. Careful architectural design is required to maximise natural light in a building while maintaining indoor temperature regulation and reducing direct light glare. The strategic placement of windows, skylights, light shafts, atriums and translucent panels in harmony with other building components, such that light is reflected evenly throughout internal spaces, is known as daylighting design.

Sunlight Transportation Systems

An emerging new technology is that of sunlight transportation. Natural sunlight is collected on roof panels and transported into a building via fibre optic cables for distances upto 15 metres. These sunlight-piping systems can be used in combination with solar panels to integrate natural and artificial light systems, so that there is always light in the home.

Energy Efficient Light Bulbs

The sustainable building industry is primarily focused on energy efficient lighting solutions. Standard light bulbs, known as incandescent bulbs, are known to be highly inefficient. Electricity is passed through a metal (tungsten) filament that heats to over 2000° celsius and glows to give off light. Only 10% of the electrical energy is converted to light; 90% is wasted as heat. Halogen bulbs are similar but instead have a small pocket of halogen gas that reacts with tungsten to produce light. They burn brighter, use less electricity and last twice as long as a standard bulb, but are still inefficient compared with other forms of bulbs.

Energy efficient light bulbs use significantly less energy than incandescent bulbs, and also last longer. There are two main kinds: Compact Fluorescent Lights and Light Emitting Diodes.

(a) Compact Fluorescent Lights (CFL)

These are small versions of full fluorescent lights, and consist of a glass tube coated with phosphor, filled with gas and a small amount of mercury. Electricity jumps off electrodes on the end of each tube, and excites the mercury molecules to emit ultraviolet light. This excites the phosphor coating, which emits visible light that shines out of the tube. CFLs give off the same amount of light as incandescent bulbs, but they are upto 80% cooler, are four times more energy efficient (to replace a 60 watt incandescent, you only need a 15 watt CFL), last

10 times longer (upto 20,000 hours), and are responsible for the emission of 70% less carbon dioxide.

CFLs come in many different configurations and wattages, and are suitable for all lighting purposes. Although more expensive to buy than a standard bulb, they easily recover their costs in energy savings. On the downside, they contain trace amounts of mercury, which is hazardous to health and the environment. Care needs to be taken to ensure the glass tube doesn't break and that the bulbs are disposed of safely.

(b) Light Emitting Diode (LED)

LEDs are small, solid light bulbs that are lit by the movement of electrons in a solid semi-conductor material as electricity is passed through it. This is also called 'solid state lighting', because it uses a solid material, as opposed to gas (CFL) or filament (incandescent). LEDs are extremely energy efficient, lasting over 100 times longer than incandescent bulbs, and upto 10 times longer than CFLs. They have low heat generation, low power requirements, and are highly durable because there is no filament or tube to break.

LED is a relatively new technology, and currently the bulbs are most suitable for track and recessed lighting, where a pointed light is required rather than radiated light. They are more expensive than CFLs, but energy savings over their lifetime means their cost is soon recouped. Because their power inputs are minimal, LEDs are readily combined with solar panels to provide reliable, energy efficient lighting day and night.

Use of Locally Available Materials

Sustainable building is an essential aspect of widening efforts to conceive an ecologically responsible world. A building that is sustainable must, by nature, be constructed using locally sustainable materials: i.e. materials that can be used without any adverse effect on the environment, and which are produced locally, reducing the need to travel. There are key criteria that can be used to judge whether a material is sustainable or not:

- To what extent will the materials used in this building cause damage to the environment? When using locally sustainable materials it is essential that those materials are renewable, non-toxic and, therefore, safe for the environment. Ideally, they will be recycled, as well as recyclable.

- To what extent will a building material contribute to the maintenance of the environment in years to come? Alloys and metals will be more damaging to the environment over a period of years as they are not biodegradable, and are not easily recyclable, unlike wood, for example.

- To what extent is the material used locally replenishable? If the material is locally sourced and can be found locally for the foreseeable future, travelling will be kept to a minimum, reducing harmful fuel emissions.

Reclaimed Materials

The construction industry is under increasing pressure to become sustainable. One way to address this is through the use of reclaimed materials. Reclaimed materials are those that have been previously used in a building or project, and which are then re-used in another project. The materials might be altered, re-sized, refinished, or adapted, but they are not reprocessed in any way, and remain in their original form. Materials that have been reprocessed and reused in the building industry are referred to as recycled materials.

Examples of materials that can be reclaimed include: bricks, slate roofing, ceramic tiles, fireplaces, doors, window frames, glass panels, metal fixtures and fittings, stairs, cobbled stones, steel sections and timber. A reclaimed material is often adapted for a different use, for example, a roof beam might be used as a mantelpiece. This is known as **re-purposing**.

Where to Find Materials

The best place to source reclaimed materials is direct from a demolition or re-modelling project. Many of these projects carefully dismantle buildings in such a way that their materials can be sold and re-used. In the building trade this is known as **deconstruction**.

Reclaimed materials can also be sourced from salvage centres, reclamation yards and other specialist companies, who buy and sell materials that they have salvaged themselves from demolished sites. There are hundreds of salvage companies, some which deal only in high-end architectural materials, and others that are more like junkyards. Good quality, rare and heritage materials can be gleamed from salvage suppliers, and while purchasing can be more expensive than those sourced direct from a demolition site, there is a much wider choice of materials available on demand.

Reclamation in Sustainable Development

Ongoing rapid development means that many historic buildings are being demolished to make way for new affordable housing and commercial space. Redirecting building materials from the waste stream of this process, and reusing them in other nearby projects is a critical component of sustainable development. There is a huge amount of construction waste, and the potential to reuse this to reduce landfill and new materials is enormous. When reclaimed materials are secured from an existing building site, the environmental impact is virtually zero. Even when they are sourced from far away, reclaimed materials are still the most environmentally friendly option for supplying materials to the building industry.

4.1.2 Salient Features of a Green Building

- Minimal disturbance to landscapes and site conditions.
- Use of recycled and eco-friendly building material.
- Use of non-toxic and recyclable materials.
- Efficient use of water with recyclable techniques.

- Use of energy efficient and eco-friendly equipment.
- Use of renewable energy.
- Quality of indoor air for human safety and comfort.
- Effective controls and building management systems.

The most important aspect is to consider many developmental alternatives and to explore opportunities to win-win design changes that further sustain building goals and reduce cost.

The efforts in this regard will start from selection of site.

In general one may consider the following points:

- **Use Appropriate Building Sites:** As a general rule, promote sensitive infill consistent with local plans and infrastructure is environmentally preferable to create a new development requiring.

- **Preserve Open Space:** Incorporate the preservation of open spaces – undeveloped land and resource areas into building project while avoiding impact on previously undeveloped open spaces. If open spaces must be developed, consider donating an equivalent amount of land elsewhere to open space status.

- **Reduce Sprawl:** Channelize the new building to previously developed areas with existing infrastructure wherever possible, while protecting green fields (natural or park areas) and preserving habitats. This is most relevant to developments in established suburban or urban environments. Even in rural areas, consolidating residential development through clustering which can produce vibrant communities with stores and services located within walking distance thereby reducing transportation needs and the potential for future sprawl patterns.

- **Develop Brown Fields:** (Rehabilitation of abandoned buildings and sites). A brown field is a real property, the expansion, redevelopment, or reuse of which may be complicated by the presence or potential presence of a hazardous substance, pollutant, or contaminant. Developing brown fields allows the cleanup and recycling of existing infrastructure while preventing degradation of undeveloped land.

- **Safeguard Endangered Species:** Avoid entirely any dry land or wet lands specifically designated as habitat for an endangered or threatened species.

- **Restore Damaged Environment:** Some building projects may provide the opportunity to restore damaged lands to a natural state, such as conservation of gravel parking lots to fields, wet lands or replanting trees or native grasses.

- **Design to optimize Sun, Wind and Light:** The beneficial impacts of designing a building around its local climate and topography is to achieve desirable sun, wind and light patterns. Can be quite impressive, also one must take into account impact of building on its surroundings.

4.1.3 Site Integration

- **Enhance Naturally Occurring Biodiversity:** To achieve this reconnect fragmented landscapes and establish continuous networks with other natural systems in and around site. Avoid major alterations, establish car free areas and develop foot traffic zones.

- **Minimize Site Disturbance:** Issues of concern include degradation of water quality through pollution or siltation, damaging soils through digging or mixing foreign materials etc. this can be minimized by proper site management plan.

- **Storm Water Management:** The problem arises because naturally porous vegetation is replaced with impervious surfaces like roads, parking lots etc. This causes far higher flows into local streams with high amounts of silt and potential pollutants from construction vehicles and building operations. Mitigate these problems by maximizing the use of porous surfaces or by capturing runoff.

- **Optimize Transportation Options:** This can be opted for maximizing convenience and minimizing transportation energy and time required by building users. Strategies include siting new buildings near public transport services, by promoting bicycles, covered bike racks etc. Parking lots can include spaces with electricity or natural gas recharging capacity in commercial buildings parking spots can be reserved for car pools.

- **Reduce Heat Islands:** These are responsible for creating detrimental impact on microclimate, human comfort and on animal habitat. It can be mitigated by providing shade from trees or roofs from highly reflective surfaces. Replace or line the constructed surfaces with vegetation or use star rated roofing material.

- **Reduce Light Pollution:** Reduce the intensity of external night lights, limit the height of the buildings and cover or partially shade the bright lights.

4.1.4 Benefits of Green Buildings

Environmental Benefits	Economic Benefits	Occupational Benefits
• Enhance and protect ecosystems and biodiversity • Improve air and water quality • Reduce solid waste • Conserve natural resources	• Reduce operating costs • Enhance asset values and profits Improve employee productivity and satisfaction • Optimize life-cycle economic performance. • Reduces future liability. Increases retail sales	• Improves air, thermal and acoustics • Enhances occupant comfort and health • Reduces healthcare costs Improves employee satisfaction and morale- less absenteeism and turnover

Green building materials are those with the least environmental impacts throughout their life cycle, whether measured in terms of energy used, scarce natural resources or air and water emissions. Reusing or recycling materials has substantial environmental benefits well beyond the weight of the material actually reused or recycled on site. Green building projects, like other building supplies, are required to meet the highest safety and performance requirements. The most significant benefits involve the reduced use of energy, reductions in air and water pollution during resource extraction and manufacturing and the safeguard of scarce natural resources.

Green Building Materials Strategies:

Prepare a Green Building Product Selection Plan

Excellent resources are available to assist with and the companies should discuss priorities with the contractors team at the earliest moment. While it is impractical to thoroughly evaluate every product alternative, it is reasonable to ask the contractor team to include green building products in the products considered at every stage.

Use of Salvaged Building Products

Salvaged products like doors, framing, windows or plumbing can save costs and sometimes allow the use of high end or antique products that can greatly add to a building's ambience. They simultaneously keep old products out of the waste stream and they eliminate the need to manufacture new products. Deconstruction firms are beginning to compete effectively in some instances with demolition firms.

Use Recycled Content Building Products

Recycled Content Products (RCP) must meet or exceed all the performance, health and safety requirements of other buildings products. Examples of products include lumber and carpet made from recycled plastics, cellulose installations made from recycled newsprint, aggregates made from recycled asphalt or glass, masonry blocks made from recycled glass and many more. For e.g. recycled plastic lumber made from 100% post consumer recycled plastics is available. This is suitable for 2 × 4 decking. Many other dimensions and products are available, such as 2 × 4 structural strength; 3/8" plywood sheet at prices comparable to the wood counterparts. These products are advertised as being maintenance free and come with a claim of no staining or rotting.

Use Locally Available Materials

Each region produces a range of construction products unique to that region. Purchasing these products from the local suppliers rather than from distant resources can substantially save on shipment costs while greatly reducing their life cycle energy use. Depending on the region, materials like straw bales, earth or cob may be available which are appropriate for some residential buildings in certain climates with adequate rebar or other fortification to meet any applicable earthquake safety specifications.

Use Rapidly Renewable

Rapidly renewable resources include agriculture-based materials like straw converted into pressed board products. Plastics can be made from agriculturally grown products. Boards can be made from sunflower seeds and wheat grass. Wool carpet is another example.

Use Certified Wood

The smart wood program evaluates and recognizes forests managed according to sustainable principles. The Hoopa lumber is also certified by the Forest Stewardship Council (FSC). Criteria for certification include, ensuring the long term health and productivity of forests for timber production, wildlife habitat protection, clean air and water supplies, climate stabilization, spiritual renewal, and social benefits.

Use Structural Insulated Panels

Structural Insulated Panels (SIPs) are high performance building panels that can be used in floors, walls and roofs, in both residential and commercial buildings. The panels are often made of Expanded Polystyrenes (EPS). SIPs are very strong, energy-efficient and cost effective. SIPs can reduce construction waste considerably and can be a very cost effective way of increasing the overall energy insulation of a building.

Commissioning of Green Buildings

Commissioning is a systematic process – beginning in the design phase and extending through a typical period – of ensuring through documented variation, that all building systems perform interactively according to the contract documents, and that the faculty staff are properly trained and system documentation has been adequately provided.

Commissioning and Green Building design share three things in common:

- They both involve a systems approach to look at the buildings and its performance.

- They both view buildings from a life-cycle perspective.

- They both involve increased attention during the design phase to ensure that the design meets the owner and occupant needs.

Benefits of Green Buildings

(I) Energy Savings:

Energy efficiency may be the foundation of green buildings. Buildings account for 36% of all energy use. Reducing energy use in buildings reduces the impacts proportionately. Increased efficiency also yields increased comforts, aesthetics, and productivity. Strategies used for energy saving result in a home or commercial space that are vastly more comfortable to live or to work in.

Energy Saving Strategies:

(a) Passive Solar Design:

- Optimize the site, design and orientation.
- Landscape to provide natural shade.
- Use natural daylight.
- Use natural heating and ventilation.

(b) Energy Management Plan:

- Evaluate tradeoffs and minimize projected energy costs
- Train building occupants
- Track and optimize performance overtime
- Employ an energy management system and commissioning

(c) Energy Efficient Products:

- Use high performance thermal insulation
- Use high performance roofing and glazing
- Use high performance lighting
- Use high performance HVAC (Heating Ventilation and Air-Conditioning) systems.

(II) Waste Reduction:

Waste reduction is one of the two approaches used to conserve materials in green buildings. The other approach being, the purchase of reused and recycled products. Waste reduction can focus on the construction site and can be part of an overall maintenance and operations plan. Rehabilitating buildings, reusing components of existing buildings or using salvaged building products may result in substantial cost saving, where it is a feasible option. They also have significant environmental benefits involving reduced use of energy, reductions in air and water pollution during resource extraction and manufacturing, and the safeguarding of scarce natural resources.

Waste Reduction Strategies:

- Prepare and implement a construction waste reduction plan
- Rehabilitate existing buildings
- Demolition / deconstruction waste management
- Design to facilitate recycling and reuse
- Specify products that can be repaired or renovated instead of replacement
- Specify environmentally preferable products and practices

(III) Health and Productivity Benefits

There is growing recognition of the large health and productivity costs imposed by poor Indoor Environmental Quality (IEQ) in commercial buildings. This is not surprising as people spend 90% of their time indoors and the concentration of pollutants is typically higher than outdoors (ten to hundred times).

Following are some relevant attributes common in green buildings that promote healthier work environments. On an average 25-30% more energy efficient, much lower source emissions from measures such as better sitting, significantly better lighting quality, generally improved thermal comfort and better ventilation, commissioning use of measurement and verification, CO_2 monitoring to ensure better performance of systems such as ventilation, heating and air conditioning.

(IV) Indoor Air Quality

Experience and research shows that these risks can be reduced or eliminated through the strategies discussed in this module. Like day lighting enhanced IAQ is a sustainable building strategy that can yield tangible benefits to users each and every day. The concept is responsible to increase the productivity at large.

IAQ Improving Strategies:

- Ensure adequate ventilation
- Designate indoor smoke free spaces
- Use low emitting building products
- Install controllable systems
- IAQ management plan

(V) Water Efficiency

Water is the most vital of all resources for all living bodies. If the water conservation strategies are integrated with landscaping, industrial use etc. it will be an important step towards reducing the pressures on pure water supply.

Strategies to Achieve Water Efficiency:

- Water use management plan
- Indoor water conservation
- Outdoor water conservation (through rain water collection, sustainable landscape technique, high efficiency irrigation technique, innovative waste water management, use waterless urinals, use biological treatments).

Green Buildings in India

The concept of GB is not new. Our ancestors worshipped the five elements of nature. Today through LEED (Leadership in Energy and Environmental Design), we are rediscovering the Indian ethos.

First GB in India: CII GODREJ GBC – PLATINUM RATING

ITC GREEN CENTER – GURGAON

WIPRO TECHNOLOGIES – GOLD RATING

GRUNDFOS PUMPS – CHENNAI- GOLD RATING

NEG MICON, CHENNAI

Standards followed: NBC guidelines, MoEF guidelines, CPCB norms, ENVIS norms etc

LEED Green Buildings Rating System-Certification Levels

Sr. No.	Credits	New building
1.	Energy and Atmosphere	17
2.	Indoor Environmental Quality	15
3.	Water Efficiency	5
4.	Sustainable Sites	14
5.	Materials and Resources	13
6.	Innovation and Accredited Professional Points	5
	Total	69

Rating	New building
LEED certified	26-32
LEED certified-silver level	33-38
LEED certified-gold level	39-51
LEED certified-platinum level	52-69

Through PMC Eco-Housing rating is set recently and if any building satisfies a particular level mentioned then many benefits will be given for the same like reduction in the Tax etc.

Science and Technology Park:

1. Science and Technology Park (Scitech Park) is one of the Science and Technology Entrepreneurship Development Parks (STEPs) promoted by National Science and Technology Entrepreneurship Development Board (NSTEDB) of Department of Science and Technology, Government of India and University of Pune with an aim to convert **"Knowledge into Wealth"**.

2. Pune Municipal Corporation has appointed Scitech Park as the Certifying, Monitoring and Evaluating agency for Eco-housing certification of residential buildings.

3. One of Scitech Park's unique initiative is the Eco-housing Certification Program for certifying residential projects using world test practices adequately modified for application to different climate conditions.

4. **The Certification Criteria:**

   - Climate specific
   - Focus on Resource Conservation
   - Site planning
   - Environmental architecture
   - Water management
   - Eco-friendly building material
   - Renewable energy
   - Solid waste management
   - Other innovative measures.

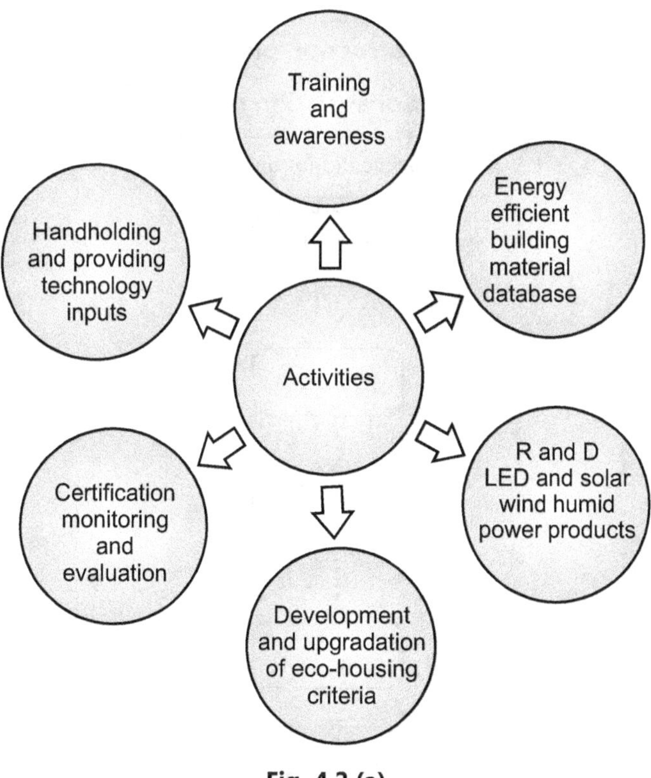

Fig. 4.2 (a)

5. **Climatic Zone Specific Criteria:** For the first time the certification criteria has been customized following different climatic zones of India which makes it more scientific.

   - Hot and Dry
   - Warm and Humid
   - Composite
   - Temperate
   - Cold.

6. **Star Rating System:**

   - 500 – 600   *
   - 601 – 700   * *
   - 701 – 800   * * *
   - 801 – 900   * * * *
   - > 900   * * * * *

Design and Pre-construction phase

Construction phase

Post Construction phase

```
+-----------------------------+
|     Certification process   |
+-----------------------------+
             |
             v
        +-------------+
        | Registration|
        +-------------+
             |
             v
        +-------------+
        | Evaluation  |
        +-------------+
             |
             v
        +-------------+
        | Provisional |
        | certification|
        +-------------+
             |
             v
        +-------------+
        |    Final    |
        | certification|
        +-------------+
```

(b)

Fig. 4.2

Star Rating	Rebate in Total Premium	Rebate offered with Provisional Certificate
*	10%	5%
* *	20%	10%
* * *	30%	15%
* * * *	40%	20%
* * * * *	50%	25%

Star Rated Projects	Star
Nyati Environ, Phase I, II, III – M/s Nyati Builders	*****
Kumar Sublime-Bldg A & B M/s Kumar Builders	*****
Crossover County M/s Darode-Jog Lagad Venture	*****
Rohan Mithila, Plot B, C, D M/s Rohan Builders and Developers (I) Pvt. Ltd.	*****
Kool Homes – Solitaire M/s Kool Homes Group	***
Kool Homes – Arena M/s Kool Homes Group	***

4.1.5 Environmentally Friendly, Non-Toxic Paint

All paints contain three main components: pigment (colour), a binder (holds the paint together) and a carrier (disperses the binder). With many modern paints these ingredients are made using toxic chemicals that are harmful to both the environment and human health. Cadmium, lead and chromium are frequently used in pigments; and petrochemicals, solvents, benzene, formaldehyde and other volatile organic compounds (VOCs) are used in binders and carriers. Toxic, environmentally harmful, chemicals are also used in modern paints as preservatives, stabilisers, thickeners and driers.

VOCs are organic (carbon based) chemical compounds that evaporate easily in the atmosphere, and are known to be a major contributor to global climate change. Many of them are highly toxic and linked with numerous health problems such as respiratory disease, asthma, dizziness, headaches, nausea, fatigue, skin disorders, eye irritation, liver and kidney damage and even cancer. Modern chemical paints continue to emit VOCs many years after their application.

Increasing concerns about the impact of chemical paints on health and the environment have led to a growing market in non-toxic paints. Environmental regulations have forced conventional paint companies to significantly reduce their VOC content, and most of the large paint companies now offer one or more varieties of non-toxic paints. However, many of these still contain VOC solvents, chemical pigments and fungicides.

Eco-Labels for Paints

Non-toxic paints are often called Low-VOC, No-VOC, VOC-Free, odourless, odour-free and green, natural or organic paints. There are no set standards for defining these labels, and they are widely misused for marketing purposes. To help consumers make informed decisions on their paint purchases, various ecological labels have been developed by different countries to indicate that the paint has fulfilled certain environmental requirements, in accordance with respective government regulations. These eco-labels can be found as logos on paint cans, and include the European Eco-Label, Blue Angel in Germany, and Green Seal and Green guard in the USA. In the UK, VOC labels are used, and indicate the content of VOCs using one of five classifications: Minimal (0-0.29%), Low, Medium, High and Very High (VOC content greater than 50%).

Low-VOC paints tend to use water as a carrier instead of petrochemical solvents, and so their emissions are minimal. Many conventional paints have achieved relatively low VOC levels. No-VOC or VOC-Free paints may still contain very low levels of VOCs in their pigments or additives. Although reducing VOC content is a move in the right direction, it is questionable whether either of these paint types can be considered non-toxic.

Natural Paints

Natural paints are the only true non-toxic paint since they contain no VOCs, and are made from natural ingredients such as water, vegetable oils, plant dyes, and natural minerals. The main binders used in natural paints are: linseed oil (from flax seeds), clay, lime, and milk protein. Lime and milk paints give an authentic period look, and are often used in antique restoration projects. Chalk is used as an extender to thicken paint; turpentine (distilled from pine trees) is used as a solvent; essential oils from citrus fruits (d-limonene) are used as a solvent and fragrance; and natural mineral and earth pigments are used as colorants.

The main benefits of natural paints are:

- **Non-toxic:** No hazardous fumes or harmful effects on health. This is significant for allergy sufferers and chemically sensitive people who are unable to tolerate chemical paints.

- **Environmentally Friendly:** Use renewable resources; are biodegradable, can even be composted.

- **Micro-Porous:** Allow walls and surfaces to breathe, preventing condensation and damp problems, and reducing associated indoor allergens. They are also less prone to paint flaking, peeling and blistering.

4.1.6 Green Roofing

Plants have been used on roofs for thousands of years, from sod roofs in Europe to the hanging gardens of Babylon. But in the last 50 years this practice has evolved into what are now called green roofs, living roofs or eco-roofs. Green roofs are those that have been planted with specific vegetation using a well researched sustainable design methodology. They are an exciting new development in the sustainable building movement, and are gaining in popularity across the world.

Types of Green Roof

While there is no standard classification for green roofs, they can be divided into two basic types:

1. **Intensive Living Roofs:** These incorporate plants from between 1 to 15 feet high, including shrubs and trees. They require deep levels of soil to support them and a weight loading roof. They support a high level of plant and wildlife diversity, but require ongoing maintenance and extensive irrigation. They are not suitable for most domestic buildings.

2. **Extensive Living Roofs:** These incorporate low-lying plants from 2 to 6 inches high. They require only a few inches of soil to support them, and only need a low weight-loading roof. They are low maintenance and can be used for any kind of roof, including sheds, garages, houses, balconies, extensions and outhouses, and also commercial buildings.

Both types of green roofs can be used for flat or pitched roof construction. Flat roofs are the most common and the easiest to establish and maintain, but green roofs can have a pitch upto 45 degrees. With sloped roofs, there are design issues affecting drainage and soil loss that need to be carefully considered.

How to Construct a Green Roof?

A green roof system consists of layers that mimic natural processes and also protects the building and roof. The basic components are: a waterproof layer, root repellent membrane, filter cloth (to allow water to drain but prevent soil escaping), moisture blanket (to ensure enough water retention for plant life), drainage system (to drain excess water), soil substrate, seeds and plants. The soil is the growing medium and should be lightweight and free draining, but also be able to hold enough moisture for the plants to survive. Recycled aggregates such as crushed porous brick are often used in the soil substrate, with the added benefit of increasing its sustainability index.

Plants suitable for extensive green roofs are low growing, rapid spreading, drought-tolerant, have a fibrous root system (to protect roof membranes), low irrigation and nutrient requirements, low maintenance requirements, use native species, and are allergen-free. Short perennials, wild flowers and succulents such as sedum (stonecrop) are commonly used. To help cut down on planting time, impregnated sedum and wild flower mats are now commercially available. These can be rolled out directly onto the soil.

Living roofs can be designed to grow native plants that might otherwise become endangered, and to encourage a wide range of important wildlife including insect species such as butterflies, bees and beetles, and local birds.

Benefits of Green Roofs:

There are a number of social, economic and environmental benefits to green roofs, including:

- Increasing home energy efficiency - cooling in summer, insulation in winter.
- Filtering and cleaning toxins from both air and water.
- Reducing carbon dioxide emissions.
- Retaining rainwater before it evaporates, reducing the likelihood of flooding.
- Reducing urban temperatures and associated smog.
- Insulating against sound and noise.
- Preserving and enhancing biodiversity.
- Providing aesthetic appeal and 'green space' recreational opportunities.
- Using recycled materials like aggregates and plastic sheets.
- Biomass roofing is the use of plant materials to build roofs.

The Different Types of Biomass Roofing:

Although hundreds of different plants have been used to roof houses, these can be classified into two main types: thatch and wood tiles.

1. Thatch

- All sorts of plants have been used for thatching in Britain: oats, reeds, broom, heather, bracken and various grasses. But today only three main thatching materials are used: water reed, wheat reed and long straw.

- Water Reed is the most popular thatching material. Both water reed and wheat reed (actually a straw but cut with a binder and combed to give the appearance of reed) gives a compact and even texture when applied to a roof. This is in contrast with long straw (wheat straw that has been thrashed so that the ears and butts are mixed up together), which gives a shaggy, rounded appearance. The lifespan of thatch is around 30 to 50 years, although this varies widely depending on the skill of the thatcher, the pitch of the roof, the local climate conditions and the quality of the materials.

- The technique for thatching is basically the same for all materials, first the thatch is fastened together in bundles about 25 inches in diameter. Each bundle is then laid down with the butt end facing outwards, secured together to the roof beams, and pegged in place with wooden rods. Successive layers are added on top of each other, working from the bottom of the roof up towards the top, with a final layer used to reinforce the ridgeline.

- Thatch roofs can withstand high winds and heavy rains, provide good thermal insulation and are easy to repair. Thatch is light and needs only a simple support structure, and is flexible so can be used for any roof shape. On the downside, thatching is labour intensive and a certain level of skill is required. The materials can be expensive as reeds are increasingly imported from Europe to keep up with demand. Like all biomass materials, thatch is flammable which means that building restrictions may apply and home insurance can be high.

2. **Wood Tiles: Shingles and Shakes**
   - Wood tiles have been used for roofs since medieval times in Britain. They are traditionally made by hand-splitting logs into small wedge shaped pieces, but today most are manufactured by machine. There are two basic types: shingles, which are sawn, and shakes, which are split. Shakes are thicker and have a more rustic, rough look, whilst shingles are thinner and smoother. Both come in a variety of lengths and are made from the heartwood of unseasoned wood. Hardwood is best, with cedar being the most popular, although any straight-grained wood can be used. Split bamboo can also be used to create Spanish-style tiles, and are popular in some countries, but bamboo has the disadvantage of decaying fast in wet conditions unless chemically treated.

   - Wood tiles are laid from the bottom of the roof to the top, with each row overlapping the previous one. A cap is placed at the roof ridge. Typically tiles are nailed onto wood strips spaced a few inches apart between the roof beams, to allow air to circulate and prevent decay.

   - Wood tiles last between 25 - 50 years. Like thatch, they give good insulation and are flexible so can cover any roof shape. They are highly resistant to wind, heavy snow and hail, but must be regularly cleaned of vegetative debris. They are also flammable, and building regulations may prohibit their use in urban areas.

Is Biomass Roofing Sustainable?

The recognised need to use renewable resources has led to a revival of traditional, natural building methods, along with a growing market for biomass roofing. Thatch and wood tiles are not only aesthetically appealing, but are durable and biodegradable. But their sustainability value is diminished if the materials have been imported or produced and treated with chemicals. Biomass roofing is only a true sustainable solution if the materials are obtained from a local, renewable source, and are grown, harvested and manufactured in an environmentally sensitive way.

4.1.7 Use of Insulating Materials

Insulation is a key component of sustainable building design. A well insulated home reduces energy bills by keeping warm in the winter and cool in the summer, and this in turn cuts down carbon emissions linked to global climate change.

In terms of energy efficiency, investing in high levels of insulation materials for your home is more cost-effective than investing in expensive heating technologies. It is worth taking the time to choose the right materials in the context of whole building design.

Insulation materials are used in roofs, walls and floors. Solid wall structures such as stone, cob and adobe cannot be insulated, but they have good thermal mass to compensate. Timber frame homes need wall insulation in the form of batts (pre-cut sections that are designed to fit between stud walls), rolls or boards. Other types of construction such as brick or concrete insulate with spray foam, loose fill or rolls. It is far easier and cheaper to install insulation in the walls and floors of a new build home, than to retrofit an existing home. However, insulating roofs is easily achieved in any home using rolls or bags of loose fill.

Insulation materials work by resisting heat flow, measured by an R-value (the higher the R-value, the greater the insulation). This R-value varies according to material type, density and thickness, and is affected by thermal bridging, unwanted heat flow that occurs at joists, studs and rafter beams.

Conventional Insulation:

Conventional insulation materials are made from petrochemicals and include: fibreglass, mineral wool, polystyrene, polyurethane foam, and multi-foils. These materials are widely used because not only are they inexpensive to buy and install, but there is an assumption from the building industry that their performance ability is higher than the natural alternatives. On the downside, almost all conventional insulation materials contain a wide range of chemical fire retardants, adhesives and other additives, and the embodied energy in the manufacturing process is very high.

Natural Insulation Materials:

The green alternative to synthetic insulation is natural insulation. There are many different types available, including:

(a) Sheep's Wool

This material usually needs to be treated with chemicals to prevent mite infestation and reduce fire risk, although some natural builders use it untreated with success. It has very low embodied energy (unless it is imported) and performs exceptionally well as an insulation material. Thermafleece is the most common commercial brand available.

(b) Flax and Hemp

Natural plant fibres that are available in batts and rolls, and typically contain borates that act as a fungicide, insecticide and fire retardant. Potato starch is added to flax as a binder. Both materials have low embodied energy and are often combined in the same product. Examples include Isonat and Flax 100.

(c) Cellulose

A recycled product made from newsprint and other cellulose fibre. It is one of the most favoured materials of natural builders because it can be blown into cavity walls, floors and roofs; used as a loose fill; and is also available in quilts, boards and batts. Like hemp and flax it contains borate as an additive. Products include: Warm cell and Eco-cell.

(d) Wood Fibre

Made from wood chips that have been compressed into boards or batts using water or natural resins as a binder. It has very low embodied energy and uses by-products from the forestry industry. Examples include: Pavatex, Thermowall and Homatherm.

Expanded Clay Aggregate

These are small fired clay pellets that expand at very high temperatures to become lightweight, porous and weight-bearing. They can be used in foundations as both an insulator and aggregate. They have excellent thermal insulation properties, but high embodied energy.

Insulating for a Better Environment

Natural insulation products have many advantages over conventional materials. They are low impact, made from renewable, organic resources and have low embodied energy. They can be reused and recycled, and are fully biodegradable. They are non-toxic, allergen-free and can be safely handled and installed. They also allow for buildings to breathe by regulating humidity through their absorbent properties, and reducing problems of condensation. This keeps the indoor environment comfortable and protects any timber structures from rot.

Unfortunately, natural insulation materials are currently upto four times more expensive than conventional materials, which can be prohibitive to builders, architects and developers. But the environmental and health benefits of natural insulation materials far outweigh their costs, and growing consumer demand combined with government regulation, and rising oil prices will inevitably drive prices down. Despite the high price, natural insulation is an energy-efficient, healthy and sustainable choice for a better indoor and outdoor environment.

Use of New Techniques: A potentially sustainable new form of concrete has been recently created that might make it the most environmentally friendly type of building material.

Concrete in its traditional form is made from cement, mixed with a range of coarse aggregates such as gravel, limestone or granite, and some finer particle aggregates such as sand or fly ash.

These are mixed together with water, to form a quick drying bonded structure, which can easily be manipulated into many forms such as the surface of roads, or driveways or footings for structures. It is the most commonly used building material in the world - some estimate that in the region of 7 cubic kilometres of concrete are manufactured each year, and that there already is 1 cubic metre of concrete for every human on earth.

Unfortunately concrete is not an environmentally friendly material, either to make, or to use, or even to dispose of. To gain the raw materials to make this material, much energy and water must be used, and quarrying for sand and other aggregates causes environmental destruction and pollution.

Concrete is also claimed to be a huge source of carbon emissions into the atmosphere. Some claim that concrete is responsible for upto 5% of the world's total amount of carbon emissions, which contribute to greenhouse gases. This is created in the heat that is needed to create the raw cement - cement is burnt at high temperatures, and materials such as limestone must be burnt to create the high temperature.

A New Form of an Old Material

Scientists at a British concrete manufacturer, the London-based Novacem, claim to have developed a new form of concrete that effectively absorbs large amounts of carbon dioxide as it hardens. Novacem's new version of concrete, uses a different raw material, magnesium sulphate, which requires much less heating. Novacem claim that each tonne of cement can absorb up to 0.6 tonnes of CO_2. This is opposed to figures that claim that each tonne of old style cement emits about 0.4 tonnes of CO_2.

Stones and Bricks

Stone is a beautiful natural material that can be cut to any size, and will enhance the exterior or interior of any building. A stone-clad building has a natural elegance to it, that gives it a timeless quality.

Brick can be made to any shape and most sizes, and because it is a man-made material, can be very flexible in its quality and potential uses. The use of red brick particularly can make a property very distinctive.

Weighing Up the Benefits of Both Materials

Whether or not one material outweighs the other is not a straight-forward case; Stone needs to be quarried, which clearly has an environmental impact, dressed, and transported. Using locally quarried stone can offset some of this impact, or you might be lucky to have stone already on-site. Using stone from the site you are building which emulates the environment, and could be said to offset the impact of having to transport materials from further distances. It is also said that a stone-built building gives the effect of anchoring the building to the land, and into the local environment. Regional stone has its own distinctive colour, texture and quality.

However, both stone walling and cladding a wall with stone is a slow, laborious job, requires a lot of skill and patience that many enthusiastic self-builders may not have, and above all, it is highly physically demanding.

Stone buildings are also notoriously colder. They are great in hot climates where the thick stones keep the inside cool, but heat doesn't get effectively trapped by stone. Creating an insulation layer of either thin wood or a rendering of lime can help this.

Brick, on the other hand, takes as much resources from the land as stone, in the different components used.

Also the heating process to cook the brick has an environmental impact. There is much more opportunity to get exactly the type, texture, size and colour of brick you need to construct with, which is a big advantage. Unfortunately, the material is likely to come from further away, so bear in mind this important environmental impact of travel. If cost is the most important factor in design and construction of your project, brick is going to be the cheaper material to use. It is easier to use, and the skills involved in building with brick are less and easier to learn.

Using the Right Material for the Job

These differences shown between the two materials show the unique possibilities of building with brick or with stone. It is possible, and quite common, to use a combination of brick and stone when designing and constructing a building. For example, using stone as a feature on an exterior wall, as a stone accent, or as a fascia, sets off a standard brick wall. Bearing in mind the sustainable element of the materials, comparing the impact of producing both, from a quarry or from a furnace, has to be specific to your project.

4.2 COST EFFECTIVE HOUSING

Every human being needs a shelter which will give him/her comfort, healthy environment to live in. Different income group requirements are different.

For any type of housing, fund management is an important task in front of the developer and/or owner.

The overall construction activity can be divided into:

- Planning and designing
- Execution and
- Maintenance.

Cost effectiveness, if worked out right from planning stage results in the requirement of less maintenance during the lifespan of any building.

Planning and Designing Stage: Following steps are necessarily to be considered for achieving economy.

(i) Crystal clear ideas to be given to the architect about the need of the owner. Economic backing, plot utility, positioning of rooms, total number of rooms etc.

(ii) Preparation of plan-elevation and section and submitting to authorities and to avoid delays in sanctioning (Use of user friendly softwares may prove to be best suitable option).

(iii) Phasing the activity and use of CPM-PERT networks. Phasing of activity in turn will reflect possible overlap between different activities. Merely observing the overlaps one can assess about the labour force, payments, administration requirement etc.

(iv) If modular units are used, repeated use of form work helps for reducing the overall cost.

(v) Selection of locally available materials. Locally available material saves the energy in transportation. Every check on feasibility, availability and strength parameters can easily be applied for the same.

(vi) **Labour Management:** For different activities different types of labours are required to be deployed like skilled, semi-skilled and unskilled labour. If the total count of these for any activity can be decided well in advance, it is useful in managing the labour. To achieve expected quality one must ensure about the interdependency of the activities and corresponding labour. Also proper training is to be provided to the labours as per requirement of the job.

(vii) **Testing of Materials:** To check for the necessary specifications. Crushing, bending, shear, tensile tests, water absorption, efflorescence tests etc. are responsible for detecting the quality of the materials to be used.

Other relevant factors which are totally dependant on area, door-windows, passages etc. are as under:

- In case of two buildings with same built-up area around 5% saving is possible if length is kept minimum.
- Minimum doors and windows.
- W.C./bath with minimum areas and provided individually for convenience for mass class.
- At entrance or exit, one combined unit for door and window may be adopted.
- Provide minimum passage width.
- Storage units within the wall in the form of cupboards will save the cost.
- Precast – Prefab units for mass class construction.
- Internal road networking, positioning of O.H. storage tank, drainage line, electric substation etc. also plays an important role in reducing the cost of the project.

Execution

- Utility of natural elements to its fullest, during planning stage itself will reduce the cost in substantial manner.

  For example: In hot climates, provide shorter walls on east-west sides, provide trees surrounding the building which will serve as shading device etc.

- Use of newer building materials which are ecofriendly, recyclable etc. Industrial waste can be recycled and reused like fly ash, waste glass, limestone waste, blast furnace slag etc.

  Ecofriendly materials which may prove to be substitute for wood or which may be available because of recycling of garbage/agro waste will be fruitful in this regard.

- Adopting superior construction techniques to save the time, labour with desired quality work.

- Use of energy saving techniques in every aspect of execution, such as solar heating panels, aerated water supply etc.

- Referring NBC, IS codes in order to prepare check lists for different items in construction.

- Assessment of the work by field experts other than those who are involved in design and execution process and to check whether it is indicating acceptable standards or tolerances.

- If superior quality bricks and blocks are used; instead of plastering, pointing may be adopted.

- R.C.C. work is to be preferred as against timber or stone work.

- Mix design for concrete will save the material and in mass work; steel forms, prefrabricated units will serve as economy boosters.

  1. Also one can use material after demolishing the structure.
  2. Special control techniques for wastage of material.
  3. Space management which is in turn controlling labour count and equipment charges, etc.

Maintenance

When there is genuineness in planning and execution processes, very less cost will be incurred in maintenance. Also if through periodical maintenance of all the building components and services, landscapes, etc. is carried out it in turn is responsible for satisfaction of the occupants; both mentally and economically.

Following factors shall be considered well in advance so that the structure will require less maintenance:

- Following solar path at a particular place.
- Due consideration to the thermal performance of the components of the structure.
- Use of solar radiation for heating etc.
- Day lighting and natural ventilation etc.

Assessment of the total cost of the project after completion:

As the softwares for drawings and calculations are readily available; in turn lot of time is saved thereby reducing the cost effectively. Modified revised estimates can also be easily worked out.

After taking the final exact measurements on site, one may easily determine the actual cost and then compare it with the estimated cost.

This will reflect all possible changes because of unavoidable site problems, owner's perceptions etc. And if the difference in these two is too large then automatically one may have the conclusion from it and prepare the construction report.

In this set of working drawings with changes, list of sub-contractors with their addresses, consultants lists, total cost, cost/m^2, labour cost, administrative changes, sundries etc. are mentioned. This would in turn be helpful for the other projects.

IMPORTANT POINTS

- Green building material strategies along with its points.
- Benefits of Green buildings i.e. energy savings, waste reduction, health and productivity benefits, indoor air quality and water efficiency.
- Types and benefits of Green roofing.
- Different types of Biomass Roofing.
- Different types of natural insulation materials.

QUESTIONS

1. State and explain various aspects which are considered to declare a building as a green building.
2. State the ratings for different levels/certification as offered by LEED and PMC.
3. Write short notes on eco-friendly buildings and cost effective buildings.
4. Mention in detail the criterion considered for an eco-friendly and cost effective buildings.

UNIVERSITY QUESTIONS

May 2014

1. Write a note on Green Buildings. Enlist various rating systems.

Chapter 5

INTRODUCTION TO ARCHITECTURAL DRAWING

(A) BUILDING DRAWING

5.1 INTRODUCTION

Drawing is a Language of Engineers. For Civil Engineers, drawing is most important part of subjects to understand the different activities for execution of work. Building Drawing is a language of communication between an Architect and Engineer, Engineer and Surveyors, supervisors and skilled labours etc.

For execution of Civil Engineering projects, at various stages, different types of drawings are required necessarily.

Various types of drawings are required in fields of work for civil engineers, architects, contractors, draftsmen, structure engineers, supervisors etc.

Building drawings are required to be prepared for approval of owner, for approval of sanctioning authority, for preparing estimates, for executing work at site etc.

In Building Drawings:

- Layout drawings and presentation drawings are prepared for owners.

- Submission plans for approval of sanctioning authority like Municipal corporation, collector, grampanchayat, development authorities etc.

- Working and detailed drawings for estimates and construction of buildings at site.

By means of graphical symbols, like lines, projections, drawings are prepared.

5.2 TYPES OF DRAWINGS

- Plan (Top view)

- Elevations (Front view)

- Side elevations (Side view)

- Sections

- Working and detailed drawings like, details of doors, windows, stairs, foundation plan, roof plan, site plan, area statement, construction notes etc.

- Isometric views

- Oblique views

- Perspective views

According to method of preparing drawings they can be classified as:

- Data drawings.
- Measured drawings.
- Structural drawings.
- Working drawings or Detailed drawings.
- Presentation drawings.

5.3 USE OF I.S. SPECIFICATIONS

For clear meaning of drawings and their purpose, it is a must to prepare drawings with clear dimensions and notes. Any wrong dimension or wrong notes can be misinterpreted and waste of time may be there.

Uniformity is achieved in drawing by adopting specification I.S. - 962 - 1967.

This codes gives sizes of drawings (scales), sizes of lettering; dimensioning methods, symbols and abbreviations, methods of projections; units of measurement in drawing, etc.

Various Standard Specifications from I.S. Code of Practice:

Lines: Various types of lines required to be drawn are:

    1. Visible line or construction line:

(0.60 mm to 1.30 mm thick)

    2. Centre line:

(4 : 1), (Thin), (0.20 mm to 0.30 mm thick)

    3. Hidden line: These lines shows the hidden portion of the object.

(Medium), (0.40 mm to 0.50 mm thick)

    4. Section line:

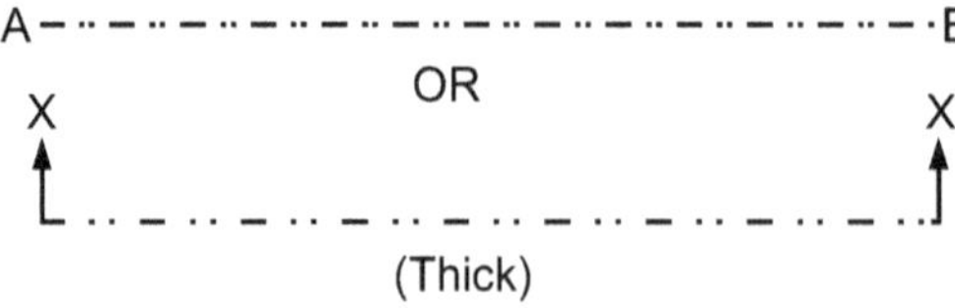

(Thick)

    5. Short break lines:

    6. Long break lines:

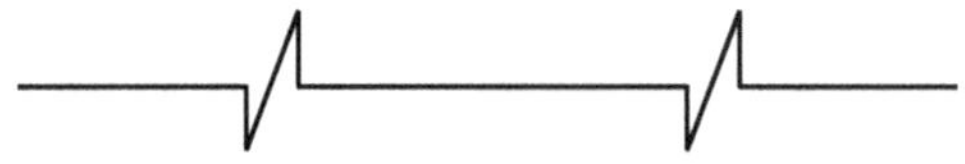

7. Dimension Lines and Extension Lines:

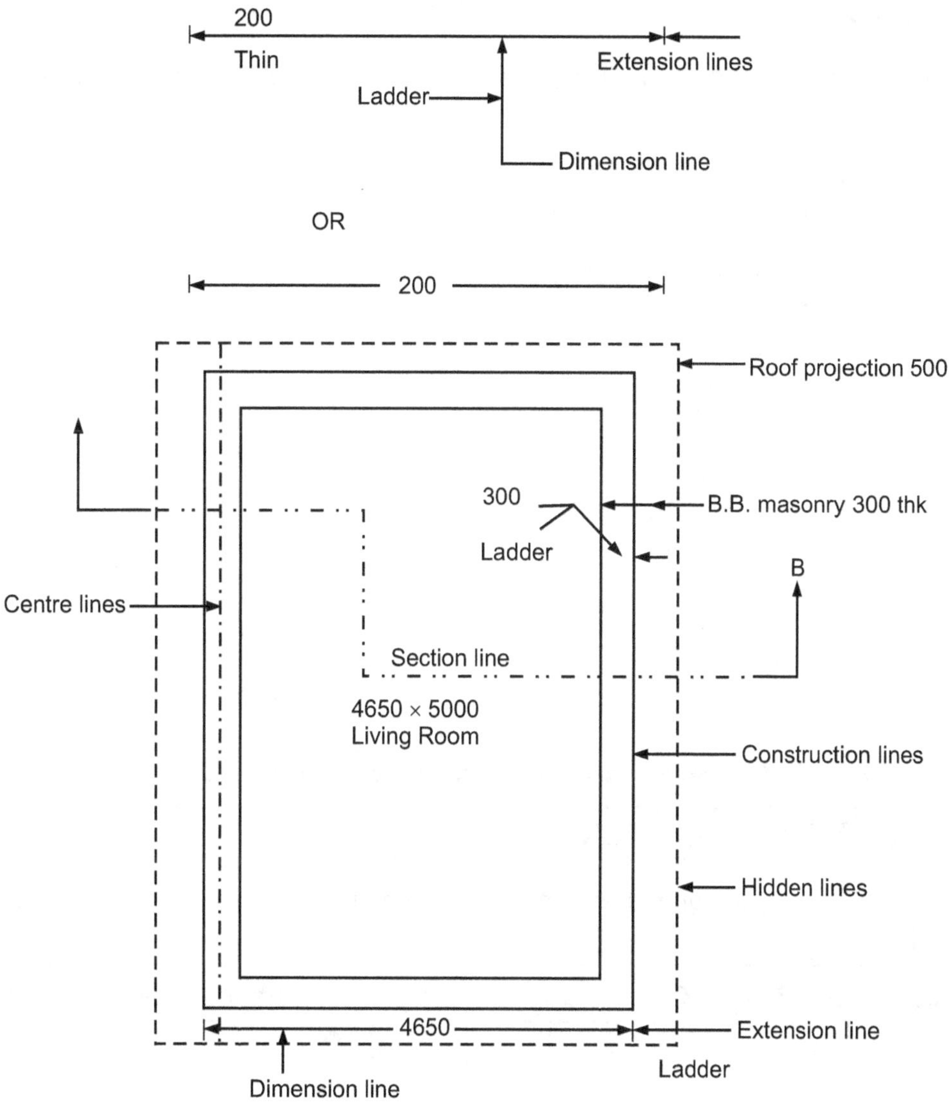

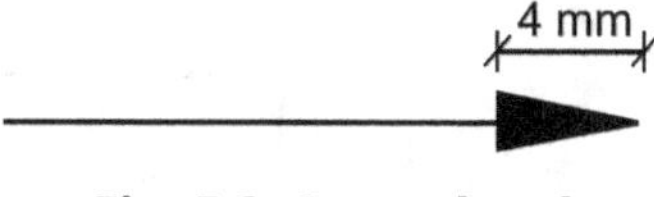

Fig. 5.1: Types of lines

- While writing dimension of units i.e. internally, in fashion 4650 × 5000, 4650 indicates (horizontal on paper) or length and 5000 indicates (Vertical on paper) or width of the unit.

- In dimension arrows should not be greater than 4 mm in length.

Fig. 5.2: Arrow head

- Dimensions of an object is not at all related with scale. It should give actual size of structure.

- All dimensions should be easily readable from the bottom or right hand edge of drawing.

- At places where it is not possible to write the note or dimension of part of object; then in such cases it is written slightly away from this, with the help of leaders.

- To show the continuity of the object, long break lines and short break lines are used as shown in Fig. 5.3.

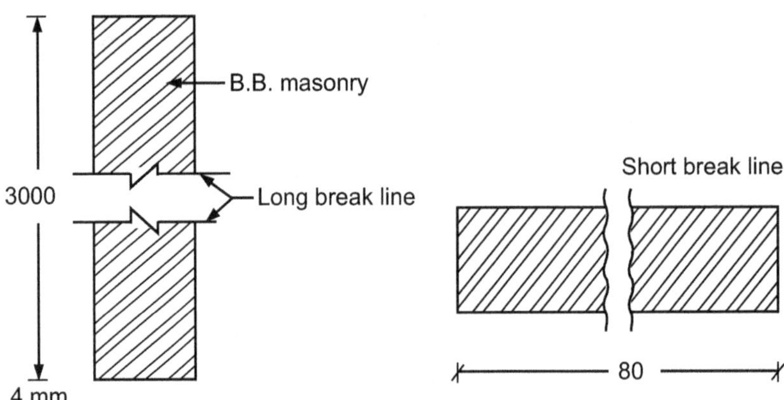

Fig. 5.3: Section of masonry with long break and short break lines

5.4 GRAPHICAL SYMBOLS

Sketches below, shows the graphical symbols for every materials of construction followed by abbreviations.

Sr. No.	Materials of Construction	Graphic Symbol
1.	Timber	
2.	Glass	
3.	Brick Masonry	
4.	UCR Masonry	

5.	Concrete	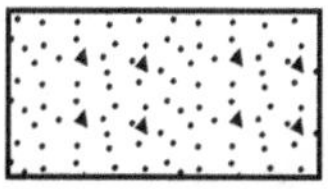
6.	Rubble	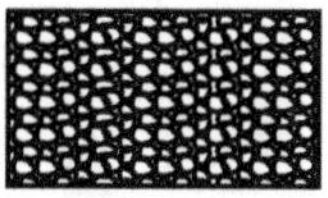
7.	Murum	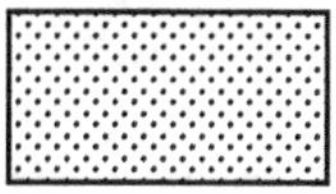
8.	Mortar	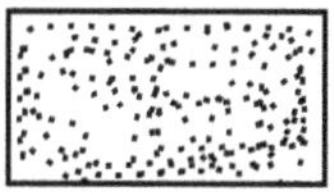
9.	Wash Basin	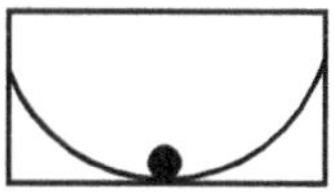
10.	W.C. (water closet)	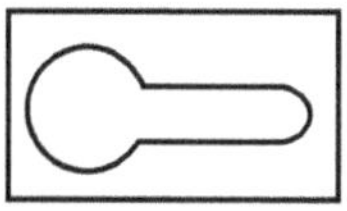
11.	Urinals	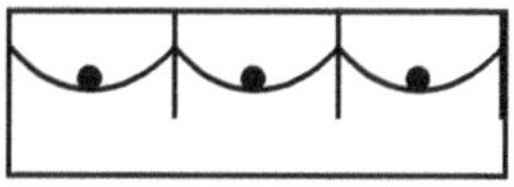
12.	Steel Bars	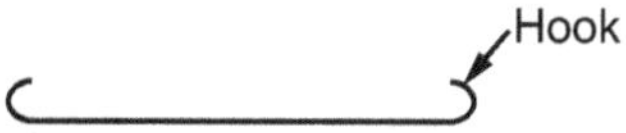 Hook
13.	Stirrups	
14.	Celling Fan	
15.	Ground Level	 G L
16.	Door: (i) Single shutter	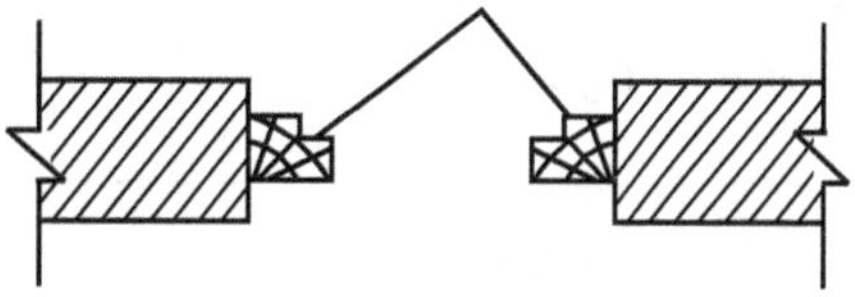
	(ii) Double shutter	

	(iii) Gate	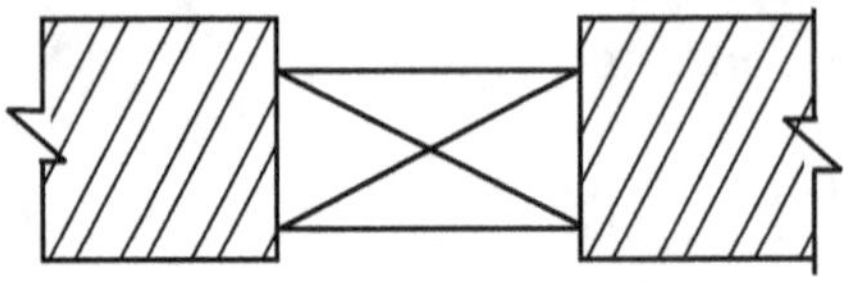
17.	Stair Case	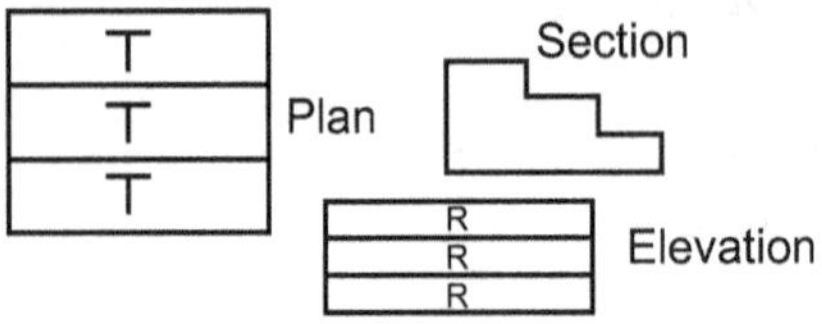 Plan · Section · Elevation
18.	Window	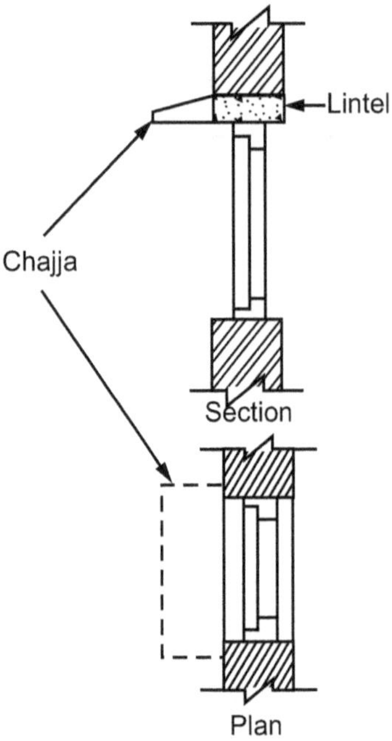 Lintel · Chajja · Section · Plan
19.	Single Leaf Double Swing Door	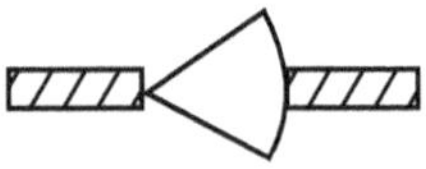
20.	Double Leaf Double Swing Door	
21.	Side Hinge	
22.	Centre Hinge	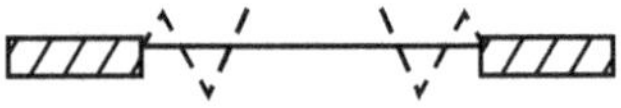
23.	Folding Double Leaf	
24.	Sliding Door	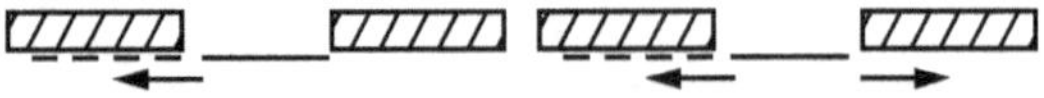

25.	Revolving Door	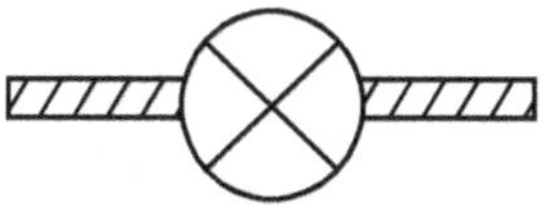
26.	Door with Projected Hinges	
27.	Rolling Shutter External	
28.	Rolling Shutter Internal	
29.	Rectangular Section	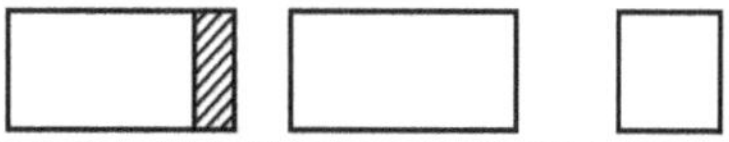
30.	Round Section	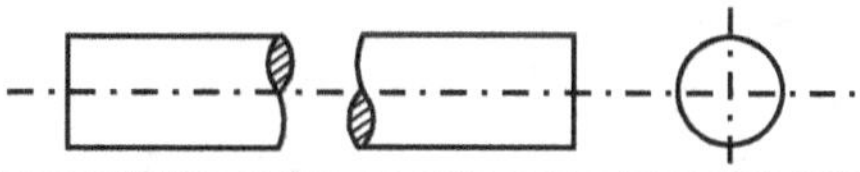
31.	Pipe or Tubing	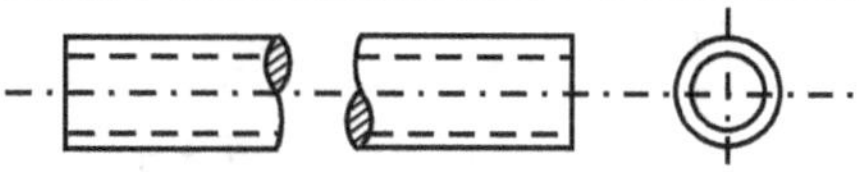
32.	Pipe or Tubing	
33.	Wood (Rectangular Section)	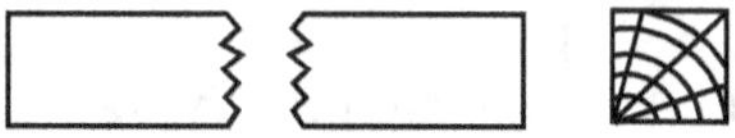
34.	Rolled Shapes	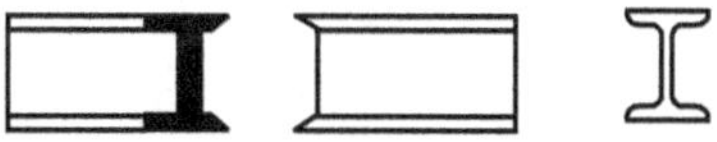

Abbreviations:

1.	B. B. M.	Burnt Brick Masonry
2.	C. M.	Cement Mortar
3.	D. P. C.	Damp Proof Course
4.	U. C. R.	Uncoursed Rubble
5.	C. R.	Coursed rubble
6.	D	Doors
7.	W	Windows
8.	V	Ventilators
9.	W. C.	Water Closet

10. F. S. I.	Floor Space Index
11. C. C. T. W.	Country Cut Teak Wood
12. T. W.	Teak Wood
13. M. H.	Man hole
14. N. T.	Nahani Trap
15. G. T.	Gully Trap
16. G. L.	Galvanised Iron
17. C. I.	Cast Iron
18. R. C. C.	Reinforced Cement Concrete
19. A. C.	Asbestos Cement

5.5 SCALES

For preparing proportionate drawings and to accommodate drawings of structures of various sizes in standard size of sheet, use of scales is done.

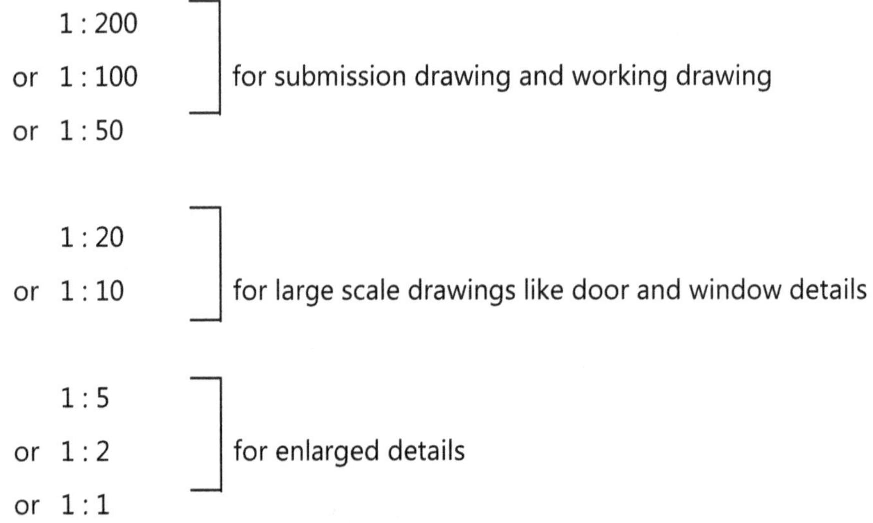

$$1 : 200$$
$$\text{or } 1 : 100 \quad \text{for submission drawing and working drawing}$$
$$\text{or } 1 : 50$$

$$1 : 20$$
$$\text{or } 1 : 10 \quad \text{for large scale drawings like door and window details}$$

$$1 : 5$$
$$\text{or } 1 : 2 \quad \text{for enlarged details}$$
$$\text{or } 1 : 1$$

5.6 TITLE BLOCK

It is prepared in every drawing sheet at right hand bottom corner of sheet before or after drawings are prepared. This block clearly states, the name of drawing, number, date of preparation, prepared by, checked by, scale, name of architect and North direction etc.

Please refer Fig. 5.4 for title block for various sizes for different sizes of sheets.

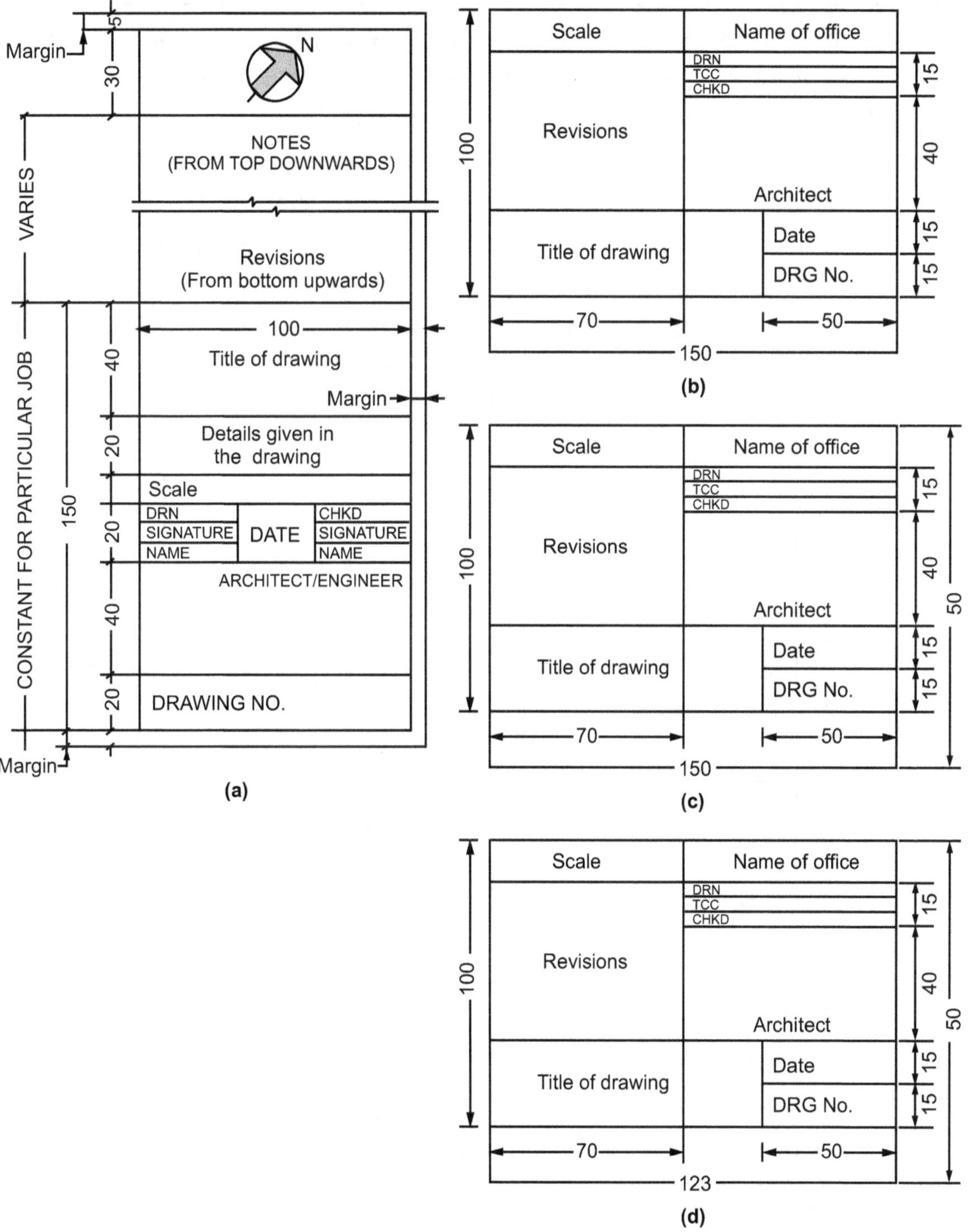

Fig. 5.4: Various types of title blocks

5.7 LINE - PLAN

It is a presentation drawing which is prepared by the architect and final plan is developed with the help of this. This plan also helps in preparing perspective drawing to be shown to the owner.

Before a plan is developed it is checked whether all the requirements of owner as well as basic requirements as per rules and bye-laws are included in line plan or not.

- This plan shows all the units and details which are to be erected while constructing the building.

- Dimension of units in this plan are clear inner dimensions.

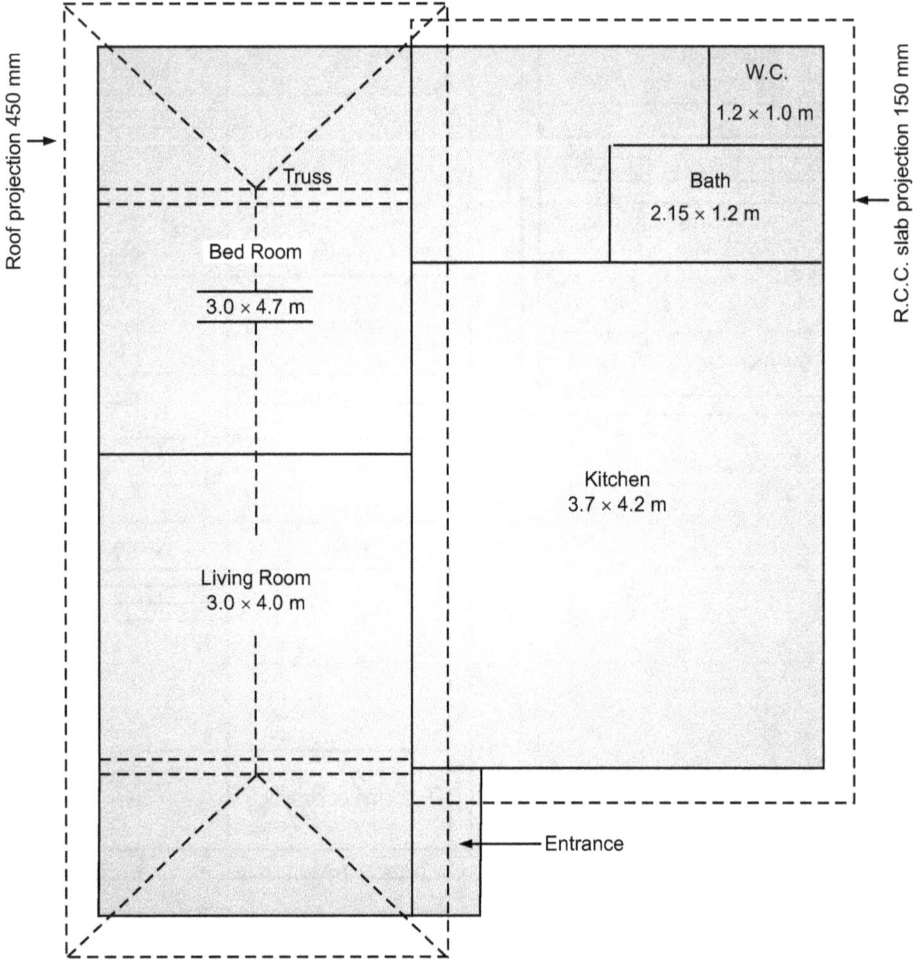

Fig. 5.5: Line – plan (not to the scale)

- It can be drawn "Not to the Scale" also.

- By trial and error, various units are placed, according to their ideal location the area if possible which suits the shape of site. Thus, line plan is prepared. Please refer Fig. 5.5.

- Line plan is also prepared by assuming that whole building to be constructed, is cut with a horizontal section plane at sill level and then viewed from top. In this plan, wall thicknesses, doors and windows, chajjas etc. are not shown.

5.8 DEVELOPMENT OF LINE – PLAN

While developing the plan, line plan which is almost finalised with respect to arrangement of units is selected.

- Now plan is developed by keeping in mind the building to be constructed is cut with a horizontal section plane at sill level and viewed from top.

- While developing plan, elevation of all sides and perspective view should be kept in mind.

- While developing plan many other factors like shape of plot, North direction, wind and rain direction, main roads etc., should be considered.

- Thickness of walls (internal and external) depth and type of foundation, Number of stories is decided by knowing the type of structure whether load bearing type or framed type.

Like:

1. R.C.C. structure have external wall 230 mm thick and internal wall 150 mm thick.

2. In load bearing structure, external and bearing walls are 300 mm thick or more and partition walls are 200 mm thick.

   Plans are drawn to the scales 1 : 50; 1 : 100 or 1 : 200.

   [Scale is always represented as Representative Fraction (R. F.)].

$$\text{R. F.} = \left[\frac{\text{Distance on map or sheet}}{\text{Distance on ground}}\right]$$

   [For drawings, R.F. is multiplied with distance on ground to know distance on map]

5.9 PLAN

This drawing shows length and width of building with rooms. A plan is prepared on a tracing paper or a sheet. A plan must include the following details:

- Wall thickness and column size.

- Area of each unit with size.

- Name of the unit.

- Location of W. C., bath, wash basin, urinals, sink etc.

- Stair case (steps with landing, with up and down directions).

- Location of door and windows (use symbols) direction of swing.

- Passages, varandah, corridor etc.

- Roof projections, slab projections, chajja projections etc.

- In presentation drawings interior arrangement of furniture can also be shown (like sofa-set, chair, table, bed, kitchen platform, cub-board etc.)

- External dimensions.

- Plinth projection (if provided).

- North direction.

- Title [i.e. plan, Ground floor plan or typical floor plan (when more than two floors are similar in all respects in a building)].

- Section lines.

- Scale.

Method of Drawing Plan

Start drawing the plan from the left-hand bottom corner. Draw all external walls and thickness of walls as per the details of construction, care should be taken that the inner dimensions of rooms should remain same as shown in line plan.

Draw the location of doors and window with symbols, as per the dimensions, from schedule of doors and windows, suitably.

Show all the details enlisted above. While giving dimensions in plan, all external dimensions and dimensions from wall surface to doors and windows should be given in load bearing structure. In framed structure dimensions should be from centre of column or centre of door and window. In case of first floor plan or other, top floors, wall thickness or column size is reduced, so these changes should be shown. Location of stairs and roof details should be shown.

5.10 ELEVATION

This drawing represents the different views looking from different direction, when building will be constructed. For drawing this, all heights i.e. plinth height, sill height, ceiling height, window height, door height, thickness of lintel, thickness of slab, height of parapet etc., must be known.

Method of Drawing Elevation

Elevation is drawn just above the plan by projecting lines from it. Now show G. L., plinth level, window sill, door and window's top level, lintel level, ceiling level, top level etc. Projected lines from plan show the location of walls, door and window steps, chajjas, roof with top of ridge, eaves, common rafters etc. After projecting doors and windows coming in elevations their detailed type should be shown. Design of grills also be shown by referring schedule of doors and windows. As far as dimensions are concerned, minimum dimensions should be shown in elevation. Because these dimensions will be shown in sections. Some dimensions can be shown like vertical heights of different levels. Title for elevation must be shown that from which side it is drawn. Along with this, notes and symbols of exterior material on the wall should be provided.

5.11 SECTIONS

For constructing a building various details are required. About the length and width, these are available from plan. Heights of different parts of building is shown in elevations. But details which are neither available in plan nor in elevations are drawn in sections by drawing suitable section lines in plan indicating all details.

Preferably section line should pass through W.C. and bath and stair-case. This gives all interior details of height of steps, height of landing, height of stair case, thickness of lintel, height of dado, height of window in W.C., details of roof etc. sections are two types generally.

1. Longitudinal section when building is imagined to be cut along the length.
2. Cross section when building is imagined to be cut along the width.

Section may be straight or offset. Section lines should be shown in ground floor plan and other floor plans also. Location of section line should be approximately at the same place. Because section line in plan represents a vertical section plane cutting the whole building.

Every section line must have arrow heads on its both ends. This arrow head shows that the building is cut and seen in the direction of arrow. The observer can stand on section line and he can see in the direction of arrows, whatever details are seen should be drawn according to type of section. These details must contain details from foundation to parapet. For section of a building with typical floor plans for number of stories, long break lines can be shown.

A very important thing is that, the dimension of each and every part should be shown clearly and notes should be mentioned wherever required.

[For plan, elevation and sections of various buildings and their component parts, refer sketchings].

Please refer Fig. 5.7, 5.8, 5.9 with reference to Fig. 5.6.

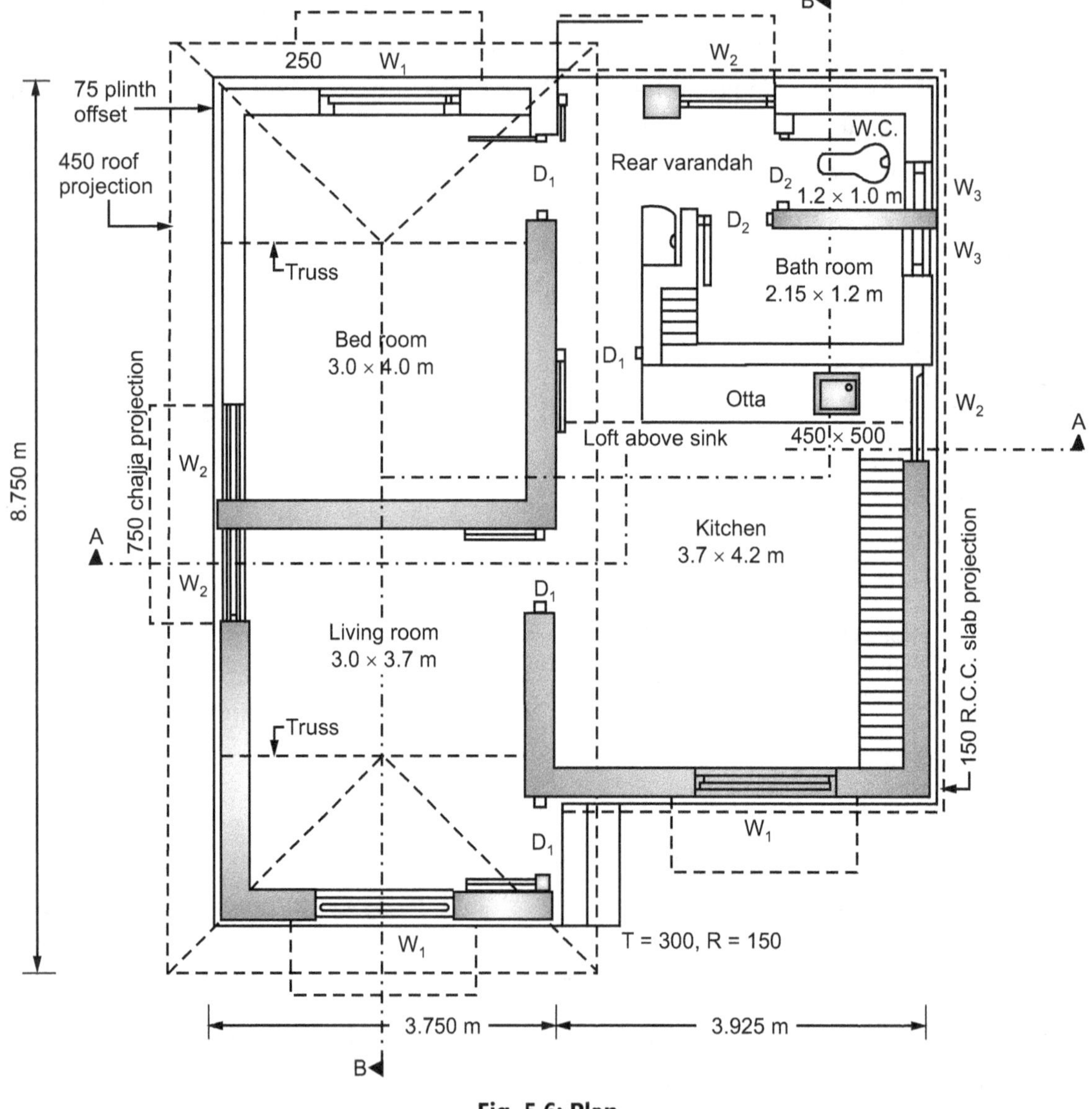

Fig. 5.6: Plan

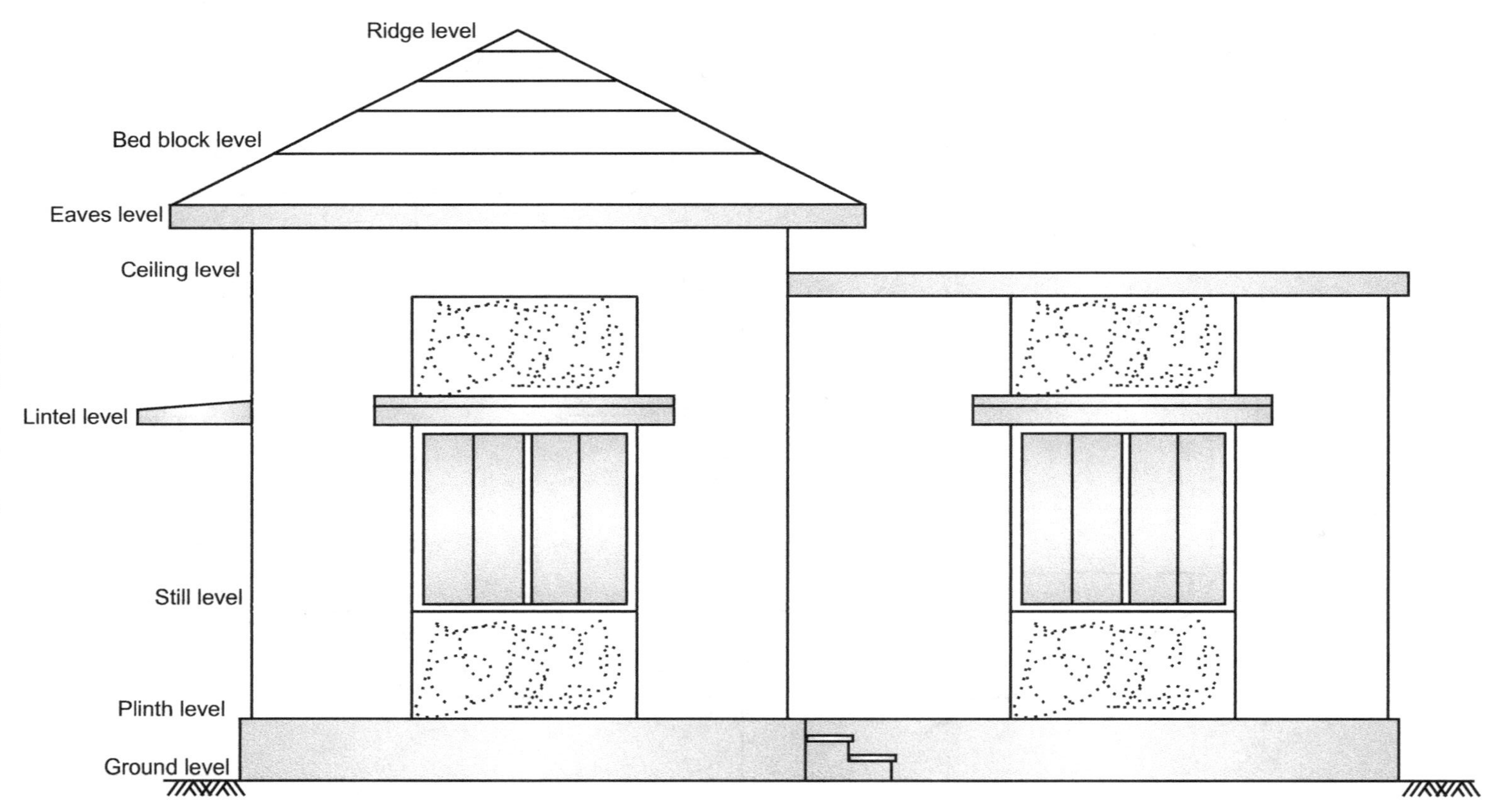

Fig. 5.7: Front elevation

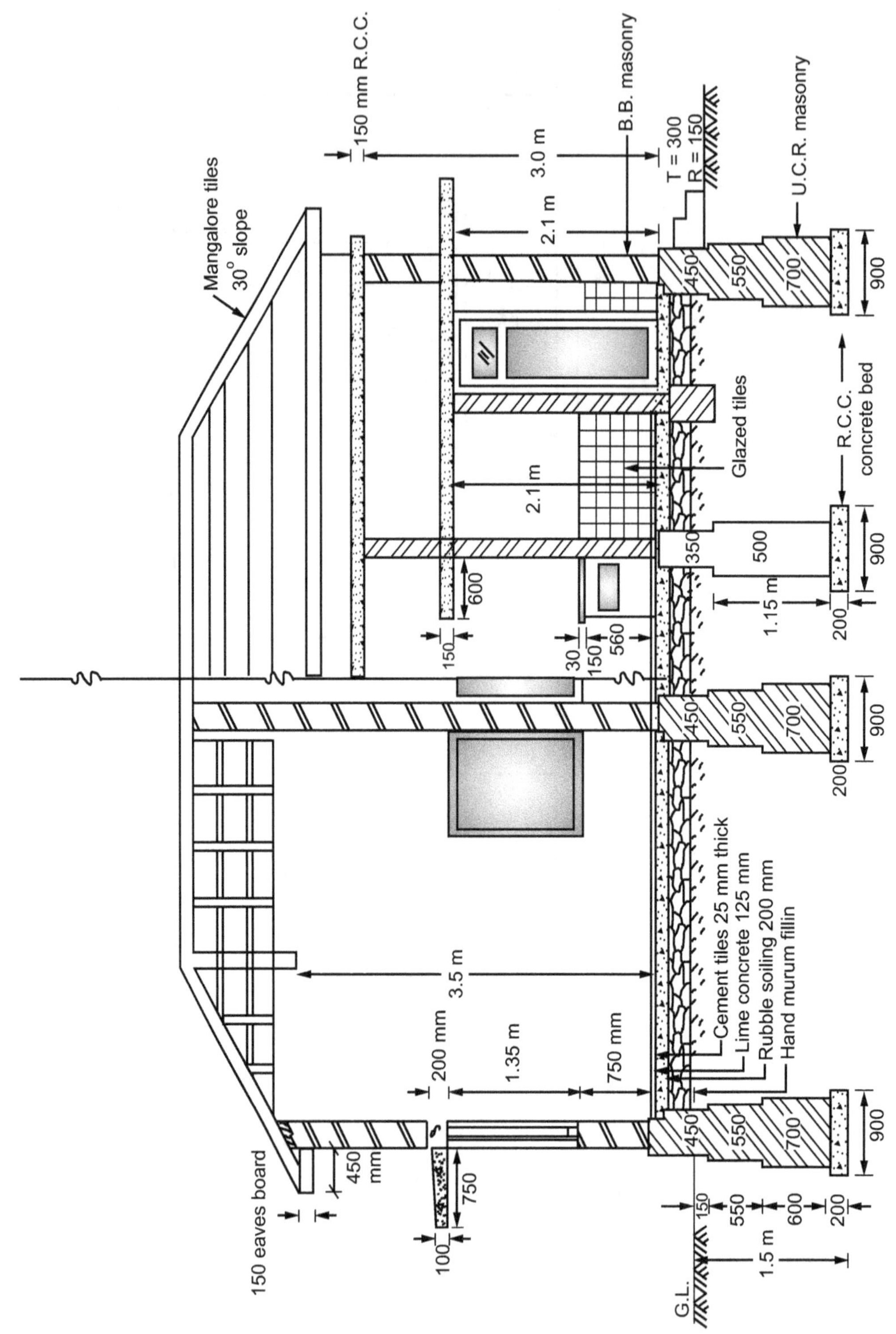

Fig. 5.8: Section B-B

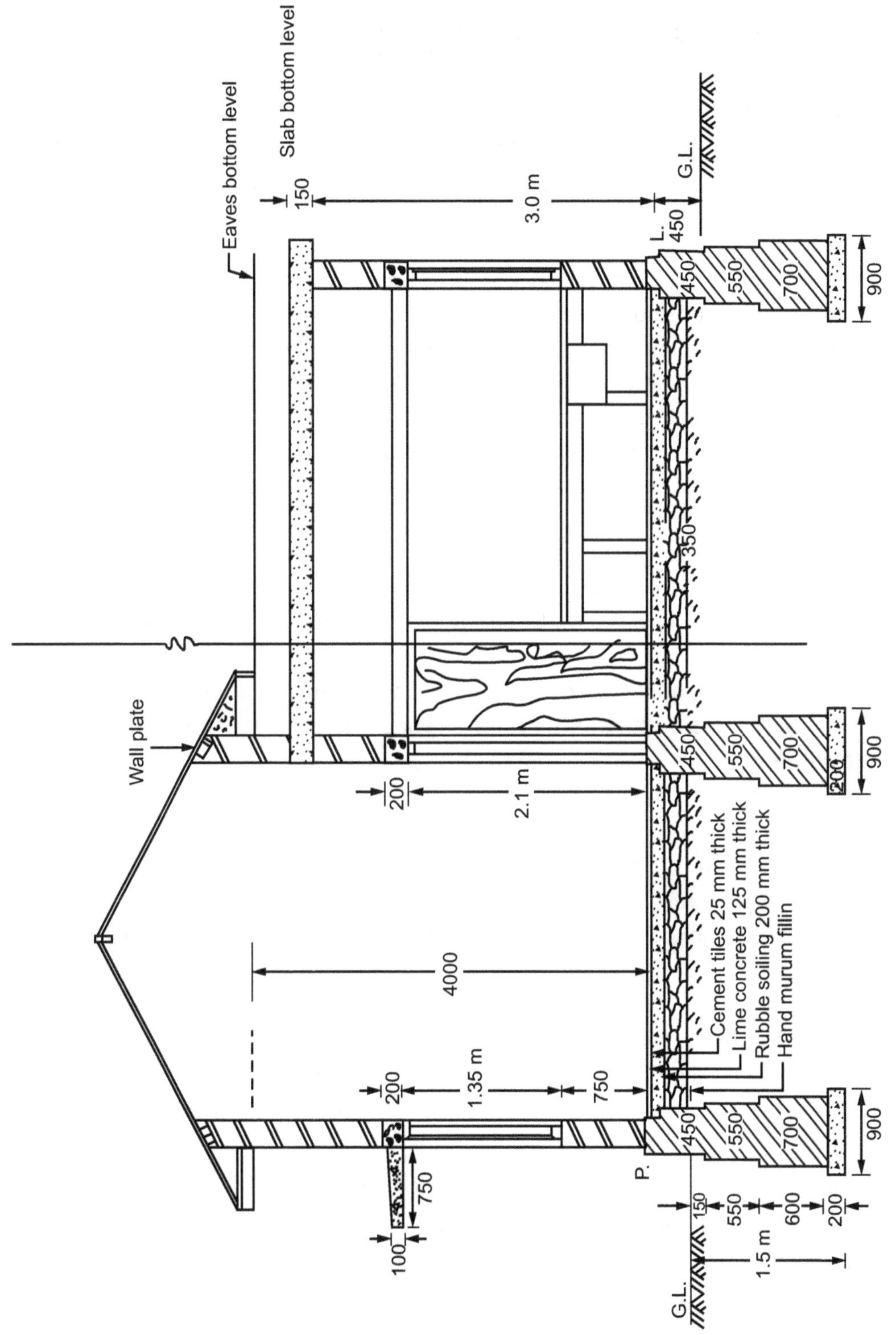

Fig. 5.9: Section A-A

5.12 SCHEDULE OF DOORS AND WINDOWS

Doors are provided in buildings for access, privacy and safety of different rooms. Windows are provided for ventilation and lightening in different rooms.

Generally, doors in a room should not be more than two and windows in each room should be provided as per the rules $\frac{1}{10}$th to $\frac{1}{20}$th of area of floor as per the climate, where building is constructed.

Types of doors which are provided in various types of buildings at different locations, like entrance, internally, shops etc. are as follows:

- Battened legged and braced (timber) single or double shutter: For low cost housing.
- Framed and paneled (timber) single or double shutter: For external and internal doors in residential building.
- Flush doors (single shutter): For external doors.
- Partly glazed and partly paneled (timber and glass) single shutter: For W.C., bath and stores.
- Fully glazed doors (glass) single or double shutters: Office buildings.
- Rolling shutter (steel): For garage, shops for large openings.
- Collapsible doors (Iron): Jewelry shops, and in balcony and at entrance, in houses for safety.
- Sliding doors (timber, iron or aluminum): Shops, offices and public buildings.
- Revolving doors: Restaurants, hotels, airports, departmental stores etc.

Types of Windows:
- Fan lights: Above the doors.
- Glazed window: Residential and public buildings.
- Casement window: In educational buildings.
- Bay window: In residential buildings.
- Louvered window: In W.C. and bath (where privacy is required as well as ventilation and light is required).
- Dormer window: In pitched roofs etc.

Fixtures and Fastenings for Doors and Windows:
Various fastening and fixtures of doors and windows are as under:

- Hinges: minimum three for each door shutter, minimum two for each window shutter.
- Tower bolts: One for each door and one for window.
- Barrel bolt: One for each door (if required) and one for window.
- Aldrop: One for each door.
- Hook and eye: One for each window shutter.
- Handle: One for each shutter of door and windows.

Preparation of Schedules:

While preparing schedule of doors and windows all details about their size, type, symbol, location and description with remarks should be there. Table 5.1 (b) showing fastenings and fixtures should also be prepared.

For schedules of doors and windows please refer Table 5.1 (a) and (b).

Table 5.1 (a): Schedule of doors and windows

Sr. No.	Item	Symbol	No.	Size	Description	Remarks
1.	Door	D	1	1000×2000	Flush door with T. W. frame, single	External door.
2.	Door	D_1	2	900×2000	Fully panelled door in T. W. frame, single shutter type.	Internal door.
3.	Door	D_2	2	800×2000	Partly panelled and partly glazed door single shutter type.	In W.C. and bath.
4.	Window	W	3	1500×1300	Fully glazed window.	In Living rooms
5.	Window	W_1	4	1000×1300	Fully glazed window. With ventilators at top	
6.	Window	W_2	2	500×800	Louvered window.	In W.C. and bath
7.	Ventilator	V	2	500×300	Pivoted at centre horizontally	In Hall, Kitchen

Table 5.1 (b): Schedule of fastenings and fixtures

Sr. No.	Item	Type and Descriptions	No.	Remarks
1.	Hinge	Butt type, brass size 100 mm long.	9 12	3 for each shutter of door, 2 for each shutter of window.
2.	Tower bolt & barrel bolt	120 mm long, Aluminium - 3, Brass - 3	6	2 for each shutter at top and bottom.
3.	Handle	1 decorative type and other ordinary type.	7	4 for external door and other for internal doors.
4.	Safety chain and night latch	Stainless steel	1 each	For door at entrance.

5.13 AREA STATEMENT

This detail is required in drawings and must, to show with every building set to state the areas utilised.

This statement of area is prepared in a table and all types of areas like plot area, built up area, permissible built up area, carpet area, plinth area, F.S.I. (Floor Space Index) should be clearly shown.

Areas should be shown in m^2. In remark column of this statement table, remarks about bye-laws should be mentioned if required. Please refer Table 5.2.

Table 5.2: Schedule of area

Sr. No.	Area heading	Area in mm^2	Remarks
1.	Plot area	300	15 m × 20 m size plot, survey no. MNG/221062, plot no. 15489.
2.	Permissible built up area	100	$1/3^{rd}$ of plot area or according to to F.S.I.
3.	Built up area	61.36	Area of all units, with wall thickness.
4.	Plinth area	61.36	Area of building at plinth level. [It is equal to built up area if building is single storeyed].
5.	Carpet area	38.64	Usable area of all units excluding wall thickness and sanitary blocks.

For preparing area statement, after knowing plot areas, by following the rules and bye-laws, margins are left around the plan of building and site plan is prepared showing all details. The plan is divided (convenient geometric figures to calculate the areas as shown in Fig. 5.10.

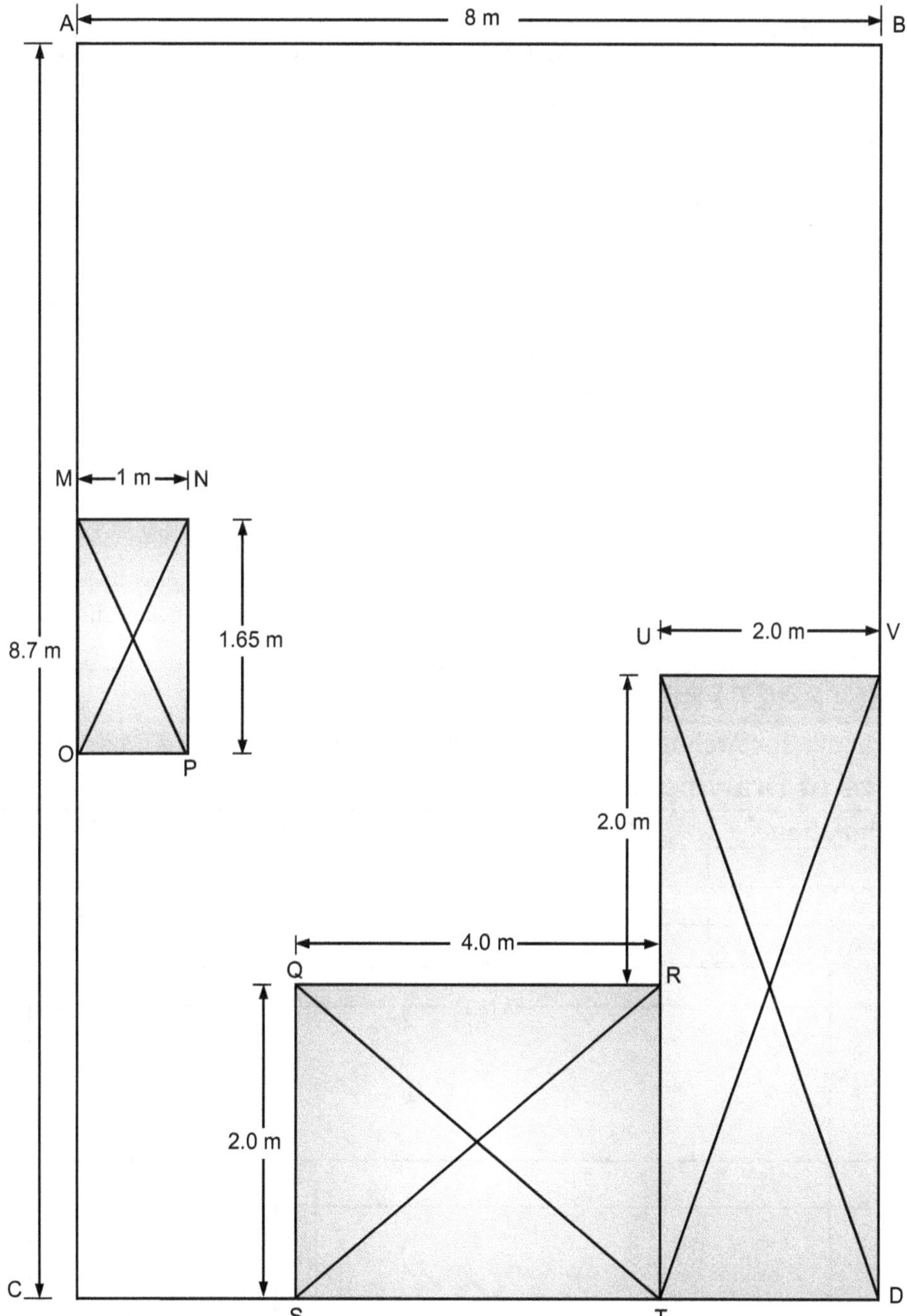

Fig. 5.10: Calculation of area of plot or building's built up area

Area of Fig. 5.10 of plan AB VU RQ SC

= Area ABCD - Area MNOP - Area QRTS - Area UTDV

= $(8 \times 8.7) - (1.65 \times 1) - (2 \times 4) - (2 \times 4) = 51.95$ m^2

Measured Drawing:

Measured drawings are prepared by taking measurements of all component parts of a building. These drawings are prepared for the following purposes:

- To be familiar with the construction details.
- To study the views like elevations from different locations.
- To study the dimensions of different parts like door, windows, roof etc., in proportion.
- To give the training to any person for knowing about plinth, stair, column, beam, slab, roof, door, window, thresholds etc.
- To give an idea of different style of architecture.

Measured Drawings are Drawn in the Following Steps:

- Visit the site and note down the construction details like type of structure, details of foundation according to trend or as per old design sheets. Write construction notes.
- Draw elevations of all sides.
- Take all internal and external measurements and draw sketch plan.
- Mark section line to give more or maximum details in section and draw section.
- It is advisable to draw plan, elevation and section on graph paper first and then on sheets.

5.14 ABSTRACT FROM I.S. - 962 – 1967

Code of Practice for Architectural and Building Drawings:

5.14.1 Size of Drawing Sheets

Designation	Size in mm	Designation	Size in mm
A_0	841×1189	A_3	594×841
A_1	420×594	A_4	297×420
A_2	210×297	A_5	148×210

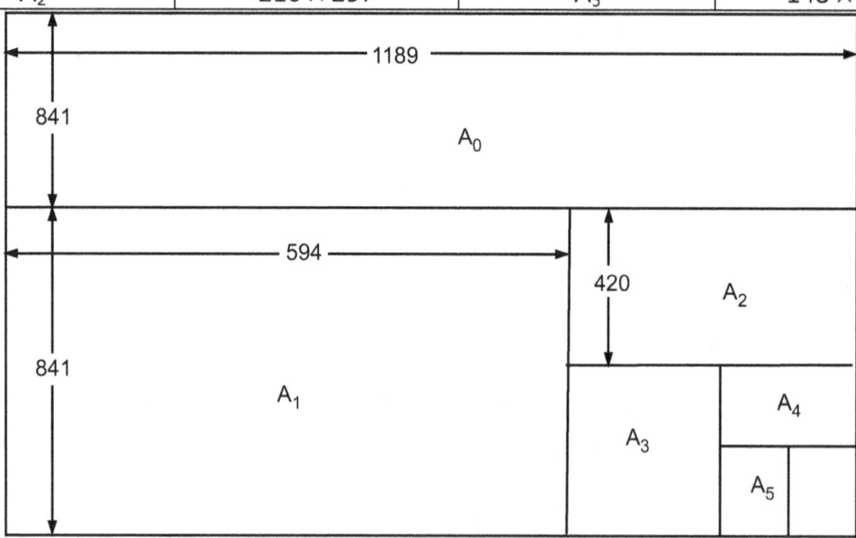

Fig. 5.11 : Sizes of drawing sheets

5.14.2 Size of Drawing Boards

Designation	Size in mm
B_0	1500×1000
B_1	1000×700
B_2	700×500
B_3	500×350

5.14.3 Margins

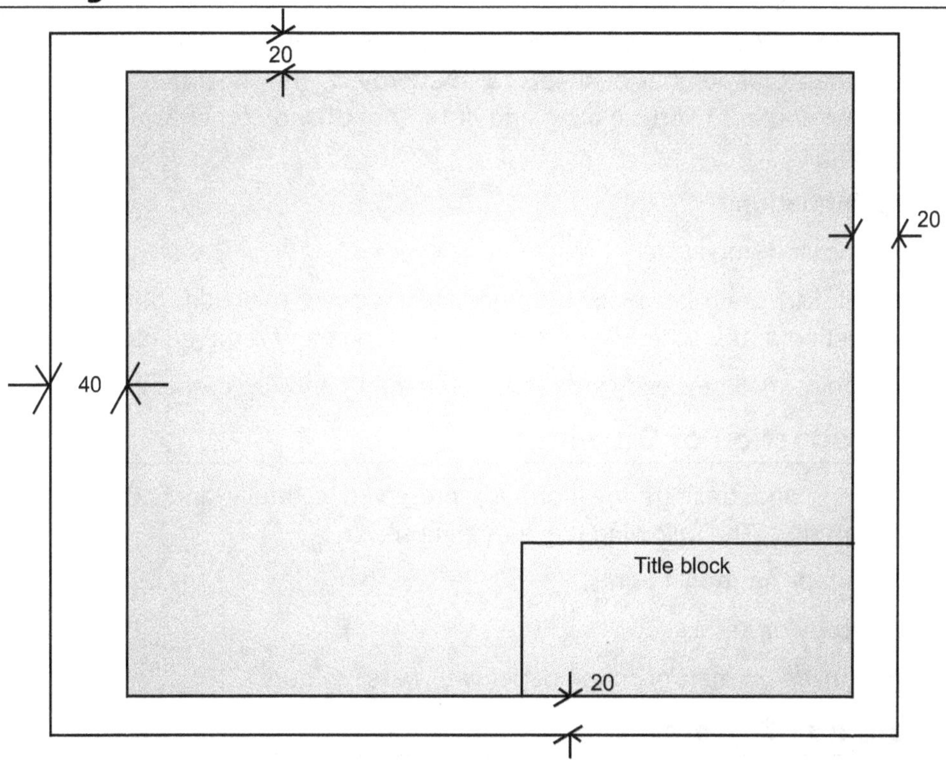

Fig. 5.12: Margins

All margins in case of full imperial size sheets are as shown in Fig. 5.12. A 40 mm margin on left hand side is left for binding in files.

In case of smaller sheets, the left hand margins may be 10 to 20 mm and remaining 10 mm.

5.14.4 Title Block

This block is very important since it presents details like title of drawing, name of organisation and firm, drawing number, scale, date of drawing etc.

It should be placed at the bottom right hand corner of the sheet where it is seen easily when the prints are folded. The title block shall have space provided for the dated initials of technical staff preparing, checking, and tracing the drawings and for the signatures of officers approving the design.

The size of the title block shall be 150 × 100 mm for large sheets, 150 × 50 mm for small sheets and also 123 × 50 mm for further small sheets.

Refer Fig. 5.4 (a, b, c, d).

5.14.5 Numbering of Drawing Sheet

In case of large civil engineering project works, where several series of drawings, for example, architectural drawings, structural drawings, construction drawings, plumbing drawings, electrical drawings and mechanical drawings are made then the drawing number shall be given either as A, B, C, D, E etc. or sheet number 3 of 10 (3/10). This gives the sheet number, as well as total number of sheets for that project. The sheet number shall be given at right hand top corner in vertical filing and at top right hand corner as well as bottom left hand corner in rolls.

Additional Information:

- Job or order number.

- Material list shall be placed immediately above the title block and includes construction notes, schedule of reinforcement, quantity required etc.

- North point shall be clearly indicated in the right hand top corner of the drawing.

5.14.6 Reproduction of Drawings

Original drawings and tracings are normally preserved carefully and copies are used in workshops or on sites. The following copies are in use:

- Blue print or Ammonia prints.

- Photo-copy or Xerox.

- Copies made on matt or rough paper with water colours.

5.14.7 Folding of Prints

The method of folding the prints of drawings is shown in Fig. 5.13 for storing in filing cases and attaching them. Following points should be observed while folding and unfolding the prints.

- All maps and plans are folded to 297 × 210 mm size for convenient record in office files.

- There is no necessity to open up the sheet to see what it refers to as the title block is visible which gives full details of it.

- Plans may be opened out easily by holding firmly the top left hand corner and pulling the bottom right hand corner.

- Always fold vertically first, fold horizontally next, and title block should be on the top most fold.

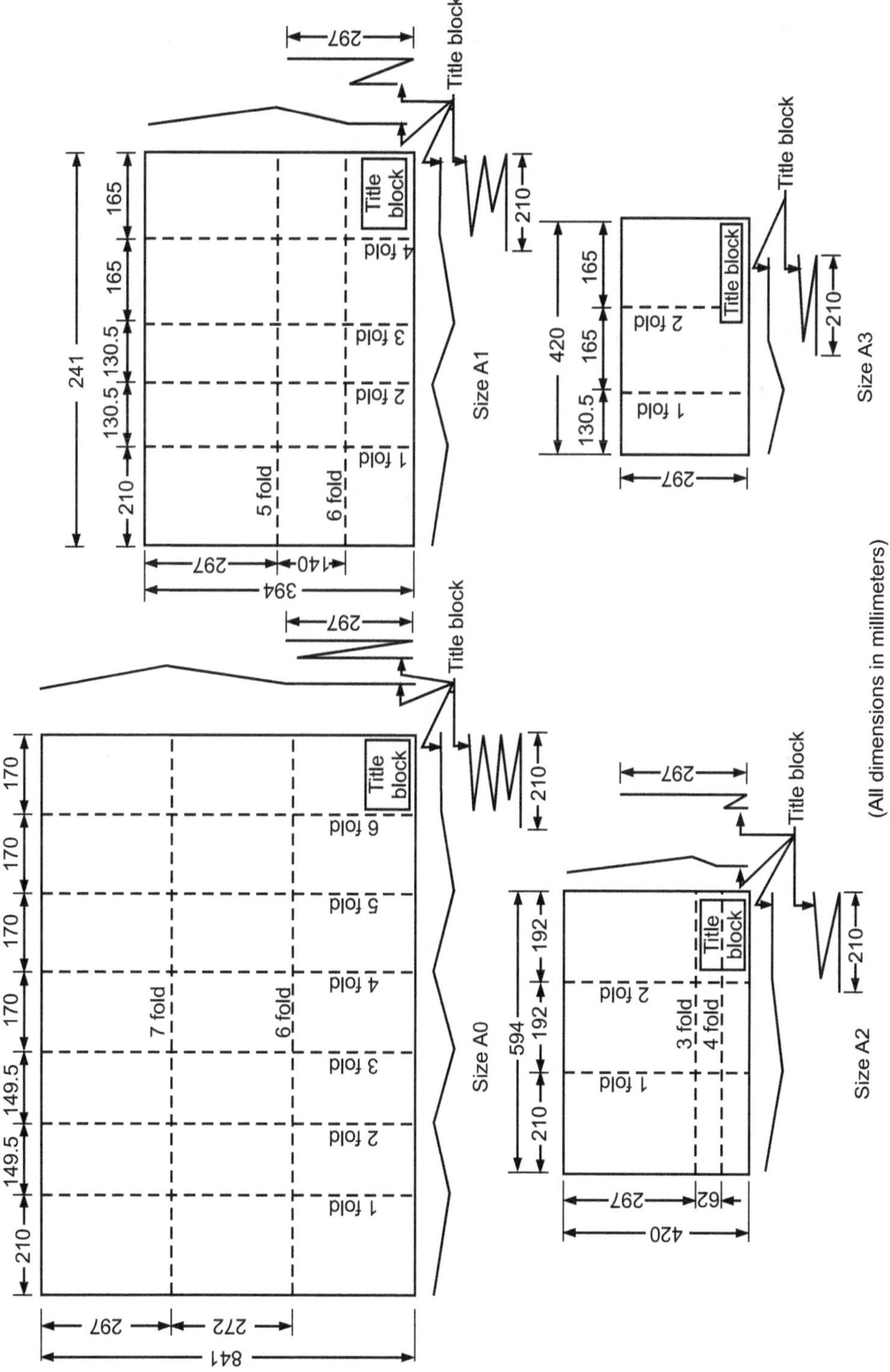

Fig. 5.13: Folding of prints

5.14.8 Reinforced Concrete Work

Numbering of beams and columns of reinforced concrete building structures shall be done, as C_1, C_2, C_3, C_4 and B_1, B_2, B_3 .... starting from right towards left. Beams shall be shown in double lines representing their width and their sizes by their overall dimensions. Beams below the slab shall be shown in dotted lines.

Slabs shall be numbered in the plan horizontally, starting at top left-hand coiner and finishing at the bottom right-hand corner.

The sizes of columns, slab thicknesses and details of stairs leading upto the level concerned shall also be indicated in the plan.

5.14.9 Colouring the Plan

Master plans, zone plans etc. may be coloured as specified in Table 5.3.

Table 5.3: Colouring the plan

Sr. No.	Item	Site Plan		Building Plan	
		Dye-Line Print	Blue Print	Dye-Line Print	Blue Print
(1)	(2)	(3)	(4)	(5)	(6)
(i)	Existing work	Black (outline)	White	Black	White
(ii)	Proposed work	Red filled in	Red	Red	Red
(iii)	Drainage and sewage work	Red dotted	Red dotted	Red dotted	Red dotted
(iv)	Water supply works	Black dotted	Black dotted	Black dotted	Black dotted
(v)	Work proposed to be dismantled	Yellow hatched	Yellow hatched	Yellow hatched	Yellow hatched
(vi)	Open spaces	No colour	No colour	–	–
(vii)	Plot lines	Thick, black	Thick, black		
(viii)	Permissible building lines	Thick, dotted black	Thick, dotted black	–	–
(ix)	Existing street(s)	Green	Green	–	–
(x)	Future street(s), if any	Green dotted	Green dotted	–	–

5.15 DETAILED DRAWINGS

Detailed drawings of various component parts of a structure are drawn and prepared to utilised them for work of supervision, preparing estimates, calculation of area for area statement, etc.

Detailed drawings are more or less related to working drawings. A complete set of submission drawings includes working drawings, detailed drawings, construction notes, area statement specification of works (if any), for execution of a building other than getting it sanctioned from the authority concerned, it is must to produce all the details of its component parts in the form of detailed drawings.

The complete set of drawings include:

- Plans: Ground floor and first floor and plan for other floors.
- Elevations of all sides (Preferably from the front side).
- Sections:
    (a) Passing through doors, windows, balcony and maximum rooms.
    (b) Passing through stairs and W.C., bath.
- Foundation plan with section of footing.
- Roof plan with schedule of roof detail or terrace floor plan.
- Site plan with area statement.
- Structural details of columns, beams, slab (If framed structure is there).
- Details:
    (a) Doors and windows drawings with fixtures and fastenings.
    (b) Staircase with all details of rise, tread, width in section and plan.
    (c) Details of chajja.
    (d) Details of dado.
    (e) Structural details of stairs.
    (f) Sanitary and water supply fixtures by drawing a house drainage plan separately showing details of drain pipes, gully traps, man holes, chambers for inspection and location of overhead tank for storage of water.
    (g) A plan showing electrical installation can also be drawn to show details of electric points in the house.
- All such drawing are drawn to the suitable scale (1 : 50, 1 : 25 or 1 : 10 etc.).
- All detailed drawings must contain each and every dimension, notes, data regarding materials used.
- Detailed drawings must be very carefully prepared as these will be used for preparing estimates as well as for site supervision. Incorrect and incomplete detailed drawings causes delay in progress of work, disputes and loss of time, also increase in expenses.

5.16 METHODS OF PREPARING DETAILED DRAWINGS

Methods of preparing drawings is explained in this chapter in details along with suitable drawings required.

5.16.1 Drawing Foundation Plan

Foundation plan is used for setting out of building, on site. Accuracy in construction depends upon the correct setting out, i.e. correct measurements of foundation plan.

For Load Bearing Structure:

Before drawing a foundation plan, depth of hard strata is determined by trial-pit results, then width of foundation. (i.e. width of foundation trench) is decided by thumb rule according to wall thickness in load bearing structure and according to loads in framed structure.

Now start drawing foundation plan:

1. Draw centre lines for all walls in plan.
2. Show width of trench equally on either side of centre line.
3. Show internal and external dimensions.
4. Mark excavation lines.
5. Mark diagonal check which is required to be checked after setting out the foundation at site.
6. Show the section of footing used with dimensions along with foundation plan.

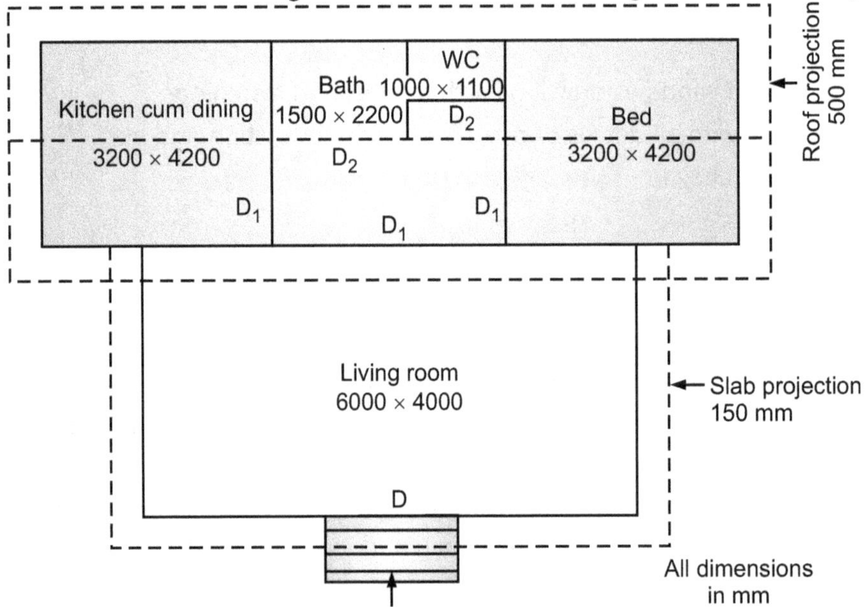

Fig. 5.14 (a): Line plan (not to the scale)

Details:

1. Depth of footing – 1100 W
2. Thickness of masonry – 300

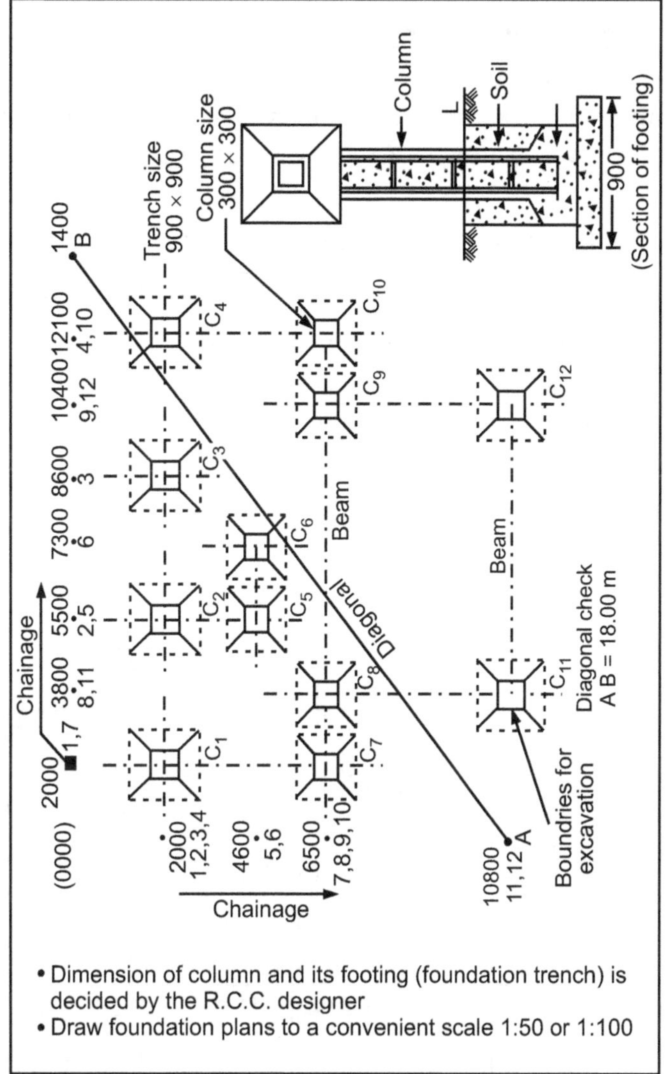

* Dimension of column and its footing (foundation trench) is decided by the R.C.C. designer
* Draw foundation plans to a convenient scale 1:50 or 1:100

Fig. 5.14 (b): Foundation plan for framed structure

- Dimension of column and its footing (foundation trench) is decided by the R.C.C. designer.

- Draw foundation plans to a convenient scale 1 : 50 or 1 : 100.

5.17 ROOF PLAN AND TERRACE FLOOR PLAN

Roof plan is prepared or drawn to get, the details of roof components - Roof for the building may be (1) Pitched roof, (2) Flat roof. For pitched roof, various types of roof covering materials are used like Mangalore tiles, A.C. sheets, G.I. sheets etc. For flat roof, materials used is R.C.C. This roof is also called slab. It can be a brick steel roof.

5.17.1 Roof Plan for Pitched Roof

A pitched roof is constructed either of wood work or steel members. In case of residential buildings it is constructed with wooden members like Trusses, Ridge, Valley, Hip, Gable, Purlins, Common rafter, Wall plates, Jack rafters, Eaves board, Gutter for drainage of rain water etc.

- In roof plan all the members should be shown clearly.

- All the members must be marked with their name and cross section.

- All external dimensions of roof plan must be shown.

- Along with this plan schedule of wood-work should be given including names of members, cross sections, lengths, quantity and number of Mangalore tiles or number of A. C. sheets required to cover the roof.

Refer Fig. 5.15 and Table: 5.1. Refer Fig. 5.14 (a) for line plan.

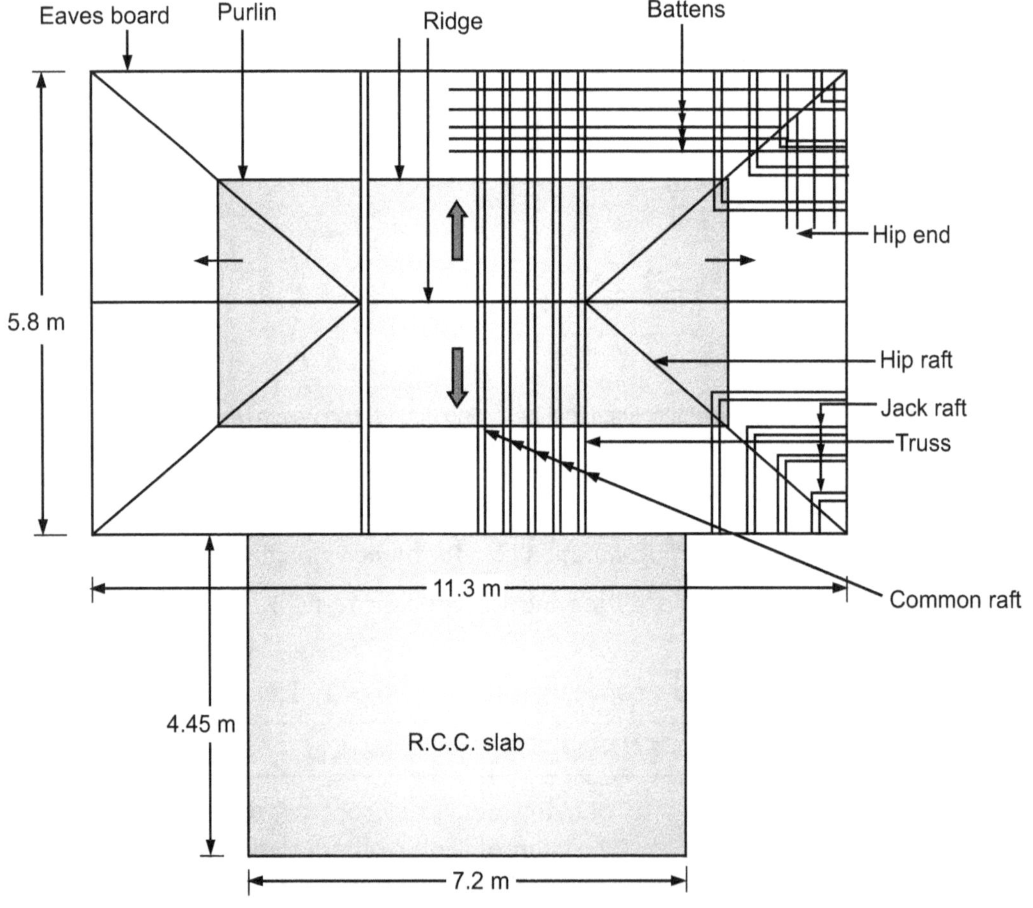

Fig. 5.15: Roof plan for pitched roof

Table 5.4: Schedule of wood work

Sr. No.	Item	Cross sections	Remarks
1.	Ridge	75×180	–
2.	Purlin	105×130	-
3.	Truss		
	(a) Tie beam	75×85	Different types of Trusses
	(b) King post	75×130	for different spans.
	(c) Strut	75×50	
	(d) Principal rafter	75×105	
4.	Hip rafter	75×135	–
5.	Jack rafter	75×155	Unequal in length.
6.	Common rafter	50×75	Equal in length 450 c/c.
7.	Battens (CCTW)	45×25	315 mm c/c.
8.	Eaves board	150×15	-

5.17.2 Roof Plan for Flat Roof

This roof is constructed as slab with R.C.C. material. Show the following details for such a roof plan:

- R.C.C. slab projection (if any) must be shown.
- Draw details of stair case room and parapet wall.
- Show the position of water tank. (Generally over W.C. and Bath).
- Show position of rain water pipes, direction of slope.
- Mark external dimensions as this gives length and width of Terrace slab.

To draw roof plan for framed structure and for R.C.C. slab, following terrace details must be shown:

- Size of terrace with slab projections.
- Rain water pipes position.
- Position of water Link.
- Position of stair case room etc.

Remaining procedure to draw this will be same as explained.

Refer Fig. 5.15 (R.C.C. slab part).

5.18 SITE PLAN

A plan showing the location of a structure with respect to some permanent features. It gives an idea of site, its location and details. It is drawn to a scale of 1 : 500 or any other convenient scale.

It include the following details:

- Shape of building with external dimensions.
- Plot size and number (SVY).
- Plots in vicinity.
- North direction.
- Marginal distance on front, rear and sides of building from plot boundary.
- Compound wall or fencing.
- Main gate, Trees, Electric poles.
- Sanitary disposed or sewer lines and water supply line.
- Roads, with width.
- Permanent structure, Temple etc. Refer Fig. 5.16 for site plan.

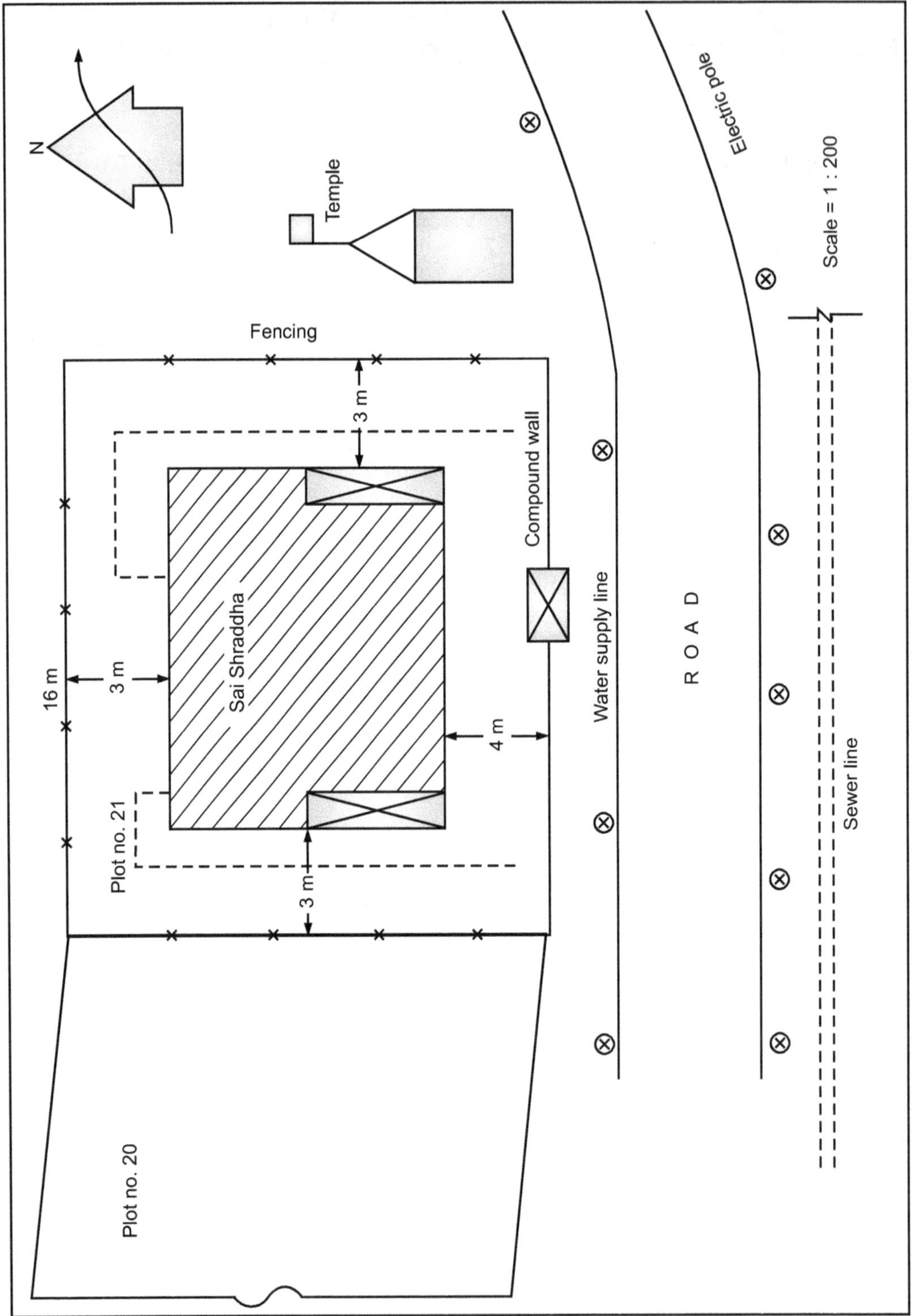

Fig. 5.16: Site plan

Area Statement:

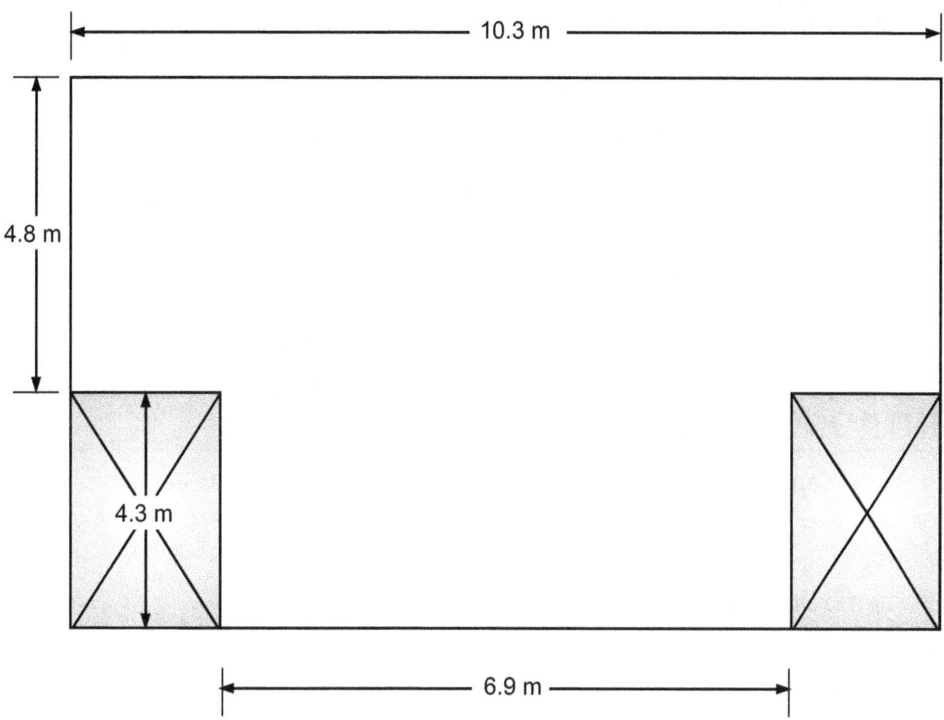

Fig. 5.17: Area plan

$$\text{Area} = \text{Complete Rectangle} - \text{Area of crossed}$$

$$\text{Plinth area} = 10.3 \times (4.8 \times 4.3) - \left[4.3 \times \left\{ \frac{10.3 - 6.9}{2} \right\} \times 2 \right]$$

$$= 93.73 - 14.62$$

$$= 79.11 \ \text{m}^2$$

Table 5.5: Area details

Sr. No.	Item	Area in m^2	Remarks
1.	Plot area	295.03	–
2.	Built-up area (permissible)	98.34	1/3 of plot area
3.	Area constructed (Built-up area)	79.11	–
4.	Plinth area	79.11	Similar to area constructed as building in single storeyed.
5.	Carpet area	60.37	Excluding W.C. bath and wall thickness.

5.19 OTHER DETAILS

Details regarding construction of various components are shown in detailed drawing like:

1. Structural details of footing, column, beam, slab etc.
2. Doors and windows, with fixture and fastenings details.
3. Stair case details with Rise, Tread, width etc.
4. Details of chajja etc.
5. House drainage plan and electrical installation plan for details of sanitary fittings and electrical fittings respectively.

(B) PERSPECTIVE DRAWING

5.20 INTRODUCTION

Drawing is a language of Engineers. Drawings give a detailed idea about the structure, as it will appear. According to the need or purpose, the drawings can be classified as:

1. Isometric Drawing.
2. Oblique Drawing.
3. Perspective Drawing.

1. Isometric Drawing

In the term isometric, prefix "iso" is taken from Greek word "isos" meaning equal. To draw isometric view, the object or structure is turned to make the three sides visible in such a way that they should lie on three equally divided axes about a centre. A pleasing view is obtained by keeping one axis vertical and other two axes at 30° angle with horizontal.

2. Oblique Drawing

The top and side view of the object is shown by projecting oblique lines from a frontal orthographic view, i.e. elevation in an oblique drawing. Angles commonly used for such drawings are 30°, 45° and 60° depending upon the desired effect.

- If 30° angle is taken from horizontal axis, it gives more detailed view of sides. (single side).
- If 45° angle is taken from horizontal axis, it gives a more clear idea of both the sides.
- If 60° angle is taken from horizontal axis, it gives a clear picture of a top view of a structure.

3. Perspective Views

The dictionary meaning of word 'perspective' is the proper relative position of objects as one perceives. Perspective is the only drawing which represents contemplated building as it would appear to spectator.

4. Perspective Drawing: It is the representation of an object on a plane surface as it would appear to eye, when viewed from a fixed position.

A picture drawn by a man on a window glass, when he is looking through a window with one eye closed and other at a fixed position would be a perspective drawing. An architect is interested in knowing how the proposed structure will really look after completion, therefore perspective would represent existing things along with all possible details of building with the knowledge of a plane and solid geometry.

5.21 IMPORTANT TERMS IN PERSPECTIVE DRAWINGS

Following is the terminology used in practice to draw perspective drawings. (Refer Fig. 5.18)

1. **Station Point (SP):** It is a point where the eye of the observer is supposed to be located when the object is viewed for perspective drawing. The position of the station point carries lot of significance as general appearance of the perspective is dependent upon it. For large objects like buildings, the station point is usually taken at the eye level of the person i.e. about 1.5 m.

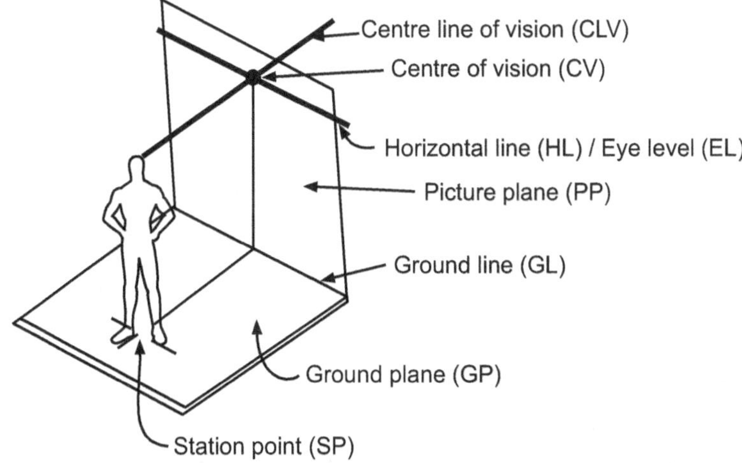

Fig. 5.18

Following general guidelines may be considered for obtaining a good position of station point:

- For small objects, the position of a station point should be such as to give a good view of top surface as well as side surface. For this, the distance of a station point from a picture plane may be taken equal to twice the greatest dimension of the object.

- For object having height and width more or less equal, the station point is so located that the angle between the visual rays from the station point to the outermost boundaries of the object is approximately $30°$.

- It is preferable that station point should be so located in front of the object that the central plane passes through the center of intersection of the object.

2. **Picture Plane (PP):** It is an arbitrary transparent plane, which is always placed in vertical position between observer (station point) and the object to be viewed. It is like a curtain which gives the relative positions of different parts of the object sighted, for different distances of the object from the station point. The position of the picture plane in relation to the object, determines the size of perspective view. Perspective view will always be shorter in size than the actual size of the object, except when picture plane coincides with the object, the size of perspective view will be same size as that of object.

3. **Line of Sight (LS):** It is the line drawn through the station point, joining to the centre of vision. It is also called as axis of vision or perpendicular axis.

4. **Horizontal Plane (HP):** It is an imaginary horizontal plane passing through the station point. It is always parallel to the ground line.

5. **Horizontal Line (HL):** It is the line formed by the intersection of a ground plane with picture plane. It is parallel to the ground line.

6. **Ground Line (GL):** It is a line developed by intersection of a ground plane with picture plane.

7. **Ground Plane (GP):** It is the horizontal plane on which the object is assumed to be situated.

8. **Centre of Vision (CV):** It is the point on picture plane. The point at which the line of sight strikes the picture plane is called the **centre of vision**. It always lies on the horizontal line.

9. **Centre Plane:** It is an imaginary vertical plane passing through centre of vision and the station point. It is perpendicular to both picture plane, and the ground plane and perpendicular axis contained in this plane.

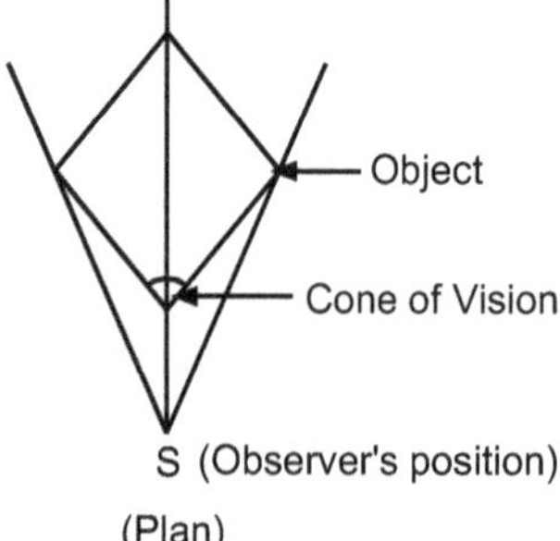

Fig. 5.19

10. **Angle or Cone of Vision:** The angle subtended at the eye, by the visible part of the object is known as cone of vision or angle of vision.

11. **Vanishing Point:** It is an imaginary point situated at infinite distance from the point. In practice, the point at which the visual rays from eye cuts the picture plane is referred as the **vanishing point**. If we stand between the parallel rails of a long stretch of railway track, it would appear as if the rails meet far away at a point. This point of converge is called vanishing point.

5.22 PRINCIPLES OF PERSPECTIVE

Perspective drawing is based upon the conception that, between the eye of the observer and the object to be drawn, there is placed a transparent plane, a sort of a window pane called a "picture plane" on which the form of the object is projected.

For example, if a window plane is selected and the keeping the hand stationary trace the images seen through pane on the window pane. The result is perspective drawing. Refer Fig. 5.20 drawing perspective the following points must be noted:

1. The lines appear to be shorter than their actual length, and this effect increases as the distance of the object increases.
2. The picture of all points and lines on the picture plane coincides with the points and lines themselves.
3. Perspective of all parallel lines which are also parallel to the picture plane are themselves parallel.
   - Vertical lines such as trees, corners of building and poles appear truely vertical. That is perspective of the vertical lines are vertical or parallel to vertical lines.
   - Perspective of horizontal lines which are parallel to the picture plane are horizontal except those at eye level, do not appear horizontal.
4. Perspective of all parallel lines; which are not parallel to the picture plane converge to a point (vanishing point).
   - Perspective of parallel line which are parallel to the vertically plane converge to a vanishing point on the vertical line.
   - Perspective of horizontal line appear to vanish on the horizontal line or converge to a vanishing point on the horizontal line. A group of horizontal lines running in one direction in the perspective drawing appear to converge to a single point. Another group of horizontal lines having different direction have different vanishing point downward which they converge.
   - Perspective of horizontal lines to the picture plane converge to the centre of vision, i.e. in this case centre of vision is the vanishing point. Refer Fig. 5.21.

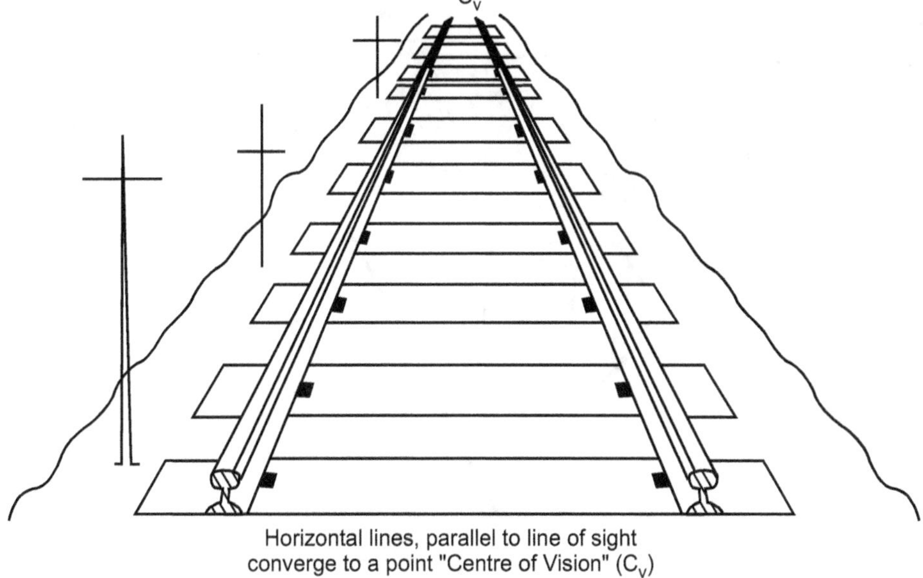

Horizontal lines, parallel to line of sight converge to a point "Centre of Vision" (C_v)

Fig. 5.20: Centre of vision

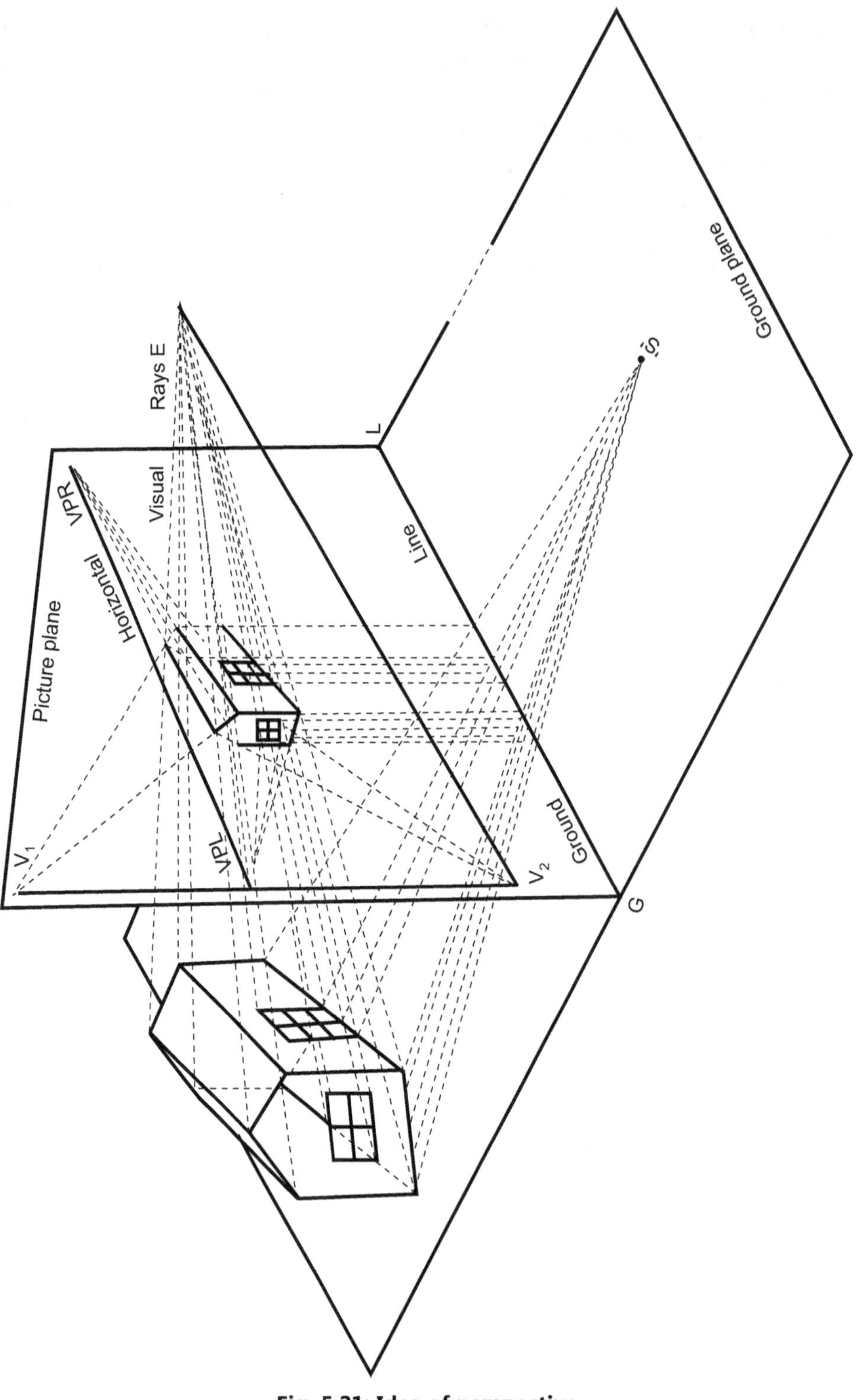

Fig. 5.21: Idea of perspective

5.23 TYPES OF PERSPECTIVE

Perspective views can be classified as:

1. Based on position of object with respect to picture plane.
2. Based on number of vanishing points.

5.23.1 Based on Position of Object with Respect to Picture Plane

1. **Parallel Perspective:** When one or more faces of an object are parallel to the picture plane, than perspective of this object is called **parallel perspective**. This is same as one point perspective. Refer Fig. 5.22.

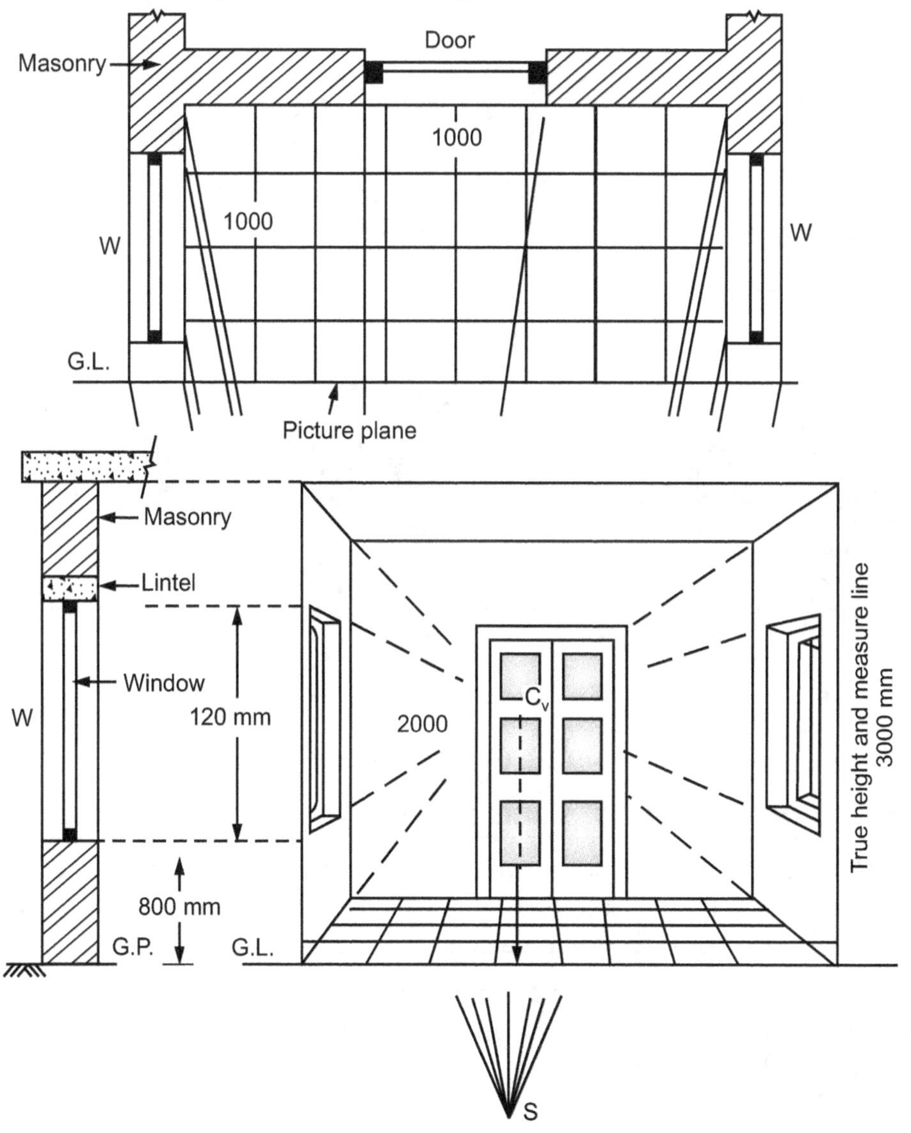

Fig. 5.22: Parallel perspective of an interior

2. **Oblique Perspective:** When the faces of the object are inclined to the picture plane then the perspective of the object is called **oblique perspective**. This is similar to two point or three point perspective. Refer Fig. 5.23.

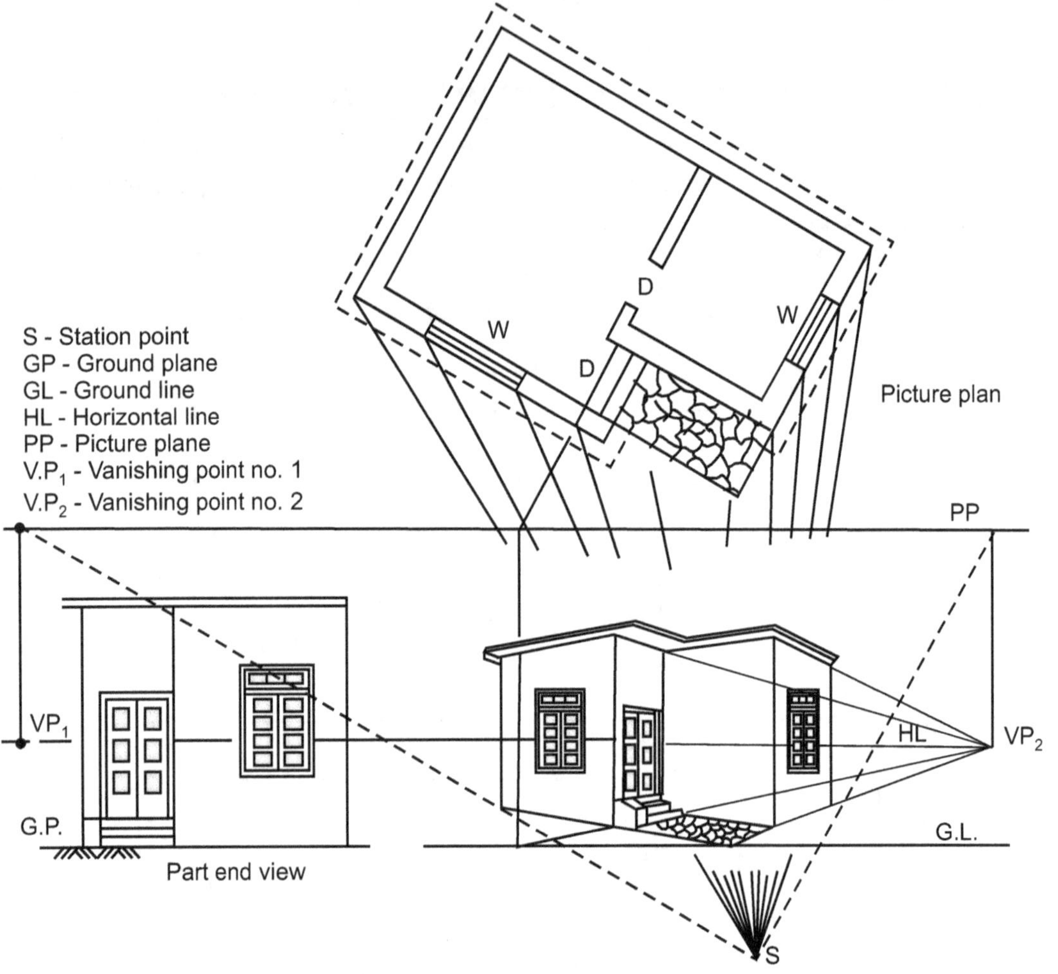

Fig. 5.23: Oblique perspective

5.23.2 Based on Number of Vanishing Points

1. **One Point Perspective:** In this perspective, there is only one vanishing point. In such views picture plane is parallel to two sets of lines out of the three sets. This perspective view drawn is called one **point perspective**.

    Here the picture plane is parallel not only to the vertical line, but also to one of the sets of horizontal lines and these horizontal lines appear as truely horizontal in the image. This perspective is used when only one plane of the object is of interest and perspective is needed only to suggest depth, like interiors of auditorium, interior decoration, front elevation. Refer Fig. 5.24.

2. **Two Point Perspective:** In this, there are two vanishing points. The picture plane is parallel to only one set of parallel lines out of these three sets of lines.

   The most general case of this is that the picture plane will be vertical and object is such that its vertical edges are parallel to the picture plane and its faces are inclined to it. In this case, vanishing points of the lines lies on the same horizontal line.

   Two point perspective is used for buildings. This is also called bird's eye view. Refer Fig. 5.25.

3. **Three Point Perspective:** In this case, the picture plane is tilted and not parallel to any of the principal lines of the object. Three point perspective is only useful when a sky-scrapper is viewed from a road or an aeroplane.

5.23.3 Shades and Shadows in Perspective Drawings

A perspective drawing is incomplete, if natural surrounding like roads, sky, garden, trees etc. are not shown.

Naturally, we observe the shadows of different object like chajjas, cantilevers, roof projections, trees, persons etc. Therefore, all these shadows are shown in perspective for pleasing appearance.

Sun rays are assumed to be parallel therefore a shadow is the part of the surface from which light is excluded by an opaque object.

Shade is the part of an object not exposed to rays of light.

Light is assumed to be appearing from upper left side of elevation of object. Therefore, shadow will fall on the right side and below the object. Shadow lines are drawn at 45° inclination in front elevation.

5.24 METHOD OF DRAWING ONE POINT PERSPECTIVE

First draw the plan of the object parallel to the picture plane as shown in Fig. 5.24. Now select a station point, S.P. at a suitable distance from the picture plane. Join all the angular points of the plan with station point, cutting picture plane at 1, 2, 3, 4. Draw vertical projections from point 1, 2, 3, 4 touching the ground line at a', b', d' and c'. Draw horizontal line parallel to ground line having the height equal to eye level. Select a vanishing point, V. P. on the line of sight EO and on horizon line. Join the point a' d' with V. P. cutting the vertical lines 2b' and 4c' at 5 and 6 respectively. Mark aa', dd' equal to h on vertical lines a 1, d' 1. Joining a, d with V. P. cutting the vertical lines drawn from b' c' at b and c. Complete the figure joining the point a, b, c and d.

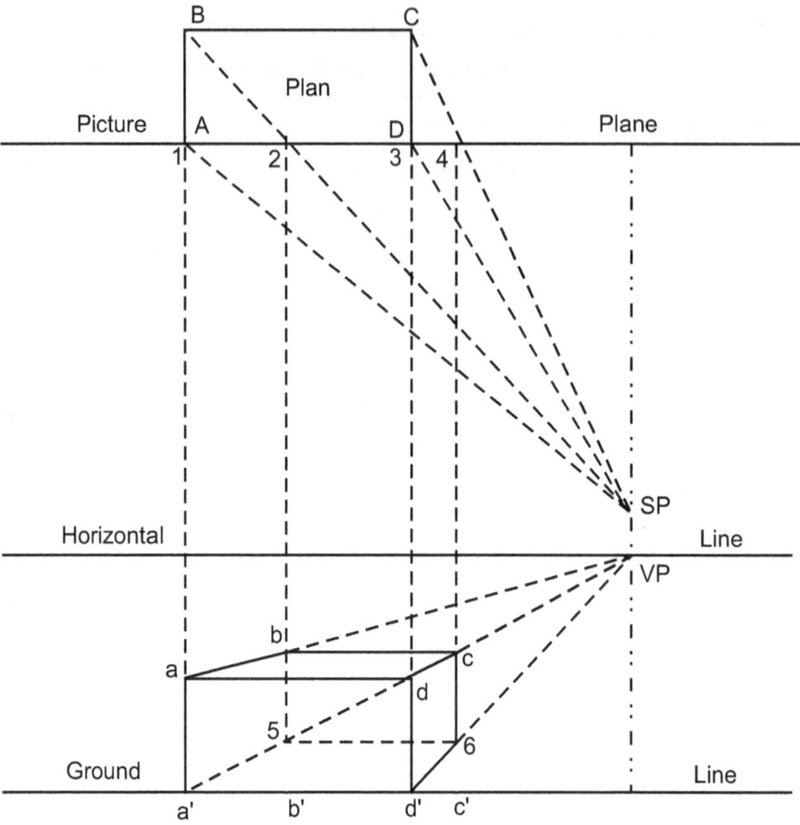

Fig. 5.24: One point perspective

5.25 METHOD OF DRAWING TWO POINT PERSPECTIVE

First draw the plan of the object making an angle of 30° or 45° with the picture plane. Draw the line of sight OE and mark the position of the station point S. P. From the station S draw lines parallel to 1, 4 and 1, 2 cutting the picture plane at V and V'. From these two points draw vertical projection cutting the horizon line which is drawn parallel to ground line and height equal to eye level at VPL and VPR. Hence, these are required vanishing points. Join the angular point of the object with station point and mark the position of these points where they pierce the picture plane. Draw vertical projection from these points. To find out depth of the object, produce the line 4, 1 cutting the picture plane. From this draw vertical projector on the ground line; on this vertical line cut the height of the object and join with the V.P.L., which gives the actual height that is 1. 1' in the vertical line drawn already. Now join 1, 4 to the V.P.L. and V.P.R. cutting the vertical line at 4, 4'. In this way complete the sketch as shown in Fig. 5.25.

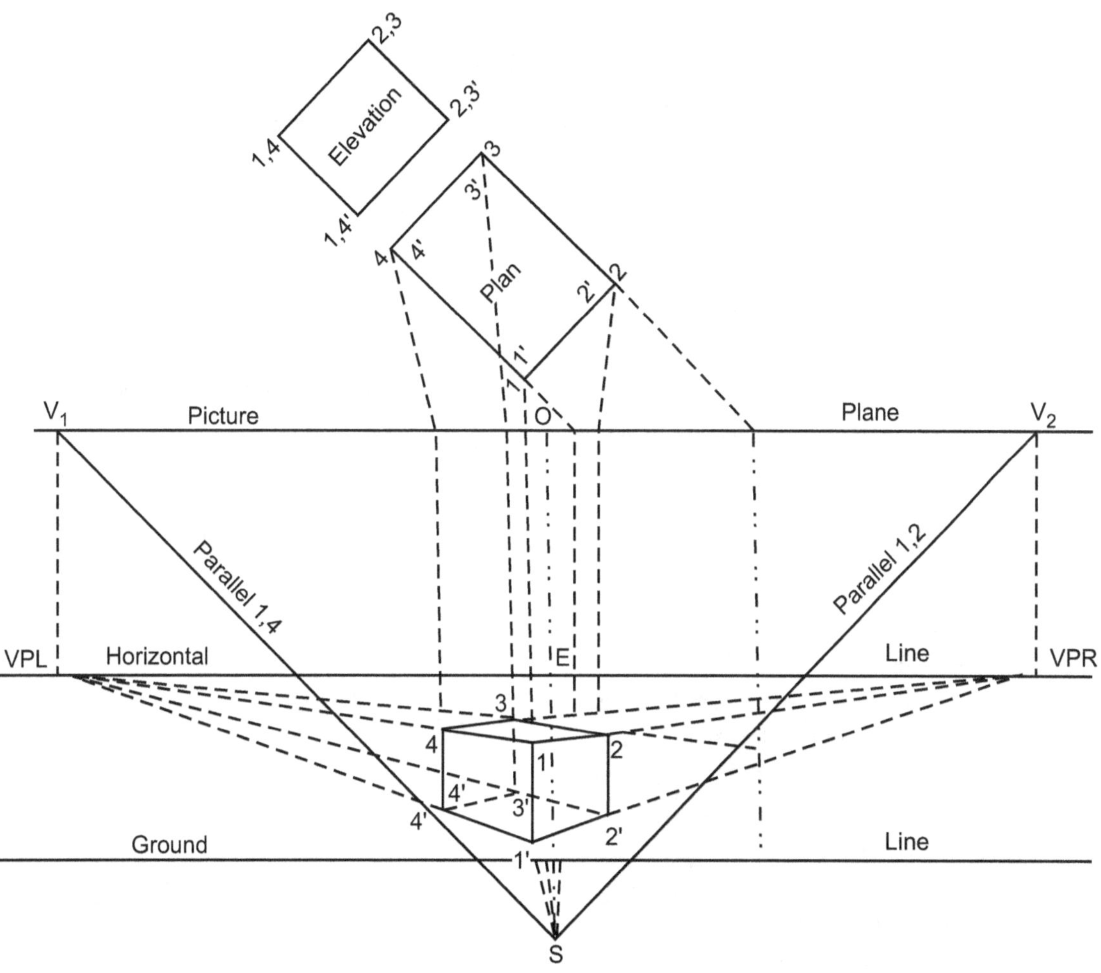

Fig. 5.25: Two point perspective

SOLVED EXAMPLES

Example 5.1 : Draw a two point perspective for a rectangular block 3 cm × 4.8 cm × 1.7 cm. The block is resting on a H.P on face 3 cm × 4.8 cm. The position of block is such that arc of the side of the plan is making 45° angle with the UP station point is 7.5 cm away from PP and height of eye is 3.5 cm. The nearest corner of block is 1 cm away from PP.

Solution:

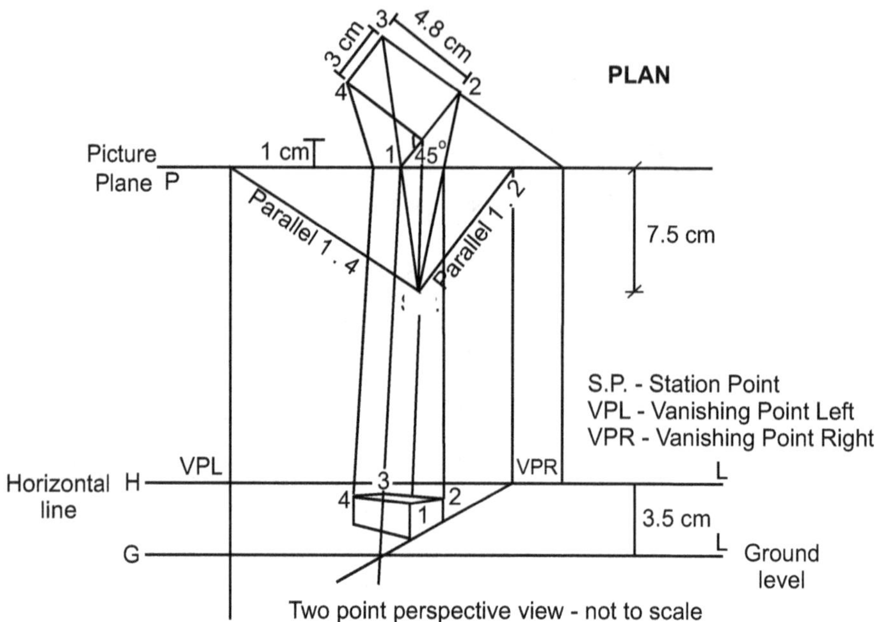

Fig. 5.26

Example 5.2: The Fig. 5.27 shows the plan and elevation of an object. It is inclined at a angle of 30 degrees to the picture plane and touches the picture plane at "B". The observer is standing at a distance of 3.00 metre from the picture plane along the central visual ray. Assuming eye level at 2.00 metre above ground level, draw the perspective view to a suitable scale.

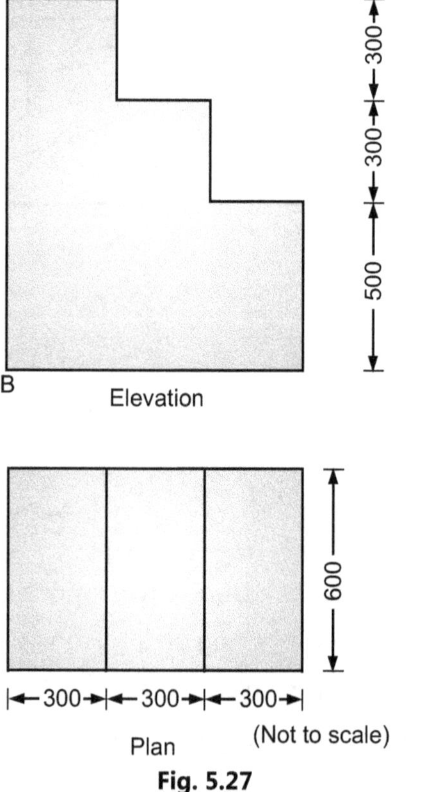

Fig. 5.27

Solution:

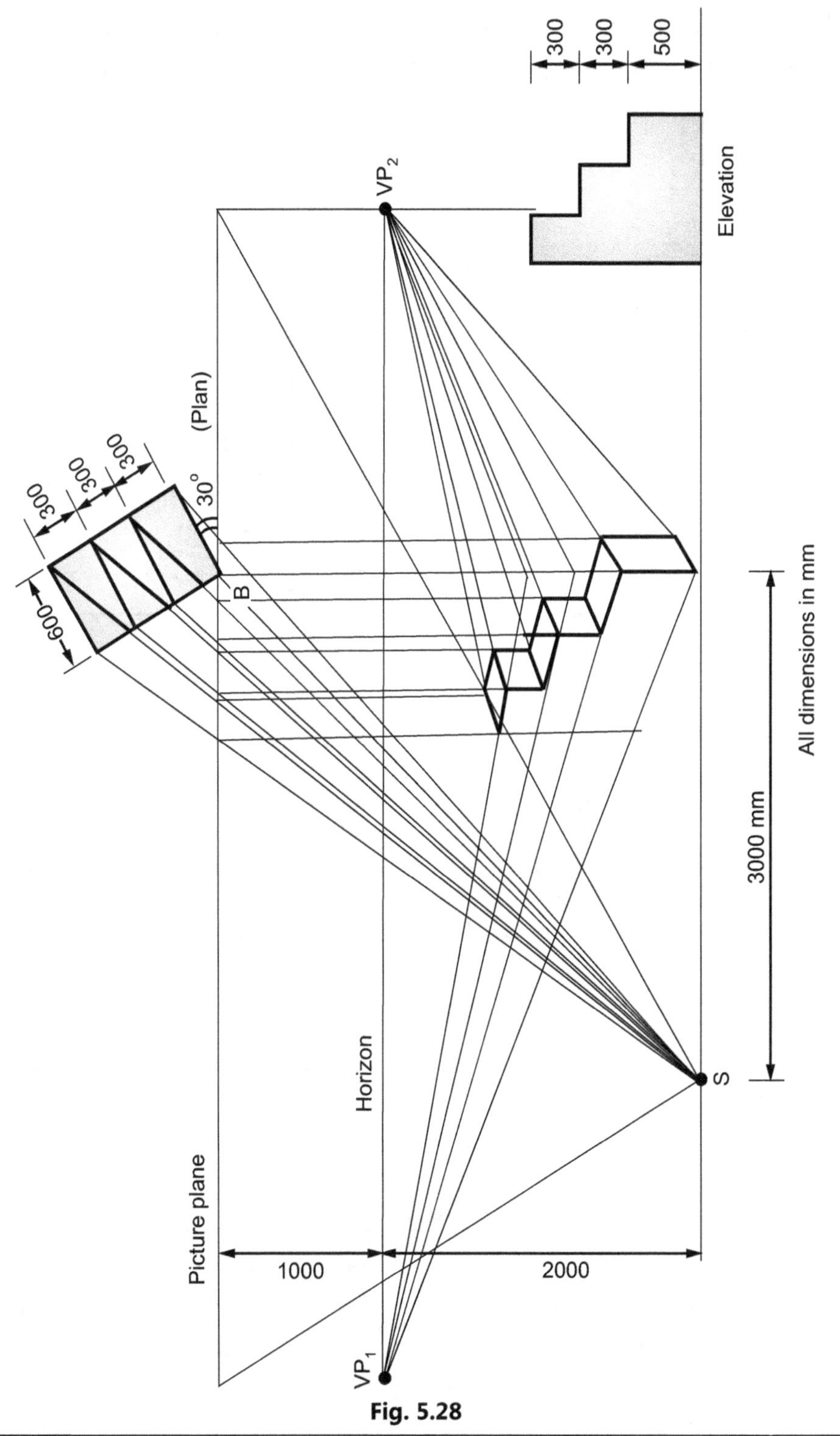

Fig. 5.28

Example 5.3: Draw parallel perspective of a cylindrical tower 4.5 metres high above plinth and 2.00 metres in diameter The tower is supported symmetrically on two square plinths $4 \times 4 \times 0.5$ metres and $3 \times 3 \times 0.5$ metres. Assume eye level 2.00 metres.

Solution:

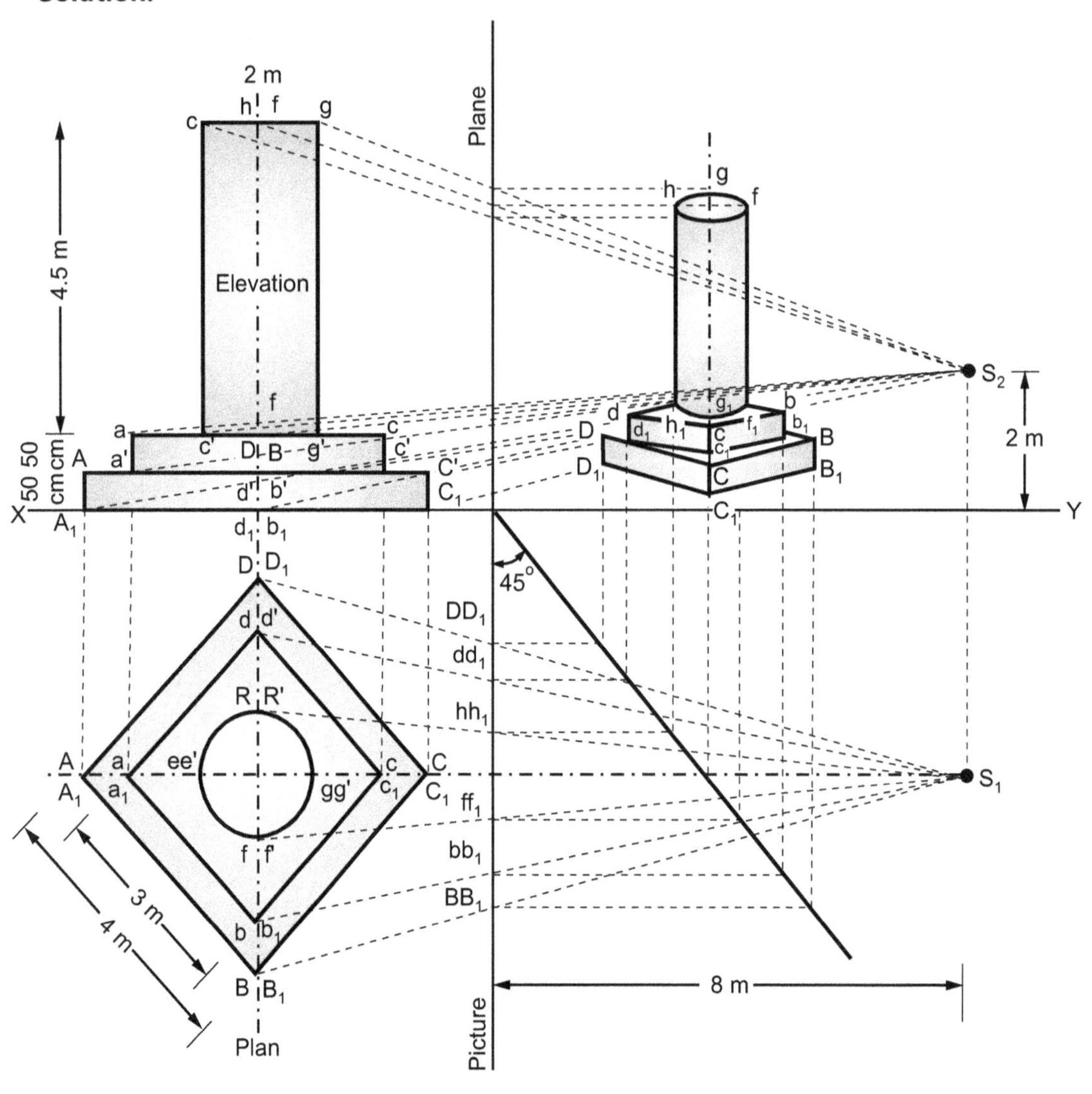

Fig. 5.29

Example 5.4: The Fig. 5.30 shows the plan of an object. Longer side of object is inclined at 30° to the picture plane and touches the same at A. The observer is at a distance of 10 m along the central visual ray. Assuming eye level at 1.5 m above G.L. Draw the perspective view of the object to some convenient scale.

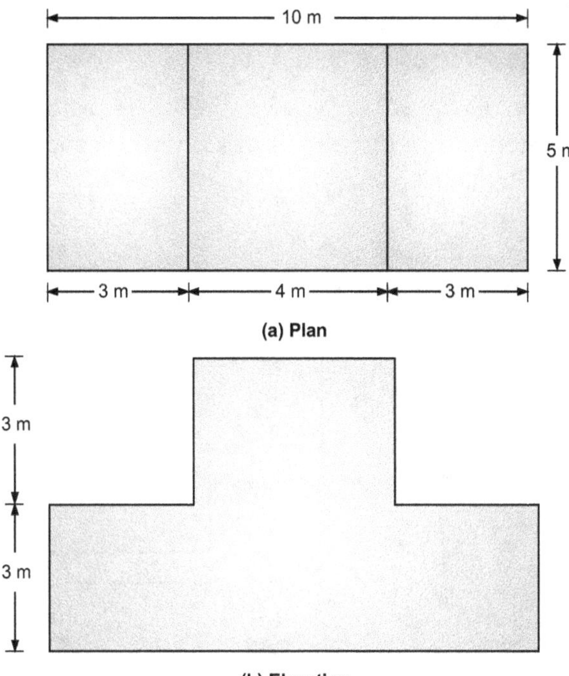

(a) Plan

(b) Elevation

Fig. 5.30

Solution:

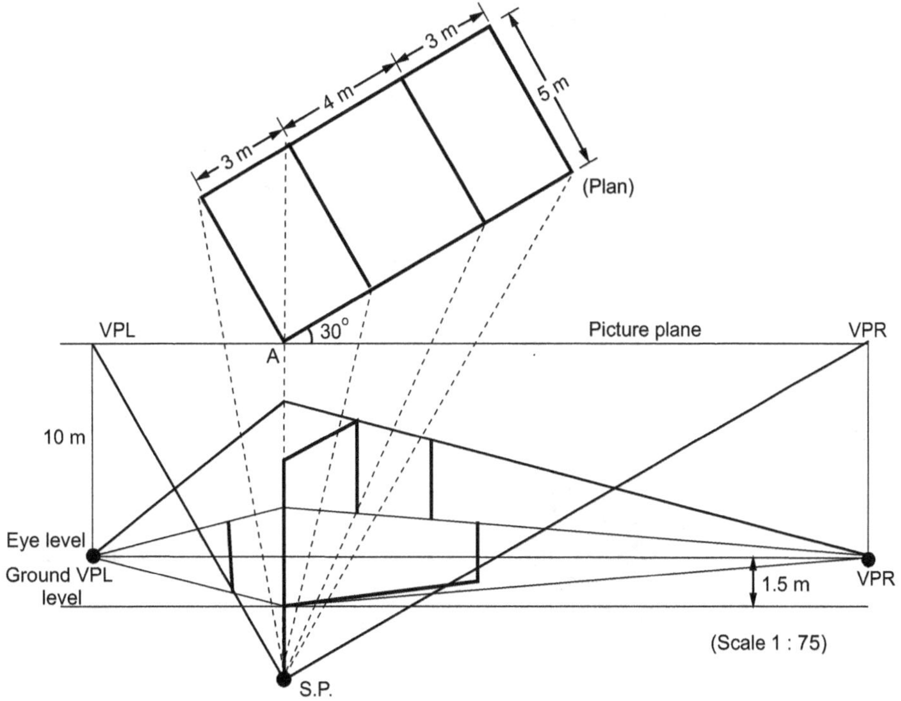

Fig. 5.31 : Perspective view

Example 5.5: Draw the two point perspective view of a stone memorial pillar shown in Fig. 5.32 to a scale 1 : 2 or to same convenient scale.

The base block of pillar makes an angle of 30° with the picture plane and touches the same at A. The observer stands at a distance 3 m along the central visual ray. Assume eye level is at 1.5 m above G.L. Retain all construction lines.

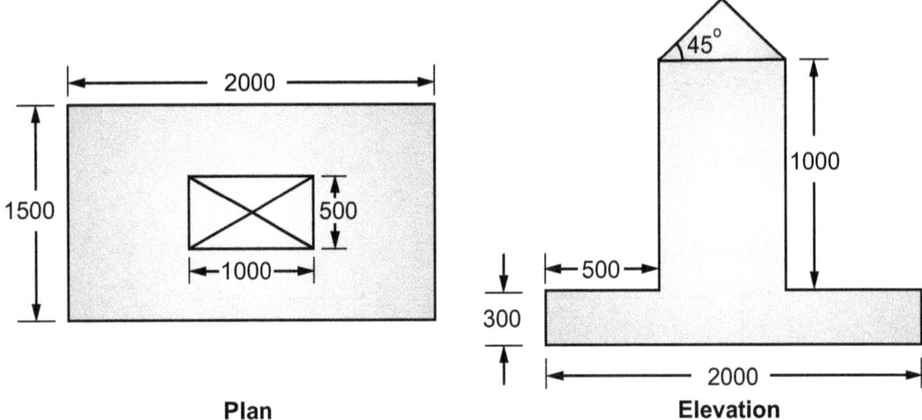

Fig. 5.32

Solution:

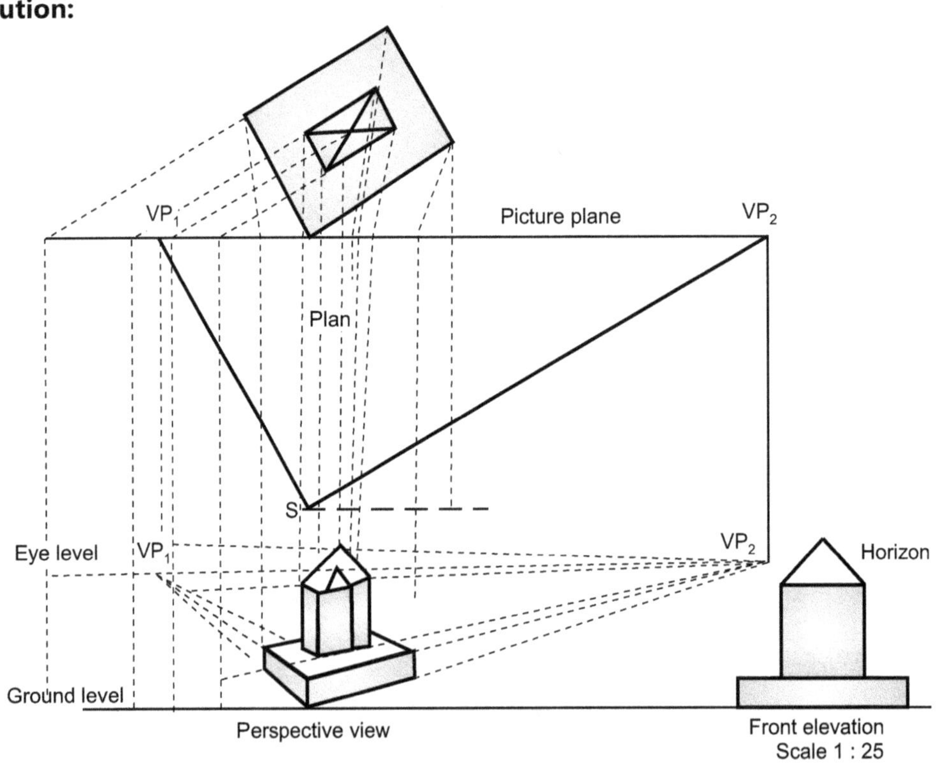

Fig. 5.33

Example 5.6: Fig. 5.34 shown below shows the plan of Thresholds, one side of which is inclined at 30° to the picture plane and touches the same at A. The observer is standing at a distance of 2 m along the central visual ray. Assuming eye level at 1.5 m above G.L. draw the two point perspective view to scale of 1 : 20.

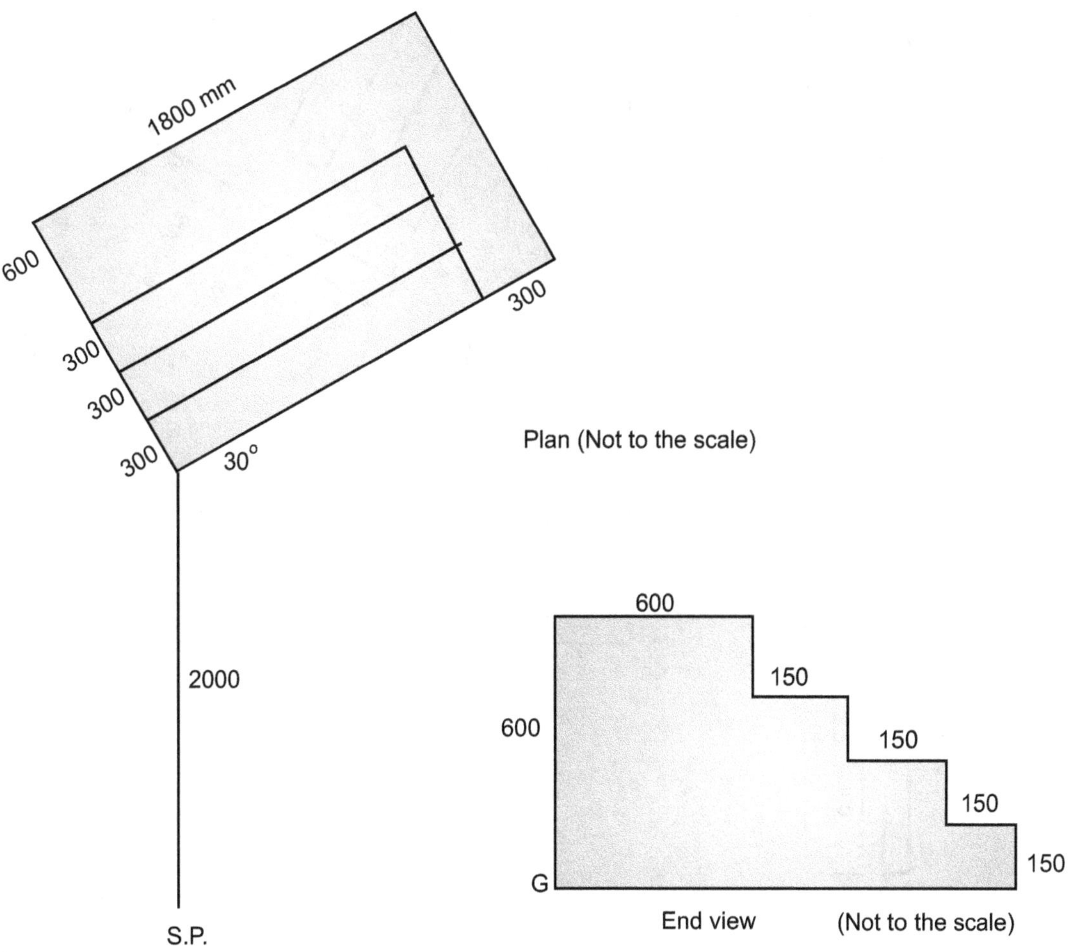

Fig. 5.34

Solution:

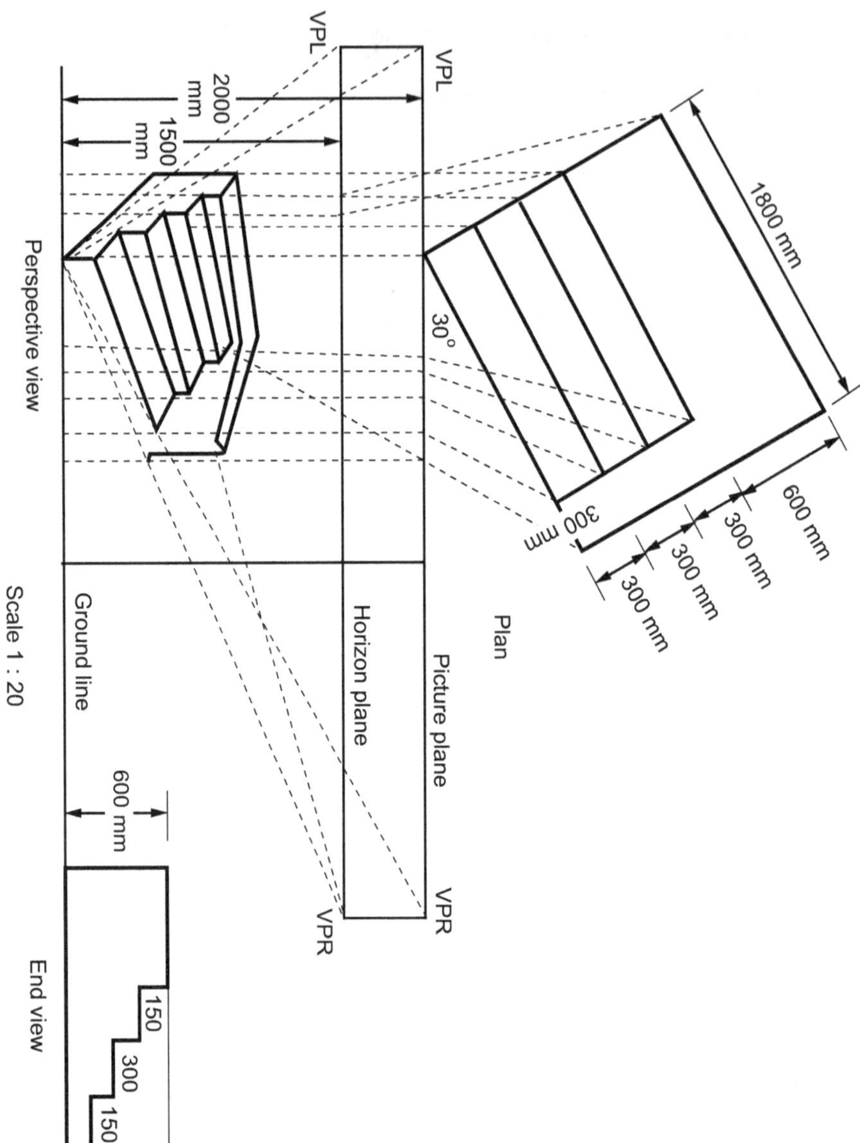

Fig. 5.35

IMPORTANT POINTS

- Various types of lines required in construction.
- Graphical symbols for construction materials.
- Abbreviations and scales.
- Title block, line-plan, elevations and sections.

- Schedule of doors and windows, types of windows and fixtures and fastenings for doors and windows.

- Detailed drawings and its set for construction.

- Methods of preparing detailed drawings, foundation plan.

- Roof plan and its types: (a) For pitched roof, (b) For flat roof.

- Perspective drawings and important terms i.e. in drawing.

- Principles of perspective and its types.

- Perspective drawing based on vanishing points i.e. one point perspective, two point perspective and three point perspective.

- Necessity of Bye-laws and basic definitions used in projects.

- Area measurement of a building :

1. Covered area 2. Plinth area 3. Floor area 4. Built-up area 5. Carpet area.

- Height of buildings for different rooms.

- Requirement of drainage and sanitation for different buildings.

QUESTIONS

1. Draw to a scale 1 : 100 or suitable a two point perspective view of an object shown below, the position of eye level is 1.8 m above ground level.

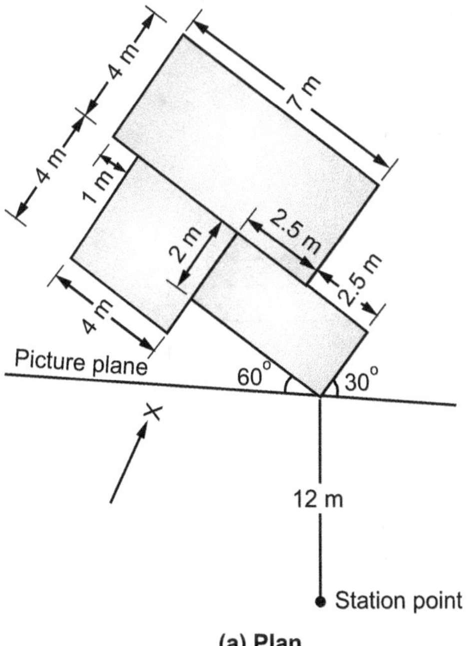

(a) Plan

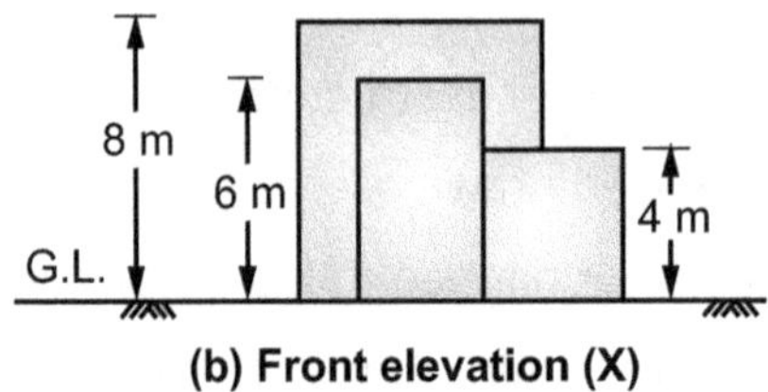

(b) Front elevation (X)

Fig. 5.36

2. Draw to a scale 1 : 100 or suitable a "Two Point Perspective" view of the overhead water tank. The plan and elevation is as shown in Fig. 5.37.

Tilt the plan to 45° w.r.t. picture plane.

Use the following details:

(a) Tilt the plan to 450 with respect to the picture plane. The corner of the tank (in plan) must be touching the picture plane.

(b) Select station point vertically below the plan from the point, where the inclined plane touches the picture plane. Take station at 7.2 m below picture plane.

(c) Select eye level = 1.90 m above Ground level.

(d) All dimensions are in mm.

(e) Retail all construction lines.

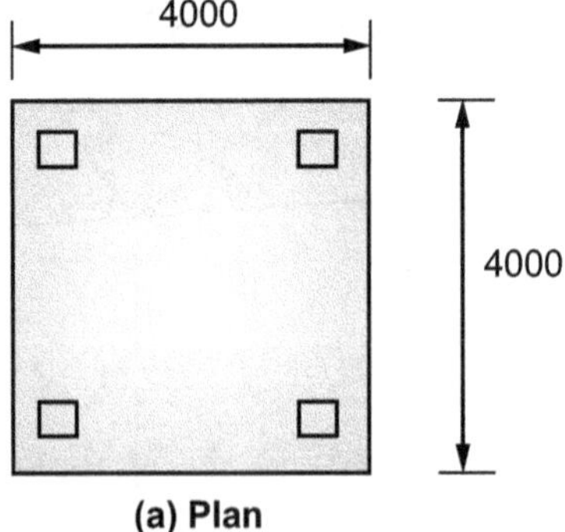

(a) Plan

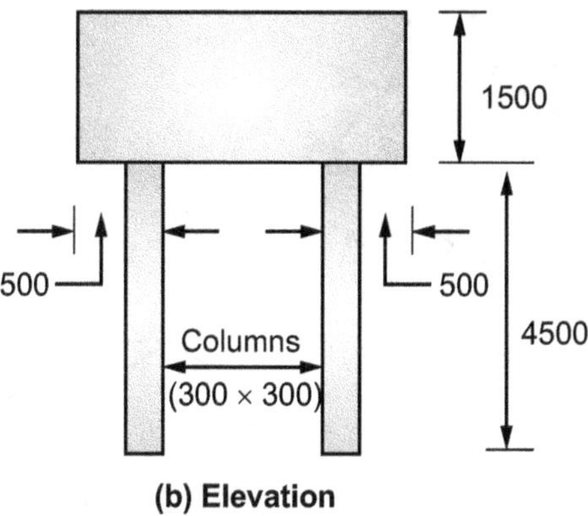

Fig. 5.37: Overhead water tank

3. Draw perspective view of the monument shown in Fig. 5.38.

   Scale 1 : 100 or suitable.

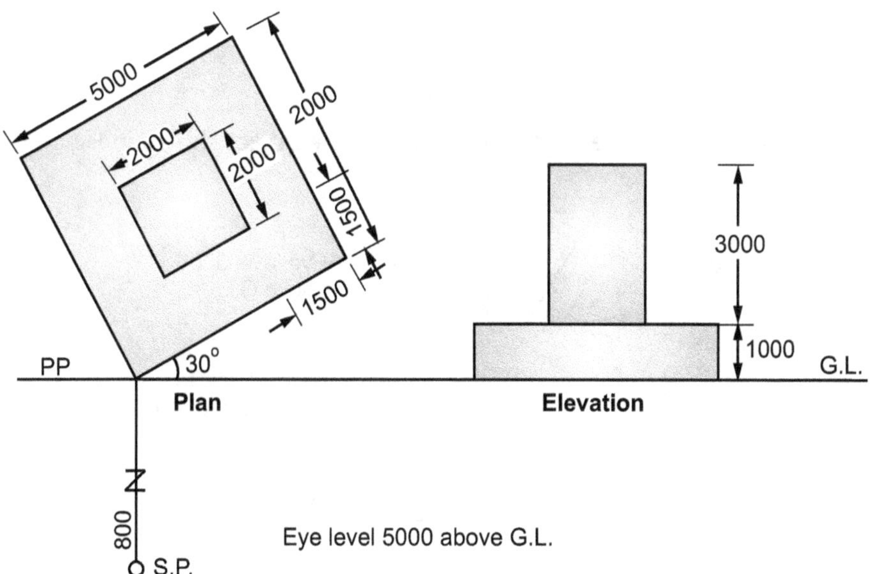

Fig. 5.38

4. Draw to a scale of 1 : 100 or suitable, a two point perspective view of the building shown in Fig. 5.39.

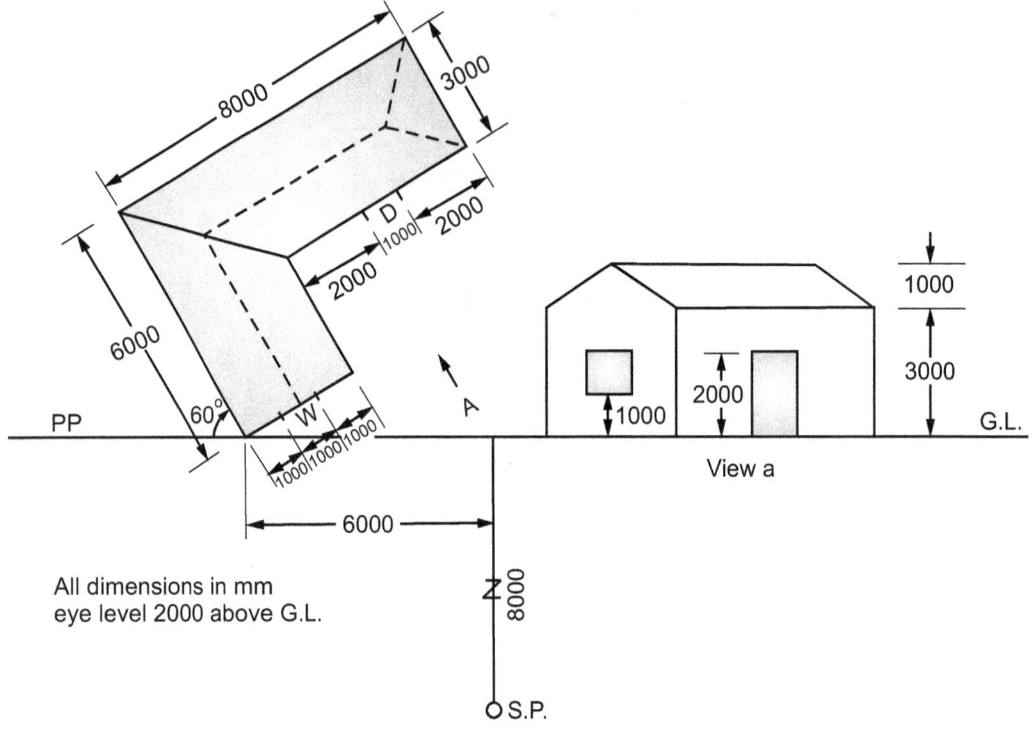

Fig. 5.39

5. Draw to a scale of 1 : 50 the perspective view of the object shown in Fig. 5.40.

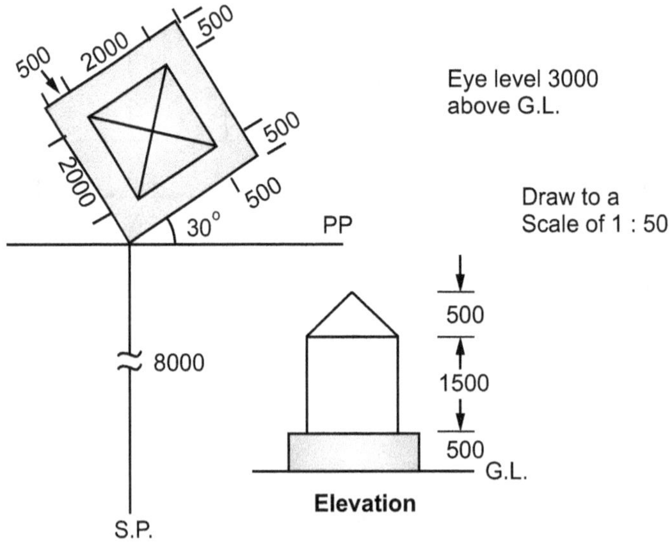

Fig. 5.40

6. Draw two point perspective view of the object shown in Fig. 5.41. Retail all construction lines.

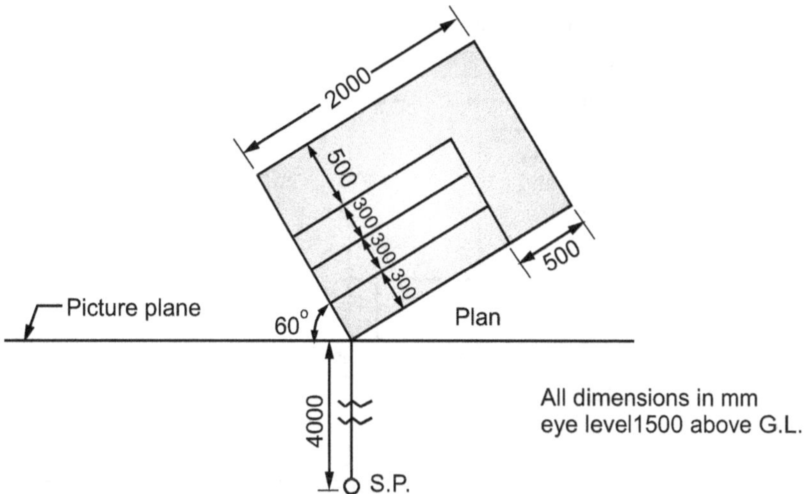

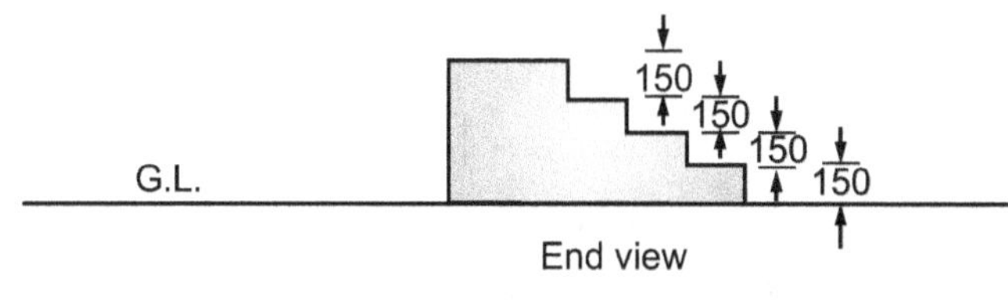

Fig. 5.41

7. (a) Explain one point and two point perspective.

(b) Draw perspective view for the block shown in Fig. 5.42 with scale 1 : 200 or suitable.

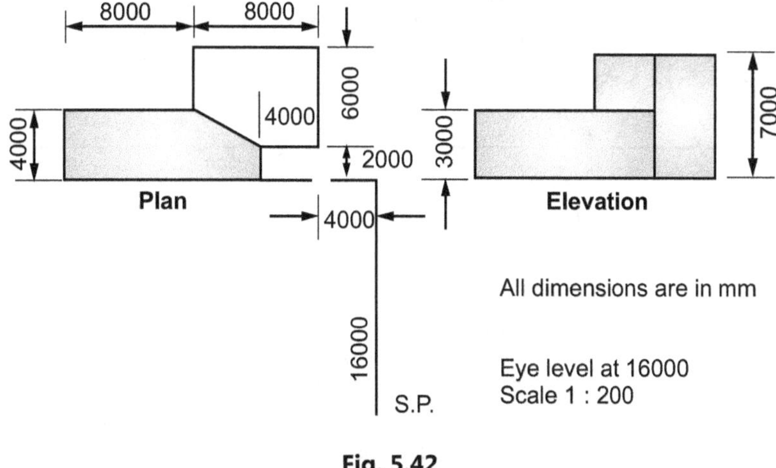

Fig. 5.42

8. Draw a one point perspective view of the blocks shown in Fig. 5.43. Assume eye level as 3 m. Scale 1 : 50 or suitable.

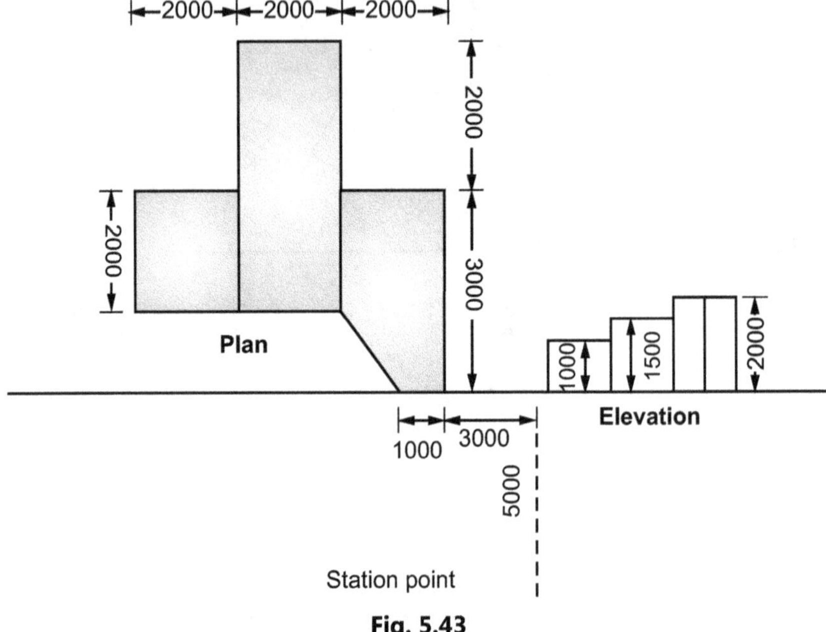

Fig. 5.43

1. Draw to a scale of 1 : 25 or suitable, a two point perspective view of the object shown in Fig. 5.44.

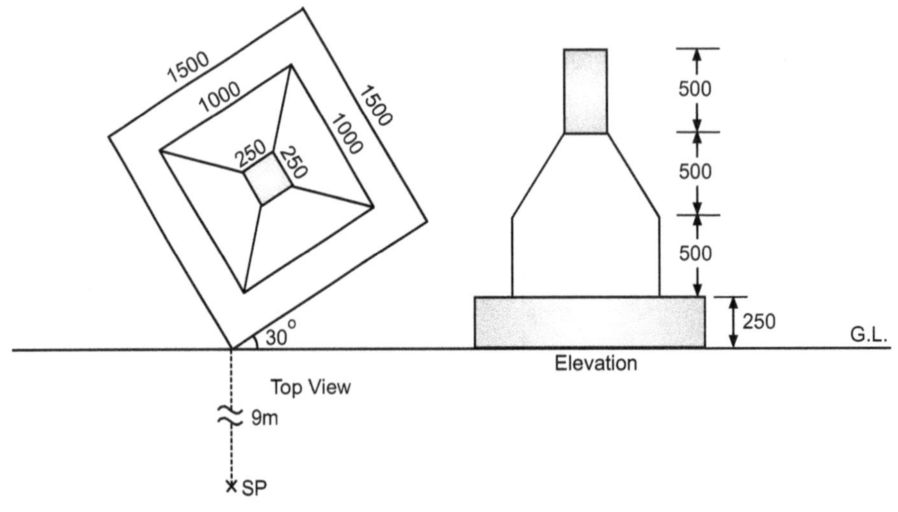

All dimensions in mm.
Eye Level 1500 mm above G.L.
Scale 1 : 25 or suitable

Fig. 5.44

2. Fig. 5.45 shows the plan and elevation of a small temple. Draw to a scale 1 : 50 a two point perspective drawing of it. Retain all construction lines.

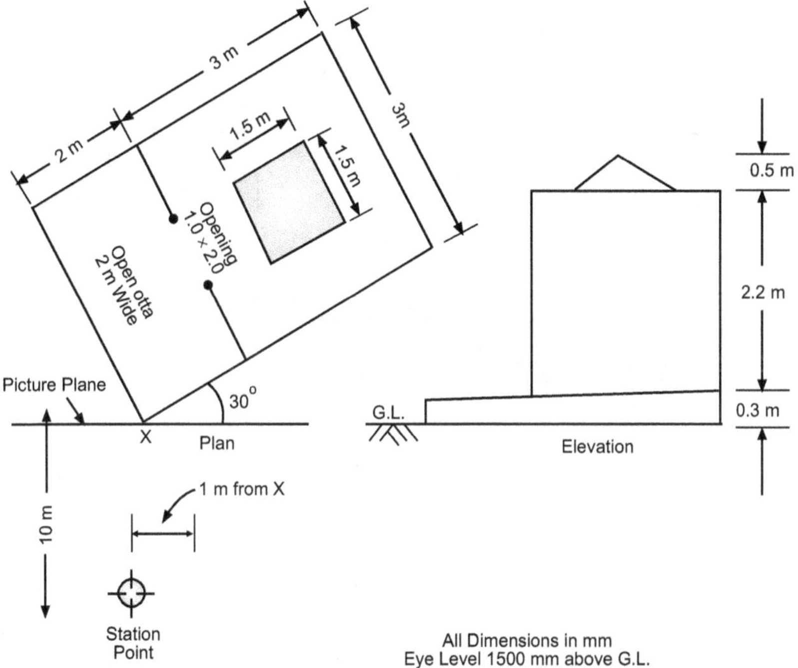

Fig. 5.45

3. Draw to a scale 1 : 50, the perspective view of the object shown in Fig. 5.46.

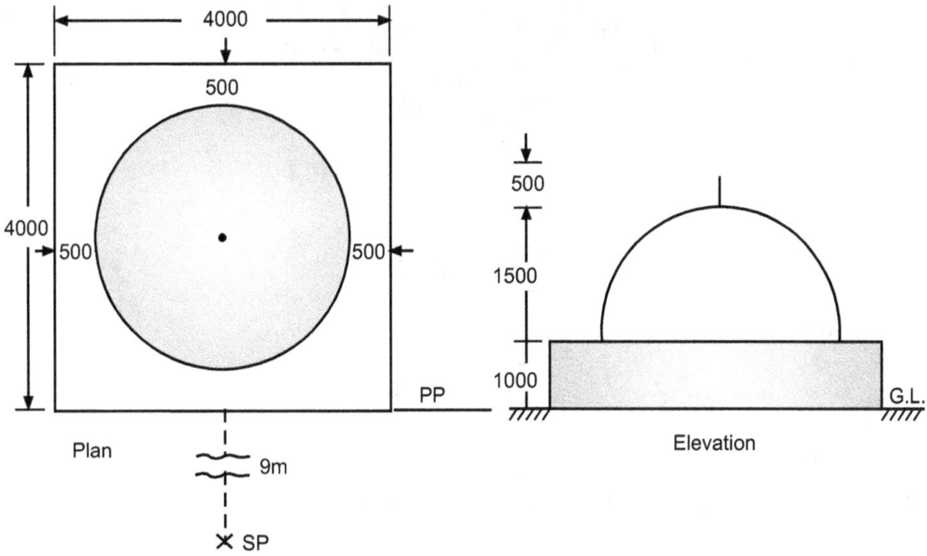

Fig. 5.46

4. Draw to a scale 1 : 100 or suitable, a two-point perspective view of the building shown in Fig. 5.47.

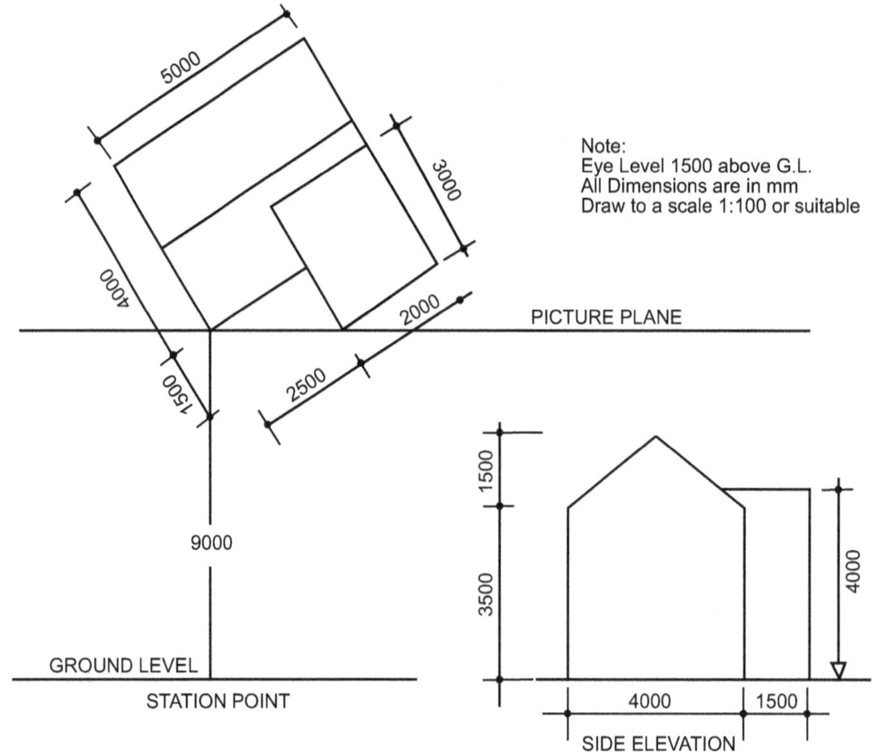

Fig. 5.47

UNIVERSITY QUESTIONS

Dec. 2014

1. Explain with sketch the following terms:

   (i) SP   (ii) VP   (iii) PP

Dec. 2015

1. Distinguish between isometric and perceptive views

Nov. 2016

1. Define the following :

   (i) Picture plane   (ii) Vanishing point   (iii) Building line

◈ ◈ ◈

Chapter 6
SAFETY ASPECTS

6.1 INTRODUCTION

Fire is an essential and integral part of our daily life but any misuse or accident in the use of fire can precipitate disaster.

Fires in buildings are nearly always man-made, resulting from error or negligence.

In olden times, dwellings were mostly timber - framed construction with thatched roofs, and within the walled townships overcrowding, narrow lanes, overhanging eaves and indiscriminate use of combustible materials provided all the necessary ingredients for the conflagrations which followed.

Towards the end of the nineteenth century, it was possible to construct large multi-storeyed buildings, the structural elements of which were of non-combustible materials. However, even today, in spite of using the most modern techniques of construction and fire resistant materials, fires still occur and cause a lot of damage to property and life.

Several rules and regulations have been drafted by government bodies to ensure the nature and quality of fire protection and safety accorded to a building.

The main purposes of fire safety legislation are:

- To impose a level of fire safety, such that it is unlikely that people occupying a building would suffer injury in the event of an unwanted fire.

- To protect the community at large from the consequences of a fire in an individual building.

Building regulations assume that if certain components of fire safety can be identified and suitable standards applied to particular building types, a satisfactory level of fire safety will be achieved.

It is assumed that if the purpose, for which buildings will be generally used, can be determined; then buildings used for a similar purpose can be classified as a particular building type. This method assumes that each building of a particular type will:

- Have the same fire loading,
- Be of similar geometry,
- Experience a similar fire scenario and
- Be exposed to a fire of similar severity.

Hence, the standards for components of fire safety can be prescribed for building types.

Thus, building classification becomes a factor in risk determination.

6.1.1 Fire Safety

"Fire Safety is defined a person in or adjacent to a building will be exposed to an unacceptable fire hazard as a result of the design and construction of the building".

In simpler terms, fire safety is the reduction of the potential for harm to life as a result of fire in buildings. Although the potential for being killed or injured in a fire cannot be completely eliminated, fire safety in a building can be achieved through proven building design features intended to minimize the risk of harm to people from fire to the greatest extent possible. Designing a building to ensure minimal risk or to meet a prescribed level of safety from fire is more complex than just the simple consideration of what building materials will be used in construction of the building.

6.2 CLASSIFICATION OF BUILDINGS BASED ON OCCUPANCY

All buildings are classified according to the use or the character of occupancy into the following groups:

Group	
A	Residential
B	Educational
C	Institutional
D	Assembly
E	Business
F	Mercantile
G	Industrial
H	Storage
J	Hazardous

Group A: Residential Buildings

These include any building in which sleeping accommodation is provided for normal residential purposes, with or without cooking or dining.

For example: residential houses, apartments, lodging and boarding houses, hotels, hostels, etc.

Group B: Educational Buildings

These include buildings for schools, colleges or day care purposes involving assembly for instruction and education.

Group C: Institutional Buildings

These include hospitals and sanatoria; homes for the aged, the convalescent and orphans; buildings for jails, prisons, mental hospitals etc.

Group D: Assembly Buildings

These are buildings in which groups of people congregate or gather for amusement, recreation, social and religious activities and also for activities related to travel.

For example: Theatres, assembly halls, auditoria, exhibition halls, museums, gymnasiums, restaurants, places of worship, dance halls, clubs, passenger stations and terminals of air, surface and marine public transportation services, stadia etc.

Group E: Business Buildings

These are buildings which are used for transaction of business, for keeping of accounts and records, professional establishments, service facilities etc.

For example: City halls, town halls, court rooms, libraries, offices, banks, laboratories, research establishments etc.

Group F: Mercantile Buildings

These are buildings which are used as shops, stores, market; for display and sale of merchandise.

Group G: Industrial Buildings

These are buildings in which products or materials of all kinds are fabricated, assembled, manufactured or processed.

Group H: Storage Buildings

These are buildings used primarily for the storage or sheltering of goods, wares or merchandise (except those that involve highly combustible materials or explosives), vehicles or animals. For example: warehouses, cold storage, truck and marine terminals, garages, grain elevators, barns and stables.

Group J: Hazardous Buildings

These include buildings which are used for storage, handling, manufacture or processing of highly combustible or explosive materials or products which are liable to burn rapidly and/or produce poisonous fumes or explosions.

For example: Storage under pressure of acetylene, hydrogen, natural gas, ammonia etc.

Storage and handling of highly inflammable materials or liquids, rocket propellants etc.

Manufacture of artificial flowers, synthetic leather, ammunition, explosives, fire crackers, match sticks etc.

6.3 FIRE LOAD

The term fire load is used to describe the heat energy which could be released per square metre of floor area of a compartment or storey by the combustion of the contents of the building and any combustible parts of the superstructure itself.

$$\text{Fire load} \ = \ \frac{M \times C}{A} \ \text{in kJ/m}^2$$

where, M = Mass of combustible materials in the compartment or storey, in kg

$\quad$ C $\ =\ $ Calorific value of materials, in kJ/kg

$\quad$ A $\ =\ $ Floor area, in m^2.

Building regulations have adopted a grouping system, which is a grading of occupancies based on assumed fire loadings. The grouping of buildings is then used as a determinant in establishing the desirable fire-resisting characteristics of the elements of the structure of the building.

Thus, it is seen that the concept of fire loading attempts is to relate the combustible contents of a building to the potential severity of a fire in that building and consequently to the fire-resisting capabilities of the elements of the structure.

Broadly, the buildings are classified into the following three groups depending upon the fire load.

Building hazard classification	Fire load in kJ/m²
Low hazard group	0 - 49
Medium hazard group	50 - 100
High hazard group	> 100

Certain rules and regulations have been framed by government bodies, which direct that all the buildings must satisfy certain requirements which contribute individually and collectively, to the safety of life from fire, smoke, fumes and panic arising from fire.

The following are Some of the General Requirements:

- Every building must be restricted in its height above the ground level regarding the number of storeys, depending upon its occupancy and type of construction.
- Open spaces around or inside a building must conform to the requirements of local development control rules and general building requirements.
- For high rise buildings (height more than 15 m), the following additional requirements must be considered.
    (a) The width of the main street on which the building abuts should not be less than 12 m.
    (b) The road should not have a dead end.
    (c) Compulsory open spaces around the building must not be used as parking spaces.
    (d) Adequate passageways and clearances required for fire fighting vehicles to enter the premises must be provided at the entrance, the width of such an entrance should not be less than 4.5 m. If an arch or a covered gate is constructed; it should have a clear head room of not less than 5 m.
- Fire detecting and extinguishing systems must be provided as per accepted standards according to the type of occupancy.
- All buildings depending upon the occupancy, use and height, should be protected by wet riser, wet riser-cum-down comer, automatic sprinkler installation, high pressure water spray or foam generating system etc. as per accepted standards.

- Static water storage Tanks: A satisfactory supply of water for the purpose of fire fighting should always be available in the form of an underground static storage tank with its capacity specified for each building.
- Automatic sprinklers can be installed in basements used as carparks; departmental stores, shops of area more than 750 m^2; godowns and warehouses on all floors of the buildings other than residential buildings, if the height of the building exceeds 45 m.
- Air conditioning and ventilating systems should be so installed and maintained as to minimise the danger of fire, smoke or fumes spreading from one floor to another or from outside into any occupied building or structure.
- For buildings over 15 m in height, fire lifts should be provided with a minimum capacity of 8 passengers and thus should be fully automated with emergency switches at ground level.

6.4 FACTORS AFFECTING FIRE DEVELOPMENT

The growth and development of a fire depend to a great extent on the geometry and ventilation of the enclosure containing fire.

A fire usually starts because a material is ignited by a heat source. The development of a fire within an enclosure depends on the following factors:

- The item first ignited is sufficiently inflammable to allow a flame to spread over its surfaces.
- The heat flux from the first ignited item is sufficient to irradiate adjacent materials which in turn begin to burn.
- Sufficient fuel exists within the enclosure; otherwise, the fire may simply burn itself out.
- The fire may burn very slowly because of a restricted supply of oxygen as in the case of a well sealed room and may eventually smoother itself.
- If there is sufficient fuel and oxygen available, the fire may totally involve the entire enclosure.

6.5 PATTERN OF FIRE

The pattern of every fire is different but the majority pass through the following stages:

Flashover is the rapid involvement of an enclosure's combustible contents as they ignite almost simultaneously. Thus, it is the time when the flames cease to be localised and flaming can be observed throughout the whole enclosure. **Flashover** is, in fact, the transition from the growth period to a steady state of combustion, or a fully developed stage in fire development.

The period A - B is known as the growth period. It is essentially the pre-flashover period during which the temperatures in the enclosure are relatively low and chances of escape are relatively high.

At B, the fire progresses rapidly through flashover to the fully developed stage upto C. During this period all the combustibles in the compartment are burning and the temperature within the enclosure is highest.

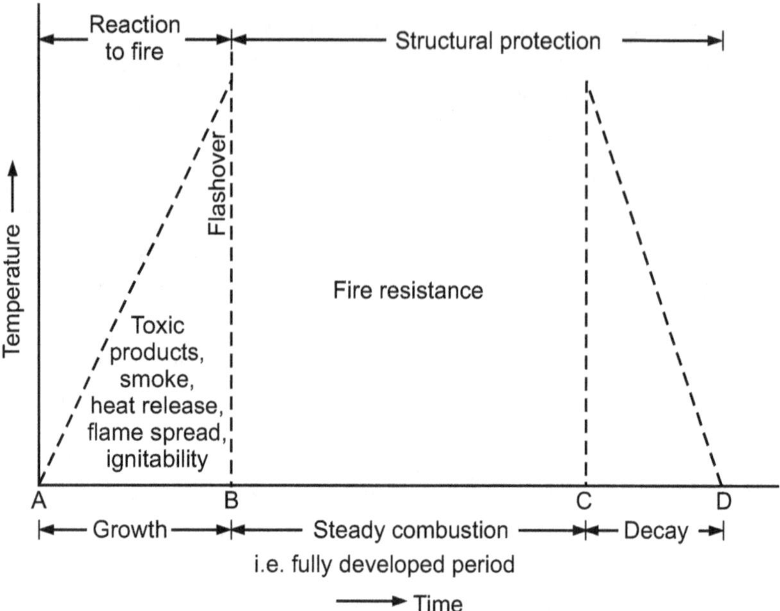

Fig. 6.1: Different phases of fire

At C, the steady combustion period ends, the temperature begins to fall and C - D is the decay period.

Though the temperatures during the growth period are low, the duration of the growth period is very important as it determines the time available for escape and for the effective operation of the emergency fire fighting services.

6.6 FIRE SEVERITY

It may be defined as the destructive potential of a fire i.e. the potential impact that a fire in a given enclosure will have upon the structural and constructional components which form the enclosure and its components. Hence, fire severity has a direct relation to the structural performance in terms of a component's fire-resisting capabilities. Therefore, the fire resistance offered by a component during the fully developed stage of a fire is extremely important in evaluating the extent of fire severity.

6.7 FIRE RESISTANCE

If a fire burns unnoticed and uncontrolled in a building, the building elements can be subjected to very high temperatures. The temperature levels and the duration of heating are dependent upon a number of factors related to the design of the building and its contents. If the building elements can withstand this exposure without the building becoming unstable or suffering collapse and without the fire spreading unrestrictedly, they are considered to have adequate fire resistance.

Thus, **fire resistance** can be defined as the ability of an element of building construction to withstand the effects of fire for a specified period of time without loss of its fire separating and load bearing functions. Therefore, a structural component should be able to:

- Endure a fire without collapse,
- Prevent the penetration of flame,
- Resist the spread of fire by conduction through the component or by radiation from the face of the component not exposed to the fire.

The factors which determine the level of fire resistance of structural components are:

- Type of occupancy,
- Height of the building,
- Floor area of the storey or compartment,
- Cubic capacity of the building or compartment and
- Location of the component

　　i.e. (a) Ground or upper storey

　　　　(b) Basement.

Unit: The fire resistance of a building or its structural elements is expressed in hours against a specified test load which is expressed in kcal/m^2 and against a certain intensity of fire.

The types of construction according to fire resistance are classified into four categories, namely, type 1, type 2, type 3 and type 4.

The following Table 6.1 gives the fire resistance ratings for various types of construction for structural elements.

Table 6.1: Fire resistance ratings of structural elements (in hours)

Structural Element		Type of Construction			
		Type 1	Type 2	Type 3	Type 4
1. Exterior walls Fire separation less than 3.7 m	Bearing	4	2	2	1
	Non-Bearing	2	$1\frac{1}{2}$	1	1
Fire separation of 3.7 m or more but less than 9 m	Bearing	4	2	2	1
	Non-Bearing	$1\frac{1}{2}$	1	1	1
Fire separation of 9 m or more	Bearing	4	2	2	1
	Non-Bearing	1	1	1	1
2. Fire walls and party walls		4	2	2	2
3. Fire separation assemblies		4	2	2	2
4. Fire enclosures of exit ways, hallways and stairways		2	2	2	2
5. Shaft other than exit ways, elevator hoist ways		2	2	2	2

6. Exit way access corridors		1	1	1	1
7. Vertical separation of tenant spaces		1	1	1	1
8. Dwelling unit separations		1	1	1	1
Non-bearing partitions		← At least half an hour →			
9. Interior bearing walls, bearing partitions, columns, girders, trusses (other than roof trusses) and framing	Supporting more than one floor	4	2	2	2
	Supporting one floor only	3	$1\frac{1}{2}$	1	1
	Supporting a roof only	3	$1\frac{1}{2}$	1	1
10. Structural members supporting walls		3	$1\frac{1}{2}$	1	1
11. Floor construction, including beams		3	$1\frac{1}{2}$	1	1
12. Roof construction, including beams, trusses and framing arches and roof deck	5 m or less in height to lowest member	2	$1\frac{1}{2}$	1	1
	More than 5 m but less than 6.7 m in height to lowest member	1	1	1	1
	6.7 m or more in height to lowest member	0	0	0	0

In relation to fire, the building materials can be classified into two categories - combustible and non-combustible. Combustible materials are those that catch fire themselves and contribute to the growth of fire. For example: wood, fibre board, straw board curtains, apparel etc.

Non-combustible materials are those that do not catch fire, but after being exposed to fire for some time, loose their inherent qualities. They may loose their shape and load carrying capacity and yield, thus resulting in the collapse of the structure For example: steel, stone.

6.8 SOME COMMON CONSTRUCTION MATERIALS

- **Timber:** Though timber catches fire and is a combustible material, it has the ability to offer resistance to fire for a period of time. It gets charred, on exposure to fire and this coating of char on timber surface functions as an insulating material and slows down the process of combustion. However, on prolonged exposure to fire, it undergoes total combustion.

- **Stone:** Stone is a non-combustible material but has very little fire resisting properties. Granite, when exposed to fire, breaks into pieces. Limestone and marble get calcined. Compact sandstone can withstand fire to some extent.

- **Bricks:** Well burnt bricks have good fire resisting properties and may withstand temperatures upto 1200°C.

- **Iron and Steel:** Though iron and steel are non-combustible materials, they are very good conductors of heat. They expand, get warped and loose their shape under exposure to prolonged fire. Thus, a steel structural component may yield under heat resulting in collapse of the structure.

- **Concrete:** Concrete, in general, is a good fire-resistant material, but this resistance will depend to a large extent on the type of aggregates used. However, RCC structure with a good cover to reinforcement offers good resistance to fire.

- **Glass:** Glass is a good fire resisting material because of its low thermal conductivity. However, it cannot tolerate sudden changes in temperature.

  For example: When it is exposed to extreme heat in the event of a fire, and the fire is doused with water, glass may crack. Reinforced glass has better fire resistance.

- **Asbestos Cement:** Asbestos cement is an excellent fire resisting material. It is a combination of fibrous material and cement and is largely used in the construction of fireproof partition walls and roofs.

6.9 FIRE RESISTANT CONSTRUCTION

Walls and Columns: Fire ratings of some types of constructions for walls are given in the following tables. Specifications of materials should be so selected; as to give these ratings.

Table 6.2 : Masonry walls : Solid (Required to resist fire from one side at a time)

Nature of Construction and Materials	Minimum Thickness (mm), Excluding any finish, for a fire resistance (Hours) of									
	Load Bearing					Non-load Bearing				
	1 hr.	$1\frac{1}{2}$ hrs.	2 hrs.	3 hrs.	4 hrs.	1 hr.	$1\frac{1}{2}$ hrs.	2 hrs.	3 hrs.	4 hrs.
1. Reinforced* cement concrete	120 (25)	140 (25)	160 (25)	200 (25)	240 (25)					
2. Unreinforced cement concrete	150	175	–	–	–					
3. No-fines concrete with : (a) 13 mm cement/sand or gypsum/sand (b) 13 mm lightweight aggregate gypsum plaster						150 150	150 150	150 150	150 150	150 150
4. Bricks of clay : (a) Without finish (b) With 13 mm lightweight aggregate gypsum plaster	90 90	100 90	100 90	170 100	170 100	75 75	90 90	100 90	170 90	170 100
5. Bricks of sand lime : (a) Without finish (b) With 13 mm lightweight aggregate gypsum plaster	90 90	100 90	100 90	190 100	190 100	75 75	90 90	100 90	170 90	170 100
6. Blocks of concrete : (a) Without finish (b) With 13 mm lightweight aggregate gypsum plaster (c) With 13 mm cement/sand or gypsum/sand	90 90	100 90	100 90	– 100	– 100	75 75 75	90 75 90	100 75 90	140 90 100	150 100 140
7. Blocks of lightweight concrete : (a) Without finish (b) With 13 mm lightweight aggregate gypsum plaster (c) With 13 mm cement/sand or gypsum/sand	90 90	100 90	100 90	140 100	150 100	75 50 75	75 63 75	75 75 75	125 75 90	140 75 100
8. Blocks of aerated concrete : (a) Without finish (b) With 13 mm lightweight aggregate gypsum plaster	90 90	100 90	100 100	140 100	180 150	50	63	63	75	100
* Walls containing at least 1 percent of vertical reinforcement. ( ) Minimum thickness of actual cover to reinforcement.										

Table 6.3 : Masonry walls, hollows (Required to resist fire from one side at a time)

Nature of Construction and Materials			Minimum Thickness (mm), Excluding any finish, for a fire resistance (Hours) of :										
			Load Bearing					Non-load Bearing					
			1 hr.	$1\frac{1}{2}$ hrs.	2 hrs.	3 hrs.	4 hrs.	$\frac{1}{2}$ hr.	1 hr.	$1\frac{1}{2}$ hrs.	2 hrs.	3 hrs.	4 hrs.
1.	Bricks of clay :												
	(a)	Without finish	170	170	170	200	200	75	100	100	170	170	200
	(b)	With 13 mm lightweight aggregate gypsum plaster	100	100	170	170	170	75	75	90	100	100	170
2.	Blocks of concrete :												
	(a)	Without finish						90	125	125	140	140	150
	(b)	With 13 mm cement/sand or gypsum/sand						90	125	125	140	140	140
	(c)	With 13 mm light weight aggregate gypsum plaster	190	200	200	–	–	75	90	90	100	125	125
3.	Blocks of light weight concrete :												
	(a)	Without finish	100	100	100	–	–	75	90	90	100	140	150
	(b)	With 13 mm cement/sand or gypsum/sand						75	75	75	100	140	140
	(c)	With 13 mm light weight aggregate gypsum plaster						63	63	75	75	90	100

Table 6.4 : Framed construction, load bearing (Required to resist fire from one side at a time)

Nature of construction and materials / Timber studs at centres not exceeding 600 mm, faced on each side with	Minimum thickness (mm) of Protection for a fire resistance of 1 hr.
1. Plasterboard layers with joints staggered, joints in outer layer taped and filled – Total thickness for each face	25
2. One layer of 12.7 mm plasterboard with a finish of lightweight aggregate gypsum plaster.	13
3. Metal lath and plaster, thickness of plaster : (a) Sanded gypsum plaster (metal lathing grade) (b) Lightweight aggregate gypsum plaster	22 13

Table 6.5 : Framed construction, non-load bearing (Required to resist fire from one side at a time)

Nature of construction and materials/ Steel or Timber frame at centres not exceeding 600 mm, facing on both sides of	Stud Construction	Minimum thickness (mm) of Protection for a fire resistance of 1 h			
		$\frac{1}{2}$ hr.	1 hr.	$1\frac{1}{2}$ hrs.	2 hrs.
(A) Dry lining with materials fixed direct to studs (without plaster finish) :					
1. One layer of plasterboard with taped and filled joints	Timber or steel	12.7			
2. Two layers of plasterboard with joints staggered, joints in outer layer taped and filled – Total thickness for each face	Timber or steel	19	25		
3. One layer of asbestos insulating board with transverse joints backed by fillers of asbestos insulating board not less than 9 mm thick or by timber	Timber Steel	9 12			
4. One layer of wood wool slabs	Timber	25			
5. One layer of chipboard or of plywood	Timber or steel	18			
(B) Lining with materials fixed direct to studs, with plaster finish : 1. Plasterboard of thickness : (a) With not less than 5 mm gypsum plaster finish (b) With not less than 13 mm gypsum plaster finish	Timber or steel	9.5	12.7		
(C) Wet finish : 1. Metal lath and plaster, thickness of plaster : (a) Sanded gypsum plaster (b) Lightweight aggregate gypsum plaster	Timber or steel Timber Steel	13	13 13	19	15

Table 6.6 : Framed external walls load bearing (Required to resist fire from one side at a time)

Nature of construction and materials	Minimum thickness (mm) of Protection for a fire resistance of 1 h
Timber studs at centres not exceeding 600 mm with internal linings of plaster board layers with joints in outer layer taped and filled, total thickness of plasterboard	31

Table 6.7 : Reinforced concrete columns

Nature of construction and materials		Minimum dimensions (mm), excluding any finish for a fire resistance of					
		$\frac{1}{2}$ hr.	1 hr.	$1\frac{1}{2}$ hrs.	2 hrs.	3 hrs.	4 hrs.
1. Fully exposed	Width	150	200	250	300	400	450
	Cover	20	25	30	35	35	35
2. 50 percent exposed	Width	125	160	200	200	300	350
	Cover	20	25	25	25	30	35
3. One face exposed	Thickness	100	120	140	160	200	240
	Cover	20	25	25	25	25	25

Table 6.8 : Concrete beams

Nature of construction and materials		Minimum dimensions (mm), excluding any finish for a fire resistance of					
		$\frac{1}{2}$ hr.	1 hr.	$1\frac{1}{2}$ hrs.	2 hrs.	3 hrs.	4 hrs.
1. Reinforced concrete (simply supported)	Width	80	120	150	200	240	280
	Cover	20	30	40	60	70	80
2. Reinforced concrete (continuous)	Width	80	80	120	150	200	240
	Cover	20	20	35	50	60	70
3. Prestressed concrete (simply supported)	Width	100	120	150	200	240	280
	Cover	25	40	55	70	80	90
4. Prestressed concrete (continuous)	Width	80	100	120	150	200	240
	Cover	20	30	40	55	70	80

Table 6.9 : Encased steel columns, 203 mm × 203 mm (Protection applied on four sides)

Nature of construction and materials	Minimum thickness (mm) of protection for a fire resistance of				
	1 hr.	$1\frac{1}{2}$ hrs.	2 hrs.	3 hrs.	4 hrs.
(A) Hollow protection (without an air cavity over the flanges) :					
1. *Metal lathing with trowelled lightweight aggregate gypsum plaster	13	15	20	32	–
2. Plasterboard with 1.6 mm wire binding at 100 mm pitch, finished with lightweight aggregate gypsum plaster not less than the thickness specified :					
(a) 9.5 mm plasterboard	10	15			
(b) 19 mm plasterboard	10	13	20		
3. Asbestos insulating boards, thickness of board :					
(a) Single thickness of board, with 6 mm cover fillets at transverse joints		19	25		
(b) Two layers, of total thickness				38	50
4. Solid bricks of clay composition or sand lime, reinforced in every horizontal joint, unplastered	50	50	50	75	100
5. Aerated concrete blocks	60	60	60		
6. Solid blocks of lightweight concrete	50	50	50	60	75
Hollow protections (with an air cavity over the flanges)					
(B) Asbestos insulating board screwed to 25 mm asbestos battens	12	19			
(C) Solid protections					
1. Concrete, not leaner than 1 : 2 : 4 mix (unplastered) :					
(a) Concrete not assumed to be load bearing, reinforced †	25	25	25	50	75
(b) Concrete assumed to be load bearing	50	50	50	75	75
2. Lightweight concrete, not leaner than 1 : 2 : 4 mix (Unplastered) concrete not assumed to be load bearing, reinforced †	25	25	25	40	60

* So fixed or designed, as to allow full penetration for mechanical bond.

† Reinforcement shall consist of steel binding wire not less than 2.3 mm in thickness, or a steel mesh weighing not less than 0.5 kg/m^3 . In concrete protection, the spacing of that reinforcement shall not exceed 200 mm in any direction.

Table 6.10 : Encased steel beam, 406 mm × 176 mm (Protection applied on three sides)

Nature of construction and materials	Minimum thickness (mm) of Protection for a fire resistance of					
	$\frac{1}{2}$ hr.	1 hr.	$1\frac{1}{2}$ hrs.	2 hrs.	3 hrs.	4 hrs.
(A) Hollow protection (without an air cavity beneath the lower flange) 1. *Metal lathing with trowelled lightweight aggregate gypsum plaster (metal lathing grade)	13	13	15	20	25	
2. Plasterboard with 1.6 mm wire binding at 100 mm pitch, finished with lightweight aggregate gypsum plaster not less than the thickness specified : (a) 9.5 mm plasterboard (b) 19 mm plasterboard	10 10	10 10	15 13	20		
3. Asbestos insulating board, thickness of board : (a) Single thickness of board, with 6 mm cover fillets at transverse joints (b) Two layers, of total thickness			19	25	38	50
(B) Hollow protection (with an air cavity below the lower flange) : 1. Asbestos insulating board screwed to 25 mm asbestos battens	9	12				
(C) Solid protection : 1. Concrete not leaner than 1 : 2 : 4 mix (unplastered) : (a) Concrete not assumed to be load bearing, reinforced ‡ (b) Concrete assumed to be load bearing	25 50	25 50	25 50	25 50	50 75	75 75
2. Lightweight concrete § not leaner than 1 : 2 : 4 (mix) unplastered	25	25	25	25	40	60

* So fixed, or designed, as to allow full penetration for mechanical bond.

† Where wire binding cannot be used, expert advice should be sought regarding alternative methods of support to enable the lower edges of the plasterboard to be fixed together and to the lower flange, and for the top edge of the plasterboard to be held in position.

‡ Reinforcement shall consist of steel binding wire not less than 2.3 mm in thickness or a steel mesh weighing not less than 0.5 kg/m^3. In concrete protection, the spacing of that reinforcement shall not exceed 200 mm in any direction.

§ Concrete not assumed to be load bearing, reinforced.

Every opening in the wall should be protected by a fire resisting door having a fire rating of not less than 1 hour.

In load bearing structures, bricks are preferred to stones because of their fire resisting properties. In framed structures, RCC frames are better than structural steel frames.

In RCC frame work the reinforcement should have proper cover to prevent it from being exposed to fire.

Partition walls also should be of fire resisting material such as hollow concrete blocks, bricks, reinforced glass, asbestos cement board etc.

All walls should be plastered with fire resisting mortar.

The use of inflammable surface finishes on walls (including external facade of the building) and ceilings affects the safety of the occupants of a building. Such finishes tend to spread the fire and even though the structural elements may be adequately fire resistant, serious danger to life may result. Therefore, the finishing materials used for various surfaces and decor should not add to the spread of fire and in addition should not generate toxic fumes and smoke.

Floors and Roofs:

The fire ratings of some floors are given in the following tables. The specifications of materials should consider these ratings.

Table 6.11: Concrete floors

Nature of construction and materials		Minimum Dimensions (mm), Excluding any finish for a fire resistance of:					
		$\frac{1}{2}$ hr.	1 hr.	$1\frac{1}{2}$ hrs.	2 hrs.	3 hrs.	4 hrs.
1. Reinforced concrete (simply supported)	Thickness	75	95	110	125	150	170
	Cover	15	20	25	35	45	55
2. Reinforced concrete (continuous)	Thickness	75	95	110	125	150	170
	Cover	15	20	20	25	35	45

Table 6.12: Concrete floors: Ribbed open soffit

Nature of construction and materials		Minimum Dimensions (mm), Excluding any finish for a fire resistance of:					
		$\frac{1}{2}$ hr.	1 hr.	$1\frac{1}{2}$ hrs.	2 hrs.	3 hrs.	4 hrs.
1. Reinforced concrete (simply supported)	Thickness	70	90	105	115	135	150
	Width	75	90	110	125	150	175
	Cover	15	25	35	45	55	65
2. Reinforced concrete (continuous)	Thickness	70	90	105	115	135	150
	Width	75	80	90	110	125	150
	Cover	15	20	–	35	45	55

Table 6.13: Timber floors - Any structurally suitable flooring of timber or particle boards

Nature of construction and materials 37 mm (minimum) timber joists with a ceiling of	Minimum thickness (mm), of protection for a fire resistance of:	
	$\frac{1}{2}$ hr.	1 hr.
1. Timber lathing and plaster, plaster of thickness	15	
2. Metal lathing and plaster, thickness of plaster for:		
(a) Sanded gypsum plaster (metal lathing grade)	15	
(b) Light weight aggregate gypsum plaster	13	19
3. One layer of plaster board with joints taped and filled and backed by timber	12.7	
4. Two layers of plaster board, with joints staggered, joints in outer layer taped and filled total thickness.	25	
5. Two layers of plaster board, each not less than 9.5 mm thick, joints between boards staggered and outer layer finished with gypsum plaster	5	
6. One layer of plaster board not less than 9.5 mm thick, finished with:		
(a) Sanded gypsum plaster	13	
(b) Lightweight aggregate gypsum plaster	15	
7. One layer of plasterboard not less than 12.7 mm thick, finished with:		
(a) Sanded gypsum plaster	15	
(b) Lightweight aggregate gypsum plaster	13	
8. One layer of asbestos insulating board with any transverse joints backed by fillets of asbestos insulating board not less than 9 mm thick, or by timber	12	

RCC floors are most suitable for fire resistance. Flat roofs are preferred to sloping or pitched roofs. A surface covering, of non-combustible and non-toxic material, should be laid directly on the incombustible floor. Flooring materials like concrete tiles and ceramic files are quite suitable.

Linings or false ceilings should not be encouraged in buildings.

In some cases, requiring provision of skylights, monitor lights or north lights in the roofs; glazings should be of glass in metal frames with a fire rating of minimum half an hour.

Staircase: All internal staircases must be of fire resisting materials such as RCC stairs. It should be constructed as a self contained unit and should be completely enclosed.

6.10 MEANS OF ESCAPE

The present method of providing means of escape from buildings is by observing specifications and rules i.e. rules that have evolved through time and are deemed to provide a satisfactory escape route.

The main objective of the provision of a means of escape is that the occupants should be able to reach a place of safety unharmed, in the event of a fire occurring.

A place of safety is normally associated with an area outside the building away from the threatened space. It may also be a protected corridor, a protected staircase or a place of refuge within the buildings.

Places of refuge are necessary in very tall buildings because the evacuation of these buildings may take two hours or more. Refuge floors may be provided every six or eight floors up the building, depending on the nature of occupancy, so that occupants of the fire floor, floors below the fire and above the fire can be evacuated to a place of safety.

Evacuation Time:

This is the time taken for a person to go from any occupied part of the building to a place of safety. Ideally this should be 2 – 3 minutes, but evacuation time will vary according to a person's speed of travel depending upon his age and general physical condition.

In fact, 2 - 3 minutes evacuation criterion is derived from studies which conclude that such a time is reasonable for people in a stressful situation, before panic conditions develop. Thus, it is highly desirable to evacuate people before a state of irrational behaviour starts.

In multistoreyed buildings, where this evacuation time of 2 – 3 minutes cannot be achieved, places of safety must be provided within the building.

Travel Distance:

Travel distance is the distance to be traversed in order to reach a place of safety from which dispersal can take place. This place of safety can be a protected escape route, an external escape route or a final exit.

A range of travel distances is given in the following table; varying relative to purpose, grouping and particular situation.

The travel distance to an exit from the dead end of a corridor should not exceed half the distance specified in the above table, except in educational, assembly and institutional occupancies, in which case it should not exceed 6 m.

Table 6.14: Travel distance for occupancy and type of construction

Sr. No.	Group of occupancy	Construction types	
		1 and 2 (m)	3 and 4 (m)
1.	Residential	22.5	22.5
2.	Educational	22.5	22.5
3.	Institutional	22.5	22.5
4.	Assembly	30.0	30.0
5.	Business	30.0	30.0
6.	Mercantile	30.0	30.0
7.	Industrial	45.0	30.0
8.	Storage	30.0	30.0
9.	Hazardous	22.5	22.5

These distances have been established by experience over many years and give guidance for particular applications. However, the distance to be travelled must be related to the risk involved i.e. the rapidity of flame and smoke spread. When a fire is in the growth stage, a great deal of smoke can be produced and this smoke can move, on occasions, more quickly than normal walking pace. It is, therefore, essential that travel distances can be such that persons can reach a place of safety before smoke-logging of the means of escape occurs.

Exit Requirements

Entrances, exits and circulation areas are provided in all buildings for normal use. Means of escape considerations should utilize existing arrangements wherever possible.

An exit may be a doorway, corridor, passageway to an internal staircase, external staircase, verandah or terrace which has access to the street or to the roof of a building or a refuge area. An exit may also include a horizontal exit leading to an adjoining building at the same level. Lifts and escalators are not considered as exits.

The primary consideration should be with regard to the sufficiency of existing exits in terms of:

(i)   disposition,

(ii) width and

(iii) number.

(i) Disposition: The position of exits as a means of escape in the case of a fire is absolutely critical. Exits should be clearly visible and the routes to reach the exit should be clearly marked and signs should be posted to guide the population of the floor concerned.

Exits should be so arranged, that they may be reached without passing through another occupied unit. They should also be located in such a way that the prescribed travel distances are not exceeded.

(ii) Width: It is essential while designing that bottlenecks i.e. areas where congestion will occur, are avoided. Thus, corridors should not become narrower as they approach a storey exit or staircase. No obstructions should be kept in the corridors which will reduce the effective width of the corridors.

Building codes have specified a unit of exit width of 50 cm to measure the capacity of any exit. A clear width of 25 cm is counted as an additional half unit. Clear widths less than 25 cm should not be counted for exit widths.

The following table gives the number of occupants discharged per minute in a single file through different exits.

Table 6.15: Occupants per unit exit width

Sr. No.	Group of occupancy	Number of occupants		
		Stairways	Ramps	Doors
1.	Residential	25	50	75
2.	Educational	25	50	75
3.	Institutional	25	50	75
4.	Assembly	40	50	60
5.	Business	50	60	75
6.	Mercantile	50	60	75
7.	Industrial	50	60	75
8.	Storage	50	60	75
9.	Hazardous	25	30	40

A width of 50 cm is not acceptable in practice. Hence, the national building code has specified that:

- Every exit doorway must have a minimum width of 100 cm and a minimum height of 200 cm.

- No door, when opened, should reduce the required width of a stairway or landing to less than 90 cm.

- Landing width of the stairway must be equal to at least the width of the door.

- Width of exit-corridor and passageways should not be less than the required aggregate width of exit doorways leading from them in the direction of travel to the exterior.

- Minimum width of stairs in residential buildings should be 1.0 m and in public buildings 1.5 m, as per NBC.
- Width of a straight flight in a fire escape stair should not be less than 75 cm and in case of a spiral fire escape, its diameter should not be less than 150 cm.

(iii) Number: Every building meant for human occupancy must be provided with exits sufficient to permit safe escape of occupants, in case of fire or other emergency.

All buildings which are 15 m or more in height and all buildings used as educational, assembly, institutional, industrial, storage and hazardous occupancies, having area more than 500 m² on each floor must have a minimum of two staircases.

6.11 FIRE DETECTING SYSTEMS

One method of increasing escape potential and reducing fire casualties would be the introduction of fire-detection systems as a component of escape route design, linked to a warning alarm system which would alert the occupants of a building to the presence of fire.

Various types of fire detectors are available for installation in buildings intended for different occupancies. Fire detectors may respond to the generation of heat, smoke and flames and accordingly there are heat detectors, smoke detectors and flame detectors.

6.12 FIRE EXTINGUISHING SYSTEMS

The method of extinguishing fire will depend on the building type, building occupancy and the nature of hazard. The following are some of the fixed fire extinguishing systems:

- Automatic water sprinkler system,
- Automatic high velocity water spray or emulsifying system,
- Fixed foam installation, and
- Carbon dioxide fire extinguishing system.

An automatic sprinkler system consists of an arrangement of pipes at a regular spacing under the ceiling or the most hazardous part of the building. This network of pipes is supplied with water from the fire tank pumps at regular intervals, depending upon the hazards. These sprinkler heads contain a fusible plug which is designed to open at a predetermined temperature. Thus, the heat of the flame raises the temperature of the nearest sprinkler to its operating point and it opens up, releasing a flow of water under pressure and dousing the fire beneath. To avoid unnecessary damage due to water, the sprinkler system can be provided with a water flow alarm to sound at some fire alarm headquarters.

6.13 INTRODUCTION TO EARTHQUAKE RESISTANT STRUCTURES

Earthquake-resistant structures are structures designed to withstand earthquakes. While no structure can be entirely immune to damage from earthquakes, the goal of earthquake-resistant construction is to erect structures that fare better during seismic activity than their conventional counterparts.

6.14 EARTHQUAKE LOADS

Earthquakes cause ground shaking

- The severity of earthquake loads is dependent on location.
- Ground shaking induces inertial loads in building elements; stronger ground shaking or heavier building elements result in greater loads.
- Earthquake loads are predominantly horizontal (there is also a vertical component).
- Earthquakes can strike from any direction.
- Earthquake loads are cyclic.

Understanding seismic load paths:

- An earthquake generates inertial forces in a building
- We must clearly define the load path to transfer these forces from all elements to the ground.
- Load paths must be continuous; all forces must be transferred to the foundations.

6.14.1 Roofs are a Major Load

- The roof structure must be braced to distribute loads to the walls (a diaphragm is a common way to achieve this).
- This load is then carried by side (in-plane) walls or moment-resisting frames to the foundations.

6.14.2 Walls are a Major Load

- Face loaded walls (walls perpendicular to the earthquake load) transfer their loads-up to the eaves (or bond beam) and down to the foundation.
- The eaves loads follow the roof load path as above.
- Some load is transferred horizontally to walls and columns.
- Side walls (parallel to earthquake) resist loads in shear (and bending).
- The total load is transferred to the foundations and back to the sub-grade.
- All loads must be carried to the foundations; foundations must transfer the horizontal loads to the sub-grade.

6.15 OTHER LOADS TO CONSIDER INCLUDE BUILDING CONTENTS, ESPECIALLY WHERE THE BUILDING IS USED FOR STORAGE, MACHINERY AND WATER TANKS

Note that as earthquakes can strike from any direction, these principles must hold for all directions.

Earthquake loads are a function of following:

- Seismic Zone and proximity to fault line.

- Building mass.
- Buildings period of vibration – generally a function of height and type of bracing element.
- Properties of foundation materials (soil or rock).
- Structural type configuration, material, degree of ductility, damping).
- Building category (Risk and Importance factors).

Need of earthquake Resistant Structures:

- Avoid the loss of lives resulting from the collapse of infrastructure or a building in a major earthquake (a design earthquake or ultimate limit state earthquake).
- Limit personal injury and building damage (including contents) in moderate earthquakes (serviceability limit state earthquake). Infrastructure/building should be fully functional after a clean-up.
- Minimize damage and disturbance to residents in moderate and minor earthquakes.
- Maintain the key function of the infrastructure/building.
- Protect the lives of those outside the building.
- Protect other property and the environment.

6.16 RESISTING EARTHQUAKE LOADS

In order to resist loads from any direction buildings must be able to resist loads from two orthogonal directions (at right angles). Designers usually consider the x and y directions separately. An earthquake load, from any direction can be resolved into x and y components which can be resisted by the structure in these two directions.

Loads can be resisted by:

- Moment-resisting frames
- Braced frames
- Shear walls
- Frames in filled with masonry (recommended for one- and two-storey buildings only).

6.17 SPECIFIC ACTIVITIES ASSOCIATED WITH EARTHQUAKE EMERGENCY RESPONSE

(a) Early Warning: Early warning refers to arrangements to rapidly disseminate information concerning imminent earthquake motion threats to government officials, institutions, and the population at large in the areas at immediate risk. While the warning systems only begin when earthquake shaking starts, it may allow actions such as moving to safer locations or shutting off of gas lines etc. as the earthquake begins.

(b) Evacuation/Migration: Evacuation involves the relocation of a population from zones at risk of an imminent disaster to a safer location, especially if structures are susceptible to damage from aftershock.

(c) Search and Rescue: Search and rescue (SAR), is the process of identifying the location of disaster victims who may be trapped or isolated and bringing them to safety and medical attention. In the aftermath of earthquakes, SAR normally focuses on locating people who are trapped and injured in collapsed buildings.

(d) Post-disaster Assessment: The primary objective of assessment is to provide a clear, concise picture of the post-disaster situation, to identify relief needs, and to develop strategies for recovery. It determines options for humanitarian assistance, how best to utilize existing resources, or to develop requests for further assistance.

The post-disaster assessment must distinguish among pre-disaster chronic conditions, the needs of disaster survivors and their resources.

(e) Emergency Relief: Emergency relief is the provision, on a humanitarian basis, of material aid and emergency medical care necessary to save and preserve human lives. It also enables families to meet their basic needs for medical and health care, shelter, clothing, water, and food (including the means to prepare food). Relief supplies or services typically are provided, free of charge, in the days and weeks immediately following a sudden disaster.

(f) Logistics and Supply: The delivery of emergency relief will require logistical facilities and capacity. A well-organized supply service is crucial for handling the procurement or donation, storage, and dispatch of relief supplies for distribution to disaster victims.

(g) Communication and Information Management: All of the above activities are dependent on communication. There are two key aspects to communications in disasters.

- The equipment essential for information flow, such as radios, telephones, and their supporting systems of repeaters, satellites, and transmission lines.
- The information management, that is, the protocol of knowing who communicates what information to whom, what priority is given to it, and how it is disseminated and interpreted.

(h) Survivor Response and Coping: In the rush to plan and execute a relief operation, it is easy to overlook the real needs and resources of the survivors.

- The assessment must take into account existing social coping mechanisms that negate the need to bring in outside assistance.
- On the other hand, disaster survivors may have new and special needs for social services to help adjust to the trauma and disruption caused by the disaster.
- Participation in the disaster response process by individuals to aid community organizations is a key to healthy recovery. Through them, appropriate coping mechanisms will be most successfully utilized.

(i) Security: Security is not always a priority issue after sudden onset natural disasters. Typically, it is handled by civil defense or police departments.

(j) Emergency operations management: None of these activities can be implemented without some degree of emergency operations management. Policies and procedures for management requirements need to be established well in advance of the disaster.

(k) Rehabilitation and reconstruction: Rehabilitation and reconstruction complete the disaster response activities and merge with the recovery phase.

6.18 EARTHQUAKE RESISTANT STRUCTURES AND TECHNIQUES

6.18.1 Shear Walls

Shear walls are vertical elements of the horizontal force resisting system. Shear walls are constructed to counter the effects of lateral load acting on a structure. In residential construction, shear walls are straight external walls that typically form a box which provides all the lateral support for the building. When shear walls are designed, and constructed properly, and they will have the strength and stiffness to resist the horizontal forces.

In building construction, a rigid vertical diaphragm capable of transferring lateral forces from exterior walls, floors, and roofs to the ground foundation in a direction parallel to their planes. Examples are the reinforced-concrete wall or vertical truss. Lateral forces caused by wind, earthquake, and uneven settlement loads, in addition to the weight of structure and occupants; create powerful twisting (torsion) forces. These forces can literally tear (shear) a building apart. Reinforcing a frame by attaching or placing a rigid wall inside it maintains the shape of the frame and prevents rotation at the joints. Shear walls are especially important in high-rise buildings subjected to lateral wind and seismic forces.

In the last two decades, shear walls became an important part of mid and high-rise residential buildings. As part of an earthquake resistant building design, these walls are placed in building plans reducing lateral displacements under earthquake loads. So shear-wall frame structures are obtained.

6.18.2 Purpose of Constructing Shear Walls

Shear walls are not only designed to resist gravity/vertical loads (due to its self-weight and other living/moving loads), but they are also designed for lateral loads of earthquakes/wind. The walls are structurally integrated with roofs/floors (diaphragms) and other lateral walls running across at right angles, thereby giving the three-dimensional stability for the building structures.

Shear wall structural systems are more stable. Because, their supporting area (total cross-sectional area of all shear walls) regarding total plans area of building, is comparatively more, unlike in the case of RCC framed structures. Walls must resist the uplift forces caused by the pull of the wind. Walls must resist the shear forces that try to push the walls over.

Walls must resist the lateral force of the wind that tries to push the walls in and pull them away from the building.

Types of Shear Walls

- RC Shear Wall

- Plywood Shear Wall

- Midply Shear Wall

- RC Hollow Concrete Block Masonry Wall

- Steel Plate Shear Wall

6.18.3 RC Shear Wall

It consists of reinforced concrete walls and reinforced concrete slabs. Wall thickness varies from 140 mm to 500 mm, depending on the number of stories, building age, and thermal insulation requirements. In general, these walls are continuous throughout the building height; however, some walls are discontinued at the street front or basement level to allow for commercial or parking spaces. Usually the wall layout is symmetrical with respect to at least one axis of symmetry in the plan.

Floor slabs are either cast-in-situ flat slabs or less often, precast hollow-core slabs. Buildings are supported by concrete strip or mat foundations; the latter type is common for buildings with basements. Structural modifications are not very common in this type of construction.

Reinforcement requirements are based on building code requirements specific for each country. In general, the wall reinforcement consists of two layers of distributed reinforcement (horizontal and vertical) throughout the wall length. In addition, vertical reinforcement bars are provided close to the door and window openings, as well as at the wall end zones (also known as boundary elements or barbells).

Fig. 6.2

6.18.4 Plywood Shear Wall

Plywood is the traditional material used in the construction of Shear Walls. The creation of pre-fabricated shear panels has made it possible to inject strong shear assemblies into small walls that fall at either side of a opening in a shear wall. As well as the use of a sheet steel, and steel-backed shear panel (i.e. Sure-Board) in the place of structural use plywood in shear walls, has proved to be far stronger in seismic resistance when used in shear wall assemblies.

Plywood shear walls consist of:

- Plywood, to transfer shear forces

- Chords, to resist tension/compression generated by the over turning moments

- Base connections to transfer shear to foundations.

Fig. 6.3

6.19 RC HOLLOW CONCRETE BLOCK MASONRY WALLS

RHCBM walls are constructed by reinforcing the hollow concrete block masonry, by taking advantage of hollow spaces and shapes of the hollow blocks. It requires continuous steel rods (reinforcement) both in the vertical and horizontal directions at structurally critical locations of the wall panels, packed with the fresh grout concrete in the hollow spaces of masonry blocks.

Reinforced Hollow Concrete Block Masonry (RHCBM) elements are designed both as load bearing walls for gravity loads and also as shear walls for lateral seismic loads, to safely with stand earthquakes. This structural system of construction is known as shear wall – diaphragm concept, which gives three-dimensional structural integrity for the buildings.

6.20 STEEL PLATE SHEAR WALL

In general, steel plate shear wall system consists of a steel plate wall, boundary columns and horizontal floor beams. Together, the steel plate wall and boundary columns act as a vertical plate girder. The columns act as flanges of the vertical plate girder and the steel plate wall acts as its web. The horizontal floor beams act, more-or-less, as transverse stiffeners in a plate girder.

Steel plate shear wall systems have been used in recent years in highly seismic areas to resist lateral loads. Figure shows two basic types of steel shear walls; unstiffened and stiffened with or without openings.

Fig. 6.4

6.21 MOMENT RESISTANT FRAMES

In order to perform well under earthquake loads, the following guidelines must be followed:

- A moment-resisting frame consists of beams as well as columns.
- Column - flat-slab systems rarely perform well in earthquakes.
- Columns must be stronger than beams (in buildings of two or more storeys).
- Columns must not be too slender (adequate stiffness is required).
- In general beams in moment-resisting frames must be deeper than gravity-load-only beams.
- Infill walls must be separated from frames.

- Beam-column joints must include ties at close centre across joints (to prevent diagonal shear failure).

- Concrete strength must be at least 20MPa, preferably 25MPa.

- If using high-strength steel ensure it is ductile and follow detailing rules (generally do not weld, thread, re-bend; comply with minimum bend radii).

- Supervise works to ensure re-bar is not omitted, and details are followed.

Cross-Braced (Tension Braced) Frames

- Tension-only bracing is frequently used in low rise buildings (max two storeys).

- Tension-only bracing makes efficient use of steel, utilizing its tensile strength.

- When subject to lateral forces only the tension member carries load; the compression member carries no load.

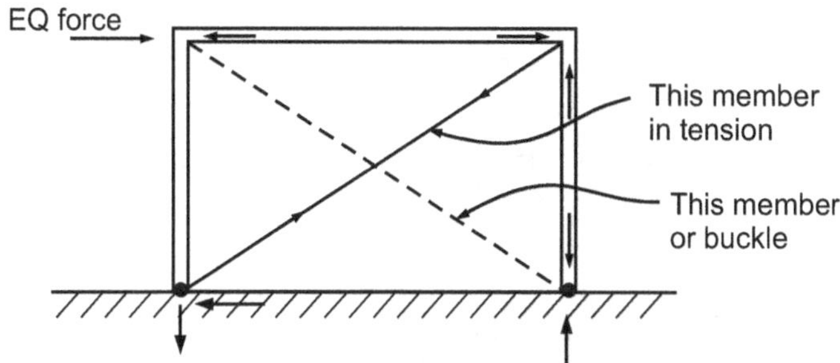

Forces in members in tension-Braced frame

Fig. 6.5

6.22 ADVANCED EARTHQUAKE RESISTANT DESIGN TECHNIQUES

Base isolation is a technique developed to prevent or minimize damage to buildings during an earthquake. It has been used in New Zealand, as well as in India, Japan, Italy and the USA.

A fixed-base building (built directly on the ground) will move with an earthquake's motion and can sustain extensive damage as a result. When a building is built away (isolated) from the ground, resting on flexible bearings or pads known as base isolators, it will only move a little or not at all during an earthquake.

The isolators work in a similar way to car suspension, which allows a car to travel over rough ground without the occupants of the car getting thrown around. Base isolation technology can make medium-rise masonry (stone or brick) or reinforced concrete structures capable of withstanding earthquakes, protecting them and their occupants from major damage or injury. It is not suitable for all types of structures and is designed for hard soil, not soft.

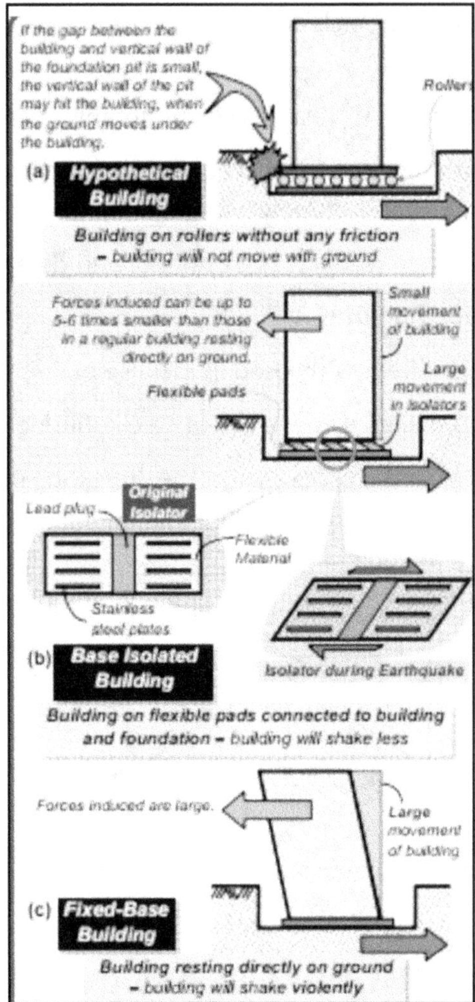

Fig. 6.6

Source: IITK-BMTPC Earthquake Tips

6.22.1 Seismic Dampers

Commonly used Seismic Dampers

1. **Viscous Dampers** (energy is absorbed by silicone-based fluid passing between piston cylinder arrangement),

2. **Friction Dampers** (energy is absorbed by surfaces with friction between them rubbing against each other),

3. **Yielding Dampers** (energy is absorbed by metallic components that yield).

4. **Viscoelastic Dampers** (energy is absorbed by utilizing the controlled shearing of solids).

Thus by equipping a building with additional devices which have high damping capacity, we can greatly decrease the seismic energy entering the building.

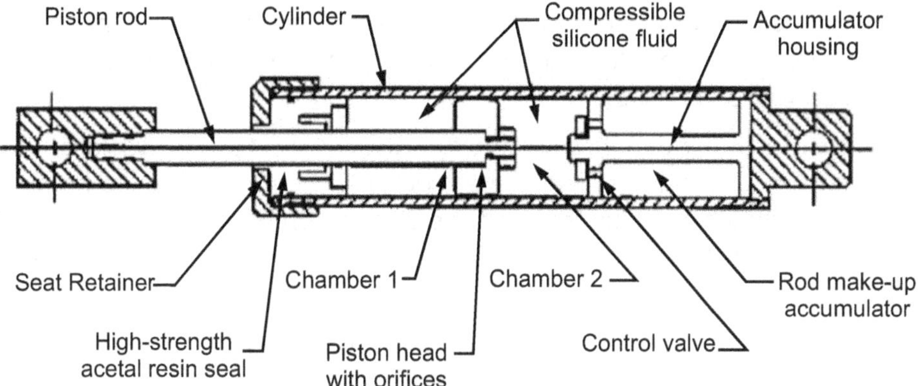

Fig. 6.7

The construction of a fluid damper is shown in (Fig. 6.7). It consists of a stainless steel piston with bronze orifice head. It is filled with silicone oil. The piston head utilizes specially shaped passages which alter the flow of the damper fluid and thus alter the resistance characteristics of the damper. Fluid dampers may be designed to behave as a pure energy dissipater or a spring or as a combination of the two.

A fluid viscous damper resembles the common shock absorber such as those found in automobiles. The piston transmits energy entering the system to the fluid in the damper, causing it to move within the damper. The movement of the fluid within the damper fluid absorbs this kinetic energy by converting it into heat. In automobiles, this means that a shock received at the wheel is damped before it reaches the passengers compartment. In buildings, this can mean that the building columns protected by dampers will undergo considerably less horizontal movement and damage during an earthquake.

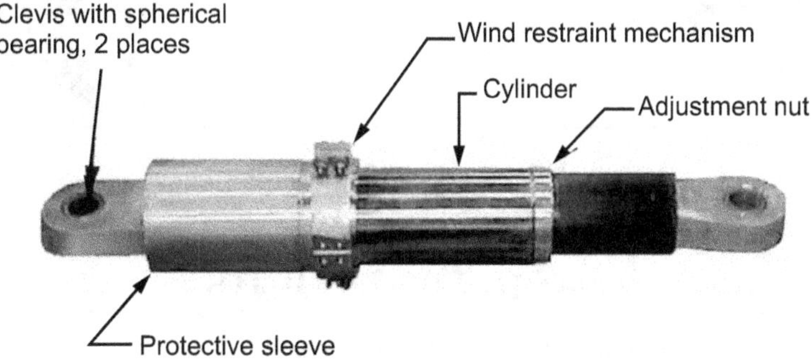

Fig. 6.8

6.22.2 New Breed of Energy Dissipation Devices

The innovative methods for control of seismic vibrations such as frictional and other types of damping devices are important integral part of seismic isolation systems as they severe as a barrier against the penetration of seismic energy into the structure. In this concept, the dampers suppress the response of the isolated building relative to its base.

The novel friction damper device consists of three steel plates rotating against each other in opposite directions. The steel plates are separated by two shims of friction pad material producing friction with steel plates.

When an external force excites a frame structure the girder starts to displace horizontally due to this force. The damper will follow the motion and the central plate because of the tensile forces in the bracing elements. When the applied forces are reversed, the plates will rotate in opposite way. The damper dissipates energy by means of friction between the sliding surfaces.

The latest Friction-Visco Elastic Damper Device (F-VEDD) combines the advantages of pure frictional and viscoelastic mechanisms of energy dissipation. This new product consists of friction pads and viscoelastic polymer pads separated by steel plates. A pre-stressed bolt in combination with disk springs and hardened washers is used for maintaining the required clamping force on the interfaces as in original FDD concept.

Fig. 6.9: Seismic Dampers

IMPORTANT POINTS

- Introduction to fire, its consequences and purpose of fire safety legislation.
- Classification of buildings based on occupancy, its types – Hazard classification for buildings.
- Fire load, its limits, certain rules and regulations for buildings.
- Phases of fire resistance of structural components.

- Fire resistant construction: Masonry walls solid, masonry walls hallow, encased steel columns etc.
- Means of escape: Evacuation time, travel distance and exit requirements.
- Fire extinguishing systems and its types.
- Resisting earthquake loads.
- Specific activities associated with earthquake emergency response.
- Earthquake resistant structures and techniques.
- Purpose of constructing shear walls.
- Advanced earthquake resistant design techniques.

QUESTIONS

1. How does fire occur in buildings? What is the purpose of fire safety legislation?
2. How are buildings classified? How does the classification become a factor in risk determination?
3. What is fire load? What are the general requirements which contribute to safety from fire?
4. What factors influence fire development in a building?
5. What is the pattern generally followed by a fire in a building?
6. What is fire resistance of a building element? What factors determine the level of fire resistance?
7. How would you plan means of escape in the event of a fire in a building?
8. Discuss different types of fire-detecting systems.
9. Explain the methods of extinguishing an accidental fire in a building.
10. Explain fire grade.
11. Explain the term fire load. How do you determine it?
12. Compare fire resisting properties of timber and concrete.
13. Explain the terms: (a) Fire load (b) Evacuation time (c) Travel distance
14. What are different fire extinguishing systems? Explain any one in detail.
15. Write a note on fire escape elements.
16. Compare fire resisting properties of: (a) Concrete (b) Store
17. What exit requirements are to be provided in a public building to escape from fire.
18. State commonly adopted fire extinguishing services. Describe any one in detail.

19. What is fire hazard. How will you carry on fire resisting construction.

20. Explain points to be observed for making walls and columns fire resistant.

21. What is fire load and how fire safety is achieved?

22. How would you plan means of escape in the event of fire in a building?

23. Discuss important considerations in fire protection.

24. State the various fire resistant materials that can be used for walls and floors.

25. Explain earthquake louds.

26. Explain new Breed of energy dissipation devices.

27. Explain types of shear walls.

28. Explain resistant structures and techniques.

UNIVERSITY QUESTIONS

Dec. 2014

1. Elaborate need for earthquake resistant structures in relation with loss of human life property and   infrastructure.

Dec. 2015

1. Explain the various safety aspects in detail.

Chapter 7
NOISE AND ACOUSTICS

7.1 INTRODUCTION

Hearing is one of man's most important communication channels, perhaps only second to vision. But, whilst the eyes can be shut when there is too much light or an unwanted scene not be viewed, the ears are open throughout life to unwanted noises as well as to wanted sounds. Protection, if necessary, must be provided in the environment.

Unwanted sound reaching the ears is called *noise*. It may be due to frequency of sound or intensity of sound or both. Noise due to high frequency sound is more unpleasant than noise due to low frequency sounds. Noisy conditions not only result in uncomfortable living conditions. Fatigue, inefficiency and mental strain, but prolonged exposure to such conditions may cause temporary deafness or nervous breakdown.

7.2 EFFECT OF NOISE

The effects of noise on man can be divided into two categories: (a) psychological and (b) physiological, and for most purposes, can be considered under the following headings:

- Causing annoyance or dissatisfaction.
- Affecting communication.
- Causing damage to hearing.
- Leads to fatigue and decreases the efficiency of persons.
- Causing permanent changes in the normal functioning of human organism, resulting in Deterioration in mental and/or physical health.
- It takes away essence of music and speech.

7.3 COMFORT STANDARDS

The comfort factors controlling noise are the acceptable noise levels in working interiors and sound insulation between rooms in the same building against air borne noise and impact noise.

Acceptable Indoor Noise Levels:

These noise levels are those which will neither cause uncomfortable conditions nor damage the acoustics of the building. Acceptable noise levels depend upon:

(a) Nature and type of noise

(b) Time of fluctuations of noise

(c) Background noise, and

(d) Type and use of building.

The acceptable noise levels inside buildings from the point of view of comfort, economy and practical considerations recommended in India are given in Table 7.1.

Table 7.1: Acceptable indoor noise levels

Sr. No.	Type of building	Noise level (dB)
1.	Radio and TV studios	25 - 30
2.	Music room	30 - 35
3.	Hospital and auditoria	35 - 40
4.	Apartments, hotels and homes	35 - 40
5.	Conference rooms, small offices and libraries	35 - 40
6.	Court rooms and class rooms	40 - 45
7.	Large public offices, banks and stores	45 - 50
8.	Restaurants	50 - 55
9.	Factories	55 - 60

7.4 PROPERTIES OF SOUND

(a) Characteristics of Sound:

There are three characteristics of sound:

1.　Intensity and loudness of sound

2.　Frequency or Pitch

3.　Quality or timbre

1.　Intensity and Loudness of Sound

Intensity of sound is defined as the amount or flow of wave energy crossing per unit time through a unit area taken perpendicular to the direction of propagation. Mathematically, the intensity at a point is proportional to the square of the amplitude of vibration of the point, i.e. $I \propto A^2$; whereas, **loudness** of a sound corresponds to the degree of sensation depending on the intensity of sound and the sensitivity of ear drums, and does not increase proportionally with intensity but more nearly to its logarithm, i.e. $L \propto \log I$. Thus, intensity of sound is purely a physical quantity, of which is independent of ear of listener. Loudness, on the other hand, is the degree of sensation which depends upon characteristics of ear and the listener.

2.　Frequency or Pitch of Sound

It is defined as the number of cycles which a sounding body makes in each unit of time. It is that characteristic by which a shrill sound can be distinguished from a grave one, even though the two sounds may be of the same intensity. The sensation of pitch depends upon the frequency with which the vibrations succeed one another at the ear; the greater the frequency, the higher the pitch and lesser the frequency, lower the pitch. The frequency scale covers a wide range varying from 20 cycles per second to 1500 cycles per second. If the frequency of sound is below 20 cycles per second, then effect of sound is lost (one can't hear such a sound).

3. Quality or Timbre

The **quality** of a sound is that characteristic which enables us to distinguish between two notes of same pitch and loudness played on two different instruments or produced by two different voices. A study of vibration curves of various musical instruments has shown that notes emitted by them are seldom pure. They contain some fundamental tones of frequency 'n' and additional tones of frequencies 2n, 3n, 4n etc. called overtones.

The quality of sound is determined by the number of overtones present along with the fundamental frequency of the wave and also their intensities.

7.5 MEASUREMENT OF SOUND

The range of variation of intensity is very high. The loudest and almost painful sound is about 10^{13} times the intensity of sound which is just audible by the human ear. If I_1 and I_0 represent the intensities of two sounds of a particular frequency and L_1 and L_0 are there corresponding measures of loudness, we have,

$$L_1 = K \log_{10} I_1$$

and

$$L_0 = K \log_{10} I_0$$

The difference in loudness of the two, technically known as intensity level 'L' between them, is given by

$$\boxed{L = K \log_{10} \frac{I_1}{I_0}}$$

In the above equations, K is the constant depending upon the units of measurements. When K = 1 (unity), the difference in loudness is expressed in *bels*, a unit named after A. G. Bel. This unit is rather large. Hence, a shorter practical unit called *decibel* (written as dB) equal to $\frac{1}{10}$ of bel, is used. Thus, the intensity level is expressed as,

$$L = 10 \log_{10} \frac{I_1}{I_0} \ dB$$

If L = 1 dB, we have,

$$L = 10 \log_{10} \frac{I_1}{I_0}$$

or

$$\log_{10} \frac{I_1}{I_0} = \frac{1}{10}$$

$$\frac{I_1}{I_0} = 1.26$$

i.e., a 26 per cent change in intensity alters the level by one decibel. This is practically the smallest change in intensity level that the ear can ordinarily detect.

Also, when $\qquad I_1 = 100\, I_0$

we get, $\qquad L = 10 \log_{10} 100 = 10 \log_{10} 10^2 = 20$ dB

Similarly, when $\qquad I_1 = 1000\, I_0,$

we have $\qquad L = 10 \log_{10} 1000 = 10 \log_{10} 10^3 = 30$ dB.

Table 7.2: Rating of intensity of sound

Common sound	Intensity level (dB)		Threshold of feeling
	Range	Average	
1. Threshold of audibility.		0	Very very faint
2. Rustle of leaves, whisper, sound proof room.	0 – 20	10	Very faint
3. Quiet living room, private office, quiet conversation, average auditorium.	20 – 40	30	Faint
4. Noisy home, average office (acoustically treated), average conversation, quiet radio etc.	40 – 60	50	Moderate
5. Noisy office, average street noise, average radio, average factory.	60 – 80	70	Loud
6. Noisy factory area, loud street noise, police whistle, truck unmuffled, train sound.	80 – 100	90	Very loud
7. Thunder, artillary, aeroplane motors, pneumatic hammers etc.	100 – 120	110	Deafening
8. Loudest sound due to pneumatic drills, or aeroplane at a distance of 4 m.	120 – 140	130	Pain and discomfort

Thus, we learn that when two sounds differ by 20 dB, the louder of them is 100 times more intense and when they differ by 30 dB, the louder one is 1000 times more intense.

To build a scale of loudness, we have to fix its zero. The loudness corresponding to the threshold of hearing is the zero of this scale; while 130 dB is the threshold of painful hearing.

The sound pressure corresponding to the threshold of hearing is about 0.0003 dynes/sq. cm and that corresponding to threshold of pain is about 300 dynes/sq. cm. Table 7.2 gives the rating of intensity of sound, in decibels.

7.6 BEHAVIOUR OF SOUND IN ENCLOSURES

When sound is generated in a room, the distance between the source and the walls is so small that there is little or no reduction due to distance. When the sound waves strike the surfaces of a room, three things happen:

- Some of the sound is *reflected* back in the room.

- Some of the sound energy is *absorbed* by the surfaces and listeners.

- Some of the sound waves set on the walls, floors and ceiling vibrating and are thus *transmitted* outside the room.

The amount of sound *reflected* or *absorbed* depends upon the surfaces, while the sound *transmitted* outside the room depends upon *sound insulation* properties of the surfaces.

7.7 REFLECTION OF SOUND

Sound waves get reflected from a large uniform plane surface in the same manner as that of light waves, the angle of incidence being equal to angle of reflection, as shown in Fig. 7.1. The reflection of sound has certain virtues in acoustics, such as the enhancement of loudness and enrichment of total quality of sound. The following characteristics of reflection of sound waves are noteworthy:

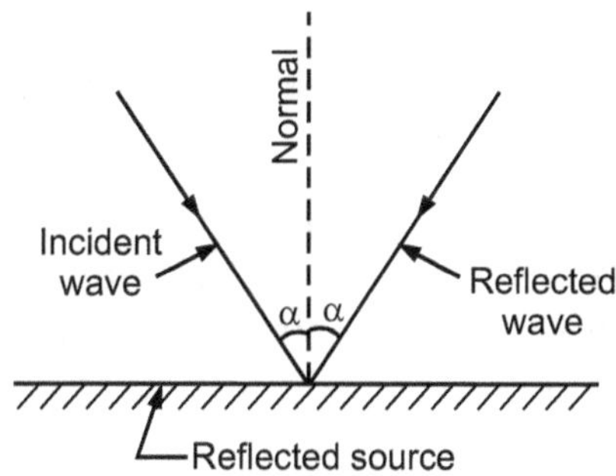

Fig. 7.1: Reflection of sound waves

1. Reflection of sound waves follow practically the same laws as that of reflection of light. However, this may not be true in some exceptional cases, hence great caution should be exercised while applying these laws.

2. The reflected wavefronts from a flat surface are also spherical and their centre of curvature is the image of source of sound [Fig. 7.2 (a)].

3. Sound waves reflected at a convex surface are magnified and are considerably bigger [Fig. 7.2 (b)]. They are attenuated and are therefore weaker. Convex surfaces may be used with advantage to spread the sound waves throughout the room.

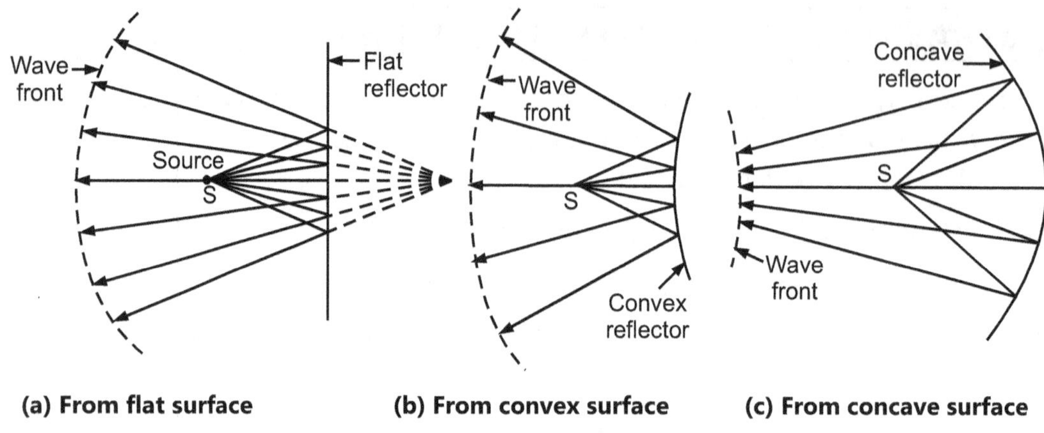

(a) From flat surface   **(b) From convex surface**   **(c) From concave surface**

Fig. 7.2: Reflection of sound waves

4. The sound waves reflected at a concave surface are considerably smaller [Fig. 7.2 (c)]. The waves are most condensed and therefore amplified. The concave surfaces may be provided for the concentration of reflected waves at certain points.

7.8 NOISE CLASSIFICATION

From the origin point of view, noises may be of two types:

(a) Outdoor noises,

(b) Indoor noises.

Outdoor noises are caused by road traffic, railways, aeroplanes, lifts, moving machinery, machines in nearby factory or building etc.

Indoor noises are those which are caused either in the same room or in the adjacent room. These are due to conversation of people, moving of people or furniture, crying of babies, playing of radios or other musical instruments, operations of cisterns and water closets, noise of type writer, banging of door, etc.

Noise may be alternatively classified as follows:

(a) Air borne noises or sounds.

(b) Structure borne noises or impact noises or sounds.

Air borne sounds are those which are generated in air and which are transmitted in air directly to human ear. Such a sound travels from one part of the building to the other, or from outside of the building to inside by (i) openings such as doors, windows, ventilators, key holes etc. or by (ii) forced vibrations set up in walls, ceilings etc. Air borne noise possesses less power, continues for a long duration and is confined to places near its origin.

Structure borne sounds or **impact sounds** are those which originate and progress on the building structure. These are caused by structural vibrations originated due to impact. The common sources of this sound are: foot steps, movement of furniture, dropping of utensils on floor, hammering, drilling, operation of machinery etc. These are more powerful, propagate over long distances and persist for a very shaft duration.

7.9 SOUND INSULATION

Sound insulation or sound proofing is a measure used to reduce the level of sound when it passes through the insulating building component. The materials and methods used for sound insulation should be such that desirable insulation is obtained. Table 7.3 gives the desirable levels of sound insulation between individual rooms (air borne).

Table 7.3: Sound insulation between individual rooms

Sr. No.	Situation	Overall insulation in dB
1.	Between living room in one house or flat and the living room and bed rooms in another.	50
2.	Elsewhere between houses or flats.	40
3.	Between one room and another in the same house or flat.	30
4.	Between teaching rooms in a school.	40
5.	Between one room and another room in an office.	30
6.	Between one ward and another ward in a hospital: (a) Normal wards. (b) Extra–quiet special wards.	40 45

For Impact Noise: The floor of a room immediately above a living room or bed room should have impact insulation which should be able to reduce the noise by 15 dB in addition to the insulating value of base concrete and by around 20 dB in the case of normal timber floor construction.

7.10 NOISE CONTROL

The levels of desired sound insulation, for different types of buildings and between the individual rooms or apartments of a building, can be achieved by the following constructional measures of noise control and sound insulation:

1. Wall insulation (i.e. Vertical barriers)
2. Floor and ceilings insulation (i.e. Horizontal barriers)
3. Windows and doors.
4. Insulating sanitary fittings.
5. Machine mounting or insulations of machinery.

1. Wall Insulation

Walls and partitions are the vertical barriers to noise. Their proper design and construction may insulate the sound to the desired level. To achieve this objective, the following methods of wall construction can be adopted:

Table 7.4: Typical insulation values for different types of walls

Type of Construction	Approx. weight in kg/m^2	Average TL in dB
1. One brick thick (i.e. 20 cm) wall	485 – 490	50
2. One and a half brick thick (i.e. 30 cm) wall	705 – 710	53
3. Cavity wall having two leaves each of half brick thickness (i.e. 10 cm) with 5 cm cavity.	485 – 490	50 – 53
4. Cavity wall having two 10 cm thick leaves of clinker block with 5 cm cavity.	310 – 312	50
5. Half brick wall with 13 mm thick plaster on both sides.	268 – 270	45
6. 20 cm thick hollow dense concrete block wall with 13 mm thick plaster in both sides.	185	45
7. Partition wall made with gypsum wall board fixed on timber frame work.	68 – 70	45
8. 76 mm thick hollow clay block wall with 13 mm thick plaster on both sides.	108 – 110	36

(a) Rigid Homogeneous Walls: A rigid wall consists of stone, brick or concrete masonry construction, wall plastered on one or both the sides. The sound insulation offered by these rigid walls depends upon their weight per unit area. The sound insulation thus increases with the increase in the thickness of the wall. Because of the logarithmic variation between weight and transmission loss, such a construction becomes highly uneconomical and bulky after a certain limit. In this type, sound is transmitted through the holes and cracks and space left due to badly fitted doors and windows.

The degree of insulation offered by different types of partition walls is shown in Table 7.4.

(b) Partition Walls of Porous Materials: The partition walls are made of porous materials, may be rigid or flexible in nature. In case of partitions of rigid porous materials such as concrete masonry, cinder concrete etc., the sound insulation increases about 10% higher than the non-porous rigid material. However, partition walls of non-rigid porous materials such as felt, mineral wool etc. offer very low sound insulation, though they can be used in combination with rigid materials with added advantage.

(c) Double Wall Partition: A double wall partition, shown in Fig. 7.3 consists of plaster boards or fibre boards or plaster on laths on both the faces, with sound absorbing blanket in between. Staggered wooden studs are provided as support, though their number should be a minimum. A double wall construction is thus a partition wall of rigid and non-rigid porous materials.

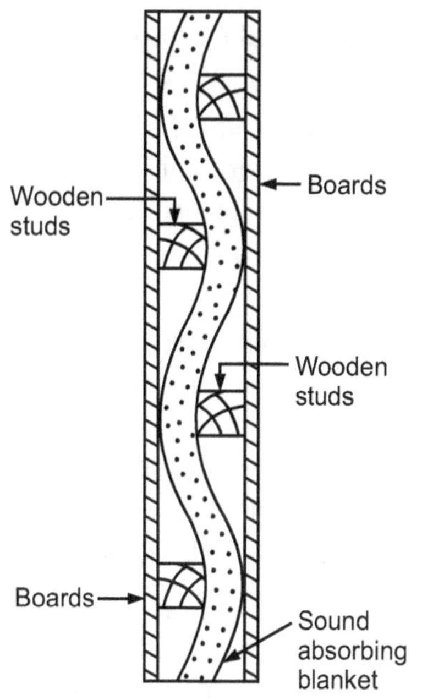

Fig. 7.3: Double wall partition

(d) Cavity Wall Construction: This is an ideal construction from the point of view of sound proofing, as shown in Fig. 7.4. The gap between the two leafs of the wall may be left air-filled or else filled with some resilient material, like quilt etc. well suspended in the gap. The two faces of the wall may be fixed with celotex or other insulating board. The width of cavity should be atleast 5 cm and the two wall leaves should be tied by use of only light butterfly wall ties.

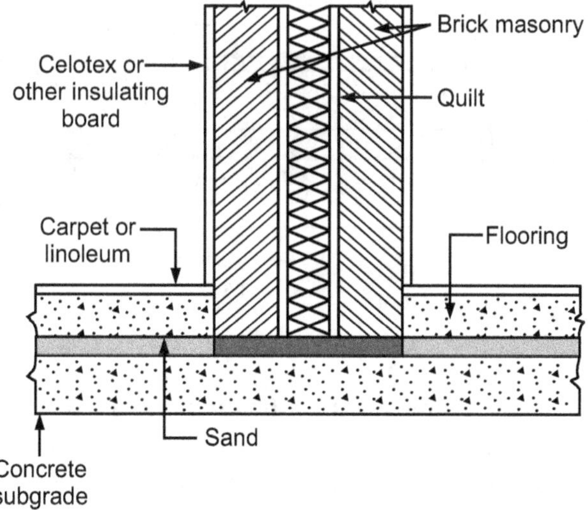

Fig. 7.4: Cavity wall or double wall construction

Table 7.4 gives typical insulation values of various types of walls.

2. Floors and Ceilings Insulation: Horizontal Barriers

Insulation or floors and ceilings act as horizontal barriers to both air borne as well as impact sounds. Normally, the rigid construction materials used for floors and ceilings offer excellent insulation against air borne noise, but they do not function well for impact or structure borne sounds. Hence, the objective of sound proofed floors and ceilings is aimed at offering good insulation against impact sounds, and this can be achieved by the following constructional features.

(a) Use of Resilient Surface Material on Floors: In this method, over the massive and rigid construction of floor slabs, a surface larger of resilient materials such as linoleum, insulation board, cork, asphalt mastic and carpet etc. are employed. By this method, insulation against impact noises to an extent of 5 to 10 dB over bare concrete floors can be obtained. The softer the materials used, greater would be the insulation value.

(b) Providing a Floating Floor Construction:

(i) Concrete Floors: This is an additional floor constructed and isolated or floated from the existing concrete floor by means of a resilient material and therefore, does not let the impacts and consequent vibration to be transmitted to the room below. It also provides useful improvement in the insulation fair borne sounds. The cement concrete used may be about 5 cm thick which is poured over a resilient material like quilted mineral or glass wool. It is important that a water proof paper be used in between and both the quilt and paper lapped so as to prevent concrete from getting through (Fig. 7.5).

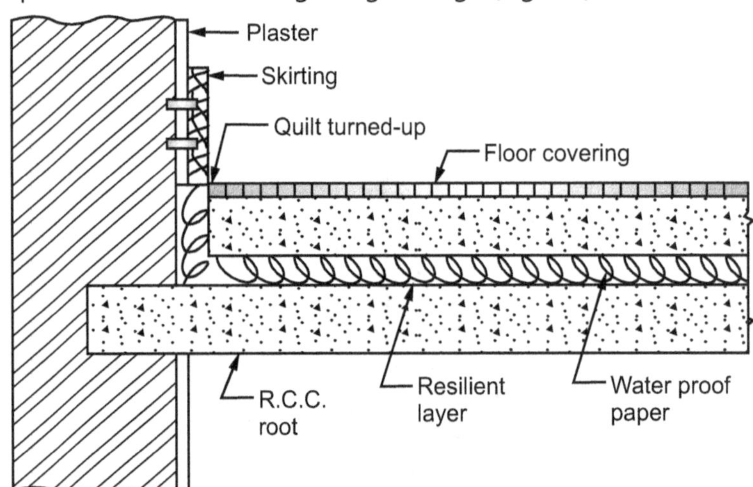

Fig. 7.5: Concrete floor floating construction

(ii) Wooden Floors: In case of floors constructed of wooden joints, the problem of sound insulation becomes more difficult, particularly in the presence of heavy mechanical impact sounds. Fig. 7.6 shows the methods of insulating such existing floors, while Fig. 7.7 shows new timber floors, employing mineral or glass wool quilt for isolation purposes. Resilient mountings may be used to obtain even more satisfactory results. A further improvement in the insulation of such floors is achieved by employing a pugging or deadening material in the air space between the wood joists. Either sound absorbent type materials like mineral wool or other materials like sand or ashes may be used, the latter are more effective because of the fact that the efficiency of pugging depends on the weight of the material used. In order to obtain useful improvement, at least 100 kg/m^2 of sand pugging is usually employed. Mineral wool pugging (at least 15 kg/m^2) is used mainly in conjunction with thin walls of 10 cm thickness or less.

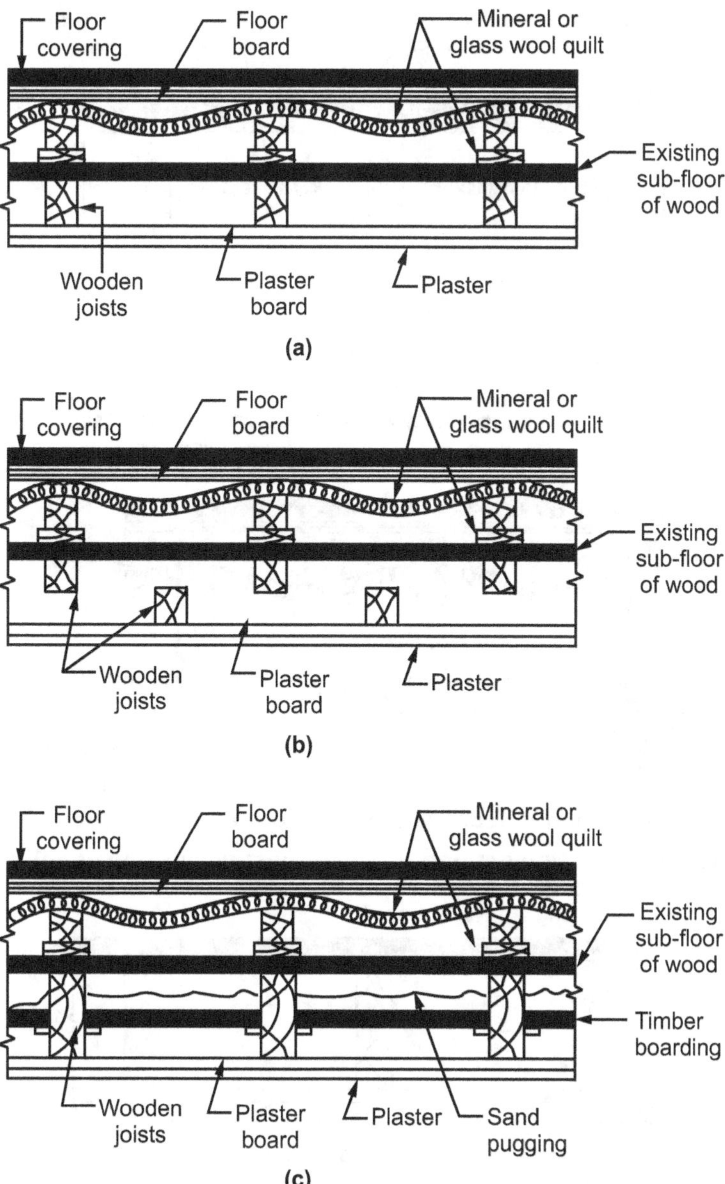

Fig. 7.6: Existing timber floors, floating construction

(c) By Providing a Suspended Ceiling with Air Space: This type of construction helps to improve the insulation of both air borne and structure borne sounds by attenuating and isolating them from room below. Typical constructions for wooden floors are shown in Fig. 7.7. For solid floors, metal hangers of acoustic clips may be used to support the ceiling below, as shown in Fig. 7.8. The extent of improvement effectively depends upon the weight of the ceiling as well as on the structural rigidity with which it is connected to the solid or wooden floor. Thus, the higher insulation could be achieved by using a very heavy ceiling which is arranged to be independent of the floor by supporting it on resilient mountings.

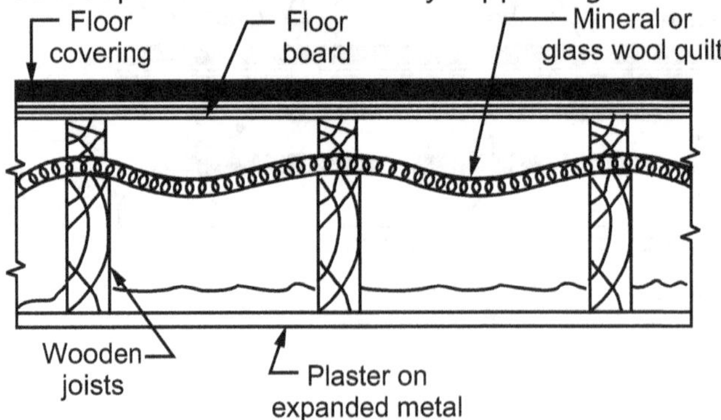

(a) When supporting walls are 10 cm thick or less

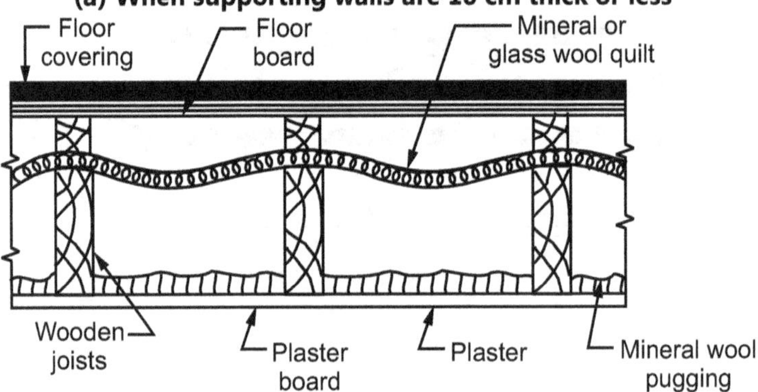

(b) When supporting walls are 20 cm thick or more

Fig. 7.7: New timber floors, floating construction with pugging

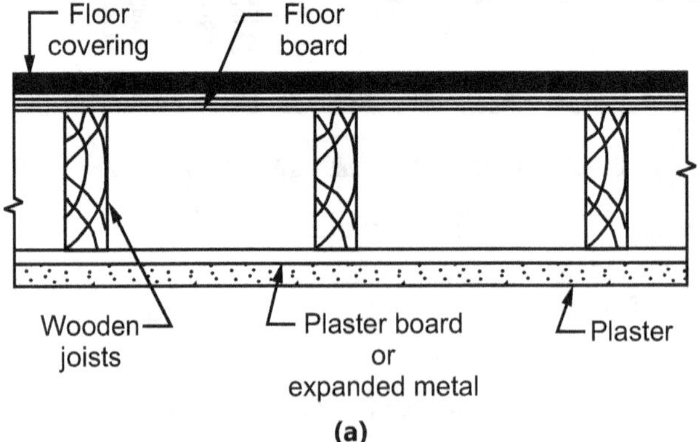

(a)

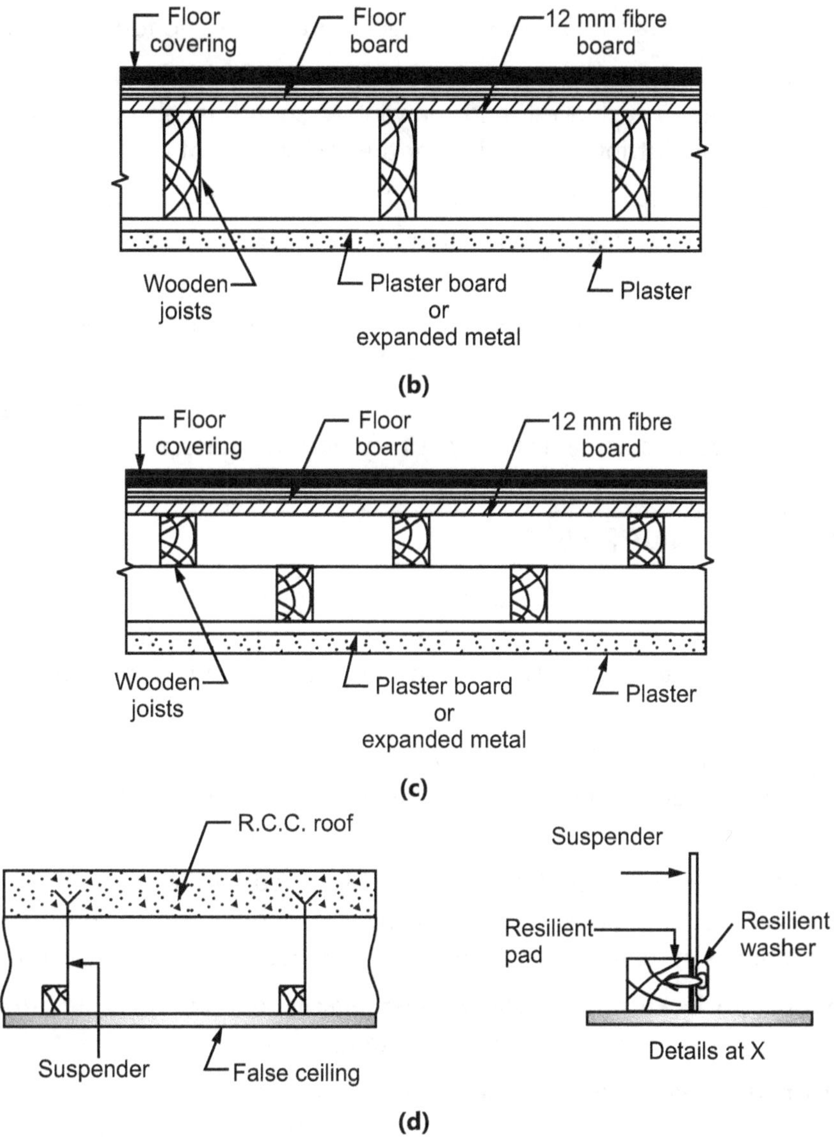

Fig. 7.8: Timber floors with suspending ceiling

7.11 REQUIREMENTS AND CONDITIONS OF GOOD ACOUSTICS

The following requirements and conditions should be fulfilled by a building having good acoustics:

- The initial sound should be of adequate intensity such that it can be heard throughout the hall. For halls of big size suitable sound amplification system should be installed.

- The sound produced should be evenly spread over the entire area so that sound foci and dead spots are avoided.

- The boundary surfaces should be so designed that there are no formation of echoes.

- The boundary surfaces of the hall should be properly designed so that the desired reverberation time is achieved and unwanted sound is absorbed. The absorbent materials should be distributed evenly over the wall surface of the hall.

- In case of conference halls, the acoustics of the halls should be so designed as to ensure proper conditions for listening, assuming that a person may speak or listen from anywhere in the hall.

- In the case of music halls, the treatment should be such that the initial sound reaches the audience with the same intensity and frequency.

- All noises (i.e. unwanted sounds) whether originating from outside or inside of the hall, should be reduced to such an extent that they do not interfere with the normal hearing of music or speech.

7.12 SOUND ABSORPTION

When a sound wave strikes a surface, a part of its energy is absorbed by friction. The sound generated in an auditorium or a hall is absorbed in four ways: (i) in the air, (ii) by the audience, (iii) in furniture and furnishing, and (iv) at the boundary surfaces such as floors, ceilings, walls etc.

(i) **Absorption in Air:** This is mainly due to the friction between the oscillating molecules when sound wave travels through it. However, this absorption is extremely small.

(ii) **Absorption by Audience:** Sound energy absorbed by the clotting of the audience. Room acoustics change perceptibly by the number of audience present. Also, absorption is more in winter, than in summer, because of heavy clottings.

(iii) **Absorption in Furnitures and Furnishings:** Furnitures, curtains, carpets etc. also absorb sound energy to a fairly good extent.

(iv) **Absorption by Boundary Surfaces:** When sound waves strike the boundary surfaces such as walls, floors, ceilings, absorption takes place due to the following factors: (a) Penetration of sound into porous materials, (b) Resonant vibration of panel materials, (c) Molecular damping in soft absorbing materials; and (d) Transmission through structures.

7.13 SOUND ABSORBENTS OR ACOUSTICAL MATERIALS

Special materials used on boundary surfaces for achieving good acoustical requirements of design by increasing their absorption are known as *absorbents*. The sound reducing effect of an absorber depends upon its area as well as on the efficiency of the materials and is indicated by a sound *absorption coefficient*. The term absorption coefficient is used to express the percentage of the incidence of sound that can be absorbed by a material.

An open window is considered to have 100% absorption as it does not interfere with the free passage of the entire sound. The *open window* has a coefficient of absorption as unity and hence the absorbing capacity of all other materials is compared with this open window unit as a standard. This open window unit is also called a *sabin*, named after the scientist who established the unit. The absorption capacity of sound and hence absorption coefficient, depends upon the frequency of incident sound. In general, low density materials have higher absorption coefficient at higher frequencies than at low frequencies. Table 7.5 gives absorption coefficient of commonly used building materials and furnishings.

Table 7.5: Absorption coefficients for building material and furnishings

Sr. No.	Materials	Absorption coefficient at		
		125 c/s	500 c/s	2000 c/s
	(a) Hangings and floorings:			
1.	Carpet, lined.	0.10	0.25	0.40
2.	Carpets, unlined.	0.08	0.15	0.25
3.	Cotton fabric, 475 g/m^2 draped to half its area.	0.07	0.49	0.66
4.	Draperies, velours 610 g/m^2	0.05	0.35	0.38
5.	Draperies, as above draped to half their area.	0.14	0.55	0.70
6.	Stage curtain.	0.19	0.20	0.23
7.	Linoleum or concrete floor.	0.02	0.03	0.04
8.	Floor, wood on solid.	0.12	0.09	0.09
9.	Floor, wood boards on timber frame.	0.25	0.13	0.15
	(b) Masonry and building materials:			
10.	Brick wall 40 cm thick.	0.02	0.03	0.05
11.	Plaster on wall.	0.03	0.02	0.04
12.	Ceiling, 50 mm plaster of paris suspended from trusses.	0.08	0.05	0.04
13.	Plyboard on 75 mm air space.	0.30	0.10	0.05
14.	Wood veneer 10 mm thick on 50 × 75 mm wood studs at 40 cm centre to centre.	0.11	0.12	0.10
15.	Glass against solid surface.	0.03	0.03	0.02
16.	Marble.	0.01	0.01	0.01

	(c) Audience, chairs etc.:			
17.	Audience seated in fully upholstered seats (per person).	0.18	0.46	0.51
18.	Chair, upholstered seat with spring.	–	0.16	0.071
19.	Seat (unoccupied) fully upholstered (per seat).	0.16	0.40	0.44
20.	Wood veneer seat and back.	–	0.023	–

Table 7.6: Absorption coefficients of indigenous acoustical materials

Sr. No.	Materials	Thickness (mm)	Density (g/cm²)	Absorption coefficient at		
				125 c/s	500 c/s	2000 c/s
1.	Fibrous (acoustic) plaster	20	0.1	–	0.30	0.50
2.	Compressed fibre board:					
	(a) Unperforated.	12	–	0.24	0.3	0.2
	(b) Perforated uniformly over part depth (rigid backing).	12.7	0.3	0.06	0.55	0.67
	(c) Perforated randomly over part depth (rigid backing).	12.7	0.3	0.15	0.52	0.76
3.	Compressed wood particle board:					
	(a) Perforated (rigid backing)	12.7	0.37	0.04	0.36	0.78
	(b) Perforated (rigid backing)	19.1	0.34	0.05	0.61	0.91
	(c) Perforated and painted (rigid backing)	12.7	0.40	0.05	0.40	0.82
	(d) Perforated and painted (rigid backing)	19.1	0.38	0.10	0.62	0.74
4.	(a) Wood wool board.	25	0.4	–	0.20	0.60
	(b) Wood wool board (50 mm from wall)	25	0.4	–	0.35	0.35
5.	Mineral glass wool quilts and mats.	25	0.06	0.09	0.17	0.50
6.	Bonded and compressed mineral/ glass wool tiles.	50	0.04	0.12	0.26	0.44
7.	Composite units of perforated hard board backed by perforated fibre board.	25	0.4	0.25	0.5	0.65

8.	(a) Mineral/glass wool with scrim mat (rigid backing)	25	0.08	0.29	0.85	0.84
	(b) Mineral/glass wool with scrim mat (rigid backing)	50	0.08	0.57	0.99	0.95
	(c) Mineral/glass wool with scrim mat faced with perforated (10% open area) hard board (rigid backing).	25	0.08	0.06	0.99	0.49
9.	Miscellaneous:					
	(a) Straw board.	13	0.24	–	0.30	0.35
	(b) Straw board spaced 50 mm from wall.	13	0.24	–	0.35	0.30
	(c) Composite panel: 5 mm perforated plywood, 50 mm mineral wool and 22 mm cement asbestos (suspended from the trusses).	–	–	0.36	0.95	0.67
	(d) Composite panel: 5 mm perforated plywood, 50 mm mineral wool and 22 mm hard board (suspended from trusses)	–	–	0.47	0.20	0.09

7.14 CLASSIFICATION OF SOUND ABSORBENTS OR ACOUSTICAL MATERIALS

The sound absorbent or acoustical materials can be broadly classified into the four groups:

1. Porous Absorbents: Absorption in porous materials is mainly due to the frictional losses which occur when the sound waves cause to and fro movement of the air contained in the material. However, their materials absorb sound mainly in the higher frequencies. Their efficiency depends upon porosity, the resistance to air flow through the materials and the thickness. Examples of absorbents under this category are rock wool, glass silk, wood wool, curtains and other soft furnishings; drilled fibre boards and acoustics plaster.

2. Resonant Panels: These are semi-hard materials in the form of porous fibre boards which absorb the sound by damping the sympathetic vibrations in the panels, caused by sound pressure waves of appropriate frequency, by means of air space behind the panel. These panels absorb sound only at lower frequencies, over a comparatively narrow frequency band ranging from 50 to 200 cycles. The frequencies, at which panels vibrate, depend upon their weight and depth of air spaces behind them.

3. Cavity Resonators: These cavity resonators consist of a container or chamber with small opening in which absorption takes place by the resonance of the air in the container which causes loss of sound energy. They can be designed to absorb sound of any frequency.

4. Composite Type-Absorbents: There are a comparatively recut developments, combining the functions of all the above three absorbents. It consists of a perforated panel fixed over an air space containing porous absorbent. The perforations in the panel should form at least 10% of the total area to allow the porous materials to absorb sound at higher frequencies.

7.15 REQUIREMENTS OF A GOOD ACOUSTIC MATERIAL

- It should have high coefficient of absorption.

- It should be efficient over a wide range of frequencies.

- It should be relatively cheap and easily available.

- It should give pleasing appearance after firing.

- It should be self supporting and should efford easy fixing.

- It should be fire resistant.

- It should have sufficient structural strength.

- It should be heat insulating and non-hygroscopic.

- It should be durable and should not be liable to attack by insects, vermits, termites etc.

7.16 ACOUSTICAL DEFECTS

To achieve perfect acoustic conditions, in practice, one has to remove or minimise all the defects in acoustics by considering suitable intensity of sound and an acceptable level of reverberation. These defects, which require due consideration for improving the acoustical conditions, are described as follows:

1. Formation of echoes,

2. Reverberation,

3. Sound foci,

4. Dead spots,

5. Insufficient loudness,

6. Exterior noise nuisance or outdoor noise effects.

1. Formation of Echoes: An *echo* is produced or formed when the reflected sound wave (from surface of walls, roofs, ceilings etc.) reaches the ear just when the original sound from the same source has been already heard. Thus, there is repetition of the sound.

The formation of echoes normally happens when the time lag between the two voices or sounds is about $1/17^{th}$ of a second and the reflecting surfaces are situated at a distance greater than 15 m. The defect usually occurs when the shape of the reflected surface is curved with smoother character. Echoes cause disturbance and unpleasant hearing. *Multiple echoes* may also be heard when a sound is reflected from a number of reflecting surfaces suitably placed, such as two parallel cliffs.

The remedy of this defect is to select the proper shape of the auditorium and surfaces, and to use the rough and porous materials for interior surfaces to disperse the energy of echoes.

2. **Reverberation:** It has been generally noticed that in public halls and auditoriums, the sound persists even after the source of sound has stopped. This persistence of sound is called reverberation. It is due to multiple reflections in an enclosed space. Reverberation is a familiar phenomenon in cathedrals and new halls/rooms without furniture, where even after sound source stops, the reverberation is heard even upto 10 seconds. A certain amount of reverberation is desirable, specially for giving richness to music, but too much reverberation is undesirable.

The time during which the sound persists is called the *reverberation time* of sound in the hall. It is the period of time in seconds, which is required for sound energy to decay or diminish by 60 dB after the sound source has stopped.

The remedy of this defect lies in selecting a correct time of reverberation known as *optimum time of reverberation*, which can be achieved by suitably using the absorbent or acoustical materials for different reflecting surfaces.

Sabine's Expression for Reverberation Time:

Prof. W.C. Sabine (1868–1919) of Hardward University studied the whole subject of architectural acoustics, particularly with reference to reverberation time. He found experimentally that the reverberation time of a room varies inversely as the effective surface area and directly as the volume of the room. He also showed that this time is independent of the position of the source and the listener and the shape of the room.

As the result of the experiments, he established the following expression for reverberation time:

$$t = \frac{0.16\ V}{\alpha_1 S_1 + \alpha_2 S_2 + \alpha_3 S_3 \ldots} \qquad \ldots (7.1)$$

$$\text{or} \qquad t = \frac{0.16\ V}{\sum \alpha s}$$

$$= \frac{0.16\ V}{A} \qquad \ldots (7.2)$$

where, t = Reverberation time in seconds

$$V = \text{Volume of the room in } m^3$$

$$\alpha_1, \alpha_2, \alpha_3 \ldots = \text{Absorption coefficient of individual units (i.e. walls,}$$
$$\text{floors, ceilings, etc.) See table 7.5.}$$

$$s_1, s_2, s_3 \ldots = \text{Areas of individual absorbing surfaces}$$

$$A = \text{Total absorption power.}$$

The total *absorbing power* is expressed in m^2 sabines.

Fig. 7.7 is also used to calculate the total absorption to be provided, in order to achieve any desired time of reverberation.

Table 7.7 gives the relation between reverberation time and the acoustics of a room.

Table 7.7: Reverberation time and acoustical quality

Reverberation time in seconds	Acoustics horizontal
0.50 to 1.50	Excellent
1.50 to 2.00	Good
2.00 to 3.00	Fairly good
3.00 to 5.00	Bad
Above 5.00	Very bad

Table 7.8 gives the optimum reverberation time and audience factors for acoustical design.

Table 7.8: Optimum reverberation time

Type of Building	Optimum Reverberation Time (seconds)	Audience Factor
1. Cinema theatres	1.3	Two-thirds
2. Churches	1.8 to 3	Two-thirds
3. Law courts, committee rooms, conference halls	1 to 1.5	One-third
4. Large halls	2 to 3	Full
5. Music concert hall	1.6 to 2	Full
6. Parliament house, Assembly hall, Council chamber	1 to 1.5	Quorum
7. Public lecture hall	1.5 to 2	One-third

Indian Standard Code IS : 2526–1963 recommends to use Fig. 7.9 for the determination of reverberation time for various size of enclosed space and for various purpose/use of the space.

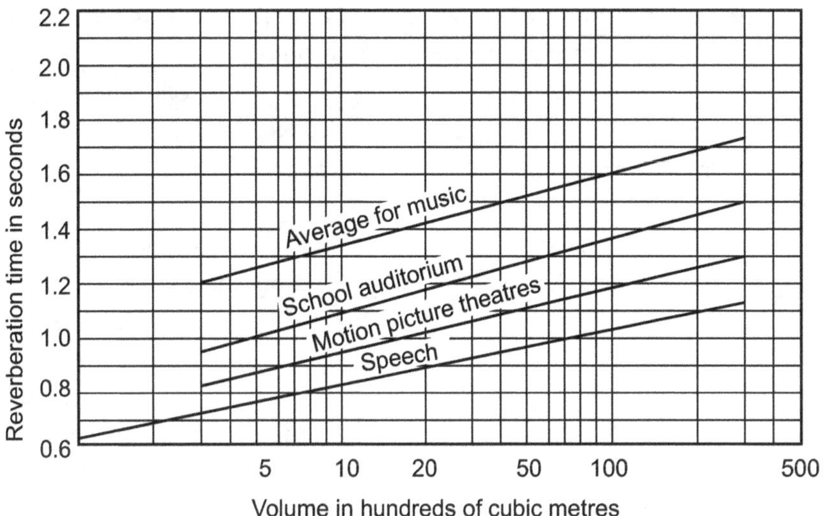

Fig. 7.9: Optimum reverberation time at 500 cycles for different types of rooms as a function of room volume

3. Sound Foci: When the interior surfaces are concave, the reflected sound waves concentrate at certain spots and produce sound of large intensity. Then spot of higher sound intensity are known as sound foci. They can be removed by avoiding concave interiors or by providing absorbent materials on focussing areas.

4. Dead Spots: This defect is an outcome of the formation of sound foci. Because of high concentration of reflected sound at sound foci, there is deficiency of reflected sound at some other points. These points are known as dead spots, where sound intensity is so low that it is insufficient for hearing. This defect can be removed by installation of suitable diffuser so that there is even distribution of sound in the hall.

5. Insufficient Loudness: This defect is caused due to lack of sound reflecting flat surface near the sound source and excessive sound absorption treatment in the hall. The defect can be removed by providing hard reflecting surface near the source and by adjusting the absorption of the hall so as to get optimum time of reverberation. When the length of hall is more, it may be desirable to install loud speakers at proper places.

6. Exterior Noise and Outdoor Nuisance: This defect is caused mainly due to poor sound insulation and partly due to poor planning and this results into bad acoustics. The exterior noise nuisance is carried inside the hall or auditorium through loose door, ventilator and window openings. This defect can be corrected or rectified by providing adequate insulation against sound for various components of the hall and through proper planning in relation to the surroundings.

Table 7.9: Summary of common acoustical defects in auditoriums and conference halls and recommended remedies

Sr. No.	Defect	Cause	Recommendations for	
			New design	**Existing building**
1.	Excessive Reverberation	Insufficient absorption	Add absorbents.	
2.	Echoes	(a) Unsuitable shape (b) Remote reflecting surfaces	Avoid unsuitable shape. Make offending surfaces highly absorbent.	
3.	Sound foci	Concave reflecting interior surfaces	Avoid curvilinear interiors.	Alter shape or use absorbents on focussing areas.
4.	Dead spots	Irregular distribution of sound	Provide even diffusion of sound.	Introduce suitable diffusers.
5.	Insufficient sound volume	(a) Lack of reflections close to source to sound (b) Excessive absorption	Disperse hard reflecting surfaces about the source of sound. Adjust absorption to give optimum reverberation.	
6.	Colouring of sound quality	(a) Selective absorption (b) Uncontrolled resonance	Use combination of absorbents to obtain uniform absorption coefficient over the required frequency range. Use wood panel absorbents which resonate over a wide frequency range and fix these on battens provided at irregular intervals. Adopt rigid construction with studs etc.	
7.	High back–ground noise	Poor sound insulation, badly fitting doors and windows or noisy air–conditioning systems.	Select construction with requisite sound insulation; provide proper fitting doors and windows with requisite sound insulation. Reduce noise from air-conditioning equipment by isolating the machine and/or treatment or plant room etc.	

7.17 GENERAL PRINCIPLES AND FACTORS IN ACOUSTICAL DESIGN

Following is the list of general planning principles and factors which are important for good acoustical conditions in a building. (Refer Art. 7.18 for details)

- Site selection and planning
- Dimensions (size)
- Shape
- Seats and seating arrangement
- Treatment of interior surfaces
- Reverberation and sound absorption.

7.18 ACOUSTICS FOR VARIOUS TYPES OF BUILDINGS

Following practical cases of buildings which deserve acoustical treatment from designer or planner will be described in short under this head.

(A) Cinema Theatres for Sound Films

The following special considerations should be made in the acoustical design and planning of the cinema theatres:

1. **Site Selection and Planning:** A noise survey of the area should be made and the site selected should be in quietest surroundings as otherwise elaborate and expensive construction may be required to provide requisite sound insulation. Depending on the ambient noise level of the site, orientation, layout and structural design should be arranged to provide necessary noise reduction so that the background noise level of not more than 40 to 45 dB is achieved within the hall.

2. **Dimensions (Size):** The size should be fixed in relation to the number of audience required to be seated, and in proportion to the intensity of sounds to be generated. The floor area of the theatre should be calculated on the basis of 0.6 to 0.9 m^2/person. The height of the hall is determined by such considerations as ventilation, presence (or absence) of balcony and type of performance etc. The ceiling of the theatre should be splayed type with a slight upward slope towards the rear-side. Total volume should be designed on the basis of 4.0 to 5.0 m^3/person.

3. **Shape:** The shape is extremely important in the acoustical design since it is a governing factor in correcting defects like echoes, sound foci, dead spots etc. A fan shaped plan with diverging side walls has been considered to be the best (Fig. 7.10).

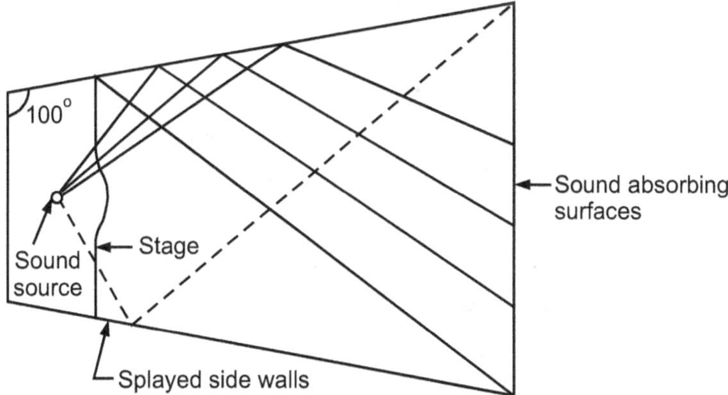

Fig. 7.10: Fan shaped plan of favourable reflection from sides

4. **Seats and Seating Arrangement:** The seats should be arranged in concentric arcs of circles drawn with the centre located as much behind the centre of the curtain line as its (curtain line) distance from the auditorium rear wall.
   - The angle subtended with horizontal at the front most observer by the highest object should not exceed 30°.

- On this basis, the distance of front row works to about 4.5 m or more for cinema theatres.
- The width of a seat should be between 45 to 56 cm.
- The back to back distance of chairs in successive rows of seats shall be at least 85 cm.
- If extra comfort is required, a higher spacing may be provided which shall vary between 85 to 106 cm.
- Seats should be staggered sideways in relation to those in front so that a listener in any row is not looking directly over the head of the person in front of him.

5. Other points:

- The surface near the source of sound should be polished hard and reflecting than those of distant or rear walls of absorbent material.
- The echo defect should be prevented at any cost, particularly by avoiding curved surfaces and using sound absorbing materials on the rear walls.
- Optimum reverberation time as per Table 7.7 should be attained finally after acoustical analysis and treatment for connection.

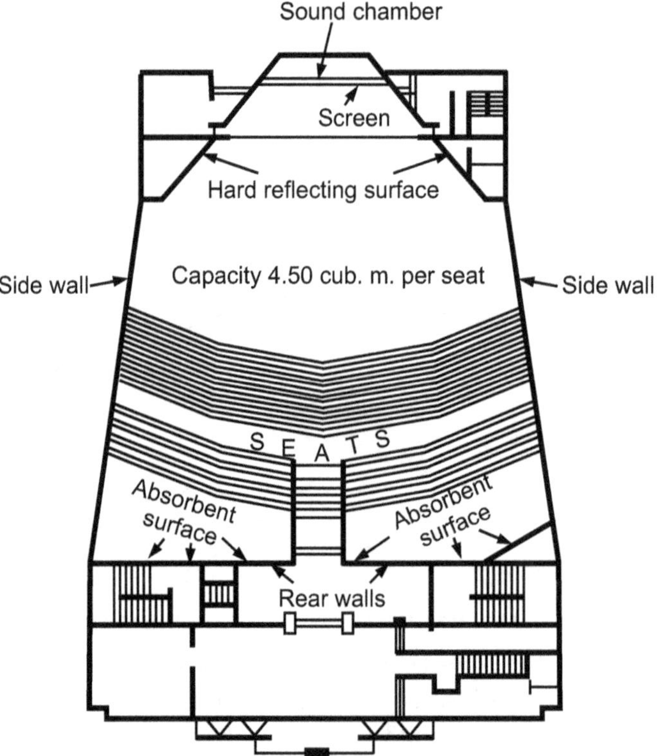

Fig. 7.11: A plan of a typical cinema theatre

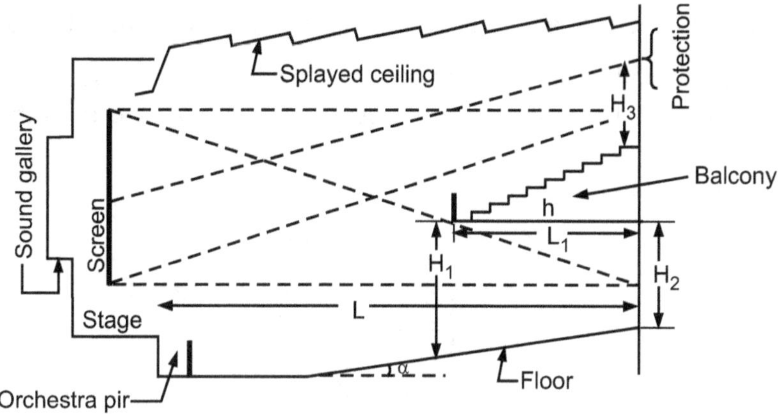

Fig. 7.12: Longitudinal section of a typical auditorium or a cinema theatre

$$\alpha \approx 8^\circ; \; L_1 > 2\,H_1; \; L_2 > L/3; \; H_2 < 3\text{ m}; \; H_3 < 2.3\text{ m}$$

(B) Radio-Broadcasting Studios

A studio is a big room or a hall where sound is picked up by a microphone, and is either recorded or broadcast. It includes radio-broadcasting station, television station and sound-recording studio.

The basic requirements of such a studio are:

- Perfect sound proofing.
- Variable reverberation time, due to variable pitch and frequency of sound produced then.

The following points are noteworthy for the acoustic design of a studio:

- The studio walls, floors and ceiling must be rigid-construction to completely insulate and exclude the external noise.
- The noise level in the studio should be brought down to 20 to 30 dB.
- The studio should be rectangular in plan with ratio of height, breadth and length as 2 : 3 : 5. The ceiling should be flat.
- The outer surface of the wall should be of reflective type, while the interior surfaces of walls, ceilings, floors etc. should be absorbent materials.
- There should be no echo formation.
- Provision of windows should be minimum, to prevent transfer noise from outside.
- Air conditioning machinery etc. should be completely isolated and their noise should be completely insulated.
- If there are more than one studios in a building, they should preferably be on the same floor. Two studios should not be located one above the other, there should be a gap of atleast one floor.

- Heavy curtains and draperies should be used to control the reverberation time.

- Variable reverberation time can be obtained by providing hinged panels or shutters, with one surface of rotable panel of absorptive material and the other of reflective material. Panels with hinge at the centre may also be used having two different absorbent materials on both the faces. (Fig. 7.13)

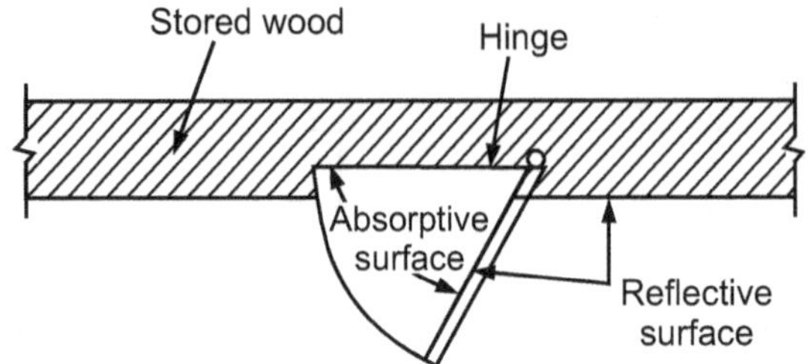

Fig. 7.13: Hinged panels on shutters in studio walls

- Reverberation time can also be varied by providing rotable cylinders in the ceiling of the studio. Each cylinder or drum has three sectors, provided with three different absorptive materials. The cylinders can be rotated by rack and pinion arrangement, thus getting the required units of absorption for the desired reverberation time.

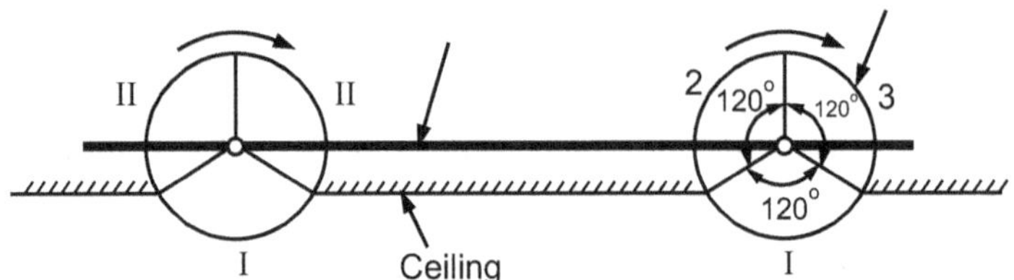

Fig. 7.14: Rotable cylinders in studio-ceiling

(C) Open Air Theatres

Open air theatre has no side walls or barriers and hence there is no reverberation. In acoustical design of open air theatre, following points require special attention:

- The selection of the site for an open-air theatre should be done very carefully considering the topographical, meteorological and acoustical properties of all available locations for the theatre. The question which is most important is the acoustical considerations thought in the selection of the site.

- The average noise level should not exceed 40 dB for a satisfactory site of a theatre.

- The slope of the seating area should not be less than about 12 degrees for good audibility and visibility.

- A properly designed orchestra shell is a must for an open air theatre. This is required for two purposes viz.

(a) The reflective power of the shell raises the average sound level throughout the area uniformly, and

(b) The shell enables the stage performers to hear each other more easily.

- A sound amplification system should be provided especially where the strength of audience will be more than 600.

- The direction of wind at the time of programme is an important factor in either helping or obstructing the passage of sound.

(D) Public Lecture Halls

The following precautions should be taken in acoustic design of a public lecture hall:

- The optimum reverberation time should not exceed 1.5 seconds, even for large halls.

- The volume per seat should be between 3 and 4 m^3.

- The hard reflecting surface on the back and around the dias or stage, including slightly outwards, should be provided.

- The rear walls facing against the dias or platform should be treated with absorbing materials.

(E) Class Lecture Rooms

The following precautions and considerations should be exercised in the acoustic design of the class rooms:

- A room with its dimensions as 7.0 m in length, 8.5 m in width, 4 m in height is considered satisfactory for a class of about 40 students.

- The noise level should be kept or brought down to 40 dB.

- The optimum reverberation time should be between 0.75 seconds at frequencies of 500 to 2000 c.p.s. and 9 seconds at frequency of 125 c.p.s.

- The volume per seat should be kept as small as possible, usually 12 m^3 or less.

- The audience should be seated near the lecture platform and seats may be arranged elevating upwards from near the platform.

- The walls and ceilings should be properly designed to give favourable reflections of sound.

- The amount of absorptive material to be used for each class room for achieving optimum time of reverberation depends upon the room size, purpose, capacity and age of the students. Hence, a class room of children having less absorption on their account, requires more absorptive material to be used for the walls and the ceiling than that would be required in rooms for adults.

7.19 SOUND LEVEL MEASUREMENTS

The human ear responds to sounds in a complex way. There is no simple relationship between the physical measurement of sound pressure levels and an individual's perception regarding the loudness of sounds. To a certain extent, the perception of relative loudness is subjective and depends on the individual's opinion. But one physical characteristic of sound (other than amplitude) that is known to have a definitive effect on the perception of loudness is the pitch, or frequency of the sound wave.

Experiments have shown that the average person with normal testing will perceive a high-pitched sound to be louder than a low-pitched sound, even though both sounds have exactly the same intensity of SPL. For example, a sound with SPL = 70 dB at a frequency of 1000 Hz is usually perceived as being louder than a 70 dB sound at a frequency of 100 Hz. In fact, a sound with a frequency of 100 Hz must have an SPL of about 76 dB for it to be judged equally as loud as a 1000 Hz sound with an SPL of 70 dB. A higher pressure level (that is, more energy) is needed at the lower frequency for the average person to perceive the same loudness, because the human ear is somewhat inefficient in detecting low-pitched sounds.

Because sounds are of the same SPL intensity, but varying frequencies are not perceived as being of equal loudness or volume, a method that allows meaningful and consistent sound or noise–level measurements is needed. One way to accomplish this is to use a chart showing equal loudness contours, as depicted in Fig. 7.15.

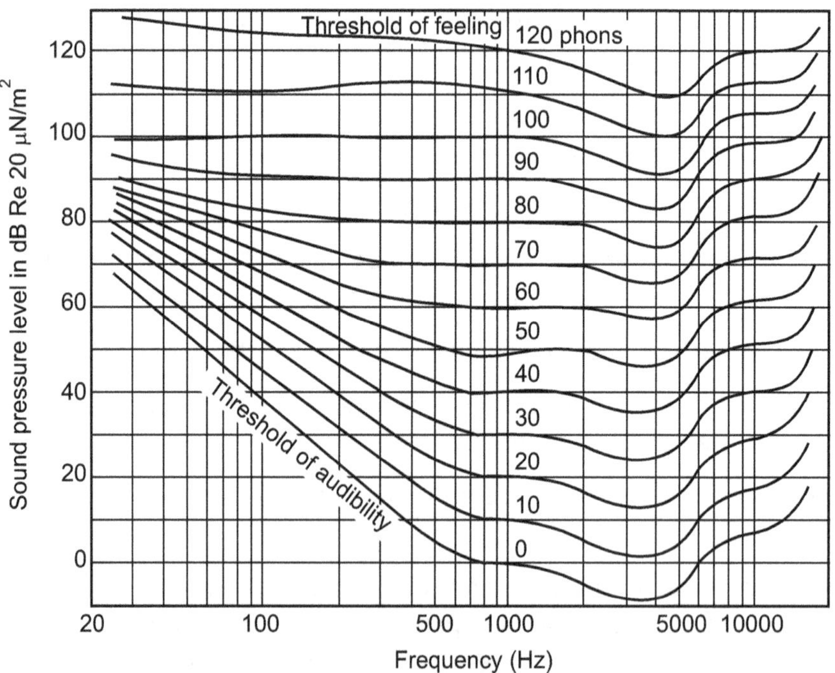

Fig. 7.15: Equal loudness contours in phons

The contour curves represent loudness or sound levels called **phons**. At a frequency of 1000 Hz, the reference pitch, sound pressure levels are the same as sound levels; both are expressed in terms of decibels. Consider, for example, a listener with normal hearing who hears a 100 Hz tone with an SPL of 70 dB. What loudness does the listener perceive? Enter the chart on the bottom axis at 100 Hz and follow the vertical line upward to a point at the 70 dB value for SPL; the closest contour curve is labelled 60. In other words, the sound will be judged to have a loudness of 60 phons. Using the same contour, it can be seen that a person hearing a 65 dB SPL sound 200 Hz would perceive the same loudness, that of 60 phons.

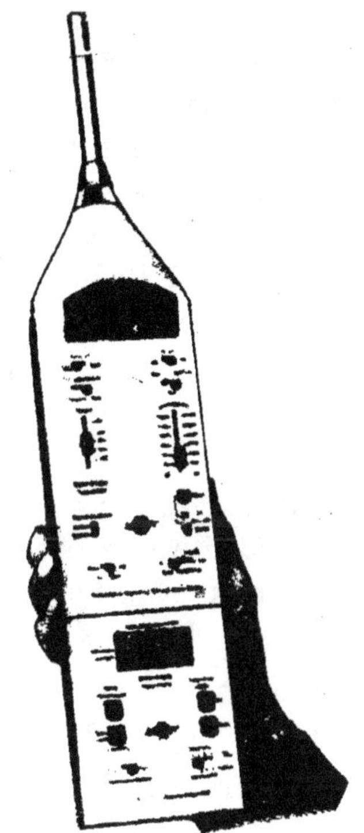

Fig. 7.16 (a): Typical hand–held sound level meter

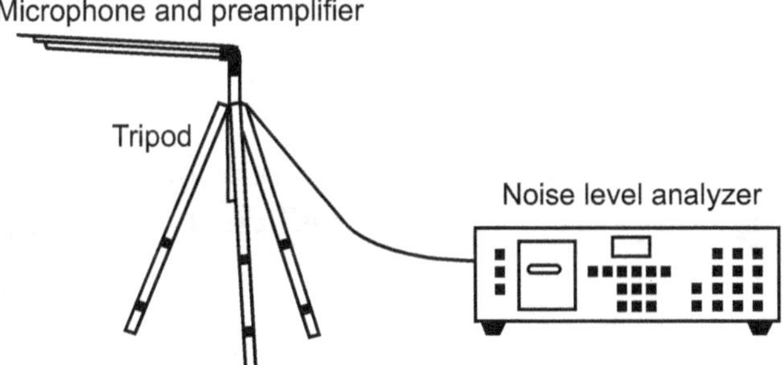

Fig. 7.16 (b): Typical measuring arrangement used for traffic noise surveys

Many other methods are used to measure apparent loudness. For example, another unit of loudness that is used is the **sone**. A loudness of 40 phons corresponds to 1 sone; each doubling of the sones increases the phons by 10. For example, a sound of 2 sones is equivalent to 50 phons, 4 sones is equivalent to 60 phons, and so on. Other units are used, as well, but a full discussion is beyond the scope of this text. The important point to note is the complexity involved in measuring both noise levels and effects.

Sound Level Meters

Many electronic instruments are available for measuring noise. The basic components of a typical noise meter includes a microphone, an amplifier, a frequency filter, and a readout device. The readings or measurements are called sound levels and take into account the variation of perceived noise or loudness with frequency. Some noise surveys can be conducted with a battery-operated, hand-held, sound level meter, as shown in Fig. 7.16 (a).

If noise measurements are to be made at one location over a relatively long period of time, such as for a traffic noise survey, meters can be mounted on a tripod, and a recording device and a frequency analyzer can be added to the system. (b) Noise meters generally cover a range of 20 to 180 dB. The selection of noise–measuring instruments depends on the type of noise, the environmental conditions and the general purpose of the survey.

SOLVED EXAMPLES

Example 7.1:

A studio has clear dimensions of length = 12 m, breadth = 8 m and height = 5 m. The ceiling is provided with acoustical tiles having absorption coefficient of 0.25. Curtains in heavy folds are provided on one of the short walls (absorption coefficient 0.5). The absorption power of other surfaces of the studio may be considered as 6.0 m² sabins.

It is desired to provide revolving panels in the studio such that the time of reverberation can be varied from 0.80 to 1 second. Calculate the following:

(a) Absorption units needed with each time of reverberation.

(b) Coefficients of absorbent materials on both the faces of the revolving panel.

(c) Area of wall panel.

Solution:

(a)

Surface	Area in m²	Absorption coefficient per m³	Absorption units in m² – Sabins
Acoustical tiles	96	0.25	24
Curtains in heavy–folds	40	0.50	20
Other surfaces	–	–	6.0
			Total 50

Volume of room = $12 \times 8 \times 5 = 480$ m³

Now, $T = \dfrac{0.16\,V}{A}$

or $0.80 = \dfrac{0.16 \times 480}{A}$

or $A = \dfrac{0.16 \times 480}{0.80}$

$$= 96 \text{ m}^2\text{–Sabins}$$

∴   Extra absorption units required

$$= 96 - 50 = 46 \text{ m}^2\text{–Sabins}$$

when $T = 0.80$

Then, $T = \dfrac{0.16\ V}{A}$

or $1 = \dfrac{0.16 \times 480}{A}$

or $A = 0.16 \times 480 = 73.6 \text{ m}^2\text{–Sabins}$

∴   Extra absorption units required

$$= 96 - 73.6$$

$$= 22.4$$

$$\approx 23 \text{ m}^2 - \text{Sabins}$$

when, $T = 1.00$

(b) From the number of extra absorption units worked out in (a), it is clear that the ratio of coefficients of absorbent materials on both the faces of the revolving panel should be equal to 2. Hence, provide hairfelt with coefficient of absorption as 0.60 on one face of the panel and perforated compressed fibreboard with coefficient of absorption 0.30 on the other face of the panel.

(c) ∴   Area of revolving panel $= \dfrac{46}{0.6} = 76.67 \text{ m}^2$

or,   Area of revolving panel $= \dfrac{23}{0.3} = 76.67 \text{ m}^2.$

Example 7.2:

An auditorium is rectangular in shape. The length is 40 metres, breadth is 30 m and height is 10 metres. The inner surfaces of the auditorium are covered by the following materials:

1. Cement plaster – 1400 m²

2. Concrete floor – 1200 m²

3. Curtains – 200 m²

4. Celotex ceiling – 1200 m²

The capacity of the auditorium is 2000 seats. Determine the following:

(a) Number of absorbing units and time of reverberation when there is (i) no audience, (ii) an audience of 1200 persons and (iii) full audience.

(b) Number of extra absorbing units required to obtain a reverberation time of 1.3 seconds when capacity of audience is 900 persons.

(c) Co-efficient of absorbing material, if the area available for fixing the absorbing material is 1800 m².

Solution:

(a)

Surface	Area or No.	Absorption coefficient m² or per No.	Absorption units in Sabins
Plaster	1400	0.02	28
Concrete	1200	0.03	36
Ceiling	1200	0.10	120
Curtains	200	0.40	80
Seats	2000	0.02	40
			Total　304

Now the absorption power in m² – Sabins of an adult is 0.46. Hence, net increase in absorption power of room due to presence of one person is obtained by deducing absorption power of seat from that of a person.

∴　Net increase in absorption power per person

$$= 0.46 - 0.02$$

$$= 0.44$$

The absorption units of the auditorium with different capacity of audience will be as follows:

Audience	Absorption unit when room is empty	Absorption units of audience	Total absorption units in m² Sabins
NIL	304	–	304
900	304	396	700
1200	304	528	832
2000	304	880	1184

Now, Volume of auditorium　　　$= 40 \times 30 \times 10$

$$= 12,000 \text{ m}^3$$

The time of reverberation for various capacity of audience is worked out by using Sabin's equation

$$T = \frac{0.16\,V}{A}$$

For no audience, $\qquad T = \dfrac{0.16 \times 12000}{304} = 6.32$ seconds

For 1200 audience, $\qquad T = \dfrac{0.16 \times 12000}{832} = 2.30$ seconds

For full audience, $\qquad T = \dfrac{0.16 \times 12000}{1184} = 1.62$ seconds

(b) $\qquad\qquad T = \dfrac{0.16\,V}{A}$

or $\qquad\qquad 1.3 = \dfrac{0.16 \times 12000}{A}$

or $\qquad\qquad A = \dfrac{0.16 \times 12000}{1.3} = 1477$ m^2 – Sabins.

Absorption power of room when audience consists of 900 persons is 700 m^2 – Sabins.

$\therefore$　Extra absorption units required

$$= 1477 - 700$$

$$= 777 \text{ m}^2 - \text{Sabin.}$$

(c) Coefficient of absorbing material

$$= \frac{777}{1800} = 0.43$$

7.20 CONSTRUCTIONAL REQUIREMENTS FOR DIFFERENT BUILDING SERVICES

While designing building (residential, commercial, institutional etc.), factors which should be considered are: (1) Elegance, (2) Safety, (3) Economy, (4) Comfort. i.e. a building should be beautiful to look at, should be safe, the owner should get maximum returns and the user should find the stay in the building comfortable. Elegance can be achieved by various architectural forms, building materials, colour schemes, etc. Safety includes structural safety, durability, health safety and fire safety. Economy can be achieved through proper use of building materials, economic design of building components etc. Necessary building services play a very important role in providing comfort to the user if environment is not suitable. These services include electrical, air handling, air conditioning, heating, ventilation, lighting and plumbing services. Other services include vertical circulation, telecommunication, entertainment services etc.

7.20.1 Electrical Services

An electrical service is very essential for any type of building to provide required power for operating various types of electrical appliances, providing artificial lighting, artificial ventilation for pumping water, etc. The installation should be carried out in a building in conformity with the requirements of Indian Electricity Act, 1910; Indian Electricity Rules, 1956 and also the relevant regulations of the electric supply authority for the area in which the building is located. For a proposed electrical work or extension of existing work or major modifications, permission of the concerned electrical local authority should be taken. The work of electrical installations shall be carried out by a licensed electrical contractor and under the direct supervision of a competent person.

The design and planning of an electrical wiring installation involves a thorough understanding of all prevailing conditions. It should consider the type of building (residential, commercial, industrial etc.) and requirements of consumers. Therefore, an architect should consult an electrical engineer during the building planning stage to provide electrical installations adequate for their intended purpose and safe and efficient in their use. While designing and planning electrical services, an architect should consider the following points:

- The type of supply, occupancy, proposed electrical load and available earthing arrangement.
- The atmospheric conditions which are likely to affect the installation adversely.
- The degree of mechanical and electrical protection necessary.
- The importance of continuity of electric supply and the possible need for stand-by supply.
- The probable operation maintenance cost and electrical supply tariffs.
- The relative costs of various alternative methods.
- Ease of maintenance and safety aspects.
- Energy conservation.
- Space required for accommodation of substation, transformer, switch rooms, service cable ducts, rising mains, distribution cables, subdistribution boards openings and chisel in floors and walls for all required electrical installations.
- Immediate requirements and requirement of services during the intended life of the building.

While planning a building site, provision should be made for space for installation of substation. As far as possible, it should be at the ground level for direct access from the street for installation or removal of the equipment. The level of the substation should be above the highest flood level. It is preferable to provide electrical substation adjacent to the air conditioning plant room, if provided.

7.20.2 Switch Room

In large installations, a separate switch room is provided. It should be located very close to the electrical load centre and suitable ducts are laid with a minimum number of bends from the point of entry of the main supply cable to the position of main switch gear. While placing the switch room, care is taken to provide rising ducts from upper floors of the building in one straight vertical line. If more than one rising duct is required, horizontal ducts are provided for running cables from the switch room to the foot of each rising main.

7.20.3 Energy Meters

Energy meters are installed in residential buildings at such a place which is accessible to the owner of the building and authority. These meters are installed at a suitable height from where meter reading can be noted. These meters are protected with a protective covering like a glass window or they are mounted inside a completely enclosed box having hinged or sliding doors with locking arrangement.

7.20.4 Layout and Installation of Wiring

An electrical layout for wiring is drawn by considering proper locations of all outlets for lamps, fans, appliances, both fixed and transportable motors etc. The exact positions of wiring and all points are marked on the plan. In the layout, wiring should be designed keeping in view disposition of the lighting system to meet the illumination levels. Power and heating subcircuits are kept separate and distinct from lighting and fan subcircuit.

Electrical installation in a new building is generally commenced immediately on the completion of the main structural building work and before finishing work such as plastering except in case of surface wiring which is carried out after the plastering work. If electrical wiring is to be concealed within the structure, the necessary conduits and ducts are positioned firmly by tying the conduit to the reinforcement before concreting.

In the building, 15 A socket outlets are provided for the use of domestic appliances such as air conditioners, water coolers, emulsion heaters, refrigerators, etc. with individual fuse or miniature circuit breaker. 5 A socket outlets are provided for lighting fittings and fans. The schedule of socket outlets depends upon the requirements of the buildings. In residential buildings normally the following schedule of socket outlet is provided.

Table 7.10: Requirements of number of socket outlets in residential buildings

Location	Number of 5 A socket outlets	Number of 15 A socket outlets
Bed room	2 – 3	1
Living room	2 – 3	2
Kitchen	1	2
Dining room	2	1
Garage	1	1
For refrigerator	–	1
For air conditioner	–	(one for each)
Verandah	1 per 10 m^2	1
Bathroom	1	1

7.20.5 Telecommunication Services

The requirements of telecommunication facilities like telephone connections, private branch exchange, intercommunication facilities, telex and telegraph lines are to be planned well in advance so that suitable provisions are made in the building plan in such a way that the demand for telecommunication services in any part of the building at any floor are met at any time during the life of the building. Once a building is completed, it is almost impossible, even with the greatest care, to carry out telephone wiring on a large scale without causing unsightliness, some damage to decoration and inconvenience to residents. Wiring for telecommunication in small buildings is undertaken by the telephone department on the surface of the walls. But in large multi-storeyed buildings intended for commercial, business and office use as well as for residential purposes, wiring for telephone connections is generally done in a concealed manner through conduits.

The following are essential requirements:

- Feed in ducts for the main cables from the public telephone distribution system, the number of intake points will depend on the design and internal arrangement of the building.

- A main distribution case or main distribution frame for connecting the lead in cables with internal wiring system.

- One or more vertical riser ducts, continuous throughout the height of the building.

- Horizontal ducts or chases for cables from the vertical duct to the telephone position in each dwelling.

It is important to discuss the above requirements with the local telephone authorities and provide for the same at the construction stage itself.

7.20.6 Entertainment Services

In multi-storeyed apartment houses and hotels where many TV receivers are located, a common master antenna system may preferably be used to avoid mushrooming of individual antennae. During the design of the building itself, local conditions should be studied to see which type of an external aerial is necessary for reception of sound and television signals. Individual installations may damage walls and also do not give satisfactory reception. Cable TV network can be integrated with the aerial system.

The master antenna is generally provided at the topmost convenient point in any building and a suitable room of the topmost floor or terrace for housing the amplifier unit etc. may also be provided in consultation with the architect or engineer. From the amplifier room conduits are laid in a recess to facilitate drawing coaxial cables to individual flats. Tap off boxes are also provided in every flat of the building or room in hotels.

7.20.7 Air Handling, Conditioning and Air Heating

Central Air Conditioning System: In this system, various units like filters, heaters, coolers, humidifiers or dehumidifiers etc. are installed at a central place. The conditioned air is supplied to various parts of the building through a duct system provided in the walls or ceiling. A duct system is a continuous passage way for the transmission of air which in addition to ducts, may include duct fittings, dampers, plenums, fans and accessories of air handling equipment.

The equipment for air conditioning consists of air filters, air heaters, refrigeration units, humidifiers, dehumidifiers, air distribution system (ducts, outlets, pumps etc.)

In a central air conditioning system, selection of location for the equipment room and provisions for duct system play an important role in the design of buildings. In selecting the location for plant room, the aspects of efficiency, economy and good practice should be considered. This room is located as centrally as possible with respect to the area to be air conditioned and should be free from obstructing columns. Wherever possible, a separate isolated equipment room should be provided. The clear headroom below soffit of beam should be between 3 – 3.6 m from the finished floor level. The floors of the equipment rooms should be light coloured and finished smooth. While designing the building, structural provisions are made for supporting water pipes on the slabs. Adequate floor-drain for disposal of waste water from the equipment room should be provided. To prevent noise transmission, no windows are generally provided in the equipment room and ventilation is provided by mechanical means. The plant machinery is founded on anti-vibratory supports.

Equipment room for air handling unit is located as centrally as possible of the area air conditioned contiguous to the corridors or other spaces for carrying air ducts. In large and multi-storeyed buildings, depending upon the design of buildings, separate air handling unit rooms are provided. Depending upon the prevailing wind directions, provision is made for the entry of fresh air.

Openings provided in external walls for inlets and outlets of air are shielded properly from weather and insects. They are fitted with corrosion resistant screens of mesh of suitable gauge. All air handling rooms should have proper arrangement for water on the floors. The floor should be light coloured, smooth and finished with terrazo tiles. If possible in the structural design, obstruction to the passage of supply and return air ducts due to beams should be avoided. Acoustical treatment to air handling equipment should be given.

When air is supplied to a number of floors by a centralised air handling unit, air risers for supply ducts and return air are provided. These risers are provided from the roof of the air handling room to the slab of the last floor. The walls of risers in passages or other spaces are constructed initially upto 1 m height and extended upto the ceiling after installation of ducts.

To supply conditioned air, supply ducts and return air ducts are provided on each floor. Provision for sufficient space should be made to accommodate these ducts. The supports which are provided for the ducts are cast with ceiling slabs. A false ceiling should be provided after the installation of the ducts. Independent supports should be provided for false ceilings and ducts. When a duct passes through a masonry wall, it should be lined from outside with felt to isolate the duct from the masonry. Openings in the walls and ceilings are provided for entry and return of air. While constructing a building, provision should be made for a shaft for condenser chilled water and refrigeration pipes from the main equipment room to the air handling unit rooms and cooling towers (if provided).

Sometimes, it is necessary to install a cooling tower on the roof of the building, as it is a source of noise. While designing the structure, load of the cooling tower should be considered. A make up water tank separate from overhead water tank is provided for the cooling tower.

To minimise the heating load and reduce energy cost, necessary precaution should be taken in glazing work. The building should be oriented suitably and minimum glazing is provided in walls subjected to heavy sun exposure. Double glazing or heat resistant glass also helps in reducing the flow of heat. Necessary sun breakers are provided to shade glazed area. Sometimes reflecting surfaces are provided on the exterior walls to reduce the heat load. The exposed roof surfaces, ceilings and floors which are not air conditioned are suitably insulated to reduce thermal transmittance.

A central air conditioning system can be used for the central heating system by providing hot water or steam boilers, heating coils, thermostat etc.

7.20.8 Vertical Circulation: Lifts and Escalators

A lift is an appliance designed to transport persons or materials between two or more levels in a vertical or substantially vertical direction by means of a guided car or platform. An escalator is a power driven inclined continuous stair way used for raising or lowering passengers. The inclination of the stair with the horizontal should not be more than $30°$ and speed of movement is 45 cm/s. Escalators are arranged in pairs one for upward movement and the other for downward movement. While designing a building, the architect should consider the following points:

- Number of lifts and size of position of lift well.
- Particulars of lift well enclosure.
- Size, position, number and type of landing doors.
- Number of floors served by the lift.
- Height between floor levels.
- Number of entrances.
- Total headroom.
- Provision of access to machine room.
- Provision of ventilation and if possible natural lighting of machine room.
- Height of machine room.
- Depth of lift pit.
- Position of lift machine above or below lift well.
- Electrical supply requirements of lifts or escalators.

The outline dimensions of machine room, pit depth, total headroom, overhead distance are shown in Tables (7.11) to (7.14).

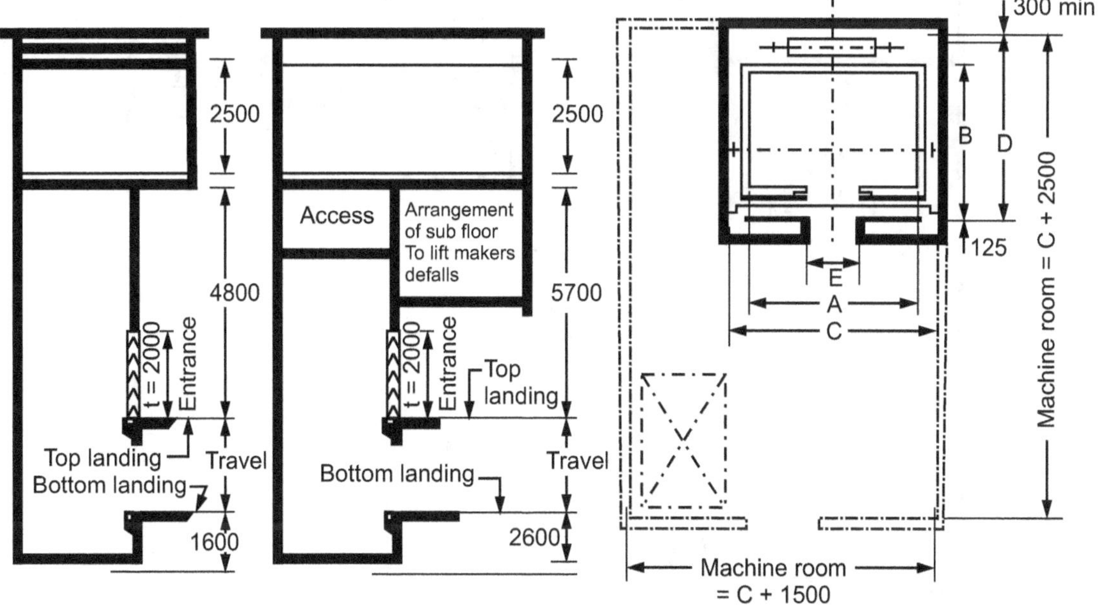

Fig. 7.17

Table 7.11: Dimensions of Passenger Lifts
(All dimensions in millimetres)

Load		Car Inside		Lift Well		Entrance
Persons	kg	A	B	C	D	E
(1)	(2)	(3)	(4)	(5)	(6)	(7)
4	272	1100	700	1900	1300	800
6	408	1100	1000	1900	1600	800
8	544	1300	1100	1900	1900	800
10	680	1350	1300	1900	2100	800
13	884	2000	1100	2500	1900	900
16	1088	2000	1300	2500	2100	1000
20	1360	2000	1550	2500	2400	1000

Notes:

1. The total headroom has been calculated on the basis of car height of 2.2 m.

2. In the case of manually operated doors, clear entrance will be reduced by the amount of projection of handle on the landing door.

3. Four and six passenger lifts are generally limited to a speed of 1 m/s.

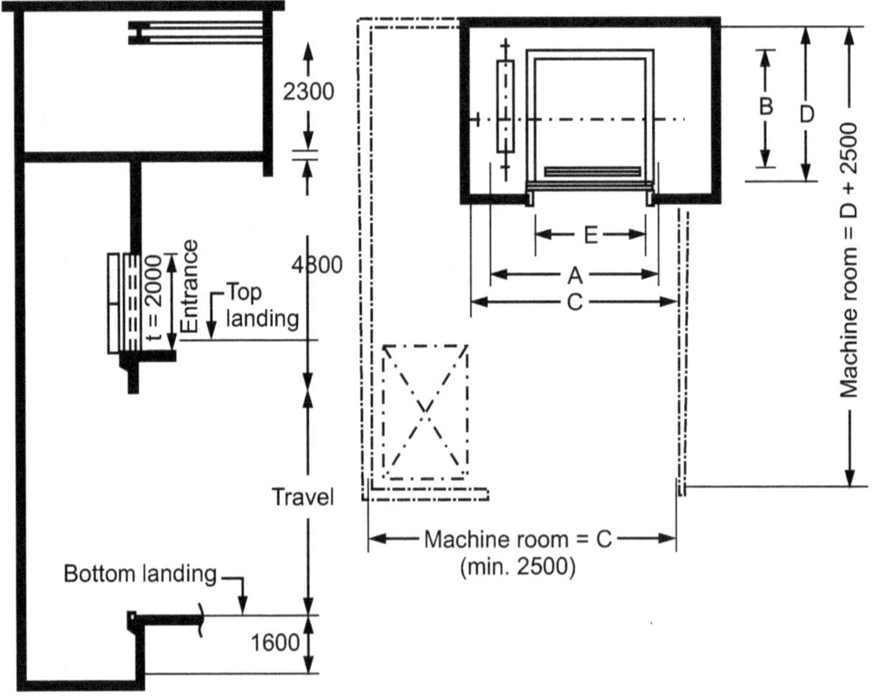

Fig. 7.18

Table 7.12: Dimensions of Goods Lifts (For speeds upto 0.5 m/s)
(All dimensions in millimeters)

Load	Car Inside		Lift Well		Entrance
kg	A	B	C	D	E
(1)	(2)	(3)	(4)	(5)	(6)
500	1100	1200	1900	1500	1100
1000	1400	1800	2300	2100	1400
1500	1700	2000	2600	2300	1700
2000	1700	2500	2600	2800	1700
2500	2000	2500	2900	2800	2000
3000	2000	3000	2900	3300	2000
4000	2500	3000	3400	3300	2500
5000	2500	3600	3400	3900	2500

Notes:

1. The width of the machine room shall be equal to the lift well width 'C' subject to a minimum of 2500 mm.
2. The total headroom has been calculated on the basis of a car height of 2.2 m.
3. Clear entrance width 'E' is based on vertical lifting car-door and vertical bi-parting doors. For collapsible mid-bar doors, the clear entrance width will get reduced by 200 mm or over, depending on the lift design.

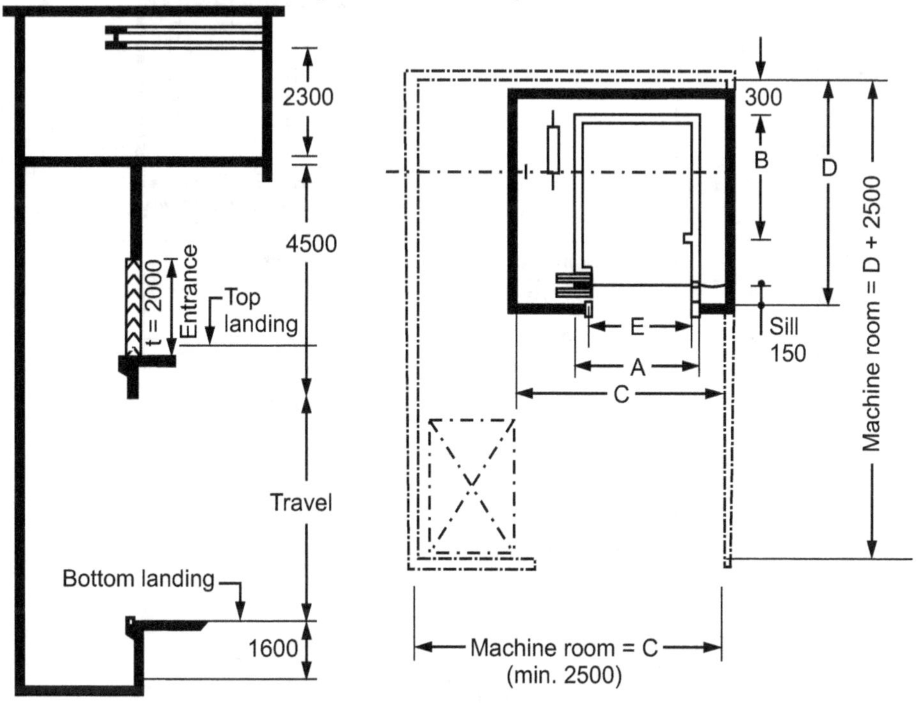

Fig. 7.19

Table 7.13: Dimensions of Hospital Lifts (For speeds upto 1.5 m/s)

(All dimensions in millimeters)

Load		Car Inside		Lift Well		Entrance
Persons	kg	A	B	C	D	E
(1)	(2)	(3)	(4)	(5)	(6)	(7)
15	1020	950	2400	1700	3000	800
20	1360	1300	2400	2200	3000	1200
26	1768	1600	2400	2350	3000	1200

Notes:

1. The total headroom has been calculated on the basis of a car height of 2.2 m.

2. In case of manually operated doors, clear entrance will be reduced by the amount of projection of handle on the landing door.

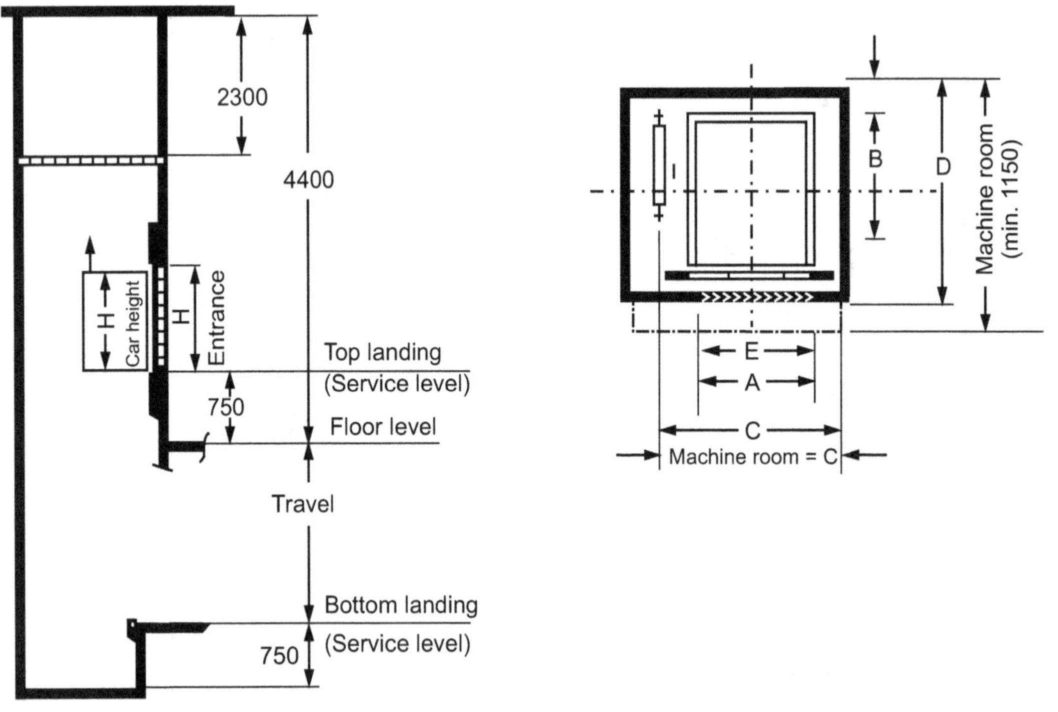

Fig. 7.20

Table 7.14: Dimensions of Service Lifts (For speeds upto 0.5 m/s)

(All dimensions in millimeters)

Load		Car Inside		Lift Well		Entrance
kg	A	B	H	C	D	E
(1)	(2)	(3)	(4)	(5)	(6)	(7)
100	700	700	800	1200	900	700
150	800	800	900	1300	1000	800
200	900	900	1000	1400	1100	900
250	1000	1000	1200	1500	1200	1000

Note: Entrance width 'E' is based on assumption of provision of vertical bi-parting doors (no car door is normally provided).

While designing a building, number of lifts and capacity of lifts is determined by considering quantity of service required and the quality of service designed. The other factors which are to be considered are number of floors to be served, number of passengers to be handled, floor area and floor to floor heights. A thorough investigation should be made for assessing the most suitable location for the lifts; the architect should consider the immediate and future requirements. The lifts should be easily accessible from all entrances to the buildings. For better efficiency, lifts are grouped near the centre of the building. The passage provided to the lift should be wide enough for providing space for waiting passengers and for through passengers. The passenger lifts in small residential buildings are placed adjoining a stair case with the lift entrances serving direct on to the landings. In commercial buildings, preferably two or more number of lifts are provided at convenient locations. Sometimes, two lifts serve alternate floors. One lift serves floor numbers 1, 3, 5, 7 etc. and the other 2, 4, 6, 8 etc. While deciding the position of goods lift, the requirements of the industrial units should be considered. The machine room is placed immediately above the lift. A lift pit is provided at the bottom of every lift. This pit should be soundly constructed and maintained in a dry condition by providing necessary drainage.

In the designing of escalators, the factors which are to be considered are:

- Floor to floor level.
- Maximum capacity required.
- The speed of the escalator.
- Available space.

The escalators should not have angle of inclination more than $30°$. The width of the step (tread) should not be less than 40 cm and the riser between treads should not be less than 20 cm. The tread surface of each step is slotted in a direction parallel to the travel of the steps. A combprate at the entrance and exit of every escalator. The combprate teeth shall be meshed with and set into the slots in the tread surface so that the points of the teeth are always below the upper surface of the treads. Combprate shall be adjustable variety.

IMPORTANT POINTS

- Characteristics of sound with its three types.
- Reflection of sound.
- Noise control and constructional measures adopted to control it.
- Wall insulation and its different types.
- Floors and ceiling insulations along with its different flooring materials:

  (a) Resilent surface material

  (b) Floating floor construction i.e. concrete floors and wooden floors.
- Absorption of sound: Four ways for the same.
- Classification of sound absorbents materials and its four types.
- Detail study for Acoustical defects with its six types.
- Describe Acoustics for various types of Buildings e.g. cinema theatres, radio studios, open air theatres, public lecture halls and class lecture rooms.
- Special considerations for acoustical design and planning of cinema theatres.
- Sound measuring instruments.
- Need of rain water harvesting, aims, advantages of RWH.
- Systems employed for effective RWH.
- Various types of RWH in India.
- Cost effectivity of building.
- Solar water heating system its need and location.
- Accessories for making solar water heaters.
- Types of solar water heaters :

  (I) Active Systems

     (a) Open-loop active systems (b) Closed-loop active systems.

  (II) Passive system of solar water heater

QUESTIONS

1. Define noise pollution. Enlist various effects of noise pollution.
2. What are different acoustical defects? Explain any one in detail.
3. Describe the various methods adopted in achieving noise control.
4. Explain:

   (a)   Sabine's formula

(b)　　Sound foci and Dead spots.

5.　How would you control noise at the stage of planning of a building?

6.　What are the courses of a excessive reverberation and formation of echoes? How do you correct for the optimum time of reverberation?

7.　Explain briefly the characteristics of an audible sound.

8.　What is reverberation?

9.　What are the design considerations for noise control?

10.　What are acoustical defects in a building? Explain any one with suitable examples.

11.　Explain briefly the characteristics of audible sound.

12.　How is reverberation time calculated? Mention the optimum reverberation time for the following buildings:

(i)　　Cinema theatres,

(ii)　　Music concert halls,

(iii)　　Assembly hall, and

(iv)　　Public lecture hall.

13.　What are the causes of excessive reverberation and formation of echoes? How do you correct for the optimum time of reverberation?

14.　Differentiate between the following:

(i)　　Acoustics and sound insulation

(ii)　　Reverberation and formation of echoes

(iii)　　Indoor noise and outdoor noise

(iv)　　Air borne noise and structure borne noise

(v)　　Sound foci and dead spots.

15.　An assembly hall, having rectangular shape, has its dimensions 40 m × 20 m × 10 m. The areas of different surfaces used are: (i) Cement plaster = 1000 m^2; (ii) Concrete floor = 800 m^2; (iii) Celotex ceiling = 800 m^2 and (iv) Light curtains = 200 m^2. The capacity of the hall is 1000 wooden seats. Assume two thirds of the audience to be present and workout the following:

(a)　　Number of absorbing units and time of reverberation.

(b)　　Number of extra absorbing units required so as to get an optimum reverberation time 1.3 seconds.

(c)　　Coefficient of absorbing material of area for fixing material is 720 m^2.

16. Write short notes on:

    (i)   Energy from night soil.

    (ii)   Storage of water in building.

17. What are the causes of excessive reverberation and formation of echo? How do you correct for the optimum time of reverberation?

18. What is reverberation time? Give the reasons for formation of echo.

19. What are the principles to be considered for noise control?

20. Describe the various methods adopted in achieving noise control.

21. Define noise. What are the effects of noise pollution? What are different methods to control noise?

22. A studio has dimensions $10 \times 7 \times 5$ m. Ceiling is provided with acoustical tiles with absorption coefficient 0.4 and curtains with heavy folds on one of short walls with coefficient 0.5. Absorption power of other surfaces of studio may be taken as 8.5 m^2 sabines. Calculate extra absorption units required for reverberation time of 1 sec.

23. What is reverberation time? Why echoes are formed?

24. Write a short note on: Rain water harvesting and future scope of it.

25. What are the different methods opted for RWH? Explain in detail.

UNIVERSITY QUESTIONS

May 2014

1. What are Acoustical defects? Explain any two in details.

Dec. 2015

1. Explain the important aspects of Noise and Acoustics.

Chapter 8
VENTILATION

8.1 INTRODUCTION

Our body produces heat continuously during its metabolic activity of converting the food we eat into living matter and energy required for doing work. Only some 20% of the energy produced is utilized by the body, the remaining 80% is to be dissipated as surplus heat from the system.

Heat may also be gained by the body from the environment by the following processes:

(i) **Conduction** by contact with warmer objects,

(ii) **Absorption** of heat from warmer enveloping air and,

(iii) **Radiation** by exposure to heat rays from the sun or hotter objects in the vicinity.

Dissipation of excess of heat, generated by metabolic activity and heat gained by the body, is very essential in order to maintain the intestinal temperature or deep body temperature constant around 37°C.

Excess body heat can be dissipated by conduction, convection, radiation and evaporation.

Heat loss by *conduction* depends upon the temperature gradient between the skin temperature and colder objects in contact with the skin.

Heat loss by *convection* is due to heat transmission from the body to the cooler air surrounding it. The heat loss increases with a faster rate of air movement around the body.

Heat loss by *radiation* is governed by the temperature difference between the skin and the objects surrounding it (but not touching it).

Heat loss by *evaporation* depends on the humidity of surrounding air and on the amount of body moisture available for evaporation. Low humidity of ambient air promotes a greater rate of evaporation.

To maintain the heat balance of the body, the excess of heat generated and gained by the body must be equal to the heat lost by the body.

In a hot environment, the heat acquired is more than the heat lost; blood circulation to the skin increases and skin temperature increases. If heat acquisition continues, the body sweats or perspires to prevent continued rise in skin temperature. In this condition, air movement close to the skin will reduce heat stress by dissipating heat from the body by evaporation of the sweat, particularly when the relative humidity is high and air temperature is near body temperature.

People consume oxygen, by inhaling air and exhale carbon dioxide. An average person, depending on his activity, inhales about 0.5 to 5 m^3/hr. In a closed environment, oxygen content is reduced and the carbon dioxide content is increased by man's presence. [Biologically the limit for comfortable existence is 0.5% CO_2 content by volume but a 0.15% increase is perceptible, because of the discomfort caused.]

The content of carbon dioxide in air rarely exceeds 0.5 to 1%. Body smells, fumes and vapours produced by a variety of processes such as combustion from the kitchen and other heating appliances, smoking etc., result in vitiating the air.

Hence, a supply of fresh air is required to supply oxygen to the human body and to maintain carbon dioxide concentration in the air within safe limits; for the control of odours, for the removal of products of combustion or other contaminants in air and to provide such a thermal environment as will assist in the maintenance of heat balance of the body to prevent discomfort and injury to health of the occupants.

Ventilation may be defined as the process of removing vitiated air from an enclosed space and supplying fresh air, either by natural or artificial means.

8.2 COMFORT FACTORS FOR VENTILATION

Where no products of combustion or other contaminants are to be removed from air, the amount of fresh air required for dilution of inside air to prevent vitiation of air by body odours depends on the air space available per person and the degree of physical activity. The amount of air requirement increases with decrease in air space per person and it may vary from 20 to 30 m^3 per person per hour.

Table 8.1

Space to be ventilated	Air changes per hour
Assembly Halls / Auditoria	3 – 6
Bed Rooms / Living Rooms	3 – 6
Bath Rooms / Toilets	6 – 12
Cafes / Restaurants	12 – 15
Cinema halls / Theatres	6 – 9
Class Rooms	3 – 6
Factories (Medium metal work)	3 – 6
Garages	12 – 15
Hospital wards	3 – 6
Kitchen (Common)	6 – 9
Kitchen (Domestic)	3 – 6
Laboratories	3 – 6
Offices	3 – 6

Requirement of air for different occupancies may be expressed in terms of air changes per hour which indicate the replacement of air in an occupancy by fresh air, expressed as the number of times such replacement is effected in an hour.

The following values of air changes are recommended by the National Building Code of India, based on maintenance of required levels of oxygen, carbon dioxide and other air quality parameters and for the control of body odours when no products of combustion or other contaminants are present in the air.

Air Change per Hour: It is the volume of outside air allowed into a room in terms of the number of room volumes exchanged, in one hour.

Thermal comfort is that condition of thermal environment, in which a person can maintain a bodily heat balance at normal body temperature without perceptible sweating.

Air movement is necessary in hot and humid weather for body cooling. A certain minimum desirable wind speed is needed for achieving thermal comfort at different temperatures and relative humidities.

As per the National Building code of India, the following wind speeds are recommended:

Case 1: Applicable to sedentary work in offices and other places having no noticeable sources of heat gain.

Table 8.2: Desirable wind speeds in m/s for thermal comfort conditions

Dry bulb	Relative Humidity (percentage)						
temperature in °C	30	40	50	60	70	80	90
28	×	×	×	×	×	×	×
29	×	×	×	×	×	0.06	0.19
30	×	×	×	0.06	0.24	0.53	0.85
31	×	0.06	0.24	0.53	1.04	1.47	2.10
32	0.20	0.46	0.94	1.59	2.26	3.04	H
33	0.77	1.36	2.12	3.00	H	H	H
34	1.85	2.72	H	H	H	H	H
35	3.20	H	H	H	H	H	H

× - None, H - Higher than those acceptable in practice

Case 2: In somewhat warmer conditions such as in godowns and machine shops where work is of lighter intensity and higher temperatures can be tolerated without much discomfort, minimum wind speeds for just acceptable warm conditions are given in the following Table 8.3.

Table 8.3: Minimum wind speeds in m/s for just acceptable warm conditions

Dry bulb temperature in °C	Relative Humidity (percentage)						
	30	40	50	60	70	80	90
28	×	×	×	×	×	×	×
29	×	×	×	×	×	×	×
30	×	×	×	×	×	×	×
31	×	×	×	×	×	0.06	0.23
32	×	×	×	0.09	0.29	0.60	0.94
33	×	0.04	0.24	0.60	1.04	1.85	2.10
34	0.15	0.46	0.94	1.60	2.26	3.05	H
35	0.68	1.36	2.10	3.05	H	H	H
36	1.72	2.70	H	H	H	H	H

× - None, H - Higher than those acceptable in practice

For normal industrial working activity for a worker with light clothing, the wet-bulb temperature may not exceed 29°C and a minimum air velocity of 30 m/min. may be provided.

In relation to the dry bulb temperature, the wet bulb temperature of air in the work room, as far as practicable, should not exceed that given in the following Table 8.4.

Table 8.4

Dry bulb temperature in °C	Maximum wet bulb temperature in °C
30	29.0
35	28.5
40	28.0
45	27.5
50	27.0

The industry should not allow the thermal conditions to go beyond the above limits, for more than one hour continuously.

Efficiency decreases with rise in the dry bulb temperature for a given wet bulb temperature attained and efforts should be made to bring down the dry bulb temperature as much as possible. Long exposures to temperatures of 50°C dry bulb and 27°C wet bulb may prove dangerous.

[**Note: Dry bulb temperature:** It is the temperature of air, read on a thermometer, taken in such a way as to avoid errors due to radiation.

Wet bulb temperature: The steady temperature finally given by a thermometer having its bulb covered with gauge or muslin moistened with distilled water and placed in an air stream of not less than 4.5 m/s.]

8.3 SYSTEMS OF VENTILATION

(I)   Natural System

(II) Mechanical System.

(I) Natural Ventilation:

It is achieved by natural means through windows and ventilators.

Natural ventilation may be achieved by:

1. **Wind effect** which depends on the direction and velocity of wind outside and sizes and disposition of openings.

2. **Stack effect** arising from difference in air temperature or vapour pressure between inside and outside the room and the difference in height between the inlet and outlet openings.

1. Ventilation due to Wind Effect

The general direction of prevailing winds is made use of, as far as possible, in the location of openings in buildings, for natural ventilation.

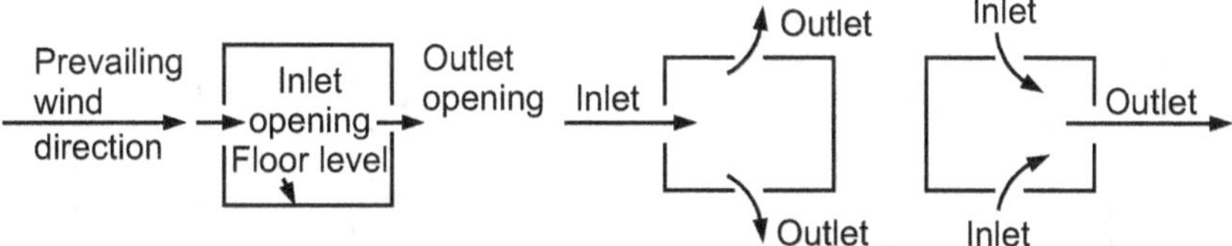

Fig. 8.1: Movement of wind through buildings

At the stage of planning itself, *orientation* of buildings with respect to the wind direction could gain some advantage in ventilation and removal of heat from inside buildings, so that the inside temperature is kept close to, if not lower than, the ambient temperature.

General Rules for Location of Windows:

•   Inlet openings in the building should be well distributed and should be located on the windward side at a low level and outlet openings should be located on the leeward side near the top, so that the incoming air passes over the occupants.

•   When outlets also serve as inlets, they should be at the same level.

•   Inlet openings should not, as far as possible, be obstructed by buildings, trees, signboards etc.

- If inlet and outlet openings are of nearly equal areas, then greater flow per unit area of openings is obtained.

- If only one wall of a room is exposed to the outer atmosphere, it is better to provide two small windows in the wall than to provide one large window.

- As per the National Building Code of India, the minimum area of openings, excluding doors should not be less than,

  (a) One-tenth of the floor area for dry hot climate,

  (b) One-sixth of the floor area for wet hot climate,

  (c) One-eighth of the floor area for intermediate climate,

  (d) One-twelfth of the floor area for cold climate.

2. Ventilation due to Stack Effect

Natural ventilation by stack effect occurs when air inside a building is at a different temperature than air outside. Thus, in heated buildings or in buildings wherein hot processes are carried out and in ordinary buildings during summer nights and pre-monsoon periods, the inside temperature is higher than that of outside, in which case, cool air will tend to enter through openings at low level and warm air will tend to leave through openings at high level. It would, therefore, be advantageous to provide ventilators as close to the ceiling as possible.

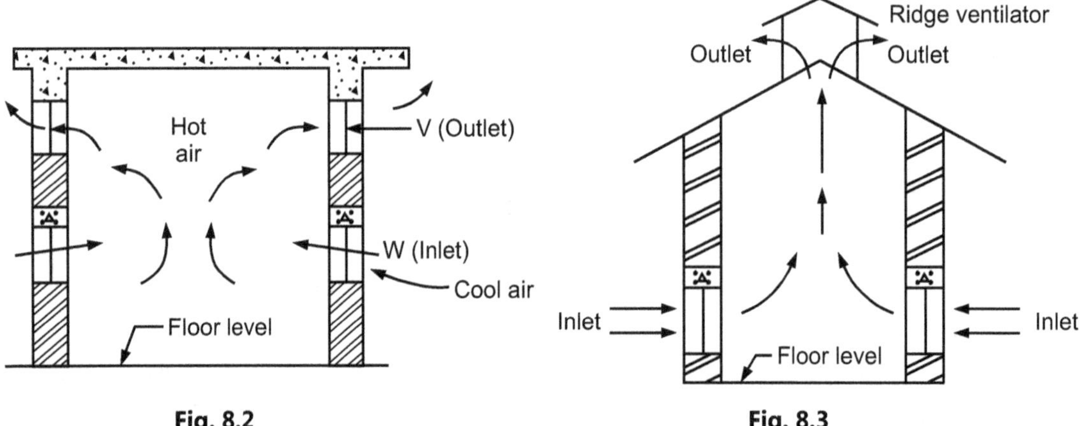

Fig. 8.2   **Fig. 8.3**

Calculation of Window Areas / Rate of Ventilation in Case of:

1. Ventilation due to Wind:

Based on the wind speed and angle of incidence of wind on the openings in buildings, the quantity of air through ventilating openings by wind action is given by,

$$Q = KAV$$

where, Q = Rate of air flow, in m^3/h

A = Free area of inlet openings, in m^2

V = Velocity of wind, in m/h

K = Coefficient of effectiveness of openings.

The effectiveness of the openings, K, depends on the direction of the wind relative to the openings and on the ratio between the areas of inlet and outlet openings. It also depends on the ratios of larger openings to the smaller openings.

When inlet openings and outlet openings are equal in area,

Value of K = 0.6 for winds perpendicular to openings and K = 0.3 for winds at an angle less than $45°$ to the openings.

SOLVED EXAMPLES

Example 8.1: Calculate the area of openings required for ventilating a living room of size 5 m × 4 m × 3 m in dry hot climate, if the wind is blowing at a velocity of 7.5 km/h perpendicular to the openings.

Solution: According to the table of number of air changes for different occupancies (Table 8.1) for a living room the number of air changes required is 3 to 6 per hour.

Assuming minimum 3 air changes / hour, (the volume of fresh outside air required in m^3/h)

$$= \text{(Number of air changes/h)} \times \text{(Volume of the room in } m^3)$$

Hence, Q (m^3/h)   = 3/h × (5 m × 4 m × 3 m)

Also, Q = KAV,   Q = 180 m^3/h, V = 7,500 m/h and

Assuming   K = 0.6 for winds perpendicular to openings,

180 m^3/h = 0.6 × A × 7500 m/h

$$A = \frac{180 \ (m^3/h)}{0.6 \times 7500 \ (m/h)} = 0.04 \ m^2 \ \text{(minimum)}$$

As per National Building Code, for dry hot climate, the minimum area of opening,

$$= \frac{1}{10} \text{ th of floor area}$$

$$= \frac{1}{10} \times (5 \times 4) \ m^2 = 2 \ m^2$$

Hence, required area of opening is 2 m^2.

(Here the local bye-laws should also be considered).

2. Ventilation due to Stack Effect:

Ventilation due to convection effects arising from temperature difference between inside and outside air is given by

$$Q = K A \sqrt{h (t_i - t_o)}$$

where,

Q = The rate of air flow, in m^3/h

A = Free area of inlet openings, in m^2

h = Vertical distance between inlets and outlets, in m

t_i = Average temperature of indoor air at height h, in $^\circ C$

t_o = Temperature of outdoor air, in $^\circ C$

K = Constant (usually 7) governed by the difference in elevation and temperature gradient between inlet and outlet openings

Example 8.2: The internal dimensions of a factory building are 30 m × 20 m × 10 m (height). The number of air changes required per hour are 3, the indoor temperature is 36°C and outdoor temperature is 30°C. Find the area of openings required, if the distance between the inlet and outlet openings is 6 m.

Solution: Volume of fresh outside air required in m^3/h

$$Q = (\text{Number of air changes/h}) \times (\text{Volume of the room in } m^3)$$

$$Q = \frac{3}{h} \times (30 \times 20 \times 10) \ m^3 = 18{,}000 \ m^3/h$$

Also

$$Q = 7 \times A \times \sqrt{h (t_i - t_o)}$$

i.e.

$$18{,}000 \ m^3/h = 7 \times A \times \sqrt{6 (36 - 30)}$$

Therefore free area of inlet openings,

$$A = \frac{18000}{7 \times 6}$$

$$= 429 \ m^2$$

Ventilation of Industrial Buildings:

The volume of air required for ventilation of industrial buildings varies with the nature of manufacturing processes, height of buildings etc.

The supply of air from outside becomes necessary in an industrial building to remove contaminants as well as to remove heat generated.

The volume of air required for removal of heat should be calculated by using both sensible heat and latent heat.

(i) Volume of Air Required for Removing Sensible Heat: Increase in sensible heat is said to occur, when there is a direct addition of heat in a building, given off by various sources; namely, the sun, manufacturing processes, machinery, occupants etc.

The volume of outside air to be provided for removing sensible heat is calculated from

$$Q_1 = \frac{2.9768 \, K_S}{t}$$

where,

Q_1 = Quantity of air, in m³/h

K_S = Sensible heat gained, in W

t = Allowable temperature rise, in °C.

Temperature rise refers mainly to the difference between the air temperatures at the outlet (roof exit) and at the inlet openings for outside air.

Table 8.5: Allowable temperature rise values for industrial buildings

Height of outlet opening, m	Temperature rise, °C
6	3 to 4.5
9	4.5 to 6.5
12	6.5 to 11

(ii) Volume of Air Required for Removing Latent Heat: An increase in latent heat is said to take place when there is an increase in the humidity of the enclosure due to the addition of water vapour emitted by humans and from various manufacturing processes.

Therefore, if the latent heat gained from the manufacturing processes and occupants is known and a suitable value for the allowable rise in the vapour pressure is assumed, then the volume of air required for removing the latent heat is given by

$$Q_2 = \frac{4127.26 \times K_l}{h}$$

where,

Q_2 = Quantity of air, in m³/h

K_l = Latent heat gained, in W

h = Allowable vapour pressure difference, in mm of mercury.

In majority of cases, sensible heat gain will far exceed the latent heat gain.

(II) Mechanical Ventilation

When natural ventilation is not sufficient for providing the required thermal environment, mechanical ventilation may have to be resorted.

Mechanical ventilation may be achieved by means of ceiling fans, exhaust fans, positive ventilation or a combination of exhaust and positive ventilation.

- **Ceiling Fans:** These are generally provided in non-industrial occupancies and serve the purpose of creating air movement. They are, however, effective only over limited areas.

- **Exhaust/Vacuum System:** It consists of mechanically removing the used air, thus creating a zone of low pressure and letting fresh air find its way in through grills and openings.

  For removing used air, exhaust fans are provided in walls on one side of the building or in the attic and roof to draw large volumes of air through the building. These fans are usually of propeller type, since they operate against little or no resistance. Adequate inlet openings should be provided on the opposite walls to let the fresh air come inside the building.

- **Plenum System or Positive Ventilation:** In this system, fresh air is supplied into a room by mechanical means and the used air is allowed to leave through the grills and ventilators.

  Positive ventilation is provided by centrally located supply fans which are usually of the centrifugal type or sometimes axial flow type, since this application requires duct work with a wide range of satisfactory and quiet operation against high pressure. The air from such centrally located fans are supplied to individual rooms through these ducts. The ductwork should be air tight and should be properly designed to allow smooth flow of air.

  Unit ventilators may be provided for individual rooms and may be placed against the outside wall. Both the central system as well as unit ventilators, besides ventilating, may also carry out the function of cooling the incoming air by evaporation or the use of cooling coils.

- **A Balanced System:** It involves both supplying and removing of air by mechanical means. The exhaust system will remove ventilated air from inside and positive ventilation will supply fresh air from outside to replace the air driven out by the exhaust system. Hence, a balanced system has the advantage of providing better control conditions and better distribution of air over the entire area of occupancy, particularly in big buildings. This system consists of supplying sufficient volumes of air in proportion to heat load generated in the respective areas, at suitable velocities, at the required areas through duct work and by extracting used air in the return ducts in proportion to the supplied air quantities and recirculating the air or a part of it after properly mixing it with cool fresh air.

- **Air Conditioning:** Air conditioning may be provided where the desired temperatures and humidities cannot be obtained by mere ventilation.

  Air conditioning is the process of treating air so as to control simultaneously its temperature, humidity, purity and distribution to meet the requirements of the enclosed space.

8.4 AIR CONDITIONING

Necessity:

In rapidly developing cities, land area available for construction of houses is progressively reducing and the cost of construction, particularly in busy localities, is steadily increasing. It is no longer possible to construct independent houses, economically, conforming with specific conditions of aspects and orientation; in order to derive maximum benefits from natural light and ventilation. Also regional or local parameters such as temperature and humidity may be inclement and not contributory to creature comfort. Hence, in congested housing complexes and also in houses in regions of extremely hot, humid, cold or polluted environment, conditioning of air is desirable to maintain living comfort and well-being of inmates.

The following are the functions of a modern heating, ventilating and air conditioning system for a building:

- Control of air temperature at desired values at all times by heating or cooling,

- Control of air humidity (water vapour content) by humidification or dehumidification,

- Control of air movement at a desirable velocity,

- Introduction of outside air as required,

- Control of air quality by removal of particles of dust and gaseous pollutants,

- Control of sound produced by the air conditioning system itself.

Air conditioning is used for two purposes, for providing comfort to people in a living space or a working space or for control of a process. Comfort refers to supply of conditioned air that provides satisfaction to people in terms of creature comforts. Process control refers to air conditions, that are required to carry out or improve some operations of a process. For example, Textile industry requires dry bulb temperature of about 25°C and relative humidity of 50 - 85%. Rubber industry requires dry bulb temperature of 25° - 35°C and relative humidity of 25 - 50%.

8.5 COMFORT AIR CONDITIONING

Design Conditions: Cooling load calculations are usually based on inside and outdoor conditions of temperature and humidity.

Table 8.6: Inside design conditions for summer

Sr.	Optimum conditions		Maximum conditions	
No.	Dry bulb temp.	Wet bulb temp.	Dry bulb temp.	Wet bulb temp.
(1)	(2) °C	(3) °C	(4) °C	(5) °C
(i)	23.3	19.4	25.9	21.8
(ii)	23.9	18.4	26.1	21.6
(iii)	24.4	17.6	26.7	20.9
(iv)	25.0	16.8	27.2	20.1
(v)	25.6	16.0	27.8	19.4
(vi)	26.1	15.2	28.3	18.8
(vii)	–	–	28.9	18.1
(viii)	–	–	29.4	17.5

Table 8.7: Inside design conditions for winter

Sr.	Optimum conditions		Maximum conditions	
No.	Dry bulb temp.	Wet bulb temp.	Dry bulb temp.	Wet bulb temp.
(1)	(2) °C	(3) °C	(4) °C	(5) °C
(i)	21.4	17.8	18.3	15.0
(ii)	21.7	17.3	18.9	13.4
(iii)	22.2	16.4	19.4	12.0
(iv)	22.8	15.3	19.7	10.8
(v)	23.3	14.4	–	–
(vi)	23.6	13.4	–	–

Inside conditions are those that provide comfort (Table 8.6 and Table 8.7).

Outside design conditions are based on dry bulb and wet bulb temperatures for summer months for different cities in India, based on a 10 year data (Table 8.8). Based on the outside design conditions and required comfort conditions inside, the amount of heat to be removed and the change in humidity can be calculated. This would require a certain rate of movement of air (Table 8.9).

Comfort Factors for Air Conditioning

For comfort air conditioning, dry bulb and wet bulb temperatures may be adopted as given in the following Table 8.8.

Table 8.8: Outside design conditions for summer

City	Temperature, °C							
	Dry Bulb				Wet Bulb			
	1%	2.5%	5%	10%	1%	2.5%	5%	10%
Ahmedabad	42.8	41.7	40.7	39.5	27.6	27.2	26.9	26.4
Amritsar	42.5	41.5	40.3	38.4	27.9	26.9	26.3	25.3
Bhopal	41.7	40.8	39.8	38.5	25.3	24.8	24.4	23.8
Mumbai	34.5	33.8	33.6	32.8	28.4	28.0	27.8	27.4
Kolkatta	39.5	38.3	37.4	35.6	29.3	29.2	28.8	28.4
Coimbatore	36.7	35.9	34.9	33.7	28.3	27.4	26.7	25.9
Delhi	43.0	41.9	41.4	40.3	28.1	27.2	26.4	25.8
Hyderabad	39.5	38.7	37.9	36.7	25.3	24.4	23.9	23.5
Jodhpur	43.5	42.5	41.3	40.0	27.9	27.2	26.5	25.8
Lucknow	42.8	41.9	41.0	39.5	28.3	27.7	27.2	26.5
Chennai	39.2	37.8	36.9	35.5	28.5	28.2	27.8	27.4
Nagpur	42.9	42.0	41.1	39.9	27.5	26.2	25.6	25.1
Patna	42.4	41.1	39.9	38.3	28.1	27.8	27.4	27.1
Roorkee	42.5	41.4	40.6	39.2	27.8	26.9	26.1	25.6
Trivendrum	32.9	32.4	31.8	31.0	27.2	26.9	26.7	26.4
Vishakhapatnam	38.4	37.0	36.0	35.1	30.4	29.7	29.3	28.8

As far as possible, thermal shock of more than 11°C should be avoided.

Adequate movement of air should be provided in an air conditioned enclosure. Air velocities in the zone between floor level and 1.5 m level should be 0.25 m/s in the case of comfort air conditioning. Air velocity in excess of 0.5 m/s in this zone should be avoided.

The total minimum outside fresh air introduced into an enclosure by an air conditioning plant or unit is related to the number of occupants in the enclosure at any time, whether they are smokers or non-smokers and to the cubic contents of the enclosed space as per the following Table 8.9.

Table 8.9: Minimum fresh air requirements

Sr. No.	Applications	Smoking	Air requirement in m^3/min.		Per m^2 of floor area
			Recommended	Minimum	
(1)	(2)	(3)	(4)	(5)	(6)
(i)	Apartments	Some	0.56	0.28	–
(ii)	Banking space	Occasional	0.28	0.21	–
(iii)	Board rooms	Very heavy	1.40	0.56	–
(iv)	Department stores	None	0.21	0.14	0.015
(v)	Directors rooms	Very heavy	1.40	0.84	–
(vi)	Drug stores	Considerable	0.28	0.21	–
(vii)	Factories	None	0.28	0.21	0.03
(viii)	Garages	–	–	–	0.30
(ix)	Hospitals:				
	(a) Operating rooms (all fresh air)	None	–	–	0.60
	(b) Private rooms	None	0.84	0.70	0.10
	(c) Wards	None	0.56	0.28	–
(x)	Hotel rooms	Heavy	0.84	0.70	0.10
(xi)	Kitchens:				
	(a) Restaurant	–	–	–	1.20
	(b) Residence	–	–	–	0.60
(xii)	Laboratories	Some	0.56	0.42	–
(xiii)	Meeting rooms	Very heavy	1.40	0.84	0.38
(xiv)	Offices:				
	(a) General	None	0.42	0.28	–
	(b) Private	Some	0.70	0.42	0.08
		Considerable	0.84	0.70	0.08
(xv)	Restaurants:				
	(a) Cafeteria	Considerable	0.34	0.28	–
	(b) Dining room	Considerable	0.42	0.34	–
(xvi)	Retail shop	None	0.28	0.21	–
(xvii)	Theatre	None	0.21	0.14	–
		Some	0.42	0.28	–
(xviii)	Toilets (exhaust)	–	–	–	0.60

The above table is to be used only when the contamination of the air in the conditioned enclosure results solely from respiratory and other physiological activities of occupants or due to their smoking.

8.6 THE COOLING LOAD

The interior of a building gains heat from a number of sources. If the temperature and humidity of the rooms are to be maintained at a comfortable level, heat must be extracted to offset these heat gains. The net amount of heat that is removed is called the **cooling load**.

The gross room heat gain is the rate at which heat is being received in the room at any time. This heat gain is made up of the following components from many sources:

- Conduction through exterior walls, roof and glass.
- Conduction through interior partitions, ceilings and floors.
- Solar radiation through glass.
- Lighting.
- People.
- Equipment and furniture.
- Heat from infiltration of outside air through openings.

Heat gains can be classified into two groups: Sensible and latent heat gains.

   (a) Sensible heat gains result in increasing the air temperature.

   (b) Latent heat gains are due to addition of water vapour, thus increasing humidity.

Items 1 through 4 are solely sensible heat gains, items 5 and 7 are partly sensible and partly latent, item 6 can be either sensible or latent or both depending on the type of equipment and the process carried out.

Procedure for Calculating Cooling Load for a Building:

1. Select inside and outside design temperatures from tables 8.6, 8.7 and 8.8.
2. Use building plans to measure dimensions of all surfaces through which there will be external heat gain for each room.
3. Calculate areas of all these surfaces.
4. Select heat transfer coefficient for each material.
5. Calculate the heat gain through structure i.e. through walls, roof, ceiling and floor by using the following equation

$$Q = U \times A \times ETD$$

where, Q = Sensible heat gain, in kcal/h

U = Overall heat transfer coefficient between the adjacent and conditioned space, in kcal/h $\times$ m^2 $\times$ °C

A = Area of the separating section concerned, in m^2

ETD = Equivalent temperature difference between outdoor and indoor, in °C

6. Calculate heat gain through glass.

Radiant energy from the sun passes through transparent materials such as glass and becomes a heat gain to the room. Its value varies with time, orientation, shading and storage effect. The net heat gain can be found from the following equation

$$Q = \text{SHGF} \times A \times \text{SC} \times \text{CLF}$$

where,
Q = Net solar radiation heat gain through glass, in kcal/h

SHGF = Solar heat gain factor, in kcal/h-m^2

A = Area of glass, in m^2

SC = Shade coefficient

CLF = Cooling load factor for glass

7. Calculate heat gain from people. This consists of two parts-sensible heat and latent heat resulting from respiration.

Following equations may be used

$$Q_s = q_s \times n \times \text{CLF}$$

and

$$Q_L = q_L \times n$$

where,
Q_s = Sensible heat gain

Q_L = Latent heat gain

q_s = Sensible heat gain per person

q_L = Latent heat gain per person

n = Number of people

CLF = Cooling load factor for people

8. Heat gain from equipment may be found directly from the manufacturers.

9. Find the heat load from outdoor air and ventilation using the following equations.

$$Q_s = V \times (t_o - t_i) \times \rho_a \times S_a$$

and

$$Q_L = V \times (W_s - W_i) \times \rho_a \times C$$

where,
Q_s = Sensible heat gain

Q_L = Latent heat gain

V = Volume of outdoor air, in m³/h

t_o = Outdoor dry bulb temperature, in °C

t_i = Indoor dry bulb temperature, in °C

r_a = Density of air

S_a = Specific heat of dry air

W_s = Outdoor humidity ratio, kg of moisture per kg of dry air

W_i = Indoor humidity ratio, kg of moisture per kg of dry air

C = Constant approximating the average kilocalories released in condensing one kg of water vapour from air

10. Add heat gains due to supply ducts, leakage in ducts, heat gain due to supply fans etc.

11. Calculate required supply air conditions. All the heat gains must be offset by supplying air at a temperature and humidity low enough so that it can absorb these heat gains. The supply air takes care of removing both sensible and latent heat gains. In order to find the outside air load, psychrometric charts are used. The psychrometric chart is a graphical representation of the properties of atmospheric air.

8.7 COMPONENTS OF AIR CONDITIONING SYSTEM

Any air conditioning system has the following basic components:

- Heating,
- Humidifying,
- Filtering and cleaning,
- Circulating,
- Dehumidifying and
- Cooling.

Depending upon the season, there are two types of air conditioning systems - (a) winter air conditioning, and (b) summer air conditioning.

(a) Winter Air Conditioning

In winter, if the air in a building is to be maintained at a comfortable temperature, heat must be furnished to the air in the rooms. This is because there is a continuous heat loss to the outdoor surroundings, that are at a lower temperature. If this loss of heat is not replenished, the room temperatures will fall rapidly. Also if the air is very dry, certain amount of moisture will have to be added to the air. Therefore, during winter, heating and humidifying equipment is used.

Heating of air may be done by using radiators.

Humidifying devices provide a means of turning water into water vapour and mixing this vapour with air in the occupied space.

This can be done by many methods:

1. Exposing a large surface of water to air being humidified, or

2. Spraying atomised water into air being humidified.

The simplest spray system passes water directly from the city water system through spray nozzles which break the water up into very small droplets. The spray humidifiers are followed by elimination plates so arranged that when the air passes over these plates, the droplets of water are removed from air.

Humidification is important because, a dry atmosphere causes dry skin which may lead to dermititis in the form of flaking or scaling of the skin; breathing dryness and loss of moisture from hygroscopic materials such as wood, natural fibres and most foods.

A simple flow diagram of the operations carried out in the winter air conditioning system can be shown as follows:

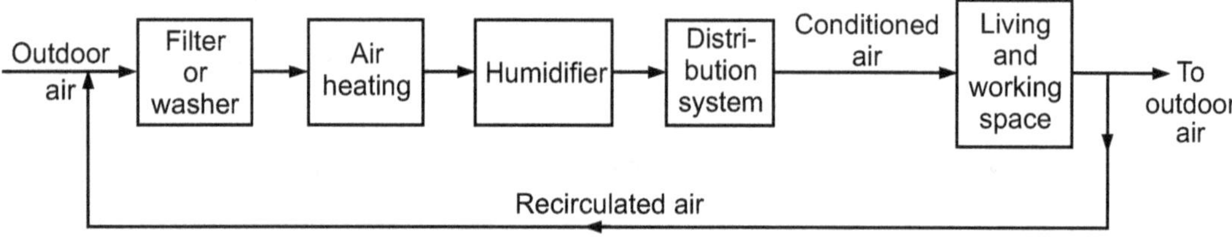

Fig. 8.4: Winter air conditioning

(b) Summer Air Conditioning

In summer, in order to maintain the room air at a comfortable temperature, there must be continuous removal of heat from the room to offset the heat gains from the surroundings. The equipment that removes this heat is called a cooling system.

Cooling of air is done by several methods:

- By mechanical refrigeration.

- By using ice.

In mechanical refrigeration, air is passed over cooled surfaces of metal coils which contain a volatile refrigerant.

In ice system of air conditioning, cooling is done by melting ice, this is a practical method for theatres and public halls that have short operating houses and relatively high peak loads. Since, mechanical refrigeration equipment is expensive for short periods, ice can be used.

In a cooling cycle, the dry bulb temperature of the air is lowered. When this happens, the relative humidity increases. Some moisture must be removed to make this air comfortable.

Excess humidity will cause condensation on window panes. Also, the rate of evaporation of perspiration being low, causes a wet and clammy feeling to the occupants. Very humid atmosphere also encourages the growth of several types of fungi and other micro-organisms. Therefore, dehumidification is carried out to remove the excess moisture.

Dehumidification may be done by two methods:

- Dehydrating the air with chemicals or

- Cooling the air to below dew point, then removing the excess moisture by condensing it on a cool surface. The air is then reheated to the desired temperature with dry heat.

In general, air filtering and circulating equipment are the same for both winter and summer air conditioning.

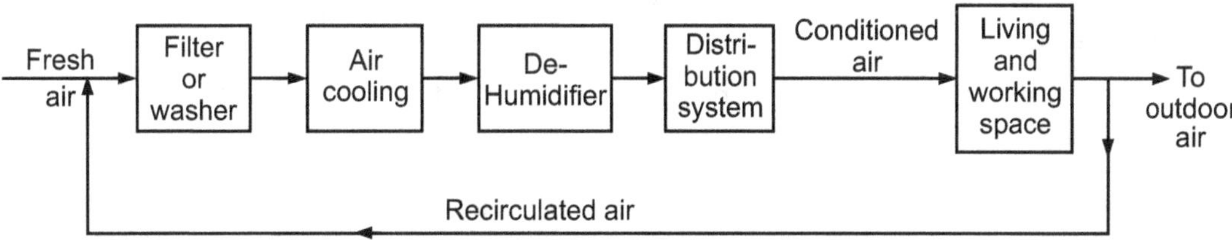

Fig. 8.5: Summer air conditioning

Air Cleaning:

Cleaning the air is a very important part of air conditioning.

Air contaminants include solids, liquids, gases and vapours. Efficient air conditioning systems will remove 75 to 95% of these contaminants.

Suspended solid particles are of the following three types:

(1) Dust which can have its origin in animal, vegetable or mineral matter.

(2) Fumes formed from materials that are ordinarily solids, but have been put into a gaseous state usually by an industrial or chemical process.

(3) Smoke caused by incomplete combination, consists of solid particles carried into the atmosphere by the gaseous products of combustion.

Liquid contaminants include the following:

(a) Mists: These small liquid particles are mechanically ejected into the air by splashing, mixing or atomizing.

(b) Fogs: These are small liquid particles formed by condensation.

Gaseous contaminants include carbon monoxide, sulphur oxides, nitrogen oxides and hydrocarbons.

The air cleaning devices must also be able to remove pollen, bacteria and molds from the air.

Removal of solid contaminants can be done by using any of the following methods:

- Centrifuging force for large particles,
- Washing the air for particles that can be wetted,
- Screens to block the larger particles.

(c) Adhesives: These are filters made of various fibres - glass, cotton, synthetic material and aluminium.

Fibres of adhesive filters are coated with adhesive liquid or oil. Air is forced to pass over these filters and the dust particles stick to the adhesive surface. When these filters get chocked with clogged dust over a period of time, they may either be washed and reused or replaced.

(d) Electrostatic Precipitators: These electrically charge the particles and make them adhere to a surface of opposite charge.

To remove liquids, liquid absorbents can be used. These are chemicals that absorb or react with the liquid contaminant.

To remove gases and vapours, the following methods can be adopted:

(i) Condensation: Cool the contaminant gas to its dew point and remove as a liquid.

(ii) Chemical Reaction: Pass the gas through a chemical which will remove the gas as a reaction product.

(iii) Dilution: Mix the gas with air.

(iv) Adsorption: Pass the gas over an adsorbent (e.g.: activated carbon).

8.8 AIR DISTRIBUTION SYSTEM

To deliver air to the conditioned space, air carriers are needed. These carriers are called ducts. They are made of steel, aluminum alloy or some non-combustible material such as clay or asbestos cement.

Ducts work on the principle of air pressure difference. Air will flow from a higher-pressure area to a lower pressure area.

There are three types of ducts:

1. Conditioned air ducts,
2. Recirculating air ducts,
3. Fresh air ducts.

Ducts may be round, square or rectangular in cross-section.

They should be made substantially air-tight throughout and should have no openings other than those required for proper operation and maintenance of the system.

8.9 SYSTEMS OF AIR CONDITIONING

1. Room Air Conditioner

It is also called unitary air conditioner and it is popular in moderate climates.

This consists of an encased assembly designed as a self-contained unit, primarily for mounting in a window or through the wall or as a console. It consists of a compressor, heat exchangers and air handling system installed in one cabinet. It is designed essentially to provide free delivery of conditioned air to an enclosed space, room or zone. It includes a prime source of refrigeration for cooling and dehumidification and means for circulation and filtering of air. It also includes means for exhausting air. It may also include means for heating, humidifying or inducting fresh air. It is factory assembled. No ducts are needed for air distribution.

2. Packaged Air Conditioners

Packaged air conditioning units come with all the needed equipments in a single cabinet and are suitable for offices, banks, shops, residences and some plants.

Window units are available upto a limited capacity. Large packaged units have ductwork for fully automatic room conditioning that is too large for one outlet.

3. Central Air Conditioning System

A central air conditioning system has all the major items of equipment like filters, air washers, fans and refrigeration machinery in one centrally located space, removed from the area to be conditioned. The conditioned air is distributed to the desired spaces through a network of ductwork.

Advantages of a Central Air Conditioning System

- The space occupied by the equipment need not be very valuable. The equipment can be located in the basement of a large building.

- For a large conditioning load the equipment may cost less.

- The maintenance and inspection of a central system does not disturb the people in the conditioned areas.

- The exhaust air can be returned and partly reused with obvious savings in heating and refrigeration.

IMPORTANT POINTS

- Types of ventilation and its two types:
  - (a) Natural system
  - (b) Mechanical system.
- Natural system in detail.

- Mechanical ventilation and its cooling types.
- Need for air conditioning for cooling with its comfort temperatures in different conditions.
- Ventilation need and factors affecting ventilation.
- Components of air conditioning system.
- Systems of air conditioning.

QUESTIONS

1. Explain with a neat diagram summer air-conditioning.
2. Explain with diagram winter air-conditioning.
3. Explain briefly the working principles of comfort air-conditioning.
4. Explain with sketches wind effects and stack effects.
5. What are the circumstances in which mechanical system of ventilation is adopted?
6. Explain in details Natural system of ventilation.
7. State different methods of mechanical ventilation. Explain only one in detail.
8. Explain with sketches various units of an air-conditioning system.
9. Differentiate between summer and winter air-conditioning.
10. Differentiate between:
    (a) Natural and Artificial ventilation.
    (b) Humidification and Dehumidification.

UNIVERSITY QUESTIONS

Dec. 2015

1. Why is the ventilation necessary? Also, explain various objectives of ventilation.

Chapter 9
LIGHTING

9.1 INTRODUCTION

The most important means of communication of man with his environment is vision. The eye is stimulated by light reflected from various surrounding objects of the man. Hence, light is essential for seeing.

The purposes of lighting are:

- To facilitate the performance of a visual task and ensure visual comfort,

- To ensure the safety of people using the building by providing well illuminated stairways passages etc. and

- To create a certain emotional effect such as a sense of well being in a pleasant environment.

Light can be obtained naturally from the sun or artificially, the major source of light being, of course, the sun.

Units:

I : The *intensity* of a light source is measured in units of *candela* (cd). This is the basic assumed and agreed unit in the System International. This is defined as the intensity of a $\dfrac{1}{60}$ cm^2 uniformly emitting black body radiator, at the melting point temperature of platinum. All other units are derived from this.

ϕ : The flux (or flow) of light is measured in lumens (lm).

One lumen is the flow of light emitted by a unit intensity (1 cd) point source, within a unit solid angle. As the surface of a sphere subtends at its centre 4π (= 12.56) units of solid angle, a 1 cd point source will emit a total of 12.56 lm in all directions.

E : Illumination is measured as the amount of flux falling on unit area, i.e. lm/m^2 which is a *lux*, the unit of illumination in the System International.

L : Luminance is the measure of brightness of a surface.

If a light source of 1 cd intensity has a surface area of 1 m^2 (i.e. 1 cd is distributed over 1 m^2), its luminance is 1 cd/m^2. This is the SI unit of luminance.

9.2 PRINCIPLES OF GOOD LIGHTING

- Visual efficiency depends strongly on lighting and it is generally measured in terms of sharpness of vision, contrast sensitivity and visual performance.
- Careful planning of the brightness and colour pattern within the working area as well as the surrounding area is necessary in order to draw attention to the important area, details are seen quickly and accurately and the room is free from any sense of gloom or monotony.
- Directional lighting should be used where necessary to assist perception of task detail and to give good modeling.
- Proper attention should be given to the colour of light as well as light distribution i.e. whether direct or different.
- Direct and reflected glare from light sources should be controlled to minimize visual discomfort.
- Excessive contrast between the illumination levels of the object and its surroundings may also cause visual discomfort. This requires attention in planning the lighting of the background as well.
- Lighting throughout the building should be correlated to prevent excessive differences between adjacent areas to prevent accidents.
- The required illumination levels vary with the age of the viewer and the condition of his eye sight. The levels of illumination also change with the nature of visual task performed in a particular area.

9.3 ILLUMINATION LEVELS RECOMMENDED BY THE NATIONAL BUILDING CODE OF INDIA, FOR VARIOUS TYPES OF VISUAL TASKS

Table 9.1

Occupancy/Visual Task	Illumination, lux
1. Residential:	
General	100 - 200
Kitchen	200
Bathroom	100
Stairs	100
Sewing and Darning	700
Reading (casual)	150
Homework and sustained reading	300

contd. ...

2.	**Hotels and Restaurants:**	
	Entrance halls	150
	Reception and accounts	300
	Dining rooms (tables)	100
	Kitchens	200
	Corridors	70
	Bedrooms – General	100
	– Dressing table	200
	– Writing table	300
	Cloak rooms and toilets	100
	– Bathrooms	100
	– Stairs	100
3.	**Shops and Stores:**	
	General areas	150 - 300
	Stock rooms	200
4.	**Offices:**	
	Entrance hall and reception areas	150
	Conference rooms and executive offices	300
	General office	300
	Business machine operation	450
	Drawing office – General	300
	– Boards & tracing	450
5.	**Schools and Colleges:**	
	Assembly halls	
	– General	150
	– Examination halls	300
	Class and lecture rooms	
	– Desks	300
	– Chalk boards	200 - 300
	Art rooms	450
	Laboratories	300
	Libraries – Shelves and stacks	70 - 150
	– Reading tables	300
	Staff rooms and common rooms	150
	Offices	300

contd. ...

6.	**Hospitals:**	
	Reception and waiting rooms	150
	Wards – General	100
	– Beds	150
	Operating theatres	
	– General	300
	– Tables	Special lighting
	Casualty and outpatients	150
	Stairs and corridors	100
	Dispensaries	300
7.	**Industrial buildings:**	
	General	100 - 150
	Assembly shops:	
	(a) Rough work e.g. assembly of heavy machinery.	150
	(b) Medium work e.g. assembly of machined parts.	300
	(c) Fine work e.g. radio and telephone equipment.	700
	(d) Very fine visual work e.g.	
	(i) assembly of very small precision mechanisms and instruments.	1500
	(ii) Minute processing in jewellery and watch making.	3000

9.4 DAYLIGHTING

The ultimate source of daylight is of course the sun, but the light reaching the earth from the sun may be partly diffused by the atmosphere and the local climatic conditions which in turn determines how this light will reach a building.

If we consider a point inside a building, light may reach it from the sun in the following ways:

- Direct sunlight along a straight path from the sun, through the window, to the given point,
- Light reflected externally by the ground or other buildings, through an opening,
- Light reflected internally from walls, ceiling or other internal surfaces and
- Diffused or skylight through an opening.

Daylight is an integral part of the design of most modern buildings. The requirements for good lighting design can be achieved by skilful application of daylighting techniques. These differ from the design methods for electric lighting because of variations in the amount of daylight, the changing position of the sun, the desire for a view of the outdoor etc.

9.4.1 Designing for Daylight

The following factors must be taken into consideration, to use daylight to advantage:

- Variations in the amount and direction of the incident daylight,
- Luminance distribution of clear, partly cloudy and overcast skies,
- Variations in sunlight intensity and direction, and
- Effect of local terrain, landscaping and nearby buildings on the available light.

The light received from the sun consists of two parts - direct solar illumination and sky radiation.

Direct solar illumination is not generally considered for the purpose of designing for daylight as direct sunlight adds to the thermal discomfort of the occupants in the form of heat and glare. Hence, only sky radiation is considered for illumination of building interiors during the day.

The amount of sky radiation depends on the position of the sun defined by its altitude, which in turn varies with the latitude of the locality, the day of the year and the time of the day. Refer to Table 9.2.

For Indian conditions, $15°$ solar altitude is assumed as the standard for design purposes. The external available horizontal illumination, which is assumed for design purpose in this country from north to south, is 8000 lux. However, the prevalent atmospheric haze which varies from place to place may necessitate a 25% increase in the design illumination value of 8000 lux.

The design sky is based on a *clear sky* at $15°$ altitude, as in India, the sky is generally clear for about 300 days in a year. Therefore, the sky is called clear sky.

In European countries, the design is for overcast sky as for most part of the year, the sky is overcast. The value of design illumination for overcast sky is taken as 5000 lux.

Clear Design Sky: The distribution of luminance of such a sky is non-uniform, the horizon is brighter than the zenith and the brightness at an altitude θ in the region away from the sun is expressed as $B_\theta = B_z \operatorname{cosec} \theta$.

where, θ lies between $15°$ and $90°$.

B_θ is constant when θ lies between $0°$ and $15°$.

B_z is the brightness of the zenith.

In India, the clear design sky is taken at $\theta = 15°$ as the luminance is uniform, more or less, from the horizon to an altitude of the sun at $15°$.

Table 9.2: Solar-altitudes (to the nearest degree) for Indian latitudes

Period of Year	22 JUNE						21 MARCH AND 23 SEPTEMBER						22 DECEMBER					
Hours of Day	07 00	08 00	09 00	10 00	11 00	12 00	07 00	08 00	09 00	10 00	11 00	12 00	07 00	08 00	09 00	10 00	11 00	12 00
(Sun or solar) Latitude	17 00	16 00	15 00	14 00	13 00	–	17 00	16 00	15 00	14 00	13 00	–	17 00	16 00	15 00	14 00	13 00	–
10°N	18	31	45	58	70	77	15	30	44	59	72	80	9	23	35	46	53	57
13°N	19	32	46	60	72	80	15	29	44	58	70	77	8	21	33	43	51	54
16°N	20	33	47	61	74	83	14	29	43	56	68	74	7	19	31	41	48	51
19°N	21	34	48	62	75	86	14	28	42	55	66	71	5	18	29	48	45	48
22°N	22	35	49	62	75	89	14	28	41	53	64	68	4	16	27	36	42	45
25°N	23	36	49	63	76	88	13	27	40	52	61	65	3	14	25	34	39	42
28°N	23	36	49	63	76	86	13	26	39	50	59	62	1	13	23	31	37	39
31°N	24	37	50	62	75	82	13	25	37	48	56	56	–	11	21	28	34	36
34°N	25	37	49	62	73	79	12	25	36	46	53	56	–	9	18	26	31	33

9.4.2 Daylight Factor

In a given building, the ratio of illumination at a certain point to the simultaneous outdoor illumination is a constant and this constant expressed as a percentage is known as the Daylight Factor (DF).

$$DF = \frac{E_i}{E_o} \times 100 \ (\%)$$

where,

E_i = Illumination indoors at the point taken

E_o = Illumination outdoors due to a clear design sky, direct sunlight being excluded

There are three components which contribute to the daylight factor.

1. Sky Component (SC),

2. Externally Reflected Component (ERC),

3. Internally Reflected Component (IRC).

$\therefore \qquad DF = SC + ERC + IRC$

SOLVED EXAMPLES

Example 9.1: Find daylight factor for an indoor illumination level of 100 lux.

Solution: E_i = 100 lux

E_o = 8000 lux - This is the assumed outdoor design illumination level in India.

Therefore, $\quad DF = \dfrac{100}{8000} \times 100 = 1.25\%$

The daylight factors on the horizontal plane only are usually taken, as the working plane in a room is generally horizontal; however, the factors in vertical planes should also be considered when specifying daylighting values for special cases, such as daylighting in class rooms, on blackboards, pictures and paintings hung on the walls etc.

Working plane is a horizontal plane at a level at which work is normally done, generally assumed to be at 85 cm above floor level unless specified otherwise.

9.4.3 Components of Daylight Factor

1. Sky Component (SC)

It is defined as the ratio (or percentage) of that part of the daylight illumination at a point on a given plane, which is received directly from the sky as compared to the simultaneous exterior illumination on a horizontal plane from the entire hemisphere of an unobstructed clear design sky.

The sky component level should be ensured generally on the working plane at the following positions:

- At a distance of 3 to 3.75 m from the window along the central line perpendicular to the window,

- At the centre of the room,

- At fixed locations, such as school desks, black-boards, office tables etc.

The daylight area of the prescribed sky component should not be less than half the total area of the room.

The magnitude of sky component depends on the area of sky visible from the point considered and its average altitude angle (i.e. the luminance of the sky at that angle). Therefore, the window size and position in relation to the point considered are essential for calculating the sky component.

Tables of sky components are given in IS 2440, which give the values of sky component due to a rectangular open unglazed window with no external obstructions. The values should be suitably corrected in the presence of window bars, glazing and external obstructions, if any. The tables are in terms of l/d and h/d ratios where l and h are the width and height of the window and 'd' is the distance of the reference point from the window on a line perpendicular to the plane of the opening through one of its lower corners. (Fig. 9.1, Fig. 9.2 and Fig. 9.3).

2. Externally Reflected Component (ERC):

It is defined as the ratio (or percentage) of that part of the daylight illumination at a point on a given plane, which is received by direct reflection from external surfaces, as compared to the simultaneous exterior illumination on a horizontal plane from the entire hemisphere of an unobstructed clear design sky.

If there are no obstructions outside the window, there will be no ERC.

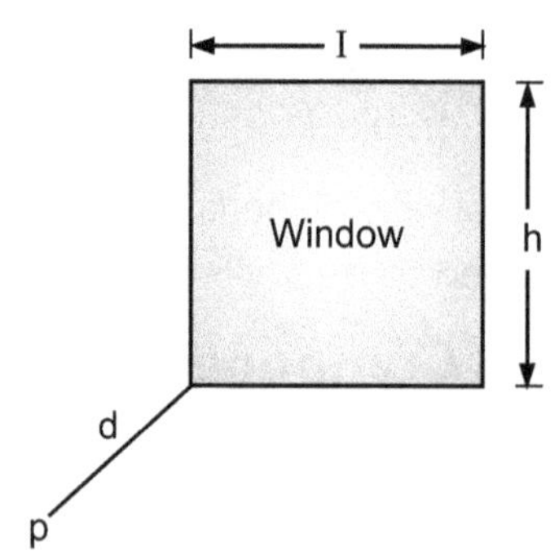

Fig. 9.1

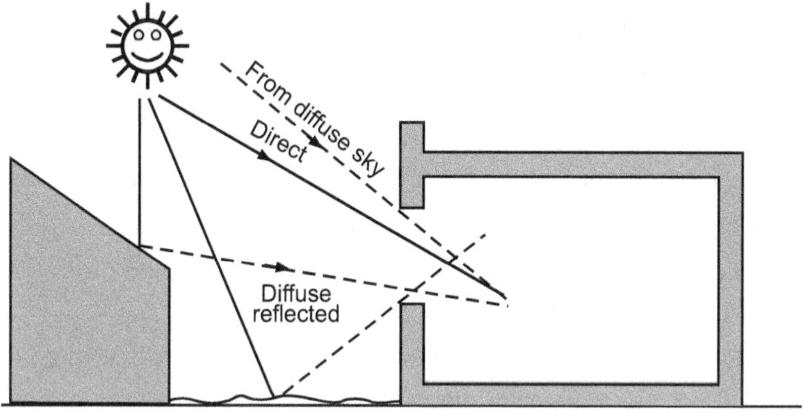

Fig. 9.2: Components of light entering a room

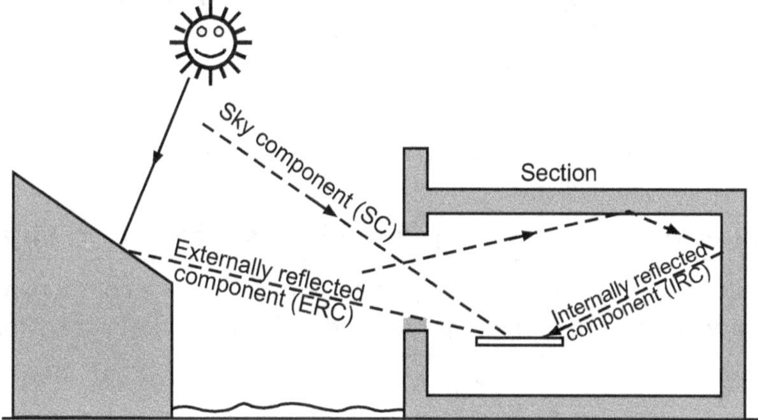

Fig. 9.3: Components of diffuse light falling on work plane in a room

3. Internally Reflected Component (IRC)

Much of the light entering through the window will reach the point considered only after reflection from the walls, ceiling, floors of other surfaces inside the room. The magnitude of this contribution to the lighting of the point considered is expressed by IRC.

It is defined as the ratio (or percentage) of that part of the daylight illumination at a point in a given plane, which is received by direct reflection or inter-reflection from the internal surfaces as referred to the simultaneous exterior illumination on a horizontal plane due to the entire hemisphere of an unobstructed clear design sky.

The portion of the light reflected by the internal surfaces is called the reflection factor. Hence, the reflection factors of various room finishes must be known, in order to calculate IRC values.

Reflection factor will be more in case of light surfaces and less in case of dark surfaces.

The values of reflection factors of the ceiling and of the walls are as follows:

White and very light colours	0.7
Light colours	0.5
Middle tints	0.3
Dark colours	0.1

IRC values can be obtained from nomograms and readily available tables.

The daylight factor (DF) will thus be obtained as a sum of SC, ERC and IRC.

$$DF = SC + ERC + IRC$$

This value of DF thus obtained, may have to be further corrected due to three factors:

(1) Glazing: If it is other than clear glass, depending upon the type of glazing used, the sky component value may have to be corrected.

(2) Framing: Depending upon the type and material of window framing, the correction factor may have to be applied. This is calculated as the ratio of net glass area to window aperture, but an average value of 0.75 may generally be used.

(3) Dirt on Glass: Correction factor will depend on the type and location of building, the pollution levels and the frequency of window cleaning, as the dirt on glass will reduce the daylight factor.

9.4.4 General Principles of Design of Windows for Good Lighting

* Generally, taller openings give greater penetrations as the sky component is more for a taller window, while broader openings give better distribution of light. (Fig. 9.4).

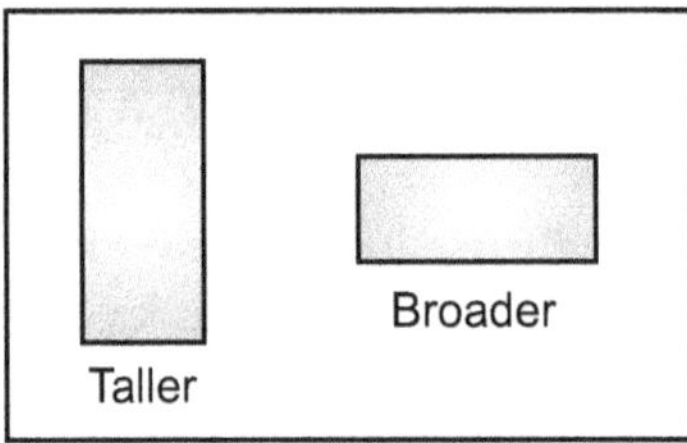

Fig. 9.4

* Broader openings may also prove to be efficient if their sills are raised by 30 to 60 cm above the working plane.

* For a given penetration, a number of smaller openings positioned along the same, adjacent or opposite walls will give better distribution of illumination than a single large opening. (Fig. 9.5).

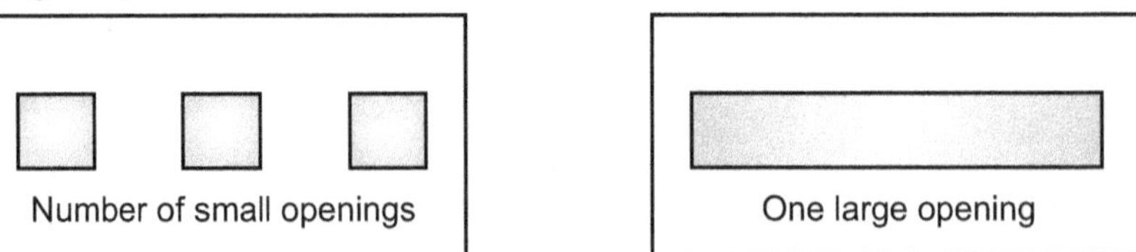

Fig. 9.5

- Unilateral lighting from side openings will, in general, be unsatisfactory if the effective width of the room is more than 2 to 2.5 times the distance from the floor to the top of the opening.

- If the room is 7 m or more across, openings on two opposite walls will give greater uniformity of internal daylight illumination. (Fig. 9.6).

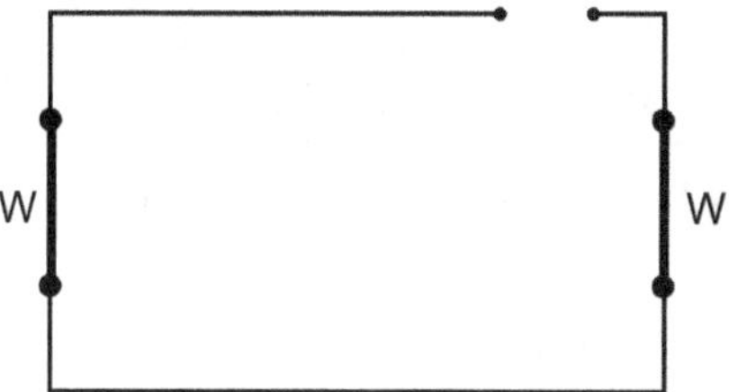

Fig. 9.6: Windows on opposite walls for room of width 7 m and above

- Cross-lighting with openings on adjacent walls, tends to increase the diffused lighting within a room. (Fig. 9.7).

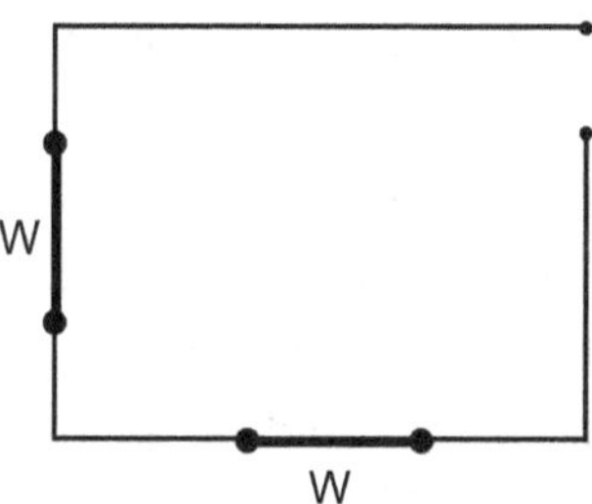

Fig. 9.7: Windows on adjacent walls

- Openings in deep reveals tend to minimize glare effects. (Fig. 9.8).

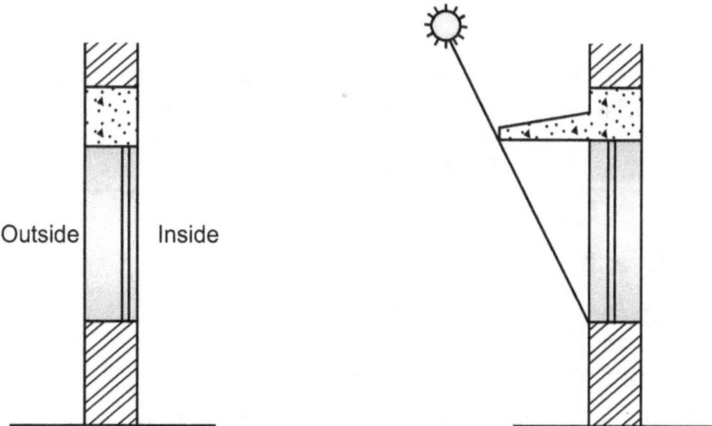

Fig. 9.8: Window with a deep reveal   **Fig. 9.9: Window with a chajja**

- Openings must be provided with chajjas, louvers, baffles or other shading devices to exclude direct sunlight entering a room. This reduces the effect of glare. (Fig. 9.9).

- Intensity of light can be controlled by making use of translucent glass panes surfaced by grinding, etching or sand blasting, configurated or corrugated glass, prismatic glass etc. The chief purpose of such fixtures is to reflect part of the light onto the roof and thereby increase the diffused lighting within, light up farther areas in the room and thereby produce a more uniform illumination throughout. They will also reduce the problem due to glare.

9.5 ORIENTATION OF BUILDINGS WITH RESPECT TO LIGHTING

From the point of view of lighting, the following climatic factors influence the optimum orientation of buildings:

(a) Solar radiation and temperature, and

(b) Clouds.

(a) Solar Radiation and Temperature

- The best orientation from solar point of view requires, that the building as a whole should receive maximum solar radiation in winter and minimum in summer. For this, it is necessary to know the duration of sunshine and hourly solar intensity on the various external surfaces on representative days of the seasons.

- Where tall buildings are built close to one another, it should be ensured, that one building does not cause obstruction to lighting of another building. Normally, the distance between two buildings should be such that the ground floors of both the buildings receive sufficient daylight.

- Sun brakers should be provided, wherever possible, to cut off direct sunlight and prevent heat radiation and effect of glare.

(b) Clouds

Clouds too, reduce direct radiation from the sun, hence it is necessary to know the period and duration of cloudy days in a year before designing shading devices.

9.6 ARTIFICIAL ILLUMINATION

When daylight is not sufficient to give the required levels of illumination, daylight will have to be supplemented by artificial means of illumination.

9.6.1 Necessity of Artificial Lighting

(a) During the day, the need for general supplementary artificial lighting arises:

- Due to reduction of daylight beyond design hours, that is, for solar altitude below $15°$ or when dark cloudy conditions occur,

- For providing artificial lighting during the day in the innermost parts of the building which do not receive enough daylight due to either improper planning, or if the external windows are not of adequate size, or when there are unavoidable obstructions to the incoming daylight and also,

- Where some visual tasks may demand during the day higher levels of illumination.

(b) During night, artificial lighting is required for extended human activities, which cannot be finished during daylight hours.

9.6.2 Types of Artificial Lighting

Two types of electric lamps are most generally used in artificial lighting:

1. **Incandescent Lamps:** In which a current is passed through a tungsten filament, which will thus be heated and its light emission will be due to thermo-luminescence.

2. **Fluorescent Lamps:** In which an electric discharge takes place between two electrodes through low pressure mercury vapour (mixed with some auxiliary gases) and the excited gas molecules emit ultraviolet radiation. This is absorbed by the fluorescent coating on the inside of the glass tube end and re-emitted at visible wavelengths.

   To achieve the same output, a much lower lamp wattage will be necessary with fluorescent than with incandescent lamps.

Comparison between the Two Types of Lamps

Incandescent Lamps:

- Provide a point source of light that can be focussed or directed over a limited area if desired.

- Most household bulbs have the same size base, thus lighting from fixtures or lamps can be increased or decreased within certain limits by a change of bulbs of different wattages.

- Most types are less expensive to buy than fluorescent tubes.

Fluorescent Lamps:

- Provide a line of light, thus in work areas the light coming from various angles tends to wipe out shadows.

- Provide three to four times as much light per watt of electricity as incandescent bulbs with less heat produced.

- Will operate about seven to ten times longer than incandescent bulbs before replacement is required.

9.6.3 Design Considerations for Artificial Lighting of Interiors

For general lighting purposes, the recommended practice is to design for a level of illumination on the working plane on the basis of the recommended levels for various types of visual tasks involved, by a method called the "Lumen method".

The selection of light sources and luminaires depends on the choice of lighting system, namely, general lighting, directional lighting and localised or local lighting.

Determination of the Luminous Flux

The luminous flux (ϕ) reaching the working plane depends upon the following:

- Lumen output of the lamps,
- Type of luminaire,
- Proportion of the room (room index) K_r,
- Reflectance of internal surfaces of the room,
- Depreciation in the lumen output of the lamps after burning their rated life and
- Depreciation due to dirt collection on luminaires and room surfaces.

Coefficient of Utilization or Utilization Factor

This is the ratio of the total luminous flux which eventually reaches the working plane to the actual luminous flux of the light sources in the interior.

The luminous flux or the illumination available due to a luminaire is calculated as,

$$E \text{ in lux} = \frac{\phi \times \mu\, d}{A}$$

where,

E = The average illumination level required on the working plane in lux i.e. lm/m^2

ϕ = The total luminous flux of the light sources installed in the room in lumens (lm)

μ = The utilization factor

d = Maintenance factor

A = Area of the working plane in m^2

The number of lamps or luminaires is calculated as,

$$N = \frac{E \times A}{\mu\, d\, \phi}$$

where,

N = The total number of lamps or luminaires

E = Illumination required in lm/m^2

A = Area of the working plane in m^2 and

ϕ = Total luminous flux of light sources in lm

Thus, with a proper design of an artificial lighting system, it is possible to achieve a working environment in which various visual tasks can be carried out, with ease and comfort.

9.7 SOLAR WATER HEATING SYSTEM

Solar water heaters, they are also sometimes called solar domestic hot water systems, may be a good investment for you and your family. Solar water heaters are cost competitive in many applications when you account for the total energy costs over the life of the system. Although the initial cost of solar water heaters is higher than that of conventional water heaters, the fuel (sunshine) is free. They are environmentally friendly. To take advantage of these heaters, you must have an unshaded, south-facing location (a roof, for example) on your property.

These systems use the sun to heat either water or a heat-transfer fluid, such as a water-glycol antifreeze mixture, in collectors generally mounted on a roof. The heated water is then stored in a tank similar to a conventional gas or electric water tank. Some systems use an electric pump to circulate the fluid through the collectors.

Solar water heaters can operate in any climate. Performance varies depending, in part, on how much solar energy is available at the site, but also on how cold the water coming into the system is. The colder the water, the more efficiently the system operates.

Solar Water Heater Basics

Solar water heaters are made up of collectors, storage tanks, and depending on the system, electric pumps.

There are basically three types of collectors: flat-plate, evacuated-tube and concentrating. A flat-plate collector, the most common type, is an insulated, weather-proofed box containing a dark absorber plate under one or more transparent or translucent covers.

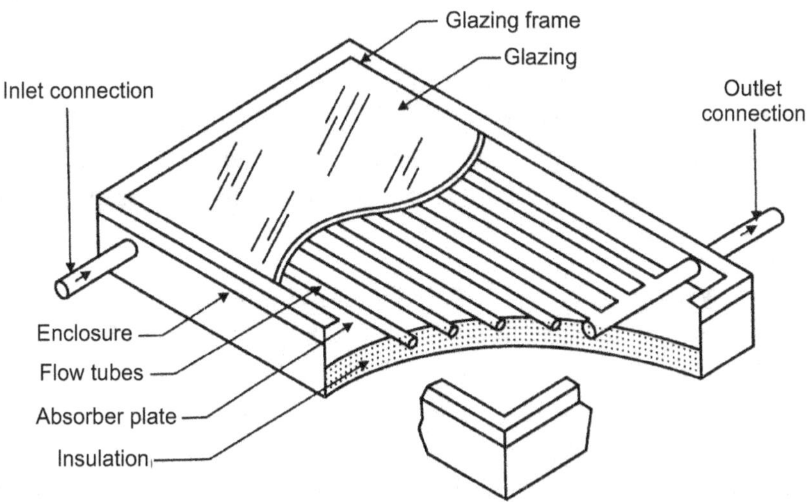

Fig. 9.10: Flat-plate collector

Evacuated-tube collectors are made up of rows of parallel, transparent glass tubes. Each tube consists of a glass outer tube and an inner tube, or absorber, covered with a selective coating that absorbs solar energy well but inhibits radiative heat loss. The air is withdrawn ("evacuated") from the space between the tubes to form a vacuum, which eliminates conductive and convective heat loss.

Concentrating collectors for residential applications are usually parabolic troughs that use mirrored surfaces to concentrate the sun's energy on an absorber tube (called a receiver) containing a heat transfer fluid.

Most commercially available solar water heaters require a well-insulated storage tank. Many systems use converted electric water heater tanks or plumb the solar storage tank in series with the conventional water heater.

Some solar water heaters use pumps to recirculate warm water from storage tanks through collectors and exposed piping. This is generally to protect the pipes from freezing when outside temperatures drop to freezing or below.

Types of Solar Water Heaters

Solar water heaters can be either active or passive. An active system uses an electric pump to circulate the heat-transfer fluid; a passive system has no pump. The amount of hot water a solar water heater produces depends on the type and size of the system, the amount of sun available at the site, proper installation, and the tilt angle and orientation of the collectors. Solar water heaters are also characterized as open loop (also called "direct") or closed loop (also called "indirect"). An open-loop system circulates household (potable) water through the collector. A closed-loop system uses a heat-transfer fluid (water or diluted antifreeze, for example) to collect heat and a heat exchanger to transfer the heat to household water.

1. Active Systems

Active systems use electric pumps, valves, and controllers to circulate water or other heat-transfer fluids through the collectors. They are usually more expensive than passive systems but are also more efficient. Active systems are usually easier to retrofit than passive systems because their storage tanks do not need to be installed above or close to the collectors.

Open-Loop Active Systems

Open-loop active systems use pumps to circulate household water through the collectors. This design is efficient and lowers operating costs but is not appropriate if your water is hard or acidic because scale and corrosion quickly disable the system.

These open-loop systems are popular in non-freezing climates such as Hawaii. They should never be installed in climates that experience freezing temperatures for sustained periods. You can install them in mild but occasionally freezing climates, but you must consider freeze protection.

Recirculation systems are a specific type of open-loop system that provide freeze protection. They use the system pump to circulate warm water from storage tanks through collectors and exposed piping when temperatures approach freezing. Consider recirculation systems only where mild freezes occur once or twice a year at most. Activating the freeze protection more frequently wastes electricity and stored heat.

Ofcourse, when the power is out, the pump will not work and the system will freeze. To guard against this, a freeze valve can be installed to provide additional protection in the event the pump doesn't operate. In freezing weather, the valve dribbles warmer water through the collector to prevent freezing.

Closed-Loop Active Systems

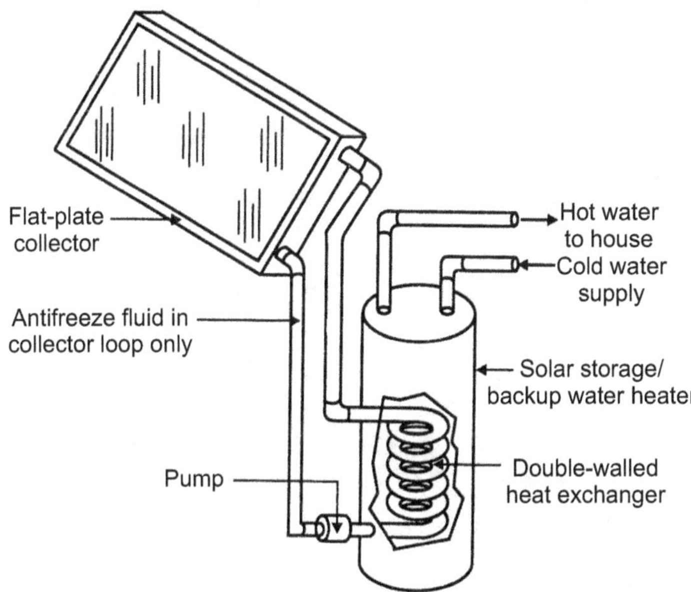

Fig. 9.11: Closed-loop Active System

These systems pump heat-transfer fluids (usually a glycol-water antifreeze mixture) through collectors. Heat exchangers transfer the heat from the fluid to the household water stored in the tanks.

Double-walled heat exchangers prevent contamination of household water. Some codes require double walls when the heat transfer fluid is anything other than household water.

Closed-loop glycol systems are popular in areas subject to extended freezing temperatures because they offer good freeze protection. However, glycol antifreeze systems are a bit more expensive to buy and install, and the glycol must be checked each year and changed every 3 to 10 years, depending on glycol quality and system temperatures.

Drainback systems use water as the heat transfer fluid in the collector loop. A pump circulates the water through the collectors. The water drains by gravity to the storage tank and heat exchanger; there are no valves to fail. When the pumps are off, the collectors are empty, which assures freeze protection and also allows the system to turn off if the water in the storage tank becomes too hot.

Pumps in Active Systems

The pumps in solar water heaters have low power requirements, and some companies now include direct current (D.C.) pumps powered by small solar-electric (photovoltaic, or PV) panels. PV panels convert sunlight into D.C. electricity. Such systems cost nothing to operate and continue to function during power outages.

2. Passive Systems

Passive systems move household water or a heat-transfer fluid through the system without pumps. Passive systems have no electric components to break. This makes them generally more reliable, easier to maintain, and possibly longer lasting than active systems.

Passive systems can be less expensive than active systems, but they can also be less efficient.

Batch Heaters

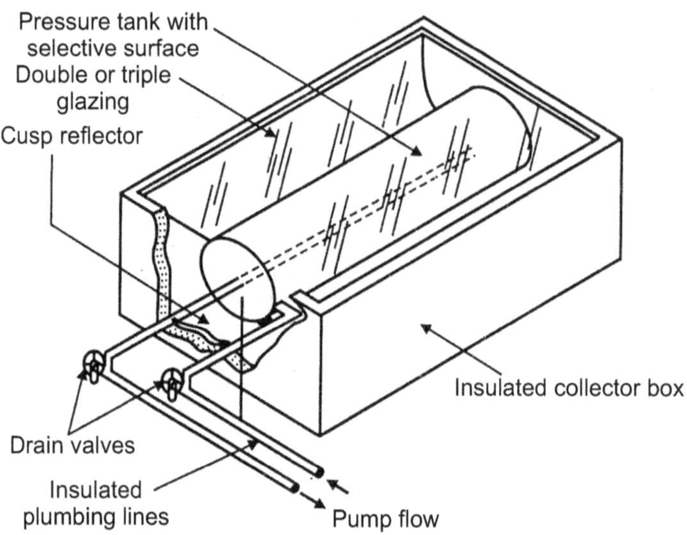

Fig. 9.12: Batch solar collector

Batch heaters (also known as "bread box" or integral collector storage systems) are simple passive systems consisting of one or more storage tanks placed in an insulated box that has a glazed side facing the sun. Batch heaters are inexpensive and have few components, in other words, less maintenance and fewer failures. A batch heater is mounted on the ground or on the roof (make sure your roof structure is strong enough to support it). Some batch heaters use "selective" surfaces on the tank(s). These surfaces absorb sun well but inhibit radiative loss. In climates where freezing occurs, batch heaters must either be protected from freezing or drained for the winter. In well designed systems, the most vulnerable components for freezing are the pipes, if located in uninsulated areas, that lead to the solar water heater. If these pipes are well insulated, the warmth from the tank will prevent freezing. Certified systems clearly state the temperature level that can cause damage. In addition, you can install heat tape (electrical plug-in tape to wrap around the pipes to keep them from freezing), insulate exposed pipes, or both. Remember, heat tape requires electricity, so the combination of freezing weather and a power outage can lead to burst pipes.

Thermosiphon Systems:

A thermosiphon system relies on warm water rising, a phenomenon known as natural convection, to circulate water through the collectors and to the tank. In this type of installation, the tank must be above the collector. As water in the collector heats, it becomes lighter and rises naturally into the tank above. Meanwhile, cooler water in the tank flows down pipes to the bottom of the collector, causing circulation throughout the system. The storage tank is attached to the top of the collector so that thermosiphoning can occur. These systems are reliable and relatively inexpensive but require careful planning in new construction because the water tanks are heavy. They can be freeze-proofed by circulating an antifreeze solution through a heat exchanger in a closed loop to heat the household water.

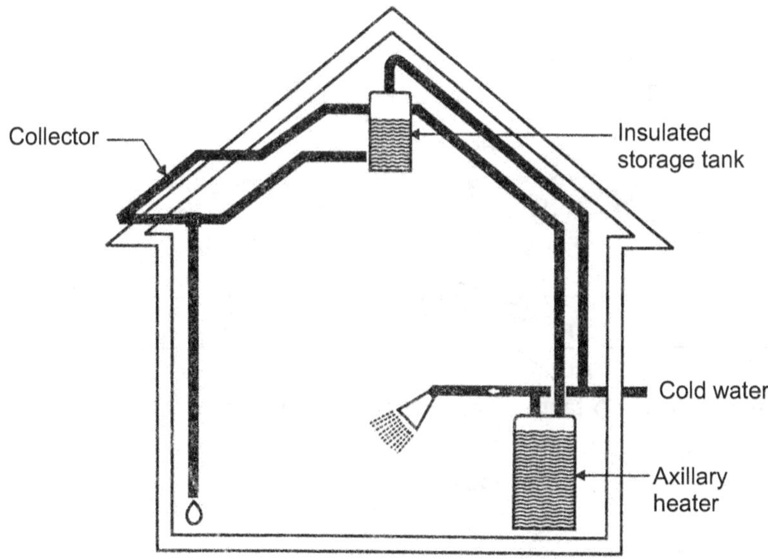

Fig. 9.13: Thermosiphon solar water heater

Benefits of Solar Water Heaters

There are many benefits to owning a solar water heater, and number one is economics. Solar water heater economics compare quite favorably with those of electric water heaters, while the economics are not quite so attractive when compared with those of gas water heaters. Heating water with the sun also means long-term benefits, such as being cushioned from future fuel shortages and price increases, and environmental benefits.

Fig. 9.14: Evacuated Tube Collector (ETC) based on solar water heater

IMPORTANT POINTS

- Purposes of lighting and its unit.
- Design of day lighting and factors considered into its design.
- Components of daylight factor and its factors.
- General principles of design of windows for good lighting.
- Design considerations for artificial lighting of interiors.
- Importance of orientation to achieve good lighting.

QUESTIONS

1. What is Artificial lighting? Give necessity of artificial lighting.
2. Explain role of lighting in planning of buildings.
3. What are the considerations for natural lighting in a residential building?
4. When artificial lighting is required? How it is provided?
5. Explain the types of solar water heaters.
6. What are the benefits of solar water heaters ?

10.1 INTRODUCTION

A plumbing system includes the water supply and distribution pipes, plumbing fittings and traps, soil, pipes, vent pipes and antisiphonage pipes, building drains and building sewers including their respective connections, devices and appurtenances within the property lines of the premises and water treating or water using equipment.

10.2 WATER SUPPLY REQUIREMENTS FOR BUILDINGS

The requirements regarding water supply, drainage and sanitation for residences shall assume, that a minimum water supply of 200 litres per head per day is assured together with a full flushing system. In case of Lower Income Group (LIG) and Economically Weaker Sections of society (EWS), the minimum value of water supply may be reduced to 135 litres per head per day. Requirements of water supply for buildings other than residences are given in Table 10.1.

Table 10.1: Water Requirements for Buildings other than Residences

Sr. No.	Type of Building	Consumption per head per day
(1)	(2)	(3) litres
(i)	Factories where bathrooms are required to be provided.	45
(ii)	Factories where no bathrooms are required to be provided.	30
(iii)	Hospitals (including laundry) per bed:	
	(a) Number of beds not exceeding 100	340
	(b) Number of beds exceeding 100	450
(iv)	Nurses homes and medical quarters	135
(v)	Hostels	135
(vi)	Hotels (per bed)	180
(vii)	Offices	45
(viii)	Restaurants (per seat)	70
(ix)	Cinema halls, concert halls and theatres (per seat)	15
(x)	Schools:	
	(a) Day schools	45
	(b) Boarding schools	135

General Requirements of Plumbing System:

* The plumbing work which is required to be carried out in a building should be executed only by a licensed plumber under the control of the authority and should be responsible to carry out all lawful directions given by the authority.
* All premises intended for human habitation, occupancy or use should be provided with the supply of pure and wholesome water.
* Plumbing fixtures, devices and appurtenances should be supplied with water in sufficient volume and at pressures adequate to enable them to function satisfactorily without undue noise under all normal conditions of use. There should be atleast a residual head of 0.018 N/mm^2 at the consumer's tap.
* Plumbing system should be designed and adjusted to use the minimum quantity of water required for proper performance and cleaning.
* Plumbing fixtures, installed in a building should be connected to a public sewer. If such a sewer does not exist near the building, suitable arrangements like septic tanks and soak pits should be made.

10.3 STORAGE OF WATER

In a building, provision is required to be made for storage of water for the following reasons:

* To provide against interruptions in supply caused by repairs to mains,
* To reduce the maximum rate of demand on the mains,
* To tide over periods of non-supply in an intermittent supply system.
* To maintain a storage for fire fighting requirement of the building (optional) minimum 10,000 litres.

As per I.S. 2065 – latest the storage capacity required, for premises occupied by tenements with common conveniences is calculated at the rate of 500 litres per tenement on each floor. For premises occupied as flats or blocks, the storage requirement is calculated as 8000 litres per tenement.

Reservoirs and tanks for reception and storage of water can be constructed of reinforced concrete, cast iron, galvanised mild steel plates. These tanks should be covered with a close fitting, dust tight, insect and fly-proof lid. These tanks are constructed either underground, above ground or above the building (overhead tanks). If the storage capacity required is more than 5000 litres, it is advantageous to arrange it in a series of tanks, so interconnected that each tank can be isolated for cleaning and inspection without interfering with the supply of water. The design of an underground storage tank is carried out with a provision for the draining of the tank when necessary.

The quantity of water to be stored is calculated by considering the following factors:

* Supply rate, pressure and water supply hours to fill up the overhead storage tanks.
* Frequency of replenishment of overhead tanks during 24 hours.
* Regularity in water supply.
* Types of building like public buildings, school buildings, hospitals etc.

The water supply system consists of municipal water supply mains, distributing pipes, consumers pipes, stopcocks, various types of taps, underground storage tanks, overhead reservoirs etc. Water is supplied to kitchen, bathrooms, W.C. etc. by service pipes and valves. The water supply arrangement in a multi-storeyed building is shown in Fig. 10.1.

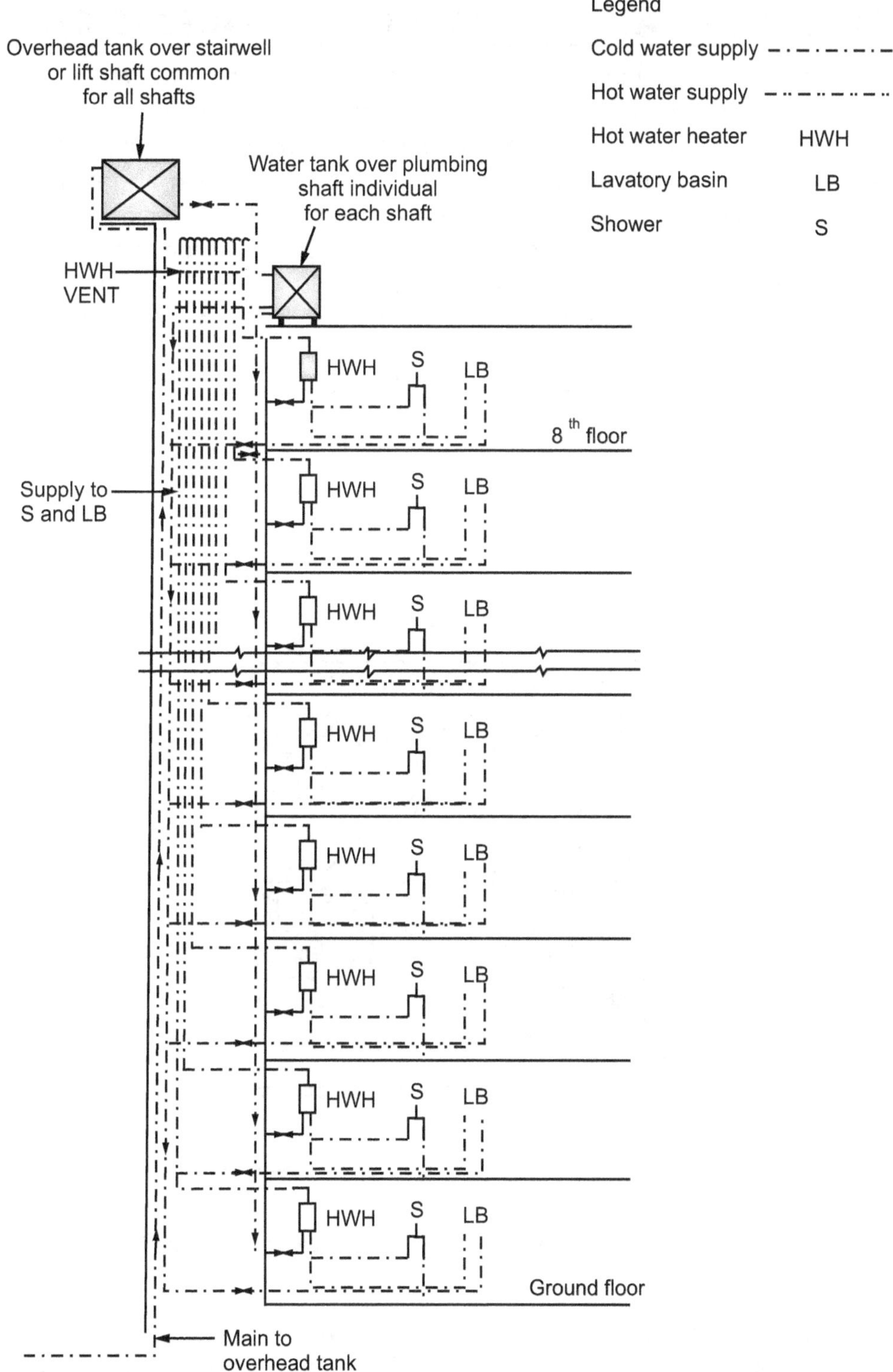

Fig. 10.1: Installation of water supply connections for 8-Storeyed Building

10.4 LAYOUT OF WATER SUPPLY AND DRAINAGE SYSTEM

Before commencing the plumbing work, a detailed layout showing the arrangements for water supply and drainage is prepared. The layout plan should contain location of service main water supply line, position of underground and overhead tanks, position of service connection depending upon various units of the building. It should also contain details regarding the drainage system which includes street sewer line, positions of manholes, inspection chambers, gully traps, drainage lines for sewage and silage and rain water. The direction of flow should also be marked on this layout. A layout for water supply and drainage system for a multi-storeyed structure is shown in Fig. 10.2 on last page.

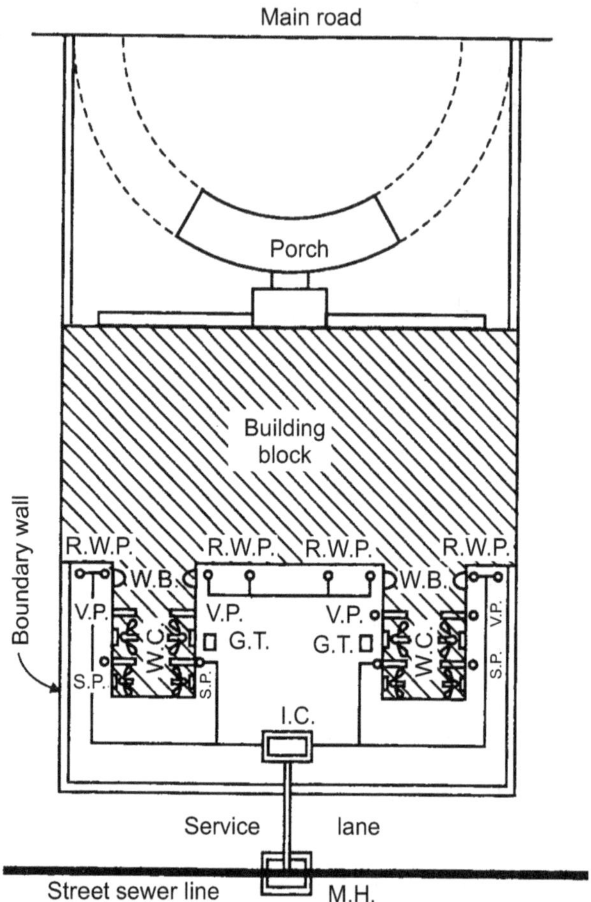

Fig. 10.2: Typical drainage layout plant of a terrace house drained at back

House Drainage Plans

Before starting the plumbing work, it is most essential first to prepare the drainage plans. In the same way detailed drawings are prepared before the starting of the construction of buildings, the detailed drainage plans should be also be prepared.

The following points should be kept in mind while preparing the drainage plans:

(i)   The drains should be laid in such a way so as to remove the sewage quickly from the building. The quick removal is governed by the fall of the pipes. The drains should be laid at such a slope that self-cleaning velocity is developed in them. The following slopes are usually sufficient:

1 in 40 for	10 cm pipe
1 in 60 for	15 cm pipe
1 in 90 for	23 cm pipe

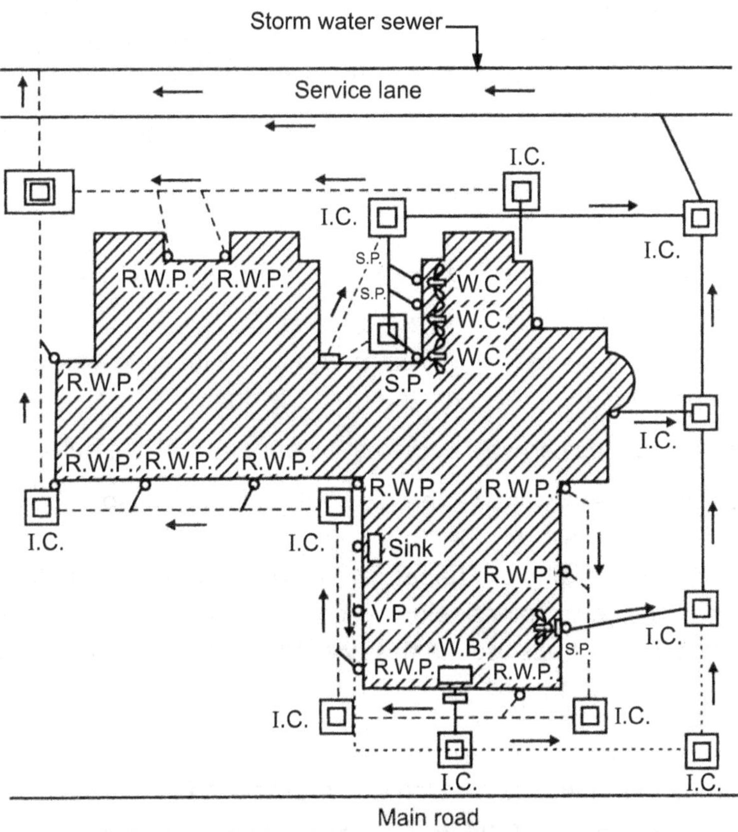

Fig. 10.3: Typical drainage layout of a large building

10.5 PLUMBING SYSTEM FOR WASTE WATER

The removal of any liquid by a system constructed for the purpose is called as drainage system. In designing a drainage system for an individual building, the aim is to provide a system of self cleaning conduits for conveyance of foul, a surface or subsurface waters. And for the removal of such waste speedily and efficiently to a sewer or other outlet without risk of nuisance and hazard to people. The different types of wastes, which are required to be removed through the drainage system, include night soil (waste from W.C.), silage from bath and kitchen and rain water collected over the building or on the premises. In the drainage system, generally, rain water is dealt with separately from sewage and silage.

Following are the main systems of plumbing for the building drainage:

(a) Two-pipe System:

- This is the most common system used in India. This method provides an ideal solution, where it is not possible to fix the fixture closely.

- All the drainage system should be properly ventilated on the house side. The ventilation pipe should be carried sufficiently high above the buildings. All the inspection chambers should provided with fresh air inlets.

- All the drains should be laid in such a way so as to ensure their safety in future.

- The drain should be laid in such a way that in future extension can be done easily if desired.

- If the quantity of sewage flowing in a pipe is small, an automatic flushing tank may be provided on its top for flushing it.

- All the rain water pipes, sweeping from house and bath water should discharge over gully traps and should be disconnected from the drain.

- All soil pipes should be carried direct to the manholes without gully traps.

In this system, two pipes are provided. One pipe collects the foul soil and lavatory wastes, whereas the second pipe collects the unfoul water from kitchen, bathrooms, house washings, rain water etc. The soil pipes (pipes carrying the soil waste) are directly connected to the drain whereas the waste pipes (pipes carrying unfoul waste water) are connected through the gully trap. All the traps used in this system are fully ventilated.

(b) One-pipe System

In this system, only one main pipe is provided which collects both the foul soil waste as well as unfoul waste from the buildings. The main pipe is directly connected to the drainage system. If this system is provided in multi-storeyed buildings the lavatory blocks of various floors are so placed one over the other, so that the waste water discharged from the different units can be carried through short branch drains.

All the traps of the W.C., basins, sinks etc. are fully ventilated and connected to the ventilation pipe.

(c) Single-stack System

This is similar to single pipe system, the only difference being that no ventilation is provided even in the traps too.

(d) Single-stack Partially Ventilated System

This system is in between the one pipe and single-stack system. In this system, only one pipe is provided to collect all types of waste water foul as well as unfoul. A relief vent pipe is provided for ventilating only the water closet-traps.

Now-a-days in modern multi-storeyed buildings one pipe system is becoming popular due to its low cost. C.B.R.I. Roorkee, after doing extensive research on this system, has recommended it in modern buildings. An analysis of this system showed that the flow from the appliance to the stack through branch is momentarily halted at the sharp change of flow of direction. Sometimes a plug of water is formed immediately at the junction, which depends upon the rate of change of discharge and the size of branch. This gives rise to unequal pressures at the seals for the lower floors of the building and sometimes this breaks the water seals of the sanitary appliances. C.B.R.I. has recommended the use of aerator and deaerator in the stack to increase its capacity.

The function of the **aerator** is to prevent the formation of the plugs of water in the vertical stack and to make a mixture of water and air of low specific gravity. The aerators are provided at every floor.

(a) For supply of water to various sanitary fittings.

(b) For collection of waste water from the sanitary fittings.

(c) For collection of rain water from the roofs, house and courtyard washings.

The fixing of sanitary appliances in the walls, floor and other places and their connected pipe works are to be done carefully for their proper functioning.

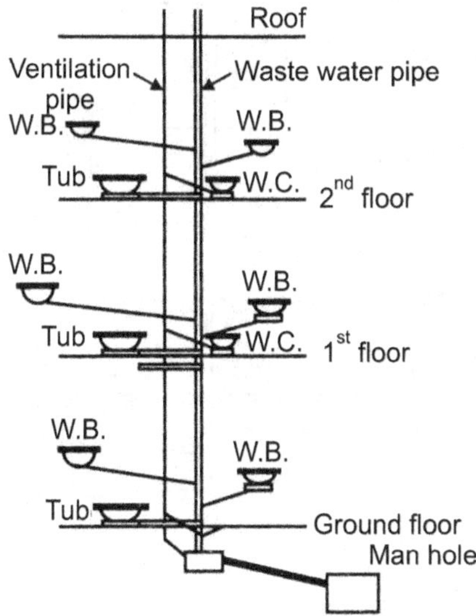

Fig. 10.4: Single stack partially ventilated system

Deaerators are provided at the foot of the stack to separate air and water to avoid excessive back pressure. Studies carried out by C.B.R.I. revealed that 100 mm diameter stack with these fittings can be safely used upto 15 storeys, whereas a single stack system without these fittings can be used only upto 5 storeys.

The two pipe system is costly as it requires much labour and material with antisyphonage pipe, as compared with single stack system of plumbing. No antisyphonage pipe is required. The single stack system is becoming popular in the modern building construction. The tests done by C.B.R.I. on 5 storeyed building shows that there was no break of water seals. As it is the common practice in India to discharge the waste water from the sinks and wash basin to the floor trap, therefore, sanitary appliance carrying, unfoul waste water do not require deeper seals. 100 mm diameter stack with two appliances at each floor can be safely used upto 5 storeyed building.

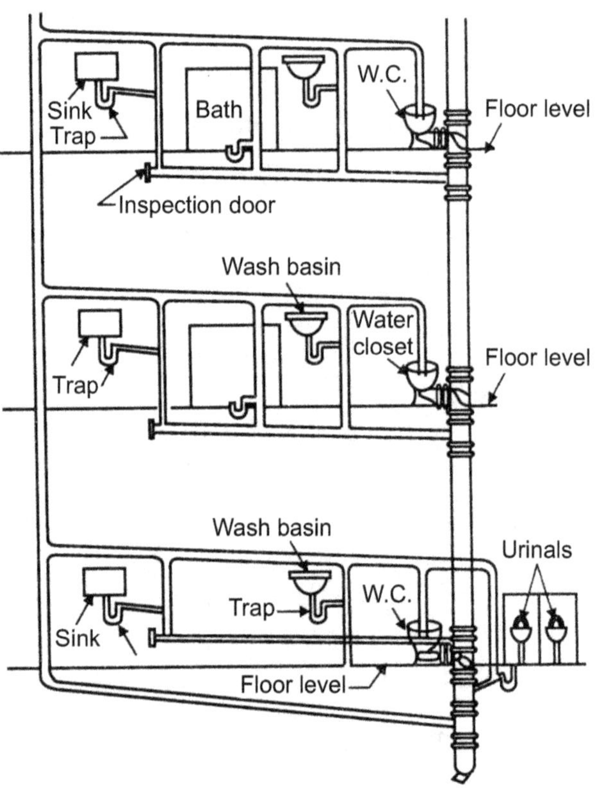

Fig. 10.5: Plumbing work of one-pipe system

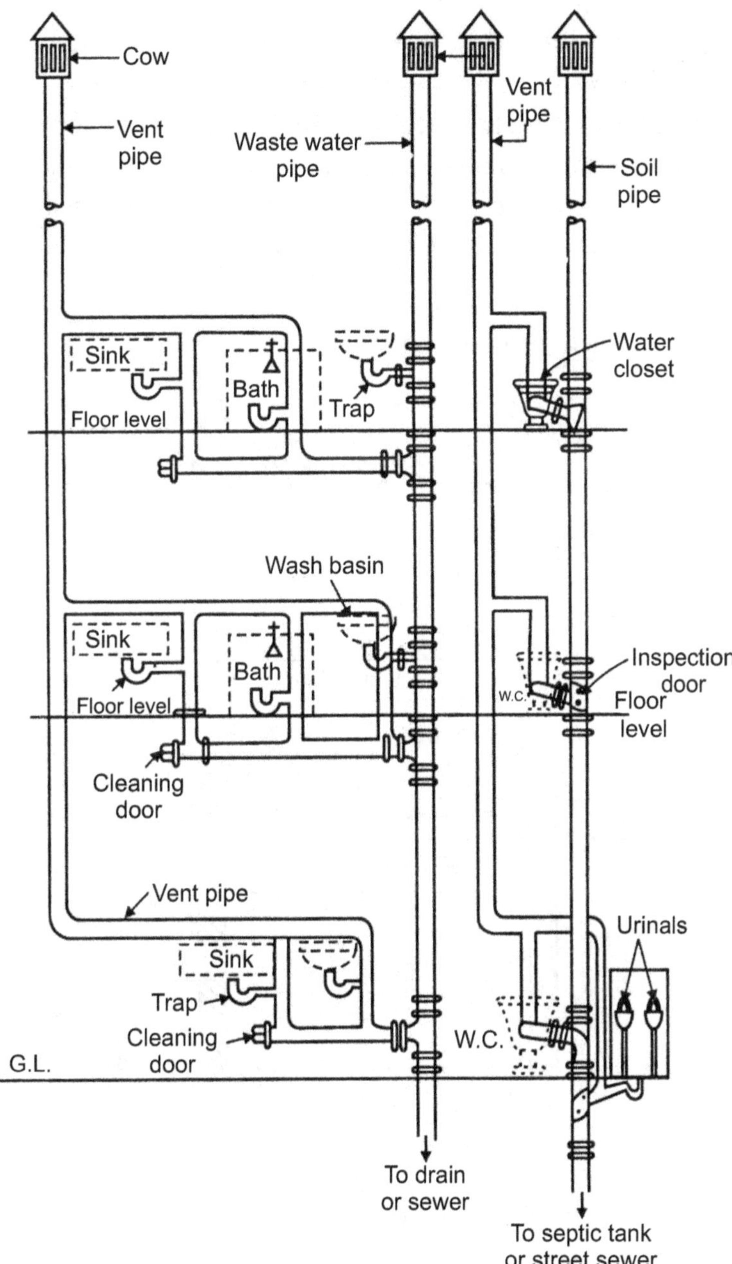

Fig. 10.6: Plumbing work of two-pipe system

Septic Tank: In the rural areas and the fringe areas of suburban towns and also in case of isolated buildings and institutions, hostels, hotel, hospital, school, small residential colonies, underground sewage system with complete treatment of sewage may be neither feasible nor economical. Under such cases septic tanks followed by subsurface disposal of effluent are provided. In the areas having porous soil, this method gives satisfactory results. The location of the septic tanks should be as far as possible away from the buildings, and should not be located in swampy areas or areas prone to flooding. In case of clayey, non-porous soils or where houses are closely spaced, suitably designed leading pits may have to be used, if septic tank cannot be avoided. The septic tank effluent should not be allowed into open drainage system, because it may cause health hazards, nuisance and mosquito breeding. If the facilities for connection to a sewer are available, the effluent from the septic tank should be connected to sewers.

Also it should be located at the lowest contour.

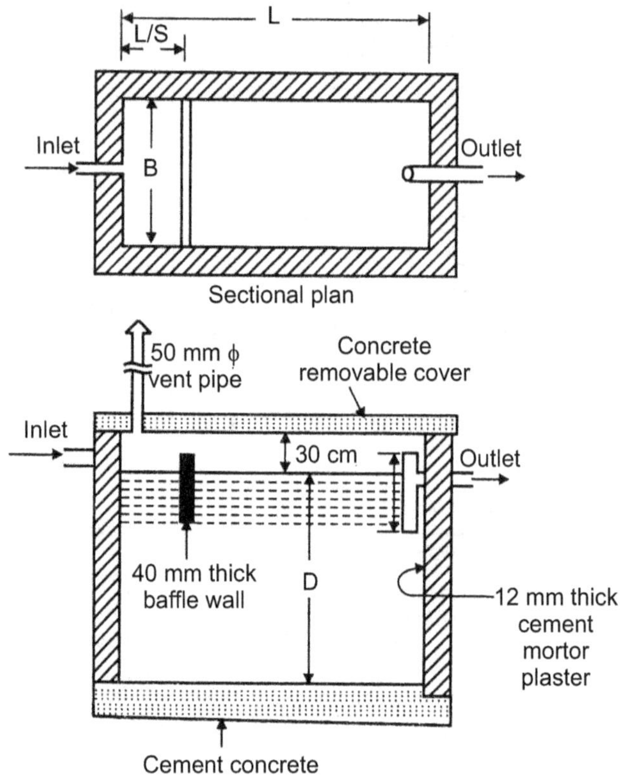

Fig. 10.7: Septic tank

Sewage Flow:

The maximum flow of sewage to the tank is based on the number of plumbing fixtures discharging simultaneously rather than the number of users and per capita waste water flow expected to reach the septic tank. For this purpose various sanitation appliances such as water closets, wash basins, bath etc. are equated in terms of fixture units as given in Table 10.2. A fixture unit is a standard receptacle which gives a discharge of 10 $l$pm when flushed.

Table 10.2: Fixture equivalents

Sanitary fixture	Equivalent fixture unit
1. Water closet	1.0
2. Bath	0.5
3. Wash basin/kitchen sink	0.5
4. Urinal with automatic flush	1.0
5. Urinal without automatic flush	0.5
6. Slope sink	1.0
7. Ablution tap	0.5
8. Dish washer	0.5
9. Combination fixture	1.0
10. Laboratory sink	2.0
11. Shower bath	1.0
12. Bath tub	2.0
13. Drinking fountain	0.5

Tables 10.3, 10.4 and 10.5 gives the estimated number of fixture units and the number of fixture units that contribute to the peak discharge in small installations-residential colonies and hostels etc.

Table 10.3: Estimated peak discharge for small establishments

Number of users	Number of fixture units	Probable no. of fixture units discharging simultaneously	Probable peak discharge *l*mp
5	1	1	10
10	2	2	20
15	3	2	20
20	4	3	30
25	5	4	40
30	6	4	40
35	7	5	50
40	8	6	60
45	9	6	60
50	10	7	70

Table 10.4: Estimated peak discharge for residential housing colonies

No. of users	No. of house holds	No. of fixture units	Probable peak discharge based on 60% fixture units discharging simultaneously in *l*pm
100	20	40	240
150	30	60	360
200	40	80	480
300	60	120	720

Table 10.5: Estimated peak discharge for casting establishments boarding schools and similar establishments

No. of Users	W.C.	Bath	Wash basin kitchen sink	No. of fixture units	Probable peak discharge based on 70% fixture units discharging simultaneously in *l*pm
50	6	6	6	12	84
100	12	12	12	24	168
150	19	19	19	38	266
200	25	25	25	50	350
300	37	37	37	74	518

Construction Details:

Following are the construction details of septic tanks:

- It is rectangular in plan, the length is usually 2 to 4 times the breadth.

- For smaller tanks liquid depth of 100 cm is provided, for larger tanks it may be upto 180 cm. Free board of 30-45 cm is provided above the level of liquid for fixing of pipes, scum, gases etc.

- An elbow pipe, usually T-pipe submerged to a depth of 15-25 cm below the liquid level is provided as inlet pipe. More number of inlet pipes may be provided for larger tanks.

- Single elbow or T-shaped outlet pipe is provided. It should also be submerged at least 15 cm below the liquid level. For very large tanks, weir type outlet similar to settling tanks are provided.

- In smaller tanks one baffle of hanging type is enough, the baffle is usually placed 20 to 30 cm from the inlet pipe and remains 15 cm above and 30 cm below the liquid level. Outlet baffle is provided only in large tanks, when weir type outlet is provided.

- Usually R.C.C. slab with C.I., manhole covers are provided.
- Ventilation pipe of usually 7.5 to 10 cm diameter of A.C. or C.I. is used for taking out the foul smells. Their tops are provided with cowls.

Table 10.6: The sizes of Septic Tanks as per I.S. 2470 (Part I) 1963

No. of Users	Length L	Breadth B	Liquid depth D min.	Liquid capacity to be provided	Free board min.	Sludge to be removed	Recommended interval of cleaning
	metre	metre	metre	m^3	cm.	m^3	
1	2	3	4	5	6	7	8
5	1.5	0.75	1.0	1.12	30	0.18	6 months
			1.0	1.12	30	0.36	1 year
			1.05	1.18	30	0.72	2 years
10	2	0.9	1.0	1.8	30	0.36	6 months
			1.0	1.8	30	0.72	1 year
			1.4	2.52	30	1.44	2 years
15	2	0.9	1.0	1.8	30	0.54	6 months
			1.3	2.34	30	1.08	1 year
			2.0	3.6	30	2.16	2 years
20	2.3	1.1	1.0	2.53	30	0.72	6 months
			1.3	3.3	30	1.44	1 year
			1.8	4.55	30	2.88	2 years
50	4	1.4	1.0	5.6	30	1.8	6 months
			1.3	7.28	30	3.6	1 year
			2.0	11.2	30	7.2	2 years

Design of Septic Tanks:

As septic tank is a settling-cum-digestion tank, it requires space for:

(i)   Settling of incoming sewage.

(ii) Digestion of the settled sludge.

(iii) Storage of digested sludge till it is taken out.

Design for Space for Settling: This is calculated for the average flow and detention period. Smaller tanks are designed on the basis of average flow and 24 hours detention period, while larger tanks are designed for 12 hours detention period.

Both surface area and detention of depth are important factors in the settling of flocculant particles such as sewage solids. For average Indian conditions at a temperature of 25°C, the surface area required will be 0.92 m^2 for every 10 $l$pm peak rate flow. This is based on 75% removal of sewage particles of 0.05 mm size and above with a specific gravity of 1.2. A minimum depth of sedimentation of 25-30 cm is necessary. The length of the septic tank is kept 2-4 times the breadth.

If only the discharge from the latrines flow is in the septic tank, the average flow per capita per day may be taken as 45 litres. On the other hand if all the waste water of the houses is to be treated in septic tank the average flow should be taken per capita per day depending on the water supply.

Design for Digestion Space: In the septic tank, the operation goes in natural way and there is no control over all it such as mixing, heating, etc. a provision of 0.0425 m^3 per capita should be done for it.

The fresh sludge stay in the tank should be long enough to undergo satisfactory anaerobic digestion so that as much of the organic matter as possible may be destroyed and the sludge may become innocuous and suitable for dewatering or drying. The time required for digestion depends on the temperature. The per capita suspended solids entering the septic tank may be taken as 70 gm/day. Assuming that 60% of the solids are removed along with fresh sludge, of which 70% is volatile, with a solid content of 5% or moisture 95%, the volume of fresh sludge works out to 0.00083 m^3 /cap./day. Now considering that 2/4 of the volatile matter is destroyed of which 1/4 is mineralised during digestion and solid content of 13% in the digested sludge, the volume of the digested sludge works out to 0.0002 m^3/cap./day. The digestion zone contains both fresh and digesting sludge. Therefore, the digestion space should provide for the average volume of the mixture of fresh and digested sludge which works out to 0.000515 m^3/cap./day. Now based on the period of digestion, the capacity required for the digestion zone can be worked out. At 25°C, the capacity for sludge digestion works out to 0.032 m^3/capita.

Design of Space for Storage of Digested Sludge: The digested sludge produced per capita in different periods is as follows:

Period of Cleaning	Storage Capacity
6 months	0.0283 m^3
1 year	0.049 m^3
2 years	0.0708 m^3
3 years	0.085 m^3

The design of space for storage of digested sludge is done on the basis of period of cleaning and the number of persons using the tank.

Adequate space should be provided in the septic tank for the storage of digested sludge and scum, otherwise their accumulation interferes with the efficiency of the tank by encroaching upon the space provided for sedimentation and digestion. A sludge storage capacity of 7.3 m^3/100 persons for an interval of cleaning of one year is provided below the sedimentation zone.

Total Capacity: The tank should also provide for a free board of atleast 30 cm, which should be sufficient to include the scum depth above the liquid surface. Addition capacity for seed sludge is not required. Care should be taken to leave 25-50 mm depth digested sludge for seed purpose. When the cleaning is yearly, at 25°C for 10 persons the tank capacity shall be 2.15 m as per details below:

(i)   Sedimentation   = Probable Peak flow 320 $l$pm

    Area required $= \dfrac{0.92 \ (m^2)}{10 \ (lpm)} = 1.84 \ m^2$

    Provided a depth of 30, volume $= 1.84 \times 3 = 0.55 \ m^3$

(ii) Digestion space $= 0.32 \ m^3$

(iii) Space for sludge storage $= 0.73 \ m^3$

(iv) Space for free board including 0.25 m^3

    for seed sludge (1.84 $\times$ 0.3) $= 0.055 \ m^3$

                Total = 2.15 m^3

A septic tank designed on the criteria given above normally provides a detention period of 24-48 hours, based on an average daily flow of sewage. But as the average daily flow varies so widely from one installation to another, detention period should not be considered as an important criterion for the design of septic tanks.

SOLVED EXAMPLES

Example 10.1: Design a septic tank for 50 users, assuming the rate of water supply as 60 litres/head/day.

Solution: Assuming the detention period as 24 hours and the time of cleaning the sludge as 3 years.

$$\text{Space required for setting} \ = \frac{50 \times 60}{1000}$$

$$= 3.0 \ m^3$$

$$\text{Space required for design} \ = 50 \times 0.0425$$

$$= 2.125 \ m^3$$

$$\text{Space required for storage of sludge}$$

$$= 50 \times 0.085$$

$$= 4.25 \ m^3$$

$$\text{Total space required} \quad = \ 3.0 + 2.125 + 4.25$$

$$= \ 9.375 \ m^3$$

$$= \ (9.5 \ m^3) \ say$$

Providing free broad of 30 cm.

Provide the septic tank of $4 \times 1.4 \times 2.0$ metres.

Garbage Disposal Arrangement:

Refuse is all the solid and semisolid waste matter of a community except night soil. It can be broadly divided into two parts:

(1) Organic matter, (2) Inorganic matter.

The organic matter of the refuse is very offensive and creates health problems. The quantity and quality of refuse depends on various factors such as season, climatic condition, geographic location, habits of people, standards of living, etc. Garbage includes all sorts of putrescible waste obtained from hotels, restaurants, kitchens etc. Garbage should be handled carefully as flies, insects, rats etc. breed in it. Garbage decomposes very quickly and produces unpleasant odours. Garbage can be used after proper processing as fertilizer.

The garbage is stored in the houses, industries and business centres, temporarily in containers and it is dumped periodically in the refuse collection boxes or chambers provided along the streets for this purpose. In multi-storeyed buildings, refuse chute system is provided for collecting and transporting in a sanitary way.

This system has three components:

1. The chutes
2. Inlet hopper
3. Collection chamber.

Occupants of the building from successive floors drop their refuse into the inlets and the refuse is collected in the collecting chamber from where the refuse is cleared at suitable intervals. The inlet hopper is located in the passage near the kitchen or at the end of a common passage. Sufficient ventilation and lighting should be provided near the inlets. The collection chamber is provided at ground level for easy clearance.

10.6 RAIN WATER HARVESTING

Introduction: Every living organism requires air and water for survival mainly in addition to other parameters. We get air in abundance but as the availability of water totally depends upon rain.

We need water for the following reasons:

- Domestic uses such as drinking, cooking, bathing, washing, flushing toilets, cleaning utensils etc.

- Agricultural practices.

- Industrial use.

- Other uses like – cleaning the roads, fire fighting, fountains etc.

Considering the asset and importance of water, towns, even in old ages, were developed nearby water bodies as mentioned in Chapter 1.

Initially the major percentage of population used to stay in rural areas but soon because of industrialization migration from rural to urban areas has set up in search of jobs. This phenomenal increase has pressurized the water supply in urban areas.

Even in the states like Assam where 1100 cm rainfall is observed, abundant surface runoff is responsible for inadequacy in water supply. Along with this in some of the areas there is depletion of water level because of many reasons. Bore wells already dug are becoming dry day by day.

In forthcoming years if we don't take proper steps for the resolution of the problem globally, we will face water scarcity. Future of water in India is in the hands of people, professionals, business sectors and the government.

Changes in atmospheric conditions, emission of CFCs, the interference of man in ecological/environmental activities is responsible for irregular and unbalanced rainfall. In turn to solve this problem we must store the rain water, recharge and replenish the water bodies. These are the only means by which sustenance for the water resources will be seen.

Need for Rain Water Harvesting:

Prior to industrialization and successive increased rate of urbanization, the natural filter for rain was the ground. This filter allows the penetration and hence the ground water was at substantial level. Continuous pumping of water for industrial use, domestic use etc., this level dropped down a lot. Also in urban areas specially, concrete pavements, foot paths, parking area etc. were responsible for less filtration and more surface runoff leading finally towards sea.

Less deposition of water in this water bank below and more withdrawal for many activities are the key factors for this depletion of water. Hence, it is the responsibility of the mankind to increase this level. In this regard, Rain Water Harvesting (RWH) is a very natural and cost effective solution which will improve the depleted water level.

Methods of RWH:

(i) Collection of rain water and utilization of the same.

(ii) Infiltration of the rain water into ground.

Aims:

- To control depletion of ground water level.
- To increase ground water table and its availability.
- To improve the quality of the ground water.
- To control the flow of sea water within the ground.
- To increase the availability of ground water as and when required at a particular place and particular time.
- To save the energy in turn.

Why RWH ?

- To supply water and satisfy the increased demand.
- To control floor in case of excessive rainfall.
- To deposit rain water in water bank below ground.
- To reduce contamination/pollution of ground water.
- To improve the quality of ground water.
- To control erosion of soil.

Advantages of RWH:

- Self sustenance in water availability.
- Saving of energy.
- Availability of soft water with high quality.
- Less erosion of soil.
- Cost effective techniques.
- Easy employment of the technique.
- It controls backflow of sea water.
- It can be employed as a very effective tool in case of islands.

It is of utmost importance to study the geological characteristics of the land to adopt best possible technique in a particular area. Financial backing and the necessary support is given by National and State Government for RWH. Government of Maharashtra also has replenished RWH in the era of Chatrapati Shivaji on his forts.

Scope of RWH:

In Pimpri-Chinchwad region where the area is 171 sq. km, average annual rainfall is 600 mm. If this entire volume is stored we will get total volume of 1,02,600 million liters of water (171 × 1000 × 1000 × 0.6 × 100). That means 338 million liters of water will be available daily and the actual requirement of Municipal Corporation is 235 million liters, that means theoretically the availability is more than the requirement.

Considering the fact that if rainfall on 50% of terrace area is collected and stored then about 27 million liters per day which is around 12% of overall consumption per day.

Also the rain falling in agricultural land can be filtered through the soil layers which will improve ground water table and avoid soil erosion. The similar techniques are effectively employed by Shri. Anna Hajare in Ralegansiddhi, Shri. Popatrao Pawar in Hivare Bajar, Shri. Vijaykumar Kedia in Aurangabad, Shri. Rajendrasingh Jain in Rajasthan.

Roof Top Rain Water Harvesting: The quantum of rainfall collected from roof top is transferred to the tank by filtration and disinfected or filtered in ground to increase water table and then utilized as and when needed.

Following are the assets of roof top RWH:

1. Catchment area

2. Pipes

3. Filtration

4. Storage.

1. **Catchment Area:** Considering runoff coefficient for a particular area, remaining part can be collected and stored, from terraces, roofs, footpaths etc.

2. **Pipes:** Normally used pipes for collection and transfer are PVC, Al, GI.

3. **Filtration:** The water collected from roofs is comparatively cleaner. But it is essential to filter it for the removal of soil particles, dust, floating objects etc. While recharging, water flowing from footpaths, roads, etc. it must be allowed to settle down in settling tank. Then this water is filtered.

4. **Storage:** After filtration, the water is stored in water tanks above or below ground which are made up of RCC, bricks, stores, ferrocrete, PVC etc.

Recharging Technique: The types for recharging based on:

(a) **Shallow structure:** In this further classification is:

- Pit method

- Trench method.

(b) Deeper Structure:

- Bore wells

- Dug wells.

Details about Filters:

(i) Roof Top Water Filter: Nearly 50,000 litres of water per annum can be stored or laid into borewell if the available roof is of area 1000 sq. ft. with annual rainfall of 600 mm.

Precautionary measures:

- Clean the roof carefully prior to rainy season.

- Do not allow the water to penetrate just after first fall.

- Filter can be cleaned by closing the valve in front of 'T' near borewell or tank and the water used for cleaning purpose is drained off from the 'T' closer to the roof side.

- For disinfection one may use TCL powder or potassium permanganate applied through 'T' section.

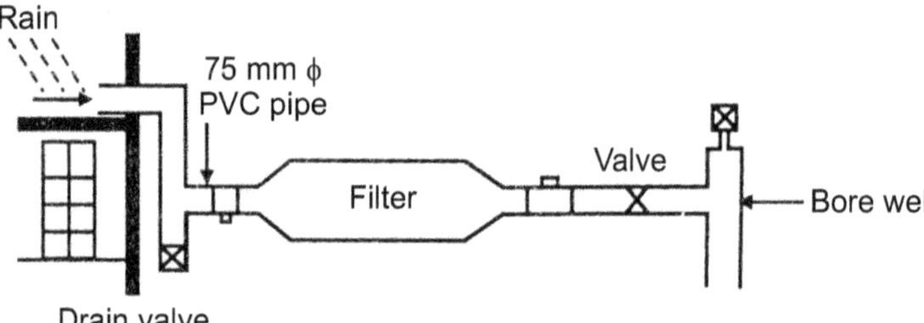

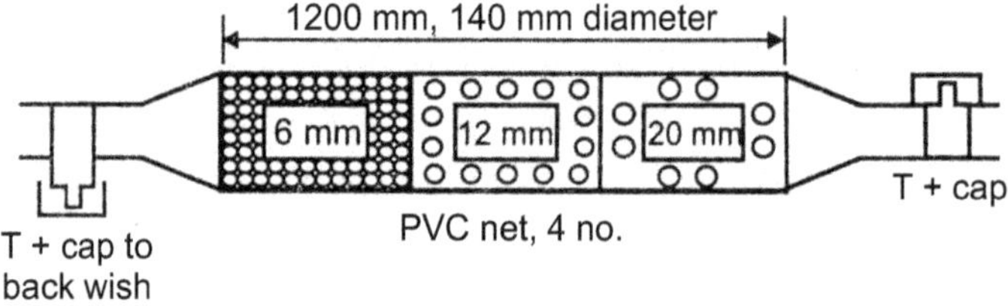

Fig. 10.8

(ii) Filter used in Case of Ferrocrete Storage Water Tanks: Filtration tank is fitted above the ferrocrete water tank and filter medium is placed inside it. The water is collected from top is collected from roof pipes and allowed to penetrate in the filter tank.

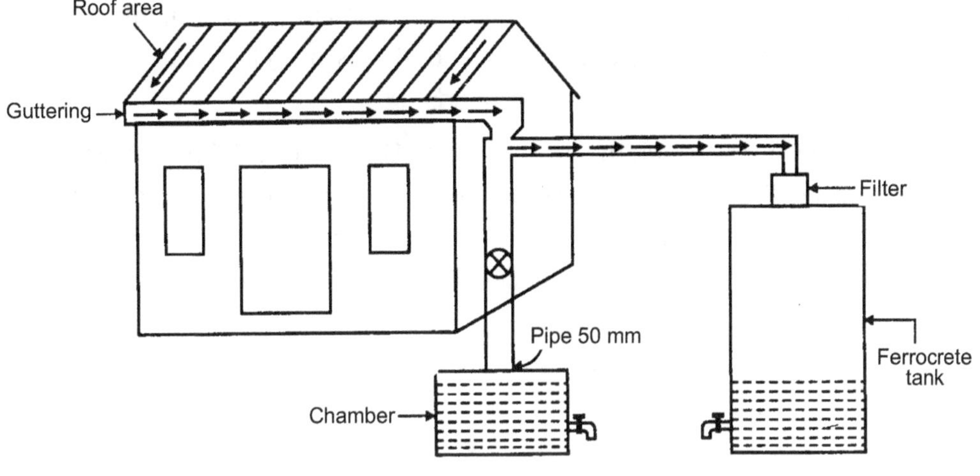

Fig. 10.9

Filter design will vary depending upon the available area and rainfall intensity.

Shallow Structure:

(a) Recharge Pits: This is used for raising the shallow level ground water table. The dimensions for pit are $1 \times 1 \times 2$, $1 \times 1 \times 3$, $2 \times 2 \times 2$ or $2 \times 2 \times 3$ m^3 (or may be circular rectangular). After excavation, the pit is filled with aggregates and stones. Care must be taken about the quality of water that will penetrate inside. It must be as clean as possible (i.e. avoid silted turbid water). The pit is to be cleaned periodically to remove silt. Normally this is to be adopted in case of 1000 sq. ft. roof top area. On the pit, grill is to be fitted to avoid any accident.

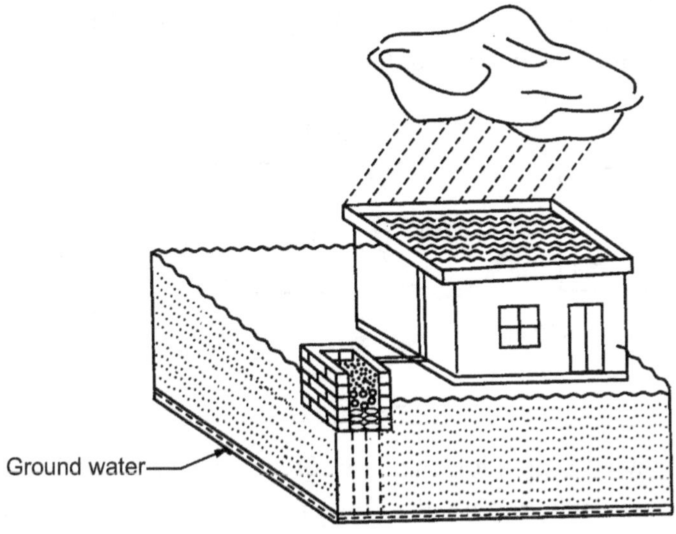

Fig. 10.10

(b) Recharge Trench: If the top layers of soil are pervious then this method is preferred. After excavating the trench sand, aggregates and stones are filled with sand at top. The trench is at 90° with respect to the slope of ground.

Normally used dimensions are: width – 0.5 to 1.00 m, Depth 1.0 to 1.5 m and length 10 to 20 m; but these are finalized only after the survey of the area in respect of available area, rainfall, character of soil etc. This method is suitable when the available roof area ranges within 200 to 300 sq.m. The trench is to be cleaned frequently and grill is to be provided on the top.

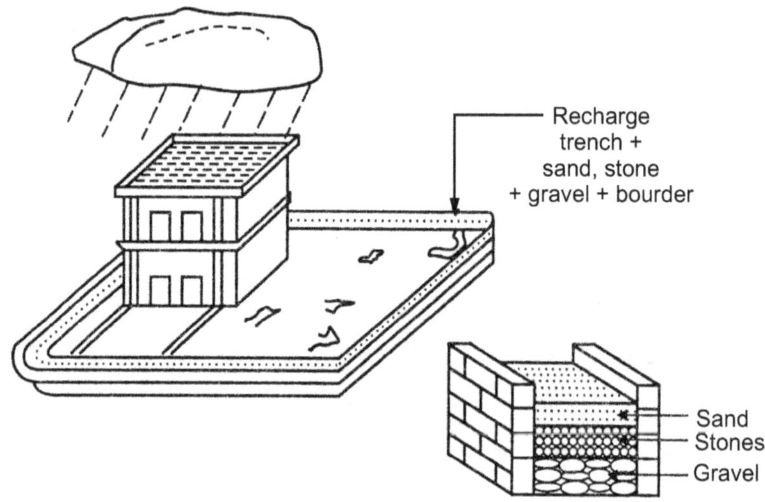

Fig. 10.11

Recharge Well: If an old well is nearby any building then directly that well can be recharged by rain water collected from roof top after filtration.

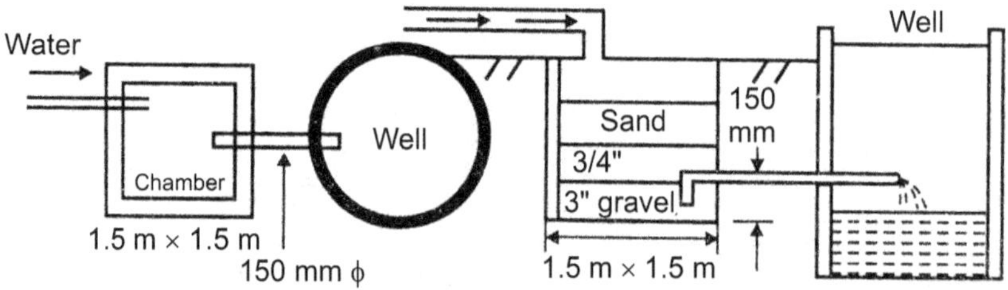

Fig. 10.12

Recharging the Borewell: Sometimes in the borewell water is discharged through Ievas filters. But if the area available is more, than the near borewell, a filter is provided and water is discharged.

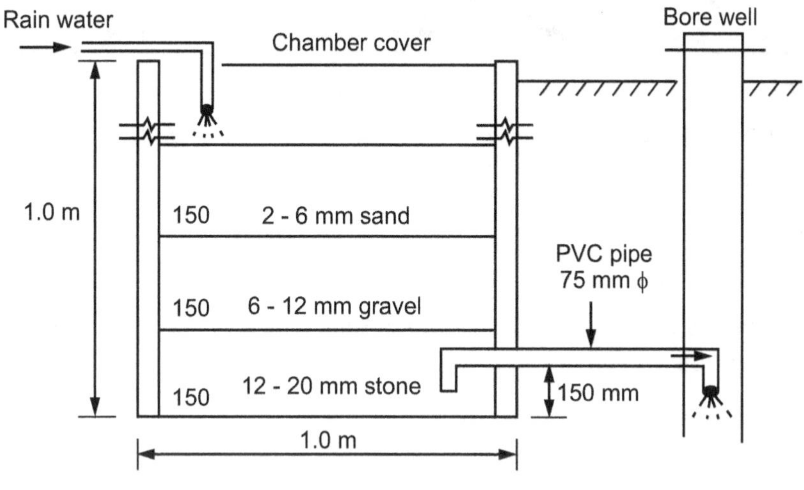

Fig. 10.13

Calculations:

Water quantity to be collected in one year (Q):

$$Q = A \times I \times R$$

where,　Q　=　Discharge in cu. m

　　　　A　=　Area in sq. m.

　　　　I　=　Average annual rainfall in mm

　　　　R　=　Runoff coefficient

(GI sheets, clay tiles, slab = 0.8)

Available quantum of rainfall (in cu.m)

RAINFALL	ROOF TOP AREA (SQ. M.)					
MM	**50**	**60**	**70**	**80**	**90**	**100**
500	20	24	28	32	36	40
600	24	28.8	33.6	38.4	43.2	48
700	28	33.6	39.2	44.8	50.4	56
800	32	38.4	44.8	51.2	57.6	64
900	36	43.2	50.4	57.6	64.8	72
100	40	48	56	64.0	72	80

Conclusion:

RWH is essentially to be employed because of increased demand of water. People participation, awareness and conscious efforts are the key factors for successful implementation of the technique. In addition to RWH, recycling techniques, if suitably considered, then more and more saving of water in best possible manner will be observed.

IMPORTANT POINTS

- Plumbing system for waste water and its types:
  - (a) Two pipe system
  - (b) One pipe-system
  - (c) Single-stack
  - (d) Single-stack partially ventilated system
- Septic tank, its need and location. Construction details of septic tank along with its three design parameters.
- Utility of septic tank.
- Garbage disposal system with components.
- Need of rain water harvesting, aims, advantages of RWH.
- Systems employed for effective RWH.
- Various types of RWH in India.

QUESTIONS

1. What are the requirements of plumbing system?
2. Explain one-pipe and two-pipe plumbing system.
3. Explain two pipe plumbing system.**[2000 (5 M), Dec. 2006, May 2006 (5 M)]**

Chapter 11

PLANNING OF RESIDENTIAL BUILDINGS

11.1 PLANNING OF RESIDENTIAL BUILDINGS

As per National Building Code of India (SP : 7-1970) Residential Buildings (Group A) are those buildings in which sleeping accommodation is provided for normal residential purposes, with or without cooking or dining or both facilities. It is a building, where one dwells or resides permanently or for a considerable time can be called as a residential building; it may be a bungalow, a block of flats, a hill side cottage or a hotel. Every type of residential building serves the purpose of dwelling in one way or the other, only there is difference of type. Buildings of group A are further sub-divided as follows:

(i) **Sub-division A-1: Lodging or Rooming Houses:** These include any building or group of buildings under the same management, in which separate sleeping accommodation for a total of not more than 15 persons, on either transient or permanent basis with or without dining facilities, but without cooking facilities for individuals, is provided.

A lodging or rooming house is classified as a dwelling in sub-division A-2 if no room in any of its private dwelling units is rented to more than three persons.

(ii) **Sub-division A-2: One or Two Family Private Dwellings:** These include any private dwelling which is occupied by members of a single family and has a total sleeping accommodation for not more than 20 persons.

If rooms in a private dwelling are rented to outsiders, these should be for accommodating not more than 3 persons.

If sleeping accommodation for more than 20 persons is provided in any one residential building, it should be classified as a building sub-division A-3 or A-4 as the case may be.

(iii) **Sub-division A-3: Dormitories:** These include any building in which group sleeping accommodation is provided, with or without dining facilities, for persons who are not members of the same family, in any one room or a management, for example, school and college dormitories, students and other hostels and military barracks.

(iv) **Sub-division A-4: Apartment Houses (Flats):** These include any building or structure in which living quarters are provided for three or more families living independently of each other and with independent cooking facilities, for example, apartment houses, mansions and chawls.

(v) Sub-division A-5: Hotels: These include any building or group of buildings under single management in which sleeping accommodation, with or without dining facilities, is provided for hire to more than 15 persons who are primarily transient, for example, hotels, inns, clubs and motels.

11.2 SITE SELECTION

In case of buildings, particularly residential, selection of a site and designs of a building before its construction, are two important aspects. Every individual has a desire to live in an ecofriendly atmosphere with a good aspect for all the natural benefits like light, air etc.

Therefore, before starting planning of any residential building, following main points should be considered by planner.

- Climate of site and its effects.

- Living habits of the owner and his requirements.

- Budget of owner.

- Bye-laws and regulations for sanctioning.

- Materials of construction and method of construction.

11.3 TYPES OF STRUCTURE

1. Load bearing structure.

2. Framed structure.

3. Composite structure.

1. Load Bearing Structure

In this method, the entire load of the structure is transmitted through the brick or stone masonry walls of a structure. The walls are supported on continuous foundations, which are resting on firm soil at shallow depth. Load bearing structure can be constructed maximum upto four storeys, but usually two storeys are constructed. In this type of structure, beam and trusses etc. rest on a load bearing walls.

2. Framed Structures

Framed structures consist of frames. These frames are formed by columns, slabs, footings and beams. The columns are created usually on independent foundations and braced together by beams at floor levels and roof levels. In some cases, instead of providing independent foundations, combined or raft foundations are provided depending on the underlying soil and load conditions.

3. Composite Structure

This is a combination of load bearing and framed structure. The outer walls can be of load bearing type, whereas column and structure can be provided internally. Thus, floors and roof are supported by walls as well as by frame. This type of construction is generally adopted for industrial buildings or ware houses where span is very large.

11.3.1 Comparison Between Different Types of Structures

The three types of structures described above can be compared with respect to the following aspects: (Refer Table 11.1)

Table 11.1

Aspect	Load bearing	Frame structure	Composite structure
Soil/Foundation strata	Soil of good S.B.C. available at shallow depth.	Can be suitable for any type of soil at any depth.	Soil of good S.B.C. available at shallow depth.
Floor space	Thick walls cause reduction in floor space.	More floor area due to thinner walls.	Intermediate floor space available.
Height (No. of storeys)	Allowed upto 4 storeys.	Multistoreyed construction possible.	Allowed upto 2 to 3 storeys.
Time of construction	Slow and time consuming construction.	Fast and speedy construction.	Intermediate time required.
Economy	Economical upto 2 storeys.	Economical for multistoreyed buildings.	Less cost than framed structure upto 2 to 3 floors.
Flexibility in planning.	Less flexible due to load bearing walls.	Flexible due to walls serving as partition only.	Internal arrangement can be modified.
Resistance to vibration	Susceptible to vibration due to machines and earthquake.	Withstand machine vibration and earthquake forces if provision is made in design.	Better than load bearing.

11.4 ARRANGEMENT OF ROOMS FOR RESIDENTIAL BUILDINGS

1. Drawing Room or Living Room:

It is the main room and living area where friends are entertained and family members relax. It can also be used as a combined drawing and dining room. It should be situated on the front entrance of a building and should not provide direct access to the bedrooms and toilet block. It should be spacious to accommodate furniture for sitting, well lighted, ventilated and adjacent to dining room.

An important factor in arranging the living room is due consideration to seating accommodation of different groups. The size and shape of the furniture depends upon the living standard of the family and allied purposes it is going to serve. The living room may be used as bed room, it may be combined kitchen-cum-living room or it may accommodate the dining space or have attached dining recess. There would be many variety of the shape and size of the living rooms to suit all types of activities which may be accommodated in them. (Refer Table 11.2). Rooms are generally more satisfactory if rectangular than square, but irregular shapes with long and narrow rooms should be avoided.

Doors and windows should be planned in view of the 'aspect', 'prospect' light and ventilation, as well as to leave good wall-spaces against which furniture can be placed. Doors should be as few as possible and not less than 0.9 m in width 1.1 m is preferable.

Table 11.2: Approximate sizes of various furniture pieces

Name	Size
(1) Large couch or settee	0.9 m × 2.1 m or 0.75 m × 2.05 m
(2) Reclining or club chair	0.75 m × 0.9 m or 0.65 m × 0.75 m
(3) Twin chair or sofa	0.75 m × 1.35 m
(4) Office chair or small chair	0.45 m × 0.45 m
(5) Chair without arms for dining	0.45 m × 0.45 m
(6) Writing table	1.35 m × 0.75 m
(7) Small desk	1.20 m × 0.60 m
(8) Bridge or card table	0.90 m × 0.90 m
(9) Coffee or card table	1.0 m diameter
(10) End table or end piece	0.60 m × 0.30 m or 0.60 m diameter

2. Dining Room

Dining room should be adjacent or attached to kitchen. For attached dining room, the activities of kitchen should be screened by a screen wall or partition. Location of drawing, dining and kitchen should be side by side. A wash basin should be provided attached or inside the dining room. It is preferred, that the dining and drawing room remain connected through connecting door. Also according to the recent trends, these two rooms are combined into one big size room.

The floor area of the separate dining room depends on the type of furniture and the minimum number of persons to be served at a time. The dining room may also serve alternative purposes such as children's study room, occasional sitting room for ladies etc. It should be well lighted and ventilated. There should be as few doors as possible, one joining either to living room or connecting passage and another for providing access to kitchen. Provision of one or two cupboards for keeping plates, crockery, glasses etc. and a wash-basin is essential for convenience.

3. Kitchen

In every house kitchen is one of the important rooms. The primary function in the kitchen is food preparation and service and may accommodate in addition to these dining, cleaning space etc.

Kitchen should be located in a corner of the house such that smoke of the kitchen does not spread in all the rooms of the house. There should be no connection with toilet block provision of cooking shelves, cupboards, storage shelves and washing utensils should be made in the kitchen. The sequence of operations needs to be taken into account while planning the kitchen. The operation in connection with meals start with collection of goods, grains, flour, vegetables, dairy and poultry products, and storing them. The food is to be prepared and cooked. The next step is to keep food in readiness to be served and then service or distribution of food. Rest of the food to be stored and preserved. The used plates and dishes need to be washed and put away.

It is essential to have good lighting in kitchens both by day and night. Windows should be planned preferably with north and east aspect to give even and adequate lighting for all working areas. A flooring of non-absorbent and smooth nature should be provided. The equipment of the working kitchen comprises of sink of size (60 cm × 45 cm × 25 cm) and at least 0.75 cm to 0.9 m height from floor level. Cooking range (chulla), working table, water storage, storage cabinets, larder and refrigerator.

4. Bed Room

This room should be located on one side of the building. It is should have at least one of its walls as an external wall so as to maintain good natural ventilation and light in the room. This room should be directly in front of the prevailing direction of wind. Attached bath and W.C. is preferable for modern planning. There should be no connection with the kitchen. The bed room should be located so as to maintain privacy. The probable bed room furniture comprises of the following pieces.

1. Double bed – size 1.35 to 1.45 m × 2 to 2.10 m.

2. Single bed – size 0.9 × 2.0 m.

3. Single cot – size 0.75 × 1.80 m.

4. Small chair – size 0.45 m × 0.45 m.

5. Small arm chair – size 0.65 m × 0.45 m.

6. Divan, port or settee – size 0.75 × 1.65 m.

7. Dressing stool – size 0.45 × 0.38 m.

8. Chest of drawers (small) – size 0.45 × 0.90 m.

9. Chest of drawers (large) – size 0.60 × 0.30 m.

10. Bed side table – size 0.60 × 0.30 m.

11. Small dressing table – size 0.45 × 0.90 m.

Above sizes are indicative of plan dimensions.

5. Store Room

For storing food grains and other articles it is preferable to place them in a store room. Ventilation and natural lightning is less important for this room. The left out space after fulfilling the requirements for all other rooms may be used as a store room.

6. Pantry

This is a small room which is attached to a dining room cooked food is kept in this room. This room should have cupboards and shelves.

7. Guest Room

This room should be located on one side of the front verandah. It may not have connection with other rooms except with the dining room. Separate toilets should be provided to the guest room to maintain privacy.

8. Dressing Room

This room should remain attached with bed room and bath and W.C. This room should have provisions of a dressing table, cupboard etc.

9. Bath and W.C.

Bath and W.C. may be separate or they combined in one room. If bath and W.C. are to be attached with a bed room, then they are generally combined. Both W.C. and bath should be well ventilated. There should be at least one separate bath and W.C. in the house, other than combined with the bed rooms. All the W.C. and bath rooms should have at least one of their wall as external walls so as to facilitate proper ventilation. Dado or glazed tiles should be provided or otherwise walls should be finished with smooth water-proof cement coat. They should also be provided with the necessary fixtures. Size and type of W.C. pans, wash basins, electrical installations for hot water, plumbing fixtures, washing machine etc. control the size of bathrooms and WC.

10. Verandah

For economic use of space the provision of verandah is becoming minimum in modern planning. But a certain amount of free space area for corridor and verandah (covered) is required to provide independent access to different rooms, seating space and for drying cloths etc. A minimum width of 1.2 m and having a length equal to that of a front room may be provided.

11. Puja or Prayer Room

A small room or space at least 1.2 m × 2.5 m should be provided for prayer by the side of bed room. This room should be lighted and ventilated.

12. Stair

Provision of a stair even for a single storeyed building is necessary for the purpose of inspection, cleaning of the roof and also as outdoor sleeping area during peak summer nights. For storied building the location of a staircase should be such that each floor or flat is separated from general movement of stair. For family use it should be located centrally and most of the rooms should have easy approach for the stair provided that their privacy of any room does not suffer.

13. Lobby

It is a hall at the entrance of which remains connected to the other parts of the building through corridors.

14. Porches

It is constructed in the front of the building. This adds to the elevation of the building. Car can be parked in it temporarily.

15. Garage and Servant's Room

These rooms are connected in the back open space of the plot. They are always made in separate blocks.

16. Corridor

It is a covered common passage in the building for independent entrance to various rooms.

11.5 SIZE OF ROOMS FOR RESIDENTIAL BUILDINGS

This depends upon the standard of living and income of the individual family. Big size rooms are generally preferred. A bed room should not be over-congested by placing too-many furnitures. For luxurious planning, the size of a drawing or living room can be made as big as possible. But considering all the points as indicated above some average dimensions for High Income Group (H.I.G.), Middle Income Group (M.I.G.); Low Income Group (L.I.G.) and maximum size as per code of practice for building bye-laws are given below for general guidance. (Refer Plate No. 1 to 16 for).

Name of the room	H.I.G. All dimension	M.I.G.	L.I.G.	Minimum (as per I.S.)
		Length × Breadth are in metres		
Drawing room	5.0 × 4.2 to 7.2 × 5.5	4.2 × 3.6 to 4.5 × 4.0	3.5 × 3.0	9.5 sq.m.
Dining room	4.0 × 3.5 to 5.0 × 4.0	3.5 × 3.1 to 7.0 × 3.1 (drawing + dining)	3.0 × 2.8	7.5 sq.m.
Bed room	4.8 × 4.2	4.6 × 3.6	3.5 × 3.0	9.5 sq.m.
Office room	4.0 × 3.6	3.5 × 3.0	–	–
Guest room	4.0 × 3.6	3.5 × 3.0	–	–
Store	3.0 × 3.0	3.0 × 2.8	2.25 × 1.5	3.0 sq.m.
Kitchen	3.5 × 3	2.0 × 2.5	2.5 × 2.2 (Breadth min.)	4.5 sq.m. (Kitchen and dinning combined 5.0 sq.m.)
Pantry	3.0 × 2.5	–	–	–
Dressing	3.5 × 3.0	3.0 × 2.5	–	–
Bath and W.C. (combined)	3.5 × 2.5	3.0 × 1.6	2.10 × 1.5	1.0 × 1.8
Bath (separate)	3.0 × 2.0	2.0 × 1.5	1.50 × 1.20	1.0 × 1.2
W.C. (separate)	2.5 × 2.0	1.8 × 1.2	1.1 × 1.0	0.9 × 1.0

Box room	1.8×1.8	–	–	–
Servant's room	3.0×3.0	3.0×2.5	–	–
Garage (min. height 2.4 m)	5.8×5.5	5.0×2.80	–	5.0×2.5
Porch	6.0×3.0 to 4.8×3.0	–	–	–

11.6 PLANNING OF A RESIDENTIAL COMPLEX

To describe various types of drawings, which are required to be drawn by the architecture, a set of different drawings is furnished here. **(For additional set of drawings refer end pages of this chapter)**

1. Plate No. 1 – Shows layout of a residential complex which includes arrangement of different buildings, internal roads, garden etc.
2. Plate No. 2 – Shows typical floor plans for first, third and fifth floors.
3. Plate No. 3 – Shows typical floor plans for second, fourth and sixth floors.
4. Plate No. 4 – Shows parking floor plan.
5. Plate No. 5 – Shows front elevation.
6. Plate No. 6 – Shows terrace floor plan.
7. Plate No. 7 – Shows floor plan for lift, machine room, and R.C.C. water storage tank.
8. Plate No. 8 – Shows section and side elevation.
9. Plate No. 9 – Shows perspective of a building.
10. Plate No. 10 – Shows perspective view of the complex.
11. Plate No. 11, 12, 13, 14 – Show typical floor plans of other buildings in the same residential complex.
12. Plate No. 15 – Shows centre line plan of a building.
13. Plate No. 16 – Shows structural drawing showing R.C.C. design details, schedule of R.C.C. footing and columns.

SOLVED EXAMPLES

Planning of Typical R.C.C. Stairs:

Example 11.1: Plan a dog legged stair for a building with the following data:

(i) Vertical distance between the floors = 3.6 m.

(ii) Size of stair hall 2.5 m × 5 m.

(iii) Thickness of the floor slab = 140 mm.

(iv) Thickness of the waist slab and landing slab = 100 mm.

Solution: Assume,   Rise = 150 mm

and   Tread = 250 mm

$$\text{Width of the flight} = \frac{2.5}{2}$$

$$= 1.25 \text{ m}$$

$$\therefore \qquad \text{Height of each flight} = \frac{3.6}{2}$$

$$= 1.8 \text{ m}$$

$$\therefore \qquad \text{Number of risers required} = \frac{1.8 \times 1000}{150}$$

$$= 12 \text{ in each flight}$$

$$\text{Number of treads in each flight} = 12 - 11$$

$$= 11$$

$$\therefore \qquad \text{Space required for treads} = 11 \times 250 = 2750 \text{ mm}$$

$$\therefore \qquad \text{Space left for passage} = 5 - 1.25 - 2.75 = 1.00 \text{ m}$$

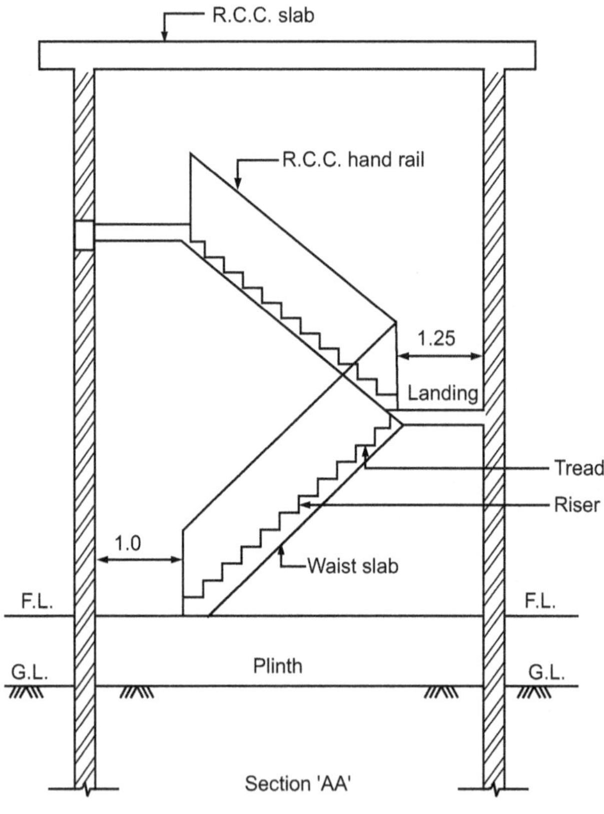

Fig. 11.1 (a)

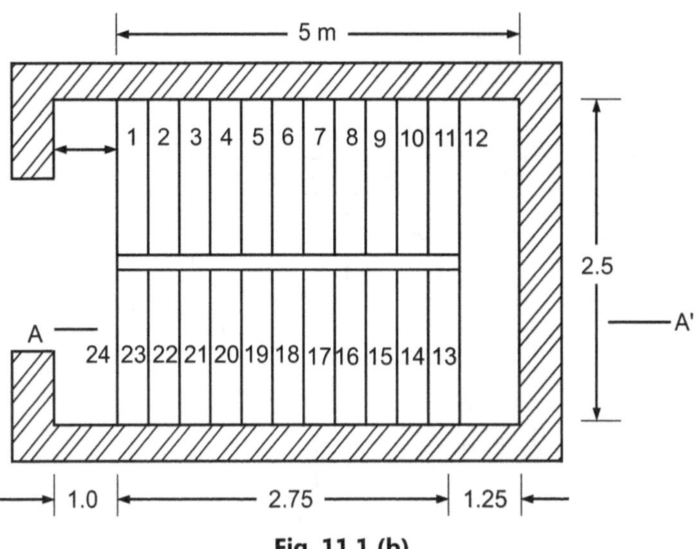

Fig. 11.1 (b)

Example 11.2: Calculate number of risers and treads in each flight for dog legged stair, floor to floor height is 3.3 m and riser is 150 mm.

Solution: Given data:

Floor to floor height = 3.3 m

Riser = 150 mm

∴ Total number of risers $= \dfrac{3300}{150}$

= 22

Assuming two flights, number of risers in each flight = 11 number and number of treads in each flight = 11 – 1 = 10 number.

Example 11.3: Plan a staircase for a residential building in which the vertical distance between each floor is 3.36 m. The size of the stair hall is limited to 4.5 × 3 m.

Solution: Given data:

(i)   Floor to floor height . = 3.36 m

Let,   Width of landing = 1.5 m

= Width of stairs

Assume,   Rise = 16 cm

∴   Total number of risers $= \dfrac{3.36 \times 100}{16}$

= 21 risers $\Rightarrow$ 11 in first flight
10 in second height

Provide 11 risers in each flight

$\therefore$ Number of treads in first flight = $11 - 1 = 0$

in second flight = $10 - 9 = 9$

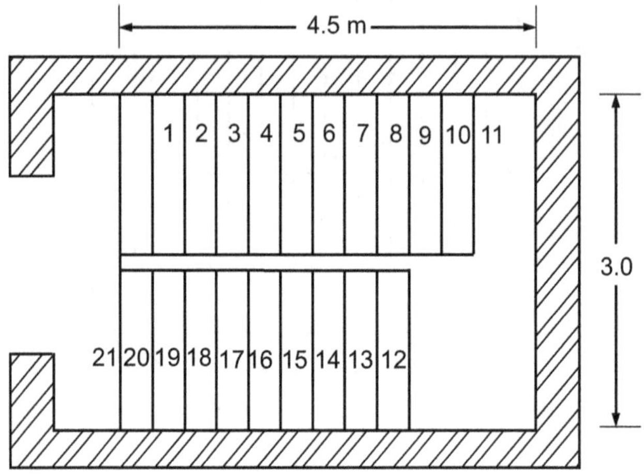

Fig. 11.2

IMPORTANT POINTS

- Types of Group-A buildings i.e.

  (a) Lodging (b) One or two family private dwellings

  (c) Dormitories (d) Flats (e) Hotels

- Arrangement of rooms for residential buildings.
- Planning and drawing as per data given.
- Planning and drawing if a line plan is given.

QUESTIONS

1. A line plan for a Residential Building is shown in Fig. 11.3.

Data:

   (a) All walls are 230 mm thick.

   (b) Walls indicated by $\otimes$ are 100 mm thick.

   (c) RCC framed structure.

   (d) Beam sizes 0.23 m $\times$ 0.38 m.

   (e) Column sizes 0.23 m $\times$ 0.30 m.

   (f) Floor to floor height 3.30 m.

   (g) Plinth height 0.60 m.

   Based on the data and Fig. 11.3:

(i)　Draw to a scale 1 : 50 detailed plan.

(ii)　Draw to a scale 1 : 50 detailed section A-A.

(iii)　Prepare schedule of openings and also show design for staircase.

(iv)　Assuming cost of construction ₹ 4000/- per sq.m., find cost of construction.

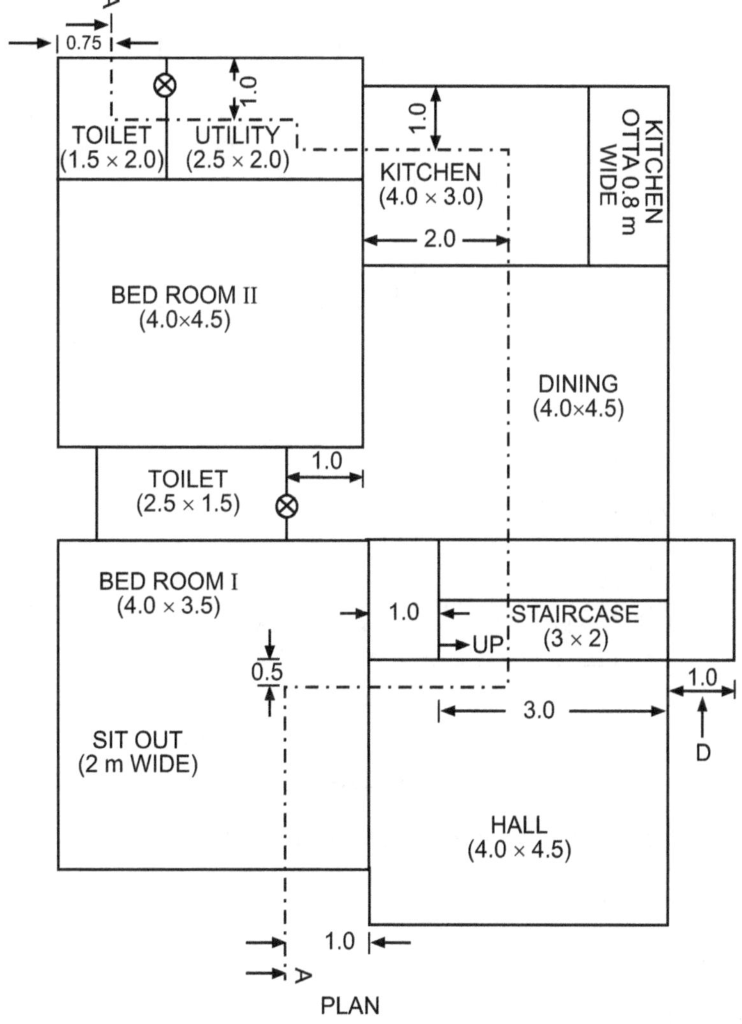

Fig. 11.3

2.　A line plan for a residential building is given in Fig. 11.4. Draw to a scale of 1 : 50 or suitable:

(a)　Detailed plan for RCC framed structure.

　　– All external walls and those marked ⊗ are 230 mm thick.

　　– All internal walls are 115 mm thick.

(b) Detailed section A-A assuming depth of foundation 1200 mm below G.L. Floor to floor height is 3150 mm. Riser – 175 mm, Tread – 250 mm.

(c) Calculate X and Y dimensions.

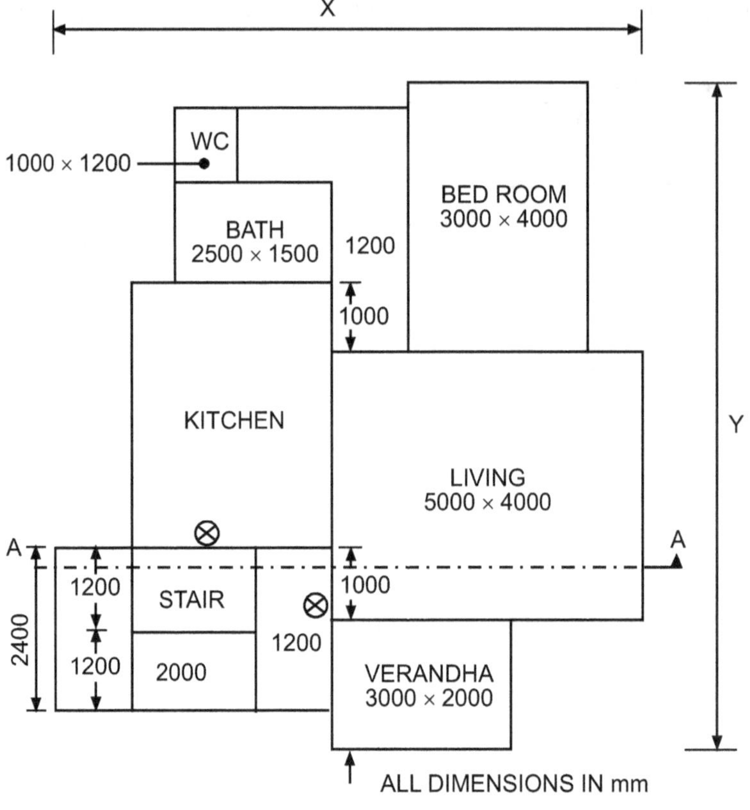

Fig. 11.4

3. Develop the line plan shown in Fig. 11.5. Scale 1 : 50.

(i) Draw detailed plan.

Wall thickness: external 230 thick.

internal 150 thick.

Doors standard size as per IS code.

Window opening 15% of room area.

Proof pitched to 30 degrees, hipped end, RCC.

Assume other relevant details.

(ii) Draw detailed section showing

(a) Stair details

(b) W.C. details

(c) Foundation details.

(iii) Prepare budget. Assume cost ₹ 5,000/- per sq.m. Calculate cost of building.

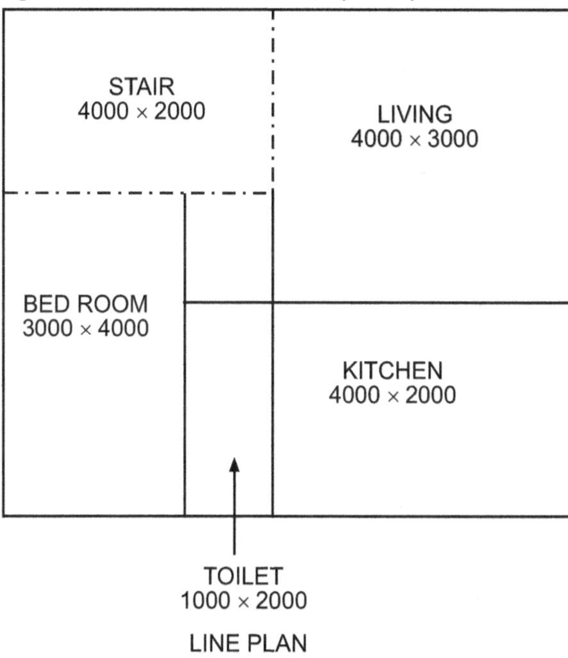

Fig. 11.5

4.   A plan for a residential building is shown in Fig. 11.6.

Draw to scale of 1 : 50

(1) Detailed plan for R.C.C. framed structure.

Take: External walls 230 thick

Internal walls 115 thick

Column size 230 × 450

(2) Detailed section S.S.

The different levels are:

- Foundation level   − 1200

- Ground level   − 450

- Plinth level   ± 000

- Sill level   − 900

- Lintel level　　　　　　　－ 2100
- Slab level　　　　　　　－ 3000
- Slab above stair　　　　－ 3900

(3) Write schedule for doors and windows.

(4) Show North direction.

(5) Calculate X and Y dimensions.

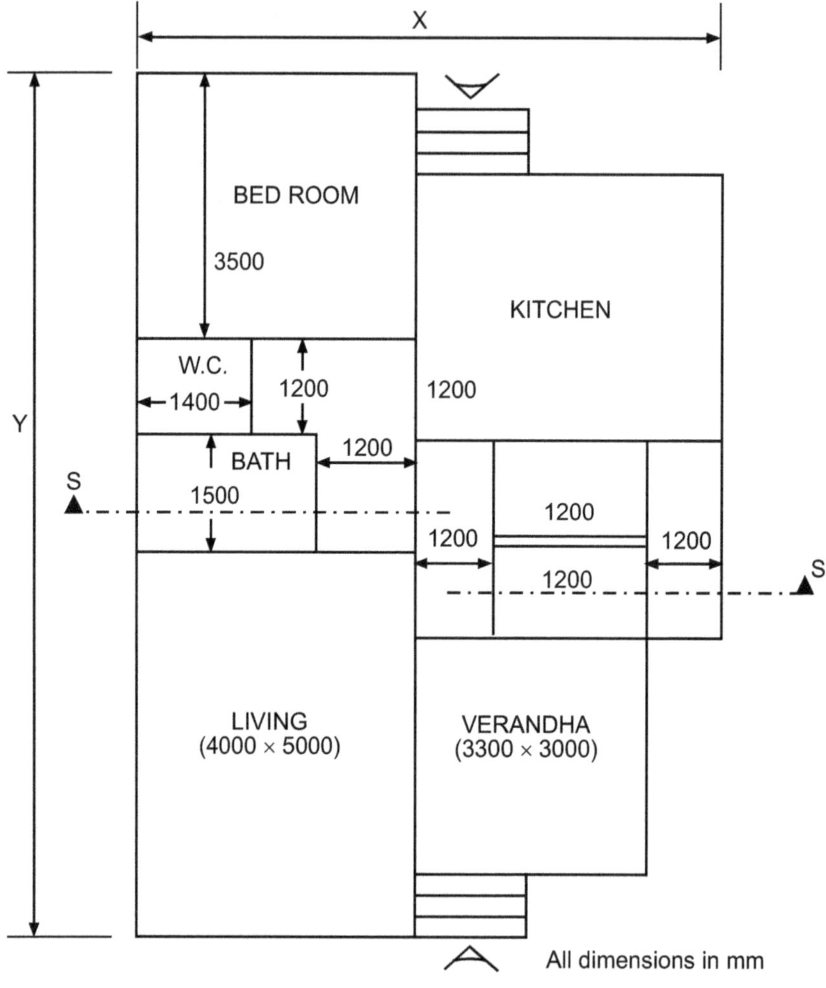

Fig. 11.6

5.　(a)　Draw a detailed floor plan to a scale 1 : 50 or suitable of a residential building for a given line plan as shown in Fig. 11.7.

Data:

1.　The structure is load bearing

2. All dimensions are in mm

3. Thicknesses of all walls are 230 mm and those marked by encircled X are 115 mm thick.

4. The building is single storey.

5. Assume proper sizes of doors and windows.

6. Consider plinth height as 900 mm (0.9 m)

7. Give the detailed dimensions.

(b) For the line plan shown in Fig. 11.7 draw the detailed sectional elevation along line XY assume suitable dimensions for the footing:

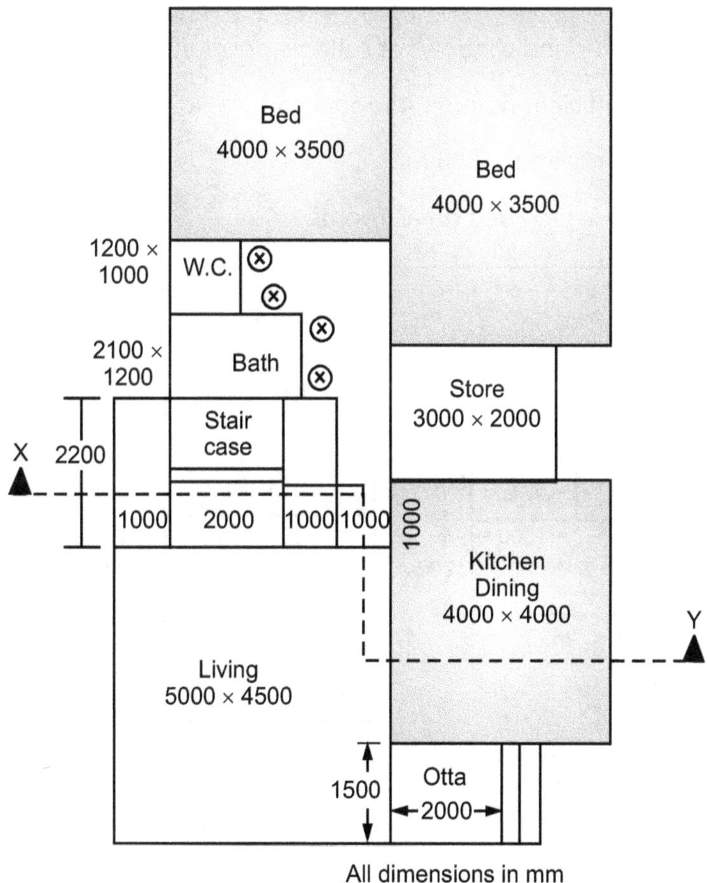

All dimensions in mm

Fig. 11.7

6. (a) Draw detailed plan to a scale a 1 : 50 of a residential building for the line plan shown in Fig. 11.8.

Fig. 11.8 is not to scale.

Refer the following guidelines:

(1) The structure is load bearing.

(2) All the walls are 230 mm thick.

(3) The building has got ground floor only.

(4) Access to the terrace is provided through staircase.

(5) All dimensions are in mm.

(6) Assume suitable sizes of doors and windows.

(7) Locate doors and windows at suitable positions.

(8) Provide sufficient number of doors and windows.

(9) Take plinth height = 600 mm.

(10) R.C.C. slab is provided on all rooms.

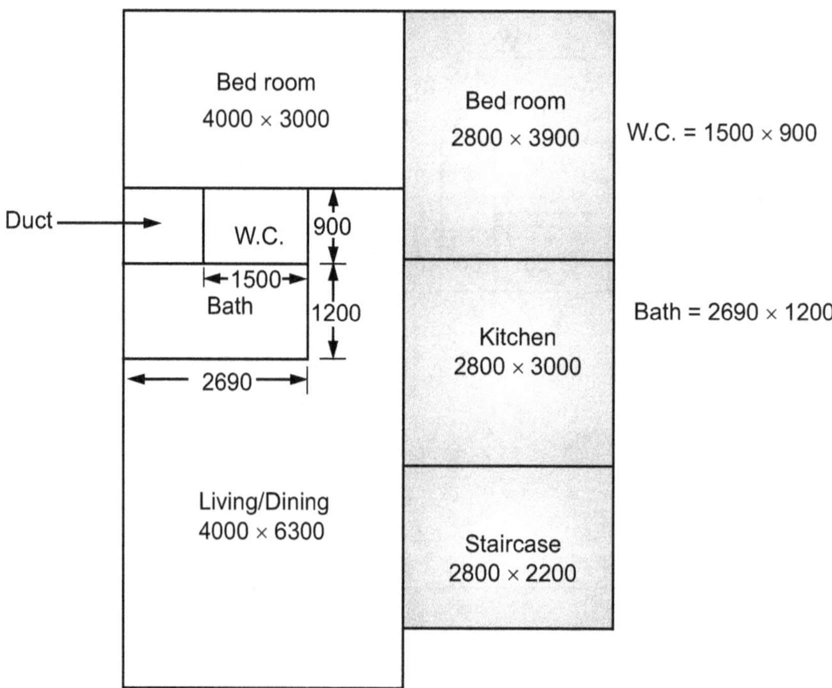

Fig. 11.8

(b) Write detailed schedule for doors and windows as per the format given:

Sr. No.	Type of door/window	No. of doors/windows	Size of opening in mm

7. Plan a residential building having G + 1 framed structure with the following requirements:

Sr. No.	Type of unit	No. of Units	Internal Area of Unit in sq. m.
1.	Living room	01	18
2.	Bed room	02	12
3.	Additional bed room with attached toilet	01	16
4.	Kitchen	01	12
5.	W.C.	01	1.5
6.	Bath	01	2.8
7.	Staircase	01	Use suitable dimensions

8. A line plan for a residential building is given in Fig. 11.9. Draw to a scale of 1 : 50 or suitable:

(a) Detailed plan for R.C.C. framed structure:

All external walls and those marked $\otimes$ are 230 mm thick:

8. All internal walls are 115 mm thick;

9. Locate doors and windows.

(b) Detailed section A-A assuming depth of foundation 1500 mm below GL and floor to floor height 3150 mm.

(c) Calculate X and Y dimensions and built-up area.

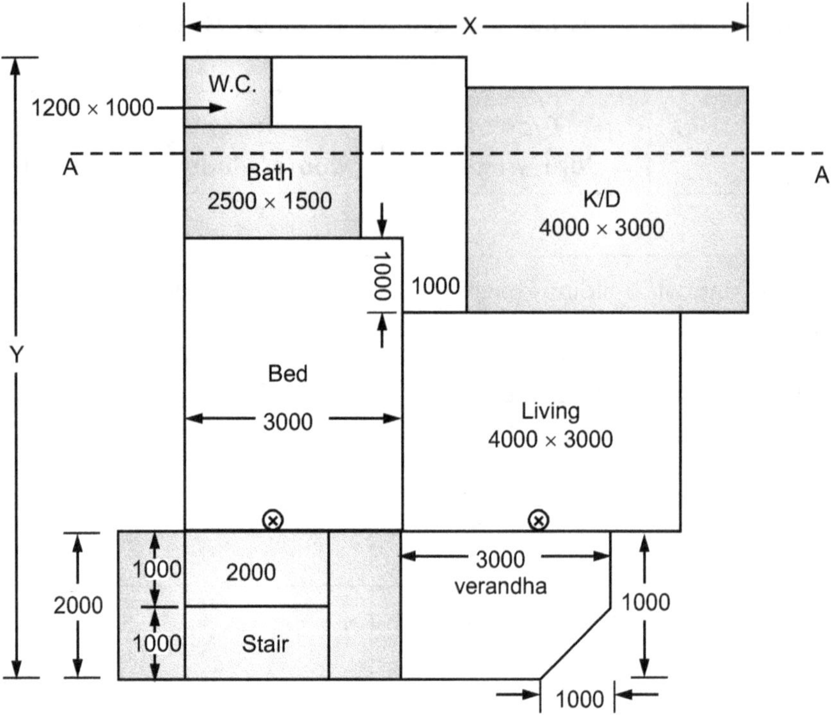

Fig. 11.9

All dimensions are in mm

All external walls and those marked ⊗ are 230 thick

All internal walls are 115 thick.

9. A line plan for a residential building is given in Fig. 11.10. Draw to a scale of 1 : 50 or suitable:

   (a) Detailed sectional plan for R.C.C. framed structure.

   - All external walls and those of the staircase room are 230 mm thick.

   - All internal walls are 115 m thick. Locate doors and windows.

   (b) Locate columns of size 230 mm × 400 mm.

   (c) Show northline to orient the building.

   (d) Detailed Section A-A, assuming depth of foundation 1000 mm below ground level. Floor to floor height is 3150 mm.

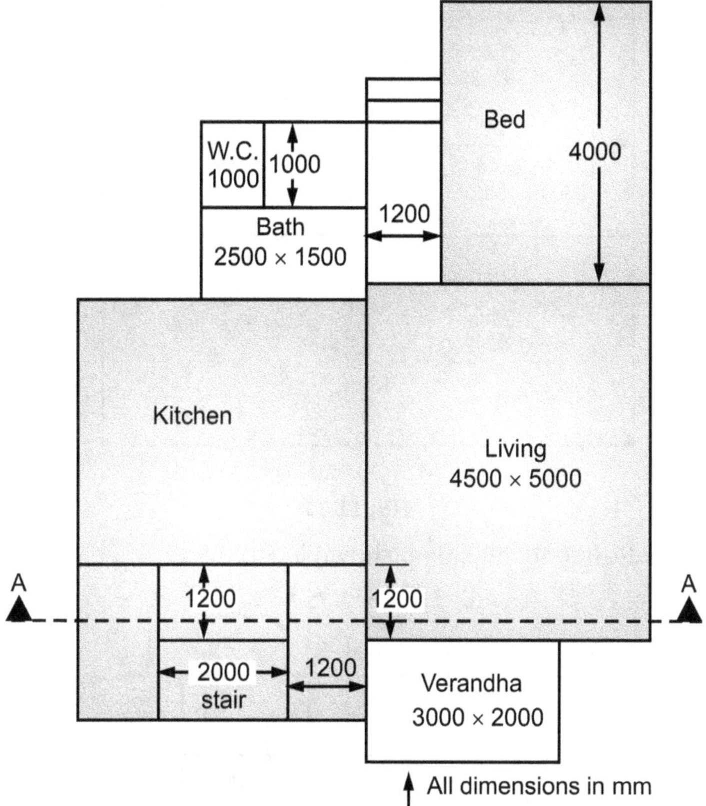

Fig. 11.10

10. Develop the line plan shown in Fig. 11.11.

    Data: Wall external BBM 230 tk.

    - Wall internal BBM 150 tk.

    - Door – As per IS code.

    - Windows – Opening 10% of floor area.

    - RCC framed structure.

    - Assume other details and state them clearly.

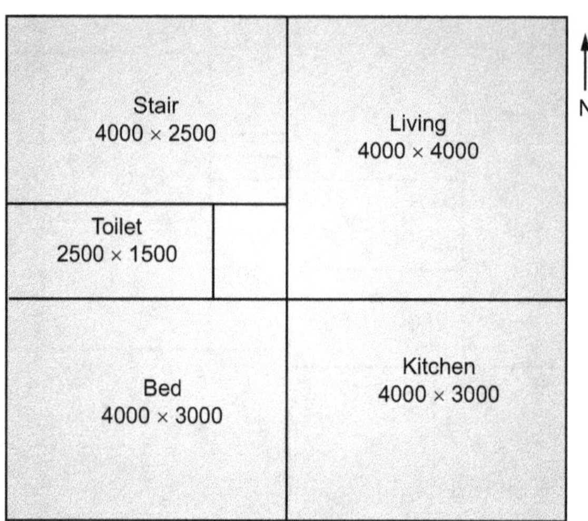

All dimensions in mm

Fig. 11.11

11. A line for a Residential Building shown in Fig. 11.12.

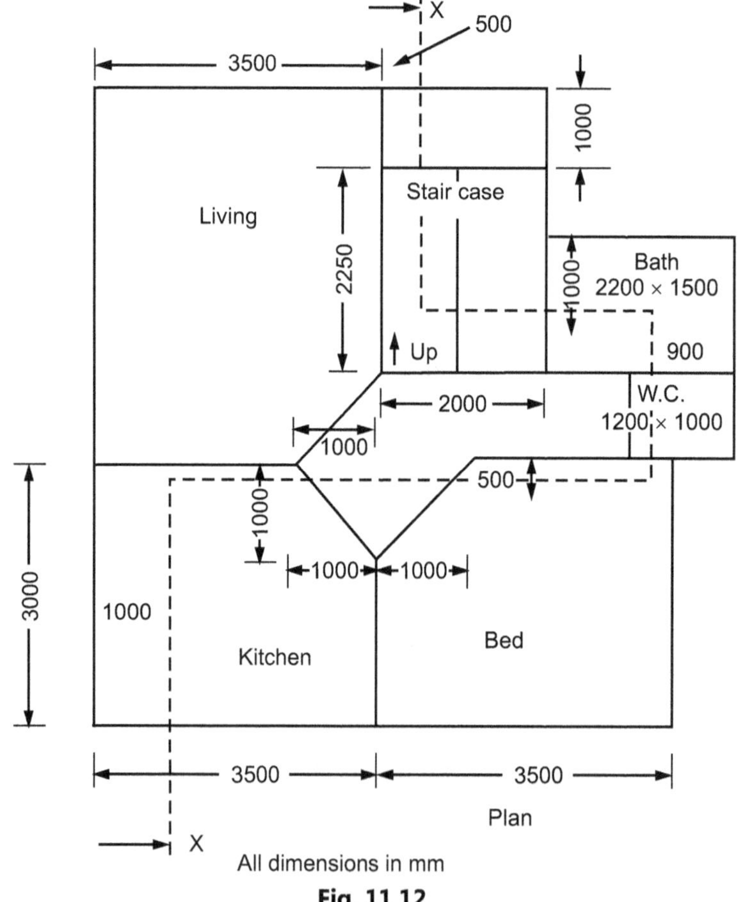

Plan

All dimensions in mm

Fig. 11.12

Data:

    (a) All walls are 230 mm thick.

    (b) Partition wall of W.C. and Bath – 100 mm thick.

    (c) Size of W.C. room – 1200 mm × 1000 mm.

    (d) Size of Bath room – 2200 mm × 1500 mm.

    (e) R.C.C. framed structure.

    (f) Beam sizes 230 mm × 380 mm.

    (g) Column sizes 230 mm × 300 mm.

    (h) Floor to floor height – 3000 mm.

    (i) Plinth height – 450 mm.

        (a) Draw to a scale 1 : 50 detailed plan.

        (b) Draw to scale 1 : 50 detailed section XX.

        (c) Calculate Built-up area.

        (d) Show design calculations for a staircase.

        (e) Show entrance steps at proper location in plan.

12. A line plan for a residential building is given in Fig. 11.13. Draw to scale of 1 : 50 or suitable:

    (a) Detailed plan for R.C.C. framed structure:

       • All external walls and those marked are 230 mm thick.

       • All internal walls are 115 mm thick

       • Locate doors, windows and columns of size 230 mm × 400 mm.

    (b) Detailed section AA assuming depth of foundation 1500 mm below ground level. Floor to floor height 3150 mm. Floor to ceiling height 3000 mm. Rise 175 mm, tread – 250 mm for R.C.C. stair.

    (c) Write schedule for doors and windows.

    (d) Calculate X and Y.

3500
Bed
1500 1000
1000
2500
Closed verandha
W.C.
1200 ×
1000
1000
2000 ×
1200
Bath
4000
All exterior Walls
and those marked O= 230 mm
All Interior Walls = 115 mm
1000
2000
1000
1000
1000
2000
A
A
1000
Living
Y
3000
4000
Open covered otta
500
X
1000
Plan

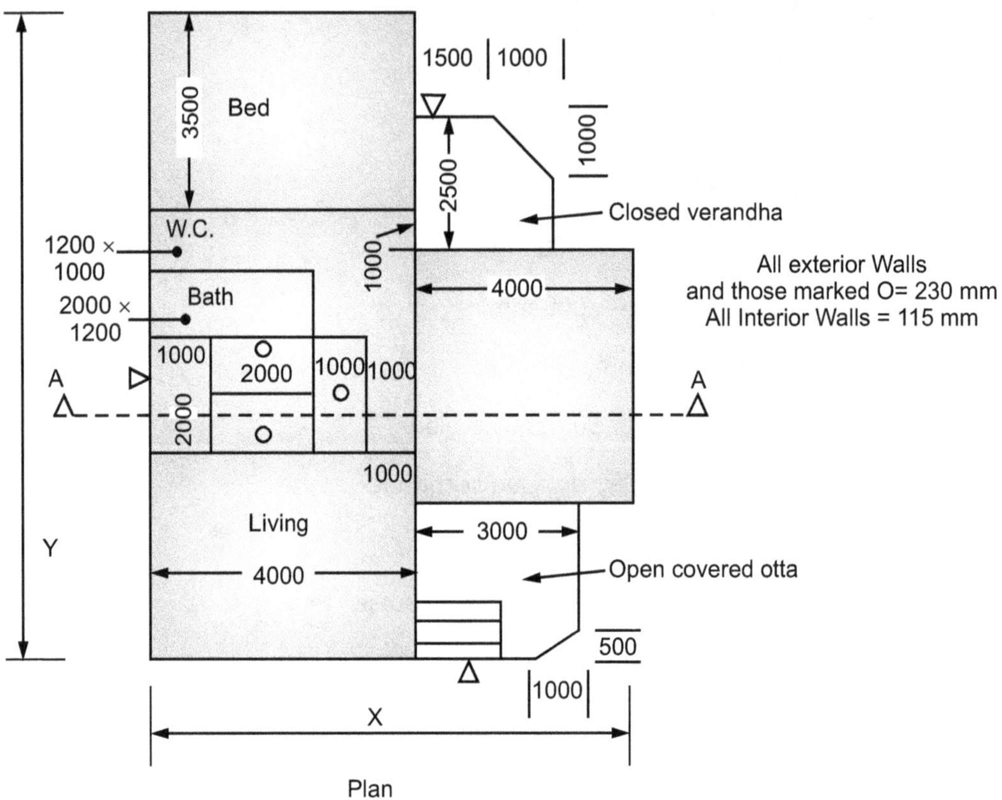

Fig. 11.13

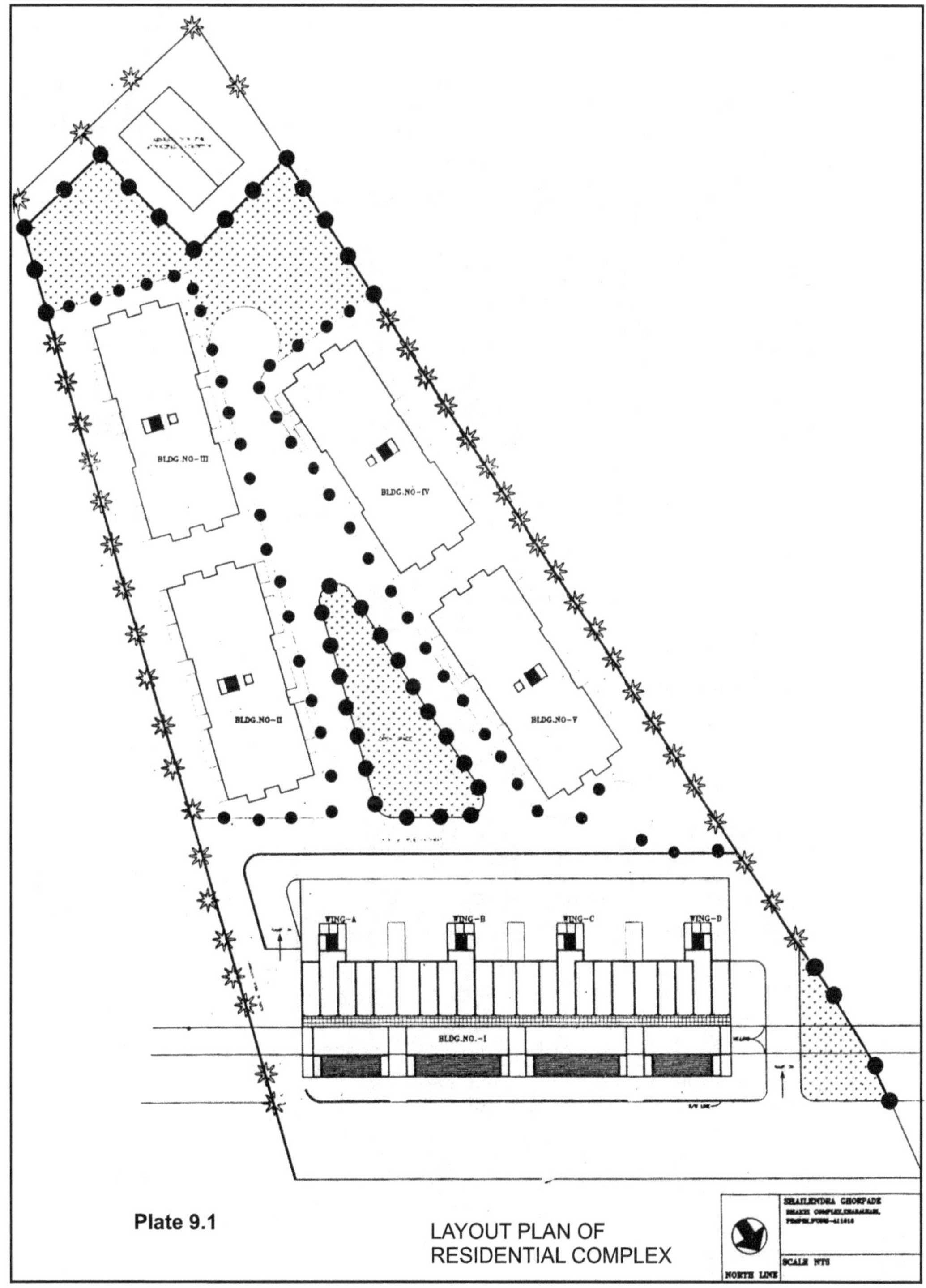

Plate 9.1

LAYOUT PLAN OF
RESIDENTIAL COMPLEX

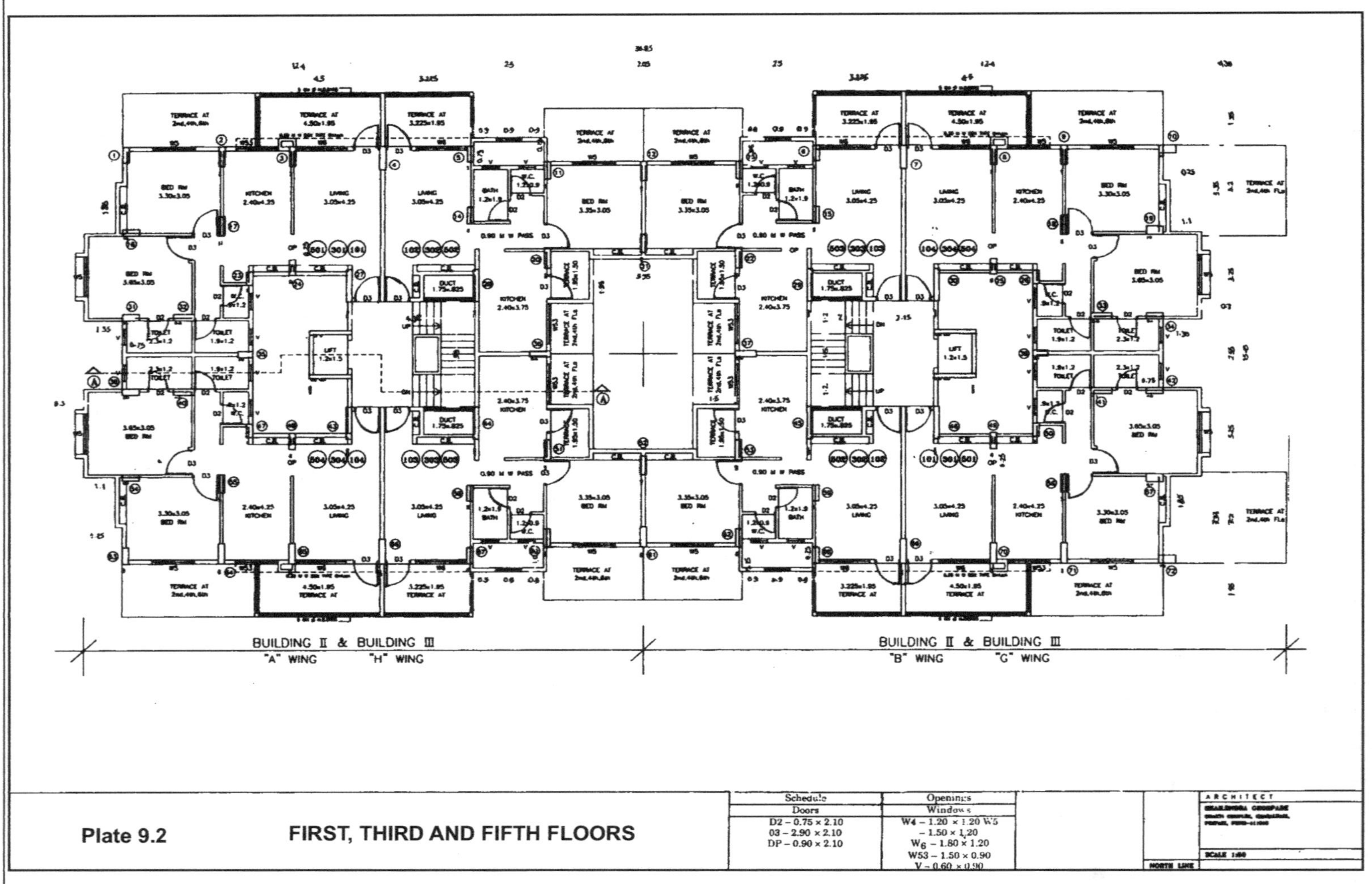

Plate 9.2   **FIRST, THIRD AND FIFTH FLOORS**

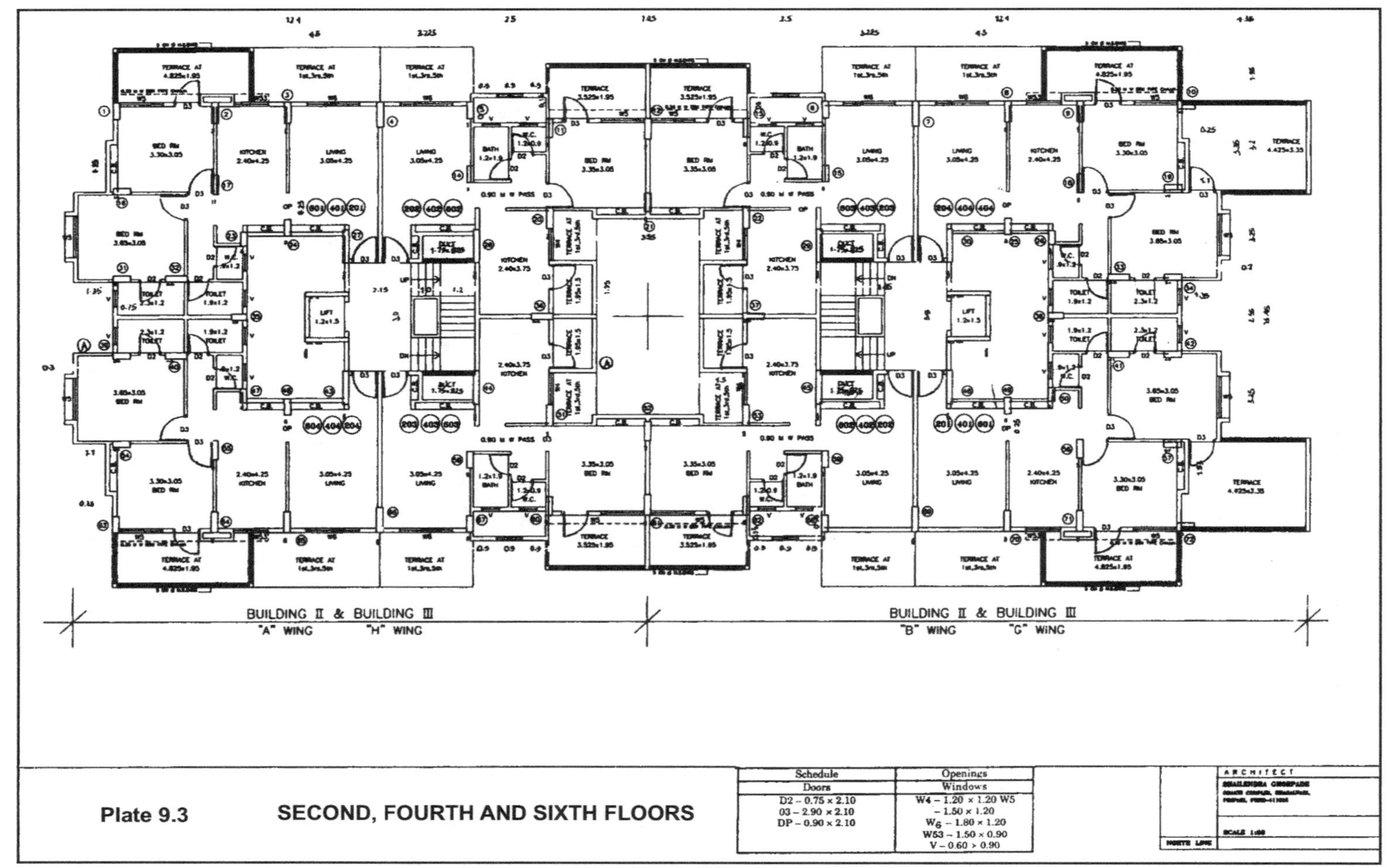

Schedule	Openings
Doors	Windows
D2 – 0.75 × 2.10 03 – 2.90 × 2.10 DP – 0.90 × 2.10	W4 – 1.20 × 1.20 W5 – 1.50 × 1.20 W_6 – 1.80 × 1.20 W53 – 1.50 × 0.90 V – 0.60 × 0.90

Plate 9.3   SECOND, FOURTH AND SIXTH FLOORS

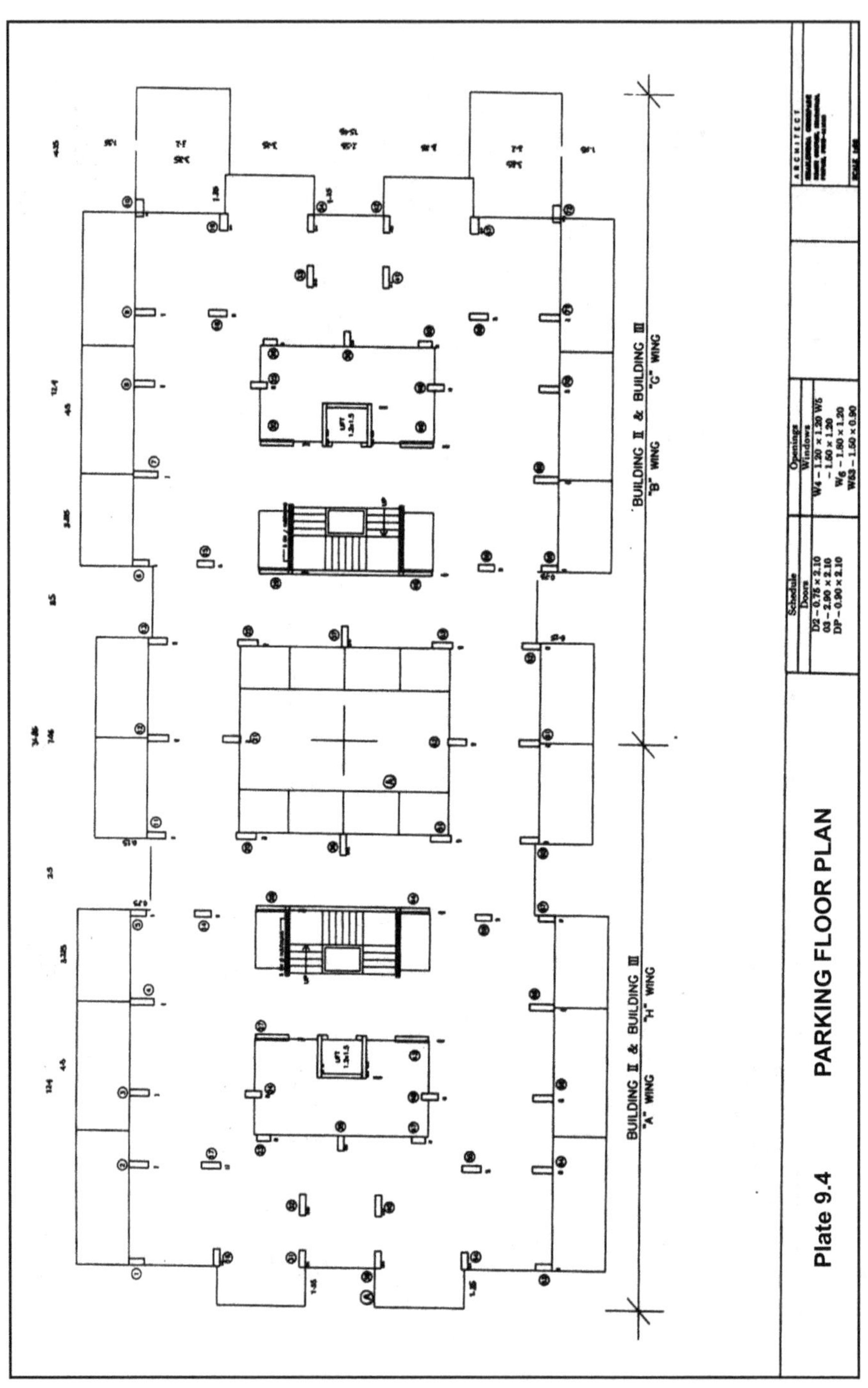
PARKING FLOOR PLAN
Plate 9.4
BUILDING II & BUILDING III
"C" WING
"B" WING
BUILDING II & BUILDING III
"H" WING
"A" WING
ARCHITECT
Schedule
Doors
Openings
Windows

Plate 9.5
FRONT ELEVATION
Schedule
Doors
D2 – 0.75 × 2.10
03 – 2.90 × 2.10
DP – 0.90 × 2.10
Openings
Windows
W4 – 1.20 × 1.20 W5
– 1.50 × 1.20
W6 – 1.80 × 1.20
W53 – 1.50 × 0.90
V – 0.60 × 0.90
ARCHITECT
SCALE 1:00
NORTH LINE

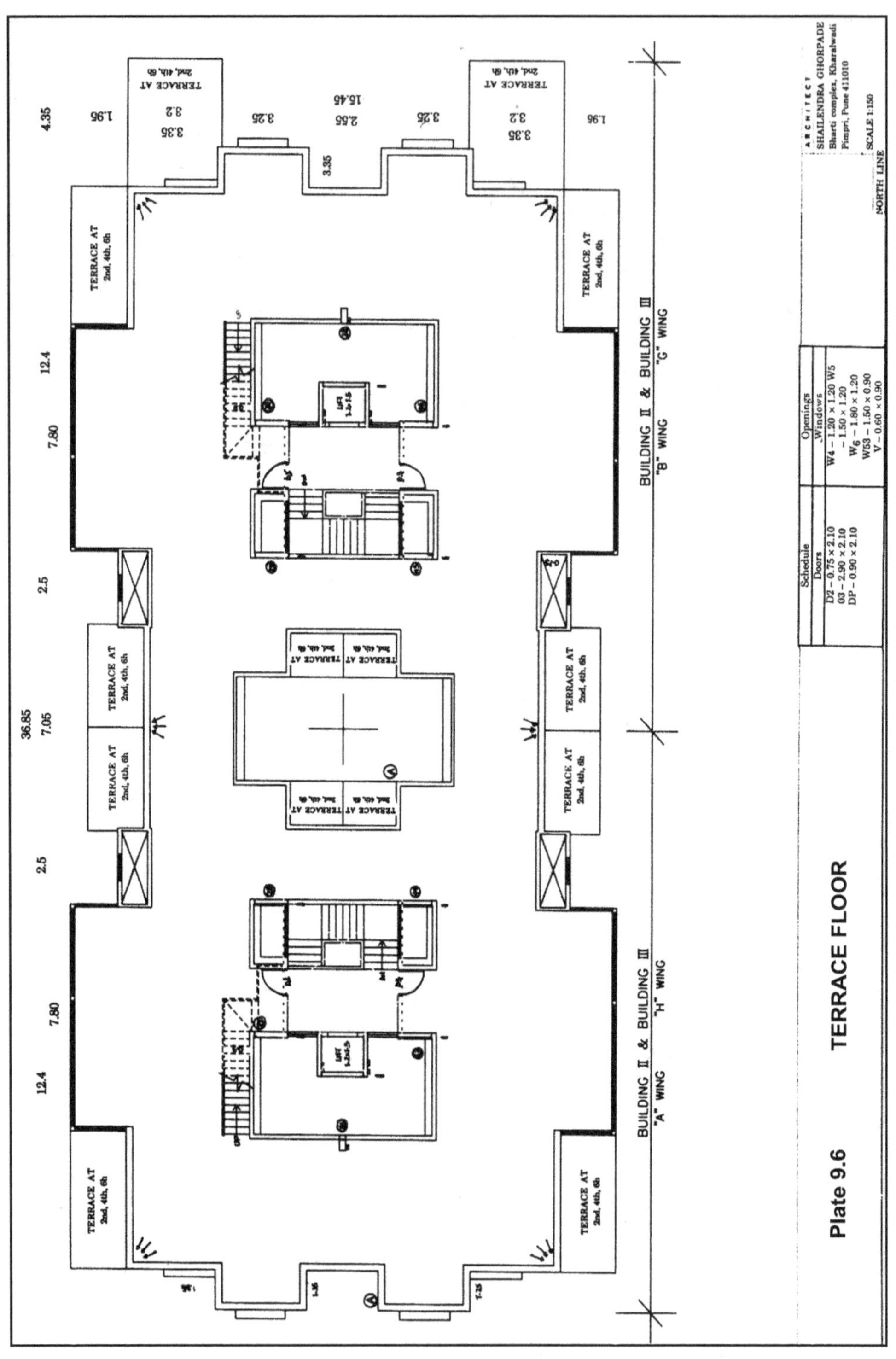

Plate 9.6 TERRACE FLOOR

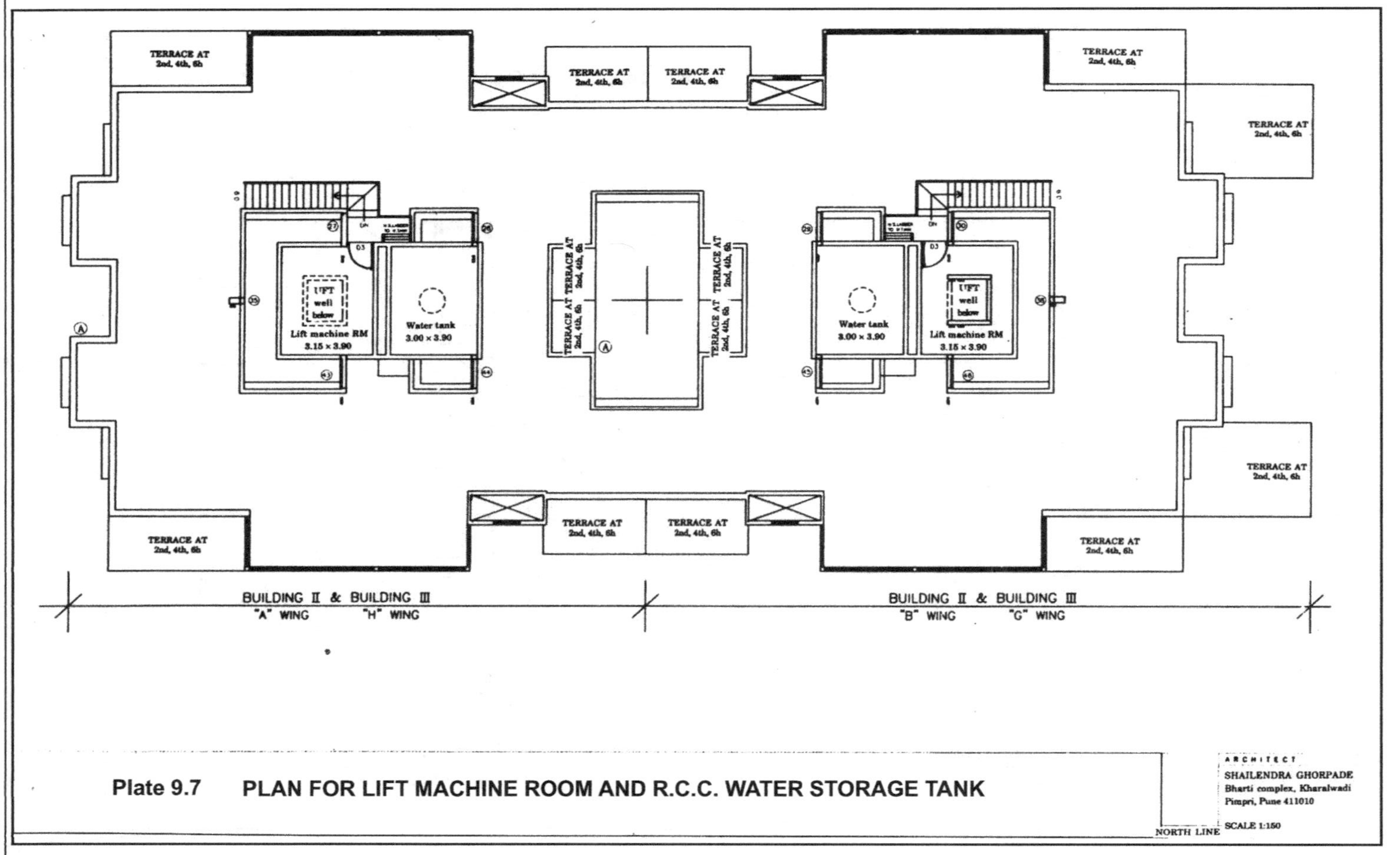

Plate 9.7   PLAN FOR LIFT MACHINE ROOM AND R.C.C. WATER STORAGE TANK

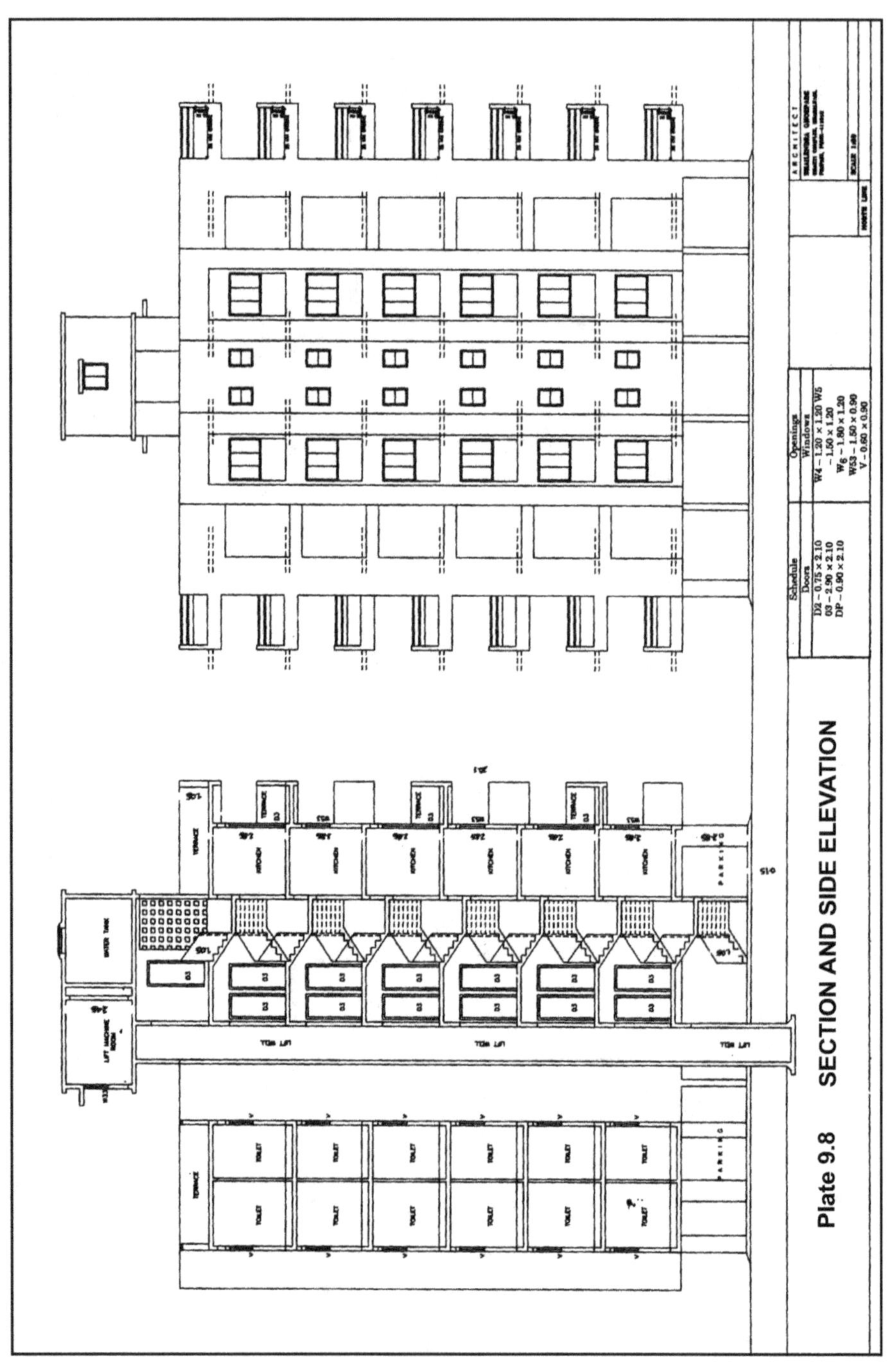

Plate 9.8 SECTION AND SIDE ELEVATION

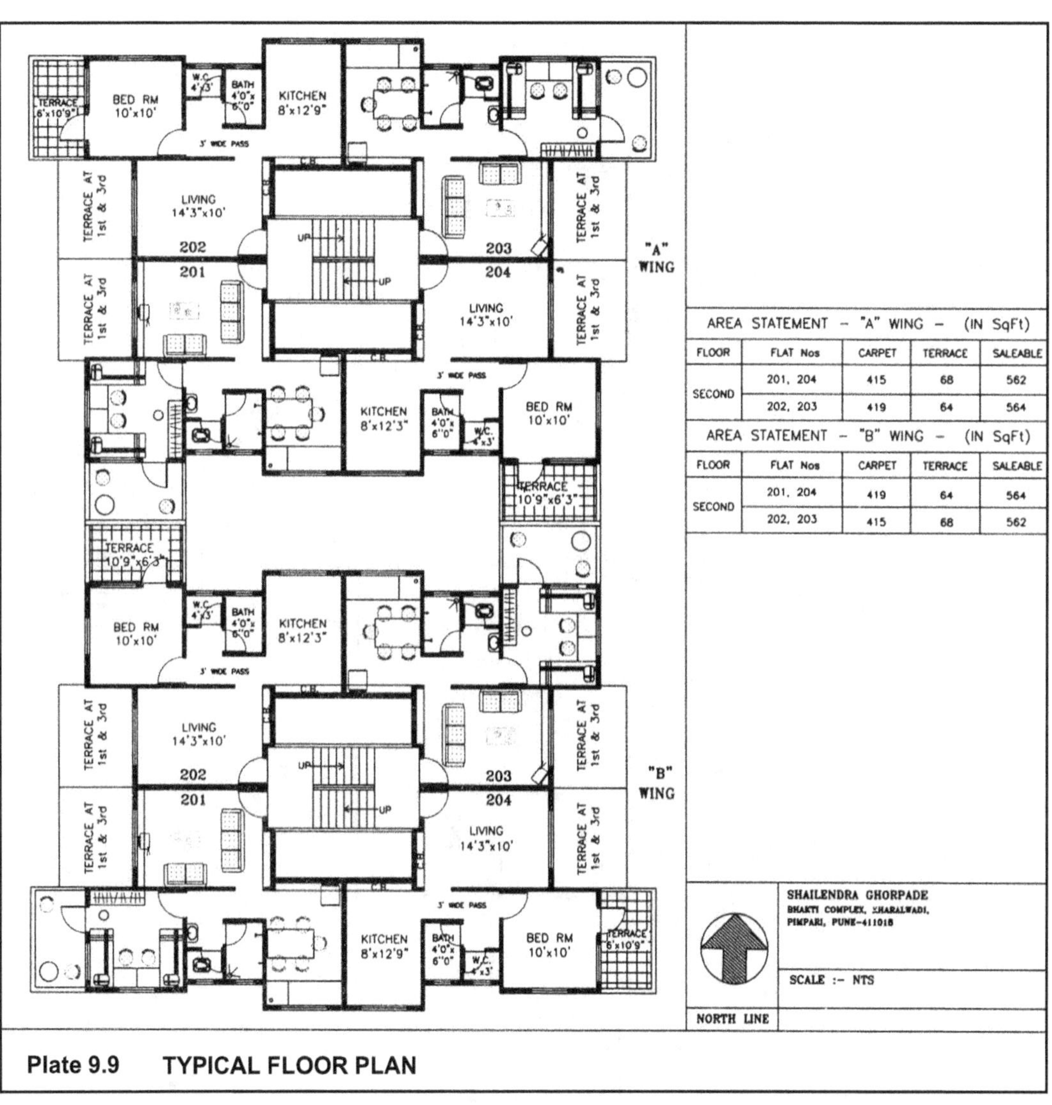

AREA STATEMENT — "A" WING — (IN SqFt)				
FLOOR	FLAT Nos	CARPET	TERRACE	SALEABLE
SECOND	201, 204	415	68	562
	202, 203	419	64	564

AREA STATEMENT — "B" WING — (IN SqFt)				
FLOOR	FLAT Nos	CARPET	TERRACE	SALEABLE
SECOND	201, 204	419	64	564
	202, 203	415	68	562

Plate 9.9　　TYPICAL FLOOR PLAN

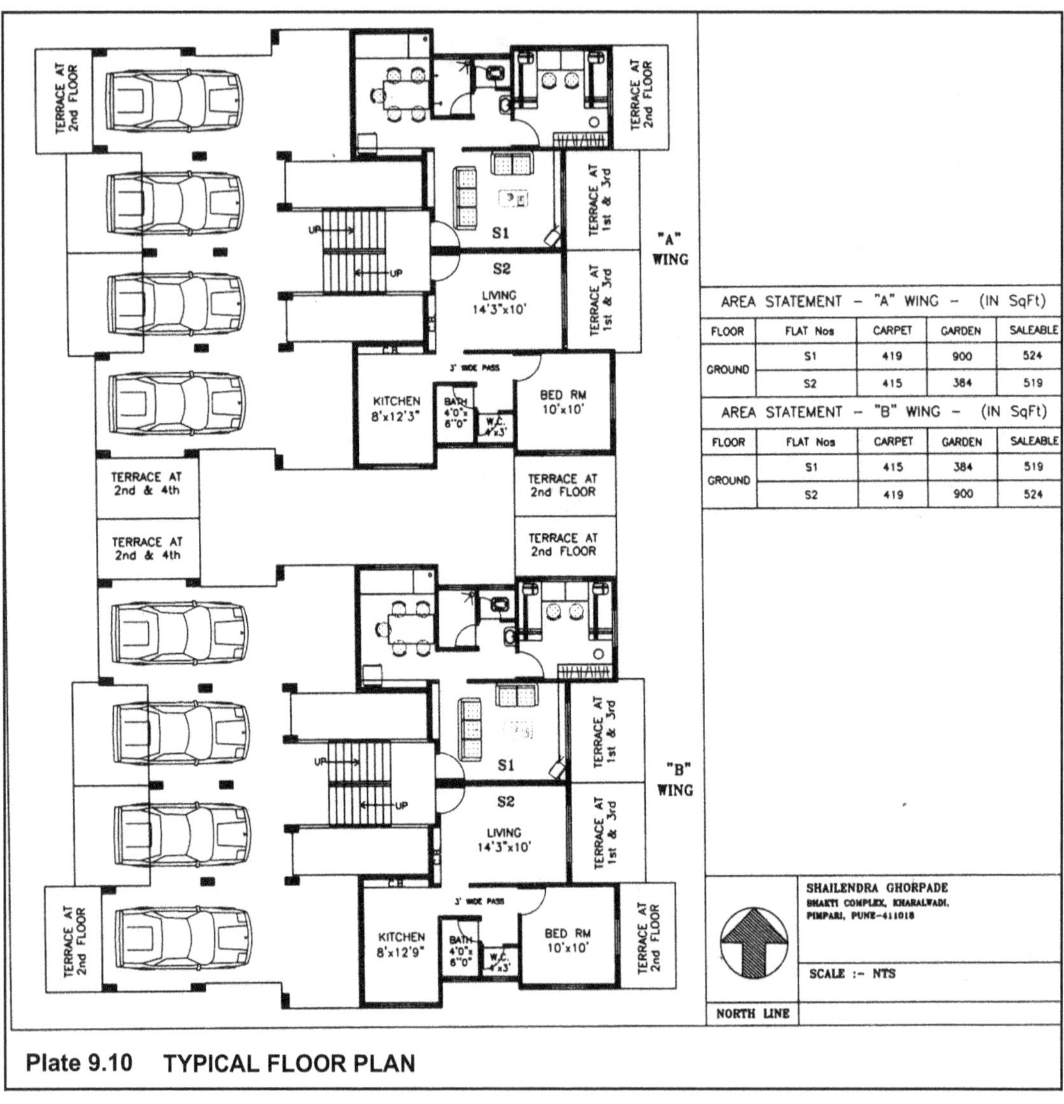

AREA STATEMENT – "A" WING – (IN SqFt)

FLOOR	FLAT Nos	CARPET	GARDEN	SALEABLE
GROUND	S1	419	900	524
	S2	415	384	519

AREA STATEMENT – "B" WING – (IN SqFt)

FLOOR	FLAT Nos	CARPET	GARDEN	SALEABLE
GROUND	S1	415	384	519
	S2	419	900	524

Plate 9.10   TYPICAL FLOOR PLAN

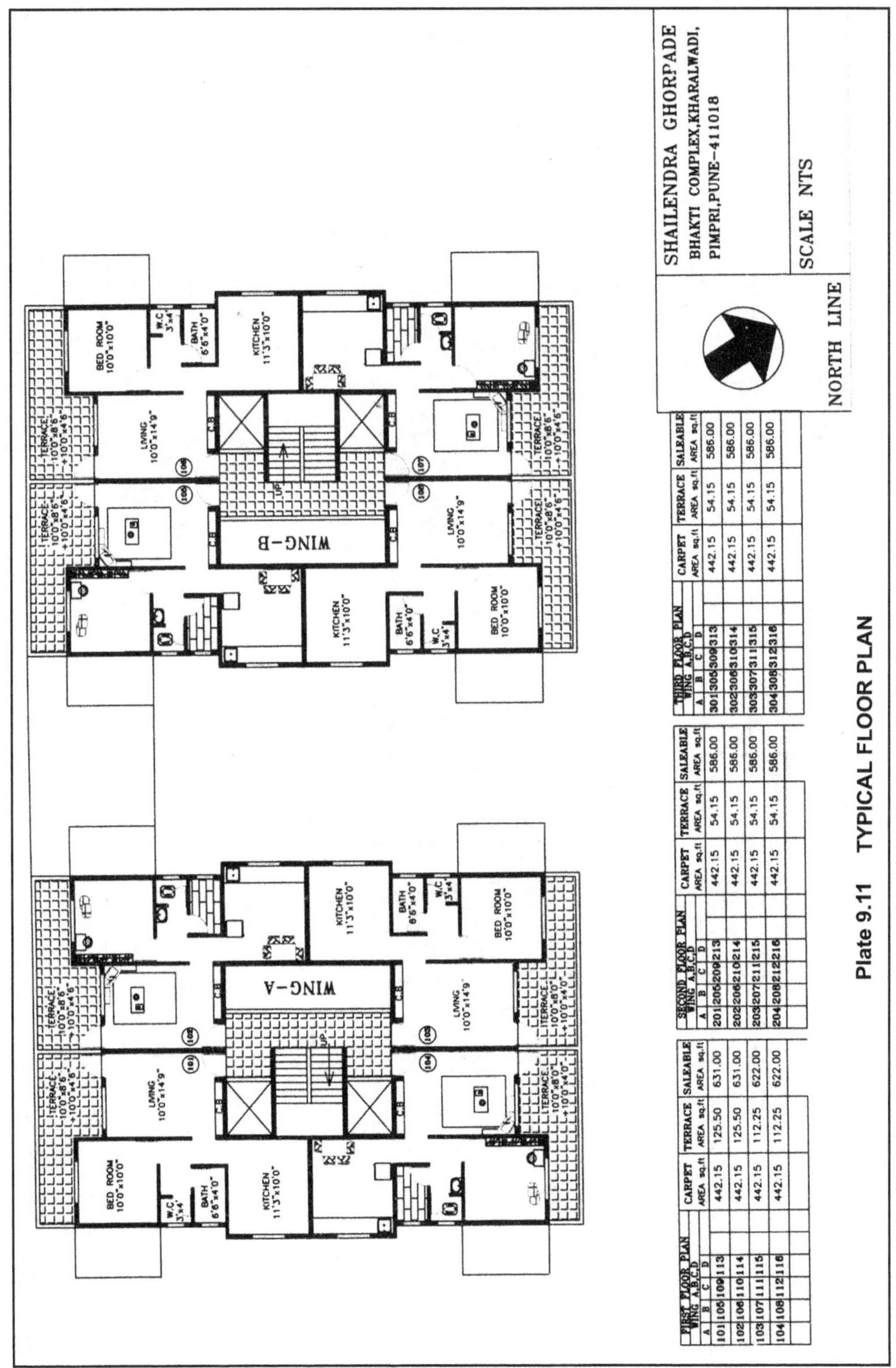

Plate 9.11   TYPICAL FLOOR PLAN

AREA STATEMENT – "A" WING – (IN SqFt)

FLOOR	FLAT Nos	CARPET	TERRACE	SALEABLE
FIRST	101, 104	415	82	570
THIRD	301, 304	415	82	570
FIRST	102, 103	419	82	575
THIRD	302, 303	419	82	575

AREA STATEMENT – "A" WING – (IN SqFt)

FLOOR	FLAT Nos	CARPET	TERRACE	SALEABLE
FIRST	101, 104	419	82	575
THIRD	301, 304	419	82	575
FIRST	102, 103	415	82	570
THIRD	302, 303	415	82	570

Plate 9.12　TYPICAL FIRST AND THIRD FLOOR PLAN

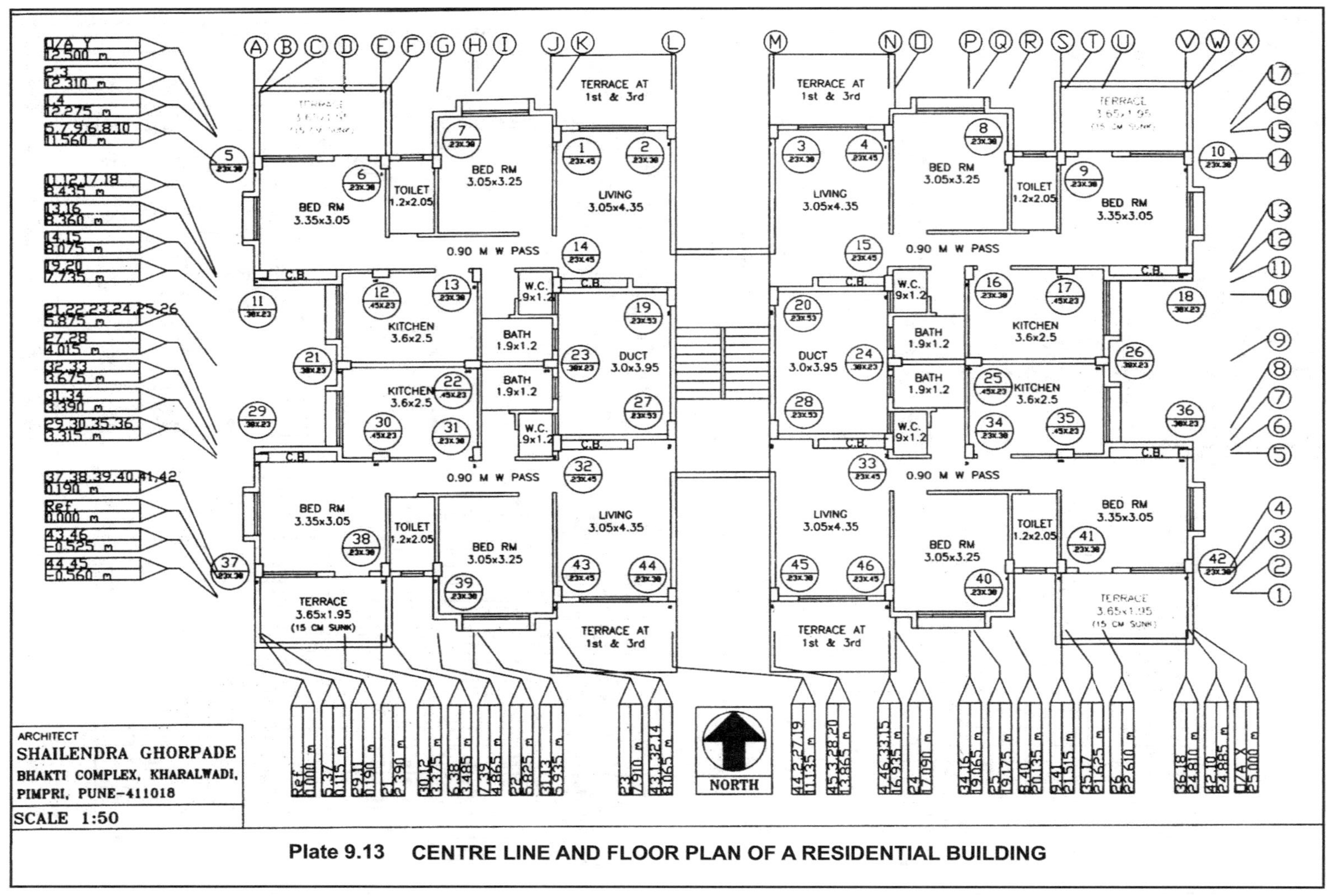

Plate 9.13　CENTRE LINE AND FLOOR PLAN OF A RESIDENTIAL BUILDING

SCHEDULE OF R.C.C. FOOTINGS AND COLUMNS

COLUMN NUMBERS	LOAD IN TONNES	150 THK P.C.C. IN 1:3:6	R.C.C. FOOTINGS SIZE	DEPTH T	DEPTH t	REINFORCEMENTS	PARKING FLOOR SIZE B	PARKING FLOOR SIZE D	PARKING FLOOR VERTICAL BARS	L
1, 5, 6, 63, 67, 68	66	1650 X 1650	1500 X 1500	530	230	10 mm Φ @ 130 c/c B/W	150	600/900	12 & 12 MM	T
2, 9, 64, 71	80	1800 X 1800	1850 X 1650	530	230	10 mm Φ @ 120 c/c B/W	150	750/750	16 & 12 MM	T
3, 8, 65, 7	86	1850 X 1850	1700 X 1700	530	230	10 mm Φ @ 120 c/c B/W	150	750/750	16 & 12 MM	T
4, 7, 66, 69	112	2500 X 1800	2350 X 1650	680	230	10 mm Φ @ 100 c/c B/W	200	900	12 & 16 MM	T
10, 19, 57, 72	112	2300 X 1950	2150 X 1800	700	230	10 mm Φ @ 100 c/c B/W	300	600	12 & 16 MM	Ds
11, 13, 60, 62	84	1850 X 1850	1700 X 1700	530	230	10 mm Φ @ 120 c/c B/W	150	750/750	16 & 12 MM	T
12, 36, 37, 61	90	1900 X 1900	1750 X 1750	550	230	10 mm Φ @ 120 c/c B/W	150	750/750	16 & 12 MM	T
14, 15, 58, 59	74	1750 X 1750	1600 X 1600	530	230	10 mm Φ @ 120 c/c B/W	150	750/750	16 & 12 MM	T
16, 31, 34, 39, 42, 54	74	1750 X 1750	1600 X 1600	530	230	10 mm Φ @ 120 c/c B/W	150	750/750	16 & 12 MM	T
17, 18, 55, 56	70	1950 X 1500	1800 X 1350	530	230	10 mm Φ @ 120 c/c B/W	200	600	8 & 16 MM	D
20, 22, 51, 53	98	2000 X 2000	1850 X 1850	600	230	10 mm Φ @ 100 c/c B/W	150	750/750	18 & 12 MM	T
21, 32	78	1800 X 1800	1650 X 1650	530	230	10 mm Φ @ 120 c/c B/W	150	750/750	16 & 12 MM	T
23, 26, 47, 50	50	1500 X 1500	1350 X 1350	450	230	10 mm Φ @ 130 c/c B/W	150	600/600	12 & 12 MM	T
24, 25, 48, 49	60	1750 X 1450	1600 X 1300	530	230	10 mm Φ @ 130 c/c B/W	200	600	8 & 16 MM	D
27, 30, 43, 46	135	2900 X 1850	2750 X 1700	750	230	10 mm Φ @ 100 c/c B/W	200	1200	16 & 16 MM	Ts
28, 29, 44, 45	110	2650 X 1850	2500 X 1500	700	230	10 mm Φ @ 100 c/c B/W	200	1200	12 & 16 MM	T
32, 33, 40, 41	80	1800 X 1800	1650 X 1650	530	230	10 mm Φ @ 120 c/c B/W	150	750/750	16 & 12 MM	T
33, 36	64	1650 X 1650	1500 X 1500	530	230	10 mm Φ @ 130 c/c B/W	150	750/750	16 & 12 MM	T
1	–	2550 X 2250	2400 X 2100	300	300	10 mm Φ @ 100 c/c B/W at bot. / 10 mm Φ @ 150 c/c B/W at top				

(The five further PARKING FLOOR column groups on the right of the schedule are left blank on the drawing.)

150 THK RCC WALL WITH 10mm Φ @ 150 C/C VERTICAL BARS ON BOTH FACES; 8mm Φ @ 200 C/C HORIZONTAL BARS ON BOTH FACES

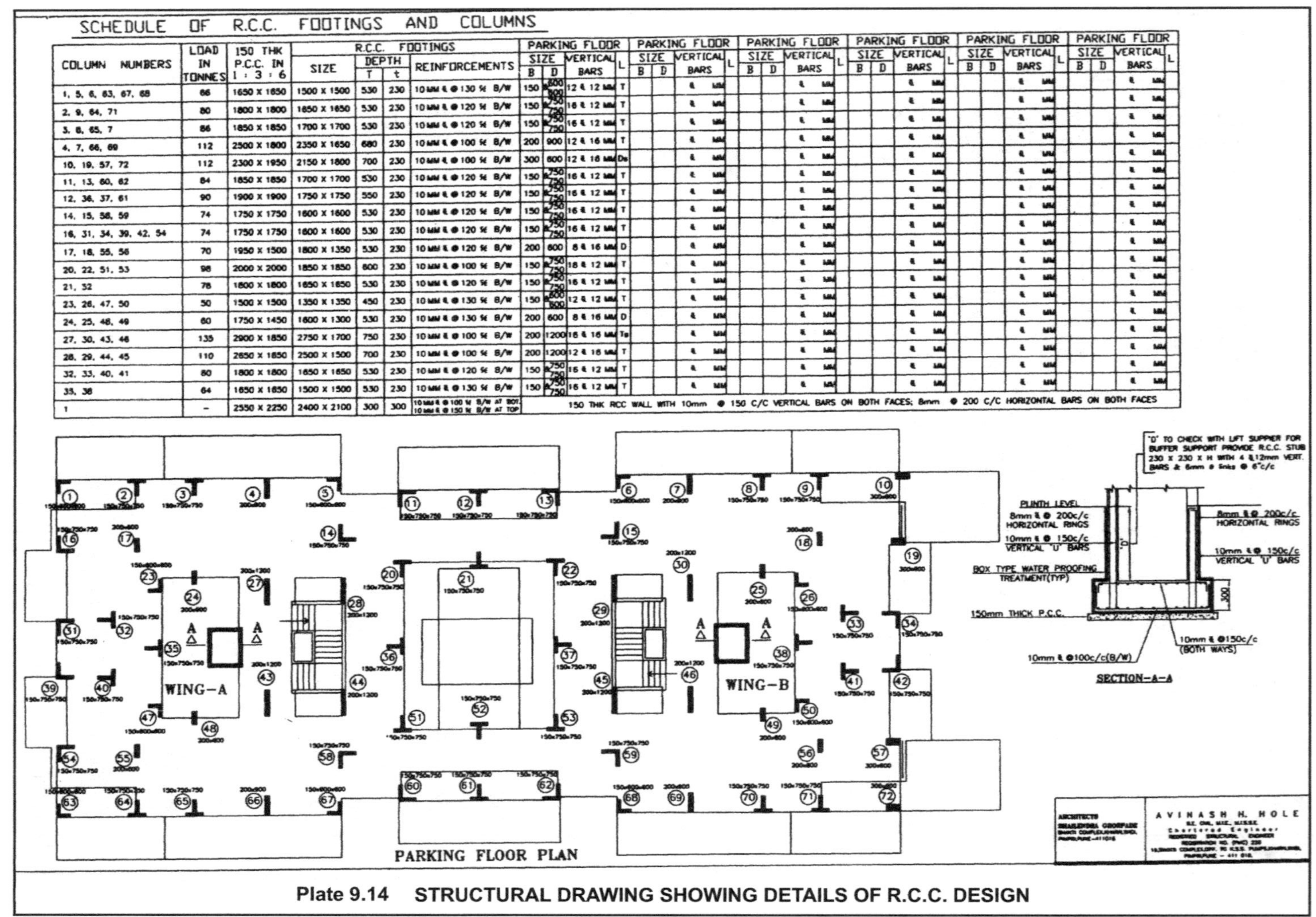

Plate 9.14　STRUCTURAL DRAWING SHOWING DETAILS OF R.C.C. DESIGN

UNIVERSITY QUESTIONS

Dec. 2014

1. Draw to a scale of 1 : 50 or otherwise, detailed plan with the following details :

2. The type of the structure is R.C.C. with wall thickness of 230 mm (external) and 100 mm (internal). Mention the schedule of openings. (Refer. Fig. 11.14)

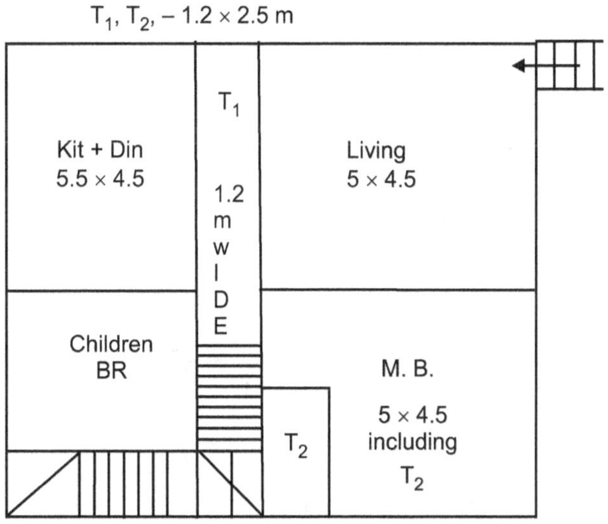

Fig. 11.14

3. Draw a detailed Floor Plan to a scale of 1 : 50 with the following data :

   (i)   Living room 1 no. approx. area 15 m^2

   (ii) Kitchen-cum-Dining 1 no. approx. area 15 m^2

   (iii) Bedrooms 2 no., approx. area 12 m^2 each

   (iv) Floor to floor height 3.3 m

   (v)   Load bearing structure

   (vi) Foundation and Plinth in UCR masonry

   (vii) Varandah, Passage, Staircase, W.C. and Bath/attached toilet etc. of suitable sizes should be provided. Indicate the North.

Dec. 2015

1. A line plan for a residential building is shown in the following Fig. 11.15. Draw detailed floor plan with 1 : 50 or suitable. Use the following data:

    (a) All external walls are of 230 mm thick

    (b) All partition walls are of 150 mm thick

    (c) RCC frame structure

    (d) Beam sizes = 0.23×0.5

    (e) Column sizes = 0.23×0.5

    (f) Floor to floor height = 3.2

    (g) Plinth height = 0.6

    (h) Toilet for M. Bed = 1.2×2.1 M (i) All dimensions are in metres.

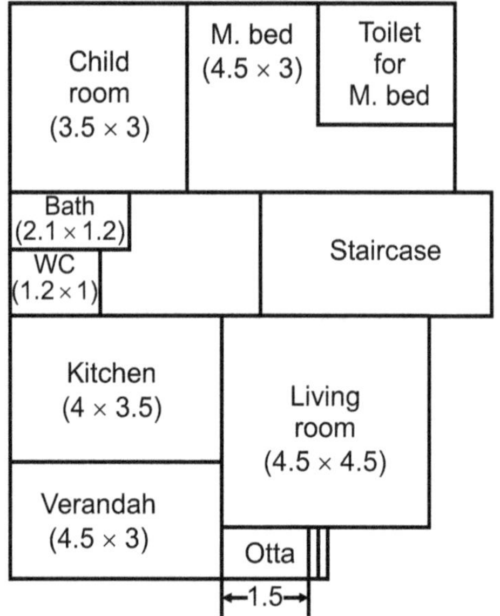

Fig. 11.15

4. It is proposed to construct a bungalow for a doctor; the following are the requirements for accommodation.

    (i) A drawing hall-25 m^2

(ii) Living room-25 m^2

(iii) Kitchen-cum-dining room-15 m^2

(iv) Guest bedroom-20 m^2

(v) Children's room-20 m^2

(vi) Master bedroom-20 m^2

(vii) Doctor's room-20 m^2

Provide adequate verandahs, passages, sanitary units, staircase etc. as per byelaws. The structure may be planned as G+1 RCC framed structure. Draw detailed ground floor plan.

Nov. 2016

1. Draw a detailed floor plan to a scale of 1 : 50 with the following data :

(i)   Living room 1 no. approx. area 15 m^2

(ii) Kitchen-cum-Dining 1 no. approx. area 15 m^2

(iii) Bed rooms 2 no. approx. area 12 m^2 each

(iv) Floor to floor height 3.3 m

(v) Load bearing structure

(vi) Foundation and plinth in UCR masonry

(vii) Varandah, passage, staircase, W.C. and Bath/attached toilet etc. of suitable sizes should be provided. Indicate the North.

May 2015

1. Draw a detailed floor plan to a scale of 1 : 50 of a residential building for the given line plan below. Use the following data : RCC framed structure, wall thickness 150 mm, single storey building, plinth height 450 mm. All dimensions in the sketch are in m. Indicate suitable locations and sizes of doors, windows in schedule of openings. Tread for the step is 280 mm.

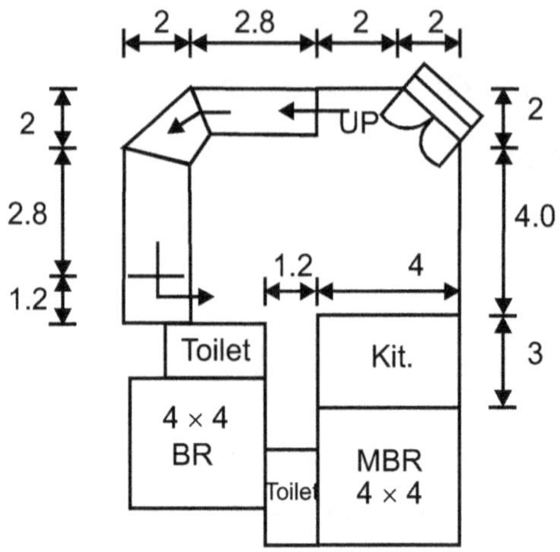

Fig. 11.16

◈ ◈ ◈

Chapter 12
PLANNING OF PUBLIC BUILDINGS

12.1 PLANNING OF PUBLIC BUILDINGS

The design of public building depends upon the nature of the building. Every building has a special character of it's own. The function of the building is to be ascertained initially. Then the different components or blocks or units are to be planned. The units are then joined together to form the whole building. The site of various units depend on the number of person that will be occupied in that room, furniture requirements, space required for circulation etc. There are no hard and fast rules to ascertain the dimension of each block or unit in these building. Minimum dimensions are needed to be fixed on the basis of space needs, thermal comfort, lightning, ventilation requirement etc. of that specified building unit.

12.2 TYPES OF BUILDINGS

National Building Code of India (Sp: 7-1970) defines the building as "any structure for what so ever purpose and of what's ever materials constructed and every part there of whether used as human habitation or not and includes foundations, plinth, walls, floors, roofs, chimneys, plumbing and building services, fixed platforms, balcony cornice or platform projection, part of a building or any thing fixed there to or any wall enclosing or intended to enclose any land or space and signs and outdoor display structures."

According to National Building Code of India (1970), buildings are classified based on occupancies, as follows.

Group A	:	Residential buildings.
Group B	:	Educational buildings.
Group C	:	Institutional buildings.
Group D	:	Assembly buildings.
Group E	:	Business buildings.
Group F	:	Merchandise buildings.
Group G	:	Industrial buildings.

Group H   :   Storage buildings.

Group I: Hazardous buildings.

In this chapter, buildings belonging to group B to group F are discussed.

12.3 GROUP B: EDUCATIONAL BUILDINGS

These include any building used for school, college or day care purposes for more than 8 hours per week. Involving assembly for instruction, education or recreation and which is not covered in Group D. This includes a primary and secondary schools, arts, science, commerce, and law colleges, technical, medical and agricultural colleges or institutes.

Codal Minimum Provisions for Various Units:

According to IS: 8827-1978:

Classrooms:

(A) For primary schools age group I-IV standards.

   (i)   For a class of 40 students per class 1.11 m^2/student.

(B) For Secondary/ Higher secondary school (Age above 10 years).

   For a class room of 40 students per class - 1.2 – 1.5 m^2/student.

   General sizes of rooms recommended are:

   4.5 m × 6 m

   5.5 m × 6.5 m

   6.0 m × 7.2 m and

   6.0 × 7.8 m

   - Teachers room   –   14 m^2
   - Drawing halls   –   Area 3-4m^2/student.
   - Ceiling height of classroom – 4.2 m or more for area upto 60 sq.m.
   - Ceiling height of classroom – 4.8 m or more for area more than 60 sq.m.
   - Assembly hall   –   0.5 – 0.6 m^2/student.
   - Laboratories   –   Area 3-4 m^2/student.
   - Library   –   area 80 – 95 m^2 for 1500 students.

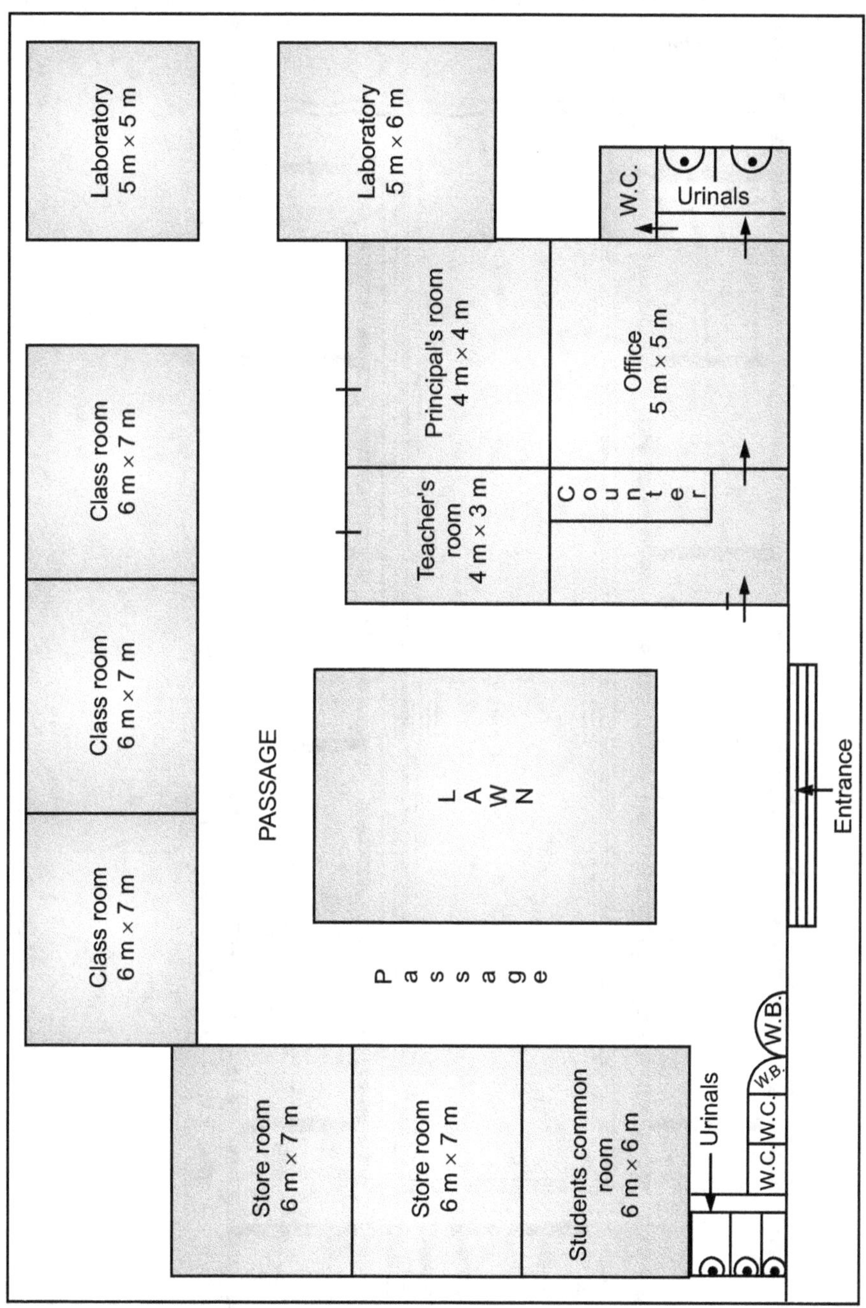

Fig. 12.1: Line plan of a School (not to the scale)

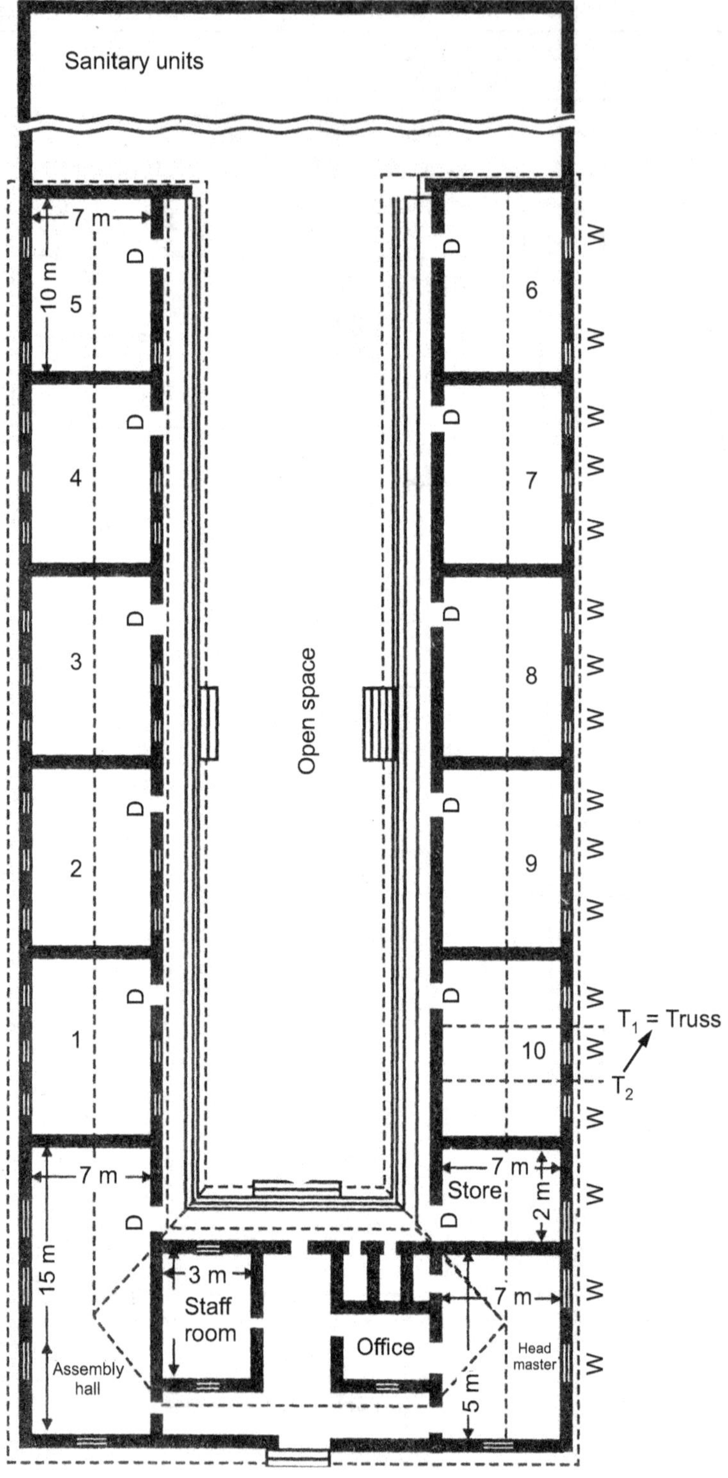

Fig. 12.2: Plan of Primary school

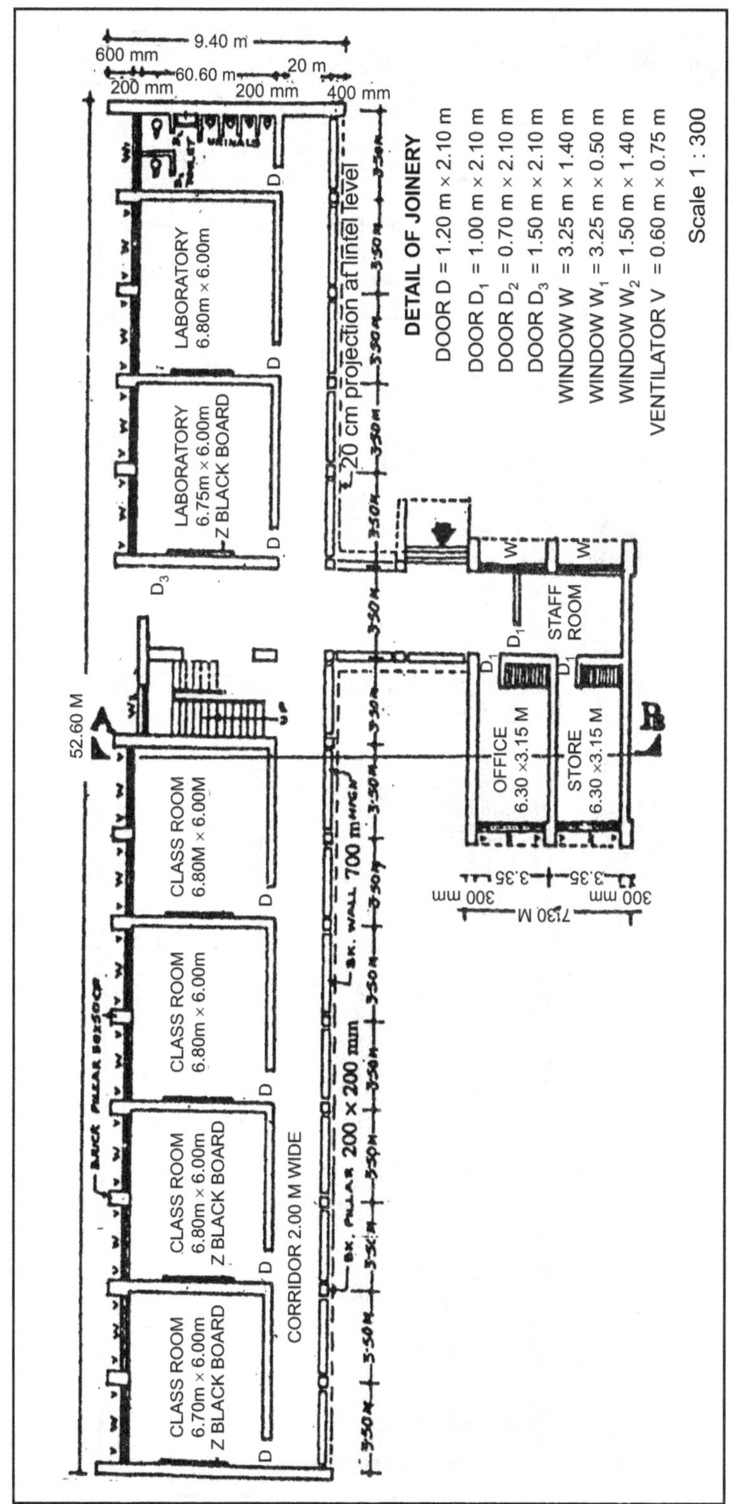

Fig. 12.3: School Building (Ground Floor Plan)

The sanitary blocks should be provided using the following rules:

Description	Male	Female
W.C.	1 for 40 students	1 for 25 students
Urinals	1 for 20 students	–
Wash Basin	1 for 40 students	1 for 40 students
Water taps	1 for 50 students	1 for 50 students

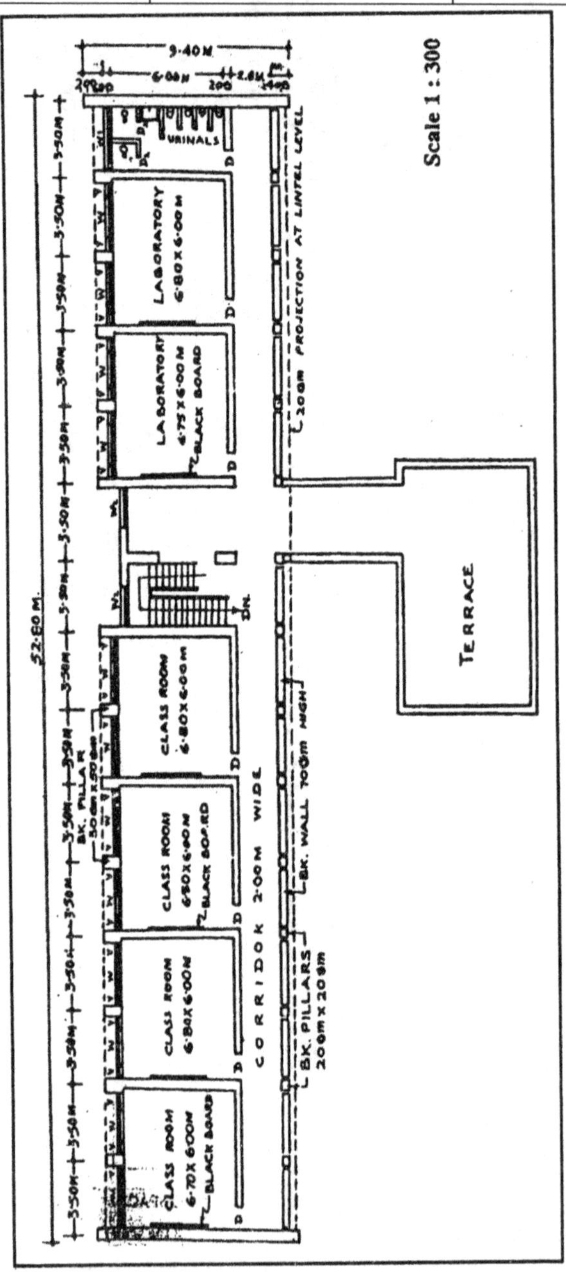

Fig. 12.4: First Floor Plan

Parking Requirements:

1. Cycles   - 1.1 m^2/student.
2. Scooters   - 3 m^2/student.
3. Cars   - 25 m^2 per car.
4. Buses   - 60 m^2 per bus.

The area of parking should be calculated after assuming some percentage of students and staff using types of vehicles. (Refer Plate 17)

Points to be Considered for Planning:

- In hot humid climate of our tropical country it is absolutely essential that the classrooms should not be constructed on two sides of a corridor and derive light from the north as far as possible.

- The classrooms and other rooms should be planned in such a manner that there is no disturbance to classrooms while the other rooms are being used.

- As far as possible, the principal's room should be located in is such a manner that classrooms are visible to him.

- The principal's room and office should be close to each other and as well as near to the main entrance.

- A common room with area 2.5 to 3.0 sq.m. per teacher would normally be provided.

- The layout of classroom can be either L-shaped or rectangular pattern.

- Care should be taken that the classroom in above fashion should form an enclosure.

- The sanitary blocks and water taps should be placed in each wing in such a manner that they are easily accessible to all units.

- Other important units are assembly hall, gymnasium, library, stackroom, administrative block and play ground.

12.4 GROUP C: INSTITUTIONAL BUILDINGS

These include any building or part there of which is used for purposes such as a medical or other treatment or care of persons suffering from physical or mental illness, disease or infirmity, care of infants, aged persons.

These buidings for health include various types of buidings from a small dispensary to a big hospital.

(A) Dispensary

A dispensary is a place where medicines are prescribed and accordingly given out to the patients. Following units are required in a dispensary:

- Entrance/waiting area – 2.5 m wide (minimum).
- Circulation area – passage, corridors etc.
- Doctor's room/consulting room – 2.5 m × 4 m.

- Dressing/Examination room/small O.T. – (3 × 4) m (one or two number).
- Drug store – 2.75 m × 3 m.

(B) Primary Health Centre:

Primary health centre is a place for medical examination and treatment. Usually, these centres are run by local bodies of government and their purpose is to provide medical advice and attention to general public.

- Entrance and waiting spaces
- Doctors room/consulting room   3 m × 3.6 m (one or two number)
- Examination room/dressing room   3 m × 4 m
- Operation theatre   4 m × 4.5 m
- Ward

  Maternity and General $8 - 10 \text{ m}^2$/bed
- Drug store   3.53 × 4.75 m
- Office 12m^2
- Residence quarters

  (i)   Doctors $60 - 90 \text{ m}^2$/head

  (ii)   Servants $40 - 60 \text{ m}^2$/head

Circulation Requirements

Provisions for Horizontal Circulation

Passage / corridor   1 – 2.5 m wide

Verandah   1.8 – 2.5 m wide

Provisions for Vertical Circulation

Stairs and lifts can be provided for the effective circulation in each building:

(i)   Stairs

    Width   1.2 m (minimum)

    Riser   130 – 150 mm

    Tread   300 – 325 mm

    Landing   1 – 1.8 m wide

Points to be Considered for Planning:

- A waiting room should be provided for the visitors in front of doctor's room and one in front of a operation theatre for friends and relatives of the patient being operated.
- The wards should be positioned in such a manner that they should have a good aspect and prospect requirements.

- Sanitary blocks should be provided at the end of the corridor to keep away any bad smell.

- Draw a line plan of primary school with the following data:

(a)	Classroom	6 m × 8 m	8 nos.
(b)	Headmasters room	5 m × 4 m	1 no.
(c)	Office	5 m × 5 m	1 no.
(d)	Staff room	6 m × 8 m	1 no.

  Assume other important details and state them clearly.

(C) Hospital

A hospital comprises of units like out patient's department, nursing units, where patients are housed and led. Nursing units are having various wards, such as medical, surgical, casualty ward, children's ward and maternity ward. A good hospital should have large nursing units. There may be separate hospital or a unit for infectious diseases.

Following are the units in a hospital building with their sizes:

Out Patient Departments

(a) Entrance and waiting space 1 – 2 m^2/person.

(b) Consulting rooms for various specialists like medicine, ENT, Eye, Dentistry, Gynaecology, Orthopeadic, Mental, Skin, Venereal diseases etc., each unit of size 12 to 15 m^2.

(c) Office   3 m × 4 m

(d) Emergency   4 m × 5.5 m

(e) Dispensary   4 m × 5 m

Sanitary Blocks

Description	Male	Female
W.C.	1 for 100	2 for 100
Urinals	1 for 50	–
Wash Basins	1 for 100	1 for 100

Operation Theatre

Operation Theatre	-	4.5 m × 5.5 m
Sterilization Room	-	3 m × 4 m
Doctor's Room	-	3 m × 4 m
Nurse's Room	-	3 m × 3 m
Waiting Space	-	3 m wide

Nursing Area (Wards)

Wards are gynecology, female, children, infectious diseases etc. The minimum sizes to be provided are as follows.

(a) Ward 8 – 10 m^2/bed and 30 cu.m space/bed

(b) Nurse's room   3 m $\times$ 4 m

(c) Sanitary Provisions:

W.C. 1 for 8 beds.

Bath 2 for 1 ward.

Wash Basin   1 for 30 beds

Other Requirements

(a) Radiology department.

(b) Laundry.

(c) Pathology laboratory.

(d) Circulation space: Horizontal and vertical circulation.

(e) Parking space.

(f) Casualty department.

(g) Kitchen and store.

(h) Drug store.

Points to be Considered for Planning of Hospital Furniture

- The numbers of beds to be accommodated in each ward varies largely with the type of wards and the total capacity of the hospital.
- For convenience a ward may contain 20 – 24 beds. But in some cases wards have been provided to contain even 30 – 40 beds.
- The space between the sides of a beds should be 0.9 m as a minimum.
- A clearance of 1.2 m between the ends of a beds should be left.
- A common size of a bed used in hospitals is 0.9 m $\times$ 2 m.
- The sill of a windows should be placed not lower than 75 cm, as height of bed is usually 0.6 m.

12.5 GROUP D: ASSEMBLY BUILDINGS

These include any building or part of a building, where group of people congregate or gather for amusement, recreation, social, religious, patriotic purpose. These type of buildings include auditorium, restaurants etc.

(A) Auditorium/Cinema Theatre

The planning requirement of such building depends on the number of audience required to be seated. Such building should have a proper sound insulation and acoustical requirements.

Following points may be kept in mind while planning for auditorium:

- The slope for floor of such halls may be towards the backside with an inclination of 8° to 15° from front side.
- Back to back spacing between two rows is about 85 – 90 cm.
- The usual width of a screen is 4.2 m. The size may vary between 3.5 m to 4.8 m.

  If any provision for a cinema scope is made, wider screens are used. Approximate screen height is 0.733 times that of width.
- The minimum distance between a screen and first row of seats should be 1.2 to 1.4 times the width of screen.
- The stage floor should be raised consistent with good sight line, usually about 1.1 m.
- The bottom of screen should be 1.65 to 1.8 m above the floor level at first row of seats.
- The rear most row of seats should not be away more than 6 times width of screen. If the distance is increased, then stage may be planned for a wider screen.
- The screens and rows of seats should be so arranged that the line of slight from first row on ground floor and the line of sight from the rearmost seat as balcony should not make an angle less than 60° with screens.
- Speaker should be usually placed 1 to 1.5 m behind the screen.
- Usually a room of size 4.5 × 3.6 m is required as a minimum for projection room.
- The area of a chairs or seats is approximately 0.8 – 1.0 m² per audience.
- Width of gallery should be 2.1 m minimum.
- Foyers, lobbies and verandah are the main circulatory elements in a plan of the theatre in addition to the staircase.

  14. Approximately a floor space at a rate of 0.05 m² per seat is provided for foyers.

Approximate Sizes of Rooms or Units:

(a) Entrance for foyer   3 m wide.

Auditorium:

Area	0.8 – 1 m²/chair or seat.
Volume	3.5 – 4.3 m²/chair.
One door	for 200 persons.
Distance between chairs	0.45 m
Stage height	1.0 to 1.2 m
Office and booking window	4 to 5 sq.m. for each clerk.
Projection room	4.5 m × 3.5 m
Snack bar, tea stall	12 m² – 15 m²
Managers office	12 m² – 15 m²
Store room	12 m²

Sanitary Provisions.

Description	Male	Female
W.C.	1 for 100 upto 400 and above 400, 1 for every 250	1 for 100 upto 200 and above 200, 1 for every additional 100
Urinary	1 for 50	–
Wash Basin	1 for 200	1 for 200

(B) Hotel

Space requirement for a hotel can be divided into (i) public area, such as entrance hall, lounges and dining halls, (ii) bed rooms, (iii) service area such as kitchen, laundries, air conditioning plant etc., (iv) restaurant attached (may or may not be).

The minimum requirements for hotels are as follows:

Entrance, reception, waiting hall.

Dining	$2.0 - 2.5$ m²/head
Kitchen	20 m² – 30 m²
Store	10 m² – 15 m²
Pantry	6 m² – 10 m²
Bed rooms:	
General bed	3.0 m × 4.5 m
Good size double bed	3.5 m × 4.5 m
General sizes	3.5 m × 5.5 m
	4.0 m × 5.5 m
Laundry	3 m × 4 m
Servant room	3 m × 4 m
Sanitary block	For servants separate

Each near dining and entrance hall

For every bed room (attached)

(C) Museums:

The approximate size be taken as

Entrance 3 m wide

Halls   4.5 m × 6.5 m to 6 m × 10 m each

Office   3 m × 4 m

Sanitary units

Circulation area

(D) Restaurants:

The approximate areas for each units of a restaurant are as follows:

Dining hall 2 to 2.5 m²/head

Pantry   4 m × 6 m

Kitchen   20 m² to 30 m²

Store   4 m × 3 m

Cook's room   3 m × 4 m

Preparation   4.5 m × 5 m

Points to be Considered for a Planning / Grouping of Units:

- The kitchen and pantry shall open out into the dining halls by means of a service counter.

- It is necessary that hygienic conditions should be maintained in the kitchen and pantry, so for this purpose sufficient light and good ventilation are needed.

- A separate service entry to be provided to the store and to the main preparation area.

- Toilets can be used by the restaurant users as well as the restaurant staff. Provisions shall be made so as to have proximity to the both area.

- A separate washing space has to be provided for washing all the utensils, vessels etc.

12.6 GROUP E: BUSINESS BUILDINGS

These include any buildings or part of a building, which is used for the transaction of business (other than covered by building in Group F) for keeping of accounts and records and similar purposes.

In such a classification, library can also be classified because the principal function of library is to keep record of books.

(A) Library:

    (a) Entrance and moving space around delivery counter   2.0 m wide (minimum)

    (b) Issue counter   Height 1.5 m – 1.8 m.

    (c) Sections in library   3 m × 3 m (minimum)

        Reference section

        Serious reading

        General reading (Magazine and Newspaper)

        Stack room

        Periodical section

    (d) Administrative area

        Librarian room

        Other staff area

        Card index area

        Record area

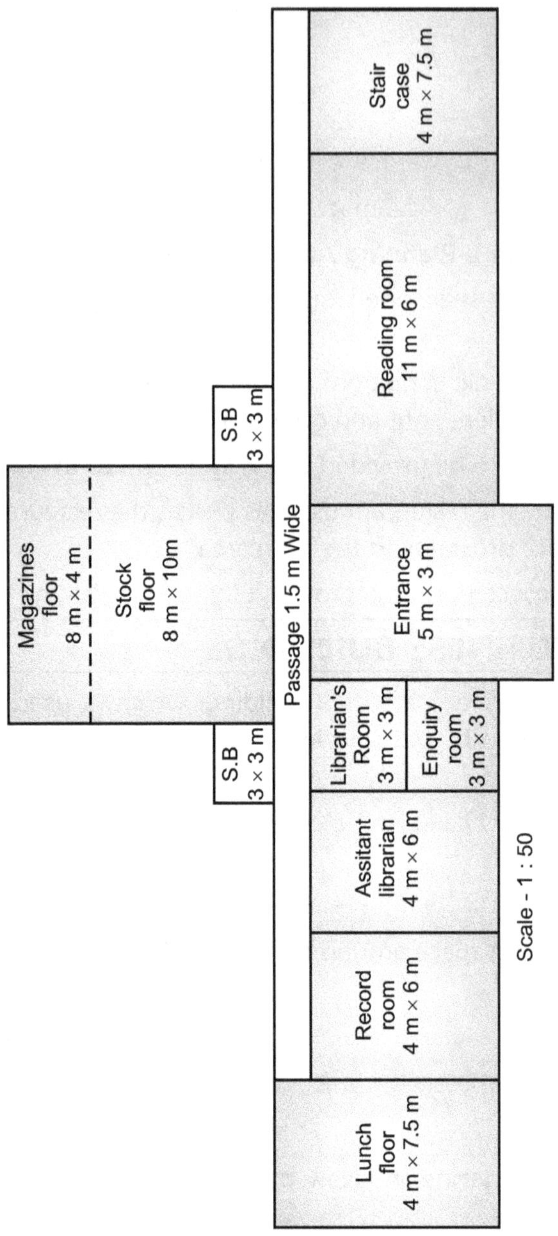

Fig. 12.5: Library building

Sanitary Blocks:

Description	Male	Female
W.C.	1 for 200, upto 400 and above 400, 1 for every 250.	1 for 100 upto 200 above 200 1 for every 150.
Urinary	1 for 50	–
Wash Basin	1 for 200, upto 450 and above 400, 1 for every 250.	above 450, 1 for every 250.

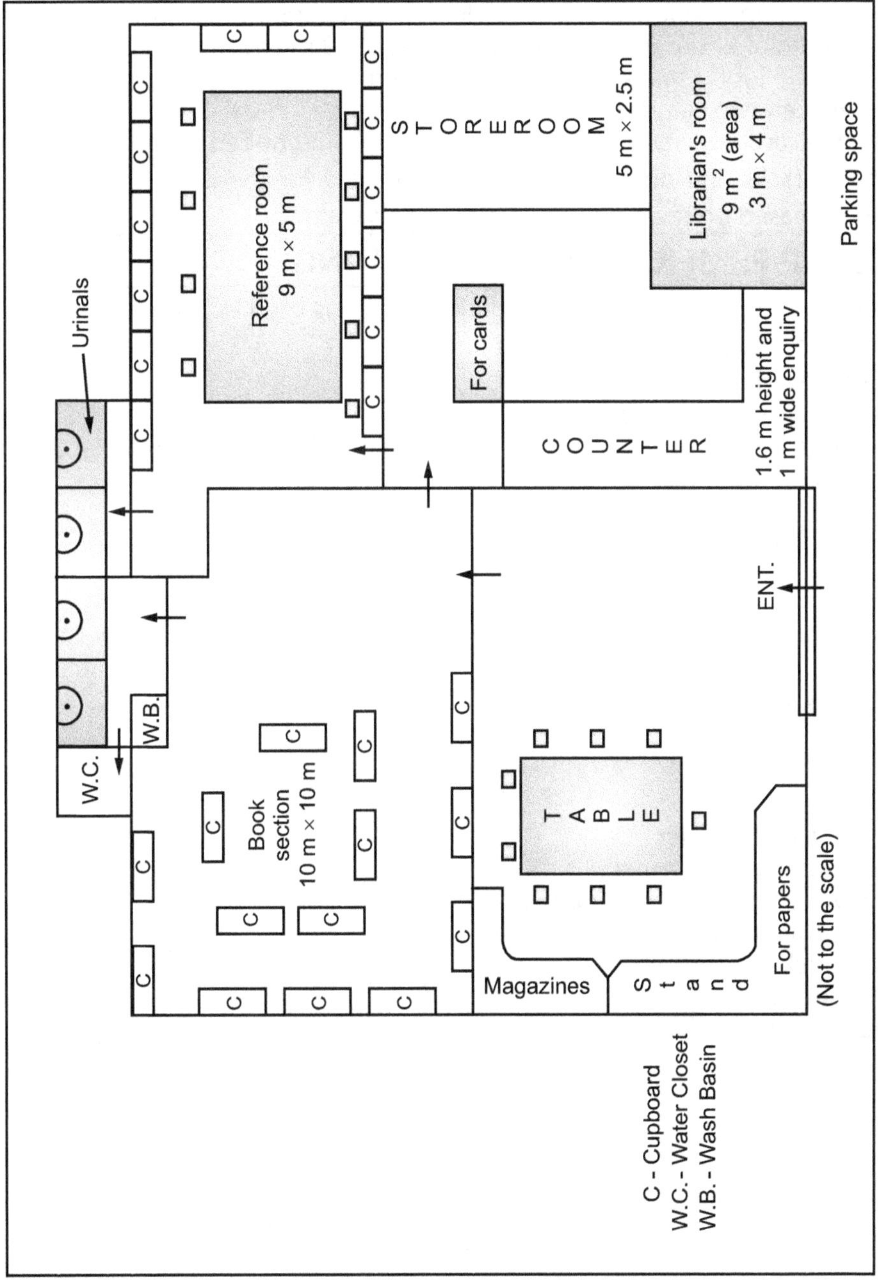

Fig. 12.6: Line plan of a library

Points to be Considered for Grouping and Furniture Arrangement:

- In reading rooms tables are designed to accommodate four to eight persons each, together on either sides.
- 0.75 m length per person is provided for table and allowing seats along both the sides it should be at least 0.9 m wide.
- Height of tables is usually 0.75 m to 0.85 m from the floor.

- Size of Newspaper stand is 1.2 m in length. The sloping face of a newspaper stand should have width of about 0.75 m and its lower end 0.9 m above ground.
- The width of a lobby space required for moving around the newspaper stand should be 0.9 m and between two stands is 1.5 m.
- Larger tables are required for reference reading than required for a periodical etc.
- The size of racks and number of sections required for the particular library should be considered based on the type of institute and its capacity.

12.7 GROUP F: MERCHANDISE BUILDINGS

These include any building or part of a building, which is used as shop, market or for display and sale or merchandise, either wholesale or retail.

(A) Vegetable Market:

Entrance Sufficient open space.	
Stalls (open/closed)	2 m × 3 m, 2.5 m × 3 m, 2.5 m × 4.0 m 2.5 m × 5 m
Cold room	12 m² minimum
Circulation space	Corridors, Staircase, lift etc.

Parking space for two wheeler, car, tempo, truck and cycle stand.
Space for collecting garbage
Administrative office
Sanitary blocks

(B) Shops or Shopping Complex:

Entrance	
Counter for customers	1.2 m – 1.6 m high
Cash counter	
Space for storing articles	
Moving spaces for customers	1.8 m minimum

Displays windows as per requirements.
Parking considerations.
Sanitary blocks.

(C) Hostel Building:

Entrance 3 m wide	
Common room	
Rector office	
Security room	
Guest room	
Rooms	
Single seated	Area 9.5 m² / head
Two seated	Area 7.5 m² – 8 m² / head
Three seated	Area 7.2 – 7.5 m² / head
Circulation	1.8 m minimum
Recreation hall	2 – 3 m² / head
Dining hall	3 – 4 m² / head
Kitchen	9.5 m² minimum
Store	2 m × 3 m
Pantry	2.75 m × 3 m
Parking space	

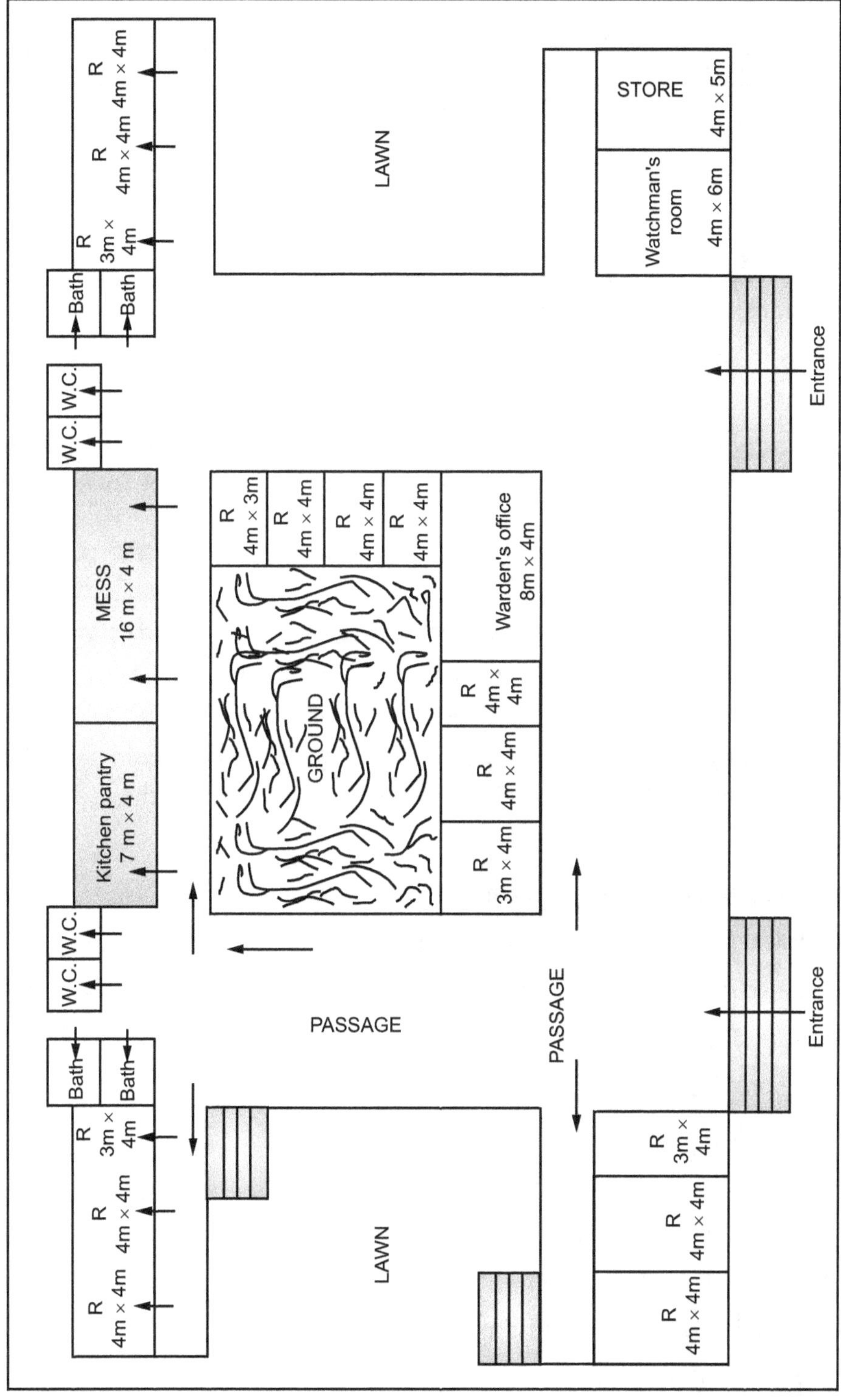

R → Room

Fig. 12.7: Line plan of a Hostel

Sanitary Blocks:

Description	Male	Female
W.C.	1 for 10	1 for 8
Bath	1 for 10	1 for 10
Urinals	1 for 25	–
Wash basins	1 for 10	1 for 10

Points to be considered for Planning:

- All rooms should be arranged or grouped in such a manner that there is a formation of an enclosure.

- The rectors room, store room, and other rooms like dining hall, common room, and kitchens area all should be taken as far as possible near to the entrance so that they do not disturb the hostel rooms.

12.8 INDUSTRIAL BUILDINGS

Industrial buildings are the structures in which various types of materials are manufactured from raw materials, fabricated and processed etc. It requires space for storage of raw materials, for installation of machinery and plant, for storage of final product.

To prevent haphazard growth of industries in cities, industrial area should be well planned. It should be located away from residential areas and preferably outside the town.

Basic Requirements:

- Raw materials available in near vicinity.
- Source of water within reasonable distance.
- Source of electric power close to railway station.
- Easy transportation facilities.
- Flexible tax policies.
- Availability of finance on easy installments.
- Land or plot with sizes for future expansion.
- Space for storage of raw materials.
- Space for installation of machineries.
- Space for parking of vehicles and circulation.

Orientation and Lighting:

- Shape of the plot and orientation of industrial building should be in close link.

- In North, saw toothed North-light roof truss can be used.

- For the regions to the South of Tropic of Cancer, North light roof truss is used.

- Proper lighting in the factory is obtained by arranging factory sheds in East and West directions and by providing glass windows in Northern walls.

- In no case, windows should be placed in Eastern and Western walls of the building.

Area of Plot and Other Spaces of Utilisation:

- Total area of plot for industrial building should be according to the requirements with future expansion.

- Area for installation of machineries of plant and storage of materials should be 60% of the total built-up area.

- Area under roads inside the factory should not be more than 20% of area of plot.

- Area of administrative building is 5% to 10% of built-up area.

- Area of open space should be 8% of total area.

- Work sheds should be of area minimum 50 sq.m to 500 sq.m.

- Minimum height of plinth is 300 mm from top of road surface.

- Height of bed block level and tie beam of roof is minimum 4.2 m from floor level.

- Flooring in cement concrete or brick flooring or rubber flooring depending on the use of industry and nature of work.

- Sizes of ventilators and windows should be according to rules of area of openings. This should be maximum 25% of floor area in hot and humid region and 15% of floor area in case of hot and dry region.

- Pitch roof in C.I. sheet or A.C. sheet should be used.

- There must be an arrangement of water supply, drainage, electricity, connection of plot with main roads at the initial stage only.

- According to the functional requirement different sizes of sheds should be constructed in 10 m to 13 m span in general cases. Standard types of trusses should be used for pitched roof.

- For small factories covered area is 50% of plot area.

- Roads should be laid in width of 3.7 m. All roads should lead to the work sheds and from there must be connected to common road.

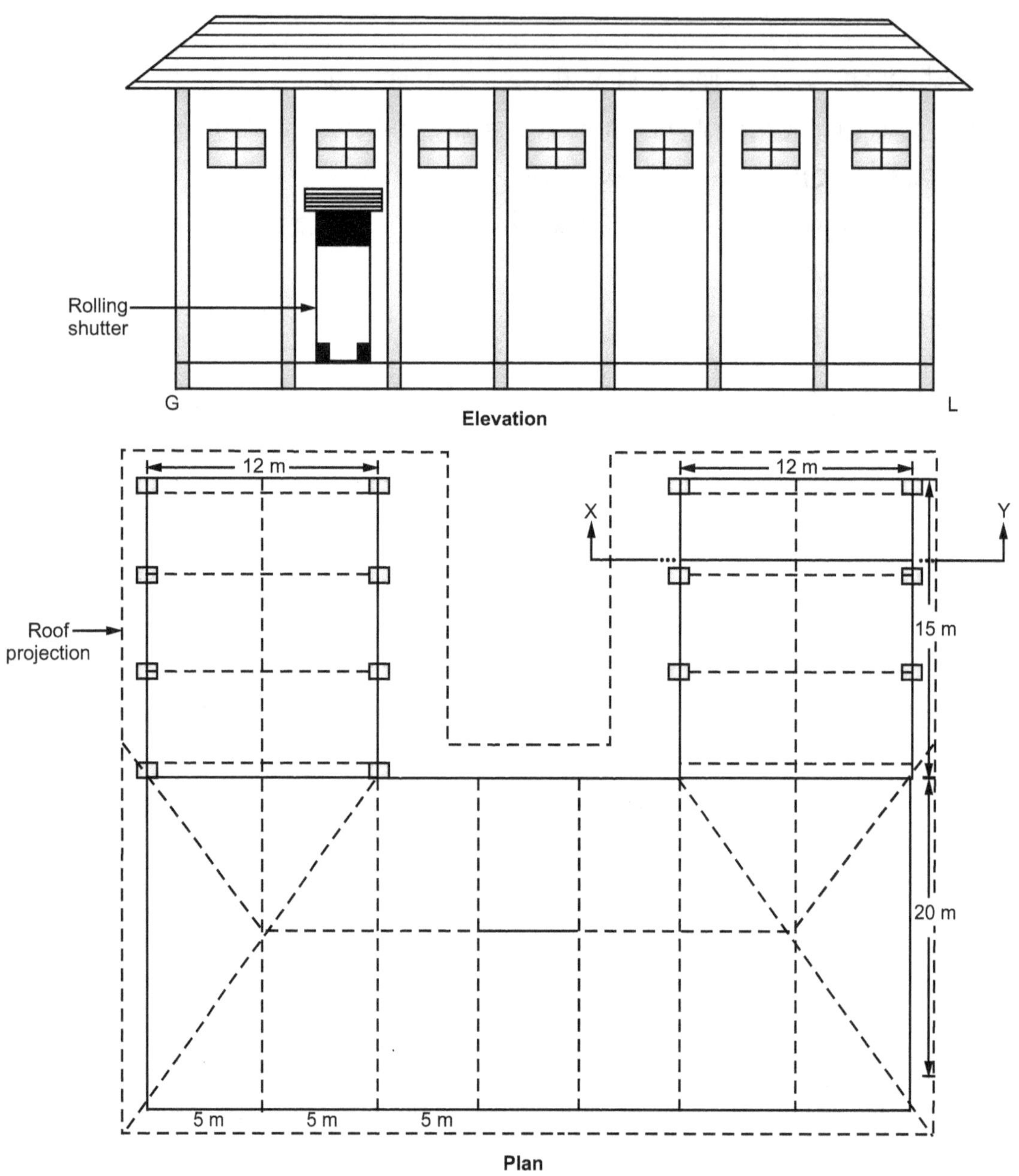

Fig. 12.8: Planning of dal mill

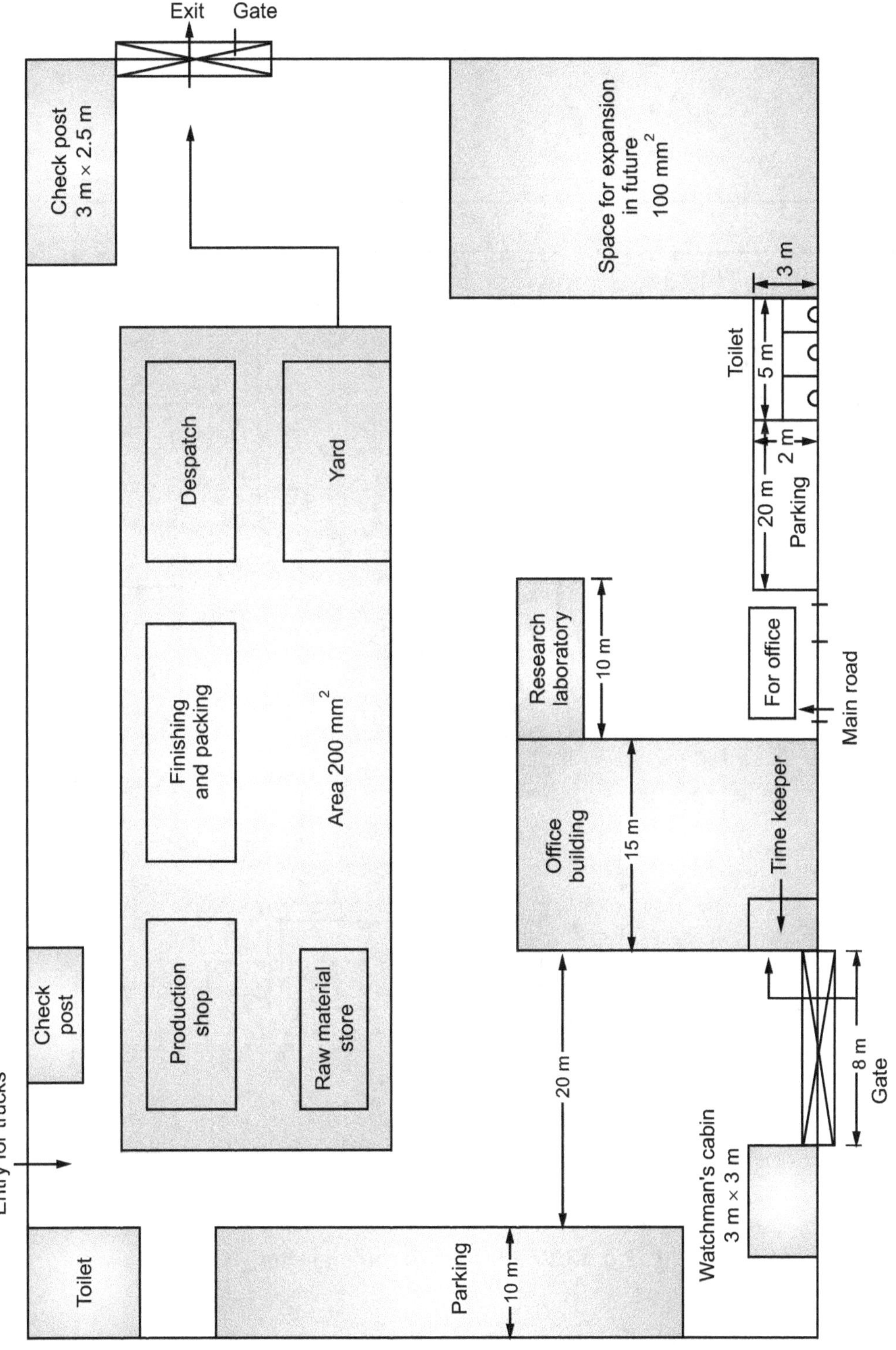

Fig. 12.9: General layout of an industrial building

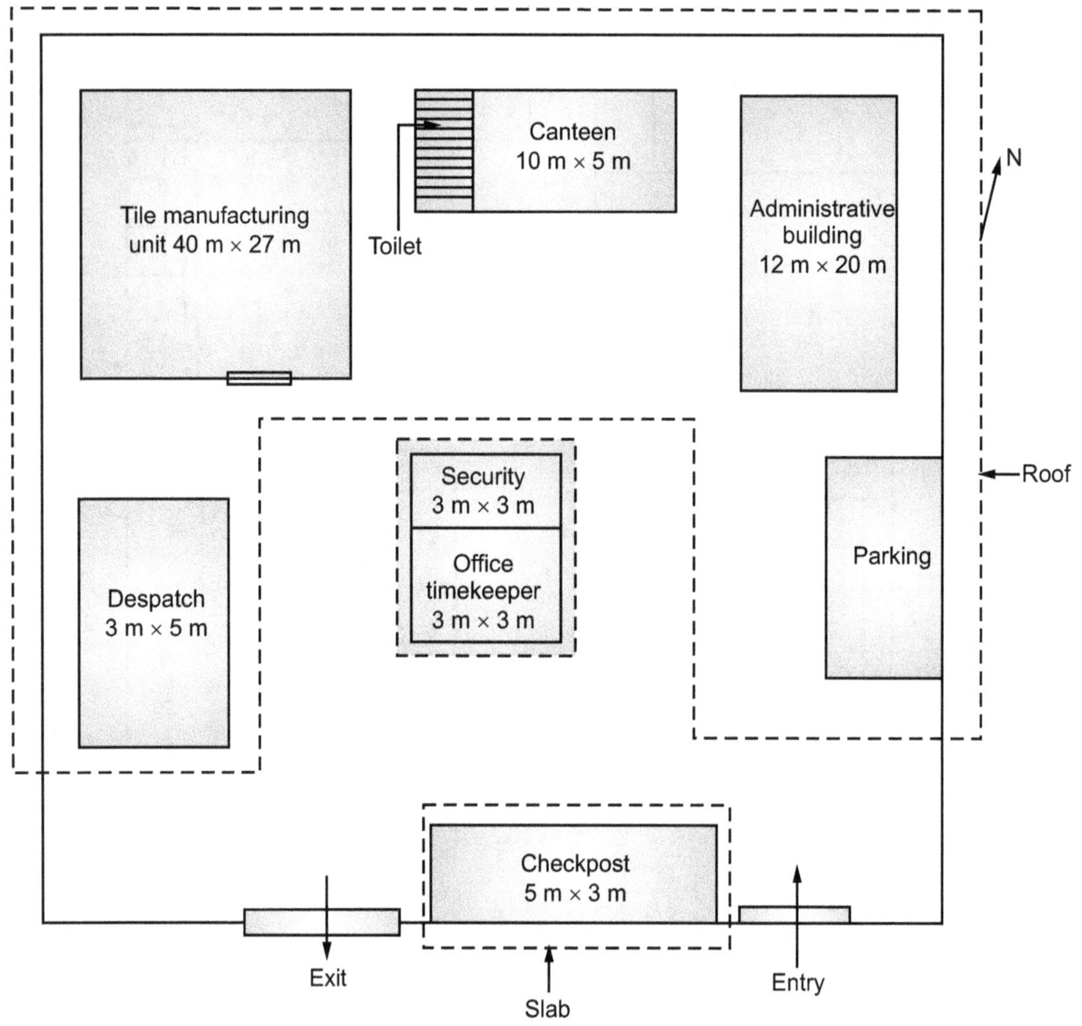

Fig. 12.10: Tile manufacturing factory

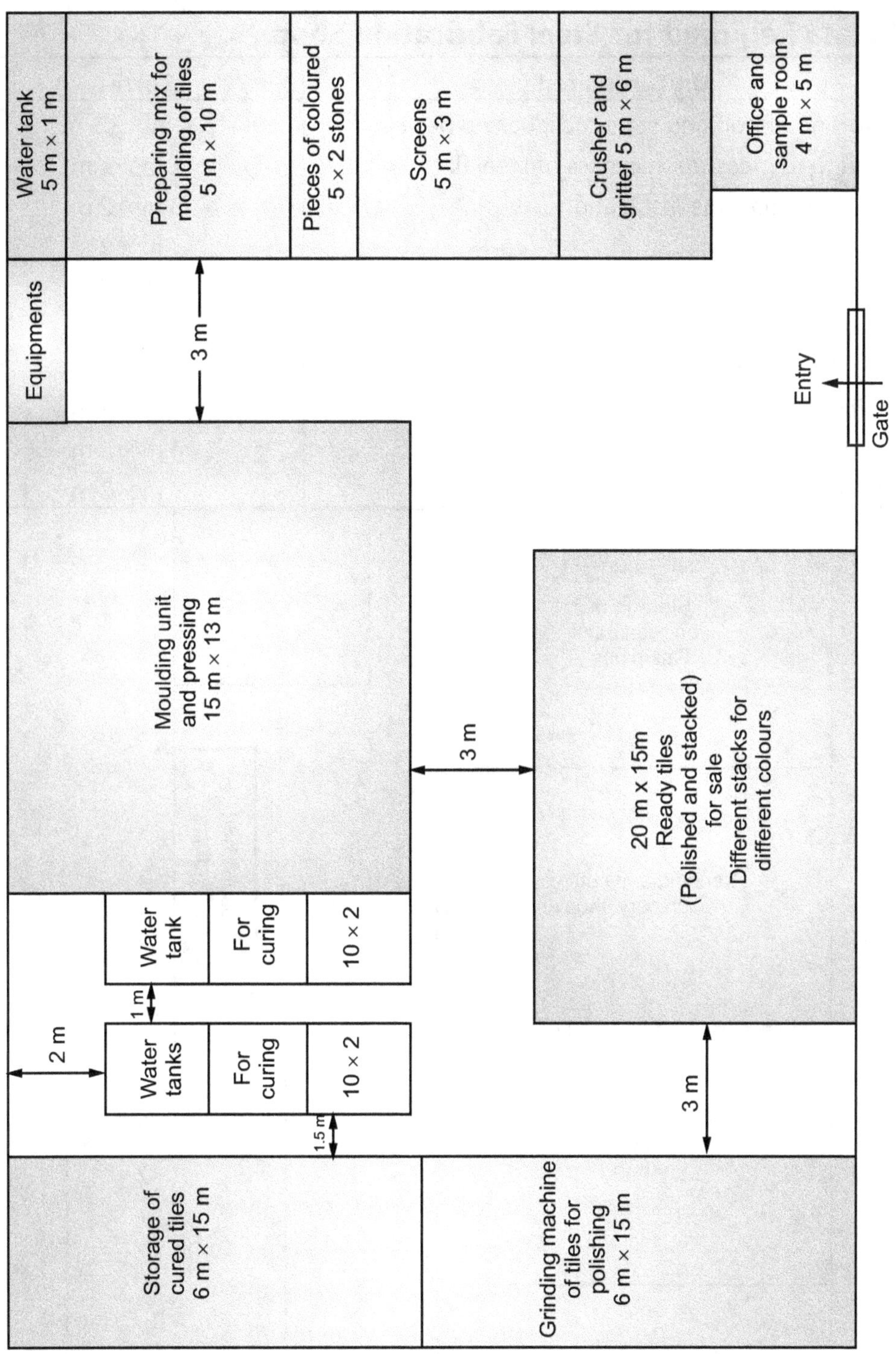

Fig. 12.11: Details of tile manufacturing unit

12.8.1 Data Required for Steel Fabrication Shop

Units required	Sizes
1. Storage of iron and steel rods, bars, pipes etc.	4 m × 3.5 m
2. Gauge to measure thickness of steel flats	1 m × 1 m
3. Bending machine installation	3 m × 2 m
4. Steel cutting unit	3 m × 2 m
5. Welding shop	10 m × 6 m
(a) Gas welding;	
(b) Electric arc welding.	
6. Office	4 m × 3 m
7. Staff room	4 m × 3 m
8. Sanitary accommodation for staff	3 m × 2 m

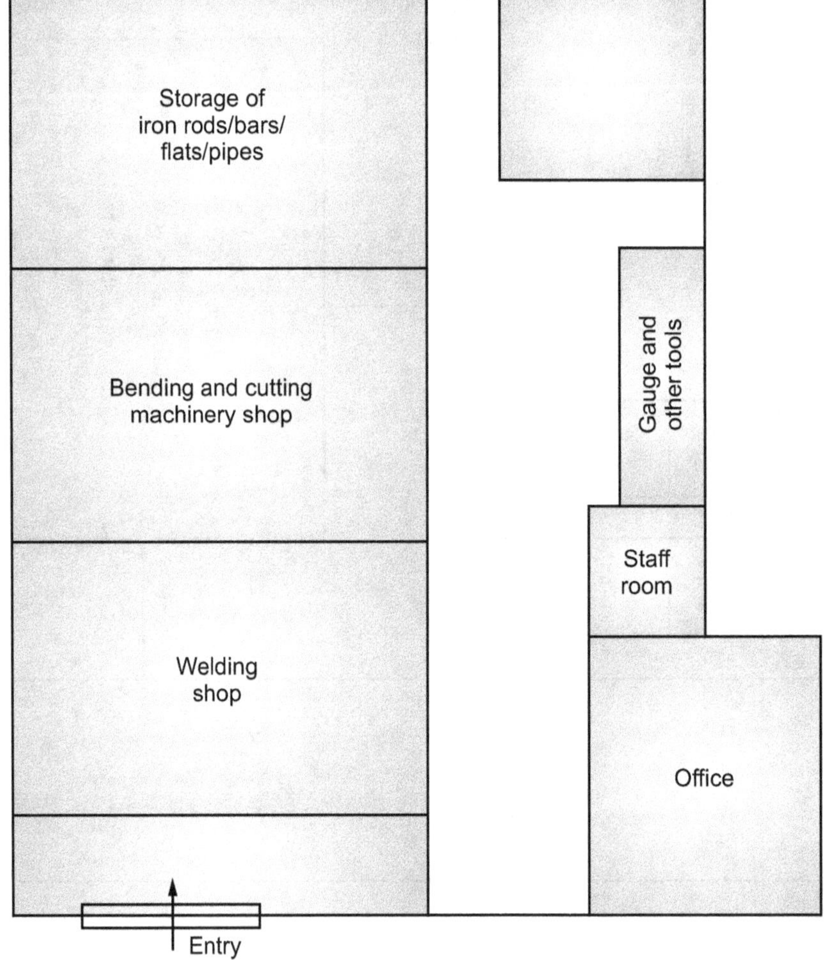

Fig. 12.12: A fabrication shop

12.8.2 Data Required for Vehicle Service Centre

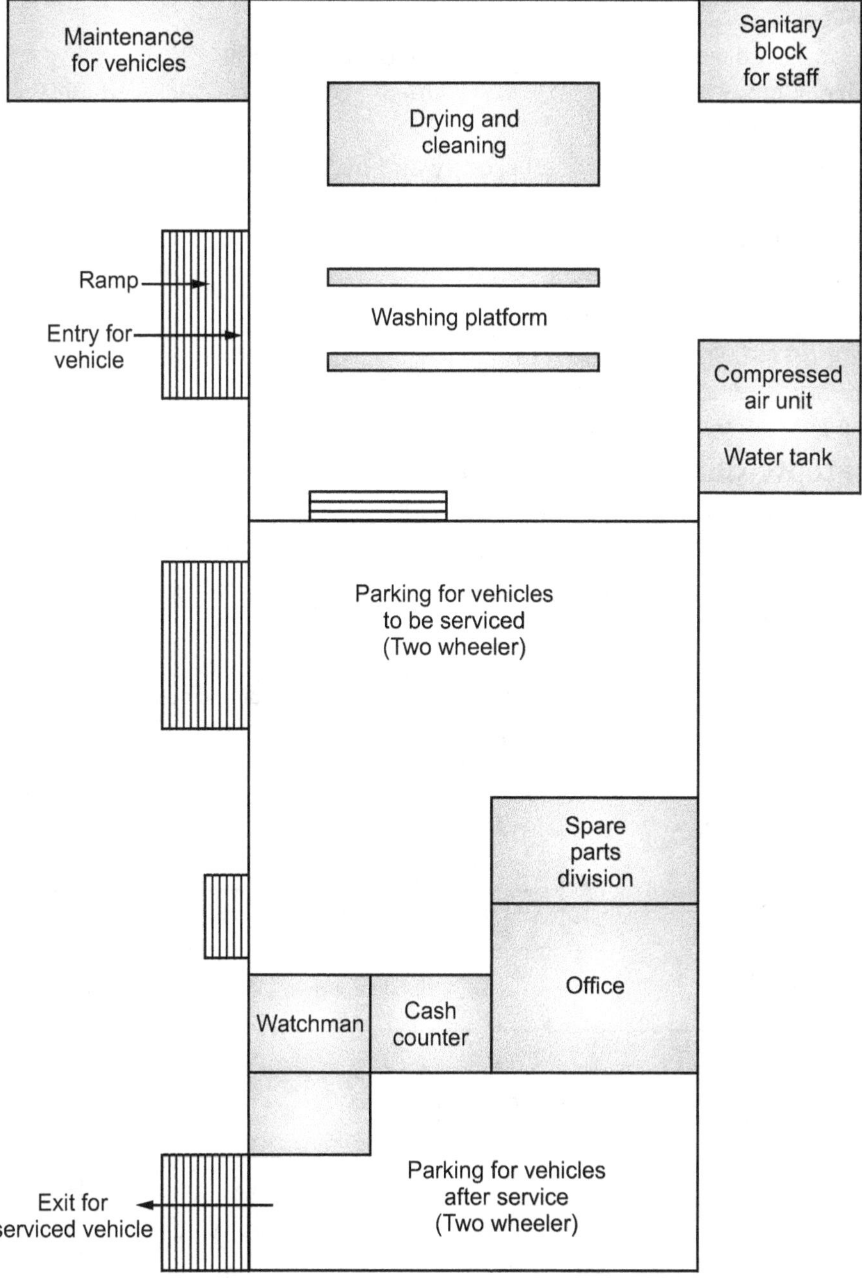

Fig. 12.13: Vehicle service centre

1. Office and cash counter.

2. Space for vehicles for servicing.

3. Space for vehicles service, i.e. maintenance, tool room, oiling, washing, cleaning etc.
4. Spare parts division.
5. Space for vehicles after servicing.
6. Delivery.

Sizes: For 25 vehicles a service centre can be provided with:

1. Office: 4 m × 3 m.
2. Cash counter: 2 m × 2 m.
3. Space for vehicles for service, i.e. entry and parking: 20 m × 6 m.
4. Servicing division: Washing - 3 m × 3 m;
   Drying, Cleaning - 4 m × 3 m;
   Oiling and Maintenance - 4 m × 3 m;
   Spare parts division - 5 m × 3 m.
5. Compressed air unit: 3 m × 2 m.
6. Parking of vehicles after service: 20 m × 6 m.
7. Delivery room with counter: 3 m × 3 m.

12.8.3 Data Required for P.V.C. Pipe Unit

P.V.C. pipes are most commonly used now-a-days in various chemical industries and food processing industries. These are popularly used in sewer pipes and in low pressure water supply pipes. General requirements are similar to other small scale industry.

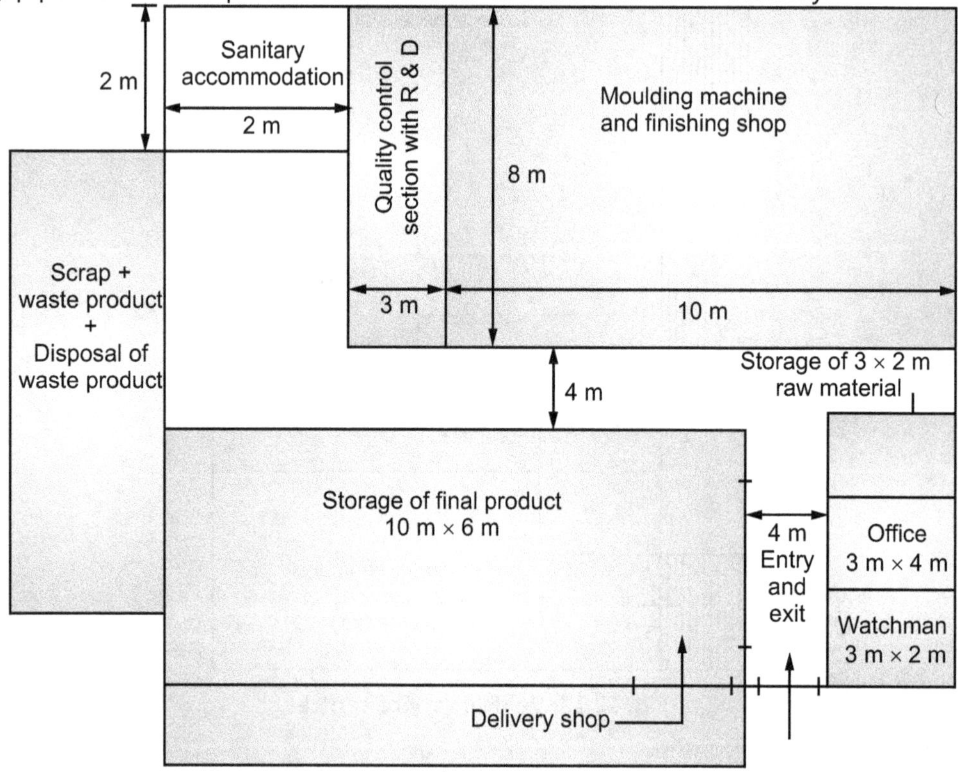

Fig. 12.14

Manufacturing of these pipes require:

- Raw material (polyethylene, poly propylene etc.)
- Crusher.
- Injection moulding machine.
- Moulds of required diameter and shape.
- Finishing, cutting, machine shop.
- Quality control section.

12.8.4 Prestressed Concrete Pole Factory

Units required for a pole factory are:

1. **Raw Material Storage:**
   - Cement
   - Steel
   - Sand
   - Aggregate
   - Water
   - Oil or grease to apply on forms.

These are stored at their appropriate places.

2. **Batching Plant (Measurement of Materials):**
   - Cement stored in godowns is batched or taken in proper proportion by weight.
   - Steel is batched by weight according to bar bending schedule (details of reinforcement).
   - Water is batched by volume.
   - Sand and aggregate are batched by weight.

   For a pole factory, a conveyor system is preferred as an automatic batching plant.

3. **Mixing Plants:** Raw materials of concrete (cement, sand, aggregate, water) are mixed in proportion by concrete mixers. Continuous type of mixers may be used for this factory.

4. **Placing Concrete in Forms:** Before placing concrete in forms, a nominal reinforcement is arranged in wooden form work or steel form work. Now a fresh concrete is placed in forms and compacted by using vibrators.

5. **Curing:** After the forms are removed, curing process is done for hardening of cement concrete.

Now poles are ready to use as electric poles or fencing poles etc.

Process layout is as below for this factory.

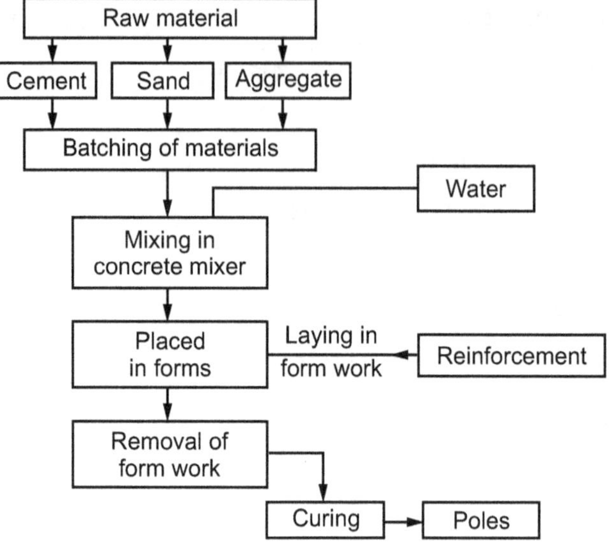

Fig. 12.15

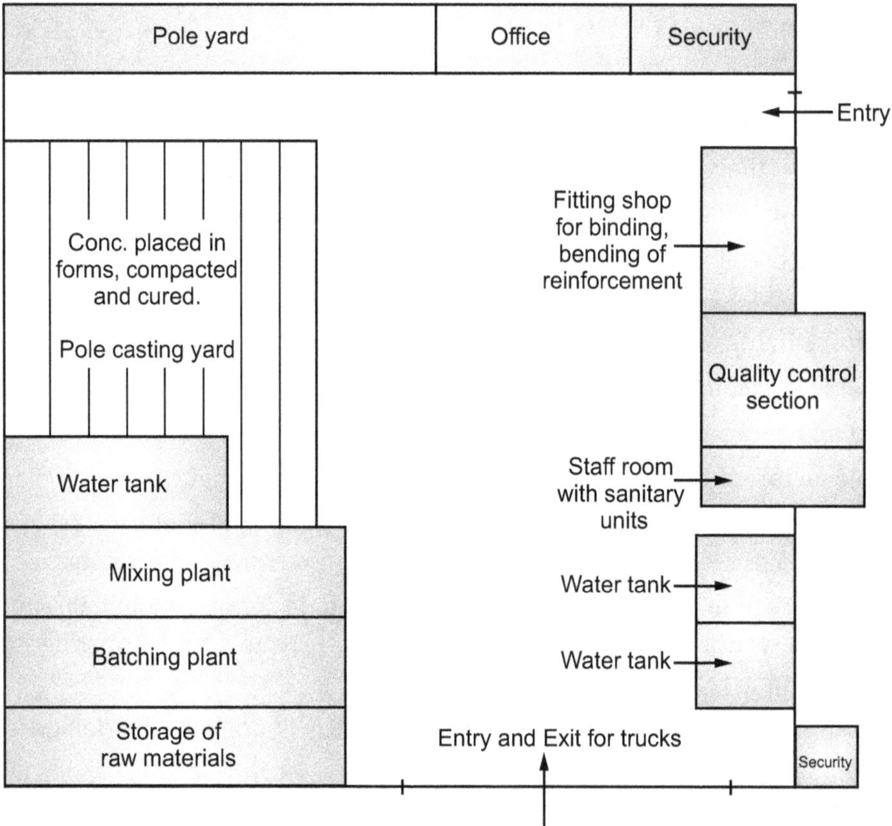

Fig. 12.16: A typical layout of a pole factory

12.9 GENERAL BUILDINGS

(A) Post Office:

Following units in a general post office should be considered.

Entrance and moving space	30 m^2
Public dealing counters	Height 1.6 m – 1.8 m, width 0.7 m – 0.95 m
Post master's room	15 m^2
Working area for other staff	30 m^2
Post separation room	30 m^2
Safe custedy area for cash	9.5 m^2
Entertainment room	12 m^2
Water room and Toilet	7.5 m^2

1. Two entrances have been provided; one main entrance for all the visitors and one service entrance for employees.

2. Entrance to post master's office should be such that it is easily accessible by both outsiders as well as employees.

3. The public dealing counters separate the waiting space from the working and post separation space.

(B) Health Club or a Club House:

Entrance	1.2 m wide
Changing room	9.5 m^2 (separate for gents/ladies)
Gymnasium	4.5 m × 4 m
Indoor game area	4 m × 5 m (each game) i.e. Table tenis, billiard etc.
Store room	2.75 m × 3 m
Parking area	

Sanitary Blocks:

Description	Male	Female
W.C.	1 for 25	1 for 15
Urinals	1 for 6 – 20	
	2 for 21 – 45	—
	3 for 46 – 70	
	4 for 71 – 100	
	1 for 25	1 for 25

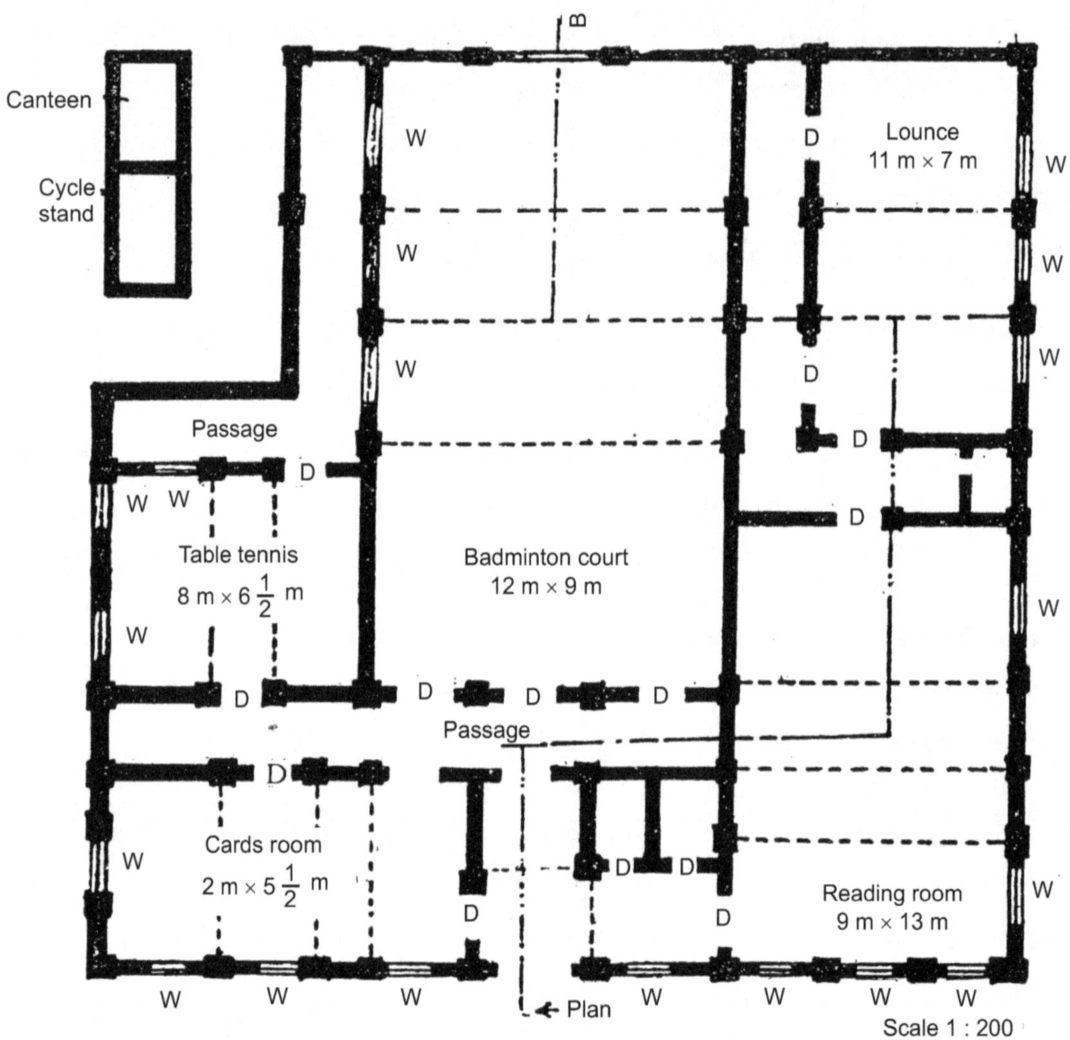

Fig. 12.17: Community centre

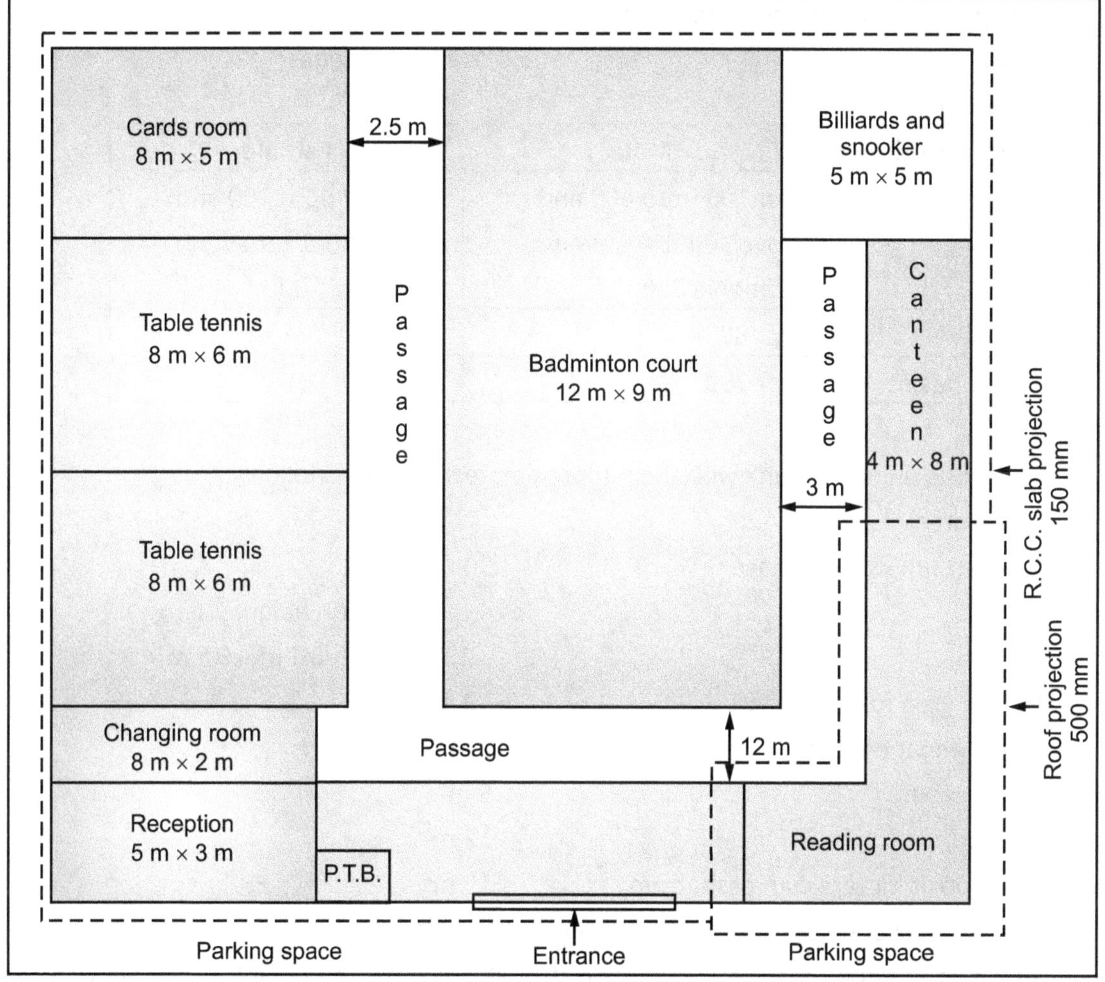

Fig. 12.18: Line Plan of a Community Centre (not to the scale)

(C) Marriage Halls:

The various units in a marriage halls may be provided as follows:

Entrance

Parking area

Kitchen $15 - 20$ m^2

Dining area

Store room $12 - 15$ m^2

Administrative office 12 m^2

Auditorium 1.1 m^2 / person

Rooms for visitors 4 m × 3 m (each)

To be provided according to requirement.

Circulation space   1.8 m wide passages

Sanitary Blocks:

Description	Male	Female
WC	1 for 100 upto 400 and above 400, 1 for every additional 250	1 for 100 upto 200 and above 200, 1 for every additional 100
Urinals	1 for 50	—
Wash basins	1 for 200	1 for 200

(D) Banks:

The various units in a bank with their approximate sizes are as follows:

Parking area

Entrance cum waiting space $30 \ m^2$

Counters $4 \ m^2$ each with height 1.6 m,
                                                            $- 1.8$ m width 0.4 m $- 0.8$ m

Working area for other staff $20 \ m^2$

Branch Managers cabin $12 \ m^2$

Cashier cabin $5 \ m^2$

Store room $12 \ m^2$

Safe Deposit lockers cum cash room $15 \ m^2$

Water and Toilet room $7.5 \ m^2$

The banks designed is a similar manner as post office, same principles may be followed in planning a bank.

(E) Lodge:

A lodge is a place where people reside for one or two days during traveling. Only provisions like sleeping arrangements are to be made. Also in some cases pantry and small canteen facilities that could only serve tea and breakfast could be provided.

The area required various units can be as follows:

Office $12 \ m^2$

Entrance   2 m wide

Rooms

(i) Single occupancy $9.5 \ m^2$/head

(ii) Double occupancy $7.5 \ m^2$/head

Pantry $2.75 \ m \times 3 \ m$

Store	2 m × 3 m
Kitchen	2.75 m × 3 m

Sanitary Provisions:

Description	Male	Female
WC	1 for 10	1 for 8
Bath	1 for 10	1 for 10
Urinals	1 for 25	–
Wash basins	1 for 10	1 for 10

(F) Factory Building with an Administrative Block:

Main factory

Office and administration block.

Store for raw material.

Store for finished goods.

Canteen.

Laboratory / Quality control Department.

Circulation space.   1.5 m to 2.0 m in width

Sanitary Blocks:

Description	Male	Female
W.C.	1 for 15	1 for 15
Urinals	1 for 6 – 20 2 for 21 – 45 3 for 46 – 70 4 for 71 – 100	–
Wash basin	1 for 25	1 for 25

- The sizes of a factory may depend on the requirement and type of the product to be manufactured.

- In case of a factory buildings care should be taken to leave sufficient space for circulations as it may be needed for shifting of materials also.

- The administrative block may be planned according to requirements.

- Departments and divisions having related functions should be located in their proper relation so that the internal circulation is compact.

- Uniform type of furniture and equipment provides greater flexibility and uniformity in appearance.

- Generally offices are provided on each side of a central corridors.

12.10 GENERAL GUIDELINES AND SOME COMMON UNITS WHICH ARE NEEDED IN PUBLIC BUILDINGS

Some of the common units required in all types of public buildings are:

1. **Sanitary Blocks:** The sanitary blocks includes bath rooms, bed rooms, wash hand basins and urinals. The number to provided in each building various according to the requirements. Common sizes adopted as a general guidelines are as follows:

   Bath rooms   1.2 m × 2.1 m, 1.9 m × 2.7 m

   Water closet   0.9 m × 1.2 m, 1.0 × 1.2 m

   Urinals   0.9 m × 0.7 5 m

2. **Circulation:** Various units are connected together by passages, corridors and verandahs. Vertical circulation can be effected by the stair and lifts.

   Common sizes adopted are as follows:

   Passage / corridor   1 – 3.0 m

   Verandah   width 1.8 – 3.5 m

   Stairs   width 1.2 m (min.)

   Riser   150 – 170 mm

   Tread   300 – 325 mm

   Landing   1 – 1.8 m wide

   Head room   1.8 m (min.)

   Floor height   2.7 m – 6 m

3. **Entrance or Reception:** Each public buildings, requires space to be provided at the entrance. The area that shall be provided at the main entry point will very slightly with the number of occupants that might enter at a time. But in any case, width of an entrance shall not be less than 2.75 m.

   General sizes to be provided can be as follows:

   3 m × 6 m   4 m × 5 m

   3.5 m × 7 m   4.5 m × 6 m

   3.75 m × 8 m   6 m × 7.5 m

                         7 m × 8.0 m

4. **Parking Space, Garages and Cycle Stands:** Open parking space is essential around any type of building the area of an parking to be provided for any public building will depend on the type of a building and number of persons visiting the building. In calculation of such area some assumptions visitor and accordingly it should be designed.

Area Required:

Vehicle	Area required
Cars	20 m² / vehicle
Scooters and Motorcycles	3 m² / vehicle
Cycles	1.2 m² / vehicle
Buses	60 m² / bus

General Guidelines for Furniture Sizes of Various Units:

A building is not complete if the necessary furniture is not provided. Whatever may be the function of the buildings and activity inside its various areas, we need furniture.

Sizes of furniture to be provided at various places are as below:

Office table	-	1.8 × 0.9 × 0.75 m
Subordinate officer	-	1.5 × 0.9 × 0.75 m
Clerk table	-	1.35 × 0.75 × 0.75 m
Chair with arms	-	0.45 × 0.05 × 0.45 m
Cupboards	-	1.10 × 0.50 × 1.8 m
Stands for books	-	1.8 × 0.45 × 2.1 m
		1.1 × 0.45 × 1.35 m

Space Left Around Furniture:

1. 50 cm length of a desk be provided in a school per student.
2. The width required from the front edge of desk to rear edge or back of the seat is about 0.85 to 0.90 m.
3. The gangway between desks should not be less than 40 cm in width preferably 45 cm.
4. At least 15 cm gap should be left between wall and a desk.
   The table to be provided in a library or a canteen shall be of a such a size that 4 to 6 persons are seated.

Approximate Sizes of Furniture:

1.	Twin sofa or Chair	-	0.75 m × 1.3 m
2.	Office chair or small chair	-	0.45 m × 0.45 m
3.	Small arm chair	-	0.65 m × 0.45 m
4.	Club chair	-	0.75 m × 0.9 m or 0.65 m × 0.75 m
5.	Writing table	-	1.35 m × 0.75 m
6.	Small desk	-	1.20 m × 0.60 m
7.	Cafee table	-	1 m diameter
8.	Bridge table	-	0.9 m × 0.9 m
9.	Single bed	-	0.9 m × 2.0 m
10.	Double bed	-	1.35 m – 1.4 m × 2 – 2.1 m
11.	Divan or setter	-	0.75 m × 1.65 m
12.	Dressing stool	-	0.45 m × 0.38 m
13.	Chest for drawers	-	0.60 m × 0.38 m
14.	Bed side table	-	0.60 m × 0.30 m
15.	Small dressing table	-	0.45 m × 0.90 m

IMPORTANT POINTS

- Types of buildings.
- Points to be considered for planning:
  - (a) Covered under residential
  - (b) Educational buildings
  - (c) Institutional buildings
  - (d) Assembly buildings
  - (e) Business buildings etc.
- General buildings:
  - (a) Post office
  - (b) Health club
  - (c) Marriage halls
  - (d) Banks
  - (e) Lodge
  - (f) Factory building
- General requirements for above mentioned buildings.

QUESTIONS

1. Design a state transport bus terminus for a Taluka place. Make suitable assumptions and mention them clearly. Clearly specify the tails of the following:
   - (i) Open space.
   - (ii) Waiting space platforms.
   - (iii) Offices.

   Draw a line plan to a suitable scale.

   Show a typical furniture arrangement plan for content buildings.

2. A hospital to serve a population of 20,000 is to be designed on a site measuring 100 m × 150 m separate word for men and women W.C., Nurses room etc. are to be provided and detailed have to be worked out. Draw a line plan to a suitable scale.

3. Design a Hostel of your college. Make suitable assumption and state them clearly. Draw a typical furniture layout of a single bed in that.

4. Plan a commercial bank in a city. Assume suitable data, clearly mention the data. Draw a line plan to a suitable scale.

5. It is proposed to construct a Public Health Centre with the following data:
   - (1) Lounge: 30 sq.m.
   - (2) Reception: 20 sq.m.
   - (3) Administration office: 20 sq.m.
   - (4) Doctor's cabins: 15 sq.m.

(5)   Nurse's room: 15 sq.m.

(6)   Labour room: 15 sq.m.

(7)   Wards two numbers: 20 sq.m each.

(8)   Store: 15 sq.m.

With the help of a connectivity matrix and bubble diagram to a scale of 1 : 50 or suitable.

(a)   Line plan showing location of doors and windows.

(b)   Schedule of openings.

(c)   Suggest suitable material for painting of walls.

6. It is proposed to construct a Post Office with the following data:

(i)   Entrance-cum-waiting space: 50 sq.m.

(ii)   Public dealing counter (six in numbers): Total 30 sq.m.

(iii) Working space for other staff 35 sq.m.

(iv)   Post master office: 15 sq.m.

(v)   Post separation room: 30 sq.m.

(vi)   Store room: 15 sq.m.

(vii) Meeting room: 20 sq.m.

(viii) Sanitary units: As per standards.

(ix)   All passages: 2000 mm wide.

(x)   Assume any additional suitable data, if necessary and mention it clearly with justification.

(a)   Draw a scale 1 : 100 or suitable, Line plan showing location of doors and windows.

(b)   Show line sketches of furniture arrangement.

7. It is proposed to construct a Single-Storeyed Shopping Complex with the following data:

(1)   Entrance: of suitable size.

(2)   Big shops: 4 nos., 30 m^2 each.

(3)   Small shops: 8 nos., 20 m^2 each.

(4)   Telephone booths: 2 nos. of suitable size.

(5)   Separate sanitary blocks for ladies and gents.

(6)   Staircase for future expansion.

(7)   All passages 2.5 m wide.

(8)   RCC framed structure.

(9)   Assume additional data if necessary.

(a)   Draw to a scale of 1 : 50 or suitable, line plan with northline.

(b)   Locate all openings and columns.

(c)   Show details of furniture arrangement with dimensions in any one shop.

8. Design a Single-Storeyed Restaurant building on a Highway. The following units are to be provided:

(1)	Entrance and general stationery shop	–	45 m^2
(2)	Dining hall	–	300 m^2
(3)	Service	–	35 m^2
(4)	Kitchen	–	45 m^2
(e)	Store-room	–	18 m^2
(6)	Cloak room for keeping baggage	–	15 m^4
(7)	Water closet for gents	–	2 nos.
	Water closet for ladies	–	2 nos.

Draw to a scale of 1 : 50 or suitable:

(a) Line plan showing location of doors and windows.

(b) Furniture arrangement in the dining hall.

9. It is proposed to construct a PWD Executive Engineer's office with the following data:

(1) Entrance and waiting	60 m^2
(2) Head clear	20 m^2
(3) Administrative office	100 m^2
(4) Gents' sanitary block	20 m^2
(5) Executive engineer's office (with attached toilet of suitable size)	35 m^2
(6) PA to executive engineer (with attached toilet of suitable size)	20 m^2
(7) Drawing, printing and Xeroxing	40 m^2
(8) Technical assistant	20 m^2
(9) Records and stationary room	30 m^2
(10) Ladies room (with attached toilet of suitable size)	15 m^2
(11) All passages	3000 mm wide

Draw to a scale of 1 : 50 or suitable.

(a) Line plan showing location of doors, widows and northline. (15)

(b) Write schedule of openings. (2)

(c) Suggest suitable flooring material for various rooms. (3)

UNIVERSITY QUESTIONS

Dec. 2014

1. Draw a Single-Storeyed Restaurant building on a Highway.

The following units are to be provided :

(1) Entrance and general stationery shop - 50 m^2

(2) Dining hall - 300 m^2

(3) Service - 35 m^2

(4) Kitchen - 45 m^2

(5) Store-room - 18 m^2

(6) Cloakroom for keeping baggage - 15 m^2

(7) Water closet for gents - 2 nos.

(8) Water closet for ladies - 2 nos.

2. Draw a line plan of a Post Office using the following data :

Entrance and moving space : 30 m^2

Public dealing counters : Height 1.6 m – 1.8 m, width 0.7 m – 0.95 m

Post Master's room : 15 m^2

Working area for other staff : 30 m^2

Post-separation room : 30 m^2

Safe custody area for cash : 10 m^2

Cash transaction room : 12 m^2

Water room and Toilet (separate for male and female) : 7.5 m^2

Dec. 2015

1. It is proposed to construct a PWD Executive Engineer's office with the following data :

    (1) Entrance + Waiting – 12 m^2

    (2) Administrative office – 15 m^2

    (3) E.E. office (attached toilet) – 18 m^2

    (4) Technical session-15 m^2

    (5) Record room-9 m^2

    (6) PA to Executive-9 m^2

    (7) Sanitary block (Ladies and Gents)–suitable

    (8) Passage-1.5 m wide

    Draw to a scale of 1 : 50 or suitable :

    (i)   Line plan showing locations of Doors, Windows

    (ii) Schedule of openings.

2. It is proposed to construct a single-storeyed shopping complex with the following data :

    (1) Entrance of suitable size

    (2) Big shops : 6 nos., 30 m^2 each

    (3) Small shops : 10 nos., 20 m^2 each

(4) Telephone booths : 4 nos. of suitable size

(5) Separate sanitary blocks for ladies and gents

(6) Staircase for future expansion

(7) All passages 2.5 m wide

(8) RCC framed structure

(9) Assume additional data if necessary

(10) Draw to a scale of 1 : 50 or suitable, line plan with north line.

May 2015

1. Design a single storey hostel building and draw only line plan with the following data

    (i)   Number of students 50

    (ii) Twenty rooms are two seated with 7.5 sq. m area per student and ten single seated with 9.5 sq. m area.

    (iii) Recreation room approx. area 35 m^2

    (iv) Gymnasium approx. area 15 m^2

    (v)   Office space approx. area 12 m^2

    (vi) Store room approx. area 10 m^2

    (vii) Varandah, passage, staircase, W.C. and Bath etc. of suitable size should be provided.

    Show North direction and mention scale.

2. Draw a line plan of a Post-office using the following data :

    Entrance and moving space : 30 m^2 with seating arrangement

    Public dealing counters : 6 in no. with 0.5 m width

    Post-master's room : 15 m^2

    Working area for other staff : 30 m^2

    Post separation room : 30 m^2

    Safe custody area for cash : 10 m^2

    Cash transaction room : 12 m^2

    Speed post delivery section : 12 m^2

    Water room and Toilet (separate for male and female) : 7.5 m^2.

SAMPLE QUESTION PAPER

Time : 2 Hours   **Total Marks : 50**

1. (a) Write a short note on land use zoning and mention the requirements of each of them. **[7]**

   (b) Explain the following principles of architectural planning with suitable sketches : unity and accentuation. **[6]**

2. (a) Write a short note on TDR. **[6]**

   (b) Elaborate need for earthquake resistant structures in relation with loss of human life property and infrastructure. **[7]**

3. (a) Write a short note on importance of use of solar energy and rain water harvesting in today's context. **[6]**

   (b) Differentiate between building line and control line by drawing a suitable sketch. **[6]**

OR

4. (a) Explain the important aspects of layout of water supply and drainage systems. **[6]**

   (b) Explain with sketch the following terms:

   (i) SP   (ii) VP   (iii) PP **[6]**

5. Draw to a scale of 1 : 50 or otherwise, detailed plan with the following details :

The type of the structure is R.C.C. with wall thickness of 230 mm (external) and 100 mm (internal). Mention the schedule of openings. (Refer. Fig. 9) **[13]**

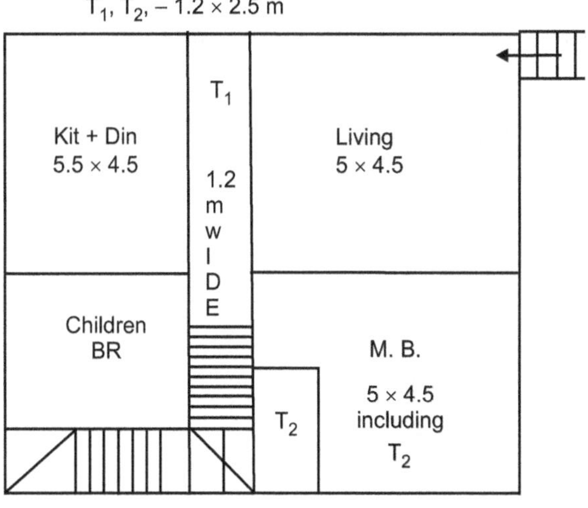

Fig. 9

OR

6. Draw a detailed Floor Plan to a scale of 1 : 50 with the following data :

    (i)   Living room 1 no. approx. area 15 m^2

    (ii)   Kitchen-cum-Dining 1 no. approx. area 15 m^2

    (iii) Bedrooms 2 no., approx. area 12 m^2 each

    (iv) Floor to floor height 3.3 m

    (v)   Load bearing structure

    (vi) Foundation and Plinth in UCR masonry

    (vii) Varandah, Passage, Staircase, W.C. and Bath/attached toilet etc. of suitable sizes should be provided. Indicate the North.

7. Draw a line plan of a Post Office using the following data :   **[12]**

Entrance and moving space : 30 m^2

Public dealing counters : Height 1.6 m – 1.8 m, width 0.7 m – 0.95 m

Post Master's room : 15 m^2

Working area for other staff : 30 m^2

Post-separation room : 30 m^2

Safe custody area for cash : 10 m^2

Cash transaction room : 12 m^2

Water room and Toilet (separate for male and female) : 7.5 m^2

OR

8. Draw a Single-Storeyed Motel building on a Highway.

The following units are to be provided :

(1) Entrance and general stationery shop - 50 m^2

(2) Dining hall - 300 m^2

(3) Service - 35 m^2

(4) Kitchen - 45 m^2

(5) Store-room - 18 m^2

(6) Cloakroom for keeping baggage - 15 m^2

(7) Water closet for gents - 2 nos.

(8) Water closet for ladies - 2 nos.

Draw a line plan with suitable scale, showing location of Doors and Windows.   **[12]**

www.ingramcontent.com/pod-product-compliance
Lightning Source LLC
Chambersburg PA
CBHW081325090726
47907CB00010B/2379